MALL GOTH

MALL GOTH

KATE LETH

dip me in chocolate and throw me to the lesbians

COLORING BY
DIANA SOUSA

LETTERING BY
ROBIN CRANK

SIMON & SCHUSTER BFYR

NEW YORK   LONDON   TORONTO   SYDNEY   NEW DELHI

SIMON & SCHUSTER BFYR

AN IMPRINT OF SIMON & SCHUSTER CHILDREN'S PUBLISHING DIVISION

1230 AVENUE OF THE AMERICAS, NEW YORK, NEW YORK 10020

FOR INFORMATION ABOUT SPECIAL DISCOUNTS FOR BULK PURCHASES, PLEASE CONTACT SIMON & SCHUSTER SPECIAL SALES AT 1-866-506-1949 OR BUSINESS@SIMONANDSCHUSTER.COM.

THE SIMON & SCHUSTER SPEAKERS BUREAU CAN BRING AUTHORS TO YOUR LIVE EVENT.

FOR MORE INFORMATION OR TO BOOK AN EVENT, CONTACT THE SIMON & SCHUSTER SPEAKERS BUREAU AT 1-866-248-3049 OR VISIT OUR WEBSITE AT WWW.SIMONSPEAKERS.COM.

THE TEXT FOR THIS BOOK WAS SET IN CC ASK FOR MERCY.

THE ILLUSTRATIONS FOR THIS BOOK WERE RENDERED DIGITALLY.

MANUFACTURED IN CHINA

FIRST EDITION

2 4 6 8 10 9 7 5 3 1

LIBRARY OF CONGRESS CATALOGING-IN-PUBLICATION DATA

NAMES: LETH, KATE, AUTHOR.

TITLE: MALL GOTH / KATE LETH.

DESCRIPTION: NEW YORK : SIMON & SCHUSTER BOOKS FOR YOUNG READERS, [2023]. | AUDIENCE: AGES 12 UP. | AUDIENCE: GRADES 7–9. | SUMMARY: "SET IN THE EARLY 2000S, MALL GOTH IS A COMING-OF-AGE STORY ABOUT GOTH LIV HOLME, WHO HAS TO NAVIGATE GROWING UP AMIDST MOVING, STARTING AT A NEW SCHOOL, AND THE DISSOLUTION OF HER PARENTS' MARRIAGE"— PROVIDED BY PUBLISHER.

IDENTIFIERS: LCCN 2021014146 (PRINT) | LCCN 2021014147 (EBOOK) | ISBN 9781534476943 (PAPERBACK) | ISBN 9781534476950 (HARDCOVER) | ISBN 9781534476967 (EBOOK)

SUBJECTS: LCSH: TEENAGE GIRLS–JUVENILE FICTION. | MOVING, HOUSEHOLD–JUVENILE FICTION. | HIGH SCHOOLS–JUVENILE FICTION. | CYAC: GRAPHIC NOVELS. | TEENAGERS–FICTION. | MOVING, HOUSEHOLD–FICTION. | HIGH SCHOOLS–FICTION. | SCHOOLS–FICTION. | COMING OF AGE–FICTION. | LCGFT: BILDUNGSROMANS. | GRAPHIC NOVELS.

CLASSIFICATION: LCC PZ7.1.L479 MAL 2022 (PRINT) | LCC PZ7.1.L479 (EBOOK) | DDC 741.5/973–DC23

LC RECORD AVAILABLE AT HTTPS://LCCN.LOC.GOV/2021014146

LC EBOOK RECORD AVAILABLE AT HTTPS://LCCN.LOC.GOV/2021014147

FOR MOMEROO

A NOTE FROM THE AUTHOR

THIS BOOK IS A WORK OF FICTION INSPIRED BY REAL EVENTS. IF
YOU OR A YOUNG PERSON YOU KNOW IS EXPERIENCING UNWANTED
ATTENTION FROM AN ADULT, SPEAK UP UNTIL SOMEONE LISTENS. YOU
CAN FIND MORE INFORMATION AND RESOURCES AT RAINN.ORG.

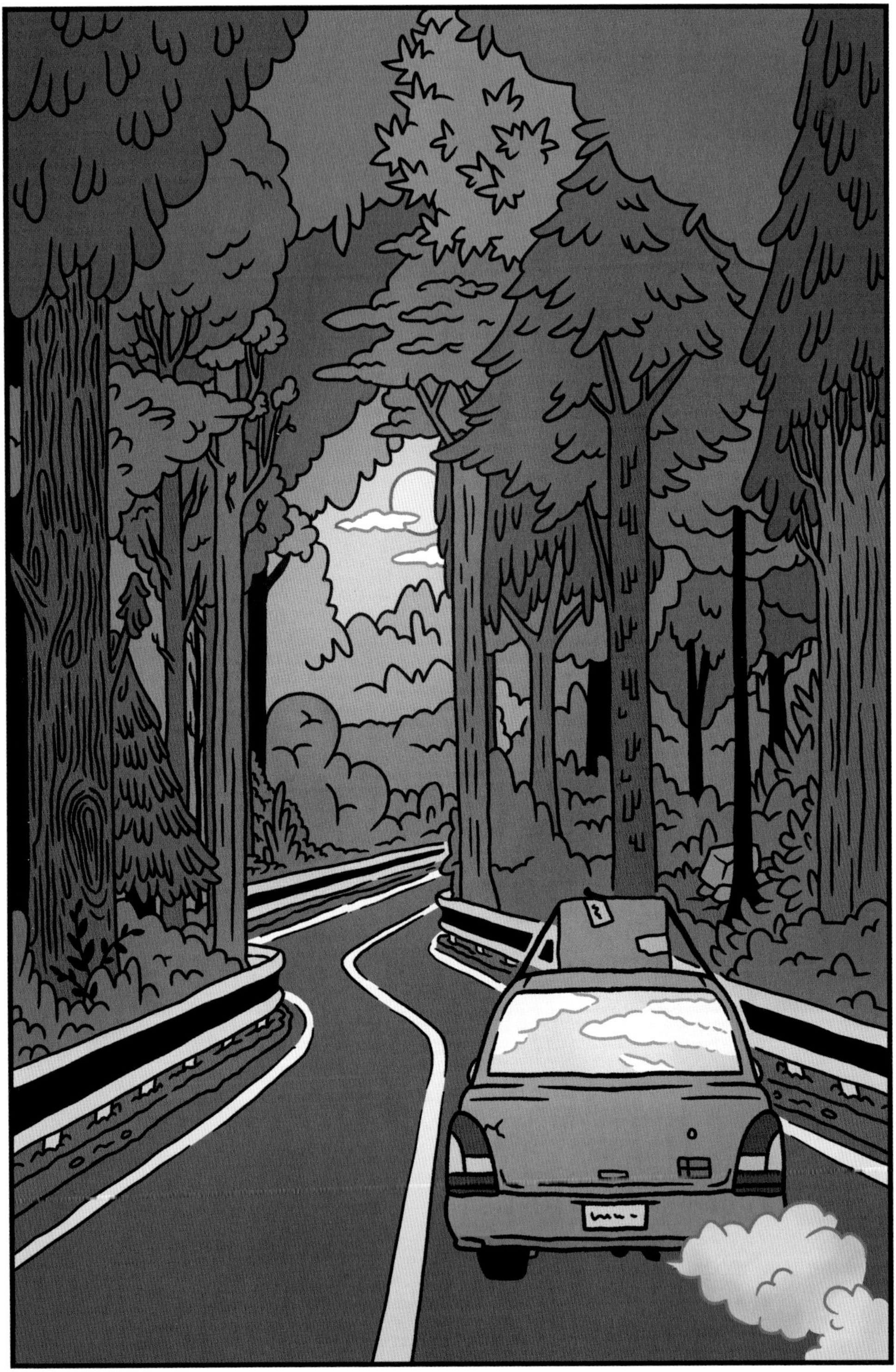

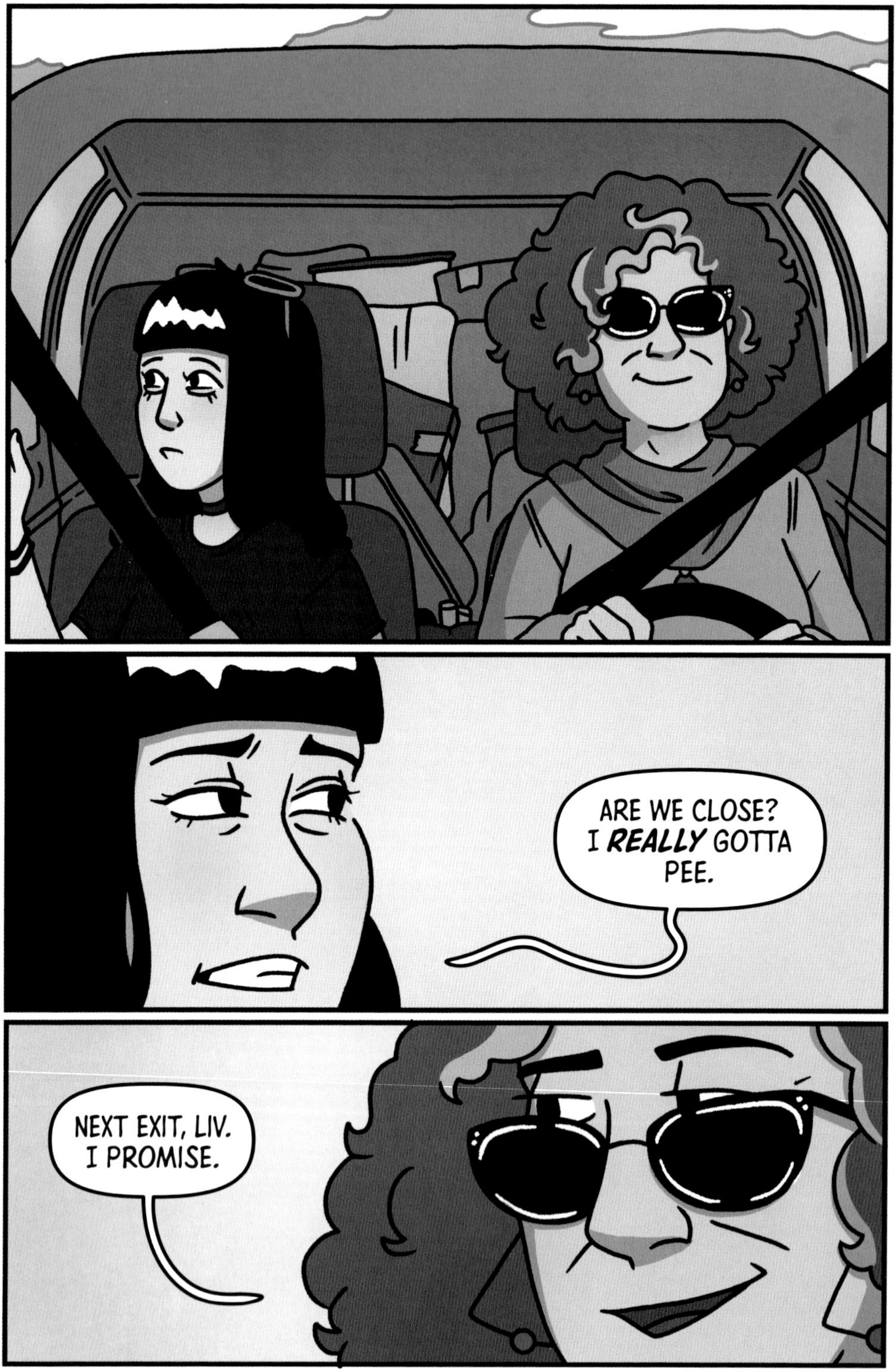
ARE WE CLOSE? I *REALLY* GOTTA PEE.
NEXT EXIT, LIV. I PROMISE.

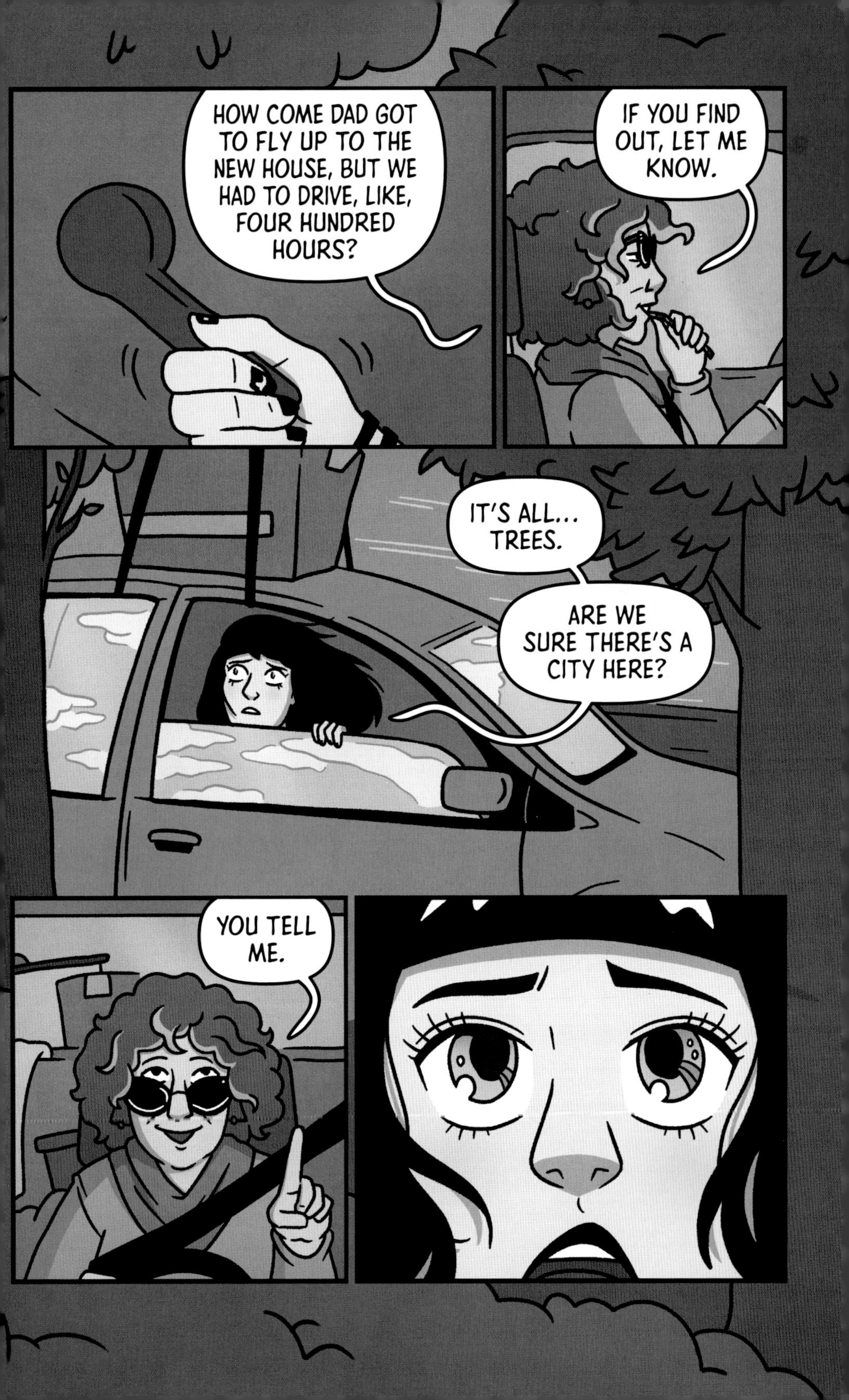
HOW COME DAD GOT TO FLY UP TO THE NEW HOUSE, BUT WE HAD TO DRIVE, LIKE, FOUR HUNDRED HOURS?
IF YOU FIND OUT, LET ME KNOW.
IT'S ALL... TREES.
ARE WE SURE THERE'S A CITY HERE?
YOU TELL ME.

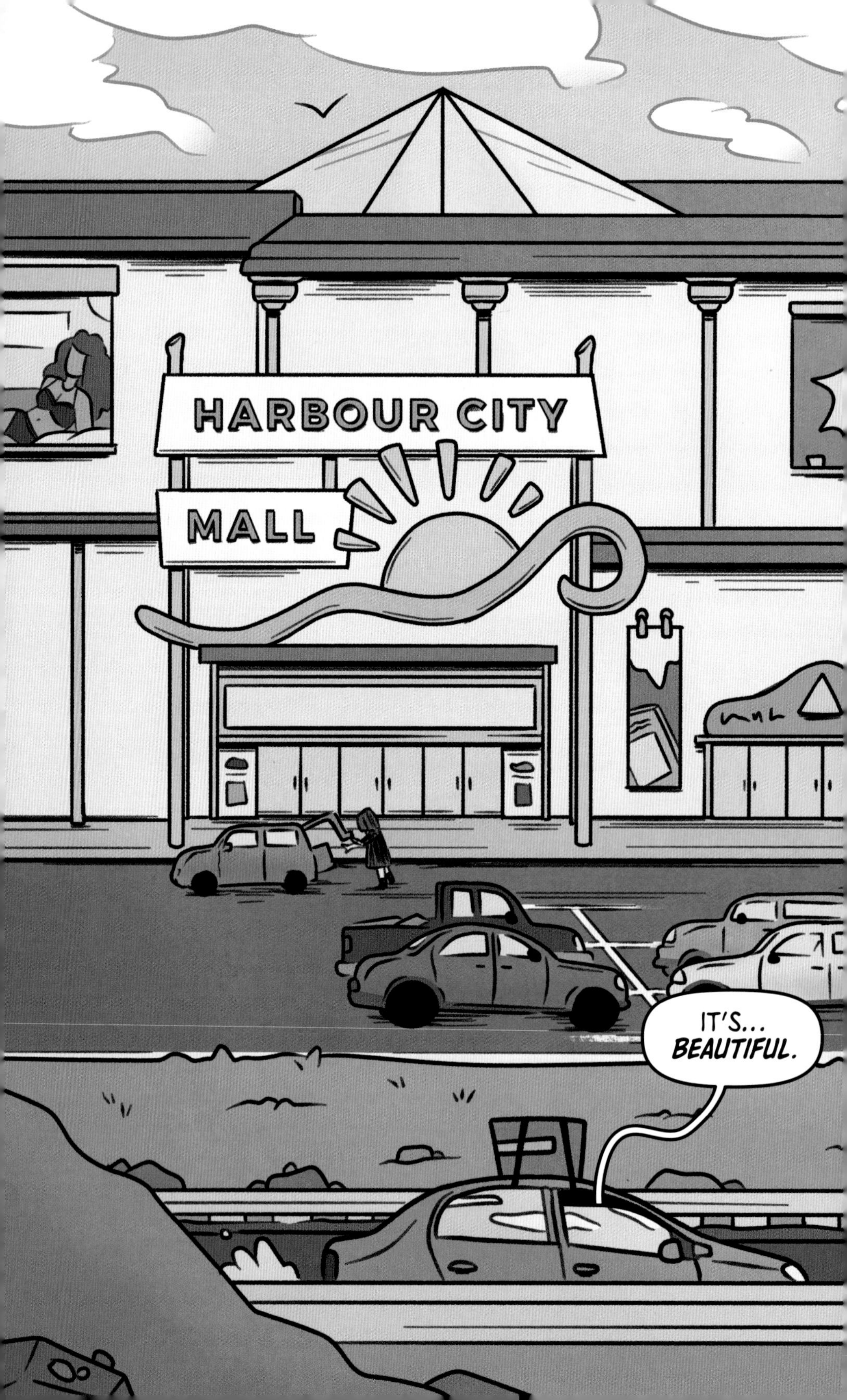
HARBOUR CITY
MALL
IT'S... BEAUTIFUL.

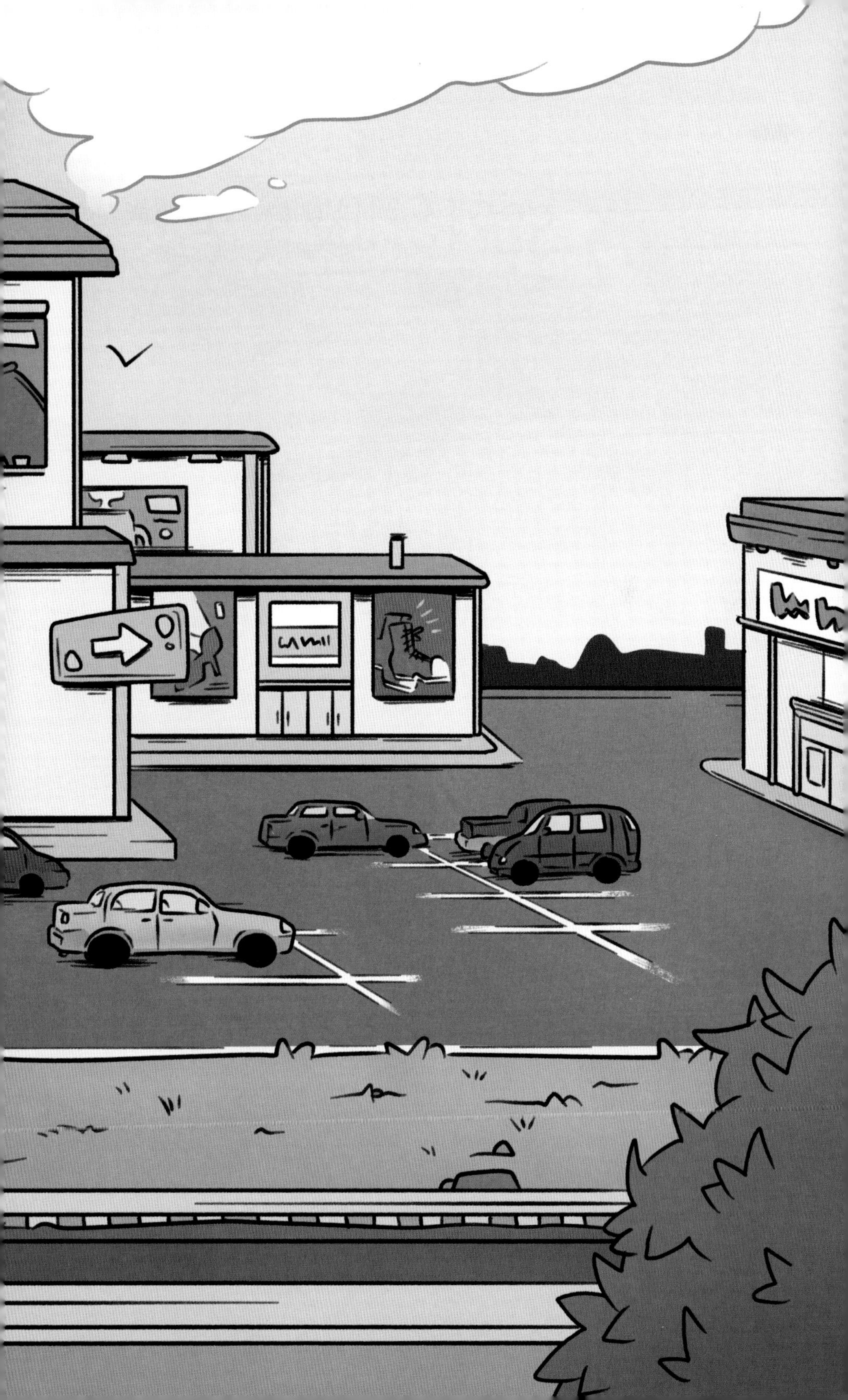

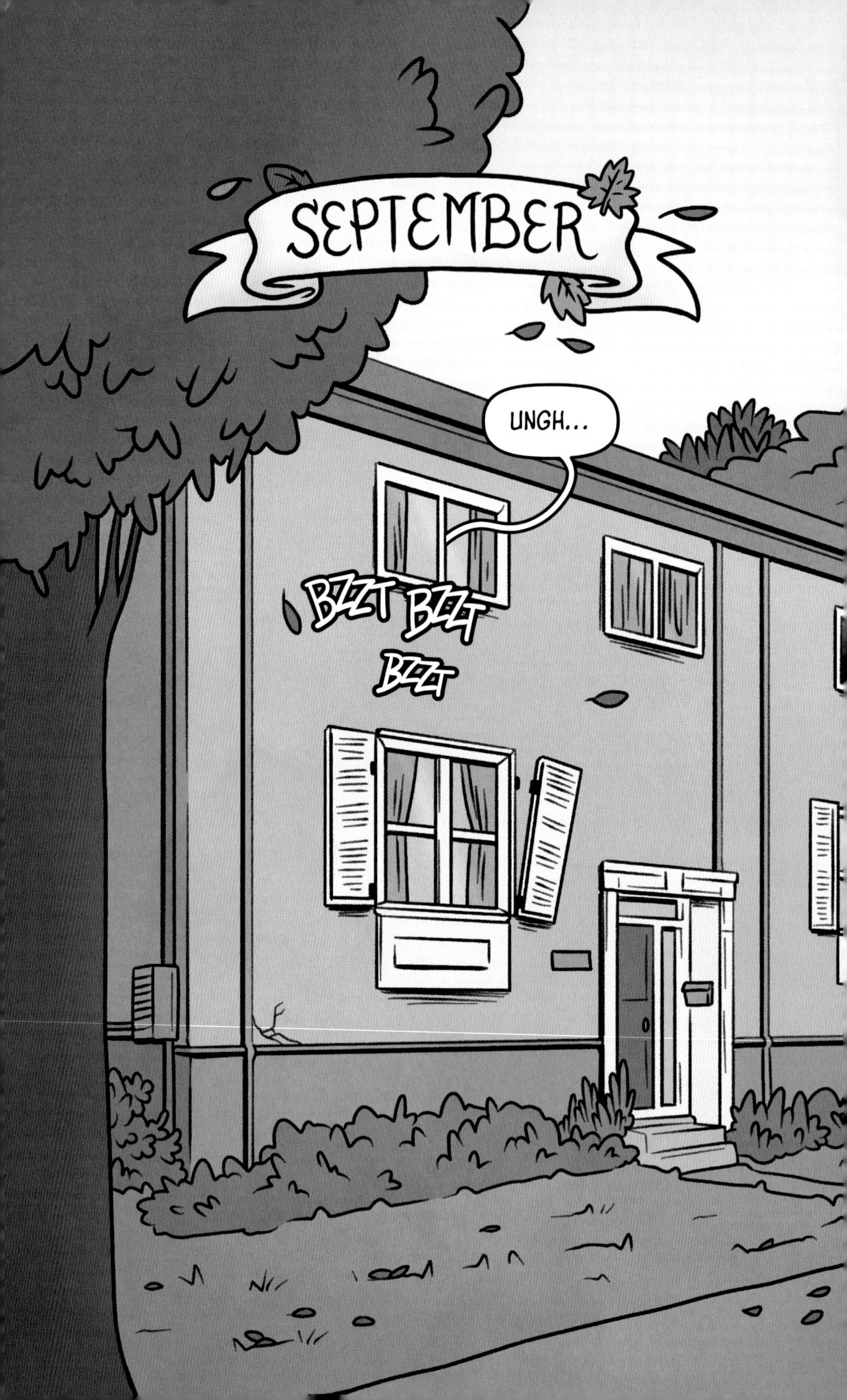
SEPTEMBER
UNGH...
BZZT BZZT
BZZT

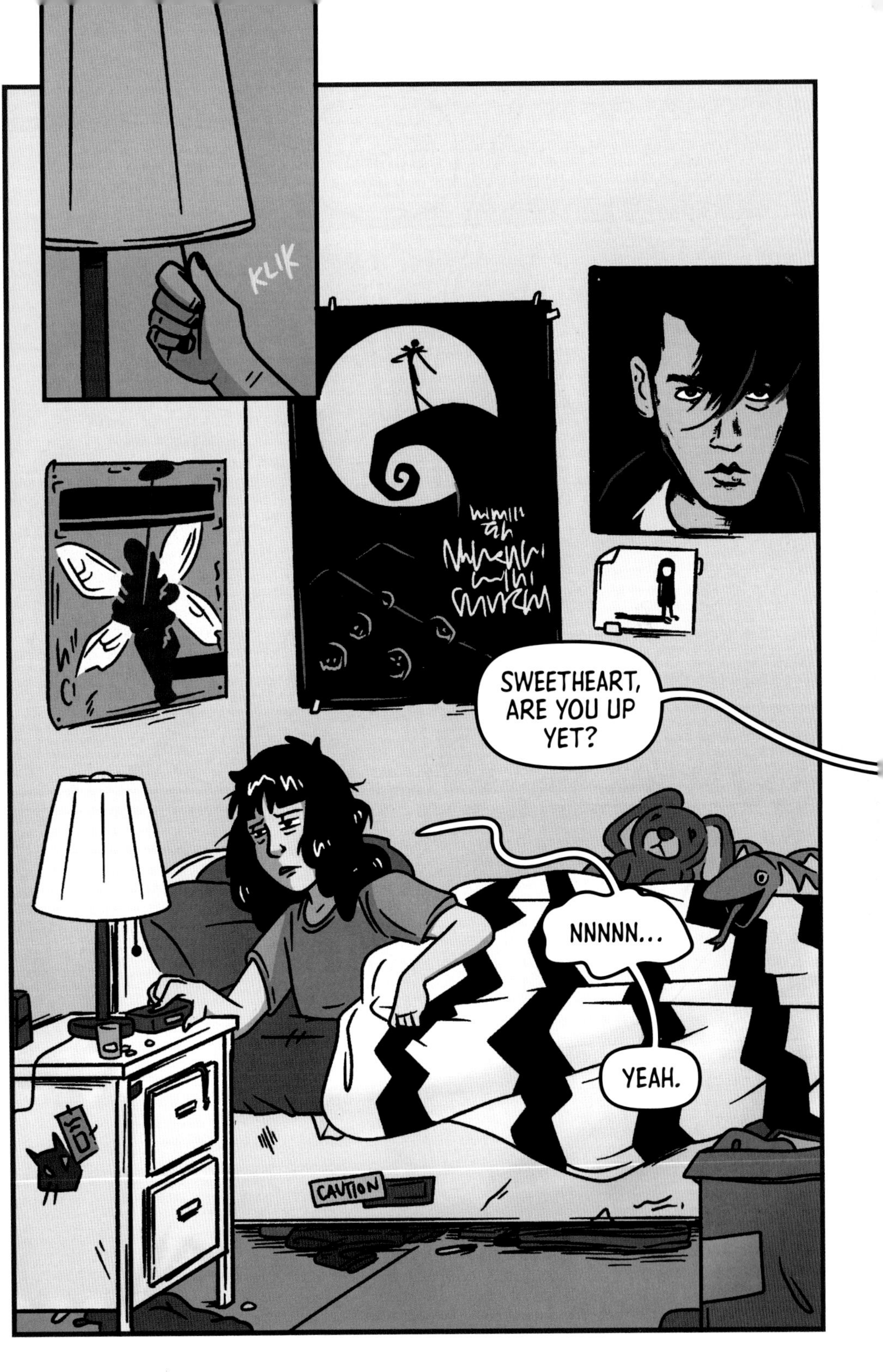
KLIK
SWEETHEART, ARE YOU UP YET?
NNNNN...
YEAH.
CAUTION

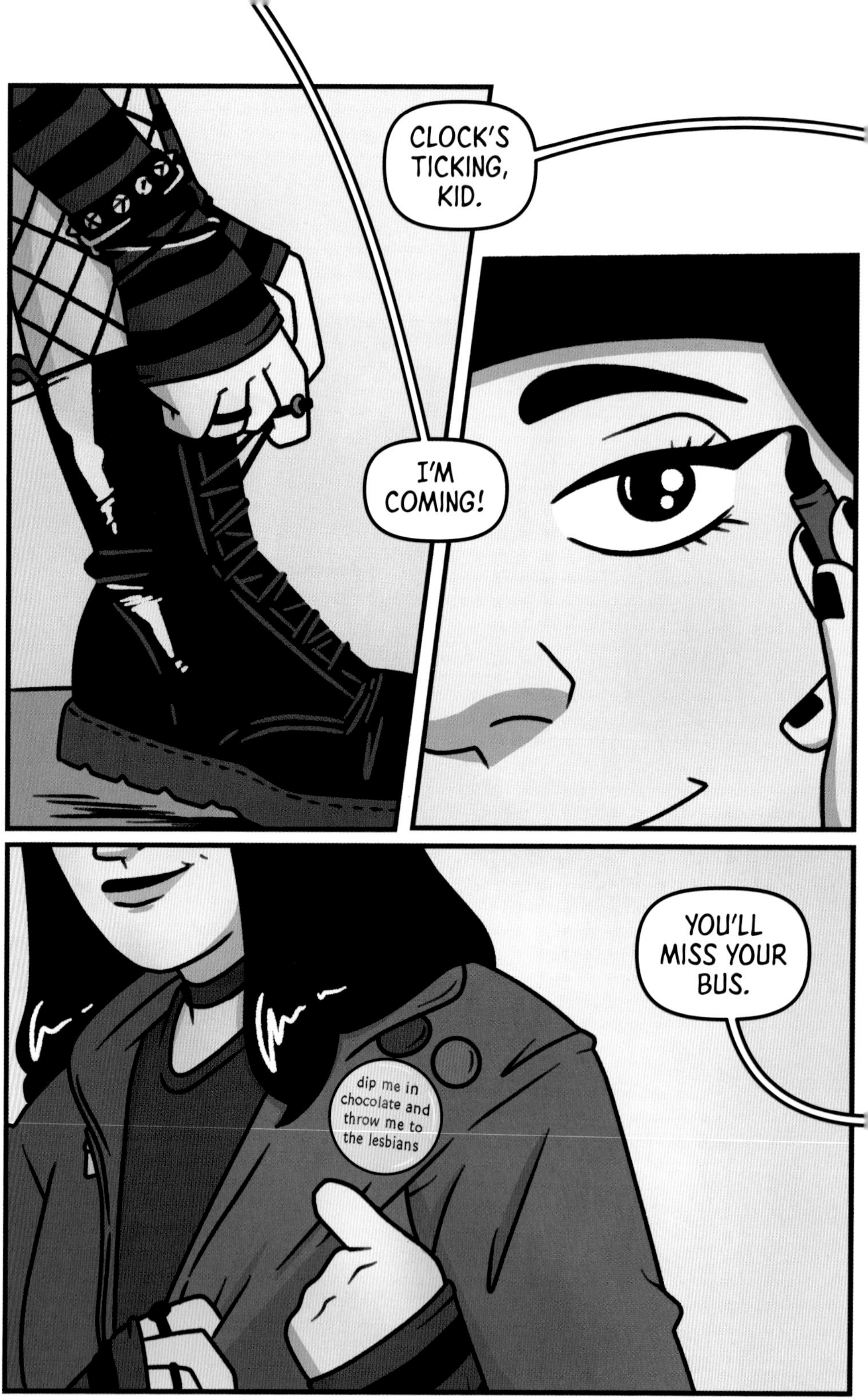
CLOCK'S TICKING, KID.
I'M COMING!
YOU'LL MISS YOUR BUS.
dip me in chocolate and throw me to the lesbians

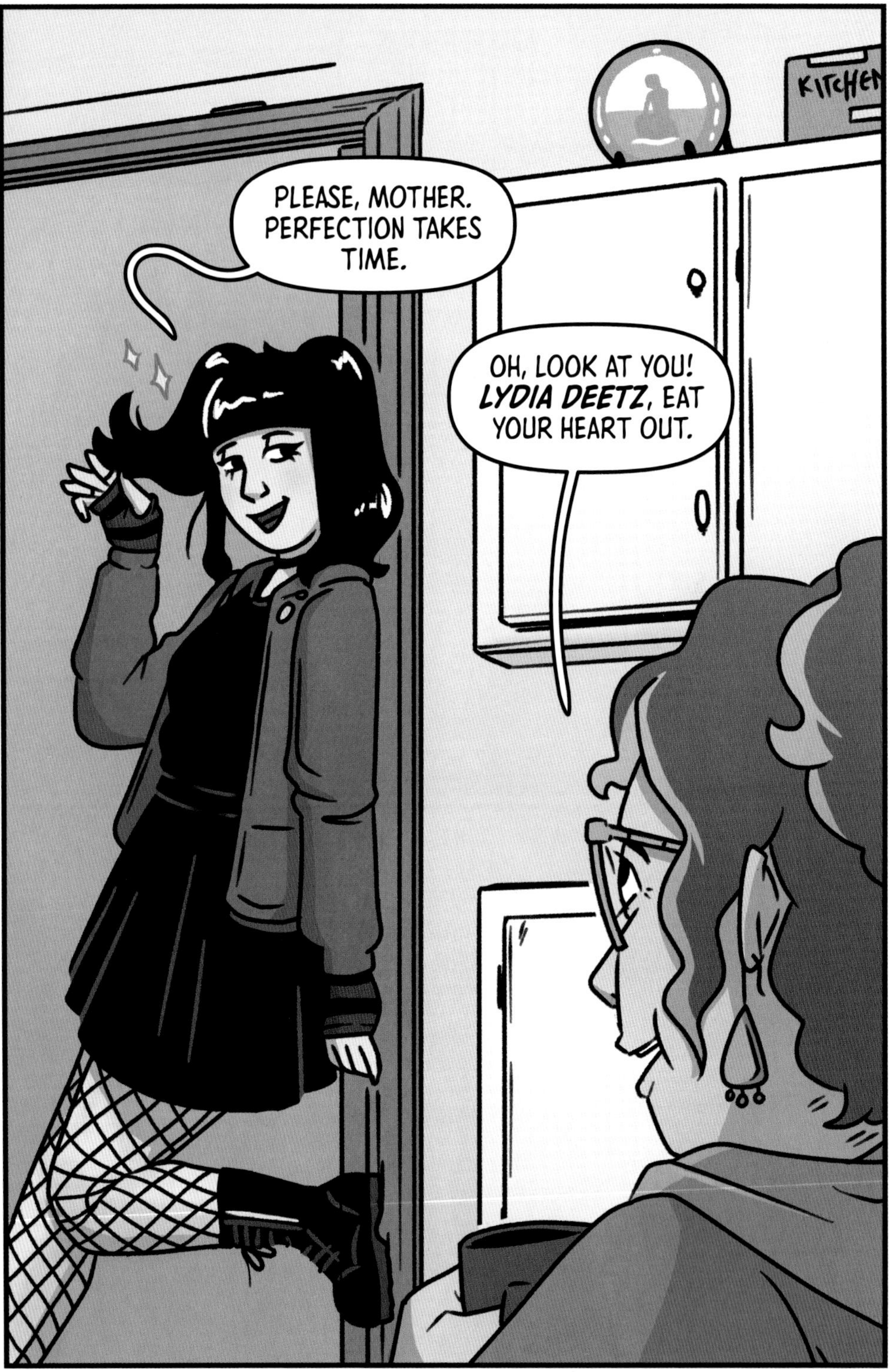
KITCHEN
PLEASE, MOTHER. PERFECTION TAKES TIME.
OH, LOOK AT YOU! *LYDIA DEETZ*, EAT YOUR HEART OUT.

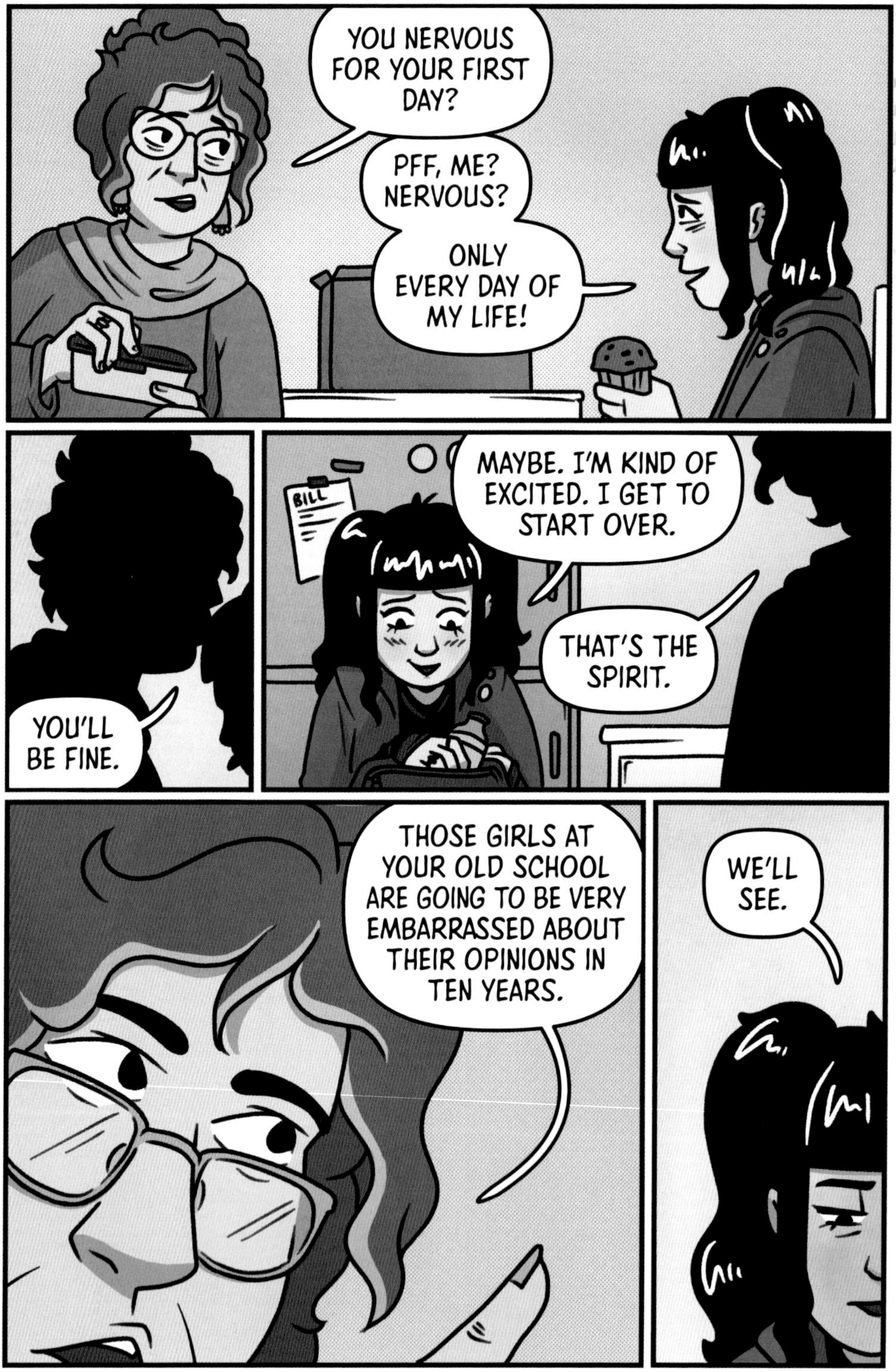
YOU NERVOUS FOR YOUR FIRST DAY?
PFF, ME? NERVOUS?
ONLY EVERY DAY OF MY LIFE!
BILL
MAYBE. I'M KIND OF EXCITED. I GET TO START OVER.
THAT'S THE SPIRIT.
YOU'LL BE FINE.
THOSE GIRLS AT YOUR OLD SCHOOL ARE GOING TO BE VERY EMBARRASSED ABOUT THEIR OPINIONS IN TEN YEARS.
WE'LL SEE.

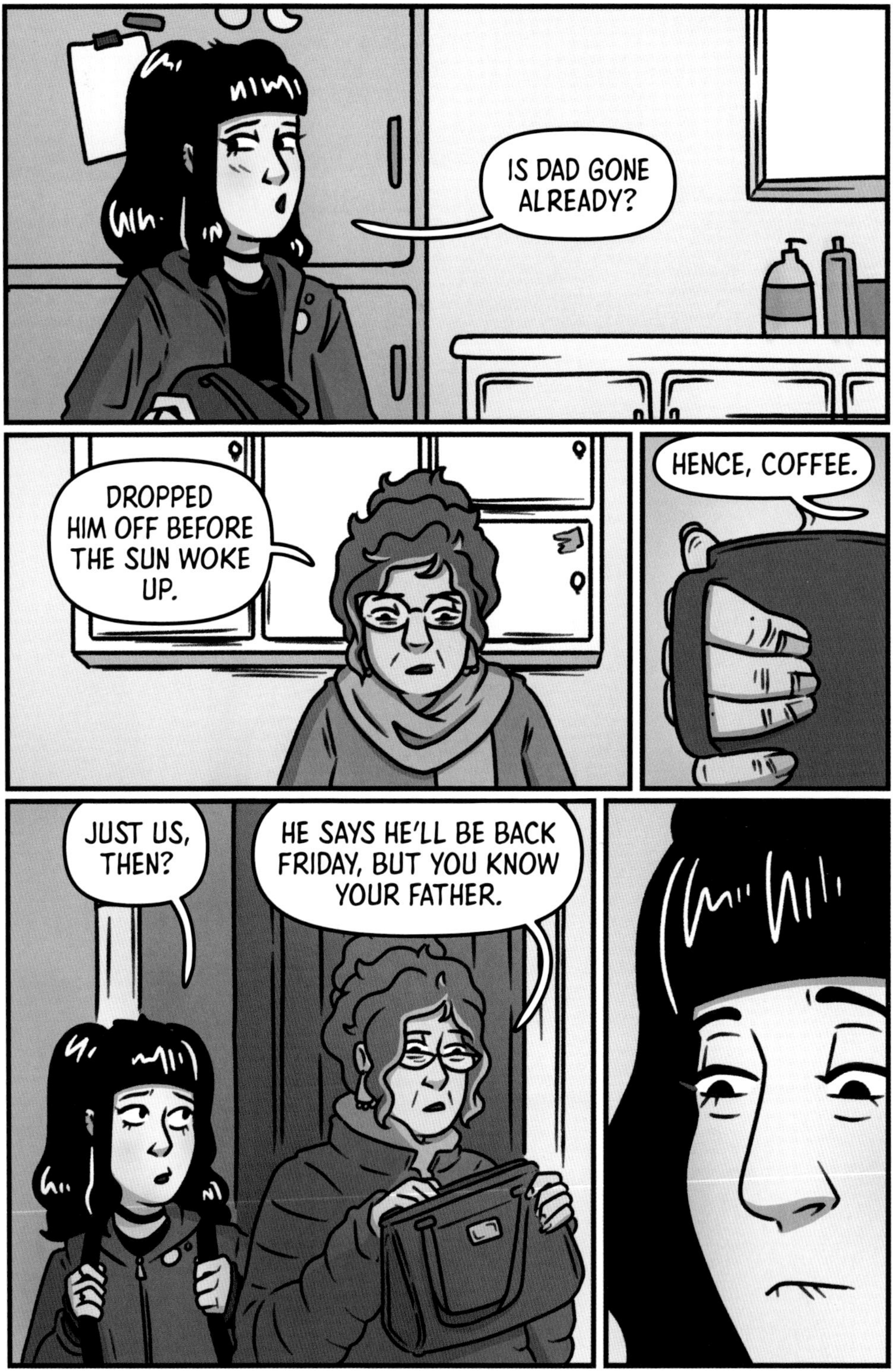
IS DAD GONE ALREADY?
DROPPED HIM OFF BEFORE THE SUN WOKE UP.
HENCE, COFFEE.
JUST US, THEN?
HE SAYS HE'LL BE BACK FRIDAY, BUT YOU KNOW YOUR FATHER.

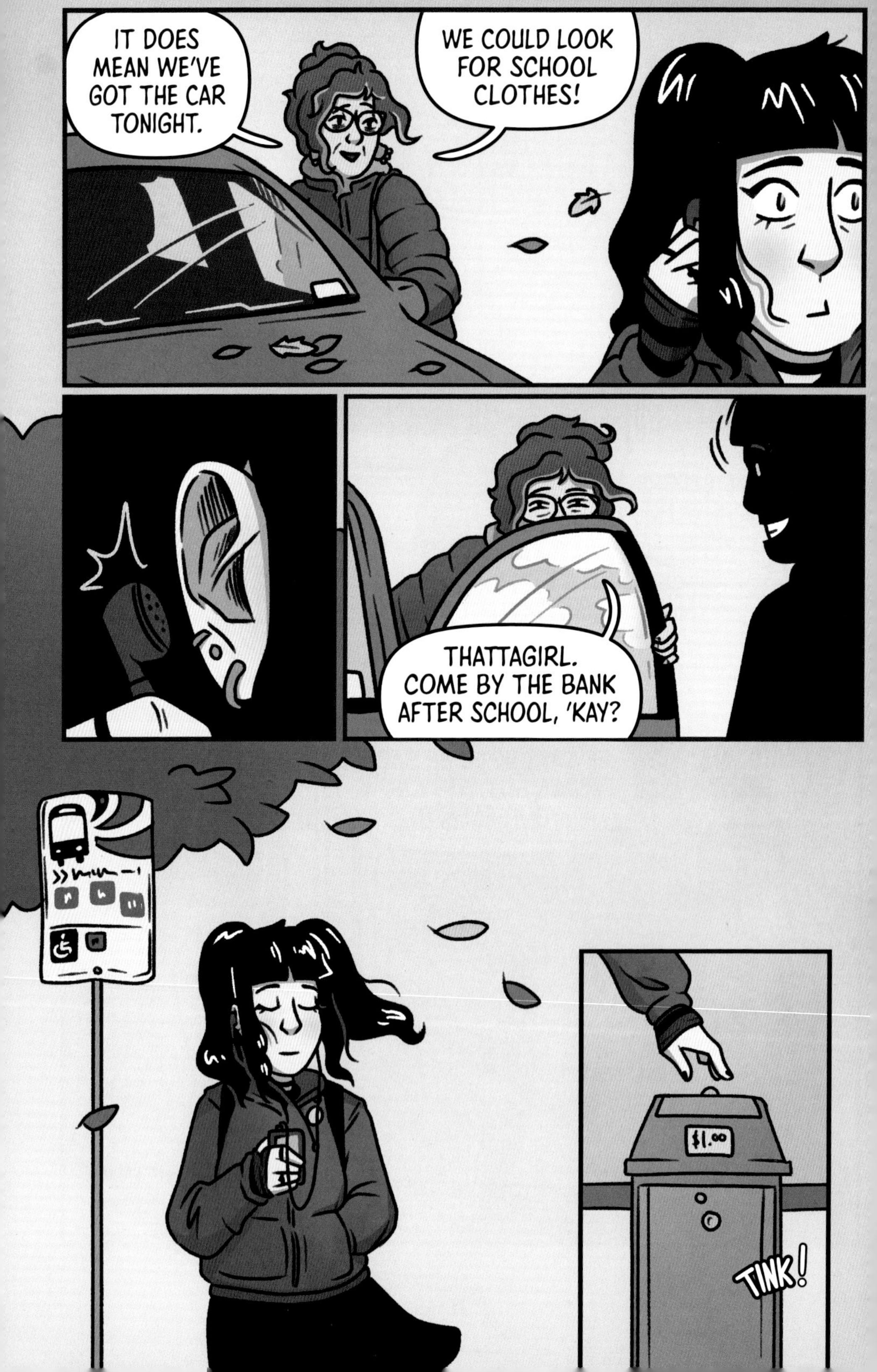
IT DOES MEAN WE'VE GOT THE CAR TONIGHT.
WE COULD LOOK FOR SCHOOL CLOTHES!
THATTAGIRL. COME BY THE BANK AFTER SCHOOL, 'KAY?
$1.00
TINK!

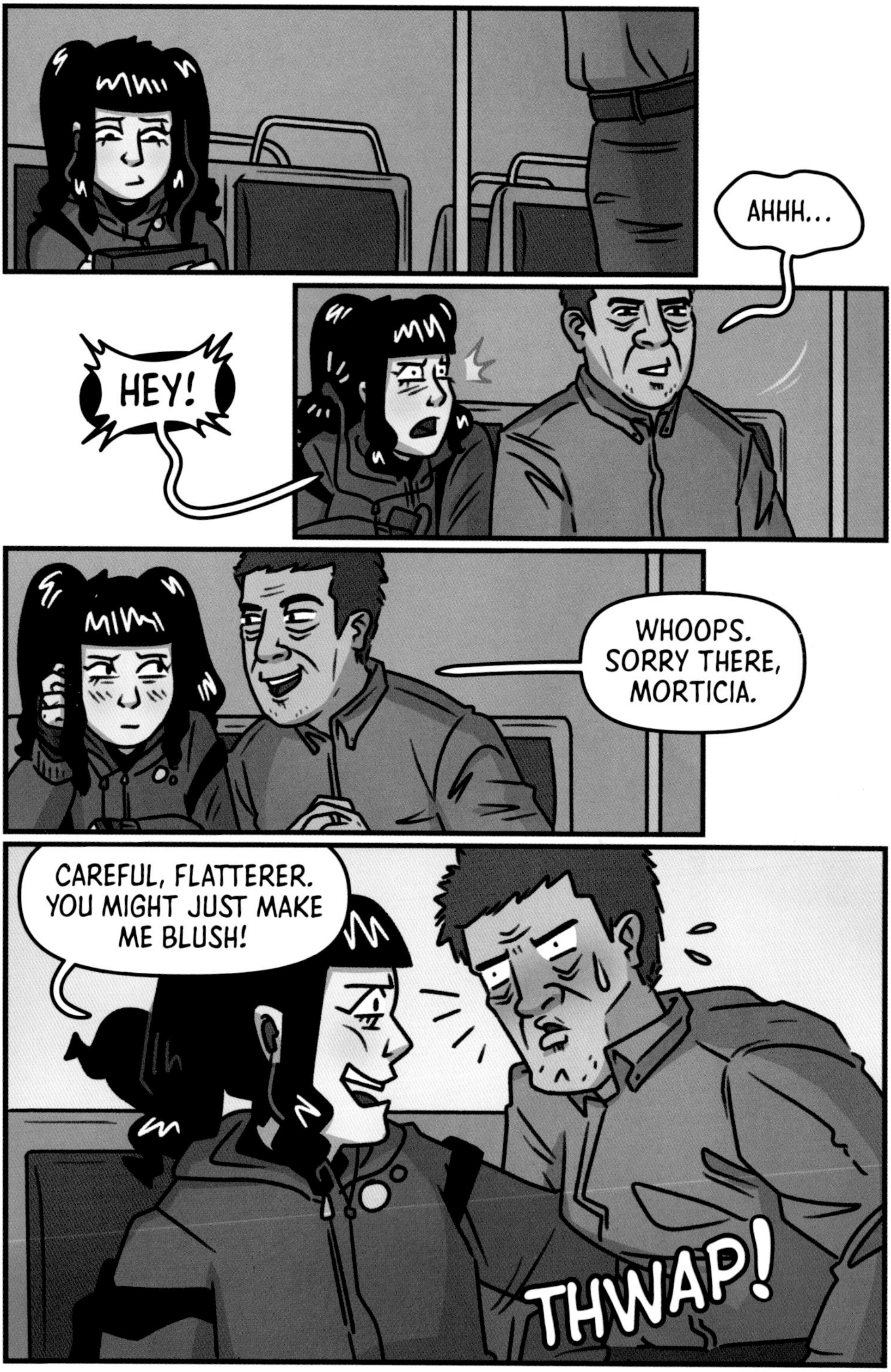
AHHH...
HEY!
WHOOPS. SORRY THERE, MORTICIA.
CAREFUL, FLATTERER. YOU MIGHT JUST MAKE ME BLUSH!
THWAP!

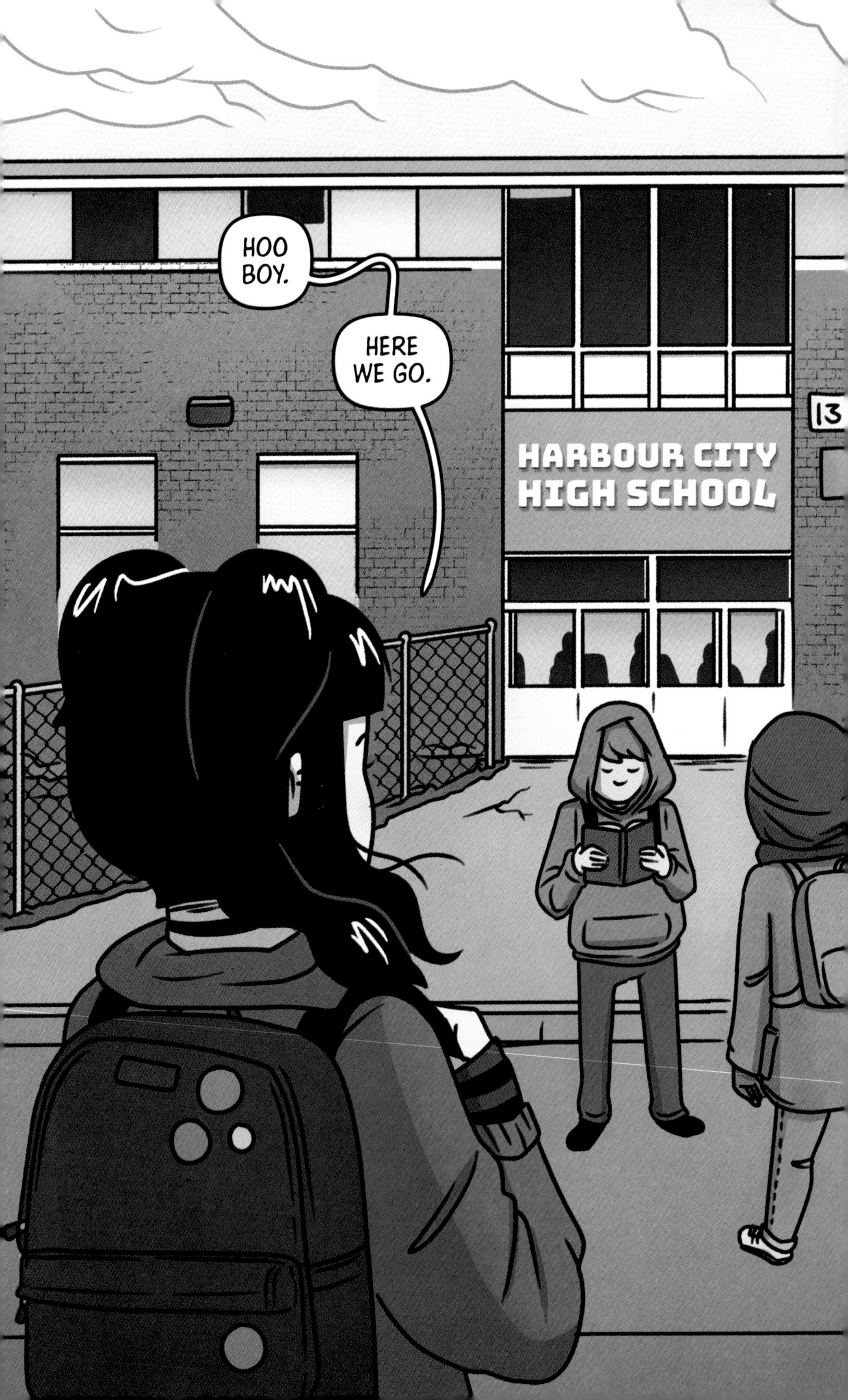
HOO BOY.
HERE WE GO.
13
HARBOUR CITY HIGH SCHOOL

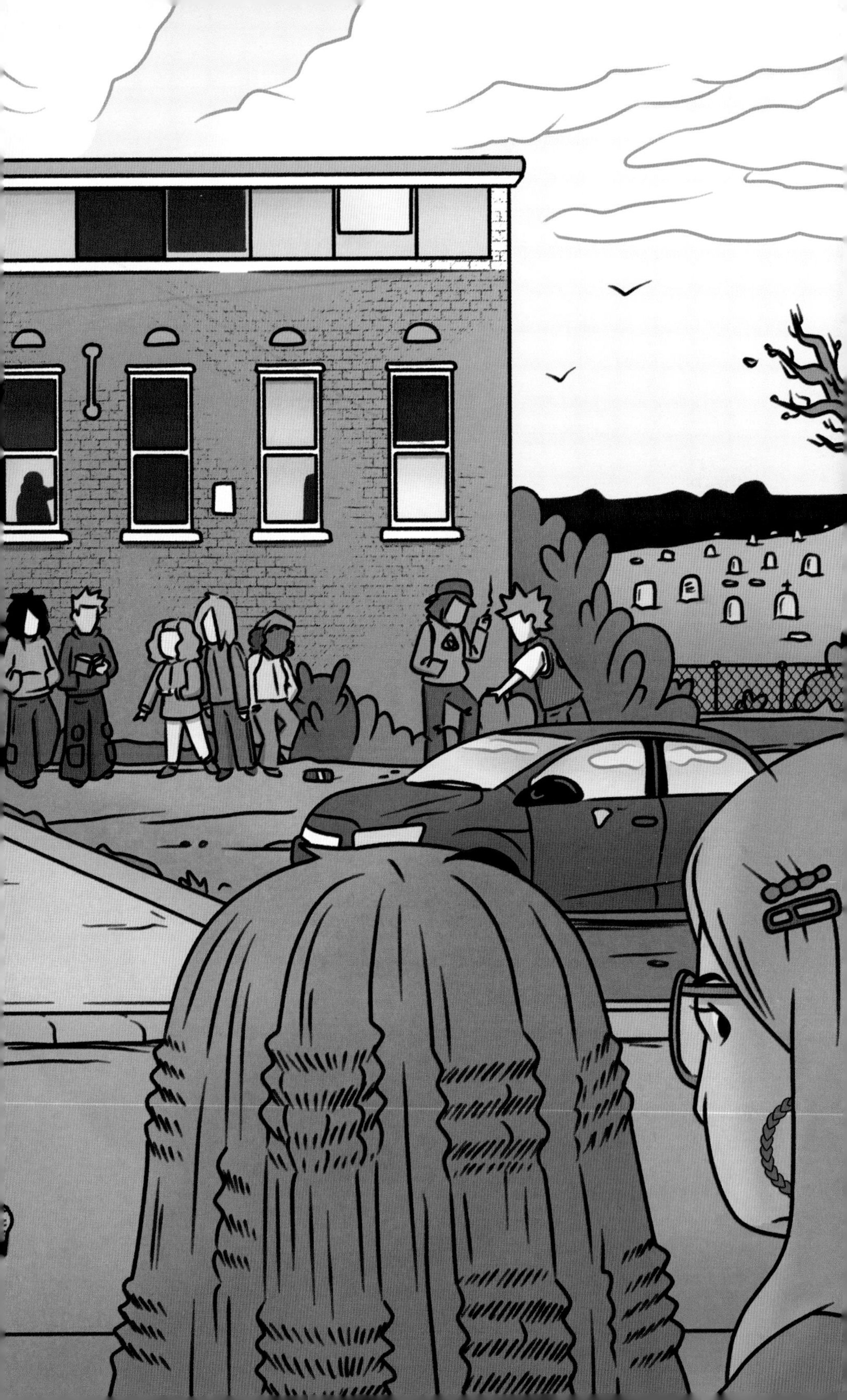

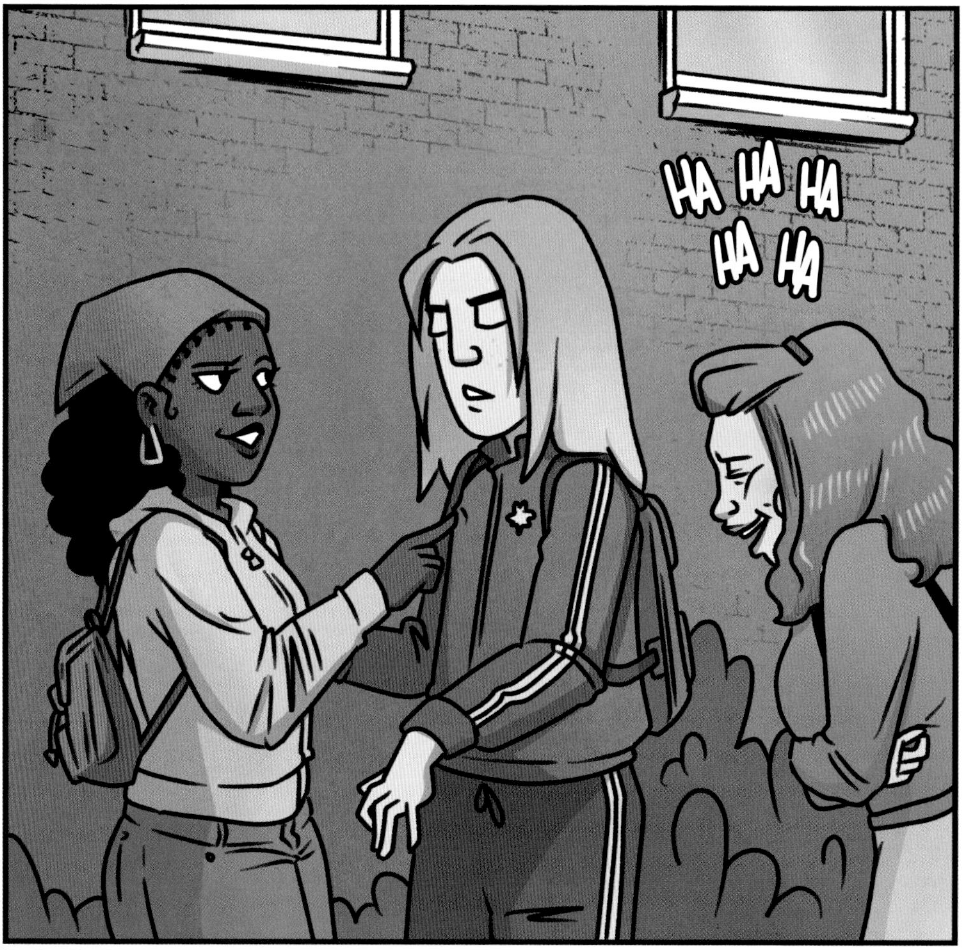
HA HA HA
HA HA

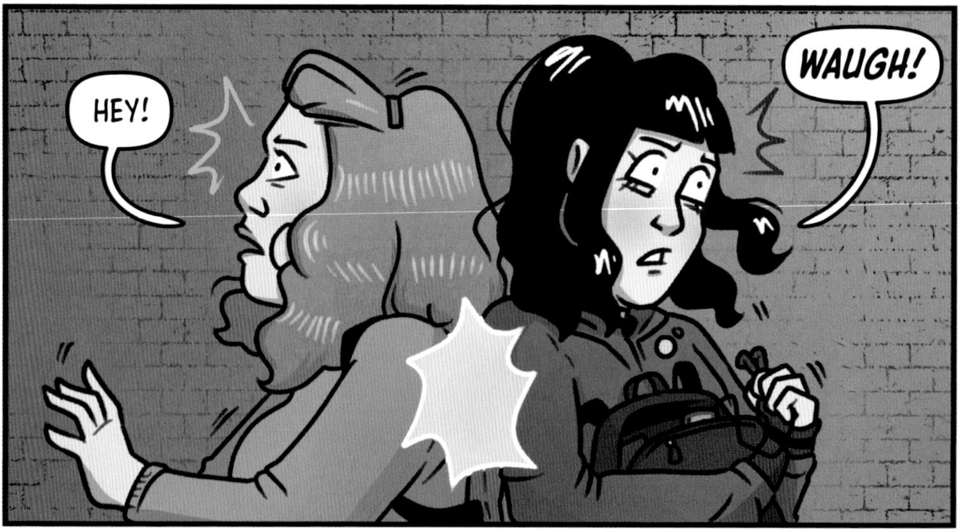
HEY!
WAUGH!

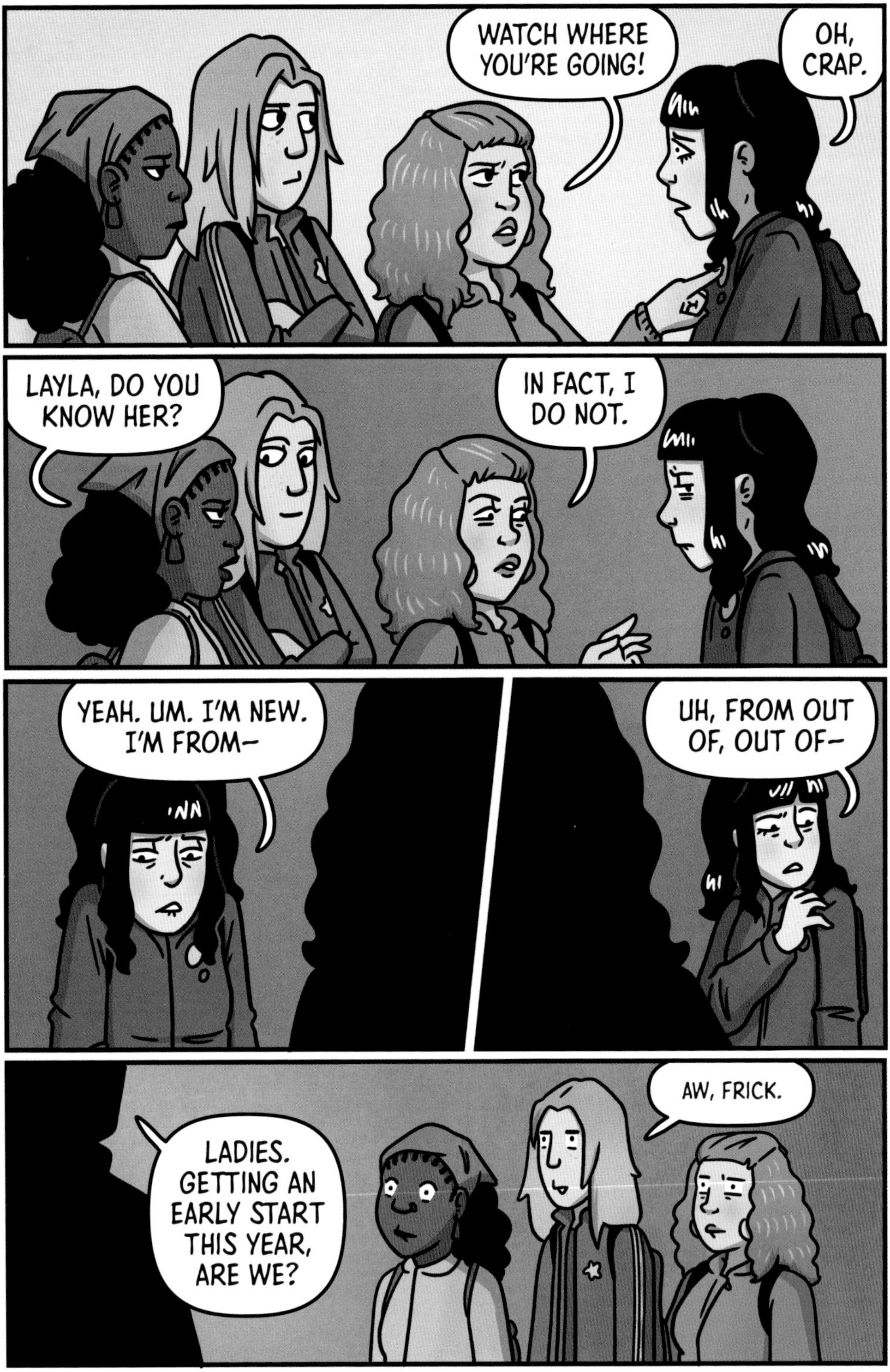
WATCH WHERE YOU'RE GOING!
OH, CRAP.
LAYLA, DO YOU KNOW HER?
IN FACT, I DO NOT.
YEAH. UM. I'M NEW. I'M FROM–
UH, FROM OUT OF, OUT OF–
LADIES. GETTING AN EARLY START THIS YEAR, ARE WE?
AW, FRICK.

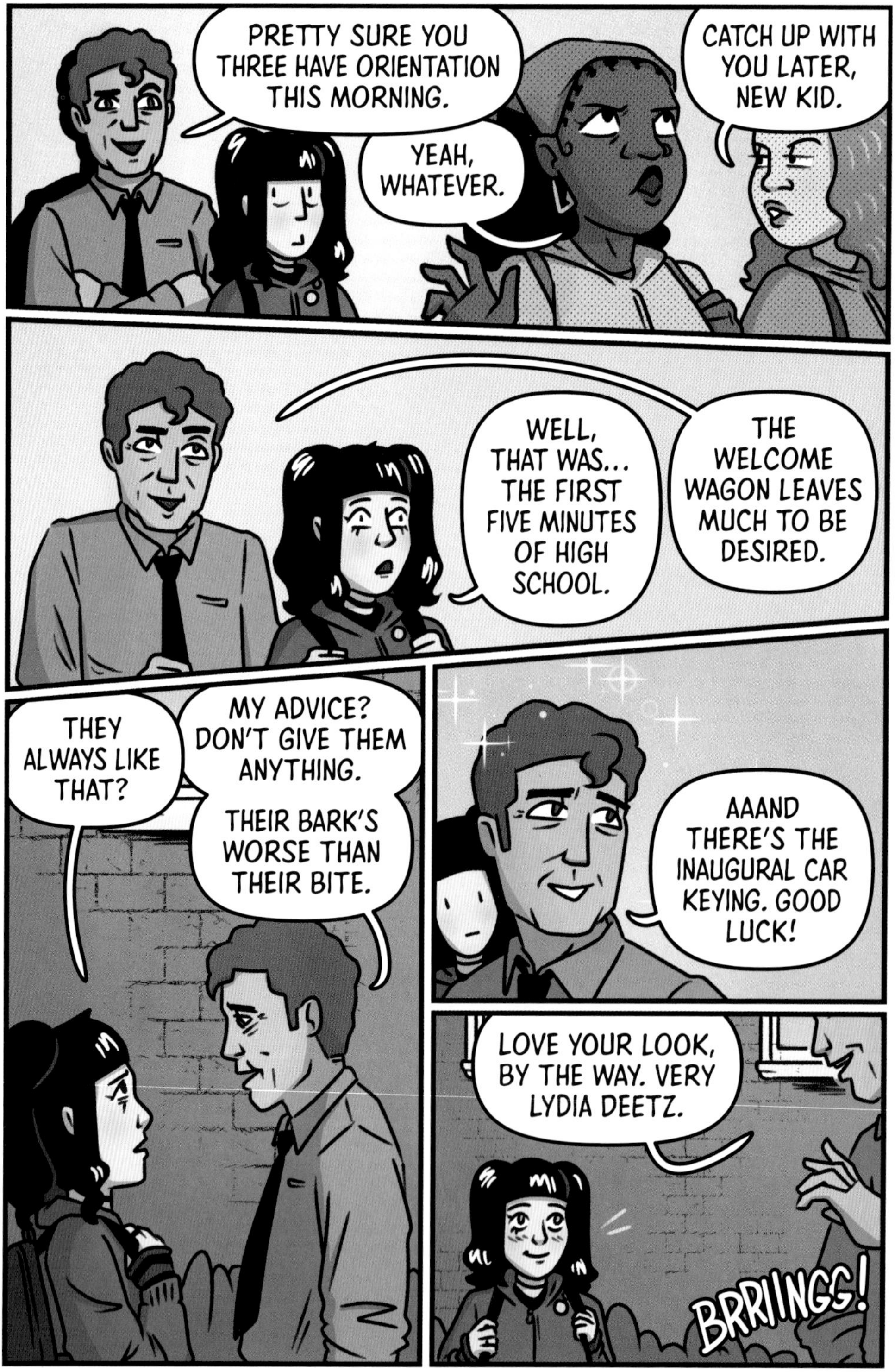
PRETTY SURE YOU THREE HAVE ORIENTATION THIS MORNING.
YEAH, WHATEVER.
CATCH UP WITH YOU LATER, NEW KID.
WELL, THAT WAS... THE FIRST FIVE MINUTES OF HIGH SCHOOL.
THE WELCOME WAGON LEAVES MUCH TO BE DESIRED.
THEY ALWAYS LIKE THAT?
MY ADVICE? DON'T GIVE THEM ANYTHING.
THEIR BARK'S WORSE THAN THEIR BITE.
AAAND THERE'S THE INAUGURAL CAR KEYING. GOOD LUCK!
LOVE YOUR LOOK, BY THE WAY. VERY LYDIA DEETZ.
BRRIINGG!

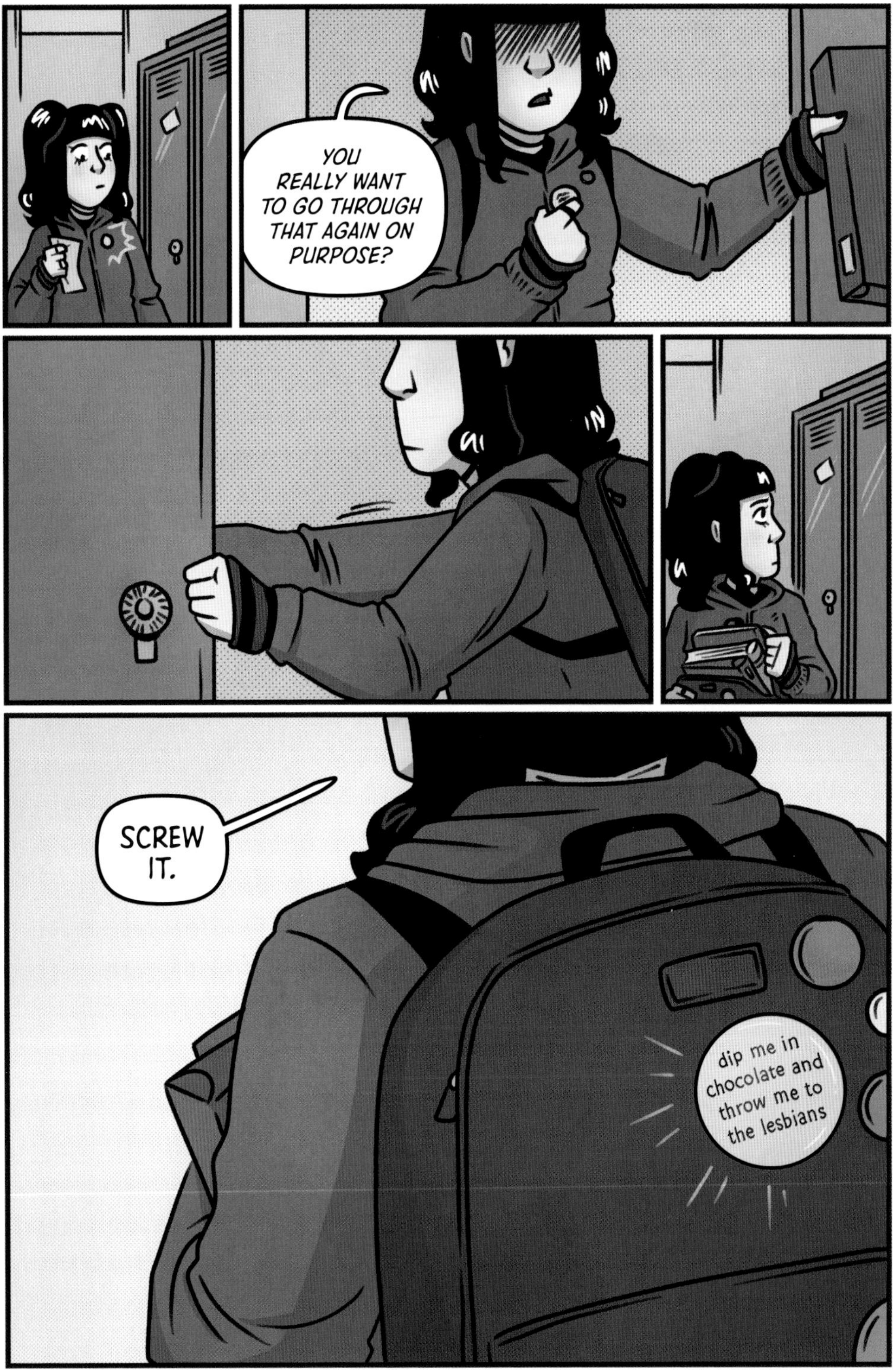
YOU REALLY WANT TO GO THROUGH THAT AGAIN ON PURPOSE?
SCREW IT.
dip me in chocolate and throw me to the lesbians

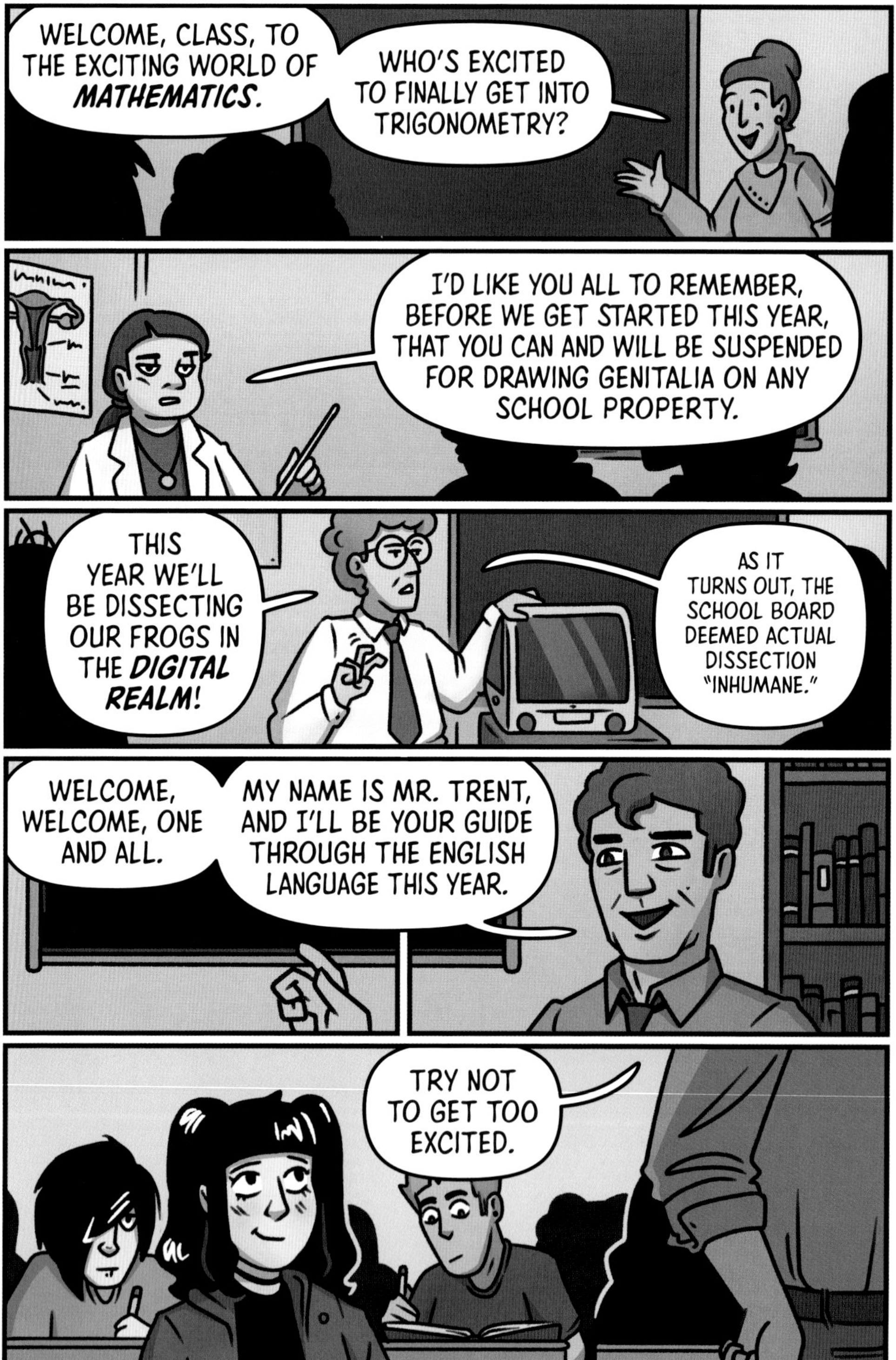
WELCOME, CLASS, TO THE EXCITING WORLD OF ***MATHEMATICS***.
WHO'S EXCITED TO FINALLY GET INTO TRIGONOMETRY?
I'D LIKE YOU ALL TO REMEMBER, BEFORE WE GET STARTED THIS YEAR, THAT YOU CAN AND WILL BE SUSPENDED FOR DRAWING GENITALIA ON ANY SCHOOL PROPERTY.
THIS YEAR WE'LL BE DISSECTING OUR FROGS IN THE ***DIGITAL REALM***!
AS IT TURNS OUT, THE SCHOOL BOARD DEEMED ACTUAL DISSECTION "INHUMANE."
WELCOME, WELCOME, ONE AND ALL.
MY NAME IS MR. TRENT, AND I'LL BE YOUR GUIDE THROUGH THE ENGLISH LANGUAGE THIS YEAR.
TRY NOT TO GET TOO EXCITED.

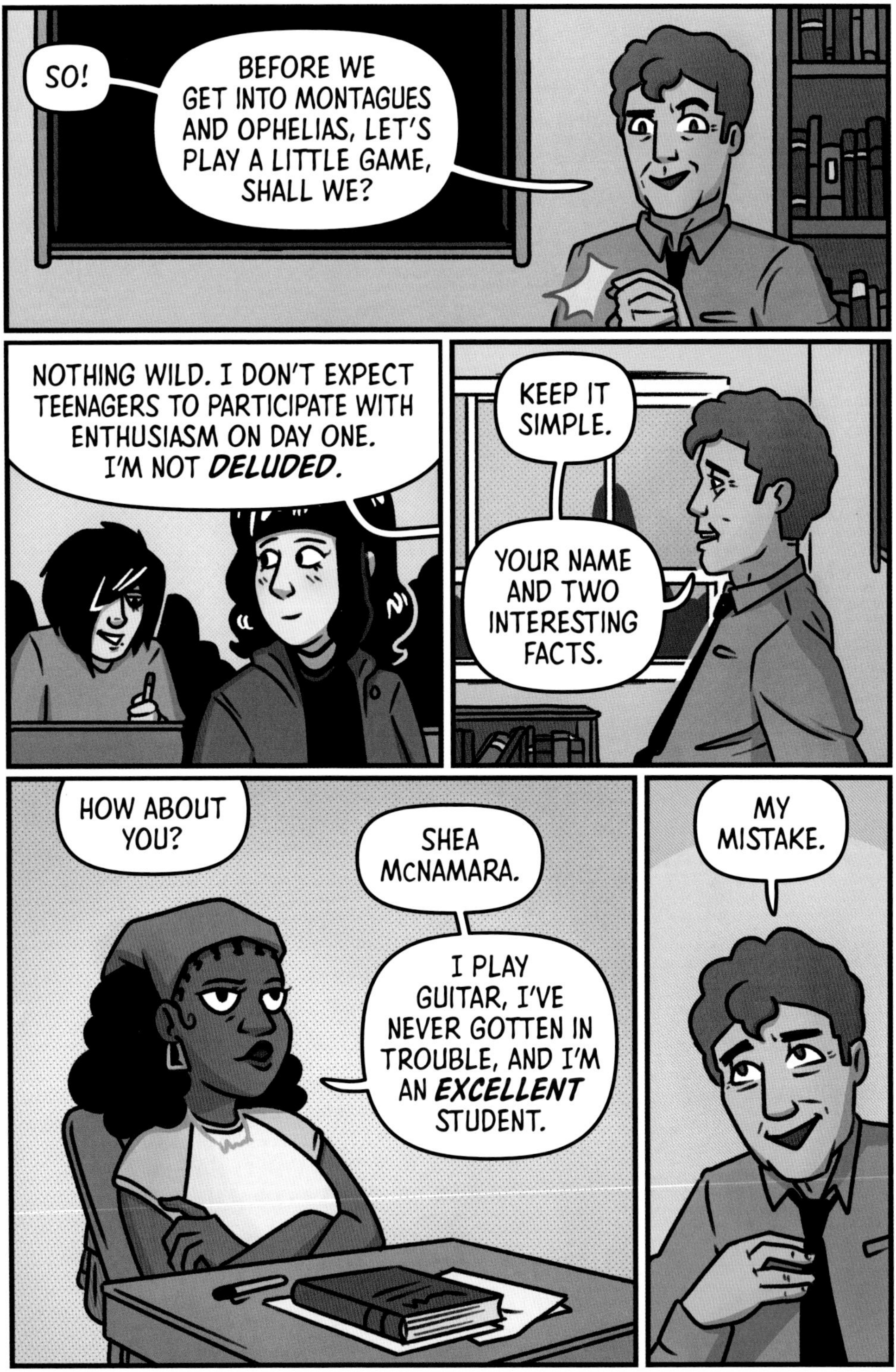
SO!
BEFORE WE GET INTO MONTAGUES AND OPHELIAS, LET'S PLAY A LITTLE GAME, SHALL WE?
NOTHING WILD. I DON'T EXPECT TEENAGERS TO PARTICIPATE WITH ENTHUSIASM ON DAY ONE. I'M NOT ***DELUDED.***
KEEP IT SIMPLE.
YOUR NAME AND TWO INTERESTING FACTS.
HOW ABOUT YOU?
SHEA McNAMARA.
I PLAY GUITAR, I'VE NEVER GOTTEN IN TROUBLE, AND I'M AN ***EXCELLENT*** STUDENT.
MY MISTAKE.

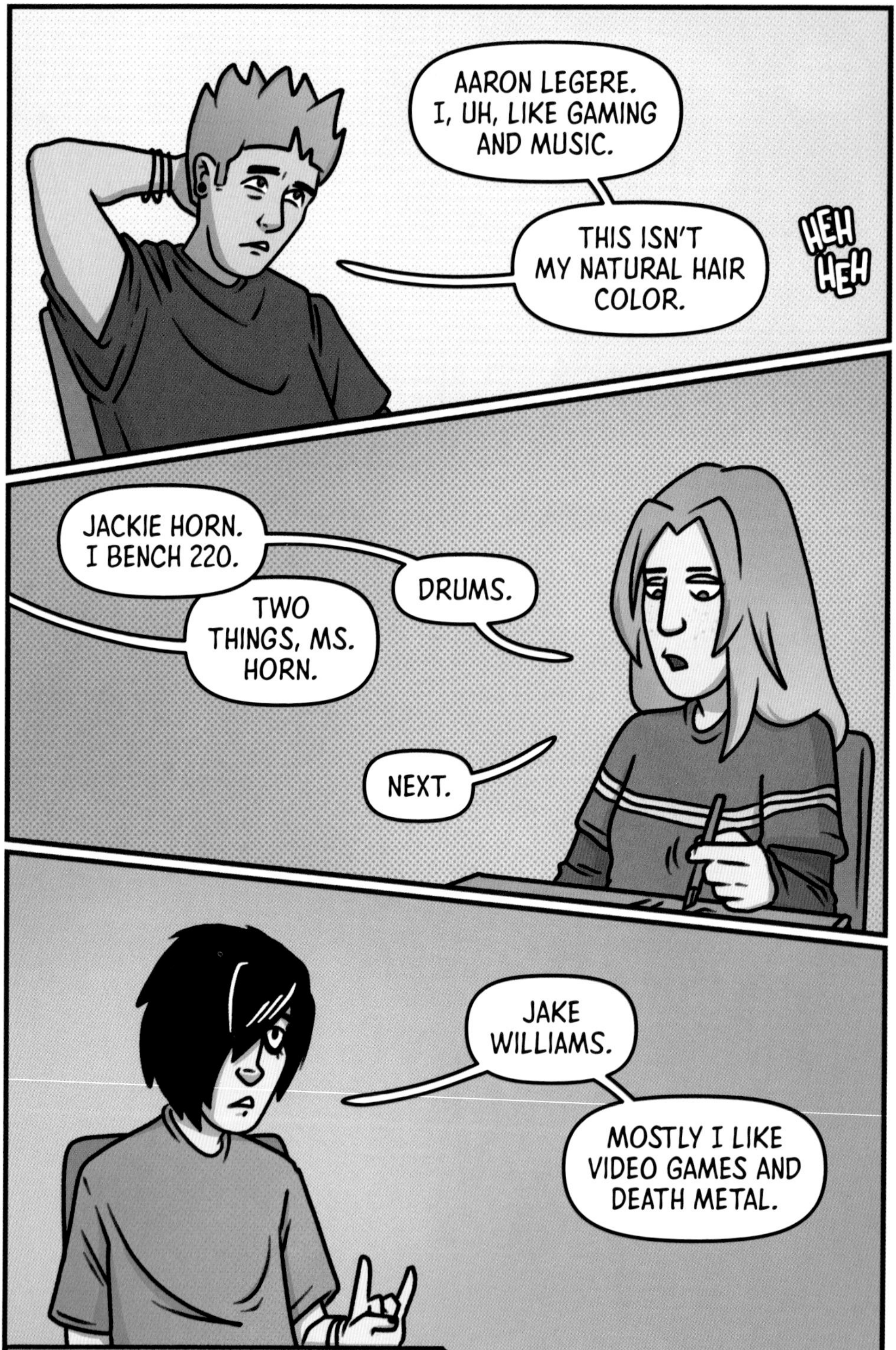
AARON LEGERE. I, UH, LIKE GAMING AND MUSIC.
THIS ISN'T MY NATURAL HAIR COLOR.
HEH HEH
JACKIE HORN. I BENCH 220.
DRUMS.
TWO THINGS, MS. HORN.
NEXT.
JAKE WILLIAMS.
MOSTLY I LIKE VIDEO GAMES AND DEATH METAL.

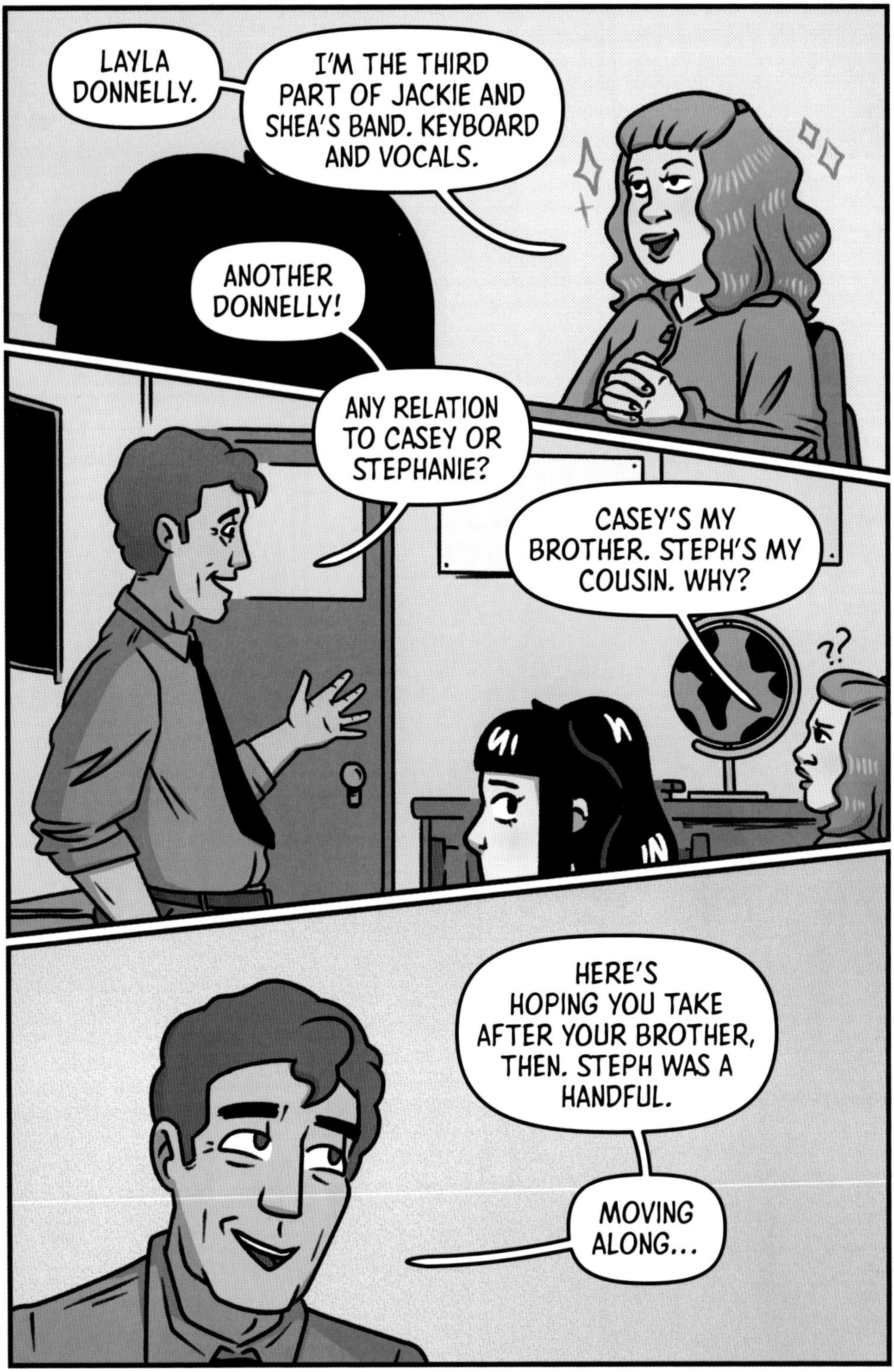
LAYLA DONNELLY.
I'M THE THIRD PART OF JACKIE AND SHEA'S BAND. KEYBOARD AND VOCALS.
ANOTHER DONNELLY!
ANY RELATION TO CASEY OR STEPHANIE?
CASEY'S MY BROTHER. STEPH'S MY COUSIN. WHY?
??
HERE'S HOPING YOU TAKE AFTER YOUR BROTHER, THEN. STEPH WAS A HANDFUL.
MOVING ALONG...

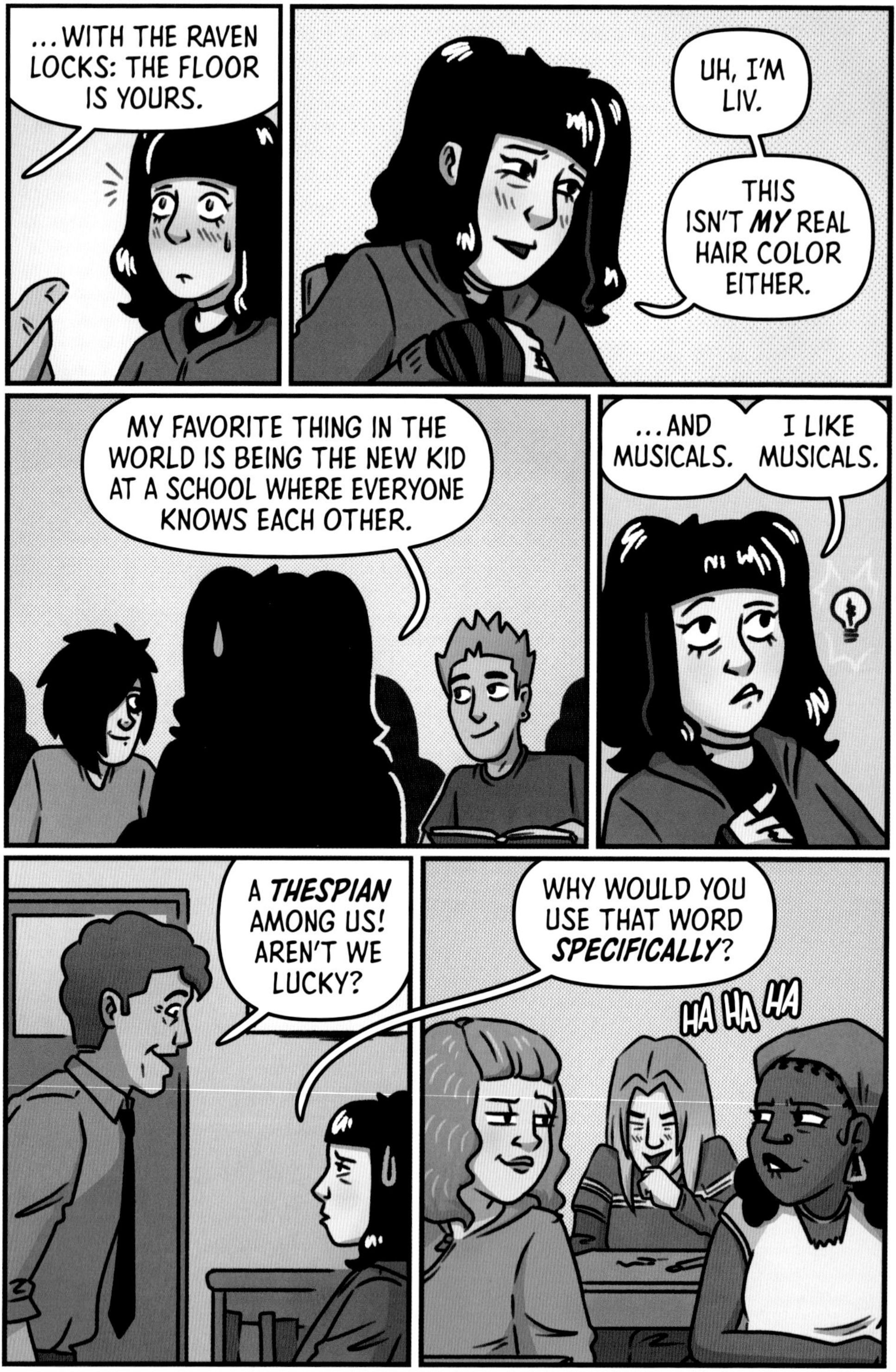
...WITH THE RAVEN LOCKS: THE FLOOR IS YOURS.
UH, I'M LIV.
THIS ISN'T *MY* REAL HAIR COLOR EITHER.
MY FAVORITE THING IN THE WORLD IS BEING THE NEW KID AT A SCHOOL WHERE EVERYONE KNOWS EACH OTHER.
...AND MUSICALS.
I LIKE MUSICALS.
A *THESPIAN* AMONG US! AREN'T WE LUCKY?
WHY WOULD YOU USE THAT WORD *SPECIFICALLY*?
HA HA HA

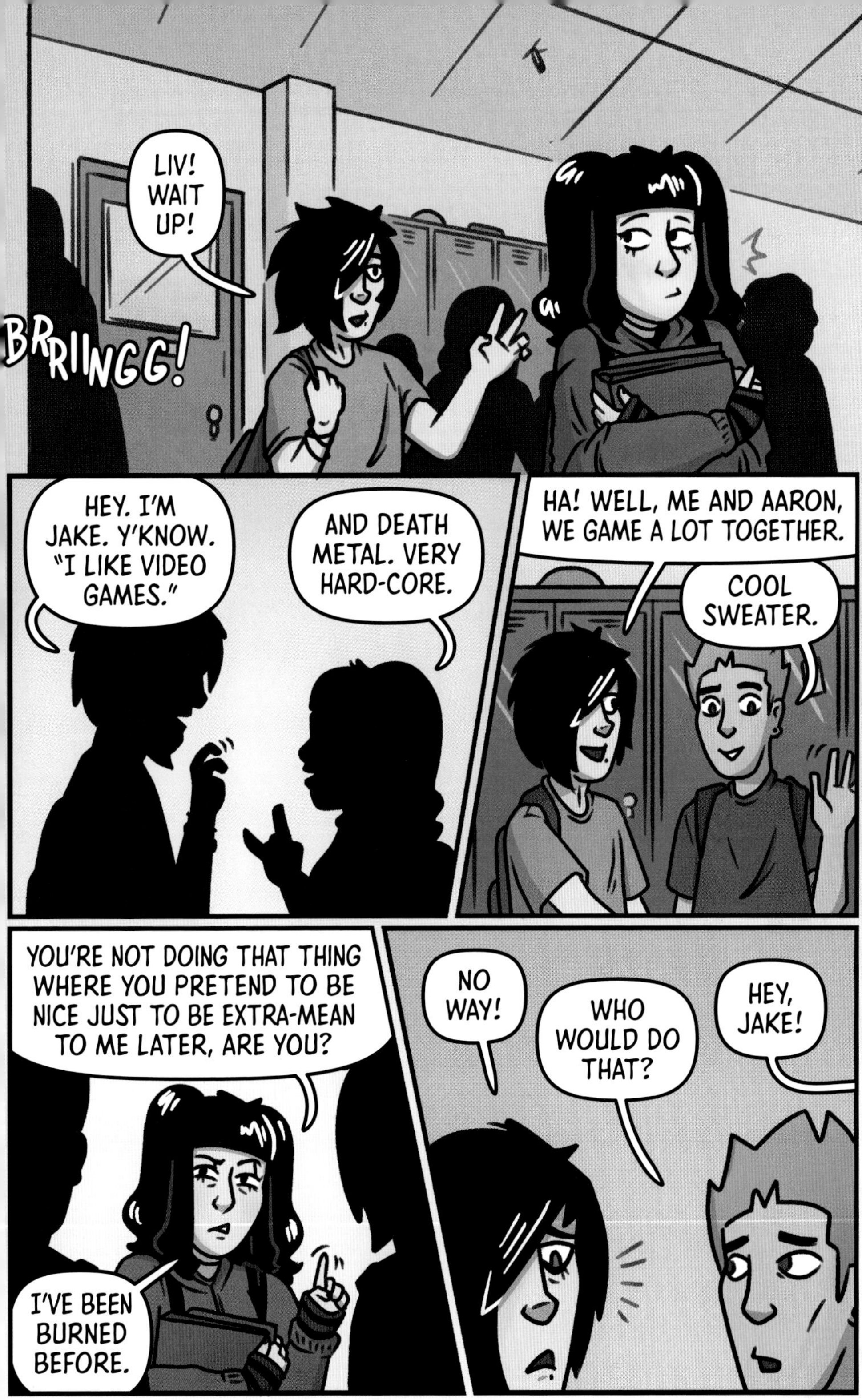
LIV! WAIT UP!
BRRIINGG!
HEY. I'M JAKE. Y'KNOW. "I LIKE VIDEO GAMES."
AND DEATH METAL. VERY HARD-CORE.
HA! WELL, ME AND AARON, WE GAME A LOT TOGETHER.
COOL SWEATER.
YOU'RE NOT DOING THAT THING WHERE YOU PRETEND TO BE NICE JUST TO BE EXTRA-MEAN TO ME LATER, ARE YOU?
I'VE BEEN BURNED BEFORE.
NO WAY!
WHO WOULD DO THAT?
HEY, JAKE!

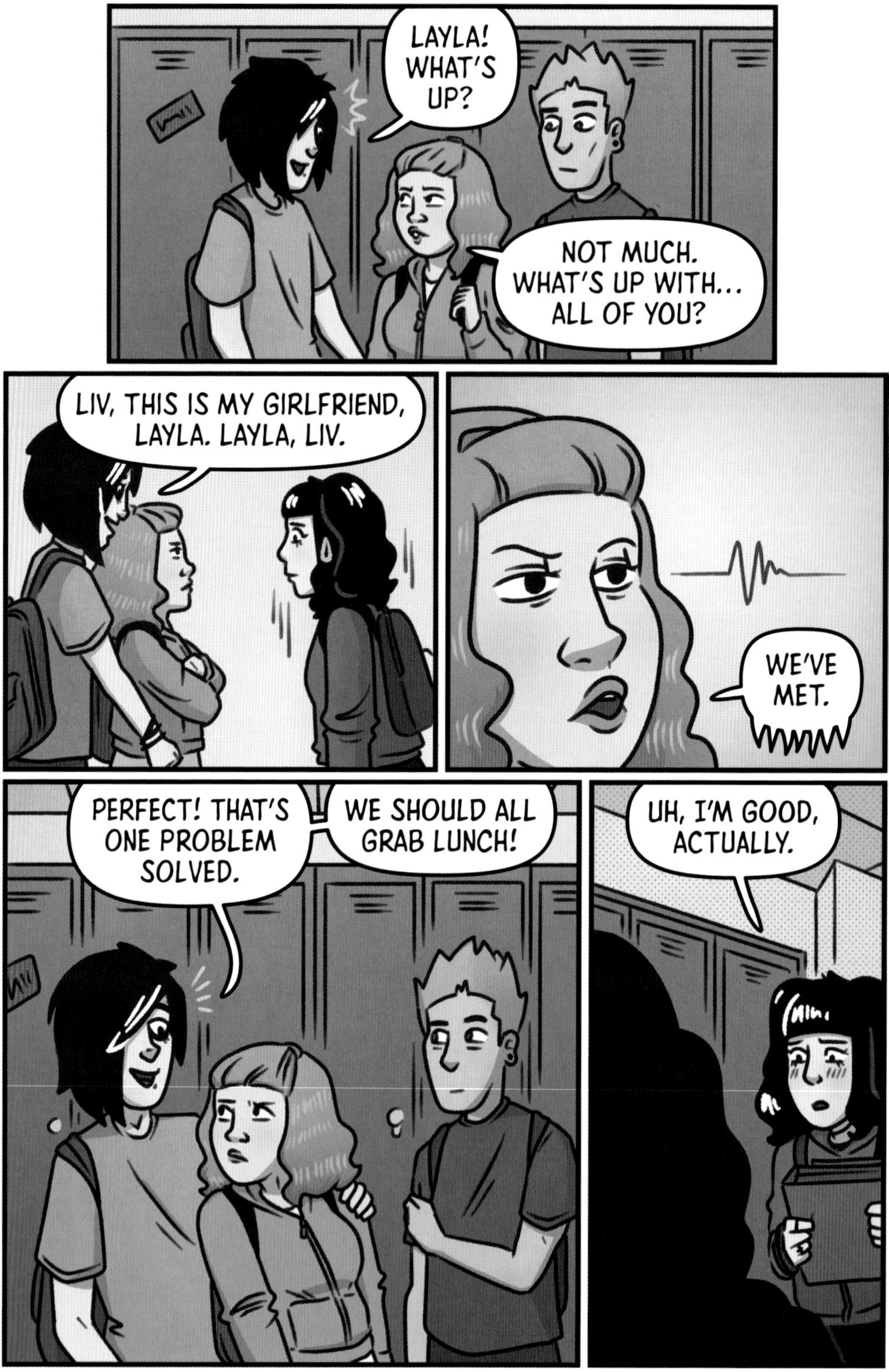
LAYLA! WHAT'S UP?
NOT MUCH. WHAT'S UP WITH... ALL OF YOU?
LIV, THIS IS MY GIRLFRIEND, LAYLA. LAYLA, LIV.
WE'VE MET.
PERFECT! THAT'S ONE PROBLEM SOLVED.
WE SHOULD ALL GRAB LUNCH!
UH, I'M GOOD, ACTUALLY.

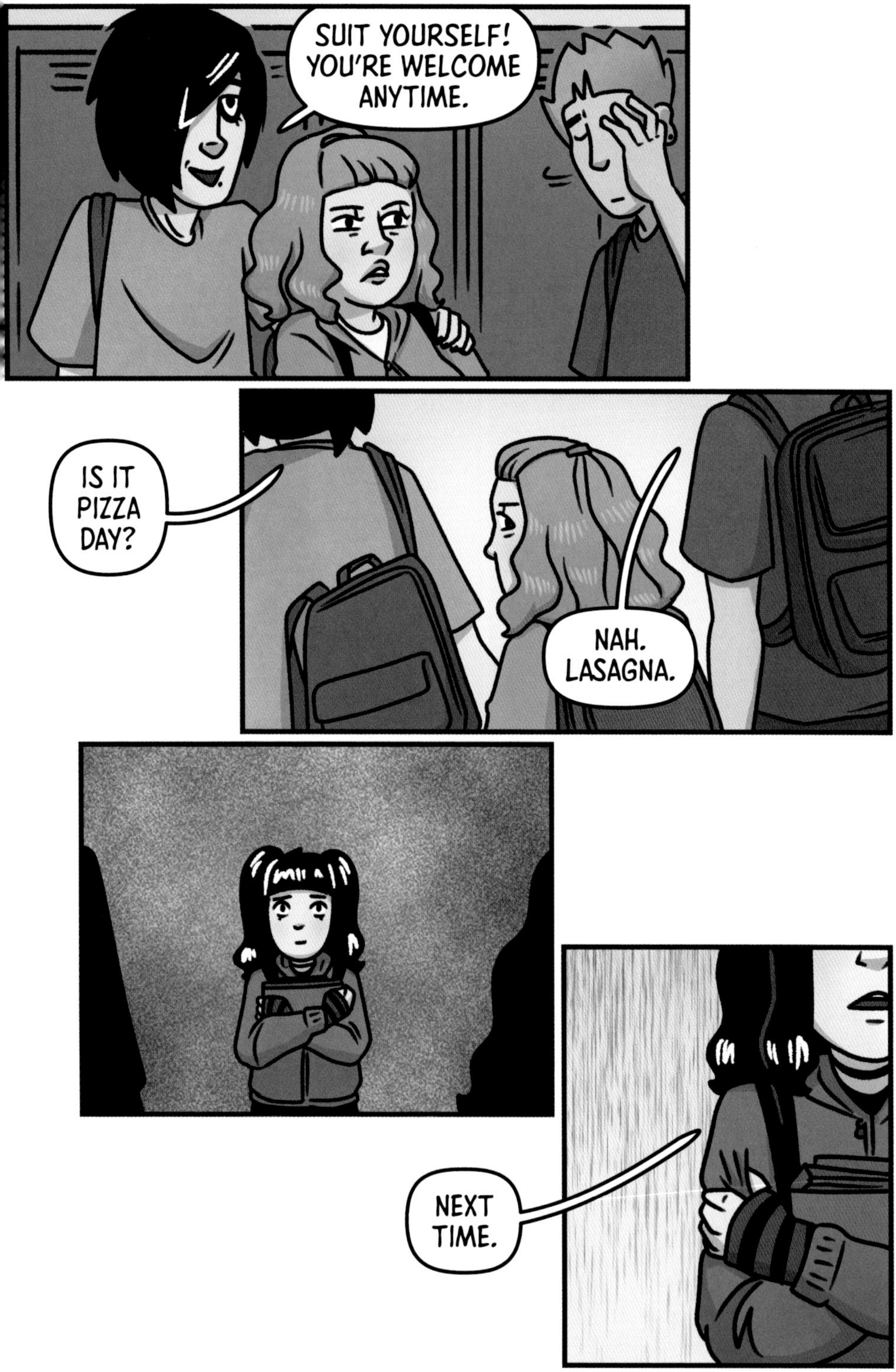
SUIT YOURSELF! YOU'RE WELCOME ANYTIME.
IS IT PIZZA DAY?
NAH. LASAGNA.
NEXT TIME.

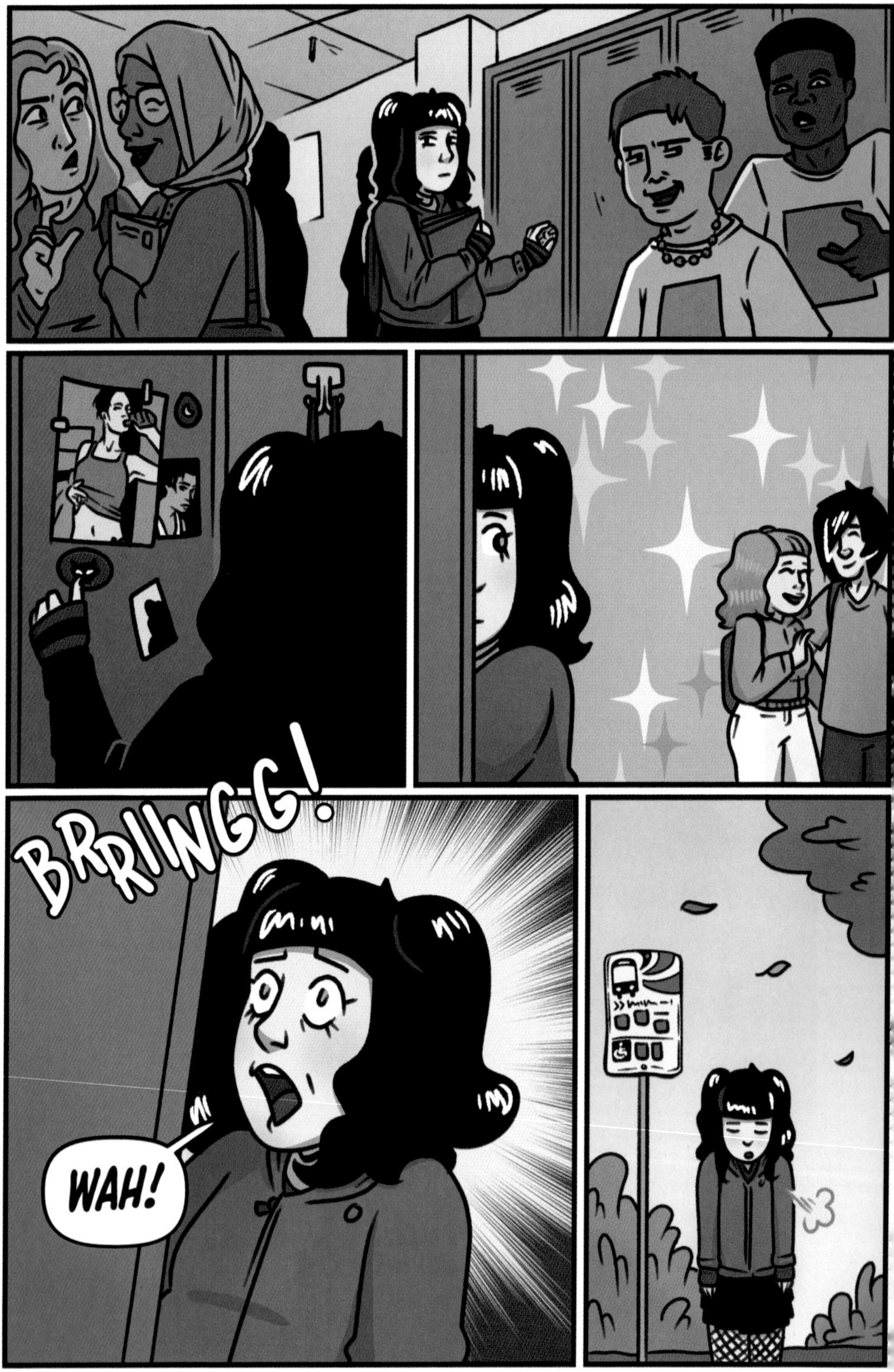
BRRIINGG!
WAH!

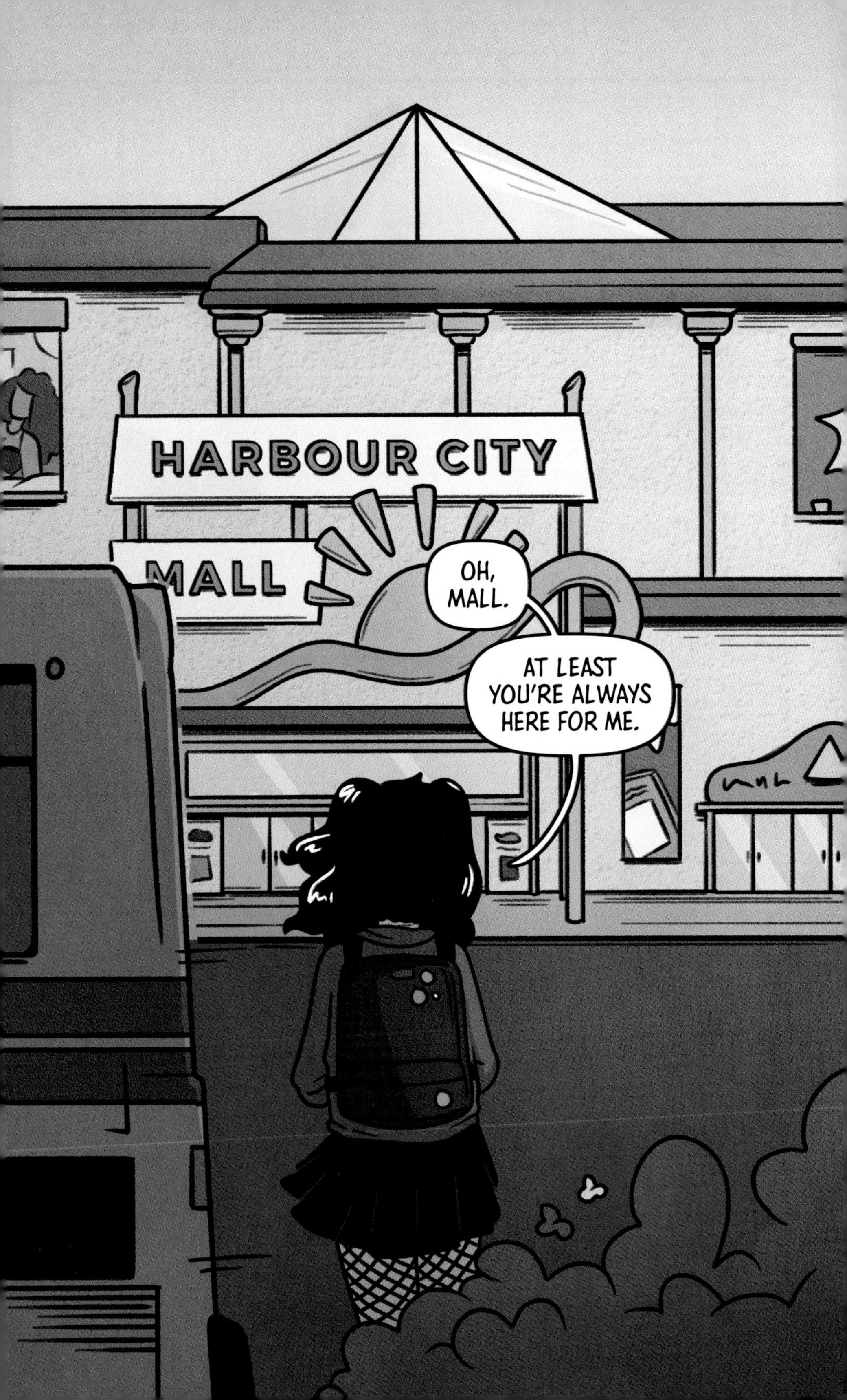
HARBOUR CITY
MALL
OH, MALL.
AT LEAST YOU'RE ALWAYS HERE FOR ME.

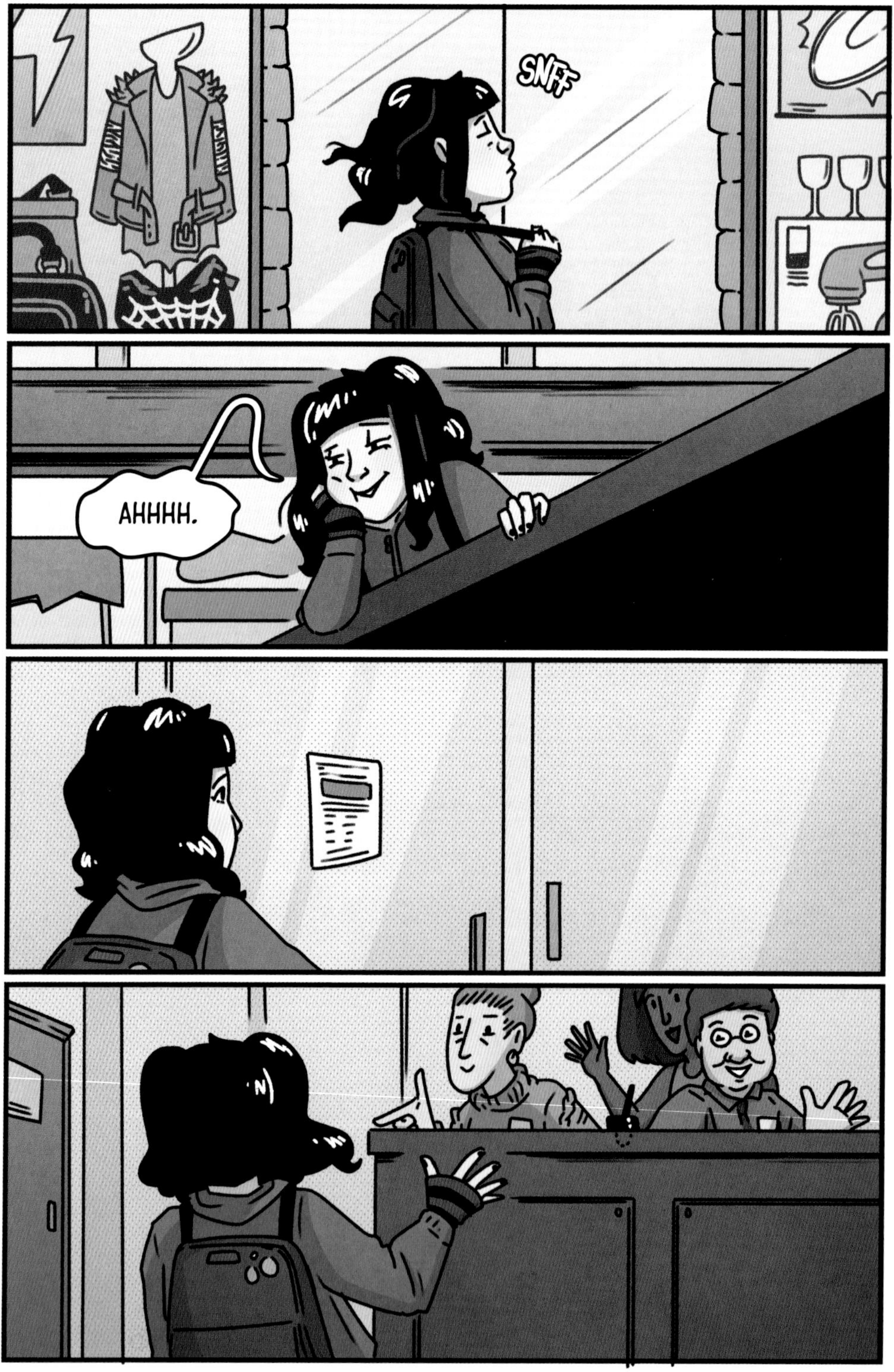
SNFF
AHHHH.

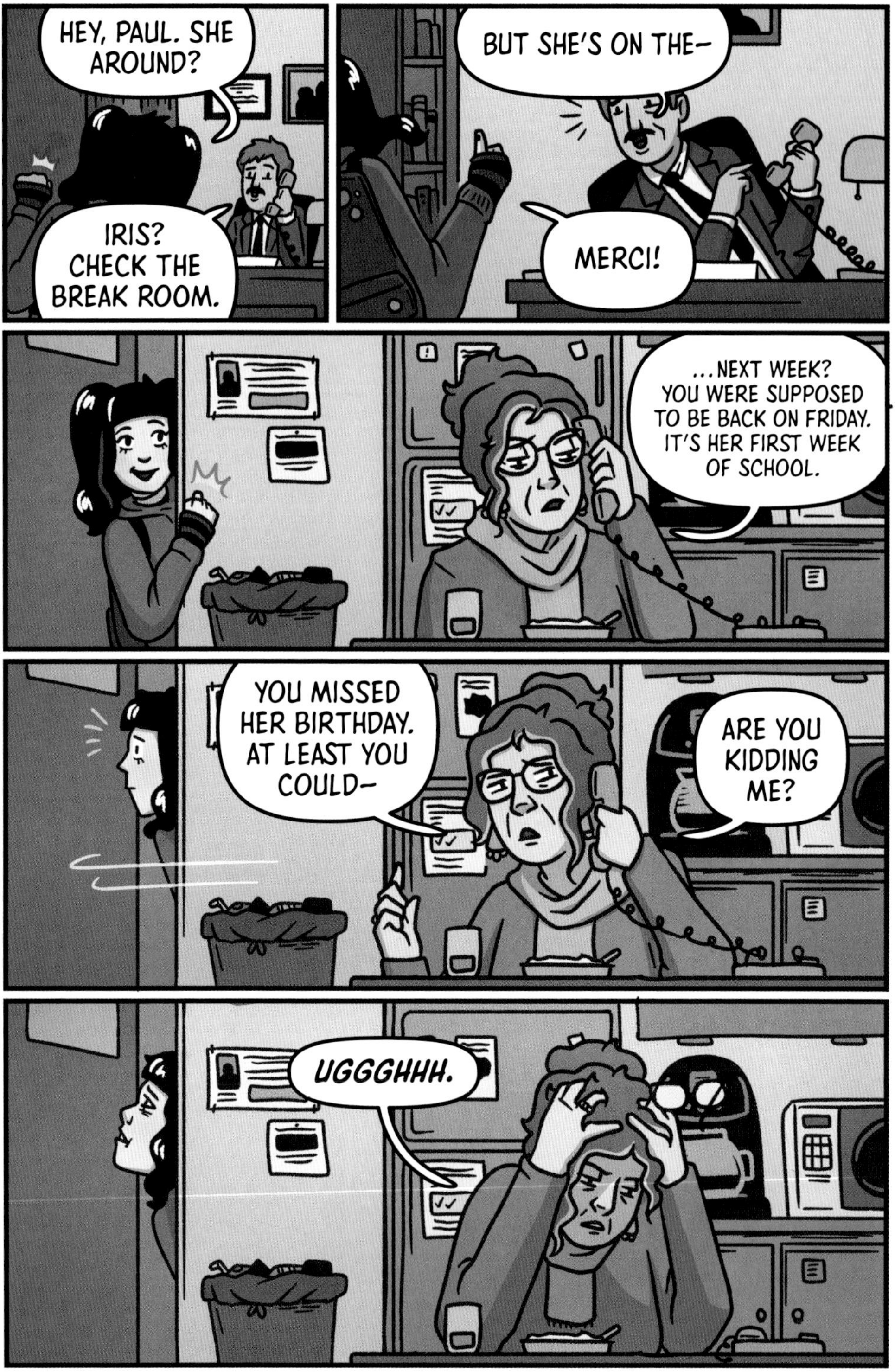
HEY, PAUL. SHE AROUND?
IRIS? CHECK THE BREAK ROOM.
BUT SHE'S ON THE–
MERCI!
...NEXT WEEK? YOU WERE SUPPOSED TO BE BACK ON FRIDAY. IT'S HER FIRST WEEK OF SCHOOL.
YOU MISSED HER BIRTHDAY. AT LEAST YOU COULD–
ARE YOU KIDDING ME?
UGGGHHH.

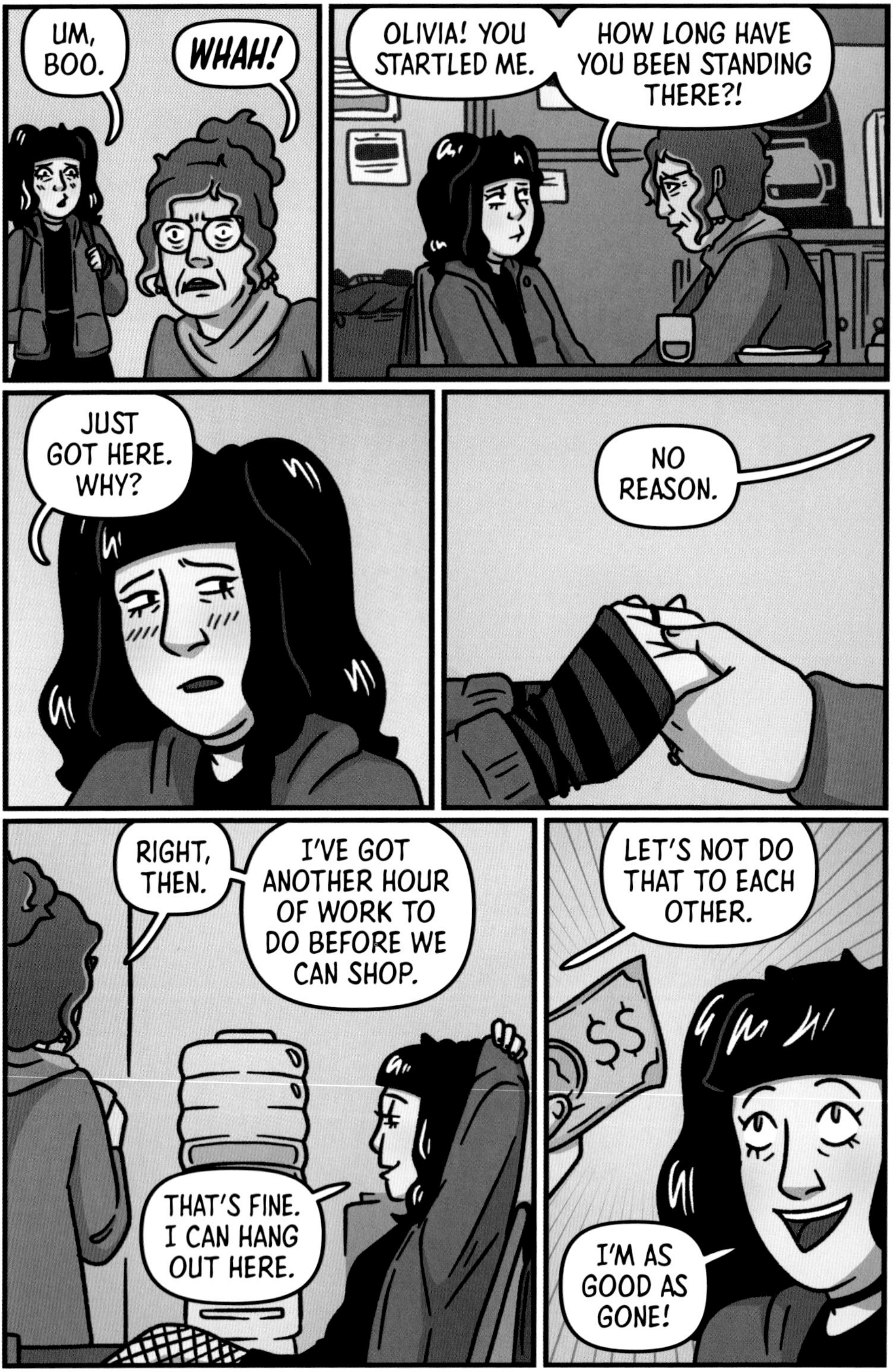
UM, BOO.
WHAH!
OLIVIA! YOU STARTLED ME.
HOW LONG HAVE YOU BEEN STANDING THERE?!
JUST GOT HERE. WHY?
NO REASON.
RIGHT, THEN.
I'VE GOT ANOTHER HOUR OF WORK TO DO BEFORE WE CAN SHOP.
THAT'S FINE. I CAN HANG OUT HERE.
LET'S NOT DO THAT TO EACH OTHER.
$$
I'M AS GOOD AS GONE!

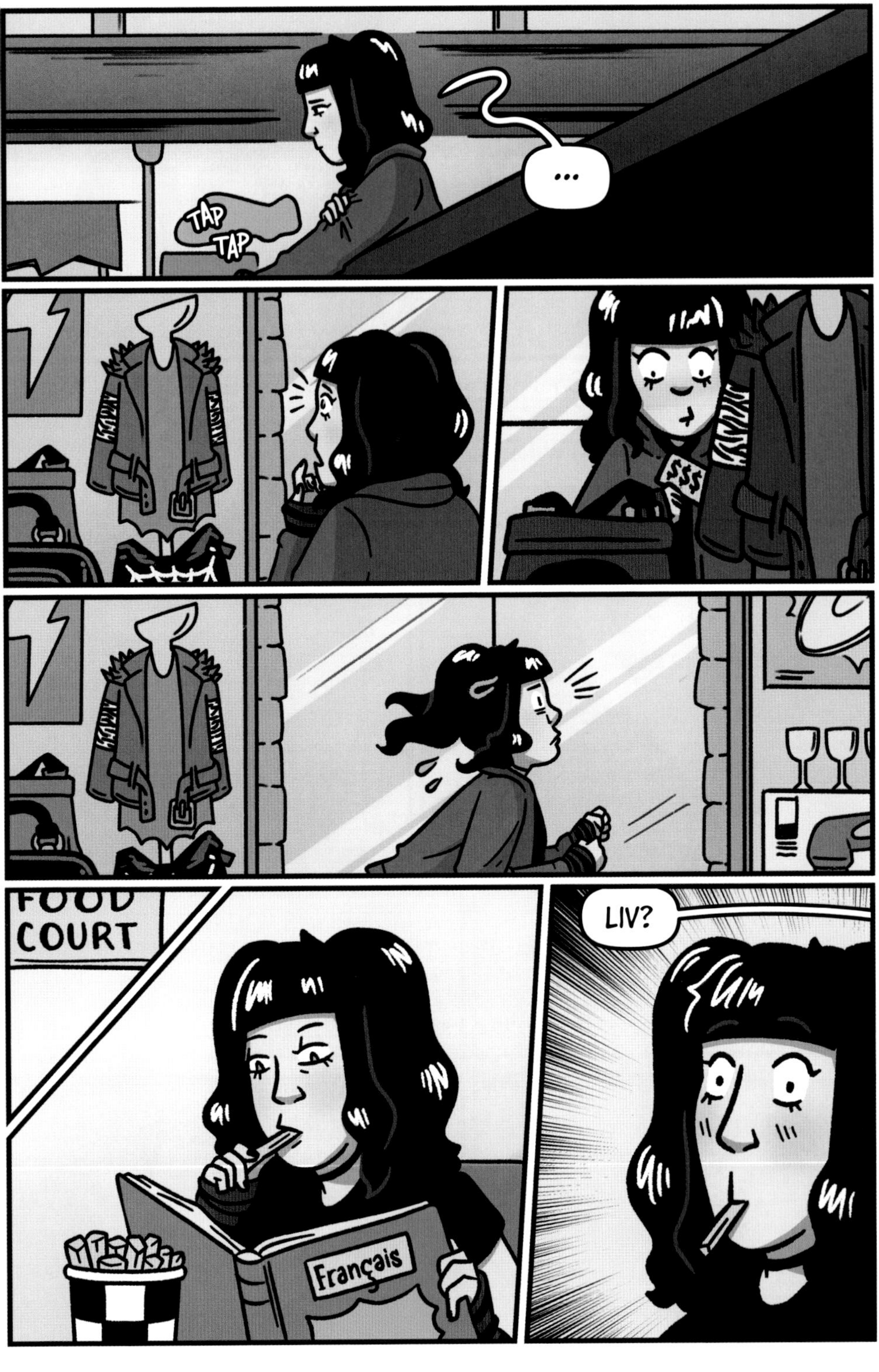
...
TAP
TAP
$$$
FOOD
COURT
Français
LIV?

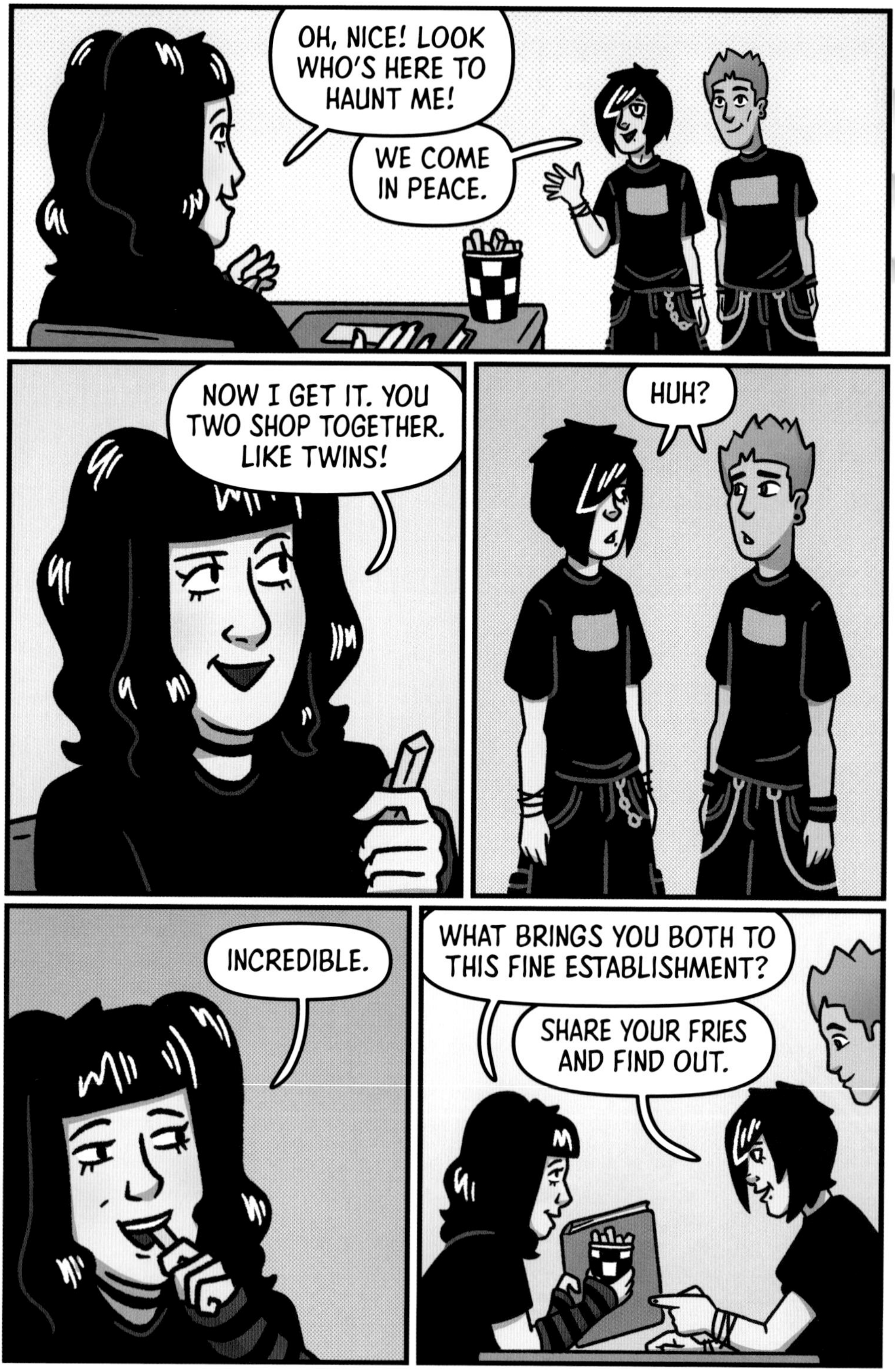
OH, NICE! LOOK WHO'S HERE TO HAUNT ME!
WE COME IN PEACE.
NOW I GET IT. YOU TWO SHOP TOGETHER. LIKE TWINS!
HUH?
INCREDIBLE.
WHAT BRINGS YOU BOTH TO THIS FINE ESTABLISHMENT?
SHARE YOUR FRIES AND FIND OUT.

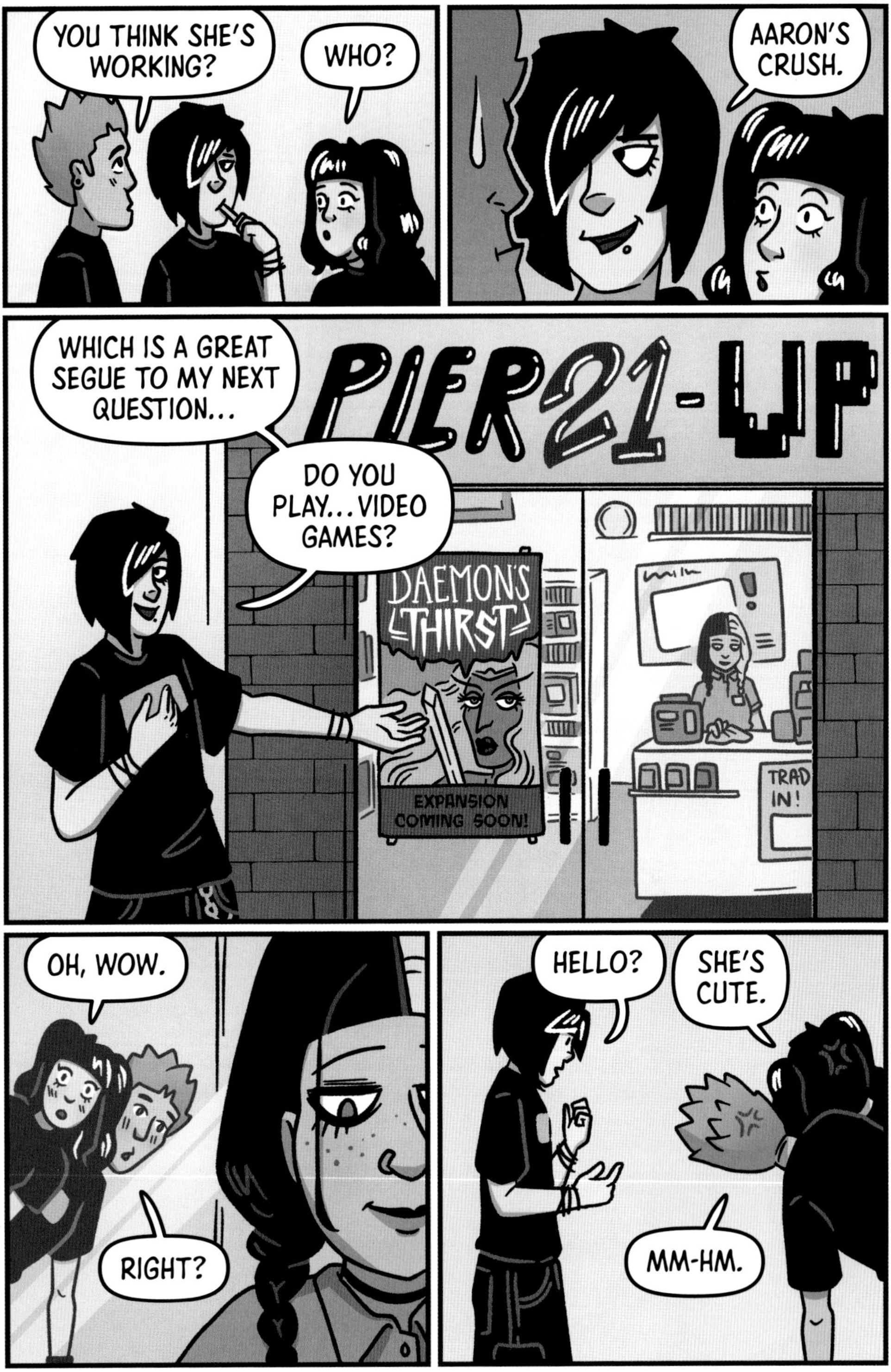
YOU THINK SHE'S WORKING?
WHO?
AARON'S CRUSH.
WHICH IS A GREAT SEGUE TO MY NEXT QUESTION...
PIER 21-UP
DO YOU PLAY... VIDEO GAMES?
DAEMON'S THIRST
EXPANSION COMING SOON!
TRAD IN!
OH, WOW.
RIGHT?
HELLO?
SHE'S CUTE.
MM-HM.

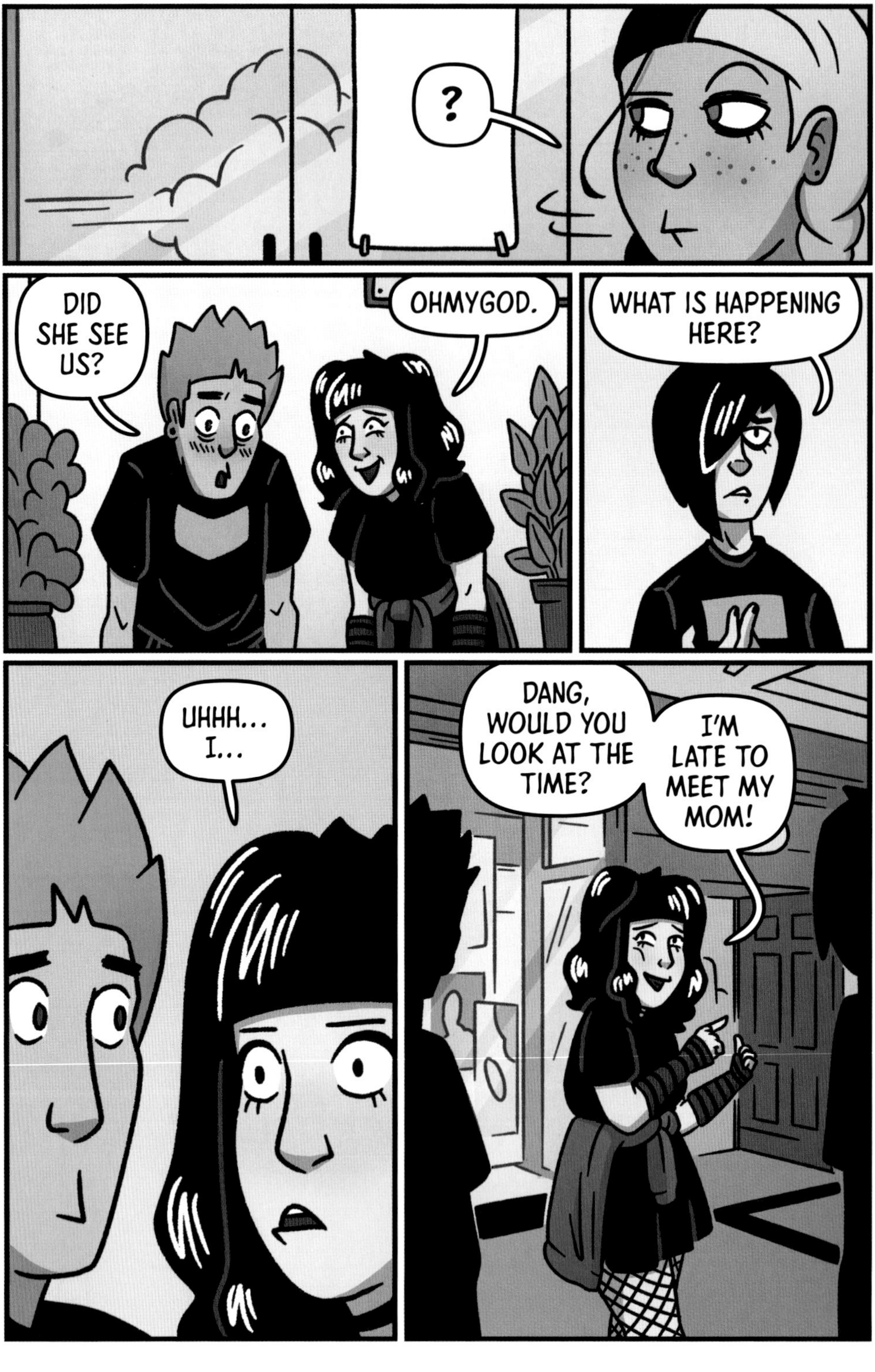
?
DID SHE SEE US?
OHMYGOD.
WHAT IS HAPPENING HERE?
UHHH... I...
DANG, WOULD YOU LOOK AT THE TIME?
I'M LATE TO MEET MY MOM!

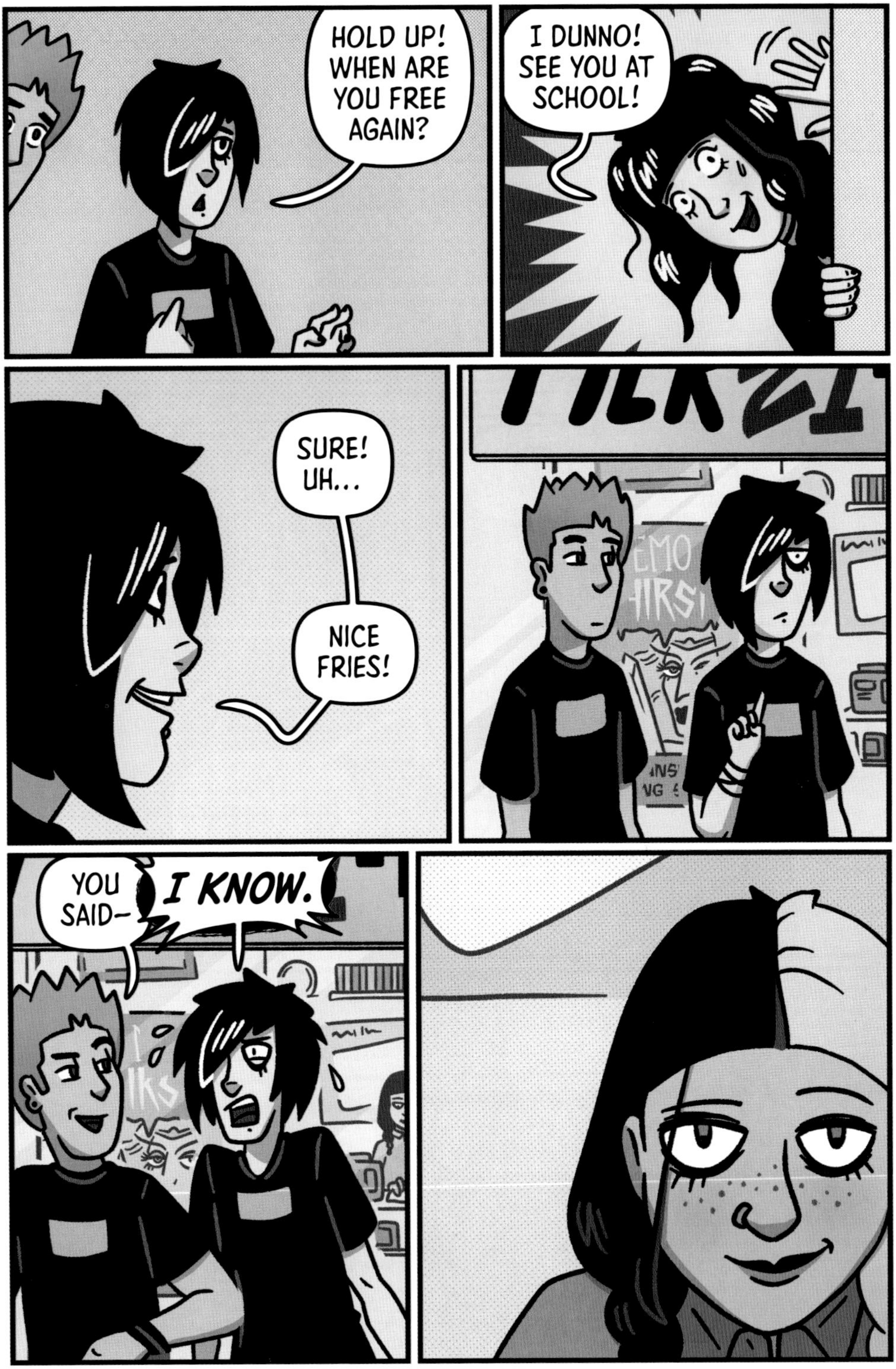
HOLD UP! WHEN ARE YOU FREE AGAIN?
I DUNNO! SEE YOU AT SCHOOL!
SURE! UH...
NICE FRIES!
YOU SAID–
I KNOW.

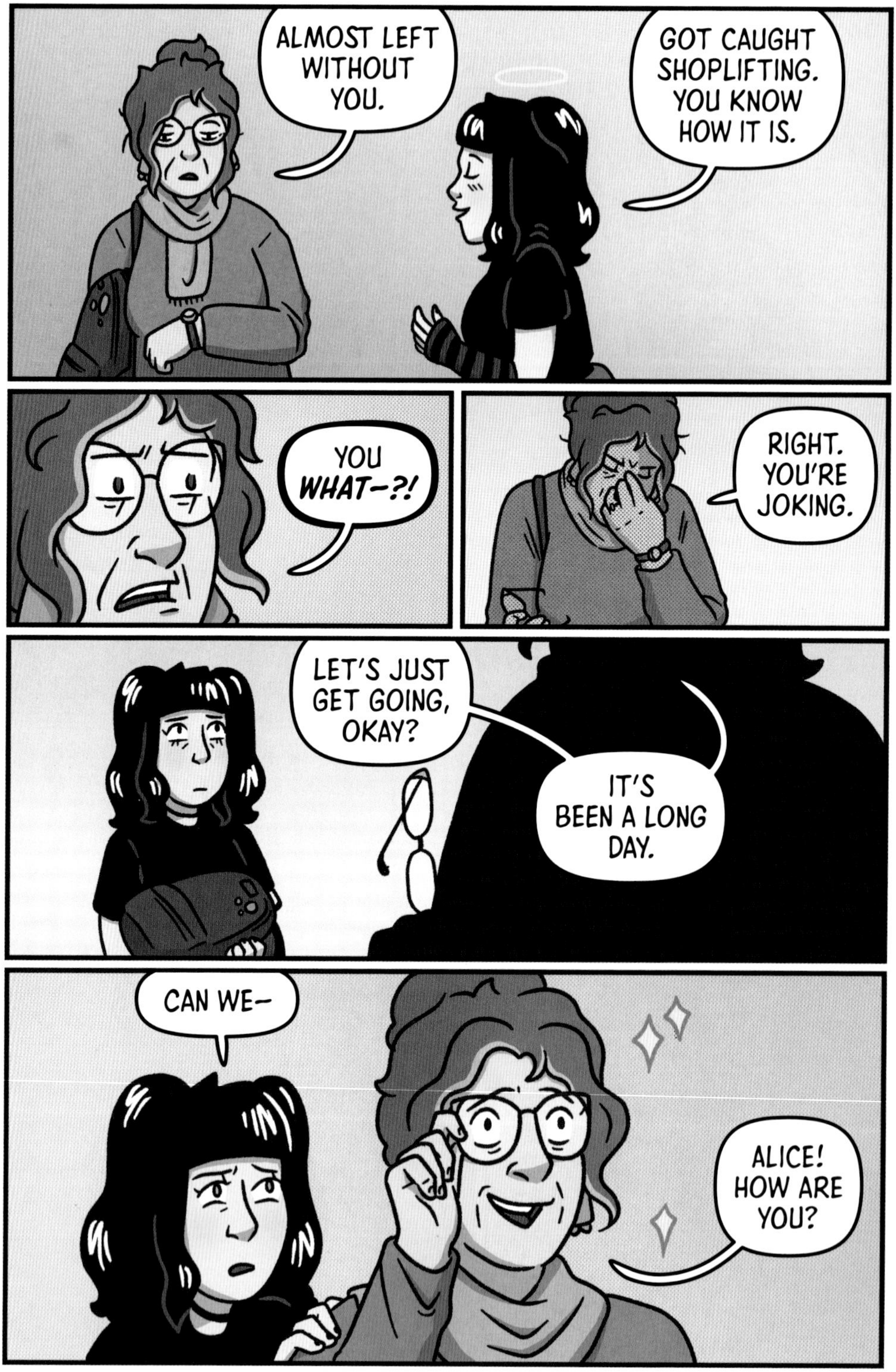
ALMOST LEFT WITHOUT YOU.
GOT CAUGHT SHOPLIFTING. YOU KNOW HOW IT IS.
YOU *WHAT*–?!
RIGHT. YOU'RE JOKING.
LET'S JUST GET GOING, OKAY?
IT'S BEEN A LONG DAY.
CAN WE–
ALICE! HOW ARE YOU?

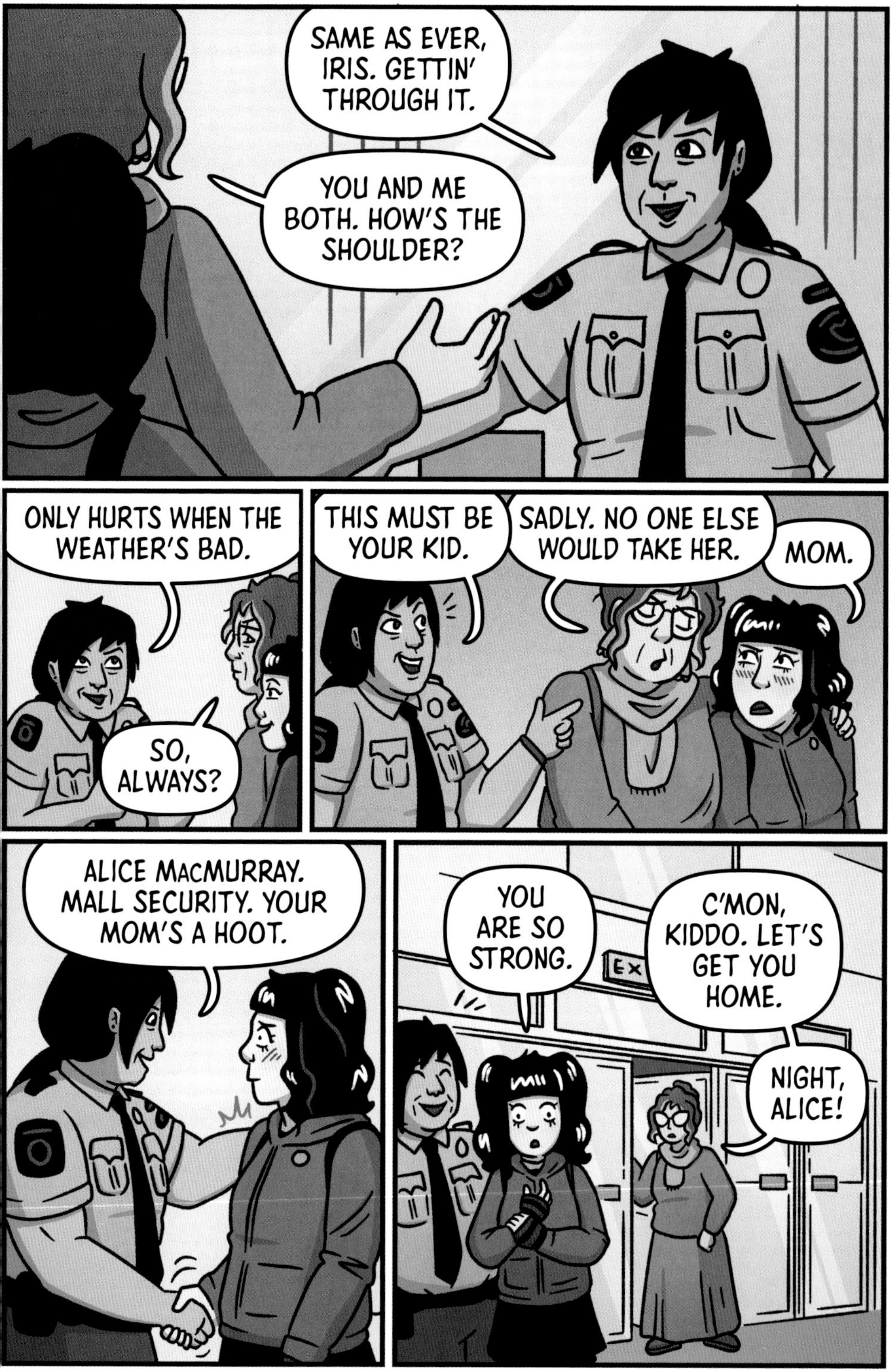
SAME AS EVER, IRIS. GETTIN' THROUGH IT.
YOU AND ME BOTH. HOW'S THE SHOULDER?
ONLY HURTS WHEN THE WEATHER'S BAD.
SO, ALWAYS?
THIS MUST BE YOUR KID.
SADLY. NO ONE ELSE WOULD TAKE HER.
MOM.
ALICE MACMURRAY. MALL SECURITY. YOUR MOM'S A HOOT.
YOU ARE SO STRONG.
C'MON, KIDDO. LET'S GET YOU HOME.
NIGHT, ALICE!

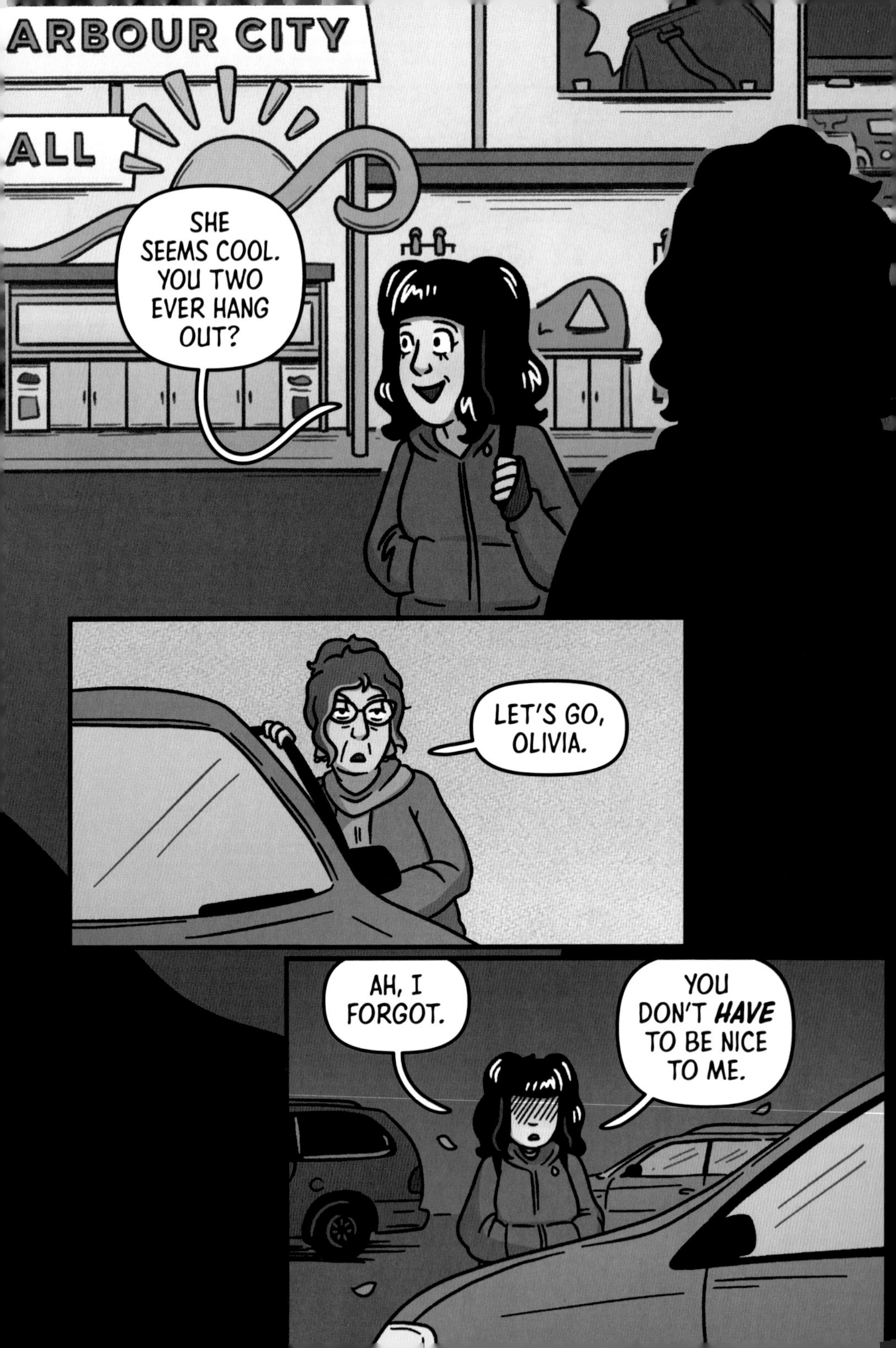
ARBOUR CITY
ALL
SHE SEEMS COOL. YOU TWO EVER HANG OUT?
LET'S GO, OLIVIA.
AH, I FORGOT.
YOU DON'T *HAVE* TO BE NICE TO ME.

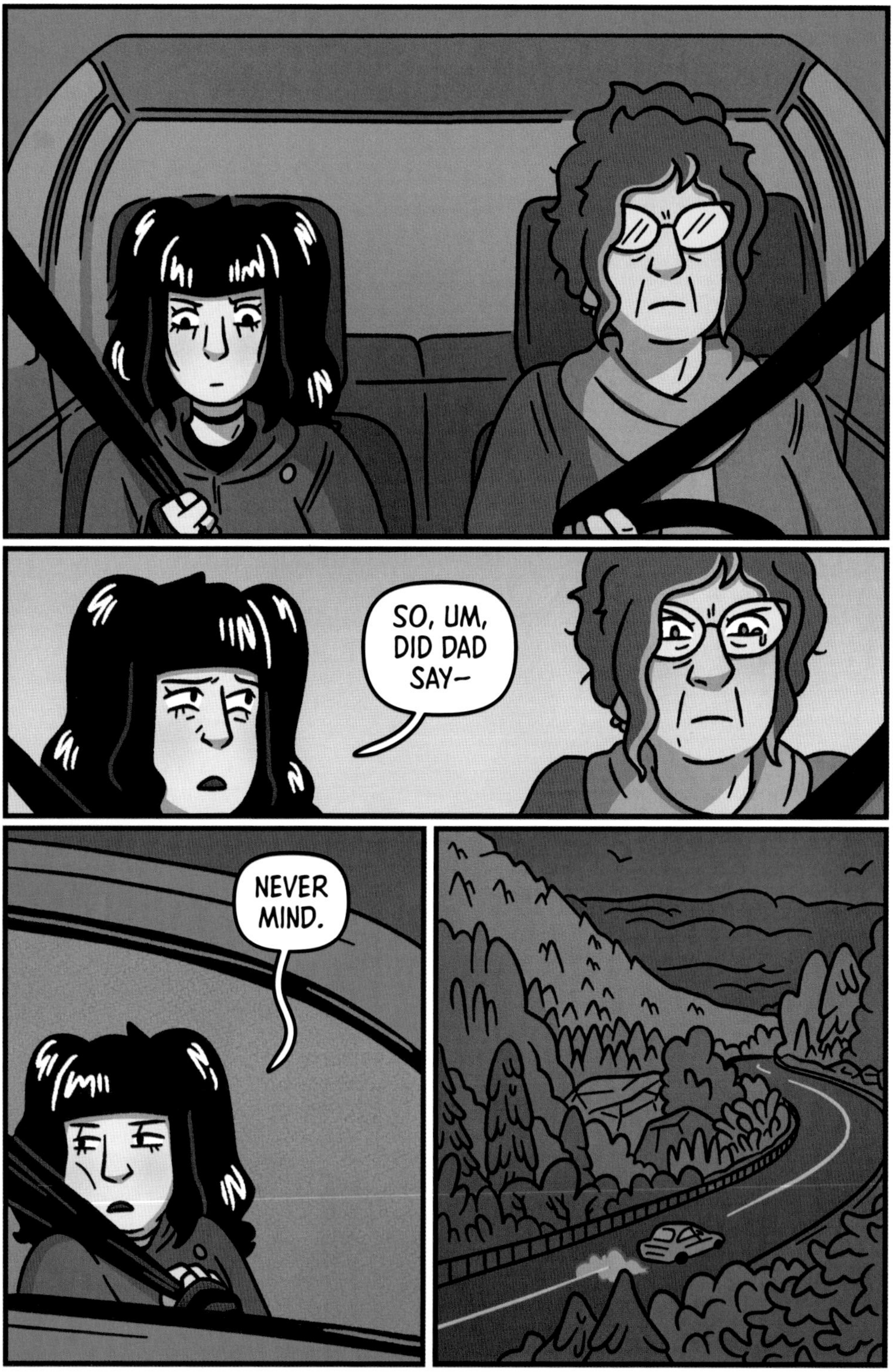
SO, UM, DID DAD SAY–
NEVER MIND.

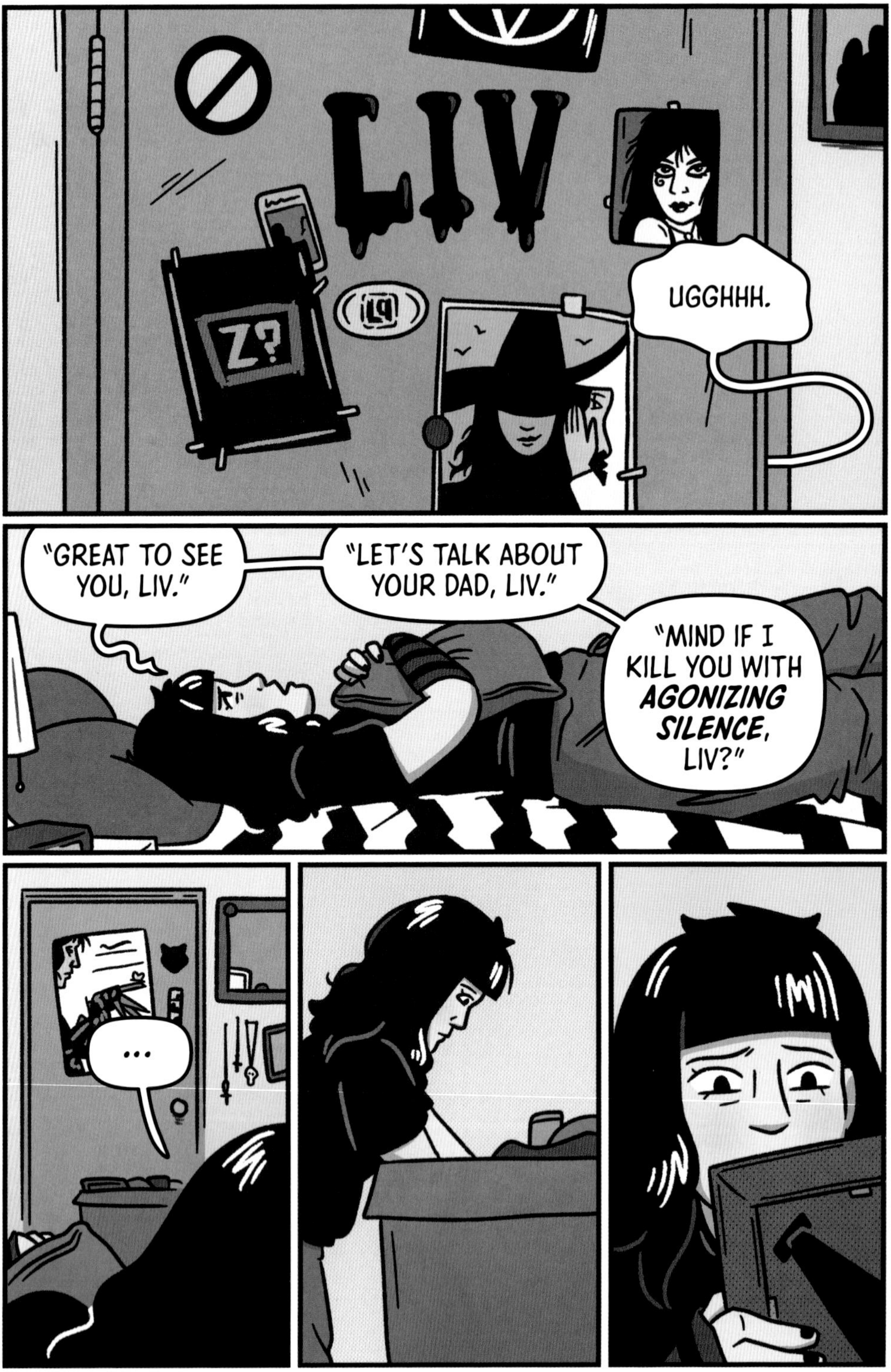
LIV
Z?
UGGHHH.
"GREAT TO SEE YOU, LIV."
"LET'S TALK ABOUT YOUR DAD, LIV."
"MIND IF I KILL YOU WITH *AGONIZING SILENCE*, LIV?"
...

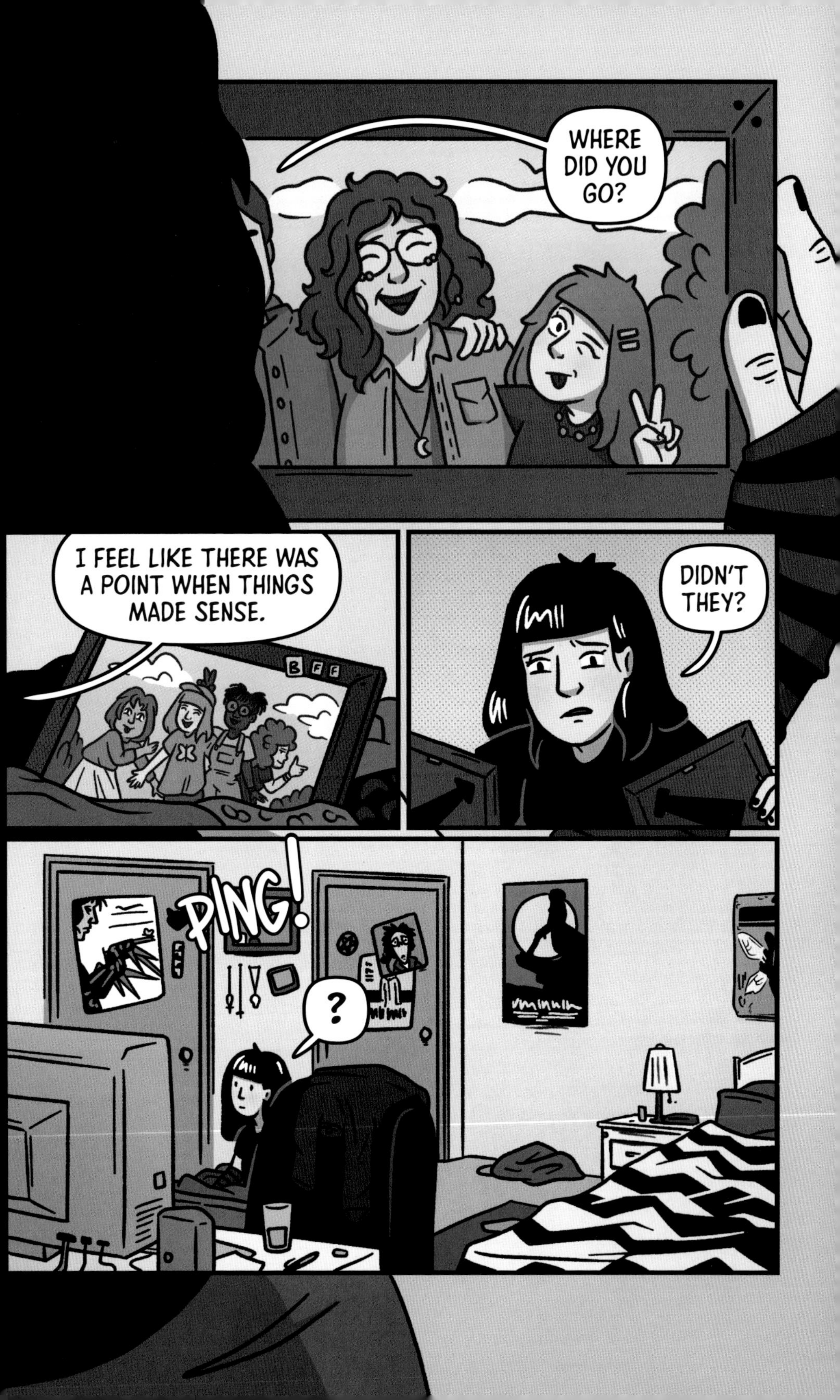

WHERE DID YOU GO?
I FEEL LIKE THERE WAS A POINT WHEN THINGS MADE SENSE.
BFF
DIDN'T THEY?
PING!
?

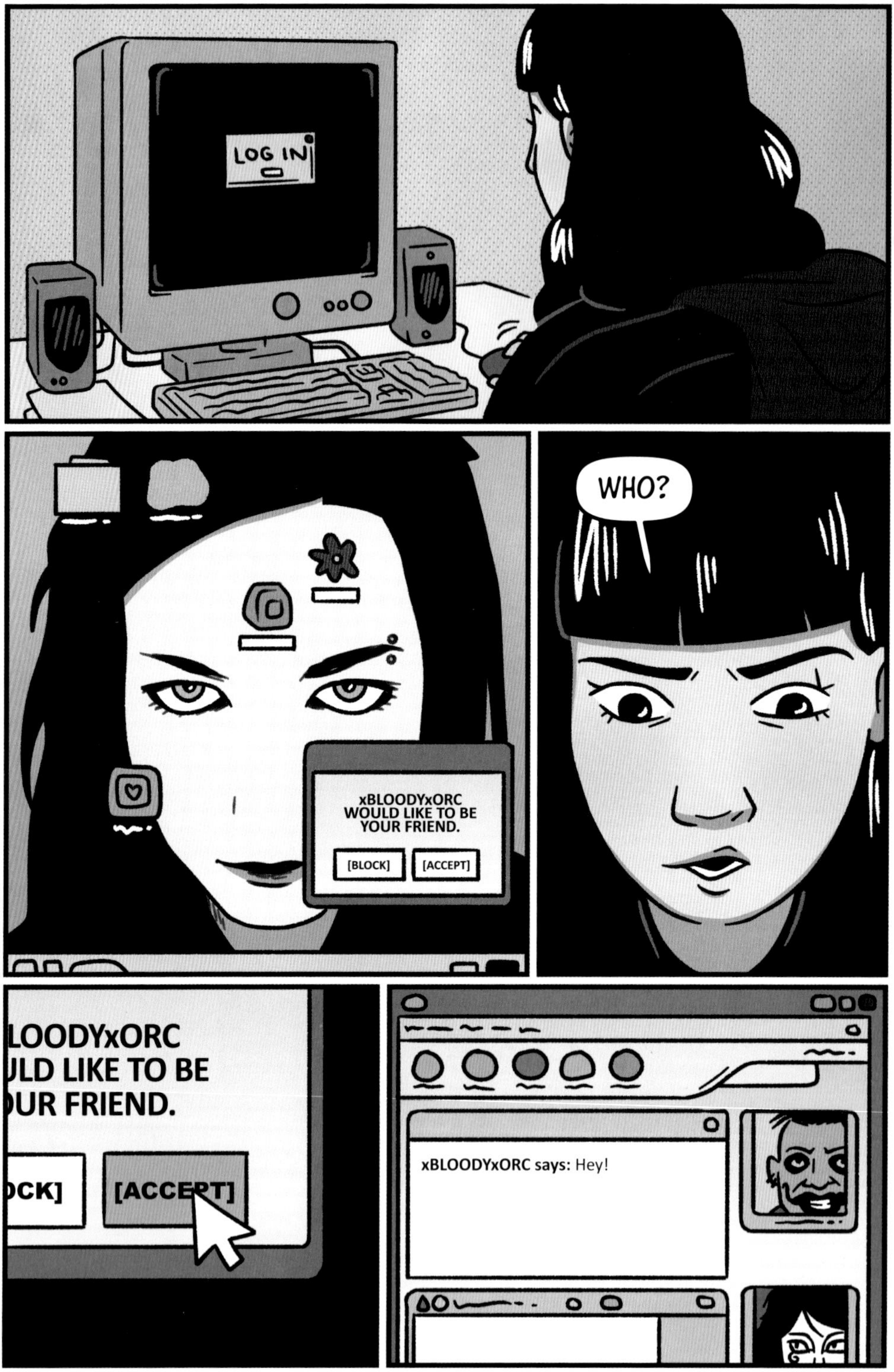
LOG IN
xBLOODYxORC
WOULD LIKE TO BE
YOUR FRIEND.
[BLOCK]
[ACCEPT]
WHO?
LOODYxORC
ULD LIKE TO BE
OUR FRIEND.
OCK]
[ACCEPT]
xBLOODYxORC says: Hey!

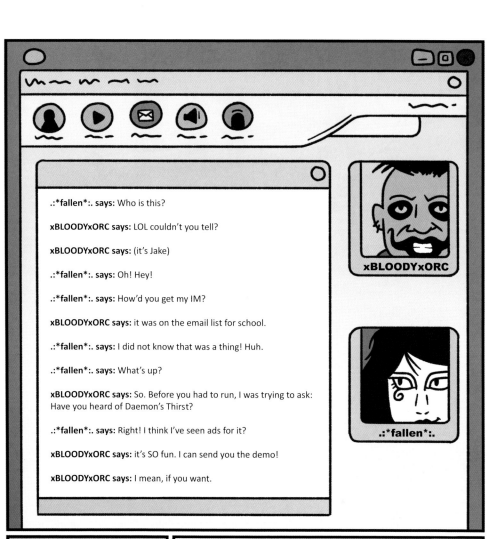

.:*fallen*:. **says:** Who is this?

xBLOODYxORC says: LOL couldn't you tell?

xBLOODYxORC says: (it's Jake)

.:*fallen*:. **says:** Oh! Hey!

.:*fallen*:. **says:** How'd you get my IM?

xBLOODYxORC says: it was on the email list for school.

.:*fallen*:. **says:** I did not know that was a thing! Huh.

.:*fallen*:. **says:** What's up?

xBLOODYxORC says: So. Before you had to run, I was trying to ask: Have you heard of Daemon's Thirst?

.:*fallen*:. **says:** Right! I think I've seen ads for it?

xBLOODYxORC says: it's SO fun. I can send you the demo!

xBLOODYxORC says: I mean, if you want.

xBLOODYxORC

.:*fallen*:.

.:*fallen*:. **says:** I'm up for whatever!

.:*fallen*:. **says:** I'm up for whatever!
xBLOODYxORC has sent you a link

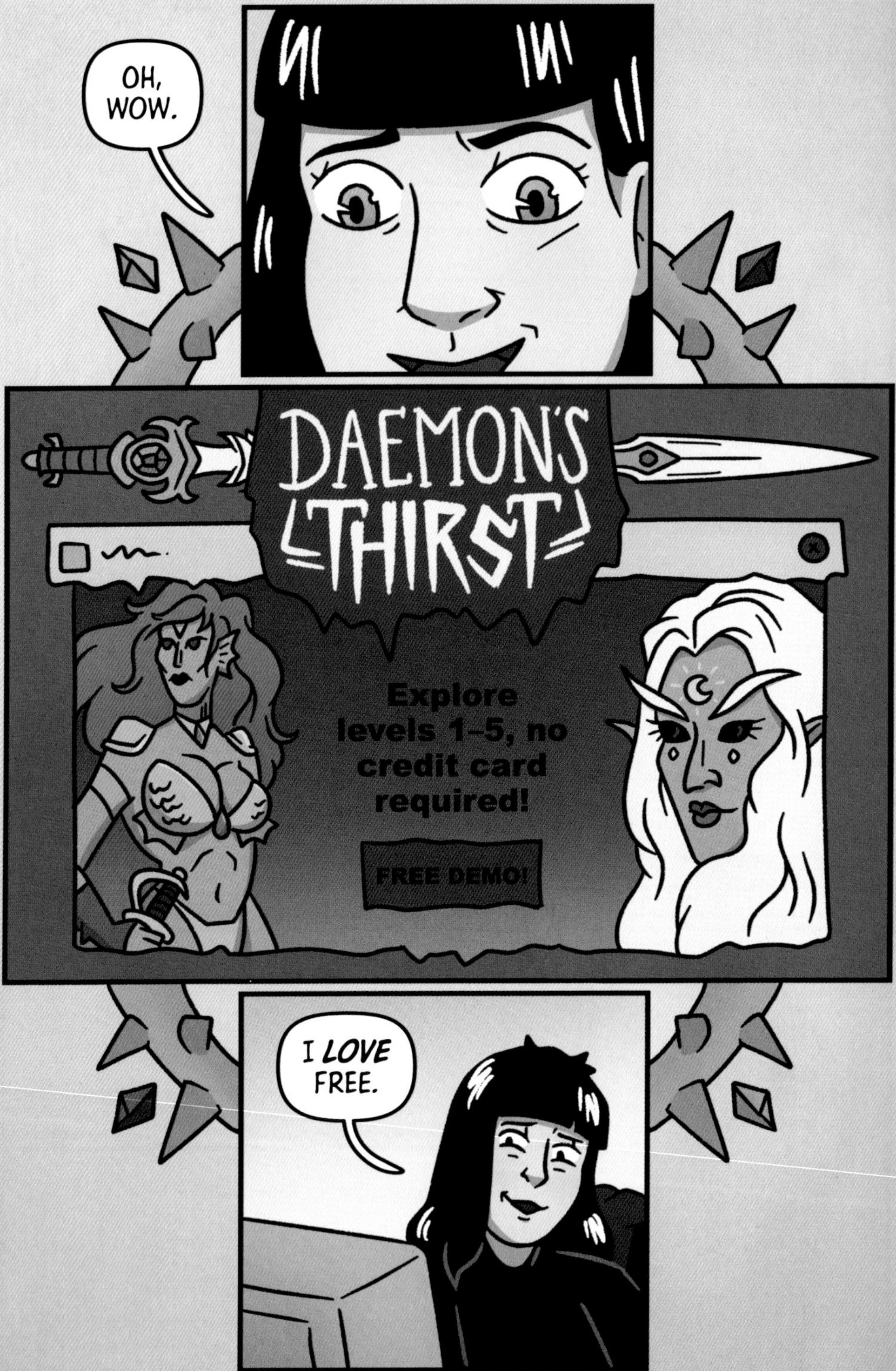
OH, WOW.
DAEMON'S THIRST
Explore levels 1–5, no credit card required!
FREE DEMO!
I LOVE FREE.

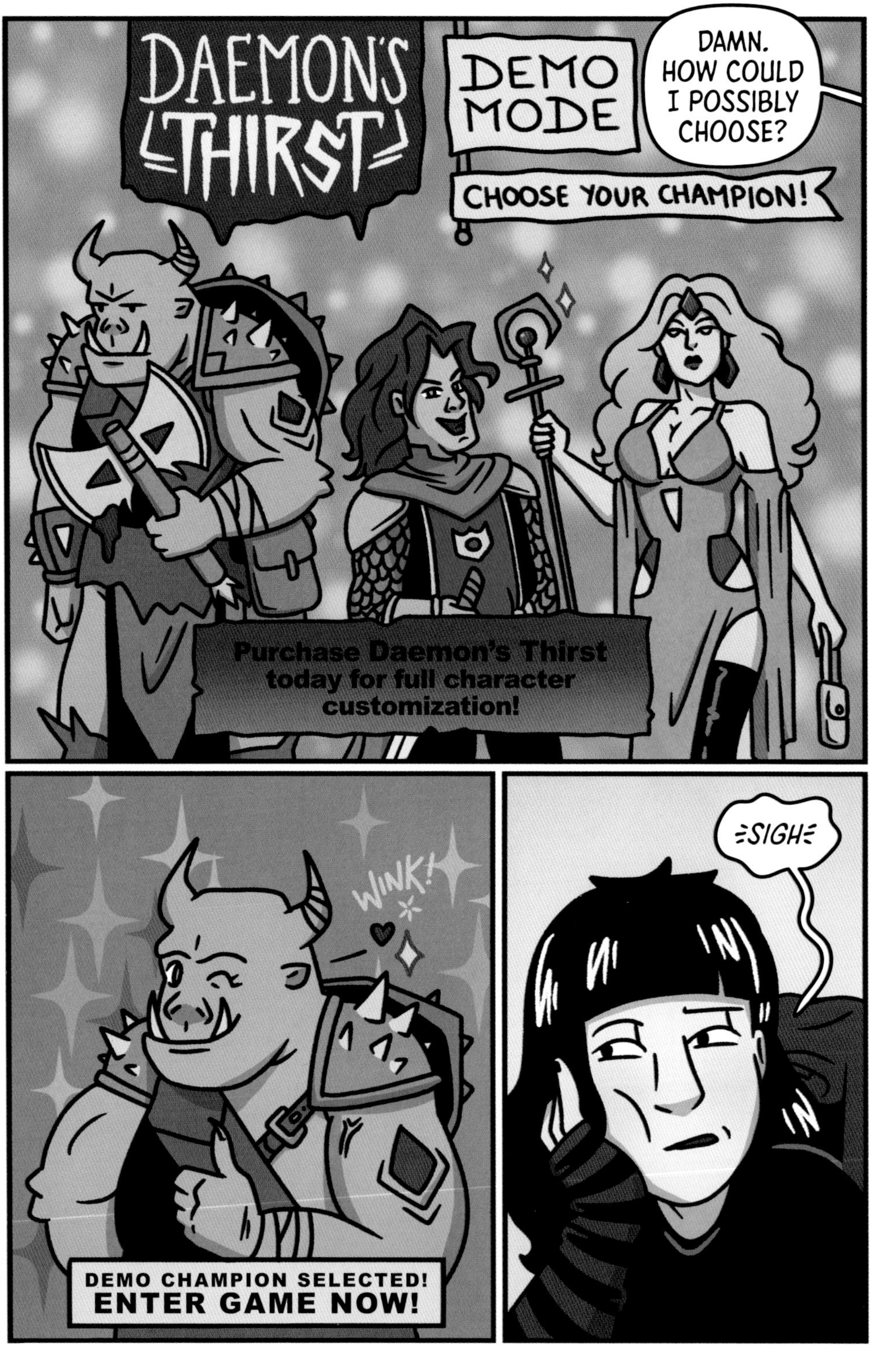
DAEMON'S THIRST
DEMO MODE
CHOOSE YOUR CHAMPION!
DAMN. HOW COULD I POSSIBLY CHOOSE?
Purchase Daemon's Thirst today for full character customization!
WINK!
DEMO CHAMPION SELECTED! ENTER GAME NOW!
SIGH

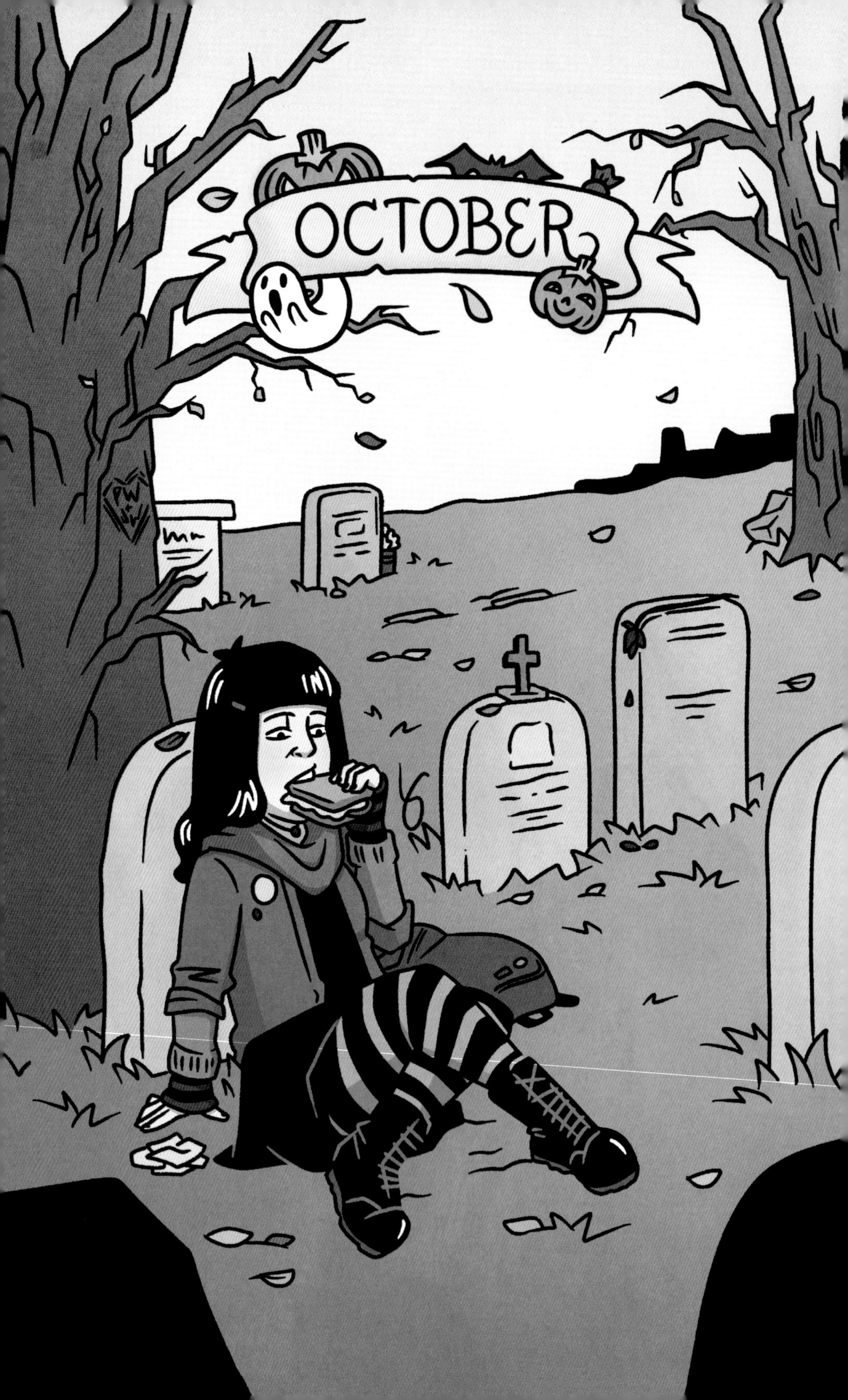
OCTOBER

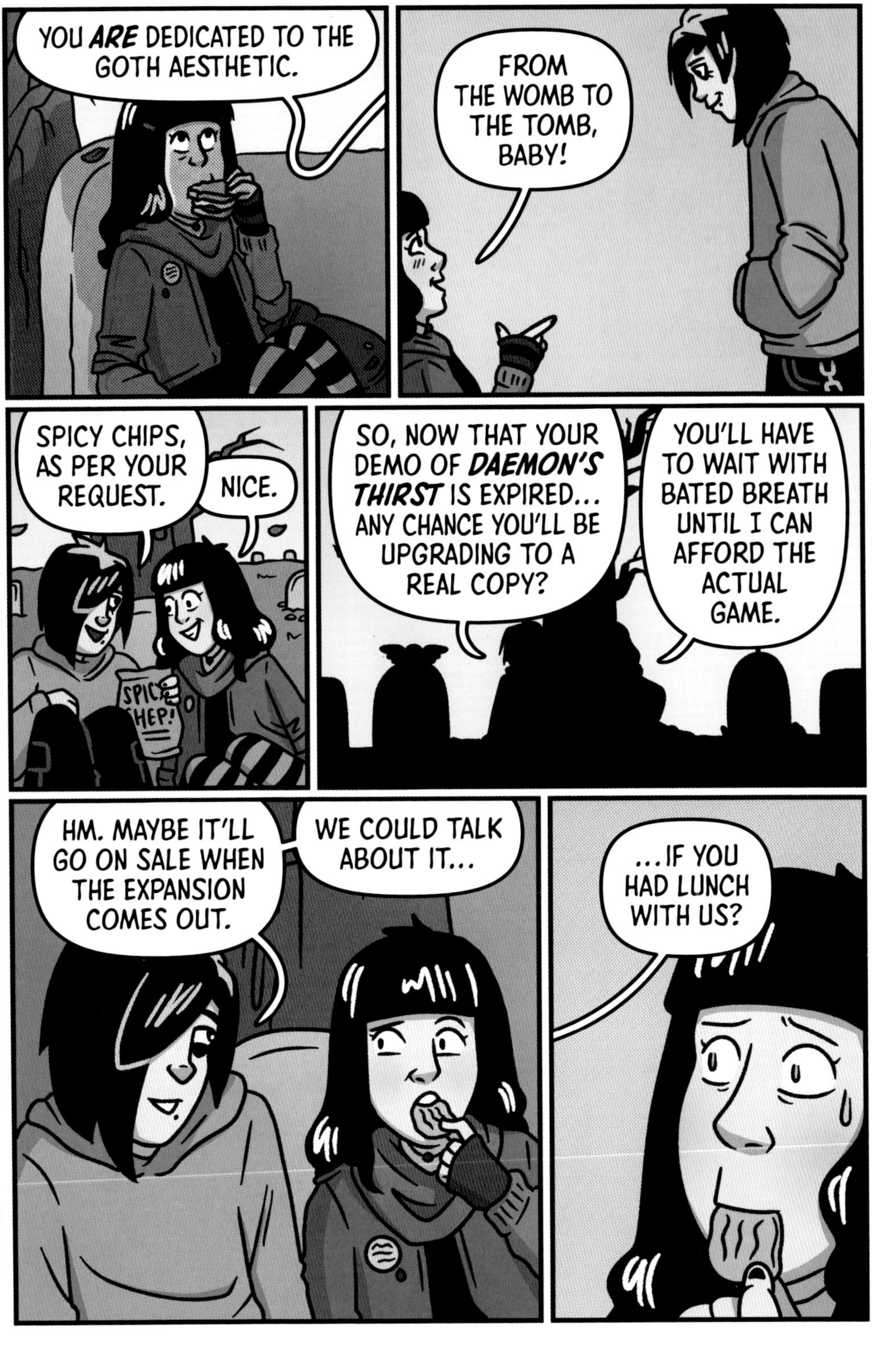
YOU ARE DEDICATED TO THE GOTH AESTHETIC.
FROM THE WOMB TO THE TOMB, BABY!
SPICY CHIPS, AS PER YOUR REQUEST.
NICE.
SPIC CHEP!
SO, NOW THAT YOUR DEMO OF DAEMON'S THIRST IS EXPIRED... ANY CHANCE YOU'LL BE UPGRADING TO A REAL COPY?
YOU'LL HAVE TO WAIT WITH BATED BREATH UNTIL I CAN AFFORD THE ACTUAL GAME.
HM. MAYBE IT'LL GO ON SALE WHEN THE EXPANSION COMES OUT.
WE COULD TALK ABOUT IT...
...IF YOU HAD LUNCH WITH US?

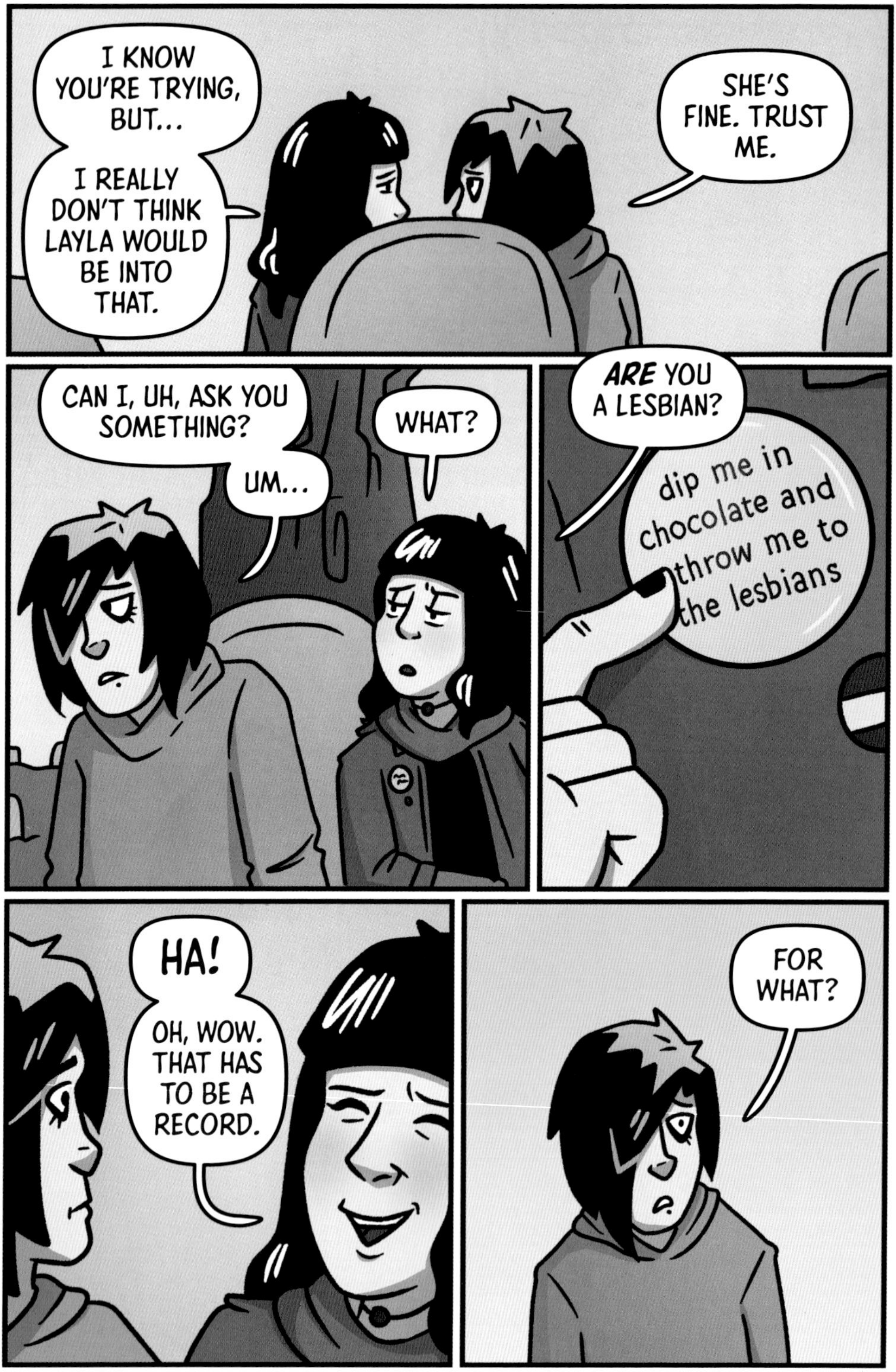
I KNOW YOU'RE TRYING, BUT...
I REALLY DON'T THINK LAYLA WOULD BE INTO THAT.
SHE'S FINE. TRUST ME.
CAN I, UH, ASK YOU SOMETHING?
UM...
WHAT?
ARE YOU A LESBIAN?
dip me in chocolate and throw me to the lesbians
HA!
OH, WOW. THAT HAS TO BE A RECORD.
FOR WHAT?

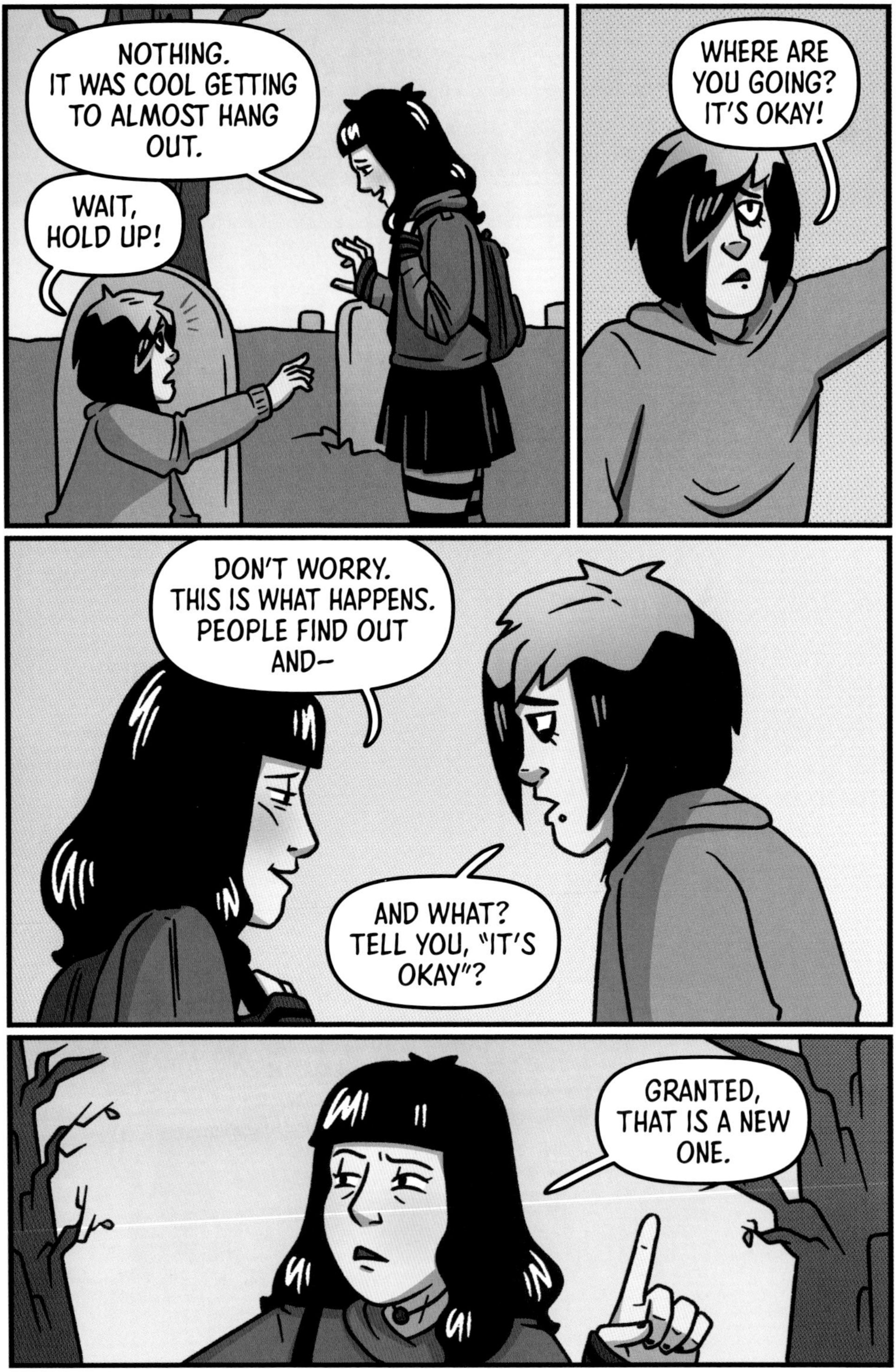
NOTHING. IT WAS COOL GETTING TO ALMOST HANG OUT.
WAIT, HOLD UP!
WHERE ARE YOU GOING? IT'S OKAY!
DON'T WORRY. THIS IS WHAT HAPPENS. PEOPLE FIND OUT AND–
AND WHAT? TELL YOU, "IT'S OKAY"?
GRANTED, THAT IS A NEW ONE.

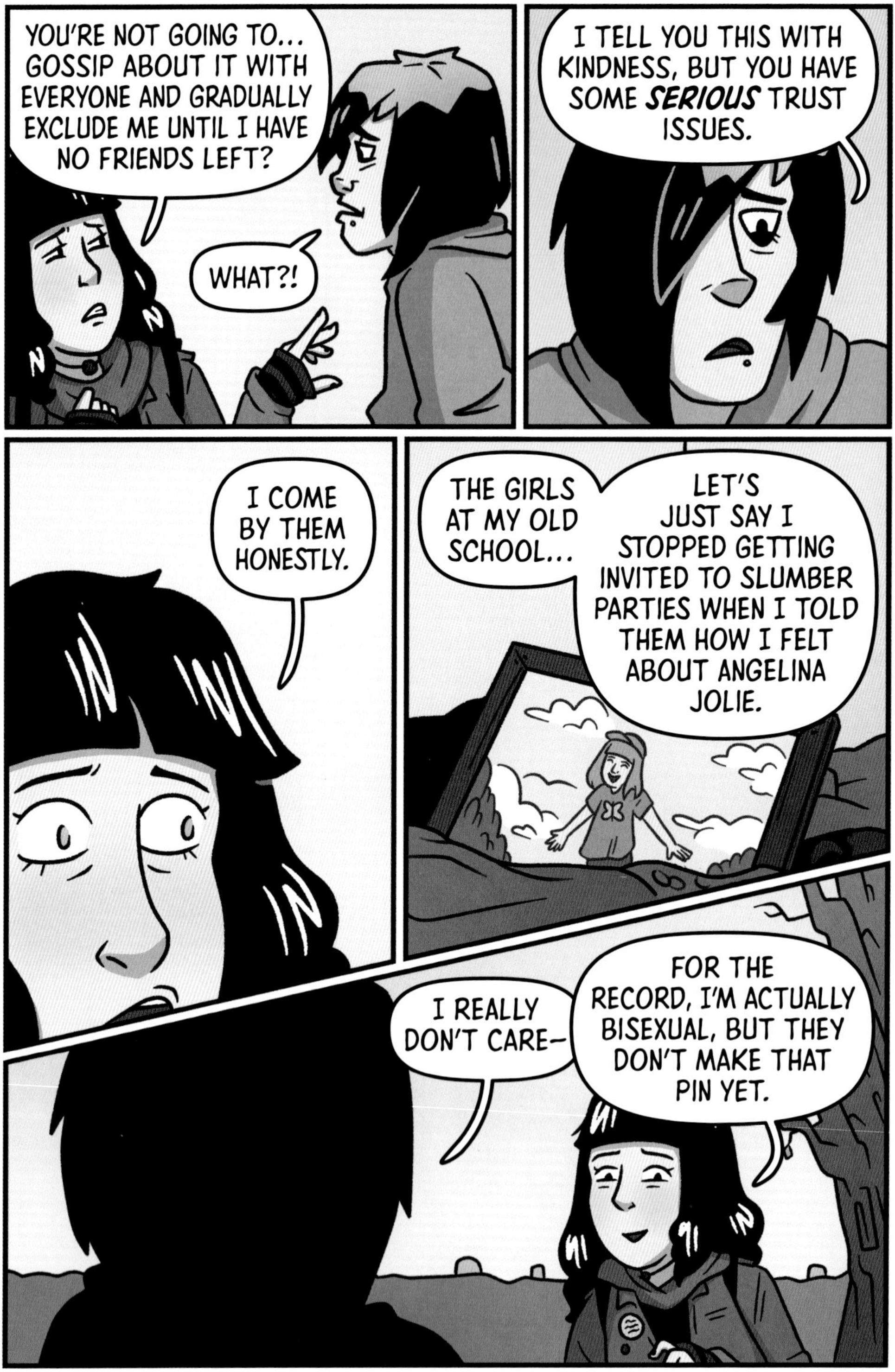
YOU'RE NOT GOING TO... GOSSIP ABOUT IT WITH EVERYONE AND GRADUALLY EXCLUDE ME UNTIL I HAVE NO FRIENDS LEFT?
WHAT?!
I TELL YOU THIS WITH KINDNESS, BUT YOU HAVE SOME *SERIOUS* TRUST ISSUES.
I COME BY THEM HONESTLY.
THE GIRLS AT MY OLD SCHOOL...
LET'S JUST SAY I STOPPED GETTING INVITED TO SLUMBER PARTIES WHEN I TOLD THEM HOW I FELT ABOUT ANGELINA JOLIE.
I REALLY DON'T CARE—
FOR THE RECORD, I'M ACTUALLY BISEXUAL, BUT THEY DON'T MAKE THAT PIN YET.

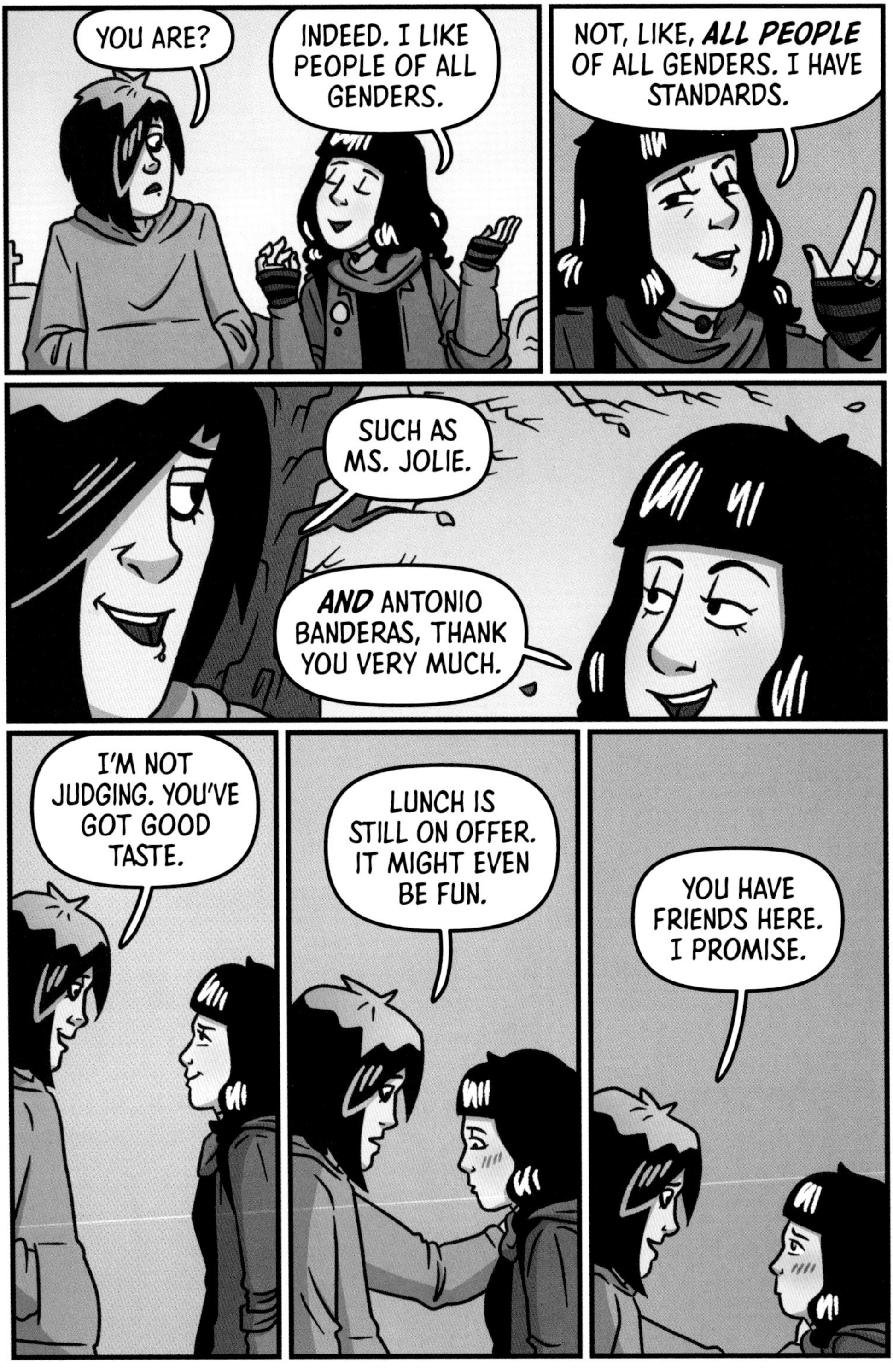
YOU ARE?
INDEED. I LIKE PEOPLE OF ALL GENDERS.
NOT, LIKE, **ALL PEOPLE** OF ALL GENDERS. I HAVE STANDARDS.
SUCH AS MS. JOLIE.
AND ANTONIO BANDERAS, THANK YOU VERY MUCH.
I'M NOT JUDGING. YOU'VE GOT GOOD TASTE.
LUNCH IS STILL ON OFFER. IT MIGHT EVEN BE FUN.
YOU HAVE FRIENDS HERE. I PROMISE.

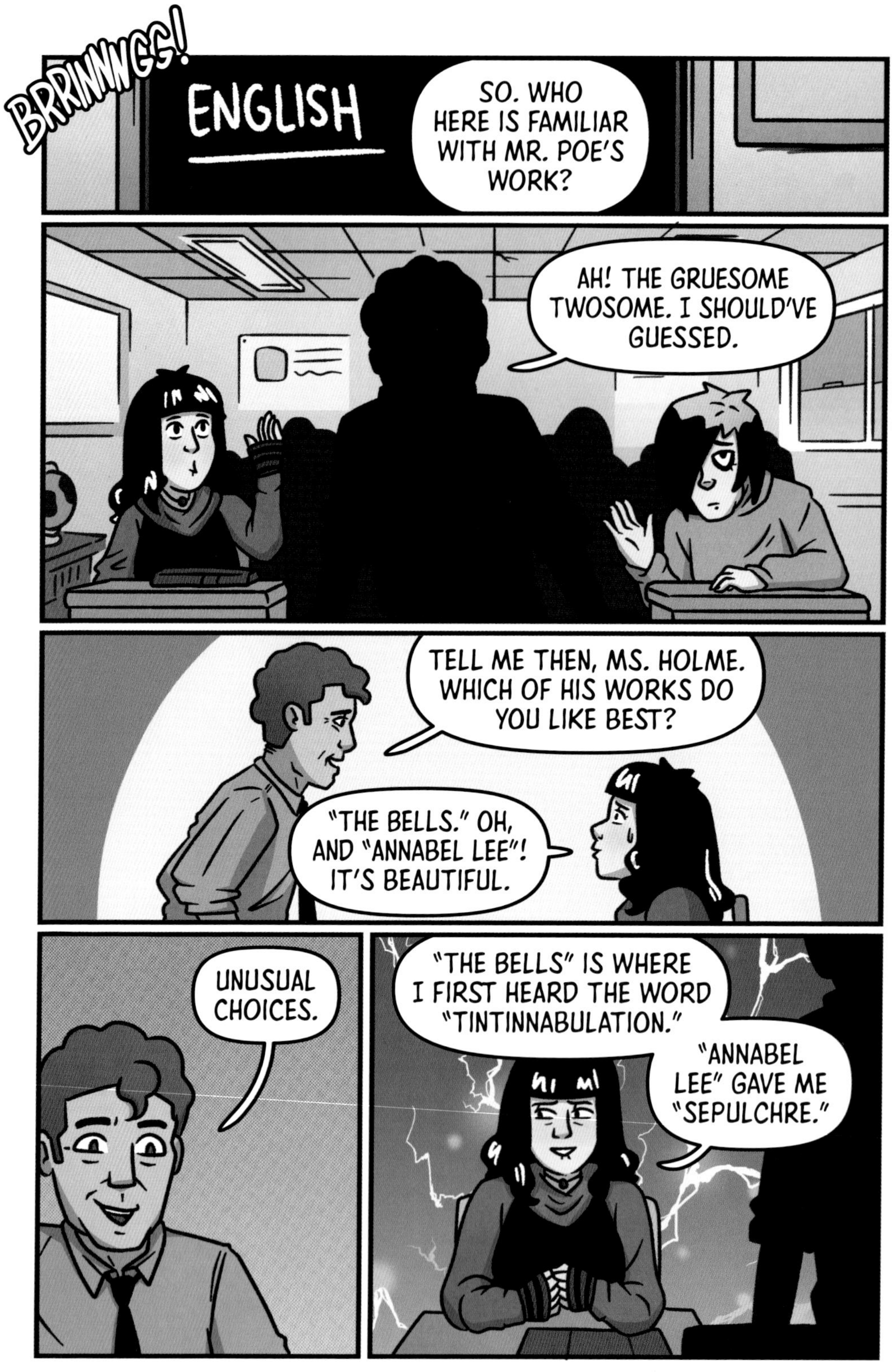
BRRINNNGG!
ENGLISH
SO. WHO HERE IS FAMILIAR WITH MR. POE'S WORK?
AH! THE GRUESOME TWOSOME. I SHOULD'VE GUESSED.
TELL ME THEN, MS. HOLME. WHICH OF HIS WORKS DO YOU LIKE BEST?
"THE BELLS." OH, AND "ANNABEL LEE"! IT'S BEAUTIFUL.
UNUSUAL CHOICES.
"THE BELLS" IS WHERE I FIRST HEARD THE WORD "TINTINNABULATION."
"ANNABEL LEE" GAVE ME "SEPULCHRE."

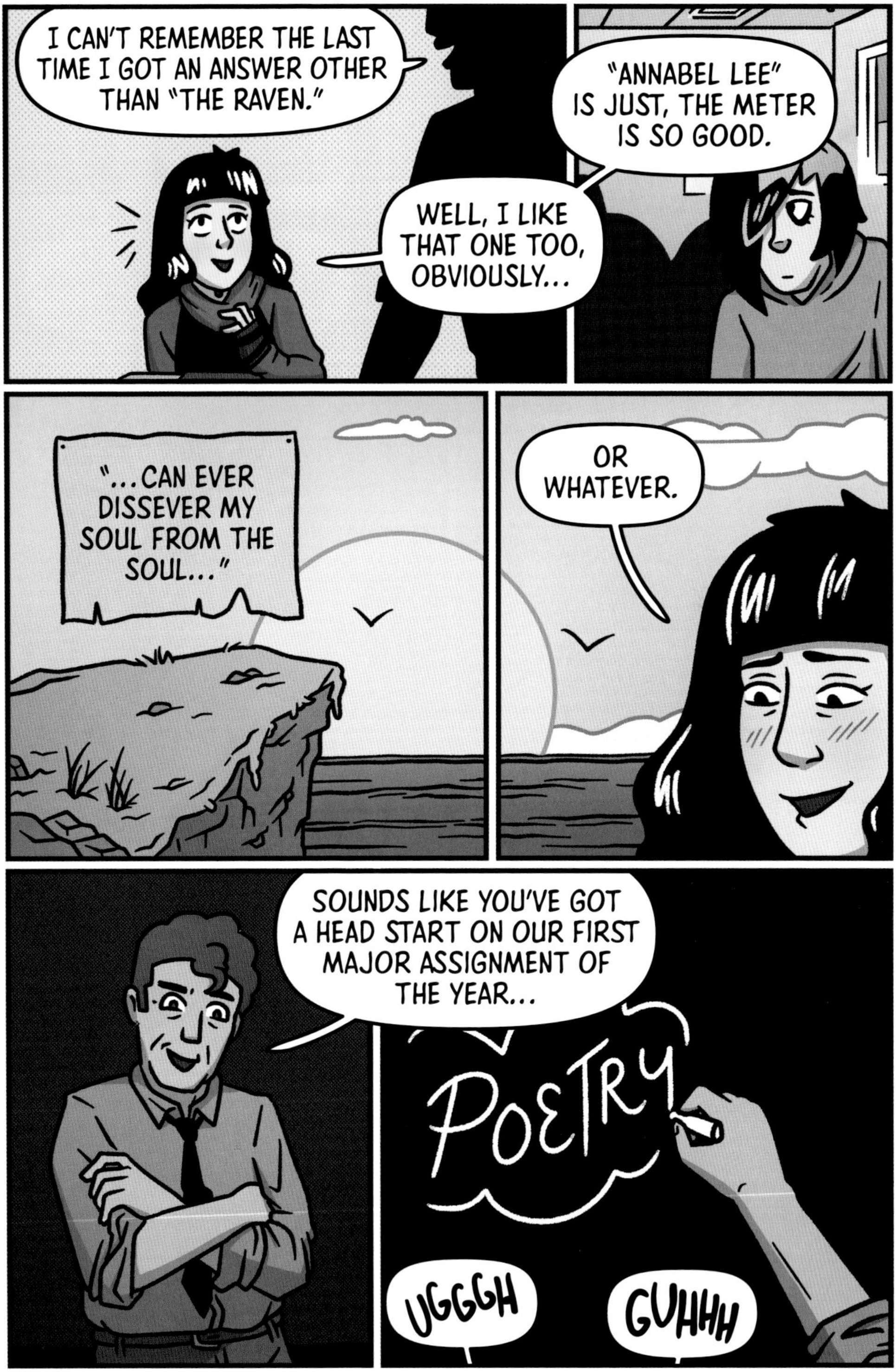
I CAN'T REMEMBER THE LAST TIME I GOT AN ANSWER OTHER THAN "THE RAVEN."
WELL, I LIKE THAT ONE TOO, OBVIOUSLY...
"ANNABEL LEE" IS JUST, THE METER IS SO GOOD.
"...CAN EVER DISSEVER MY SOUL FROM THE SOUL..."
OR WHATEVER.
SOUNDS LIKE YOU'VE GOT A HEAD START ON OUR FIRST MAJOR ASSIGNMENT OF THE YEAR...
POETRY
UGGGH
GUHHH

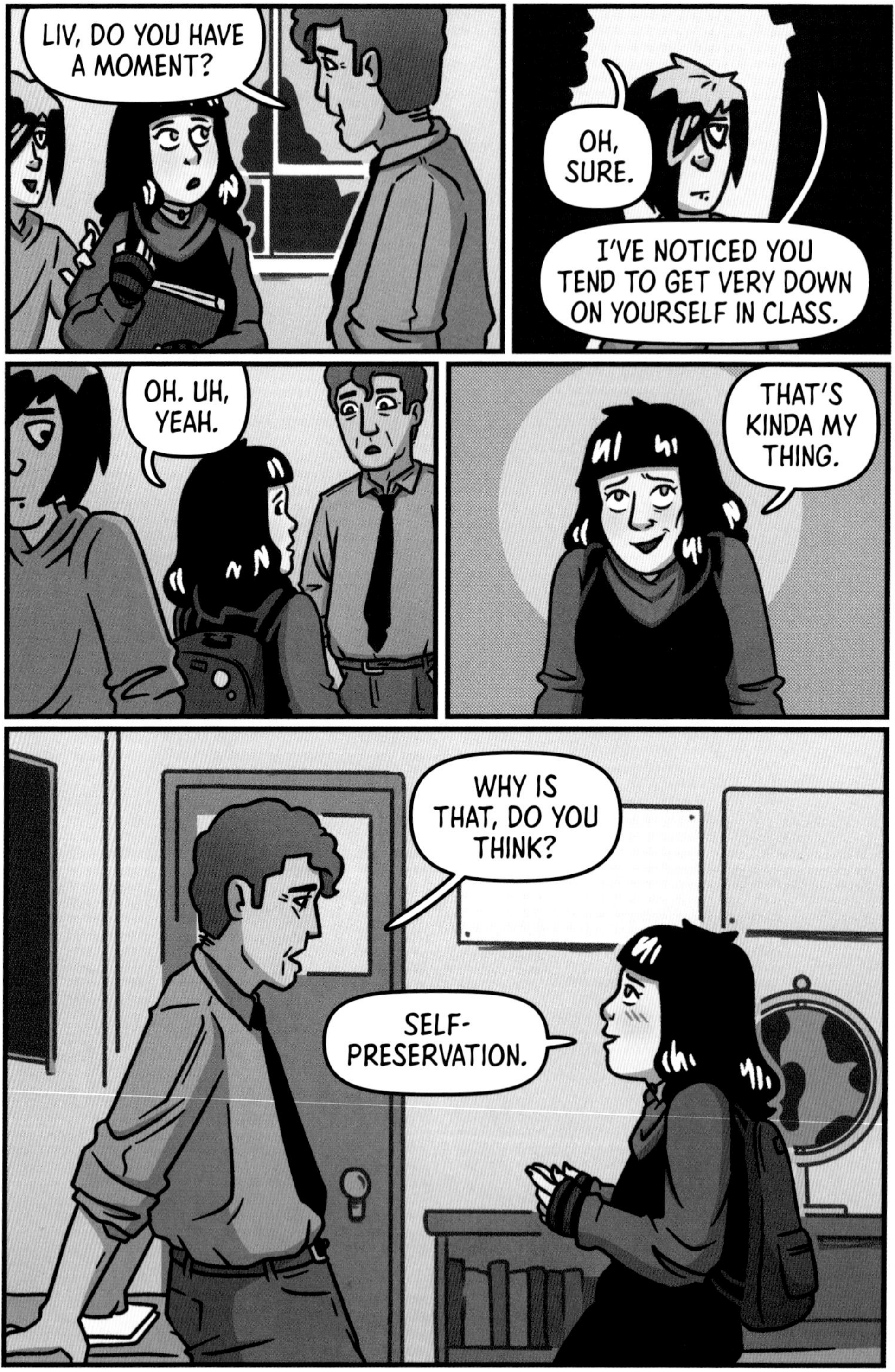
LIV, DO YOU HAVE A MOMENT?
OH, SURE.
I'VE NOTICED YOU TEND TO GET VERY DOWN ON YOURSELF IN CLASS.
OH. UH, YEAH.
THAT'S KINDA MY THING.
WHY IS THAT, DO YOU THINK?
SELF-PRESERVATION.

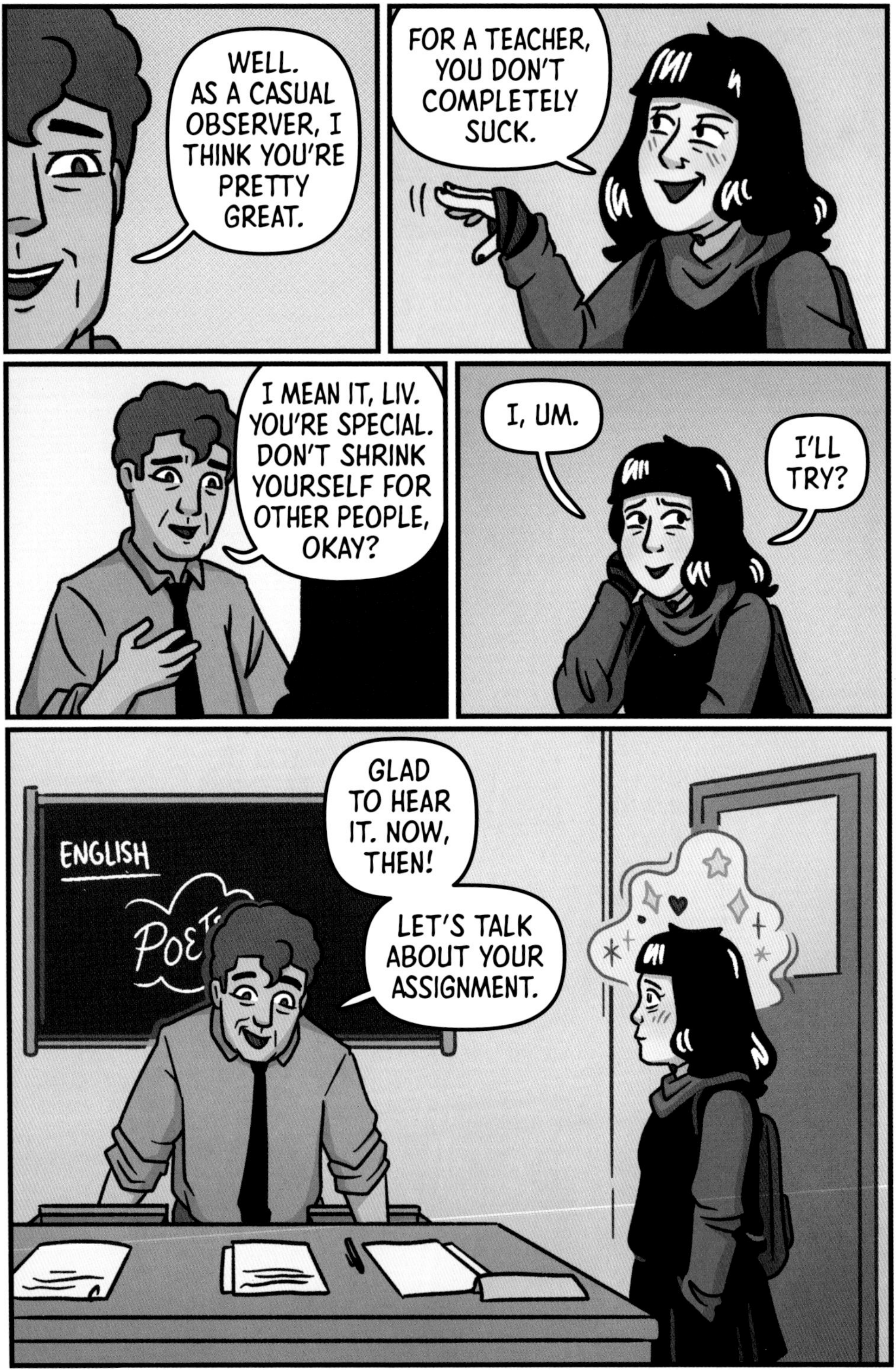
WELL. AS A CASUAL OBSERVER, I THINK YOU'RE PRETTY GREAT.
FOR A TEACHER, YOU DON'T COMPLETELY SUCK.
I MEAN IT, LIV. YOU'RE SPECIAL. DON'T SHRINK YOURSELF FOR OTHER PEOPLE, OKAY?
I, UM.
I'LL TRY?
ENGLISH
GLAD TO HEAR IT. NOW, THEN!
LET'S TALK ABOUT YOUR ASSIGNMENT.

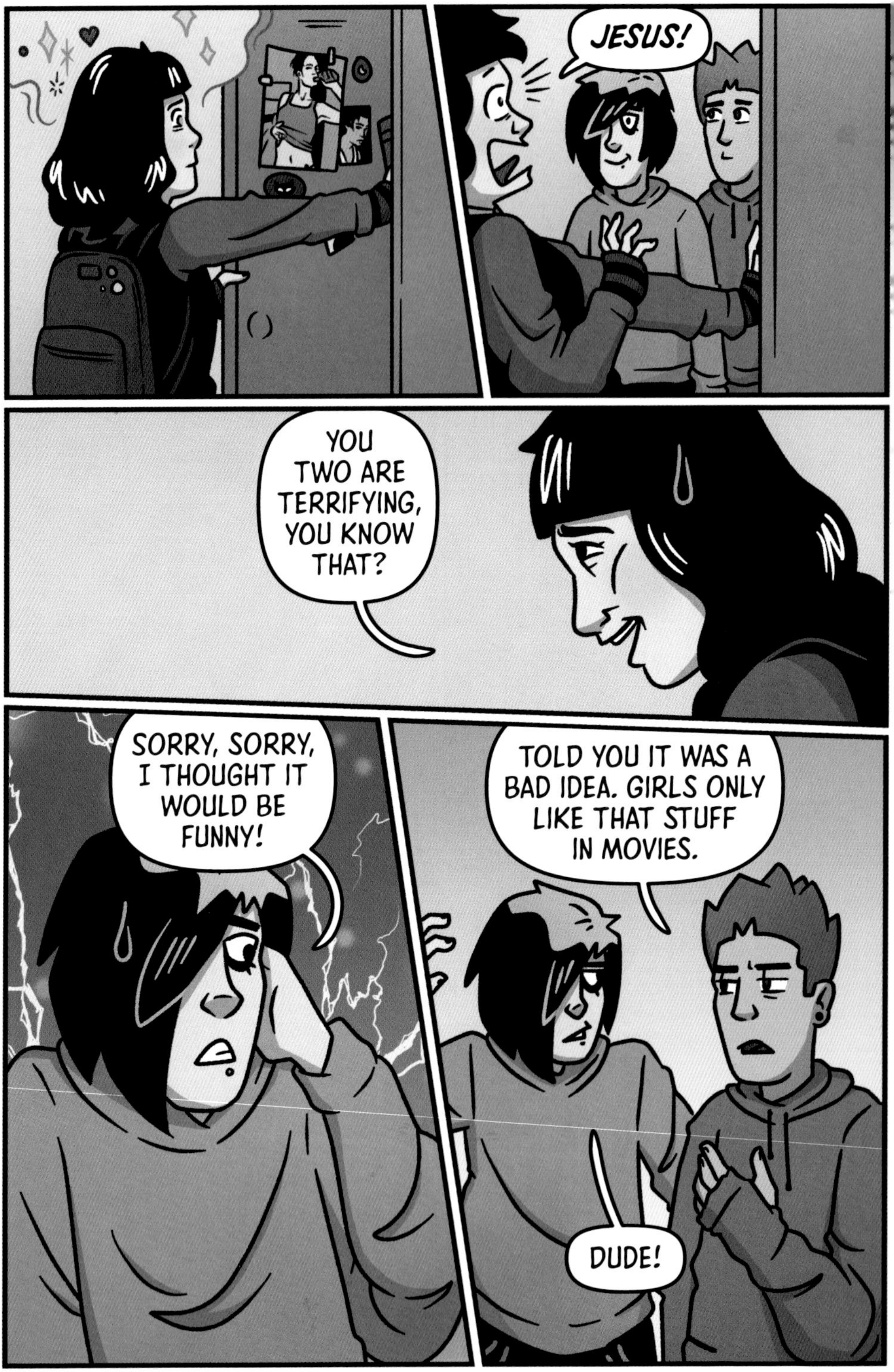
JESUS!
YOU TWO ARE TERRIFYING, YOU KNOW THAT?
SORRY, SORRY, I THOUGHT IT WOULD BE FUNNY!
TOLD YOU IT WAS A BAD IDEA. GIRLS ONLY LIKE THAT STUFF IN MOVIES.
DUDE!

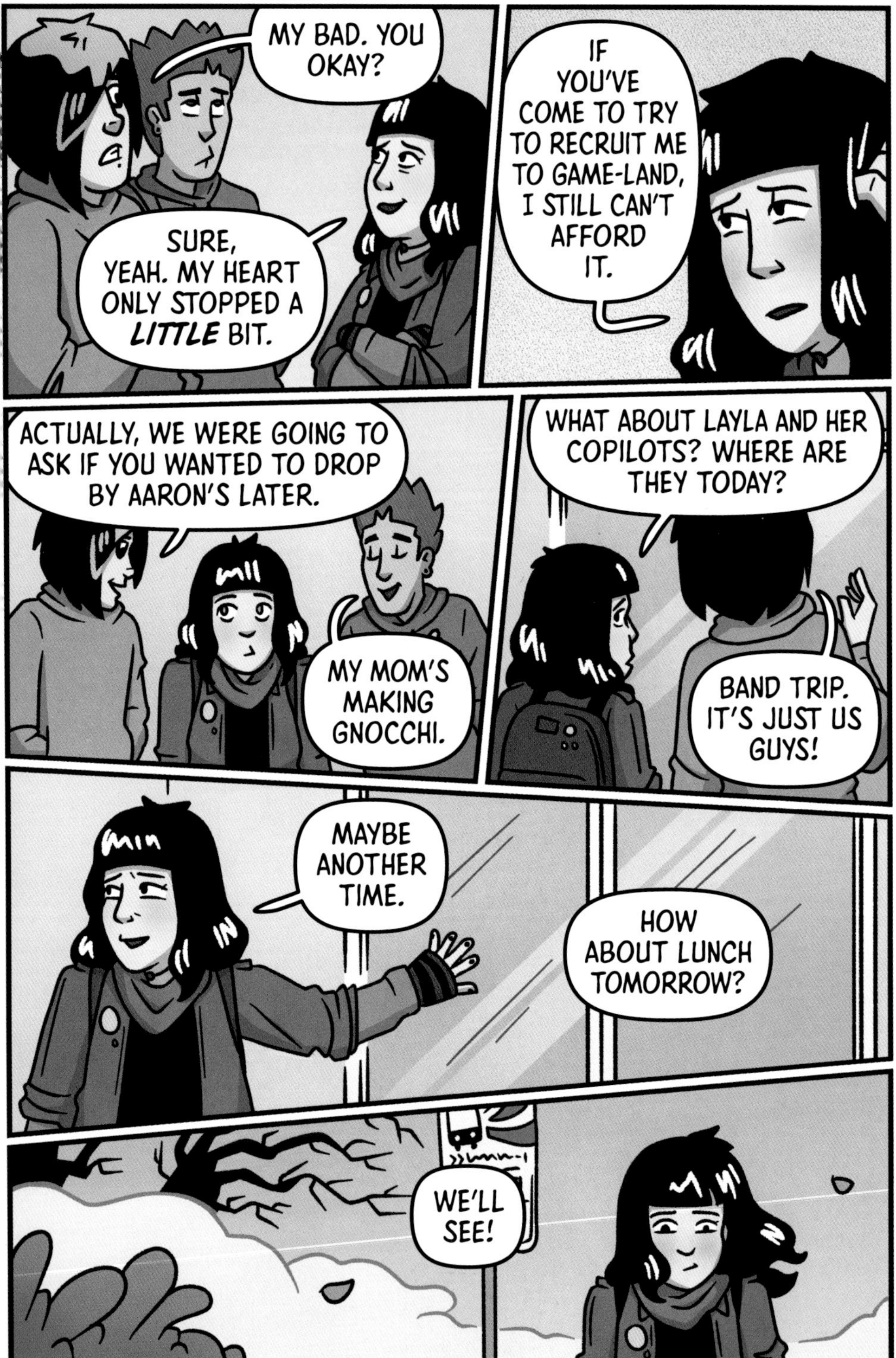
MY BAD. YOU OKAY?
SURE, YEAH. MY HEART ONLY STOPPED A *LITTLE* BIT.
IF YOU'VE COME TO TRY TO RECRUIT ME TO GAME-LAND, I STILL CAN'T AFFORD IT.
ACTUALLY, WE WERE GOING TO ASK IF YOU WANTED TO DROP BY AARON'S LATER.
MY MOM'S MAKING GNOCCHI.
WHAT ABOUT LAYLA AND HER COPILOTS? WHERE ARE THEY TODAY?
BAND TRIP. IT'S JUST US GUYS!
MAYBE ANOTHER TIME.
HOW ABOUT LUNCH TOMORROW?
WE'LL SEE!

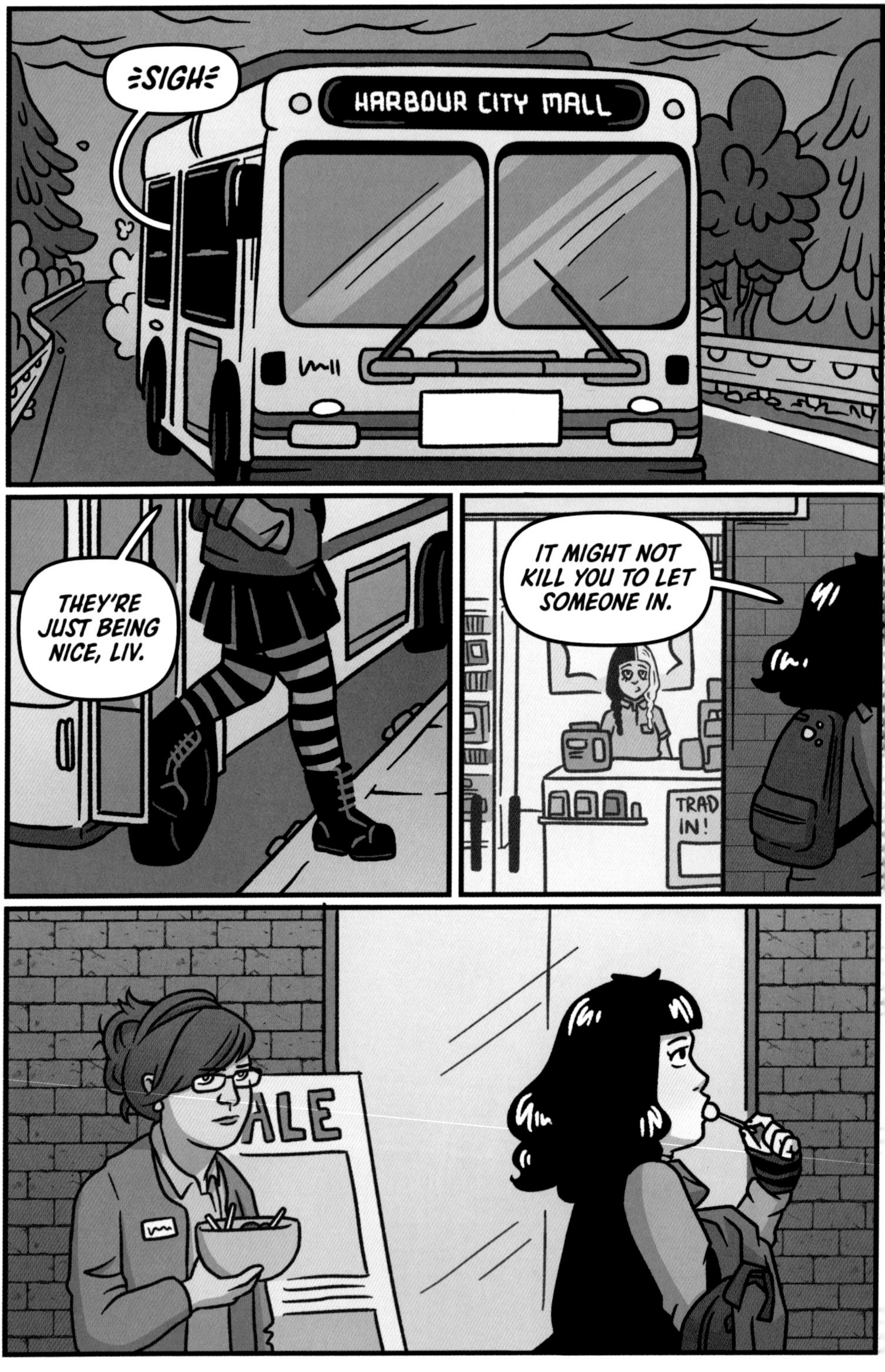
SIGH
HARBOUR CITY MALL
THEY'RE JUST BEING NICE, LIV.
IT MIGHT NOT KILL YOU TO LET SOMEONE IN.
TRAD IN!
ALE

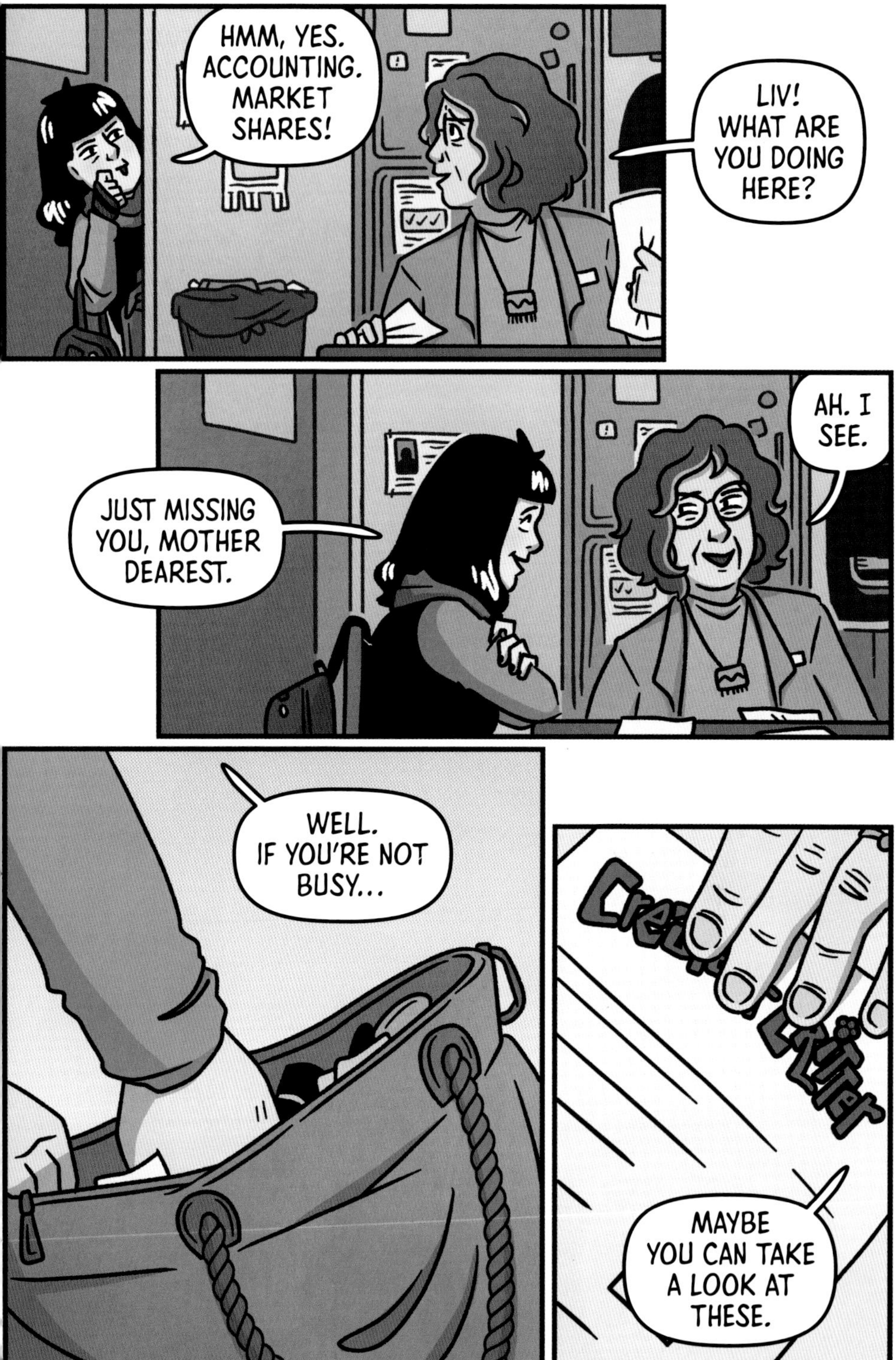
HMM, YES. ACCOUNTING. MARKET SHARES!
LIV! WHAT ARE YOU DOING HERE?
JUST MISSING YOU, MOTHER DEAREST.
AH. I SEE.
WELL. IF YOU'RE NOT BUSY...
MAYBE YOU CAN TAKE A LOOK AT THESE.

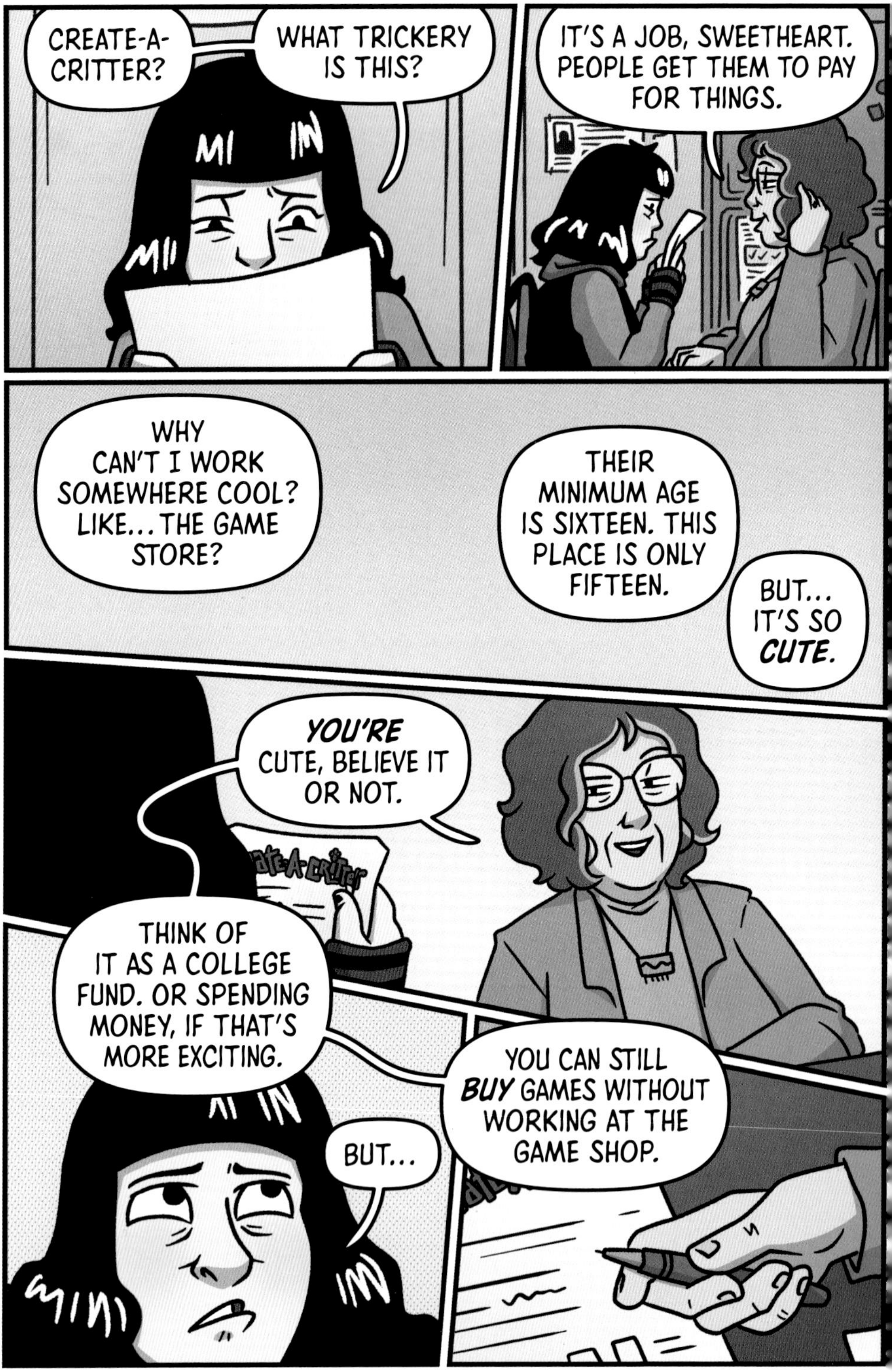
CREATE-A-CRITTER?
WHAT TRICKERY IS THIS?
IT'S A JOB, SWEETHEART. PEOPLE GET THEM TO PAY FOR THINGS.
WHY CAN'T I WORK SOMEWHERE COOL? LIKE... THE GAME STORE?
THEIR MINIMUM AGE IS SIXTEEN. THIS PLACE IS ONLY FIFTEEN.
BUT... IT'S SO *CUTE.*
YOU'RE CUTE, BELIEVE IT OR NOT.
THINK OF IT AS A COLLEGE FUND. OR SPENDING MONEY, IF THAT'S MORE EXCITING.
BUT...
YOU CAN STILL *BUY* GAMES WITHOUT WORKING AT THE GAME SHOP.

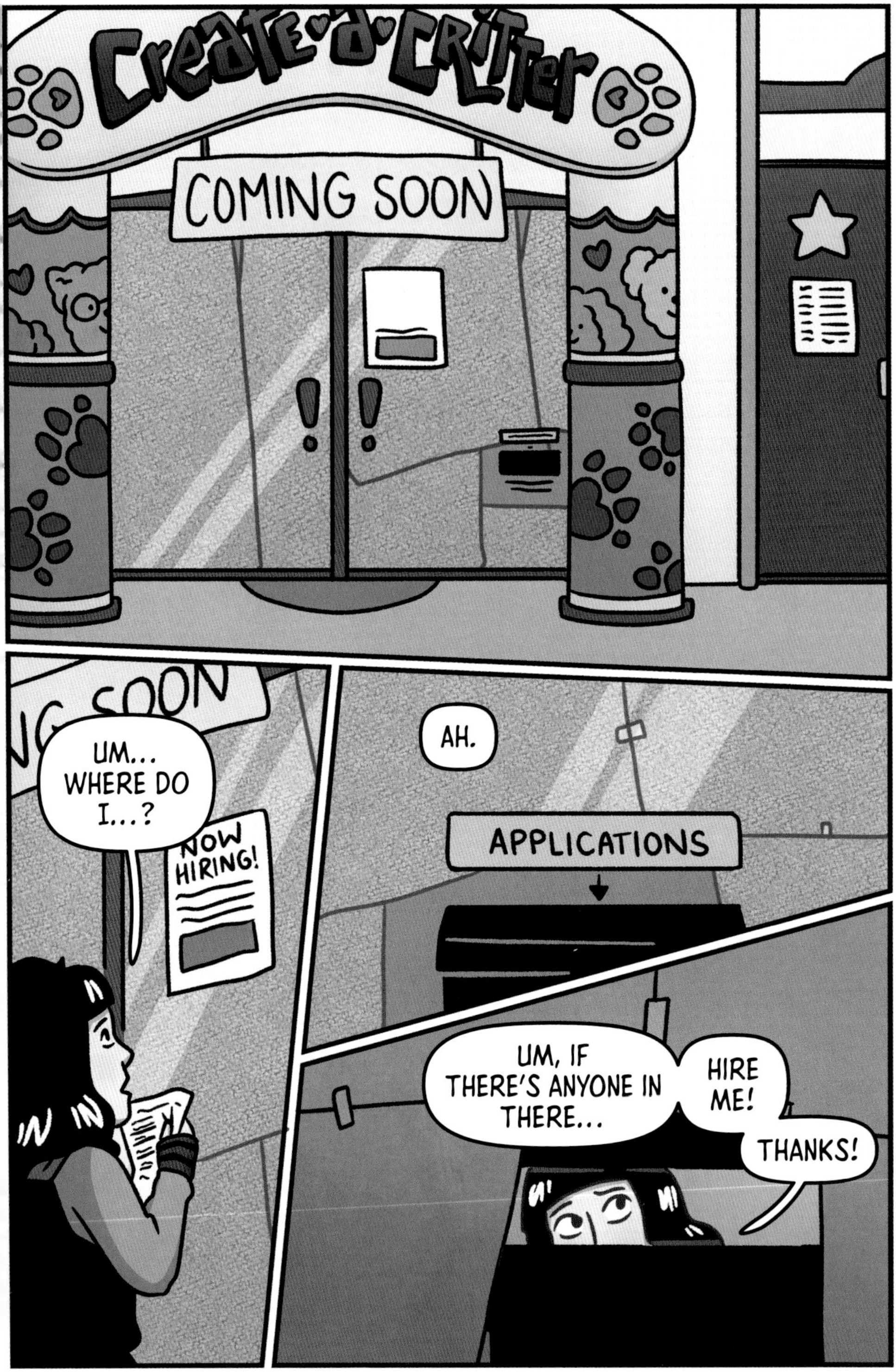
Create-a-Critter
COMING SOON
NG SOON
UM... WHERE DO I...?
NOW HIRING!
AH.
APPLICATIONS
UM, IF THERE'S ANYONE IN THERE...
HIRE ME!
THANKS!

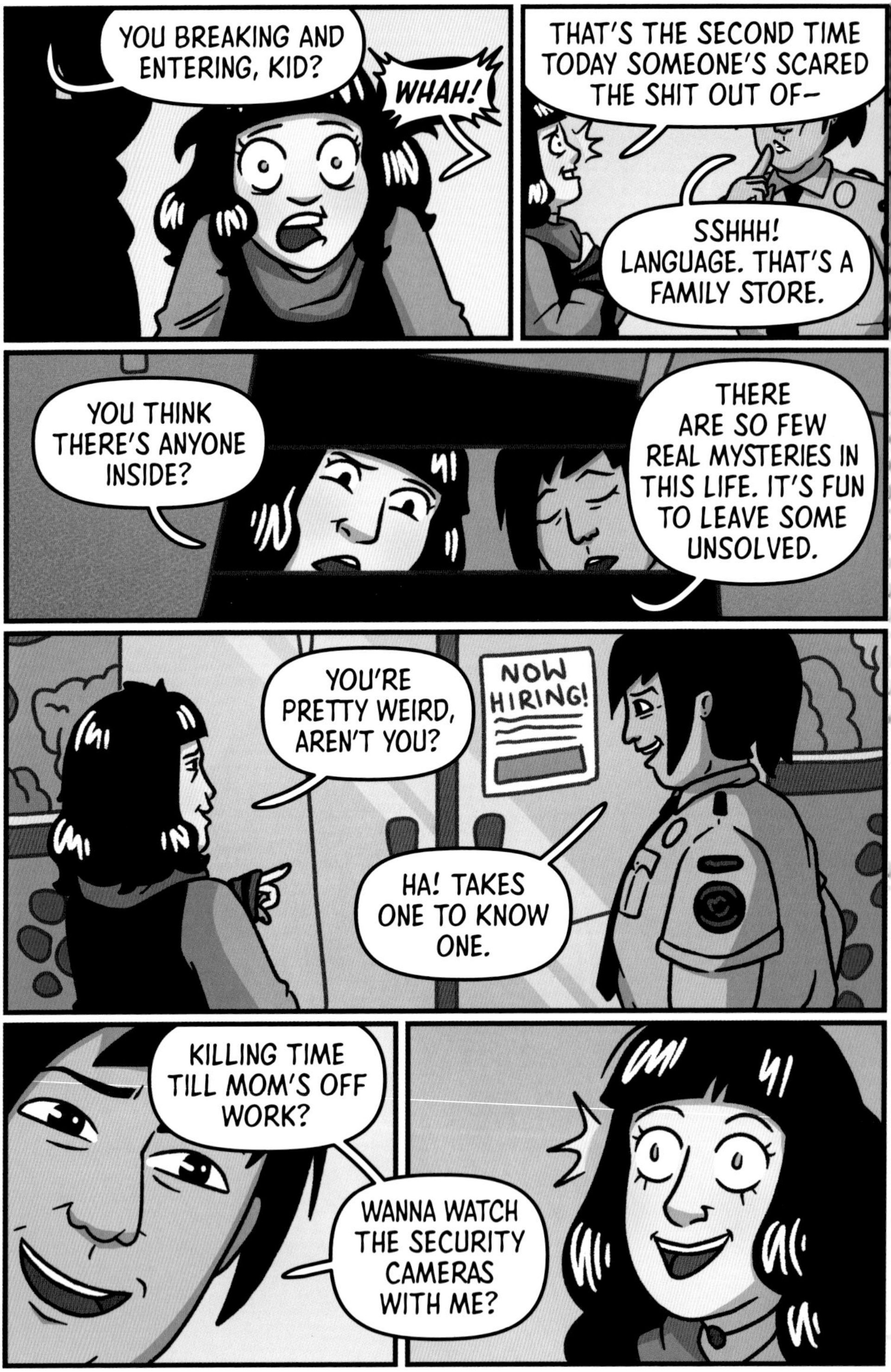
YOU BREAKING AND ENTERING, KID?
WHAH!
THAT'S THE SECOND TIME TODAY SOMEONE'S SCARED THE SHIT OUT OF–
SSHHH! LANGUAGE. THAT'S A FAMILY STORE.
YOU THINK THERE'S ANYONE INSIDE?
THERE ARE SO FEW REAL MYSTERIES IN THIS LIFE. IT'S FUN TO LEAVE SOME UNSOLVED.
YOU'RE PRETTY WEIRD, AREN'T YOU?
NOW HIRING!
HA! TAKES ONE TO KNOW ONE.
KILLING TIME TILL MOM'S OFF WORK?
WANNA WATCH THE SECURITY CAMERAS WITH ME?

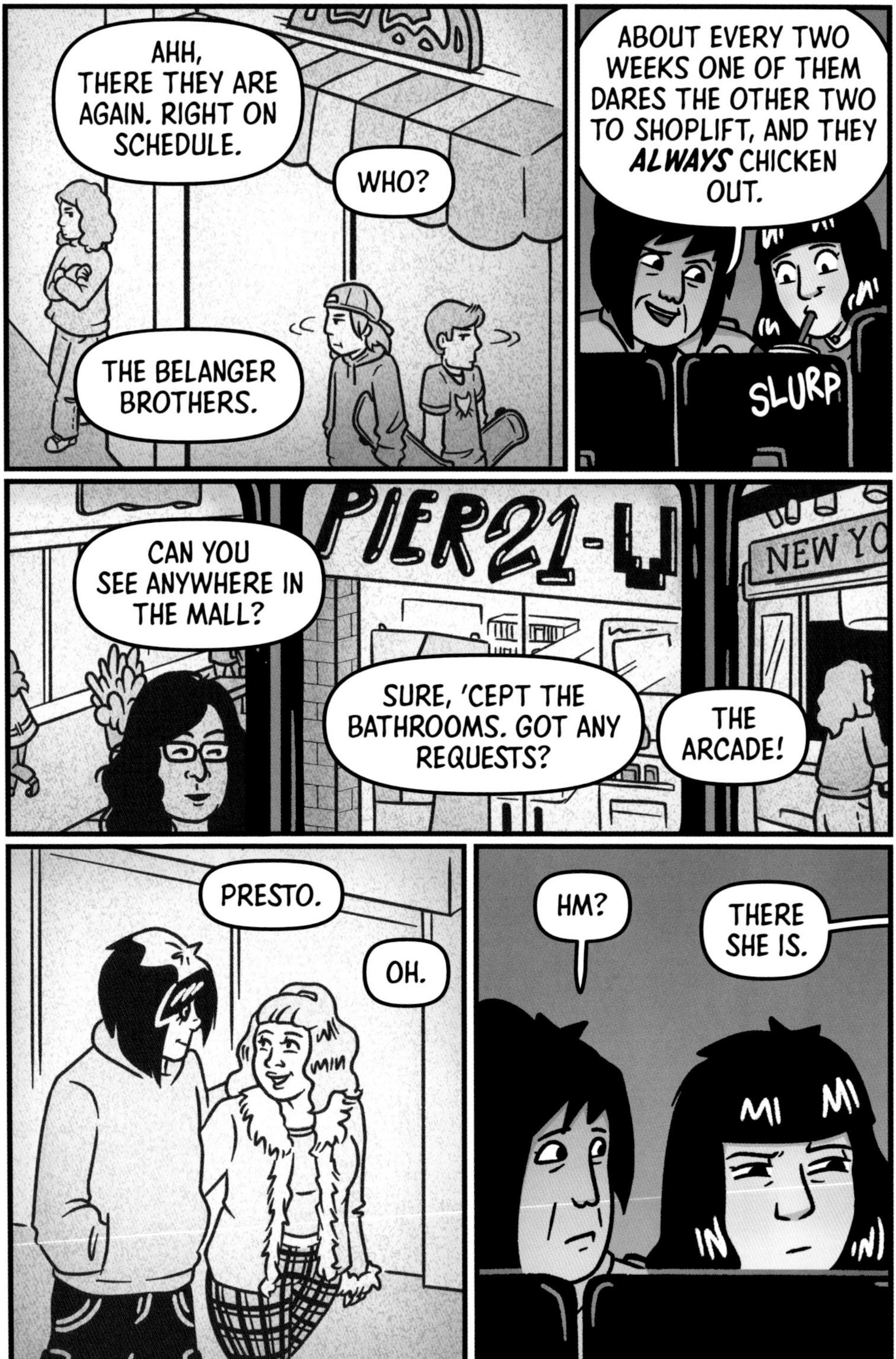
AHH, THERE THEY ARE AGAIN. RIGHT ON SCHEDULE.
WHO?
THE BELANGER BROTHERS.
ABOUT EVERY TWO WEEKS ONE OF THEM DARES THE OTHER TWO TO SHOPLIFT, AND THEY *ALWAYS* CHICKEN OUT.
SLURP
PIER21-U
NEW YO
CAN YOU SEE ANYWHERE IN THE MALL?
SURE, 'CEPT THE BATHROOMS. GOT ANY REQUESTS?
THE ARCADE!
PRESTO.
OH.
HM?
THERE SHE IS.

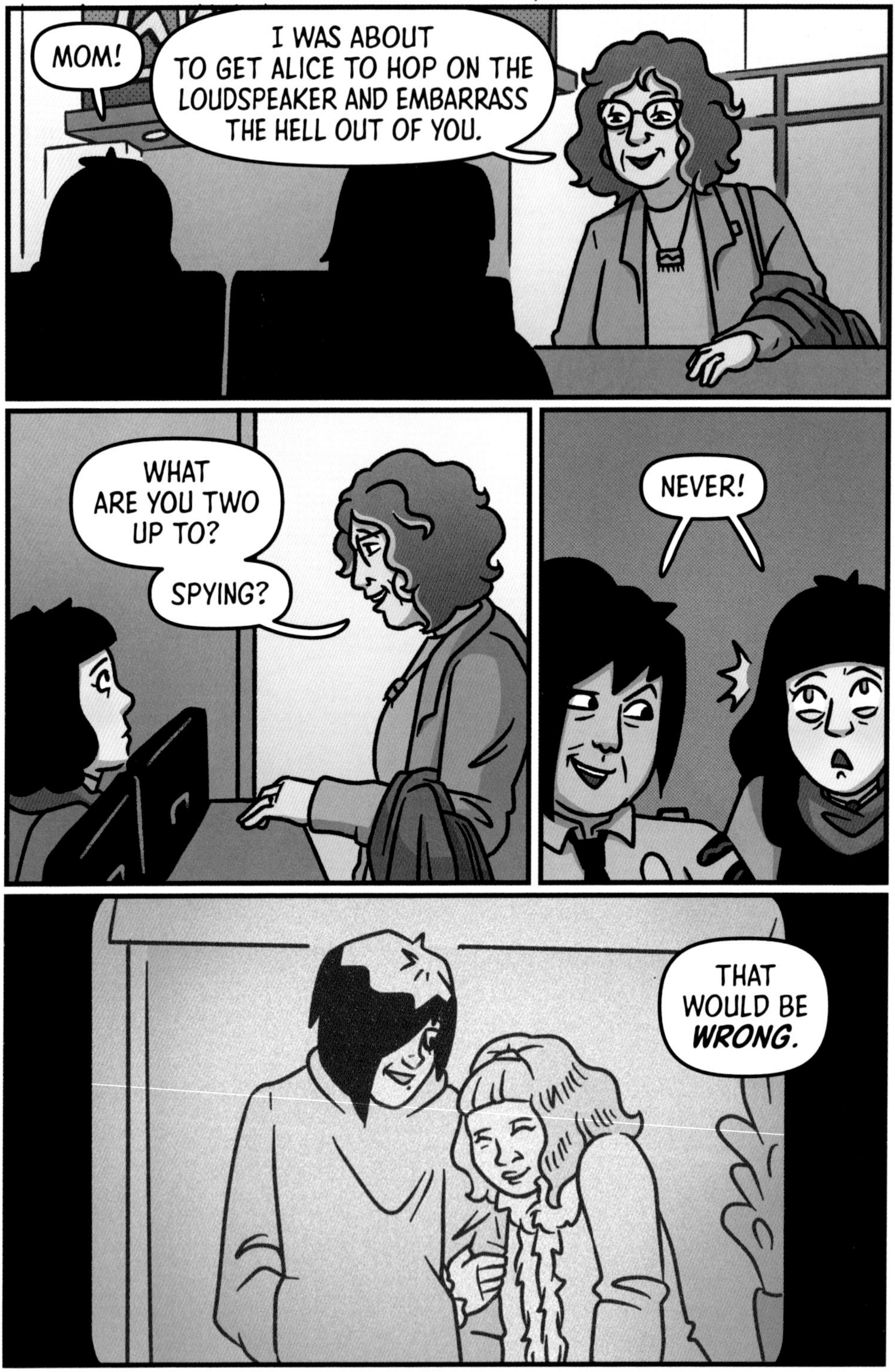
MOM!
I WAS ABOUT TO GET ALICE TO HOP ON THE LOUDSPEAKER AND EMBARRASS THE HELL OUT OF YOU.
WHAT ARE YOU TWO UP TO?
SPYING?
NEVER!
THAT WOULD BE *WRONG*.

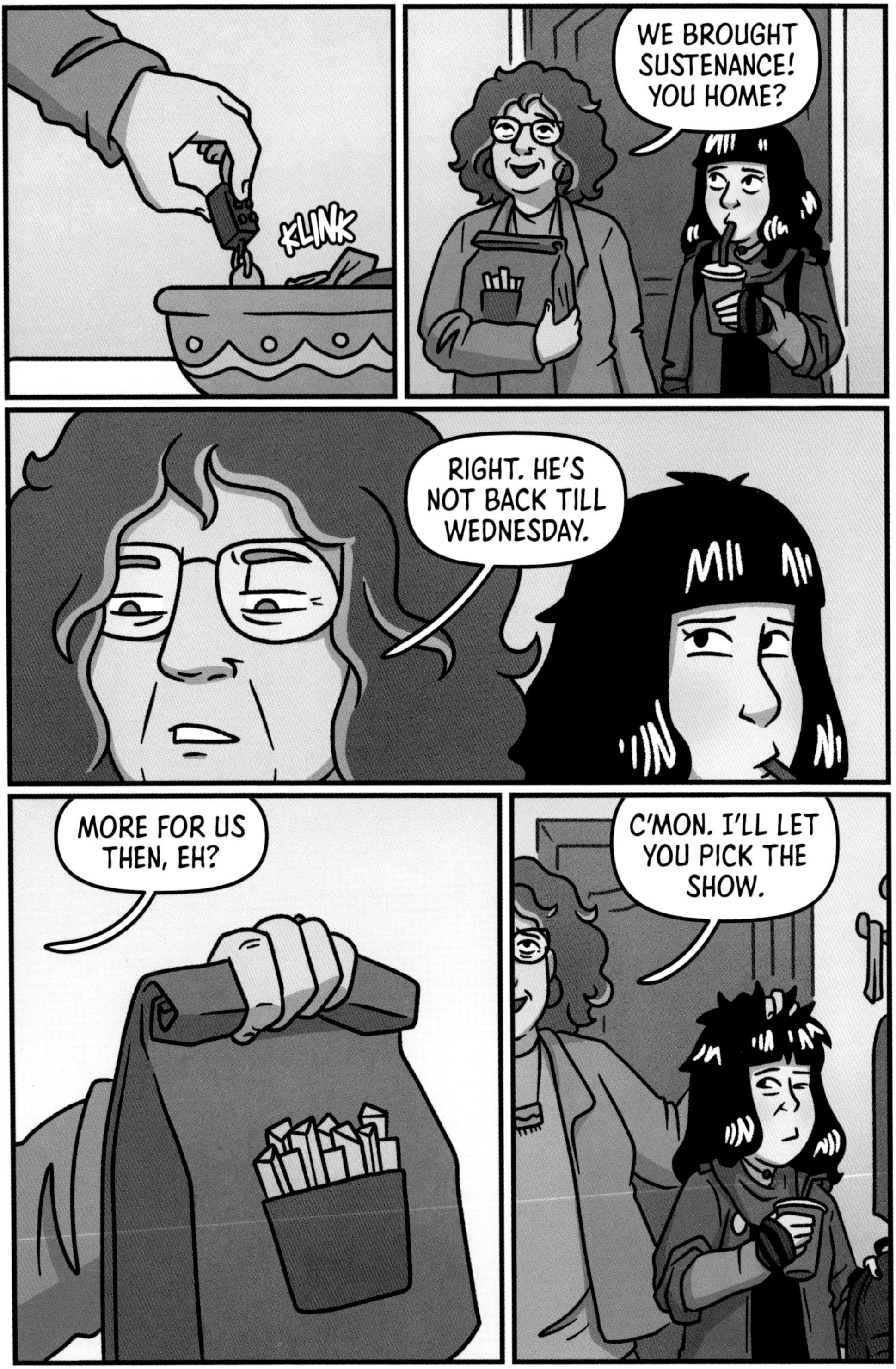
KLINK
WE BROUGHT SUSTENANCE! YOU HOME?
RIGHT. HE'S NOT BACK TILL WEDNESDAY.
MORE FOR US THEN, EH?
C'MON. I'LL LET YOU PICK THE SHOW.

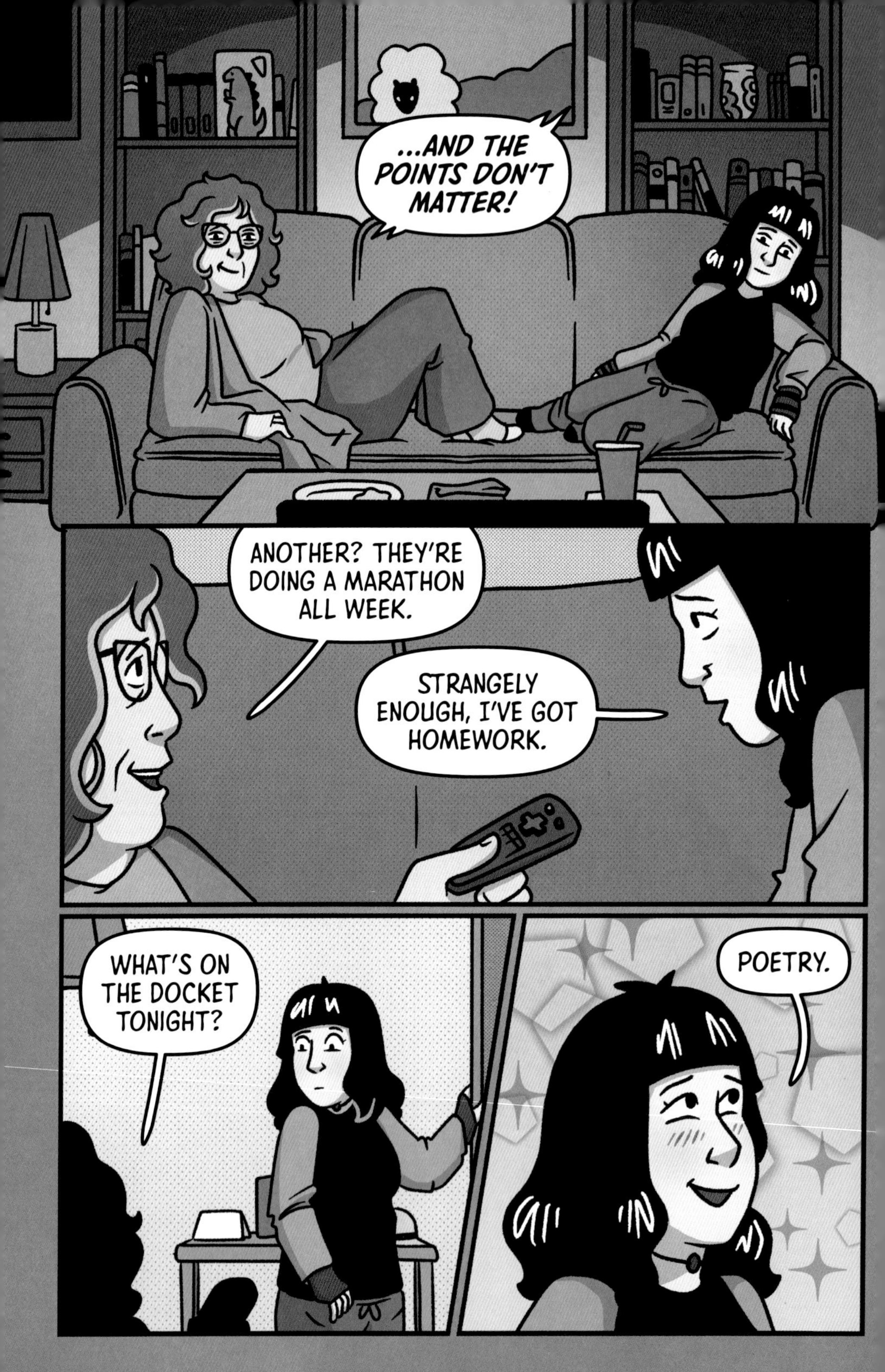
...AND THE POINTS DON'T MATTER!
ANOTHER? THEY'RE DOING A MARATHON ALL WEEK.
STRANGELY ENOUGH, I'VE GOT HOMEWORK.
WHAT'S ON THE DOCKET TONIGHT?
POETRY.

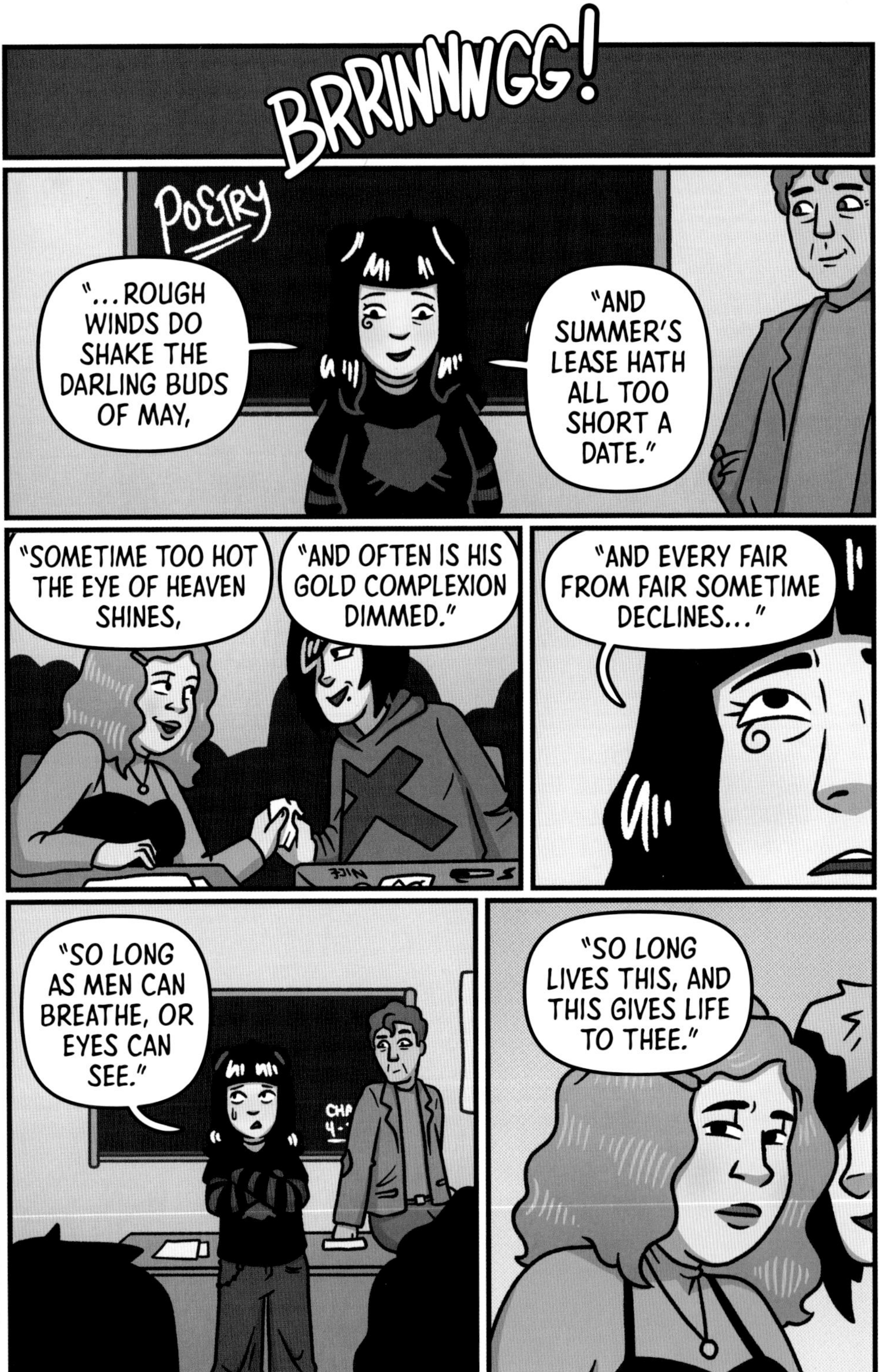
BRRINNNGG!
POETRY
"...ROUGH WINDS DO SHAKE THE DARLING BUDS OF MAY,
"AND SUMMER'S LEASE HATH ALL TOO SHORT A DATE."
"SOMETIME TOO HOT THE EYE OF HEAVEN SHINES,
"AND OFTEN IS HIS GOLD COMPLEXION DIMMED."
"AND EVERY FAIR FROM FAIR SOMETIME DECLINES..."
"SO LONG AS MEN CAN BREATHE, OR EYES CAN SEE."
"SO LONG LIVES THIS, AND THIS GIVES LIFE TO THEE."

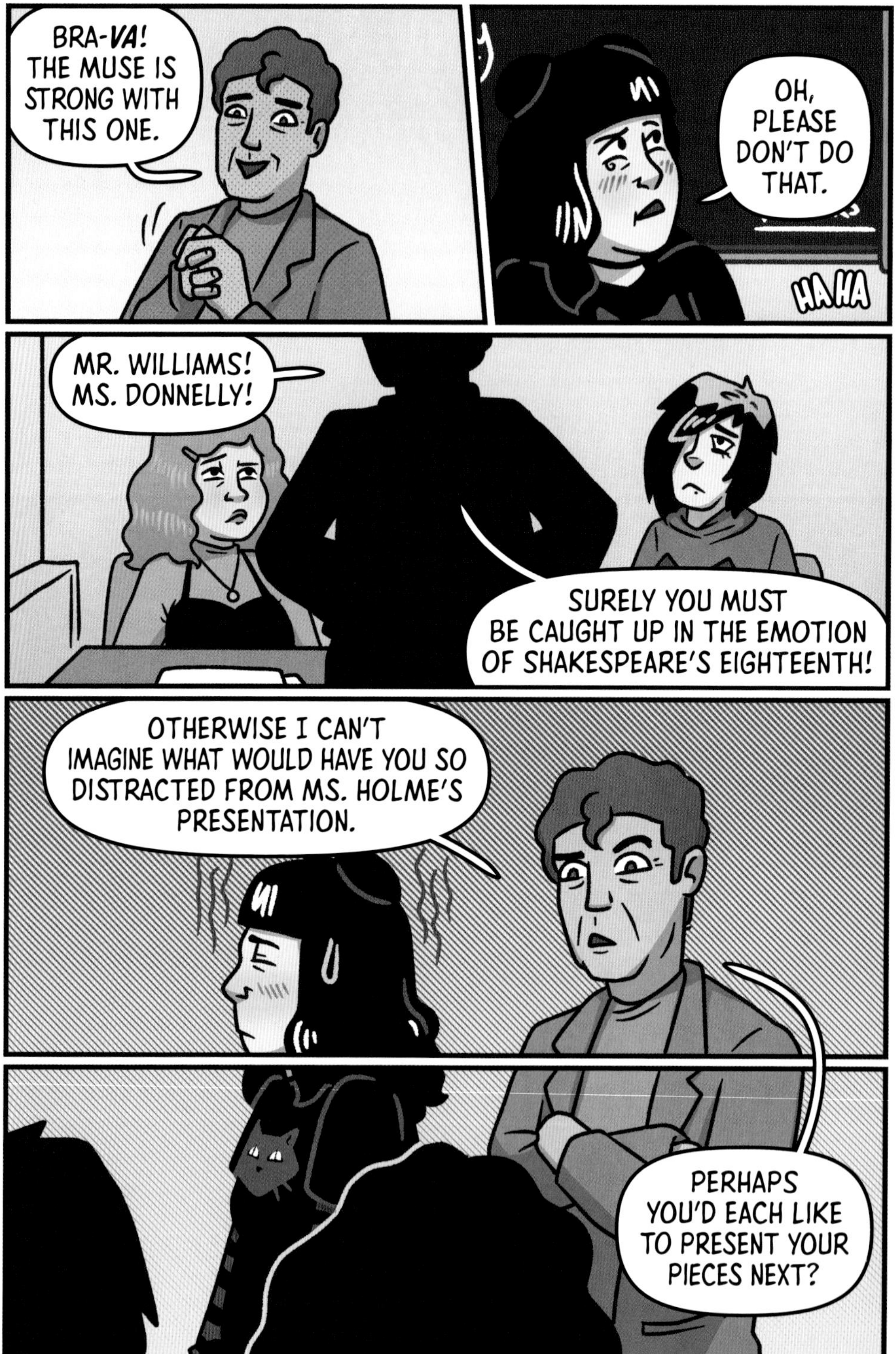
BRA-VA! THE MUSE IS STRONG WITH THIS ONE.
OH, PLEASE DON'T DO THAT.
HA HA
MR. WILLIAMS! MS. DONNELLY!
SURELY YOU MUST BE CAUGHT UP IN THE EMOTION OF SHAKESPEARE'S EIGHTEENTH!
OTHERWISE I CAN'T IMAGINE WHAT WOULD HAVE YOU SO DISTRACTED FROM MS. HOLME'S PRESENTATION.
PERHAPS YOU'D EACH LIKE TO PRESENT YOUR PIECES NEXT?

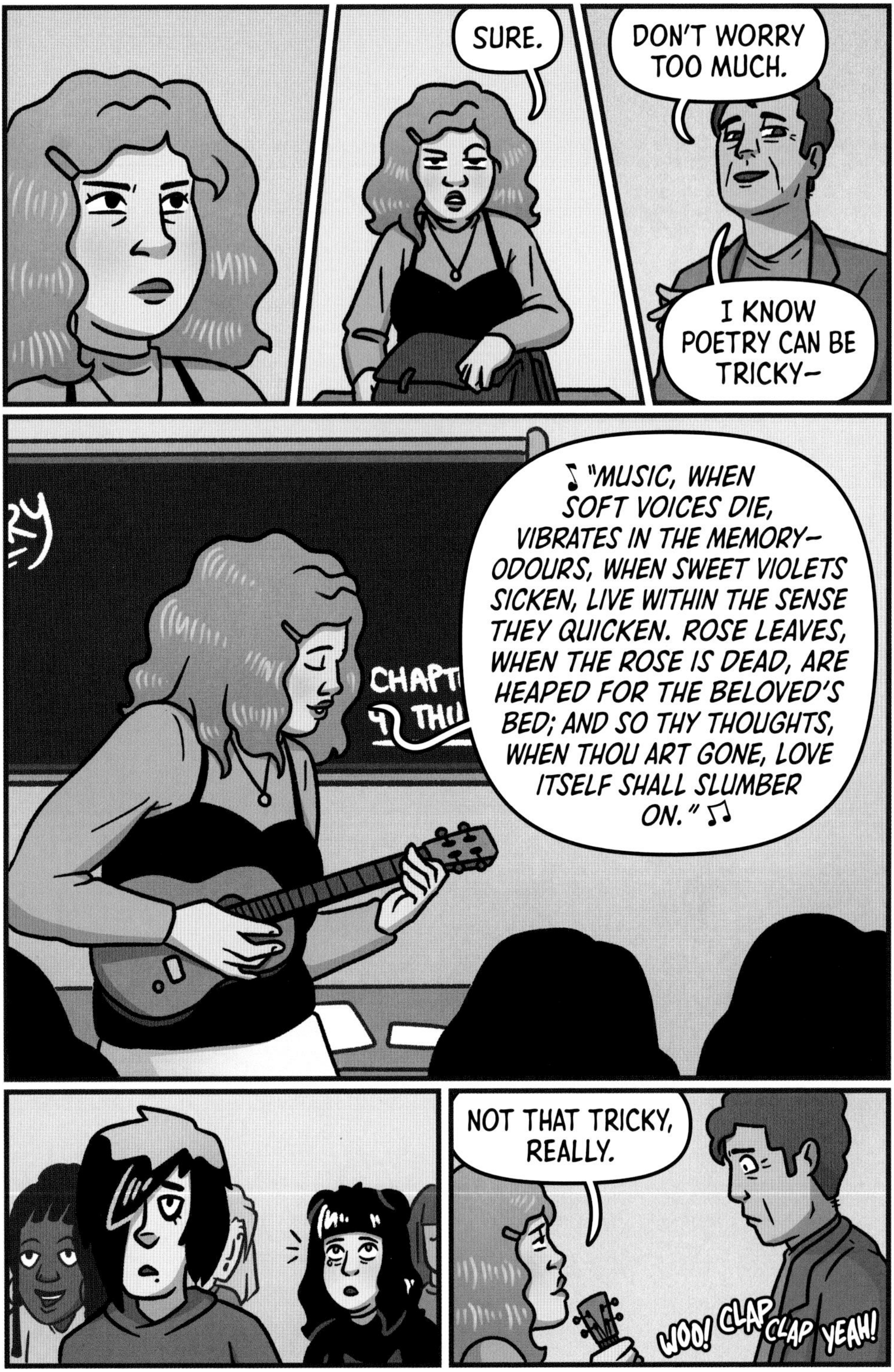
SURE.
DON'T WORRY TOO MUCH.
I KNOW POETRY CAN BE TRICKY—
"MUSIC, WHEN SOFT VOICES DIE, VIBRATES IN THE MEMORY— ODOURS, WHEN SWEET VIOLETS SICKEN, LIVE WITHIN THE SENSE THEY QUICKEN. ROSE LEAVES, WHEN THE ROSE IS DEAD, ARE HEAPED FOR THE BELOVED'S BED; AND SO THY THOUGHTS, WHEN THOU ART GONE, LOVE ITSELF SHALL SLUMBER ON."
NOT THAT TRICKY, REALLY.
WOO! CLAP CLAP YEAH!

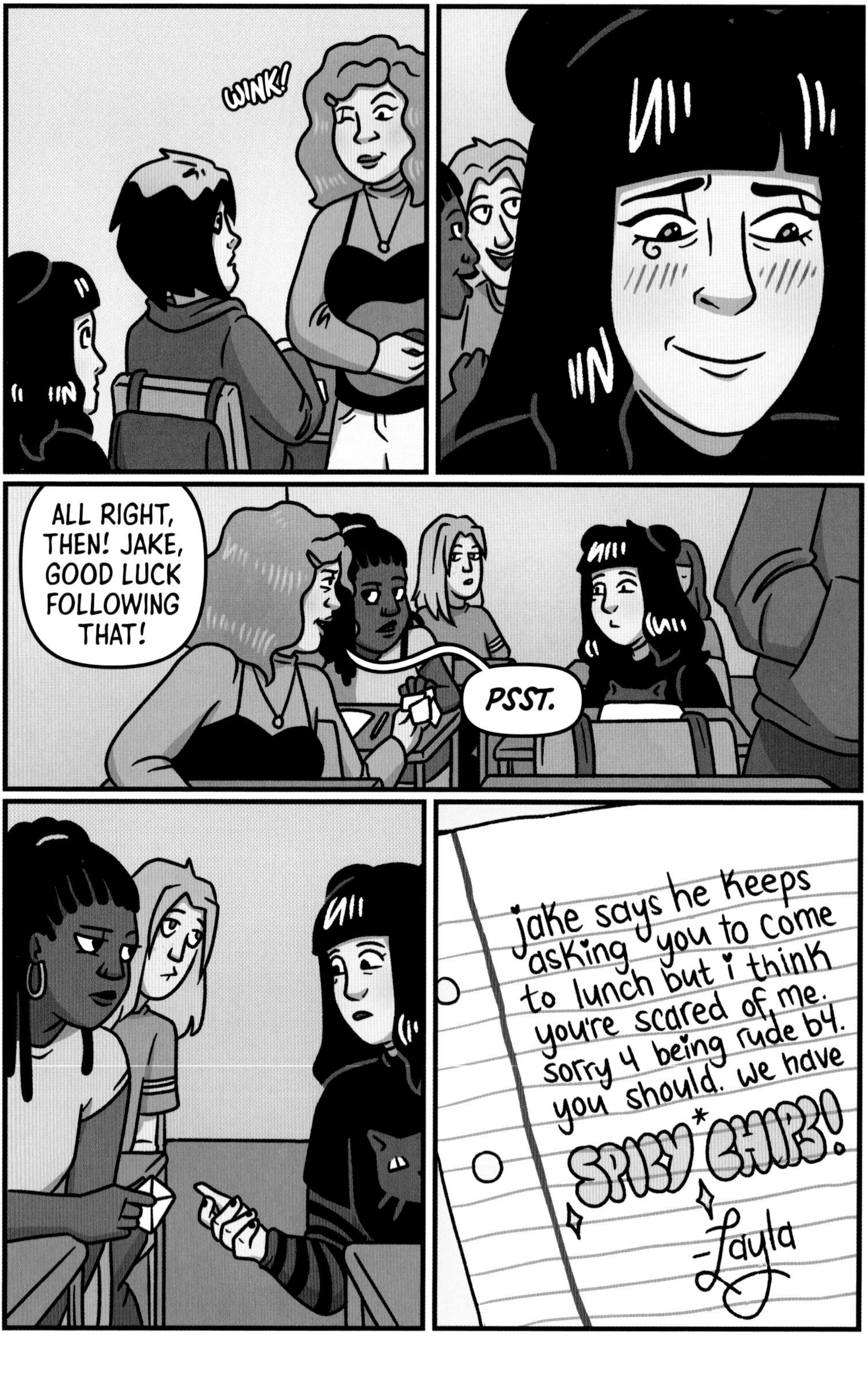
WINK!
ALL RIGHT, THEN! JAKE, GOOD LUCK FOLLOWING THAT!
PSST.
jake says he keeps asking you to come to lunch but i think you're scared of me. sorry 4 being rude b4. you should. we have
SPICY CHIPS!
-Layla

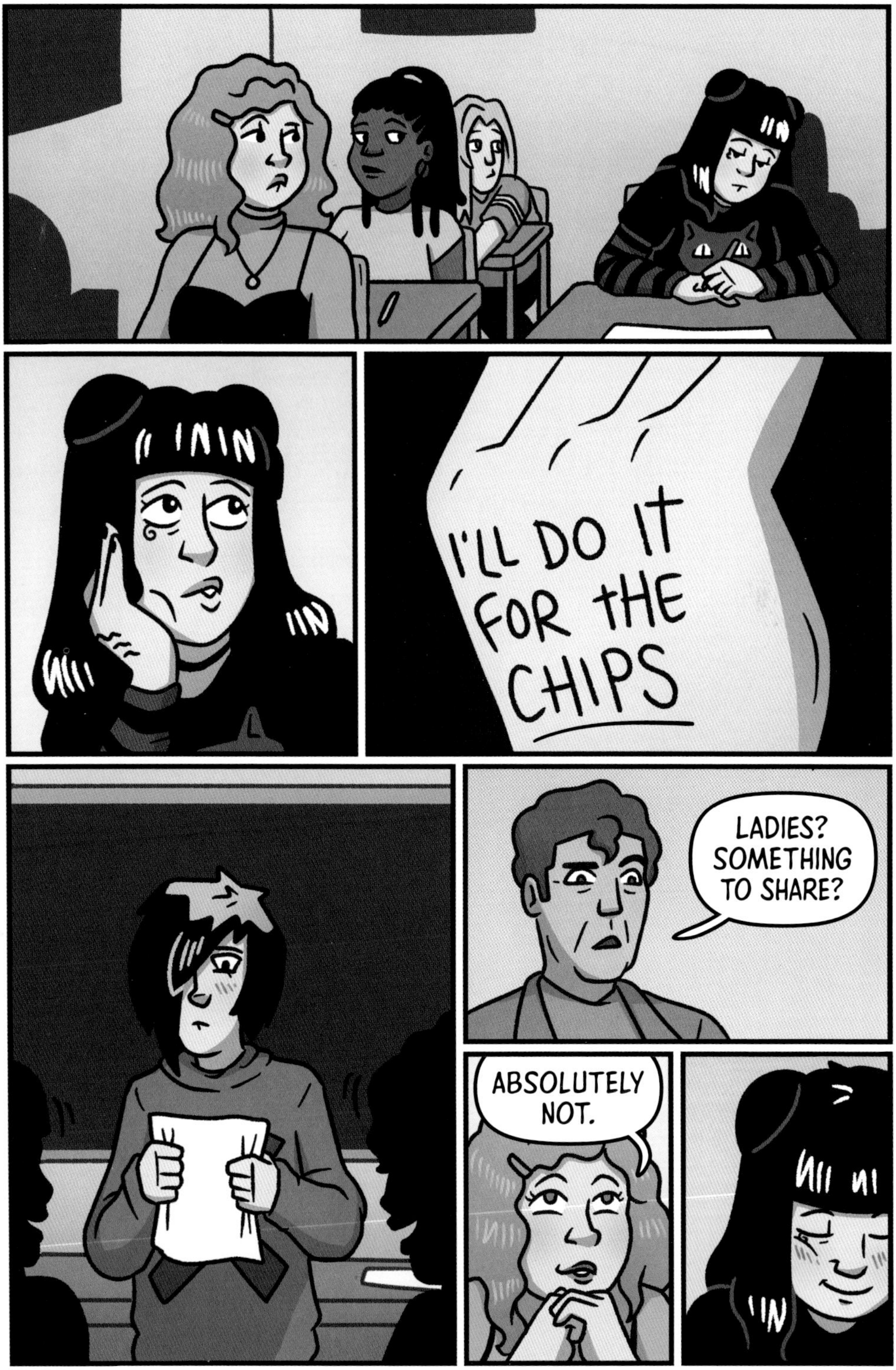
I'LL DO IT
FOR THE
CHIPS
LADIES? SOMETHING TO SHARE?
ABSOLUTELY NOT.

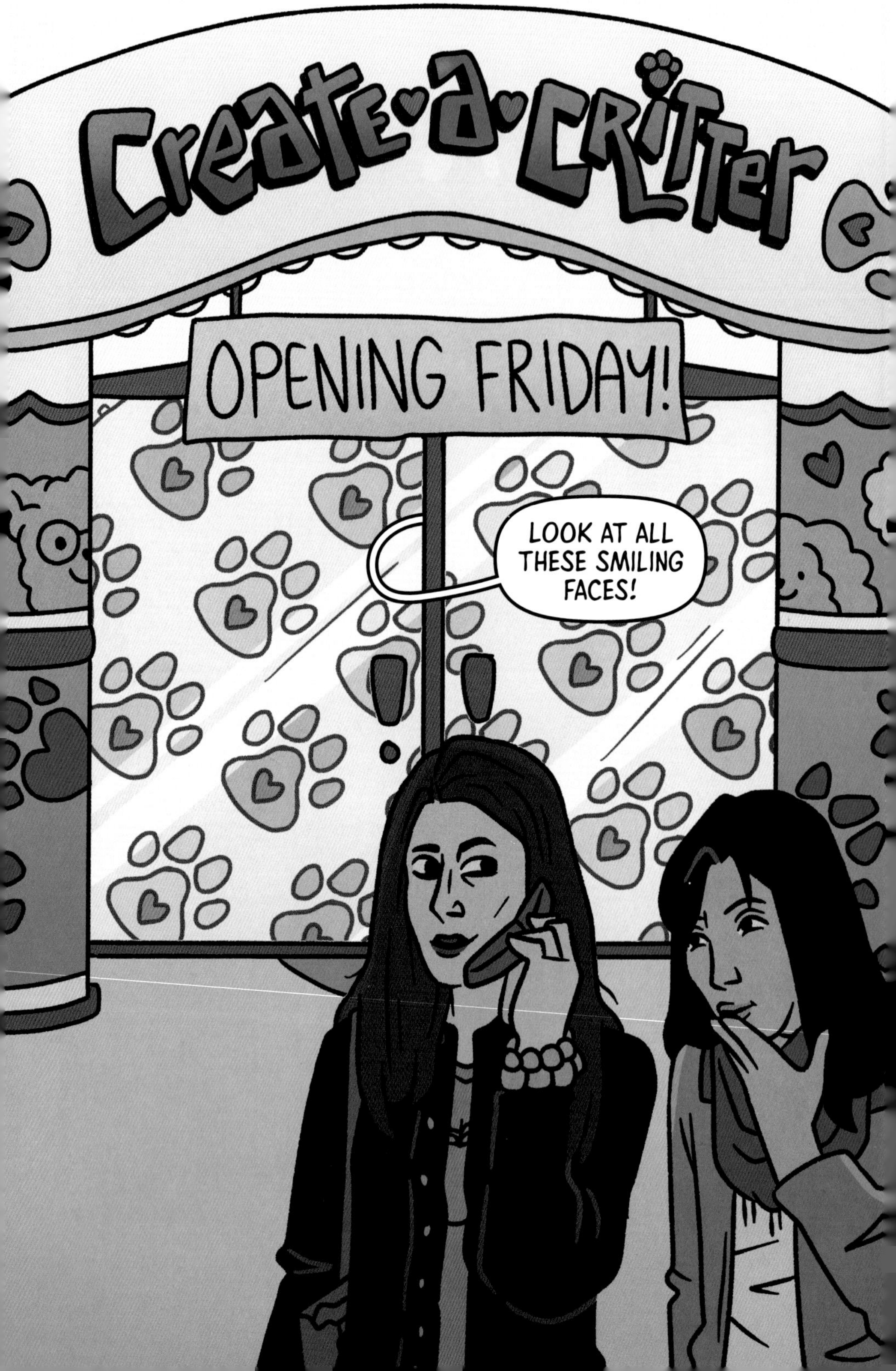
Create-a-Critter
OPENING FRIDAY!
LOOK AT ALL THESE SMILING FACES!

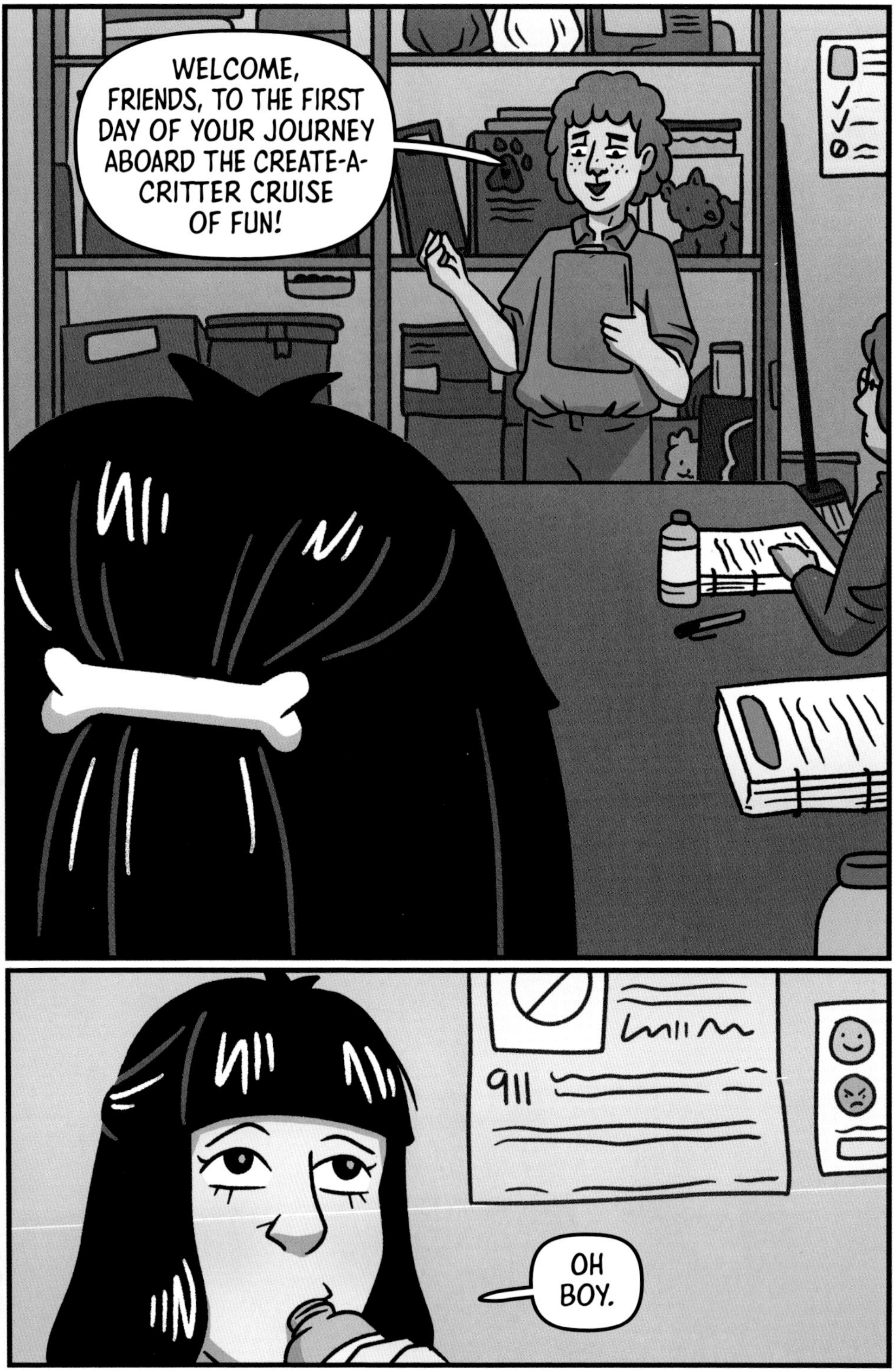
WELCOME, FRIENDS, TO THE FIRST DAY OF YOUR JOURNEY ABOARD THE CREATE-A-CRITTER CRUISE OF FUN!
OH BOY.

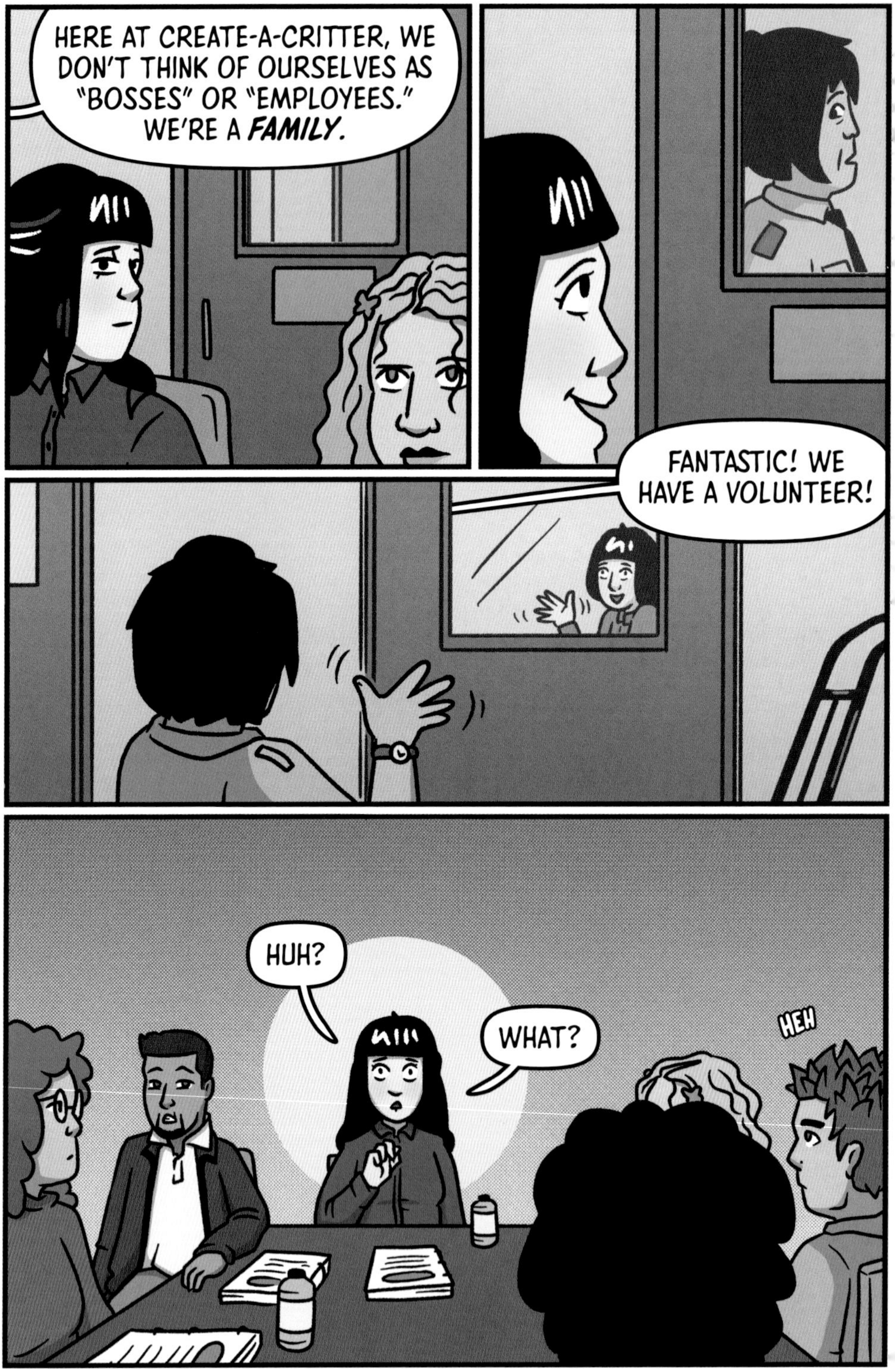
HERE AT CREATE-A-CRITTER, WE DON'T THINK OF OURSELVES AS "BOSSES" OR "EMPLOYEES." WE'RE A *FAMILY*.
FANTASTIC! WE HAVE A VOLUNTEER!
HUH?
WHAT?
HEH

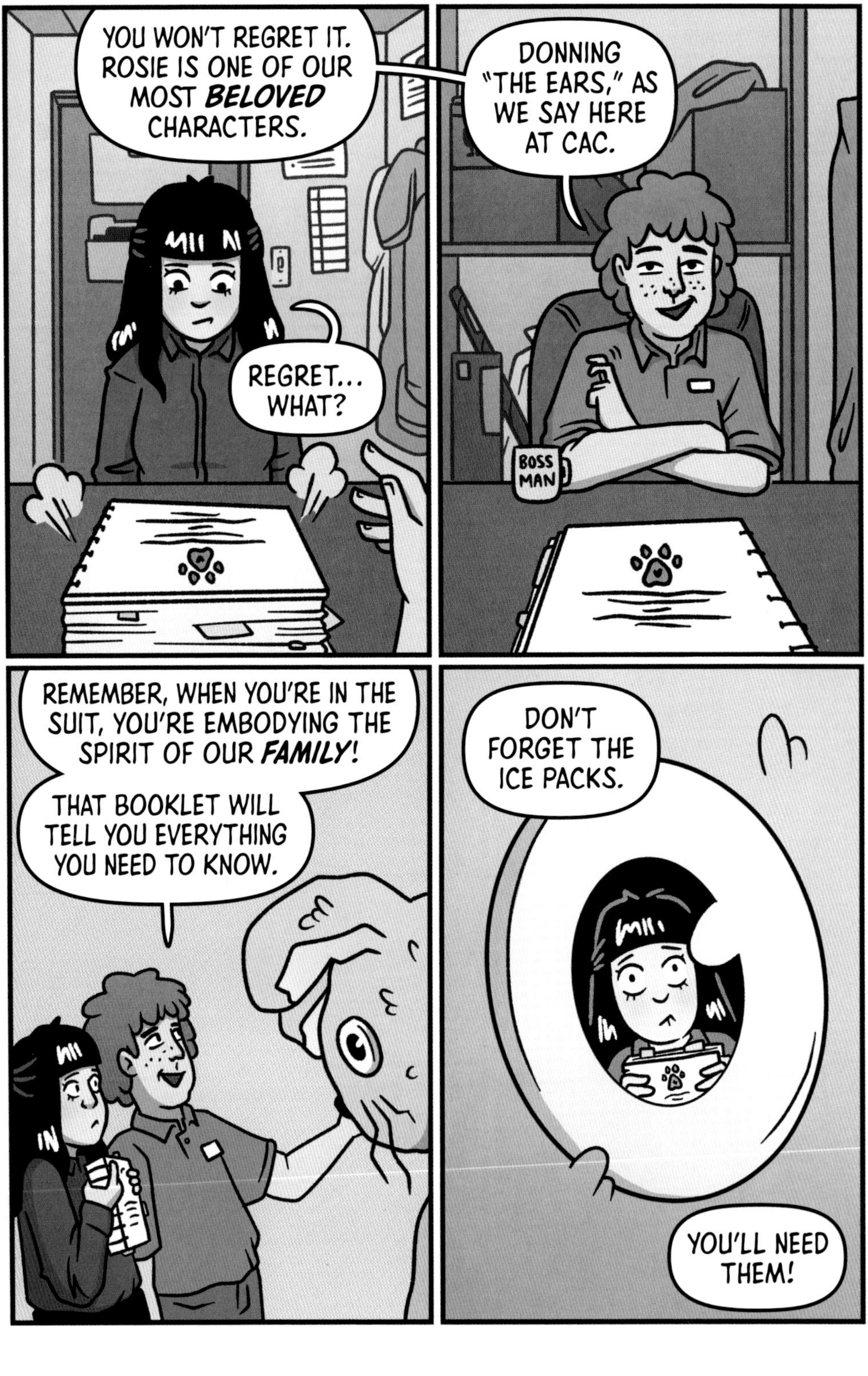
YOU WON'T REGRET IT. ROSIE IS ONE OF OUR MOST ***BELOVED*** CHARACTERS.
REGRET... WHAT?
DONNING "THE EARS," AS WE SAY HERE AT CAC.
BOSS MAN
REMEMBER, WHEN YOU'RE IN THE SUIT, YOU'RE EMBODYING THE SPIRIT OF OUR ***FAMILY***!
THAT BOOKLET WILL TELL YOU EVERYTHING YOU NEED TO KNOW.
DON'T FORGET THE ICE PACKS.
YOU'LL NEED THEM!

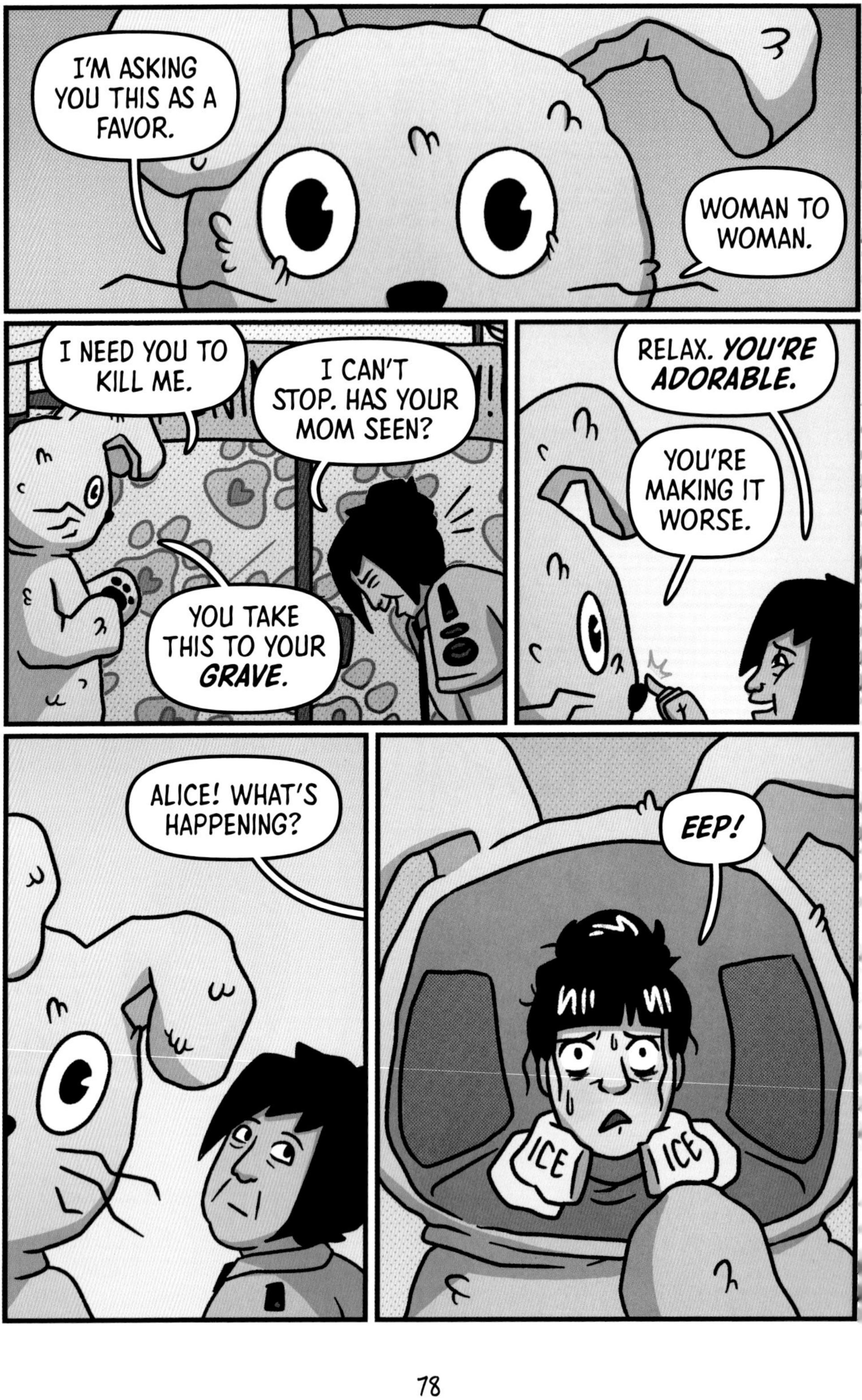
I'M ASKING YOU THIS AS A FAVOR.
WOMAN TO WOMAN.
I NEED YOU TO KILL ME.
I CAN'T STOP. HAS YOUR MOM SEEN?
YOU TAKE THIS TO YOUR *GRAVE.*
RELAX. *YOU'RE ADORABLE.*
YOU'RE MAKING IT WORSE.
ALICE! WHAT'S HAPPENING?
EEP!
ICE
ICE

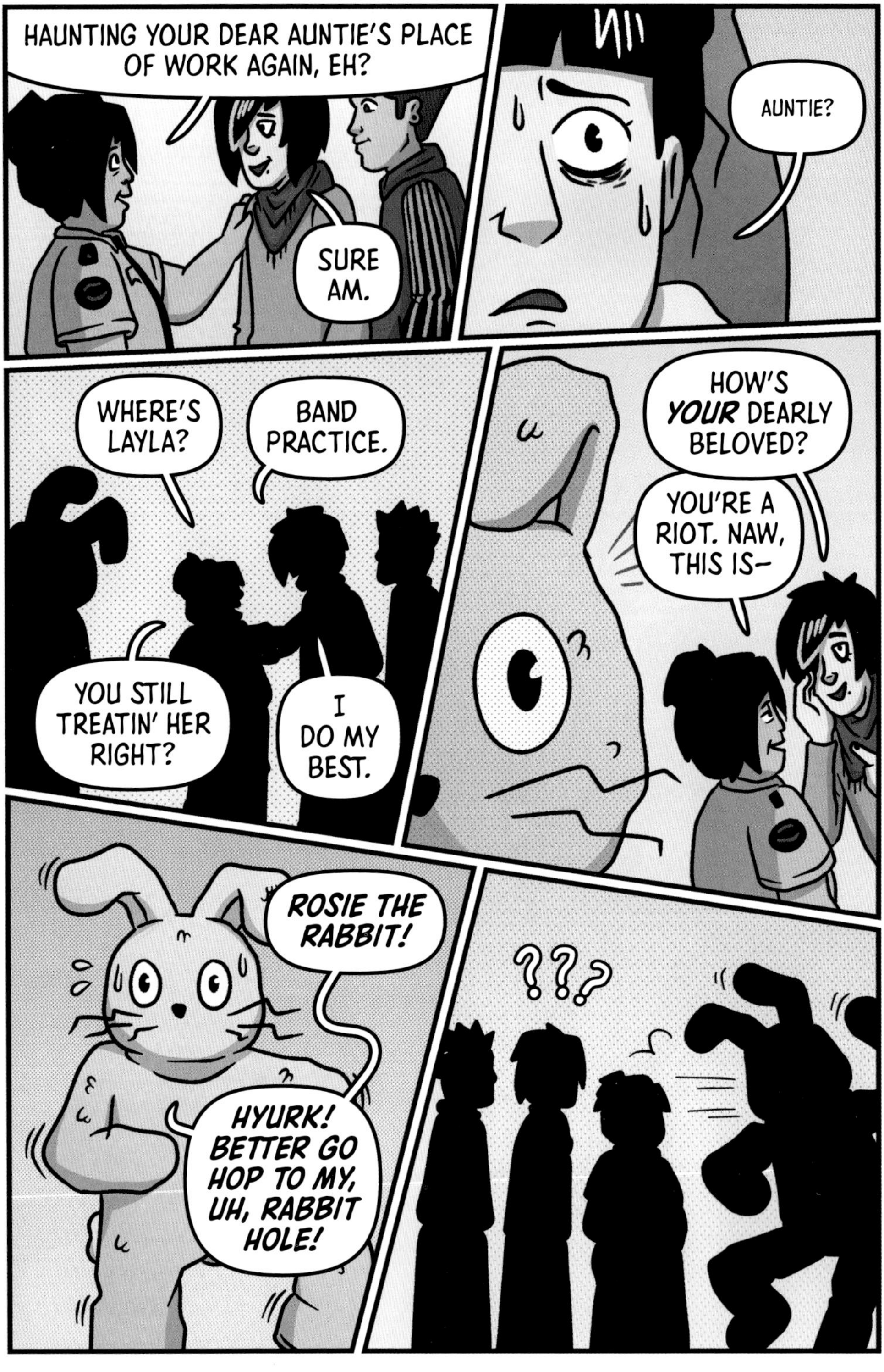
HAUNTING YOUR DEAR AUNTIE'S PLACE OF WORK AGAIN, EH?
SURE AM.
AUNTIE?
WHERE'S LAYLA?
BAND PRACTICE.
YOU STILL TREATIN' HER RIGHT?
I DO MY BEST.
HOW'S *YOUR* DEARLY BELOVED?
YOU'RE A RIOT. NAW, THIS IS–
ROSIE THE RABBIT!
HYURK! BETTER GO HOP TO MY, UH, RABBIT HOLE!
???

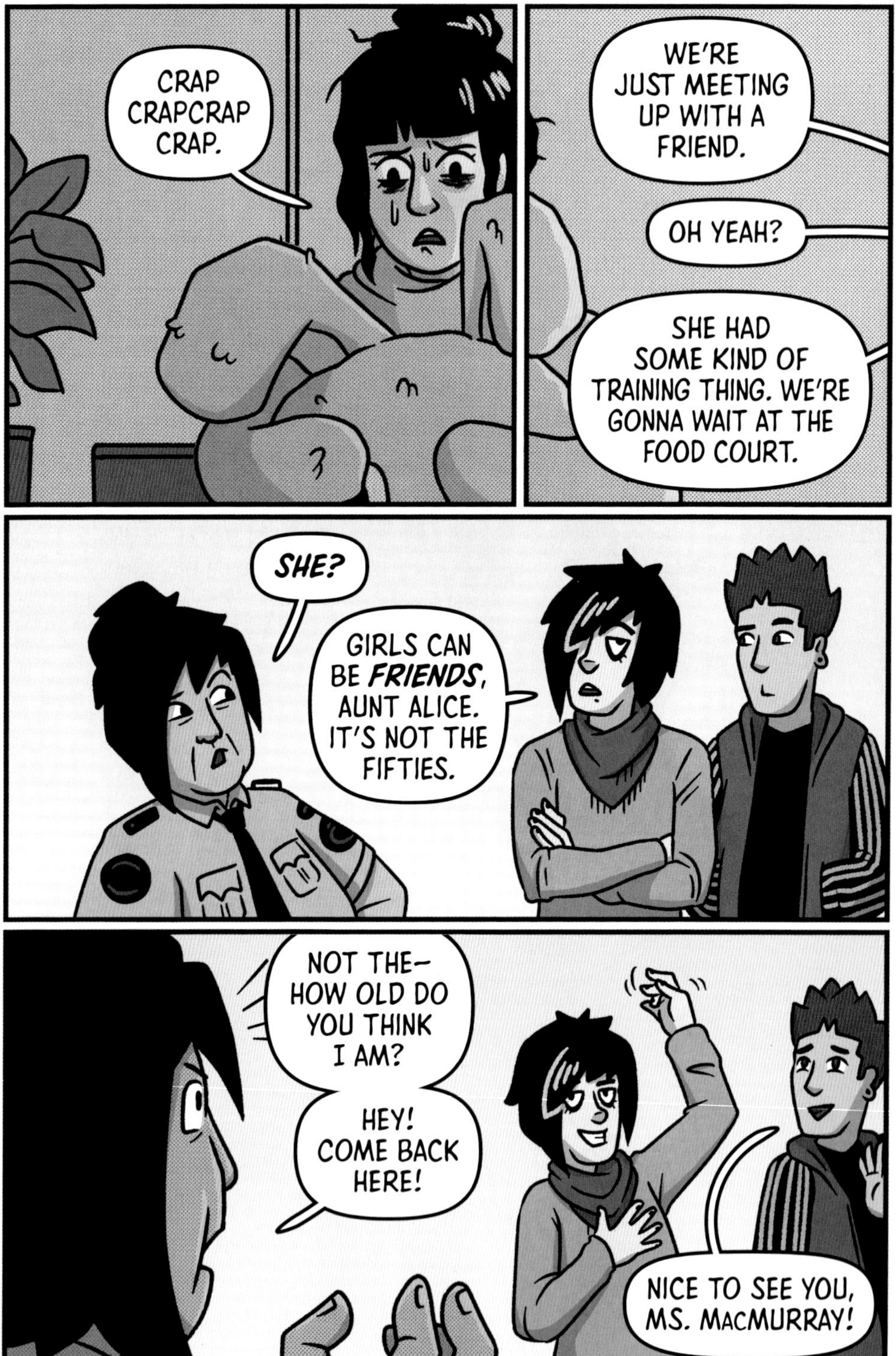
CRAP CRAPCRAP CRAP.
WE'RE JUST MEETING UP WITH A FRIEND.
OH YEAH?
SHE HAD SOME KIND OF TRAINING THING. WE'RE GONNA WAIT AT THE FOOD COURT.
SHE?
GIRLS CAN BE FRIENDS, AUNT ALICE. IT'S NOT THE FIFTIES.
NOT THE— HOW OLD DO YOU THINK I AM?
HEY! COME BACK HERE!
NICE TO SEE YOU, MS. MACMURRAY!

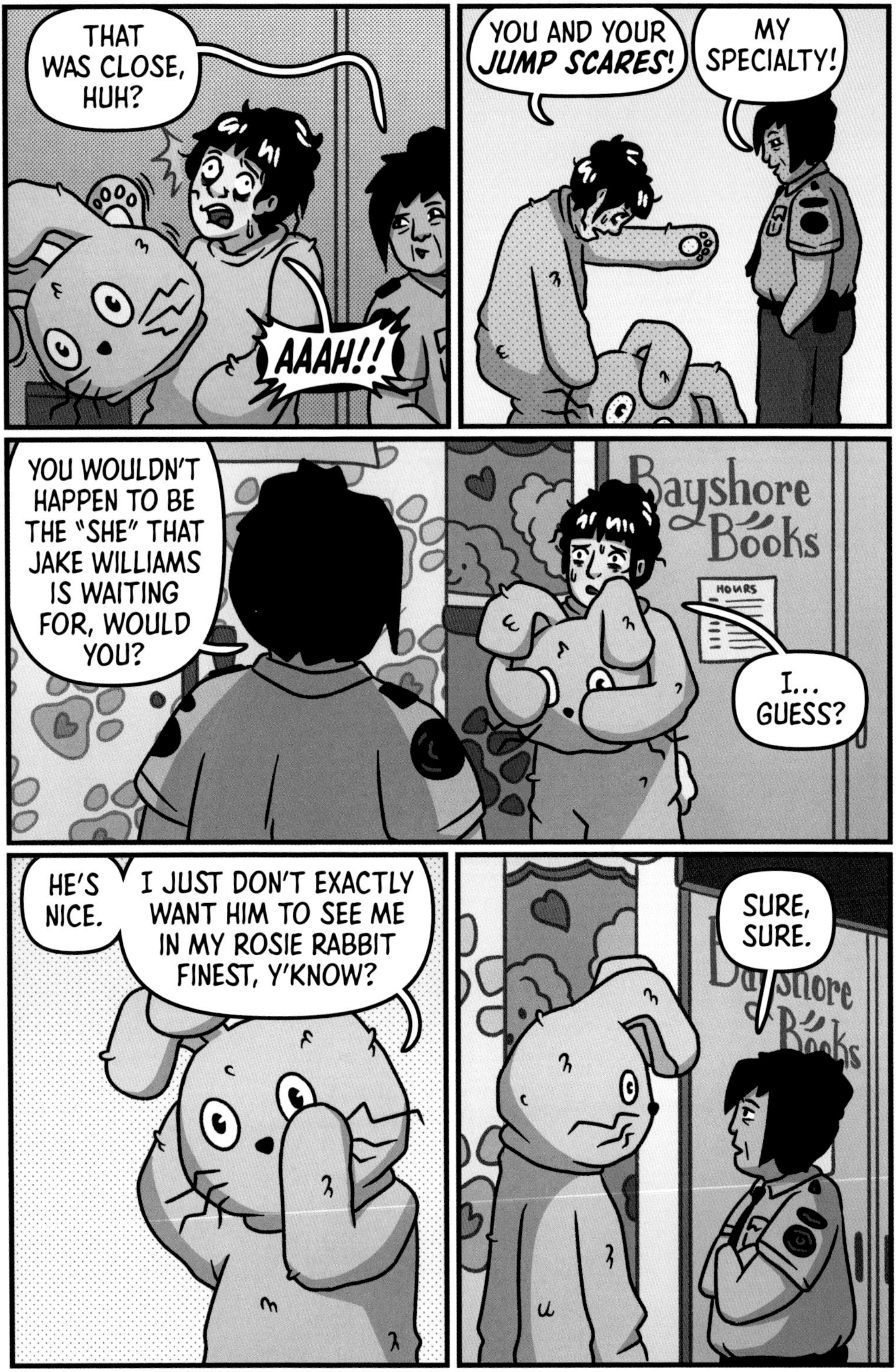
THAT WAS CLOSE, HUH?
AAAH!!
YOU AND YOUR JUMP SCARES!
MY SPECIALTY!
YOU WOULDN'T HAPPEN TO BE THE "SHE" THAT JAKE WILLIAMS IS WAITING FOR, WOULD YOU?
Bayshore Books
HOURS
I... GUESS?
HE'S NICE.
I JUST DON'T EXACTLY WANT HIM TO SEE ME IN MY ROSIE RABBIT FINEST, Y'KNOW?
SURE, SURE.

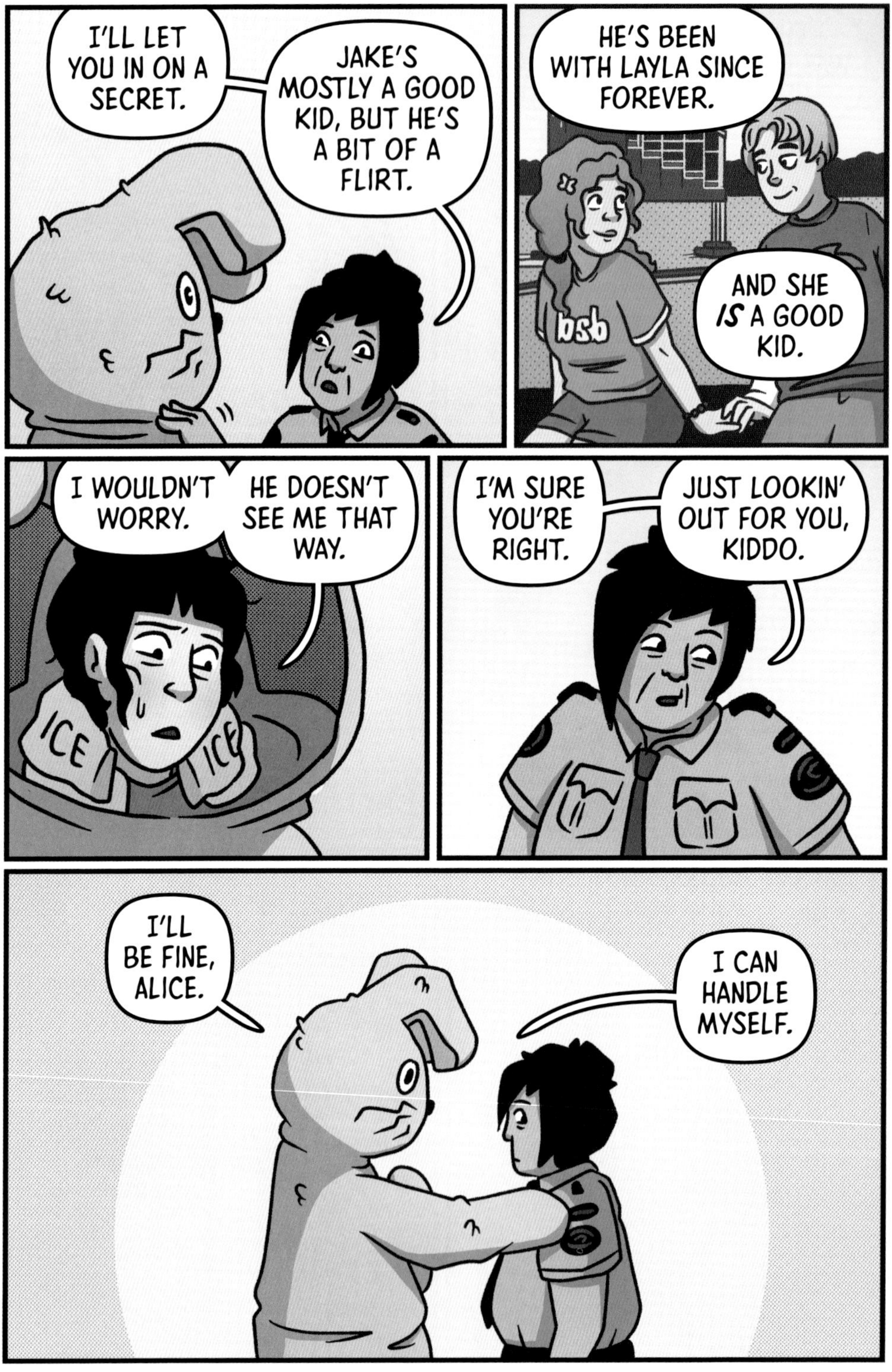
I'LL LET YOU IN ON A SECRET.
JAKE'S MOSTLY A GOOD KID, BUT HE'S A BIT OF A FLIRT.
HE'S BEEN WITH LAYLA SINCE FOREVER.
bsb
AND SHE *IS* A GOOD KID.
I WOULDN'T WORRY.
HE DOESN'T SEE ME THAT WAY.
ICE
ICE
I'M SURE YOU'RE RIGHT.
JUST LOOKIN' OUT FOR YOU, KIDDO.
I'LL BE FINE, ALICE.
I CAN HANDLE MYSELF.

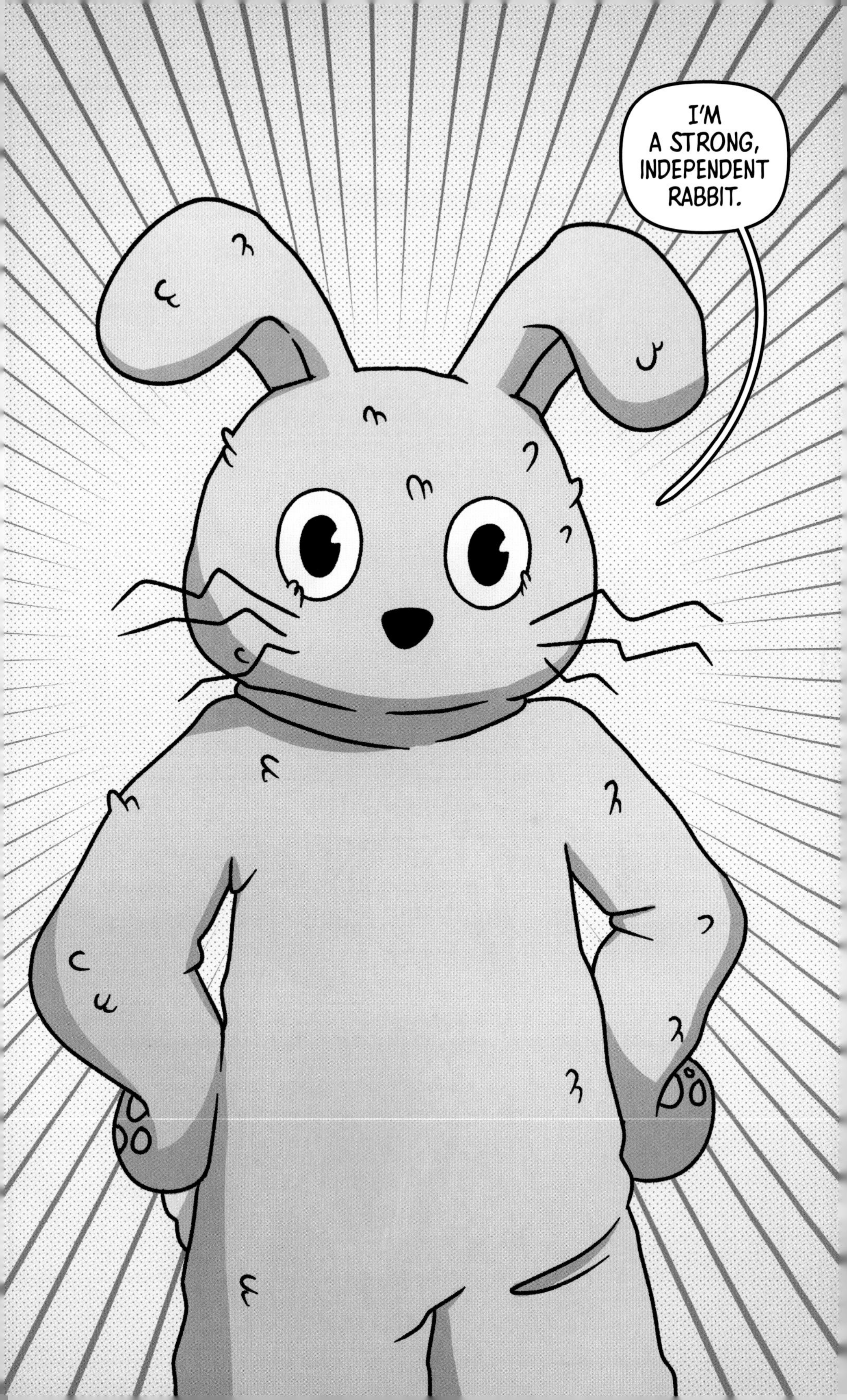
I'M A STRONG, INDEPENDENT RABBIT.

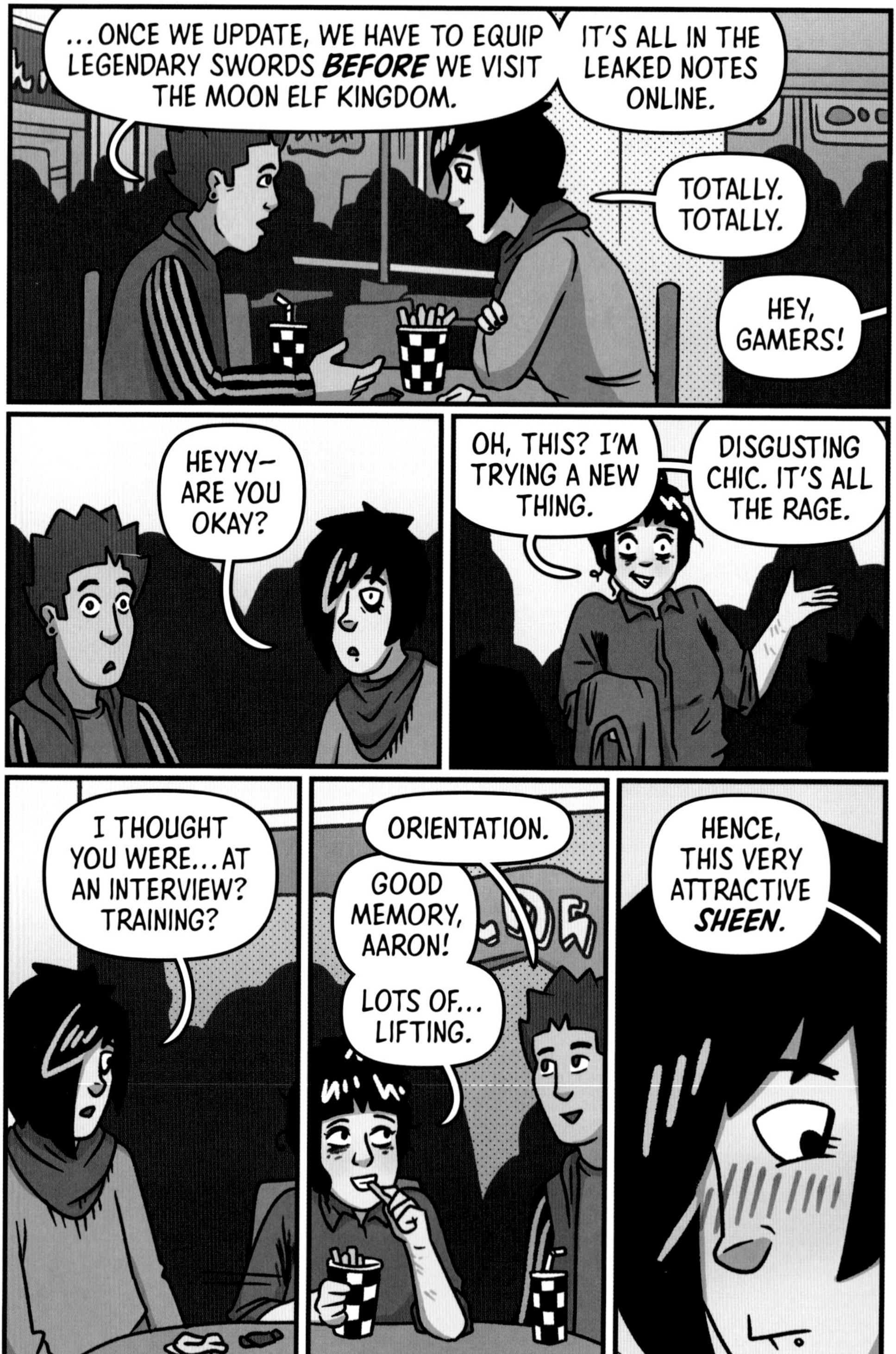
...ONCE WE UPDATE, WE HAVE TO EQUIP LEGENDARY SWORDS **BEFORE** WE VISIT THE MOON ELF KINGDOM.
IT'S ALL IN THE LEAKED NOTES ONLINE.
TOTALLY. TOTALLY.
HEY, GAMERS!
HEYYY– ARE YOU OKAY?
OH, THIS? I'M TRYING A NEW THING.
DISGUSTING CHIC. IT'S ALL THE RAGE.
I THOUGHT YOU WERE...AT AN INTERVIEW? TRAINING?
ORIENTATION.
GOOD MEMORY, AARON!
LOTS OF... LIFTING.
HENCE, THIS VERY ATTRACTIVE **SHEEN.**

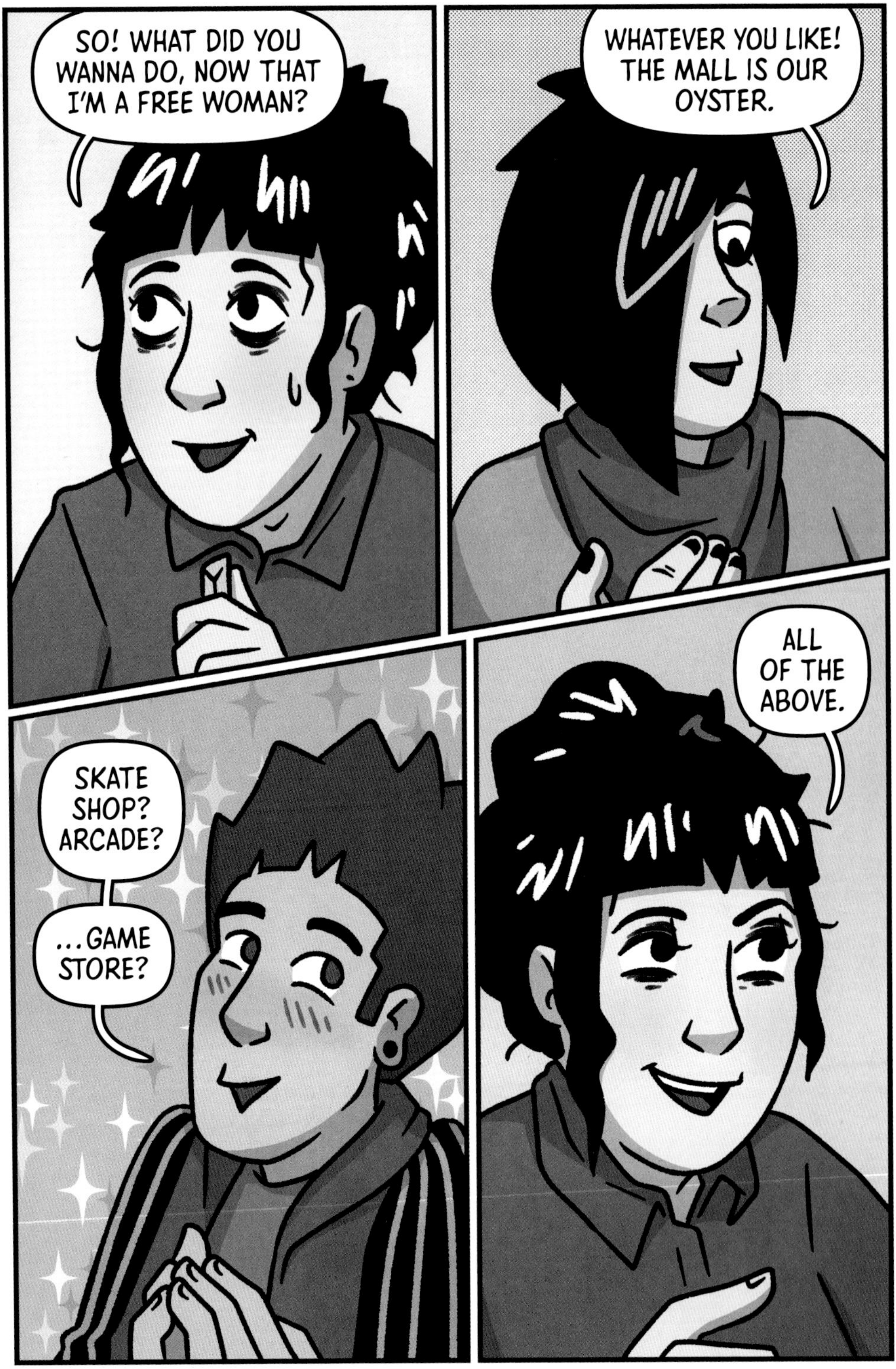
SO! WHAT DID YOU WANNA DO, NOW THAT I'M A FREE WOMAN?
WHATEVER YOU LIKE! THE MALL IS OUR OYSTER.
SKATE SHOP? ARCADE?
...GAME STORE?
ALL OF THE ABOVE.

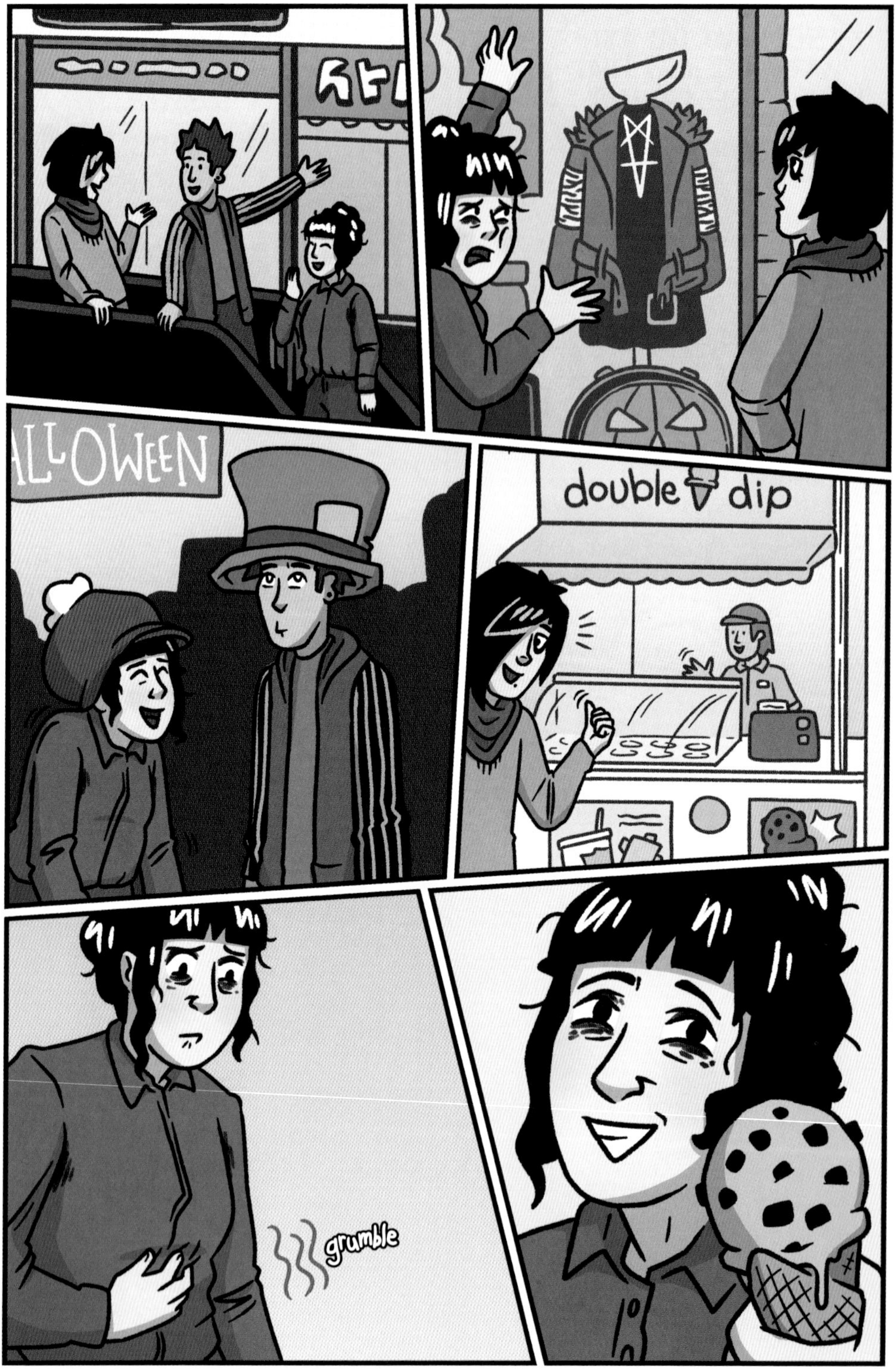
ALLOWEEN
double dip
grumble

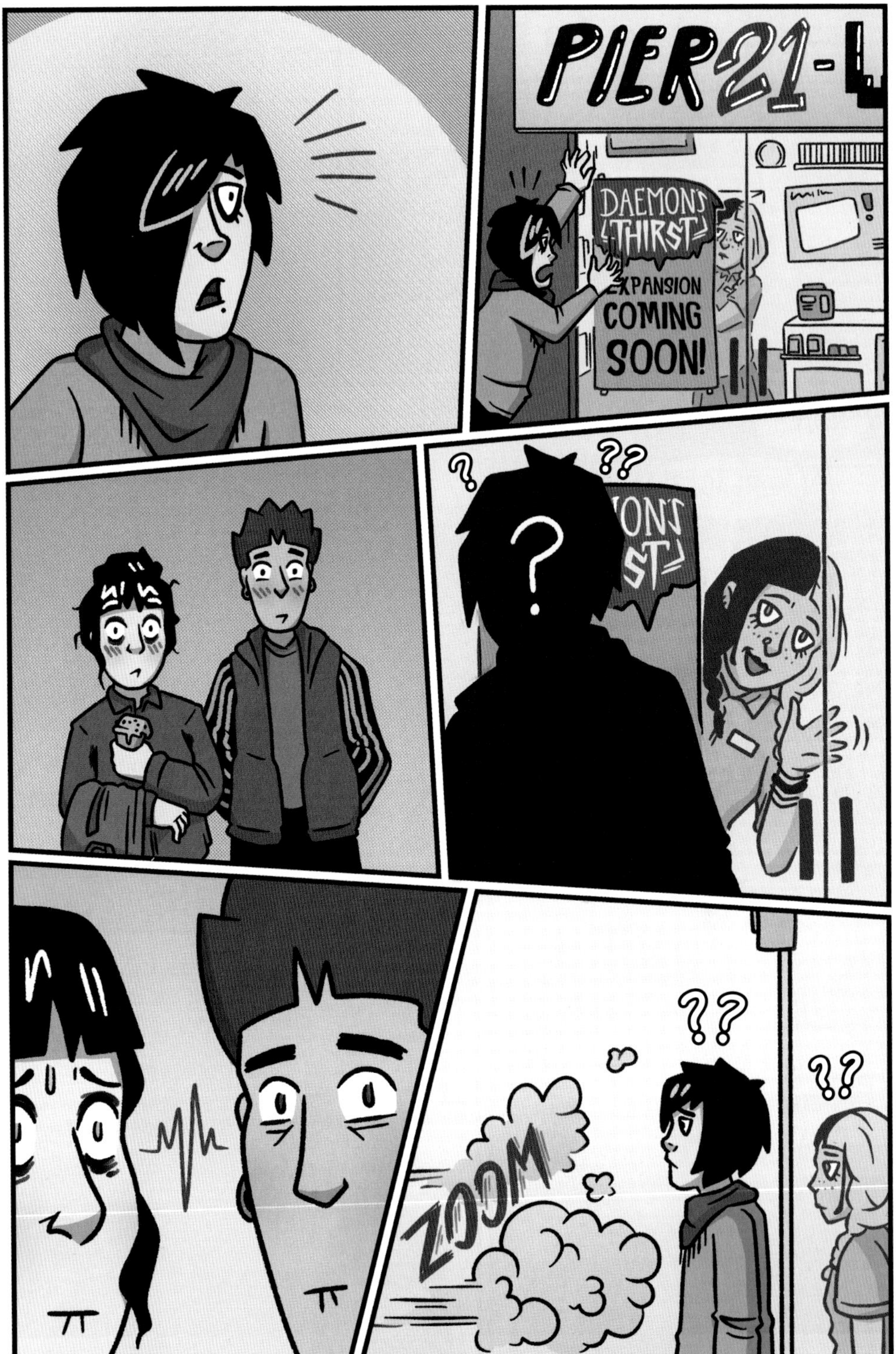
PIER 21-
DAEMON'S THIRST
EXPANSION COMING SOON!
??
??
??
ZOOM
??
??

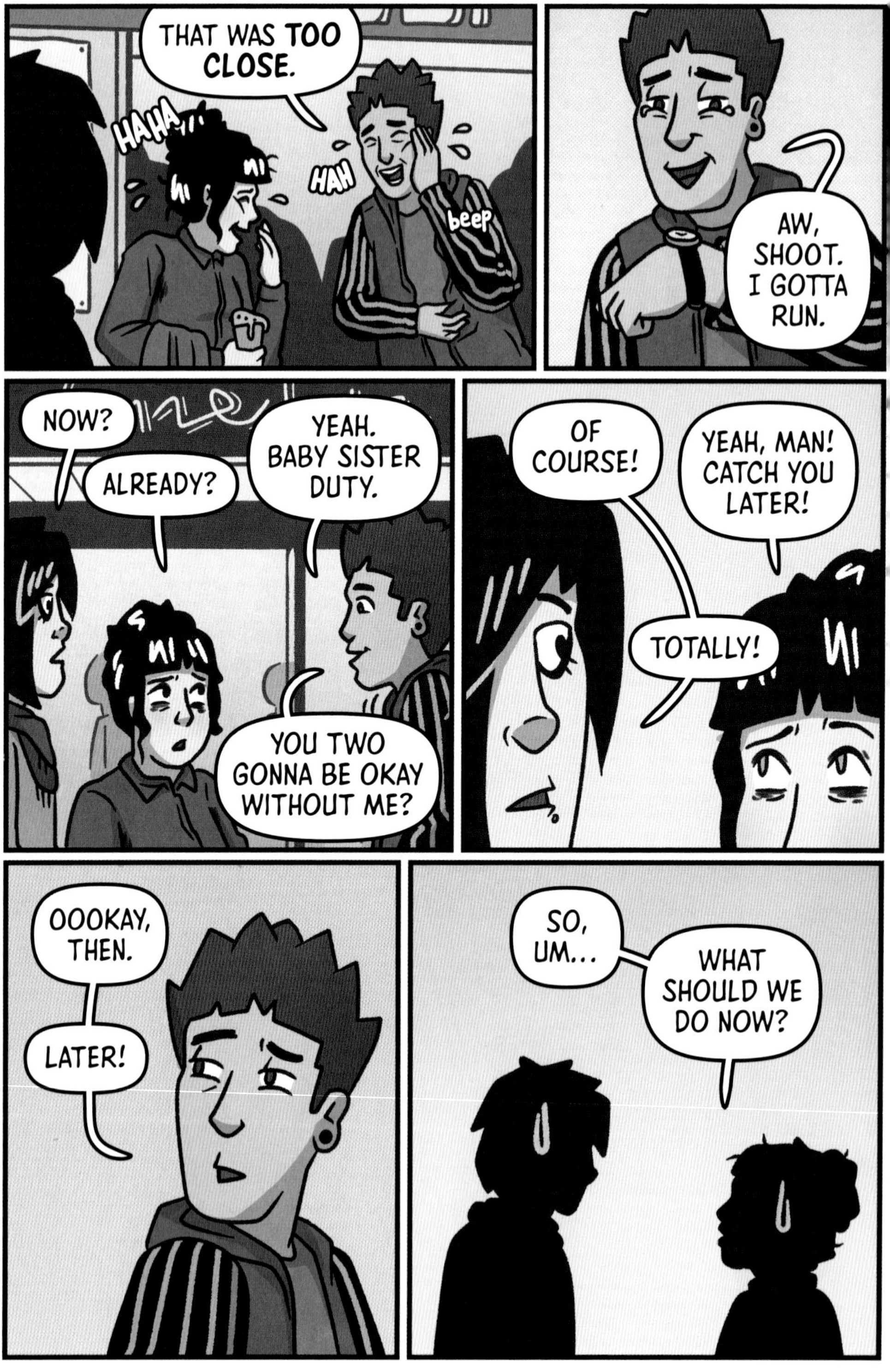
THAT WAS **TOO CLOSE.**
HAHA
HAH
beep
AW, SHOOT. I GOTTA RUN.
NOW?
ALREADY?
YEAH. BABY SISTER DUTY.
YOU TWO GONNA BE OKAY WITHOUT ME?
OF COURSE!
YEAH, MAN! CATCH YOU LATER!
TOTALLY!
OOOKAY, THEN.
LATER!
SO, UM...
WHAT SHOULD WE DO NOW?

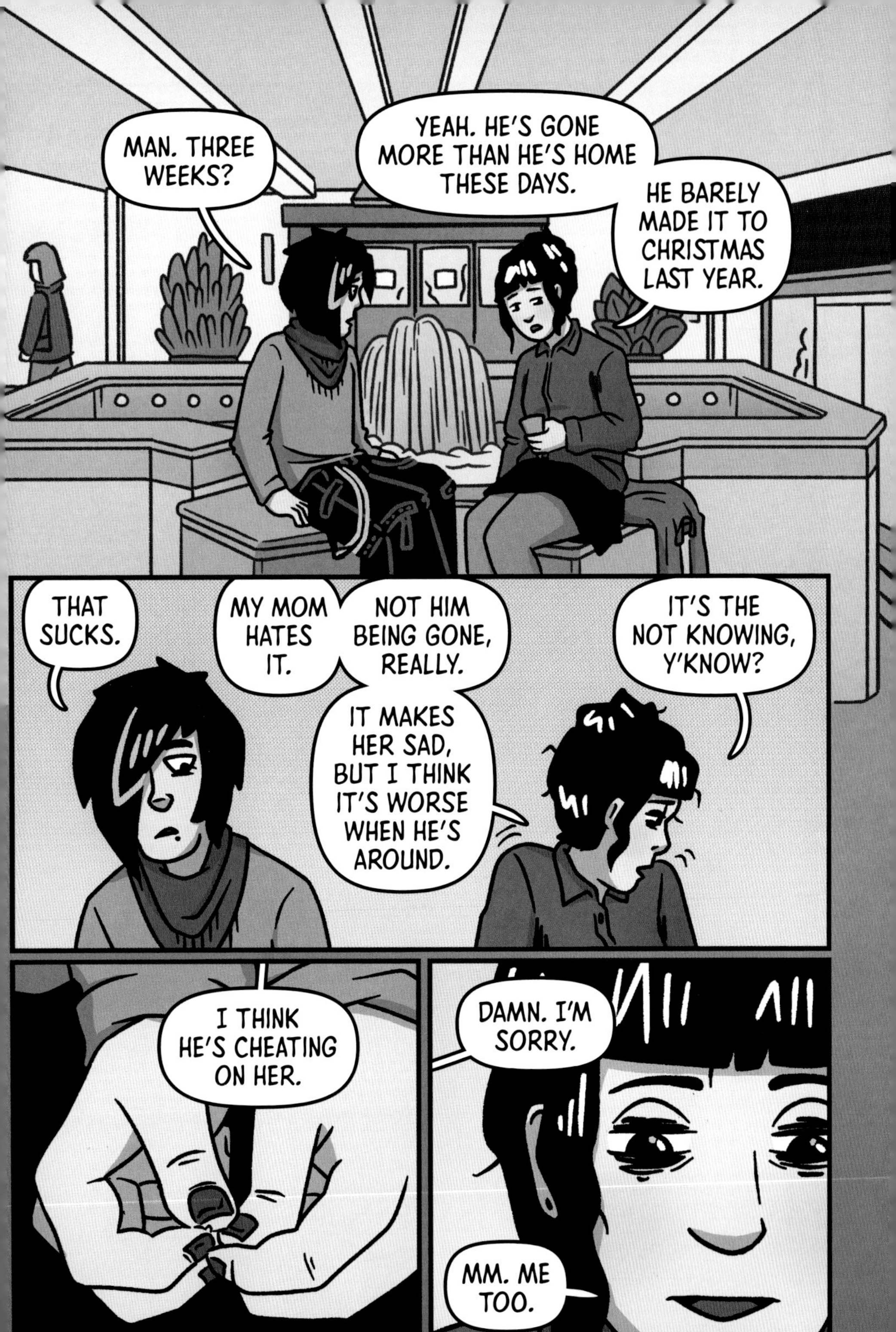
MAN. THREE WEEKS?
YEAH. HE'S GONE MORE THAN HE'S HOME THESE DAYS.
HE BARELY MADE IT TO CHRISTMAS LAST YEAR.
THAT SUCKS.
MY MOM HATES IT.
NOT HIM BEING GONE, REALLY.
IT'S THE NOT KNOWING, Y'KNOW?
IT MAKES HER SAD, BUT I THINK IT'S WORSE WHEN HE'S AROUND.
I THINK HE'S CHEATING ON HER.
DAMN. I'M SORRY.
MM. ME TOO.

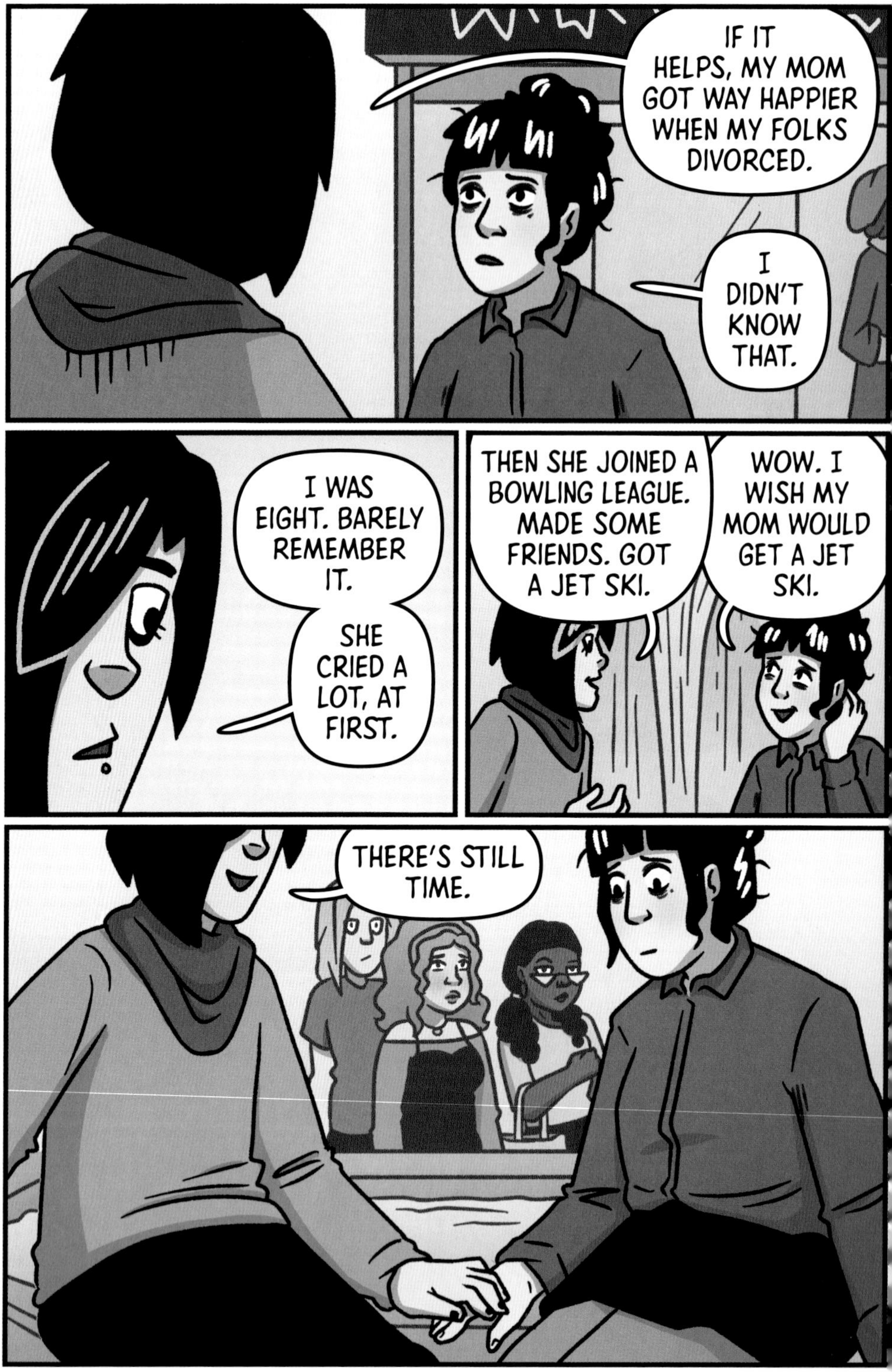
IF IT HELPS, MY MOM GOT WAY HAPPIER WHEN MY FOLKS DIVORCED.
I DIDN'T KNOW THAT.
I WAS EIGHT. BARELY REMEMBER IT.
SHE CRIED A LOT, AT FIRST.
THEN SHE JOINED A BOWLING LEAGUE. MADE SOME FRIENDS. GOT A JET SKI.
WOW. I WISH MY MOM WOULD GET A JET SKI.
THERE'S STILL TIME.

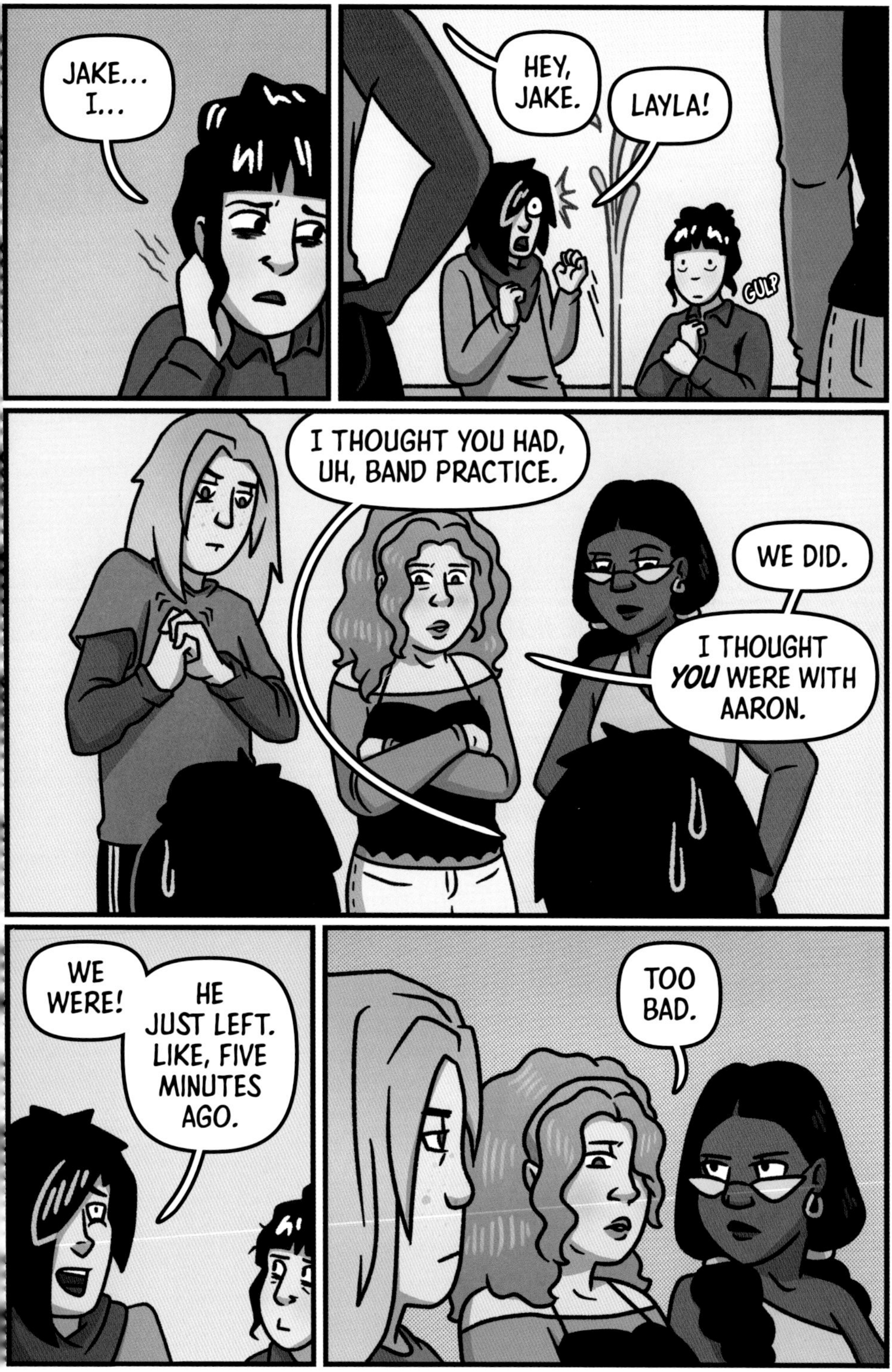
JAKE... I...
HEY, JAKE.
LAYLA!
GULP
I THOUGHT YOU HAD, UH, BAND PRACTICE.
WE DID.
I THOUGHT *YOU* WERE WITH AARON.
WE WERE!
HE JUST LEFT. LIKE, FIVE MINUTES AGO.
TOO BAD.

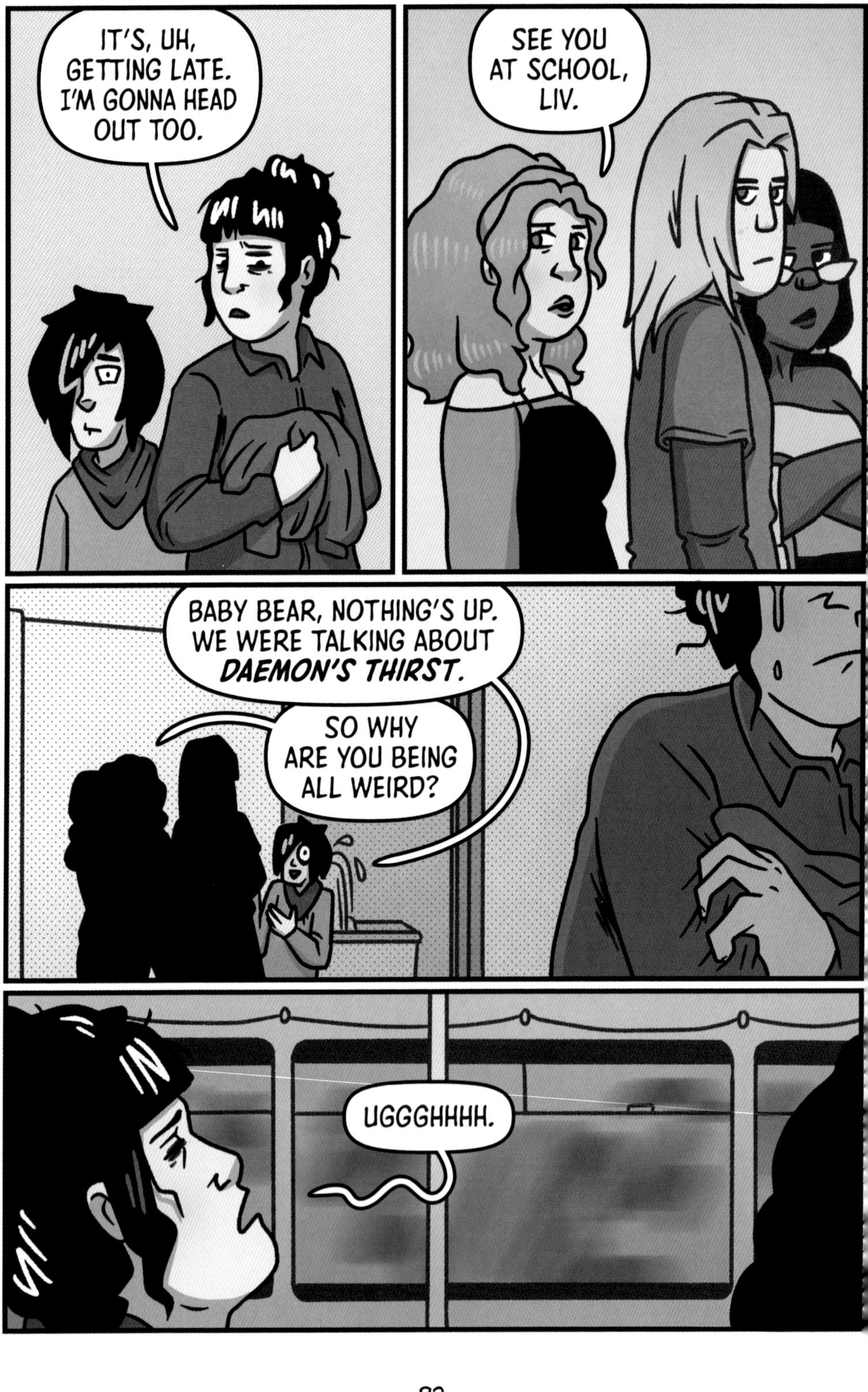
IT'S, UH, GETTING LATE. I'M GONNA HEAD OUT TOO.
SEE YOU AT SCHOOL, LIV.
BABY BEAR, NOTHING'S UP. WE WERE TALKING ABOUT *DAEMON'S THIRST*.
SO WHY ARE YOU BEING ALL WEIRD?
UGGGHHHH.

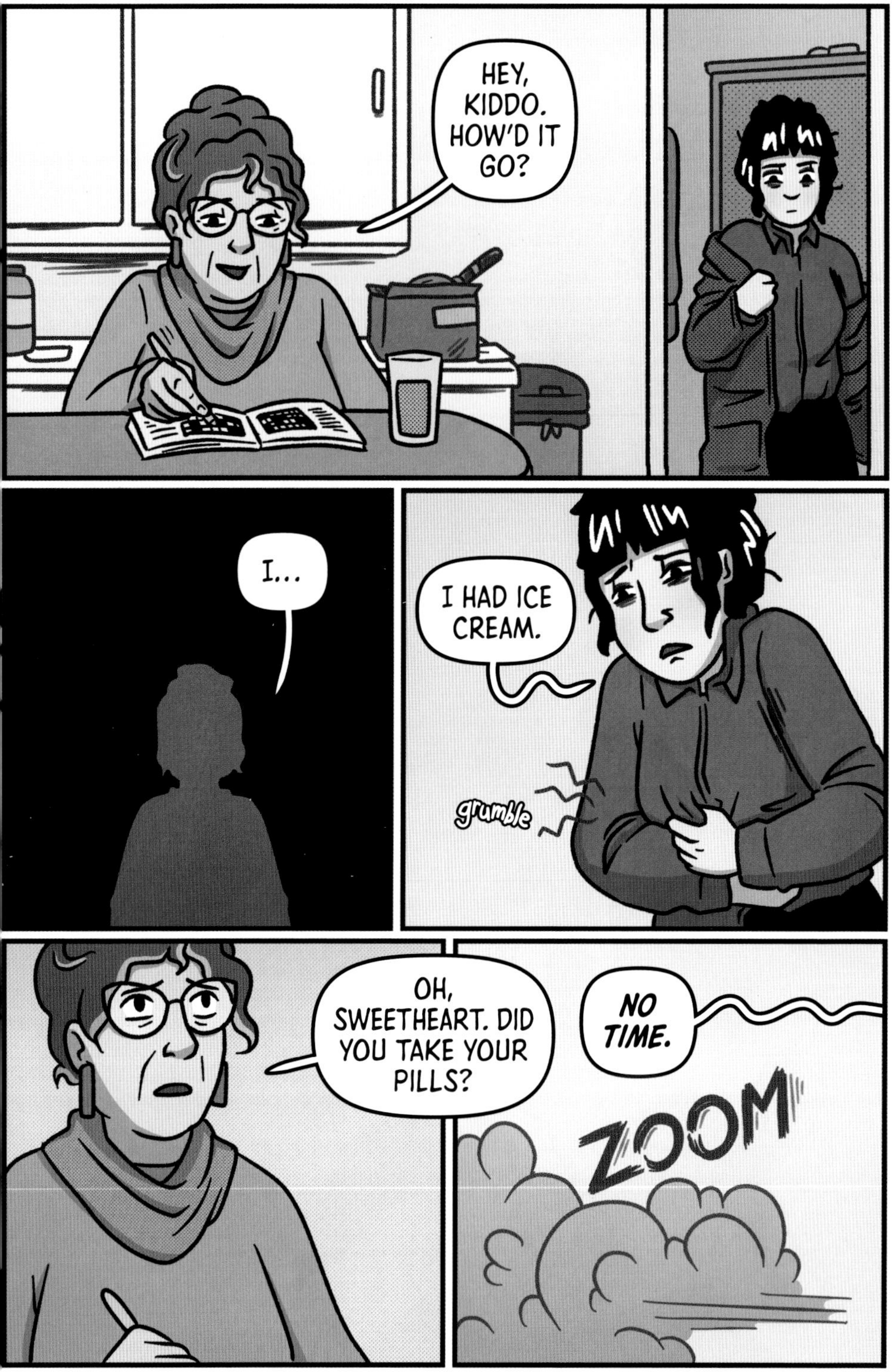
HEY, KIDDO. HOW'D IT GO?
I...
I HAD ICE CREAM.
grumble
OH, SWEETHEART. DID YOU TAKE YOUR PILLS?
NO TIME.
ZOOM

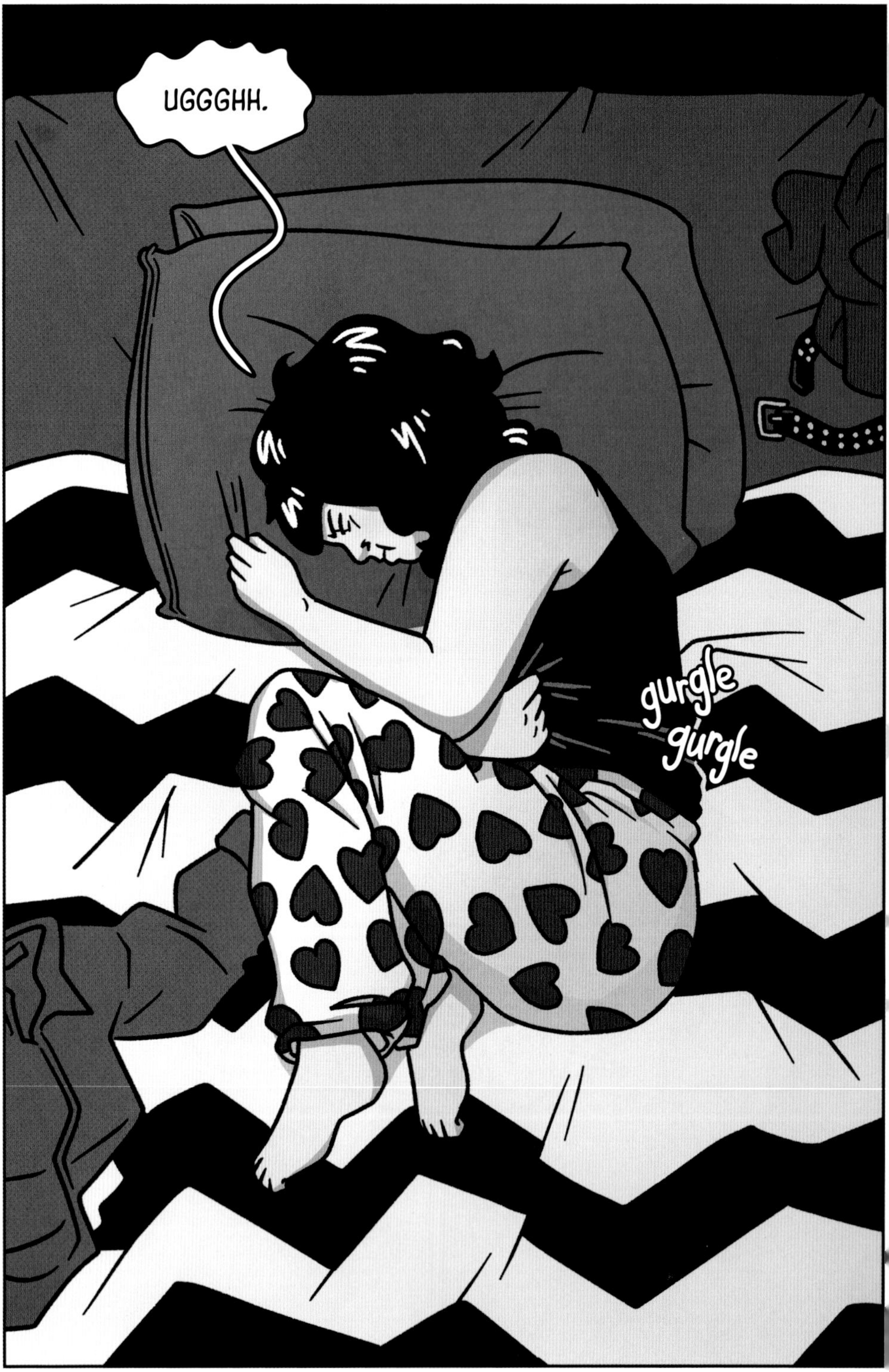
UGGGHH.
gurgle
gurgle

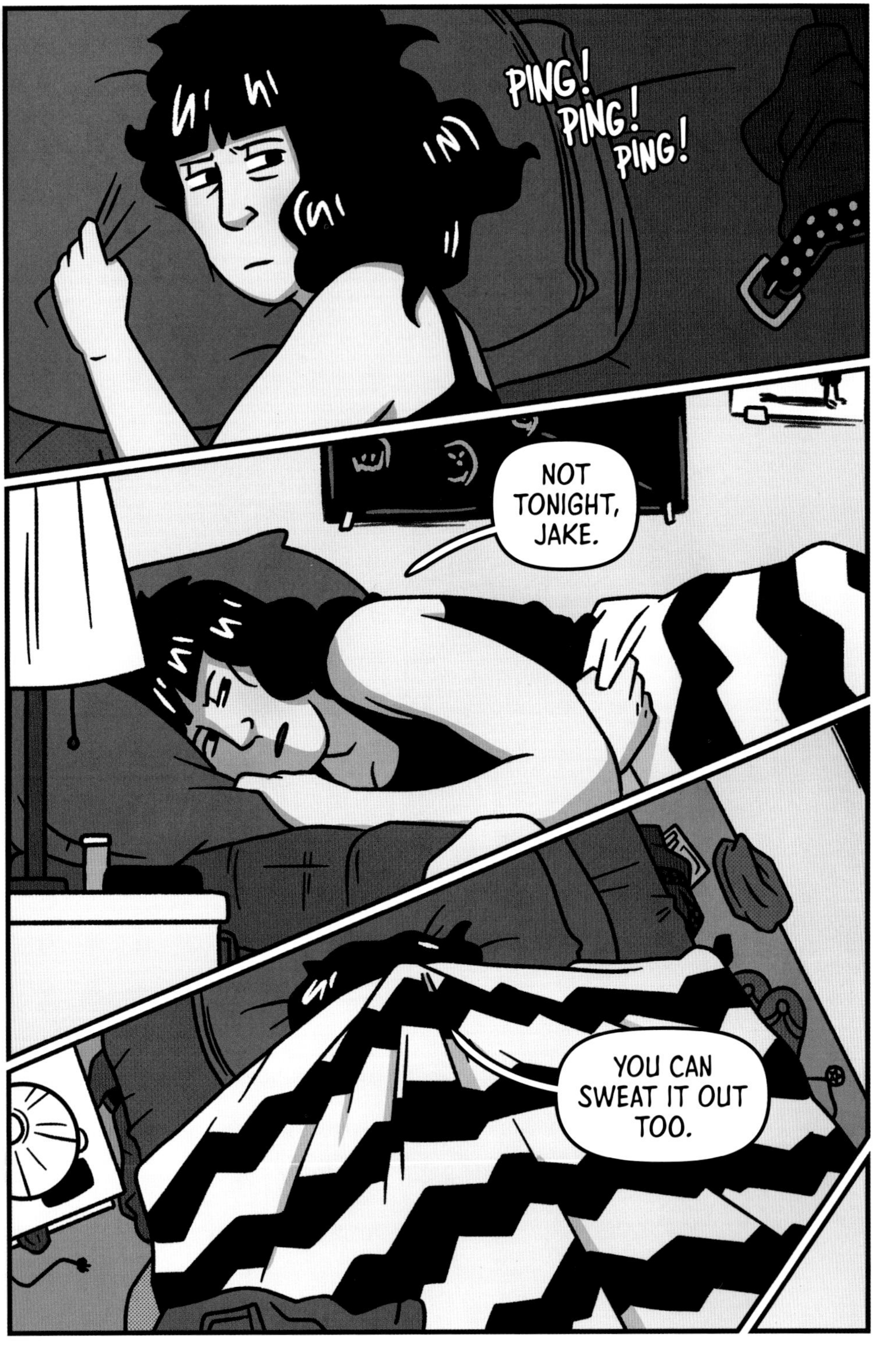
PING! PING! PING!
NOT TONIGHT, JAKE.
YOU CAN SWEAT IT OUT TOO.

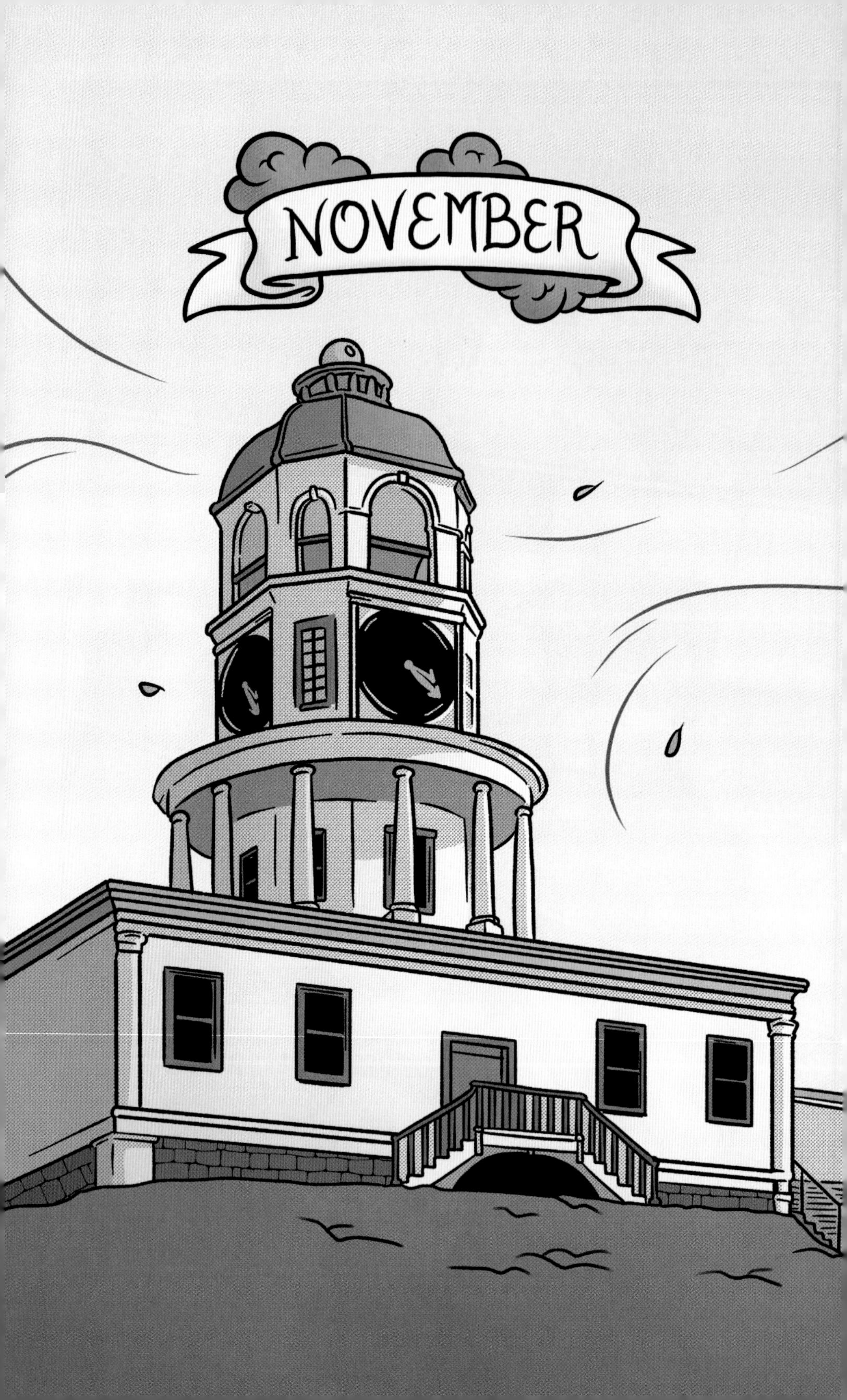
NOVEMBER

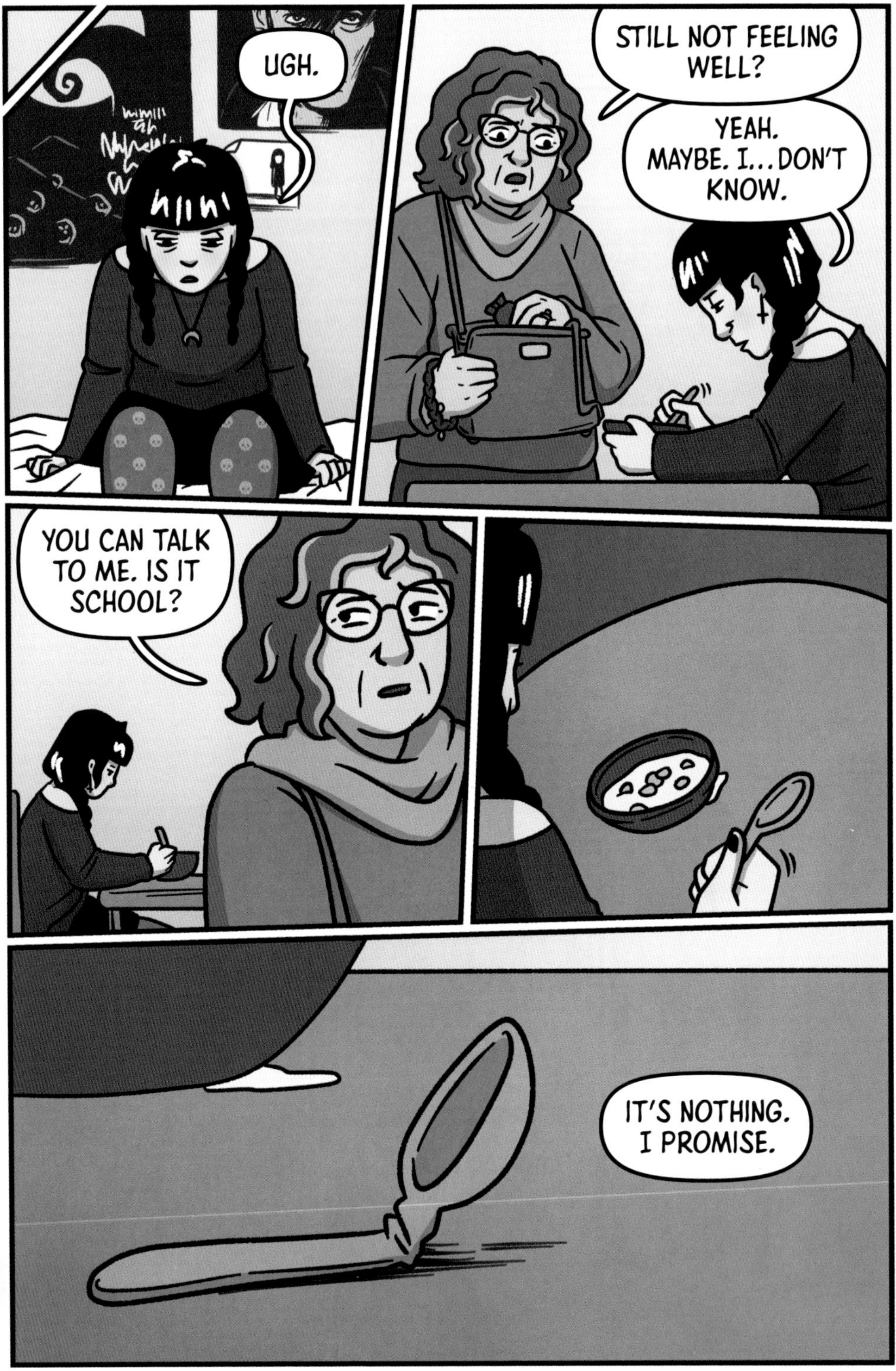
UGH.
STILL NOT FEELING WELL?
YEAH. MAYBE. I...DON'T KNOW.
YOU CAN TALK TO ME. IS IT SCHOOL?
IT'S NOTHING. I PROMISE.

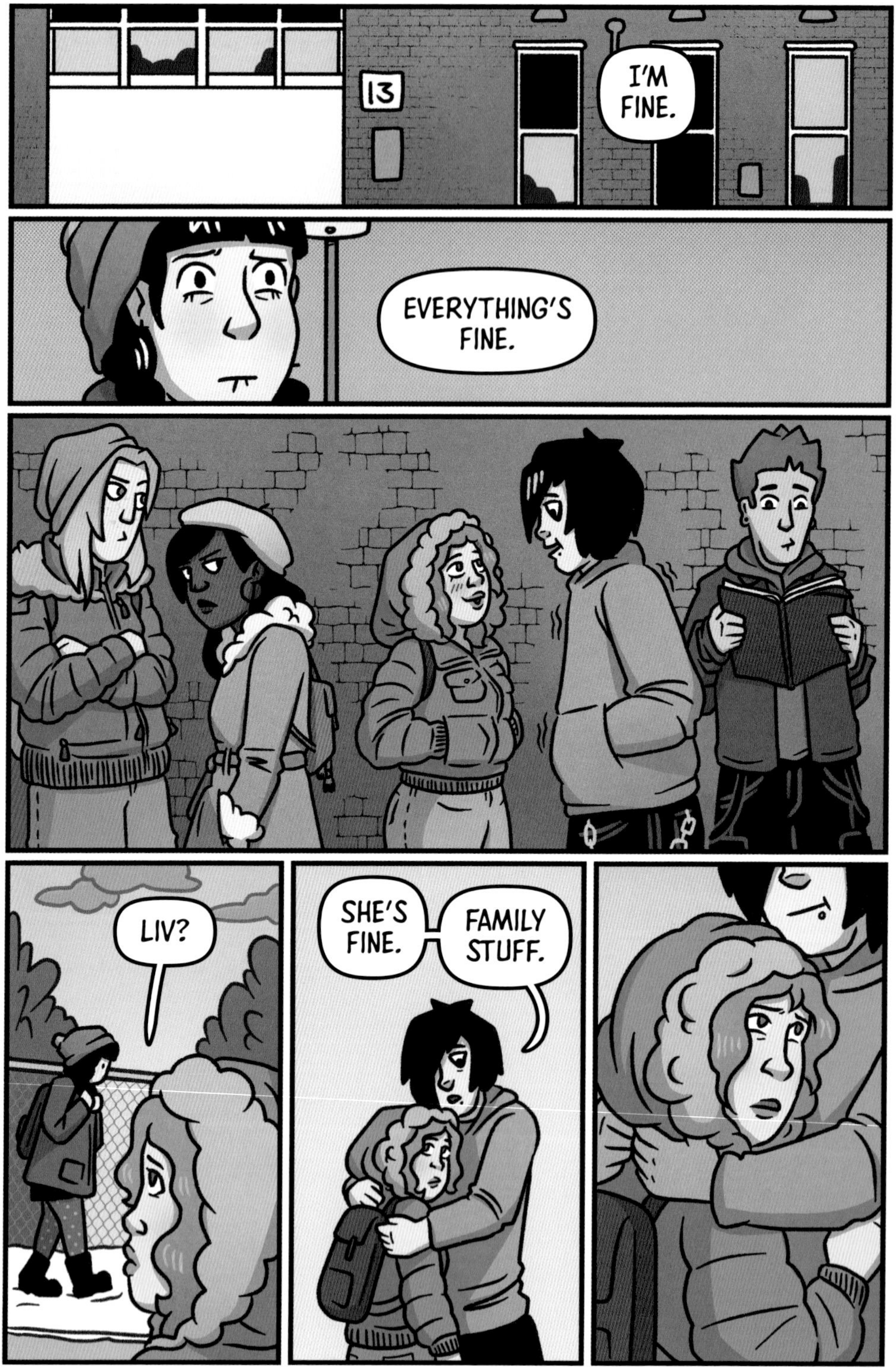

13
I'M FINE.
EVERYTHING'S FINE.
LIV?
SHE'S FINE.
FAMILY STUFF.

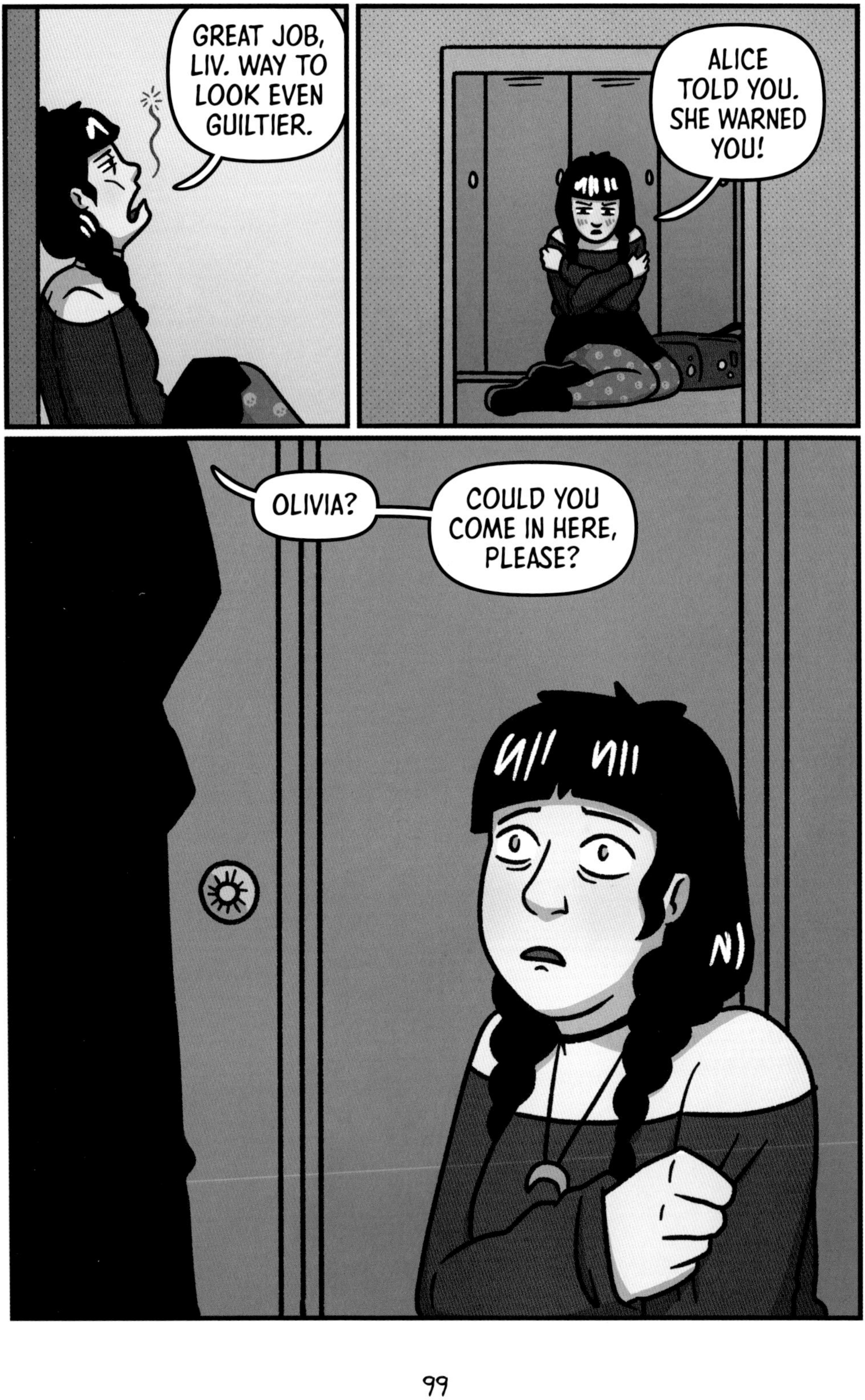
GREAT JOB, LIV. WAY TO LOOK EVEN GUILTIER.
ALICE TOLD YOU. SHE WARNED YOU!
OLIVIA?
COULD YOU COME IN HERE, PLEASE?

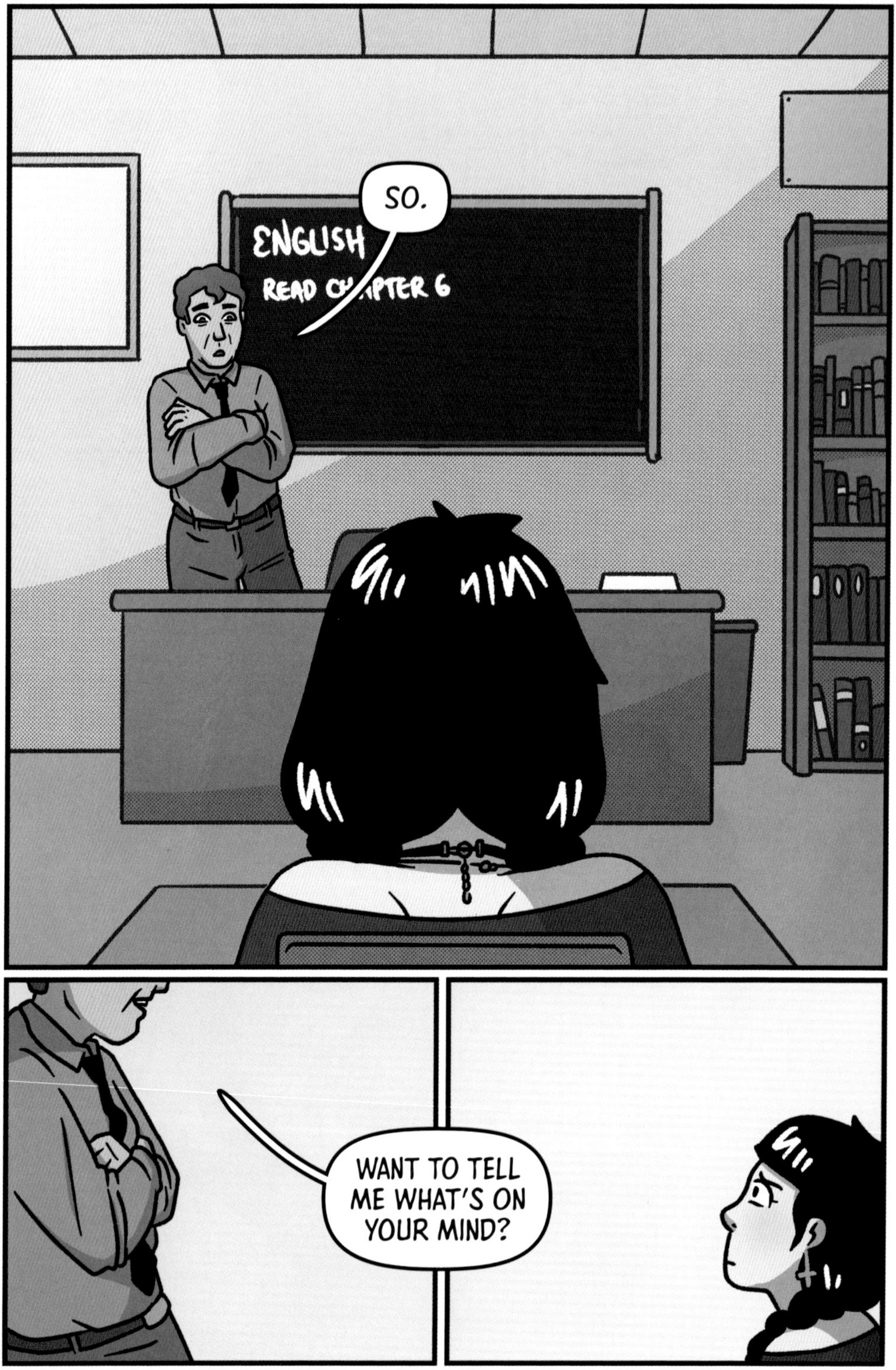
SO.
ENGLISH
WANT TO TELL ME WHAT'S ON YOUR MIND?

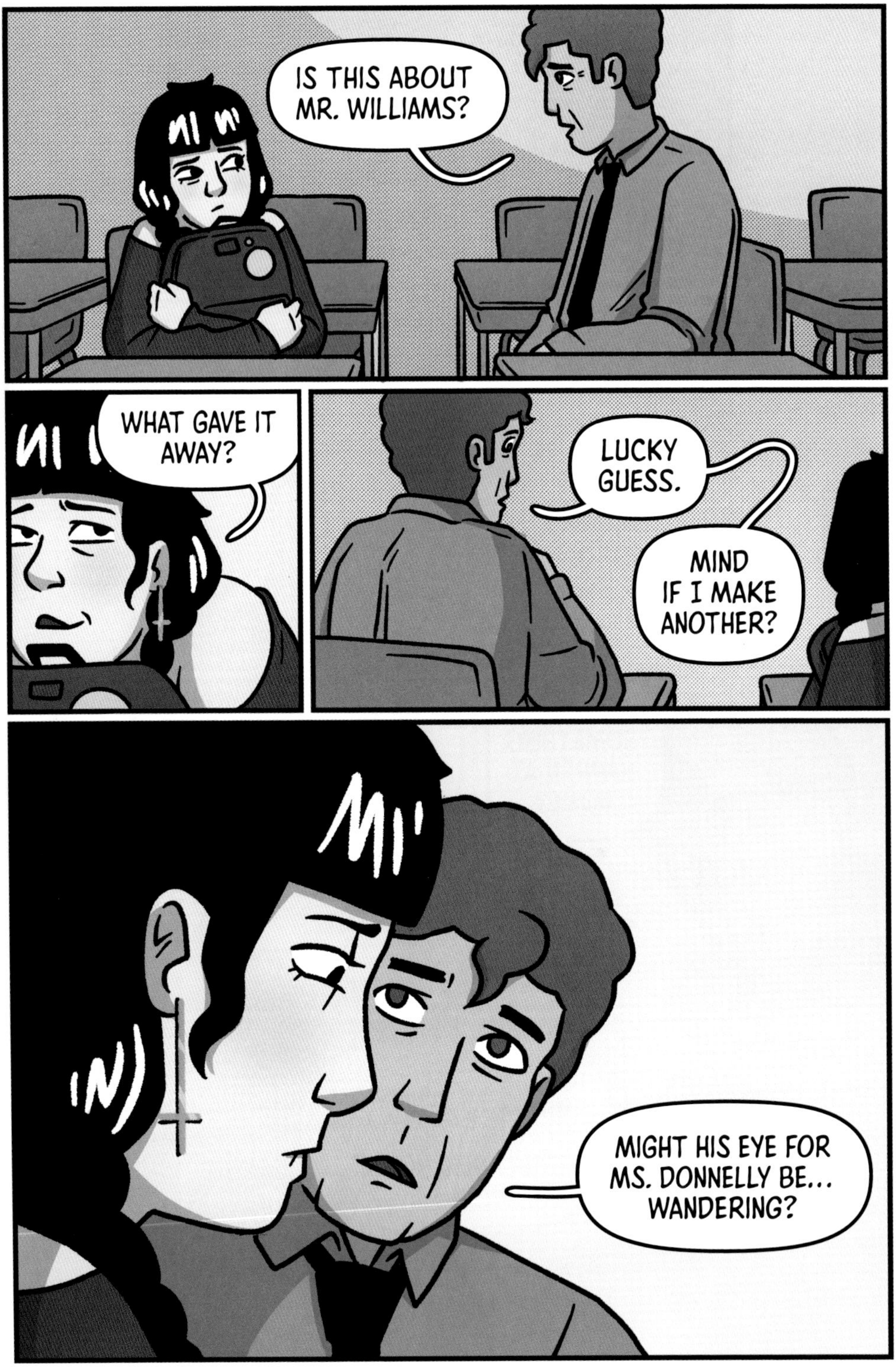
IS THIS ABOUT MR. WILLIAMS?
WHAT GAVE IT AWAY?
LUCKY GUESS.
MIND IF I MAKE ANOTHER?
MIGHT HIS EYE FOR MS. DONNELLY BE... WANDERING?

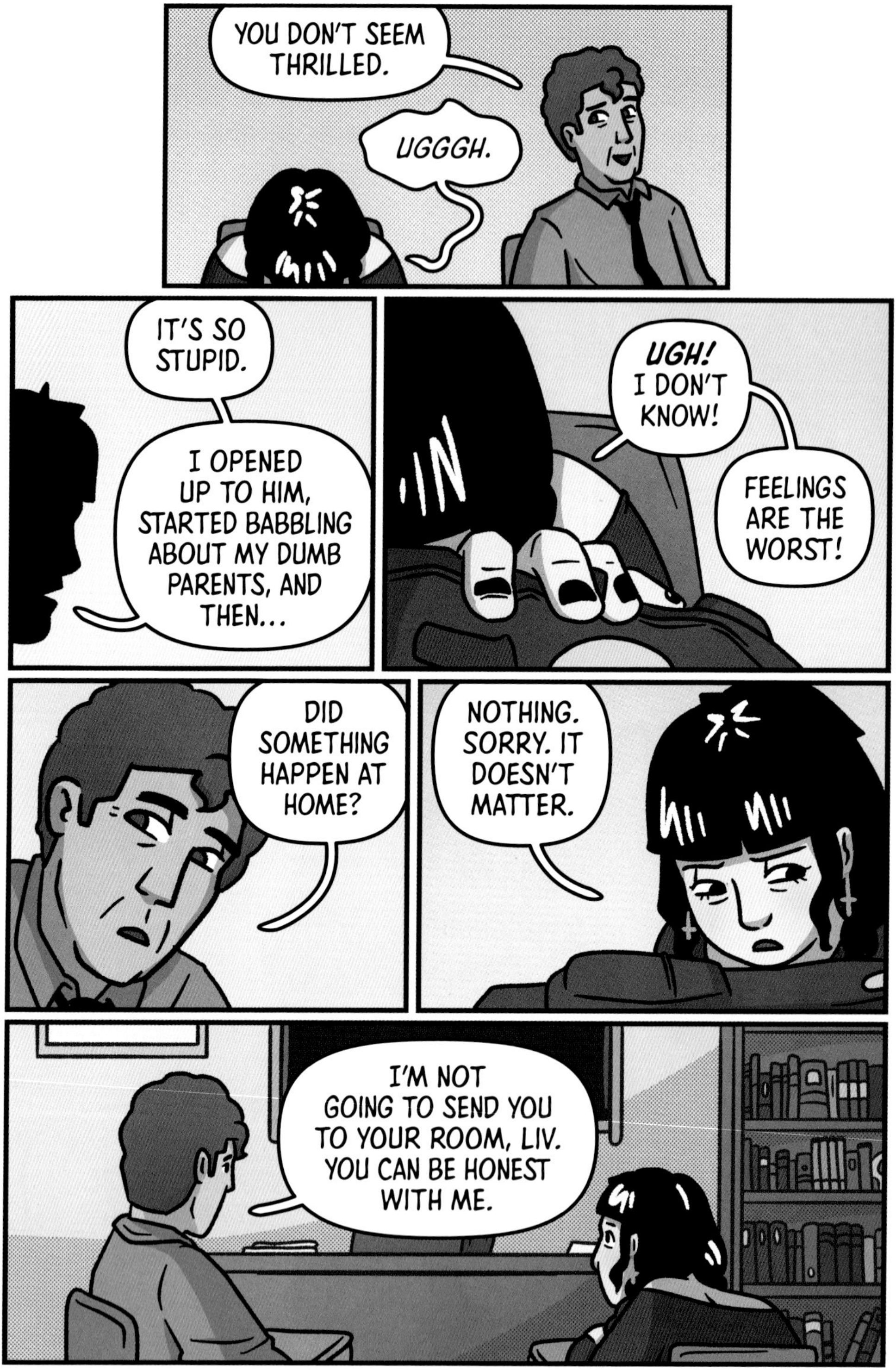
YOU DON'T SEEM THRILLED.
UGGGH.
IT'S SO STUPID.
I OPENED UP TO HIM, STARTED BABBLING ABOUT MY DUMB PARENTS, AND THEN...
UGH! I DON'T KNOW!
FEELINGS ARE THE WORST!
DID SOMETHING HAPPEN AT HOME?
NOTHING. SORRY. IT DOESN'T MATTER.
I'M NOT GOING TO SEND YOU TO YOUR ROOM, LIV. YOU CAN BE HONEST WITH ME.

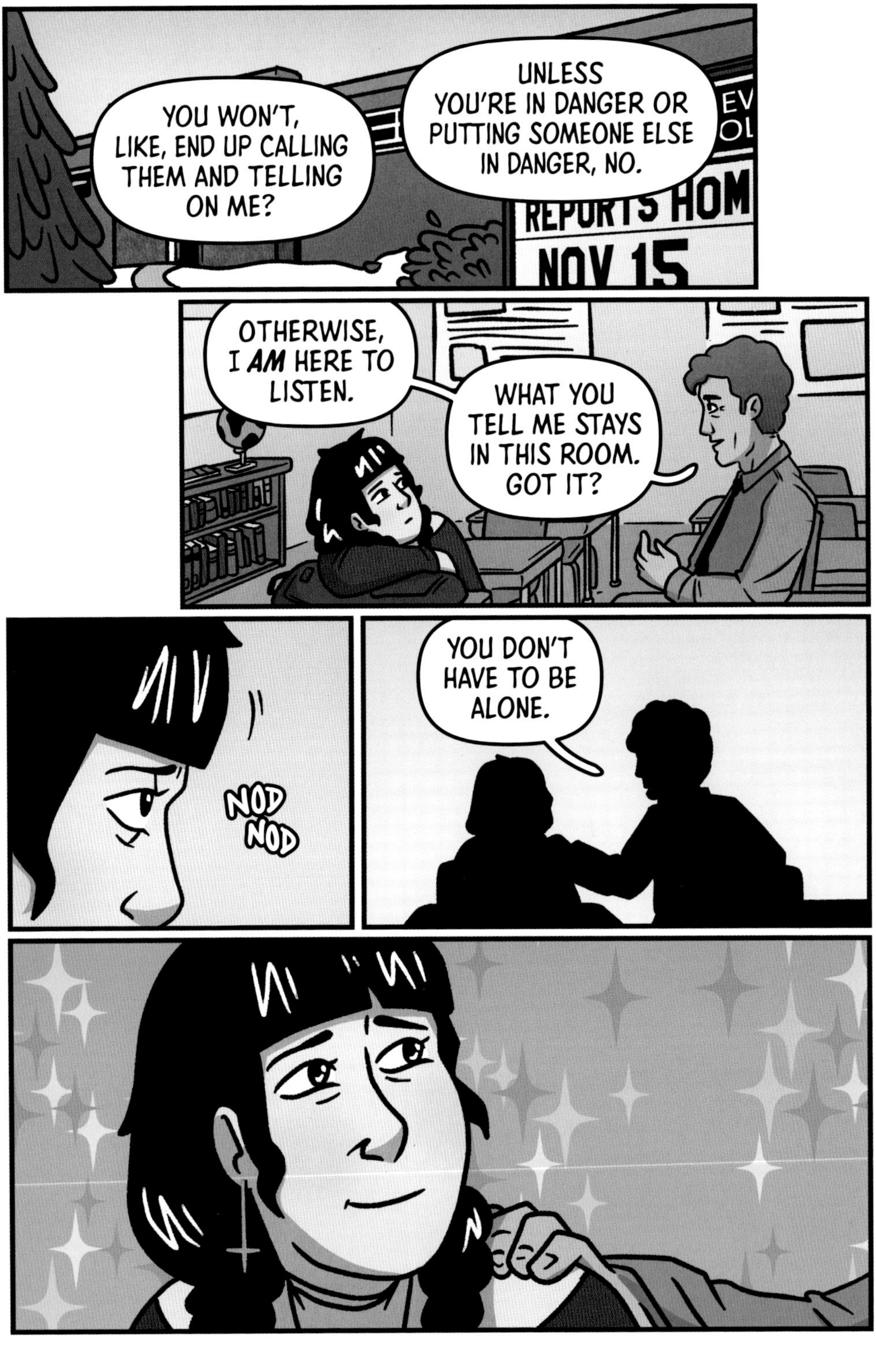
YOU WON'T, LIKE, END UP CALLING THEM AND TELLING ON ME?
UNLESS YOU'RE IN DANGER OR PUTTING SOMEONE ELSE IN DANGER, NO.
REPORTS HOM
NOV 15
OTHERWISE, I *AM* HERE TO LISTEN.
WHAT YOU TELL ME STAYS IN THIS ROOM. GOT IT?
NOD NOD
YOU DON'T HAVE TO BE ALONE.

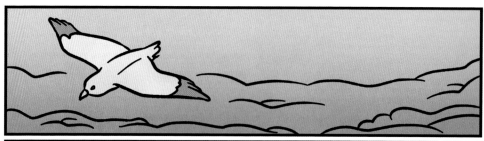

—AAAHCK!

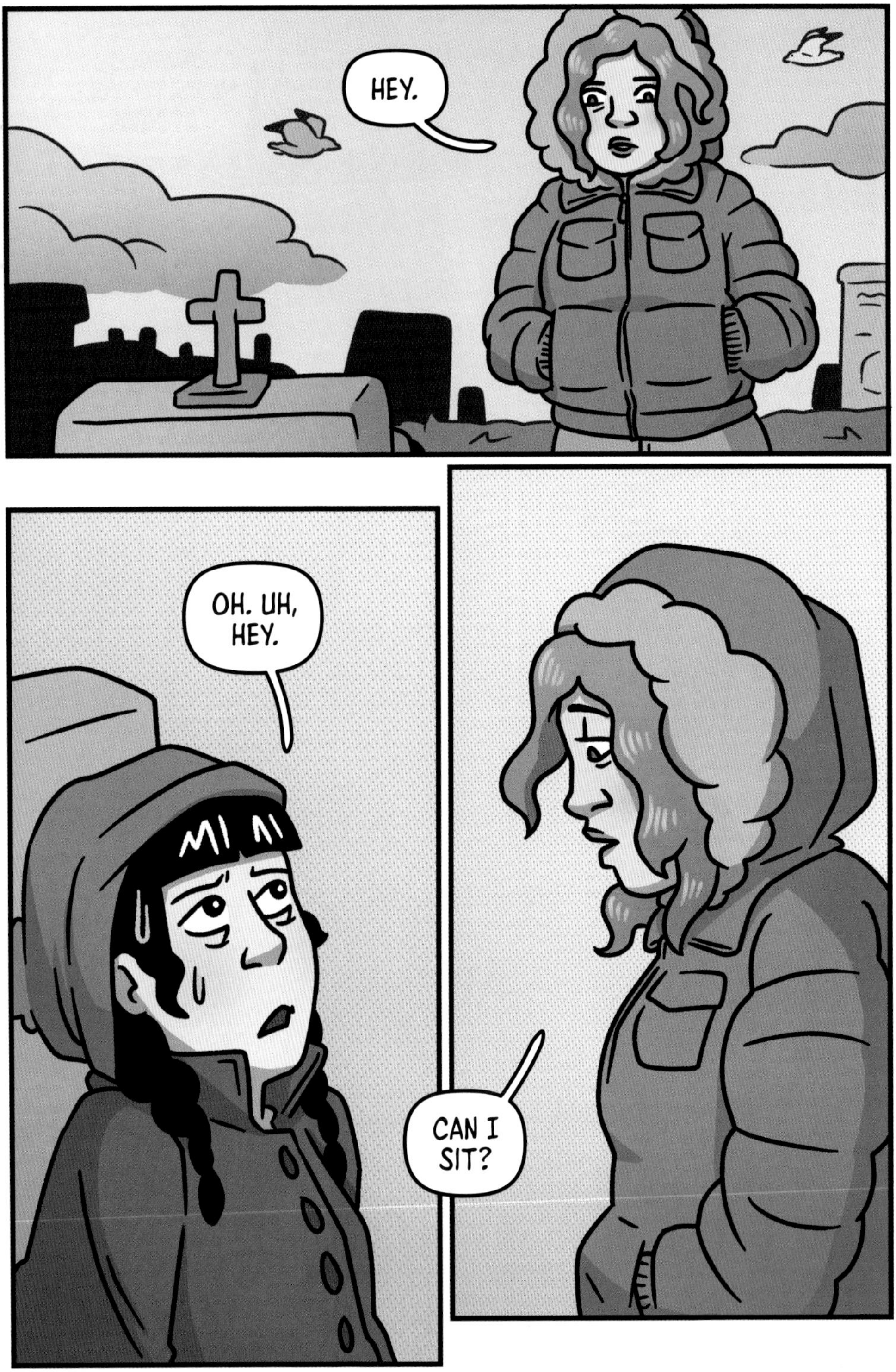
HEY.
OH. UH, HEY.
CAN I SIT?

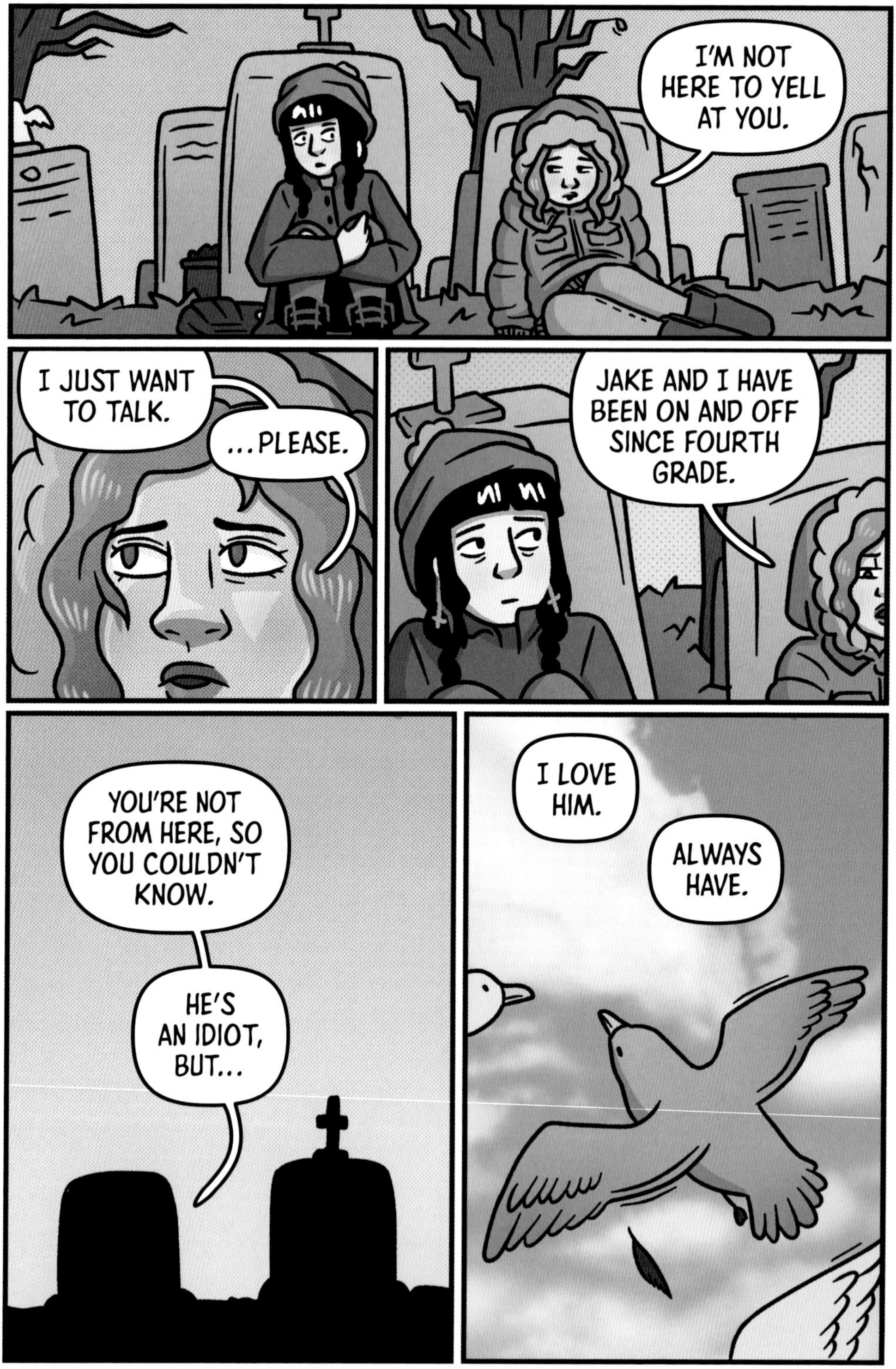
I'M NOT HERE TO YELL AT YOU.
I JUST WANT TO TALK.
...PLEASE.
JAKE AND I HAVE BEEN ON AND OFF SINCE FOURTH GRADE.
YOU'RE NOT FROM HERE, SO YOU COULDN'T KNOW.
HE'S AN IDIOT, BUT...
I LOVE HIM.
ALWAYS HAVE.

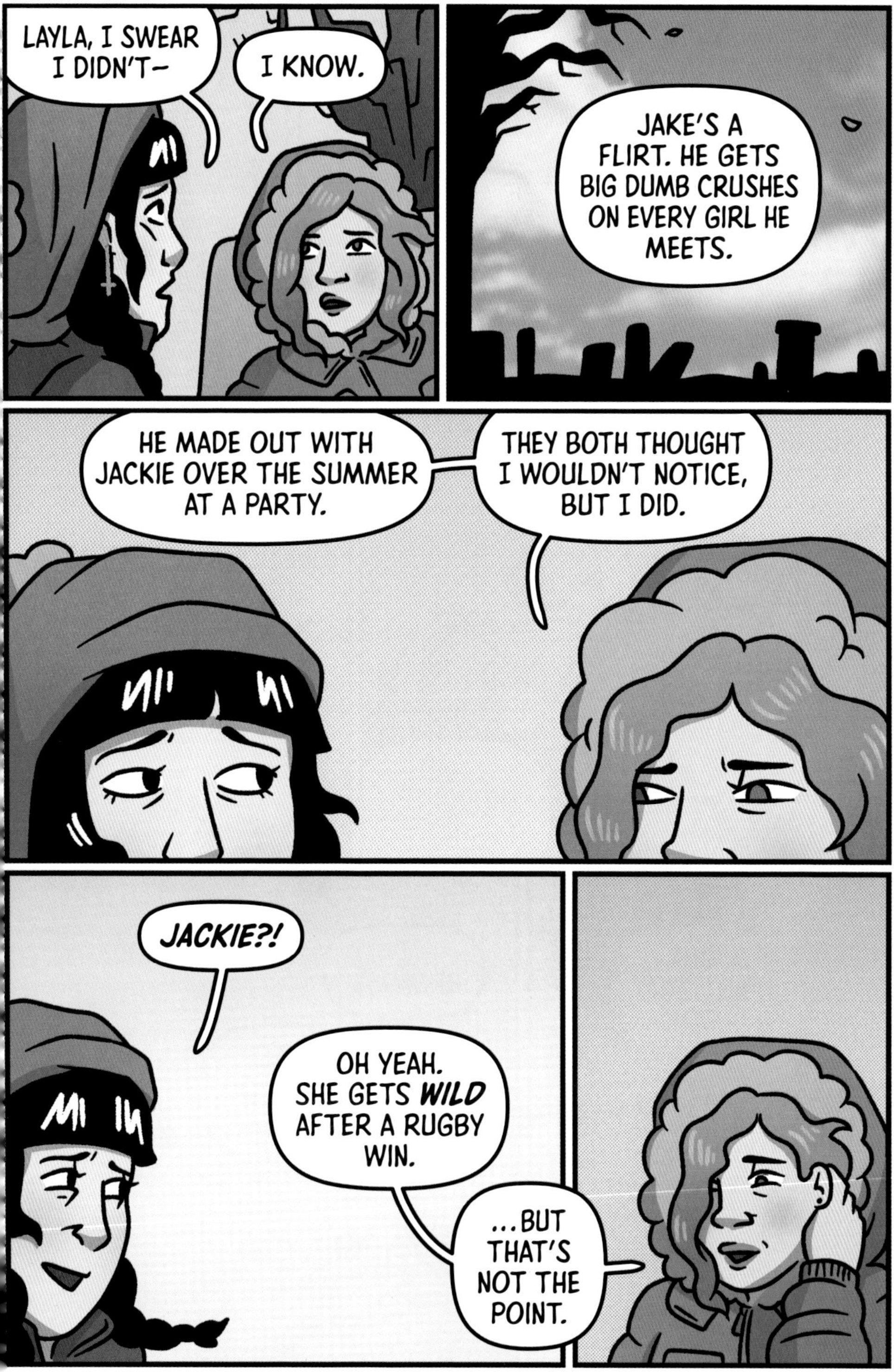
LAYLA, I SWEAR I DIDN'T–
I KNOW.
JAKE'S A FLIRT. HE GETS BIG DUMB CRUSHES ON EVERY GIRL HE MEETS.
HE MADE OUT WITH JACKIE OVER THE SUMMER AT A PARTY.
THEY BOTH THOUGHT I WOULDN'T NOTICE, BUT I DID.
JACKIE?!
OH YEAH. SHE GETS WILD AFTER A RUGBY WIN.
...BUT THAT'S NOT THE POINT.

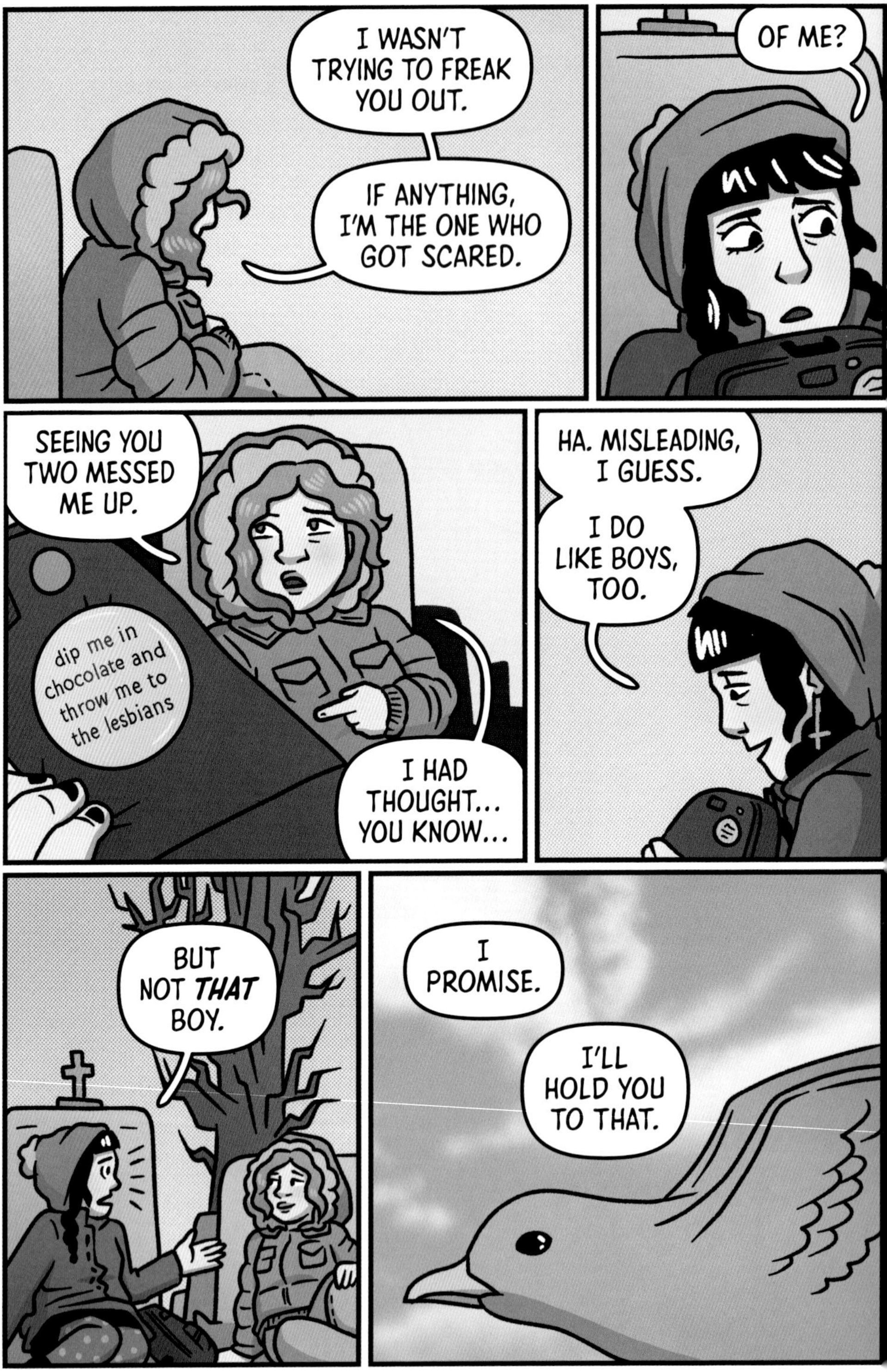
I WASN'T TRYING TO FREAK YOU OUT.
IF ANYTHING, I'M THE ONE WHO GOT SCARED.
OF ME?
SEEING YOU TWO MESSED ME UP.
dip me in chocolate and throw me to the lesbians
I HAD THOUGHT... YOU KNOW...
HA. MISLEADING, I GUESS.
I DO LIKE BOYS, TOO.
BUT NOT ***THAT*** BOY.
I PROMISE.
I'LL HOLD YOU TO THAT.

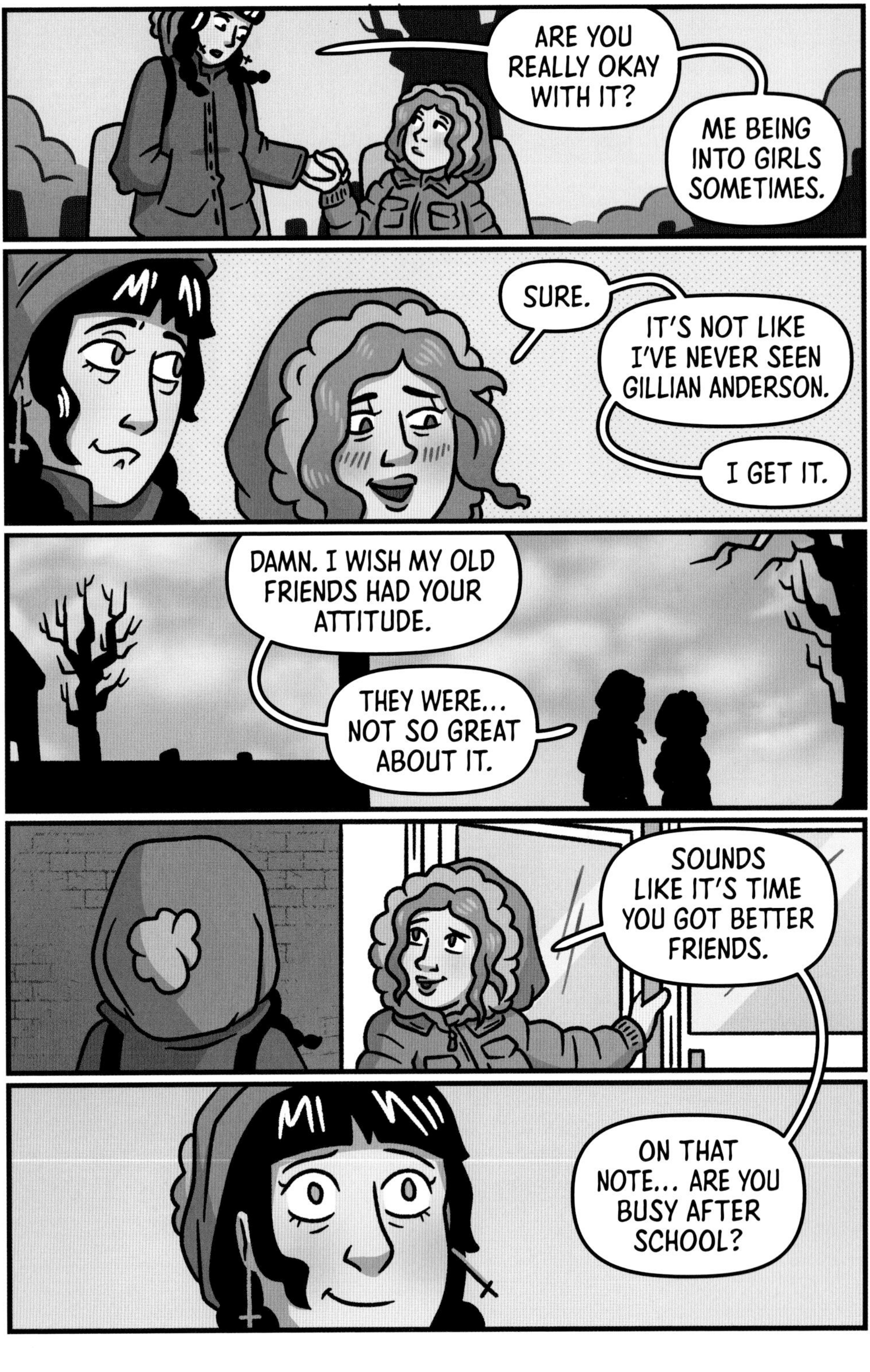
ARE YOU REALLY OKAY WITH IT?
ME BEING INTO GIRLS SOMETIMES.
SURE.
IT'S NOT LIKE I'VE NEVER SEEN GILLIAN ANDERSON.
I GET IT.
DAMN. I WISH MY OLD FRIENDS HAD YOUR ATTITUDE.
THEY WERE... NOT SO GREAT ABOUT IT.
SOUNDS LIKE IT'S TIME YOU GOT BETTER FRIENDS.
ON THAT NOTE... ARE YOU BUSY AFTER SCHOOL?

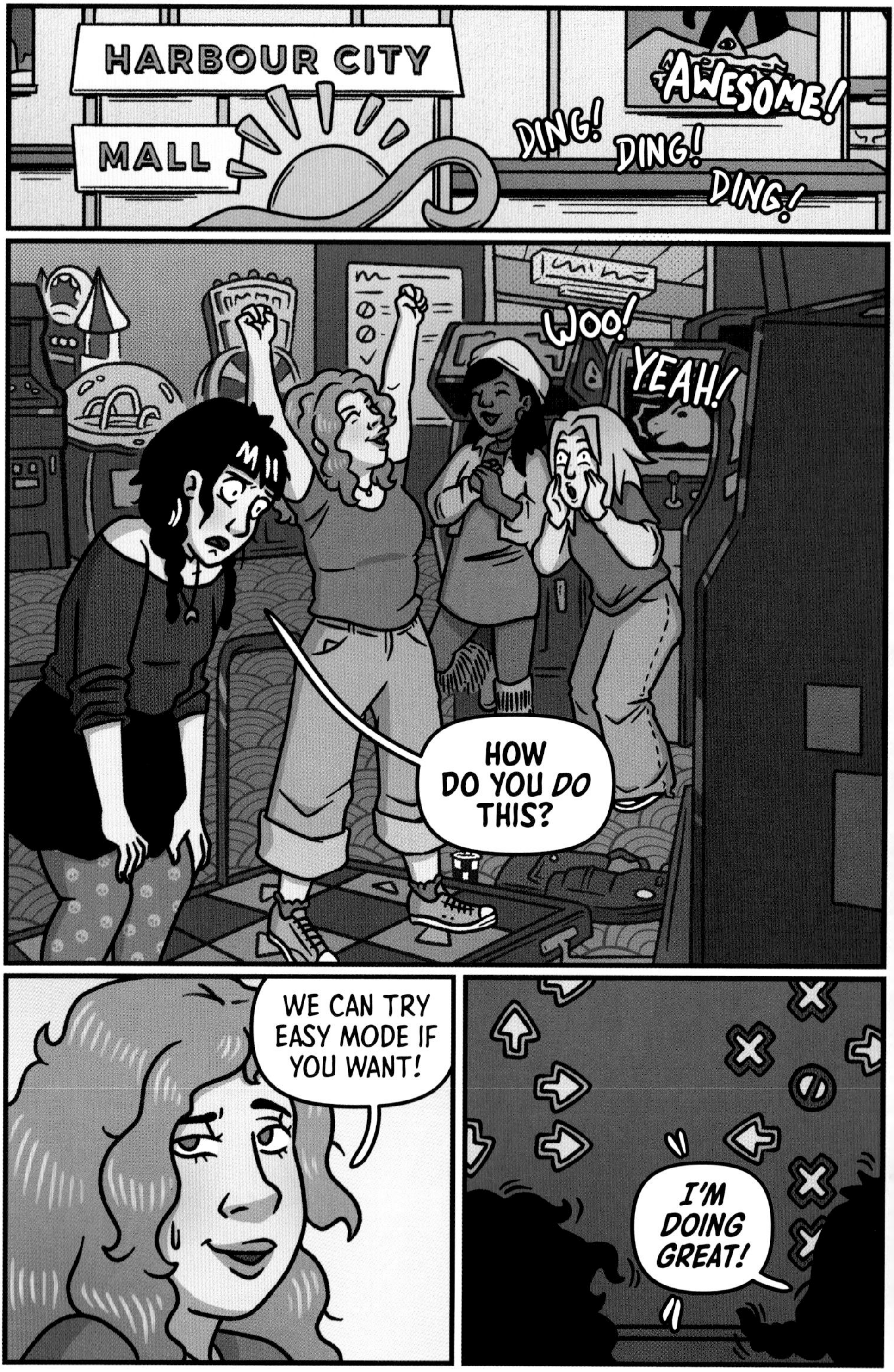
HARBOUR CITY
MALL
DING!
DING!
DING!
AWESOME!
WOO!
YEAH!
HOW DO YOU *DO* THIS?
WE CAN TRY EASY MODE IF YOU WANT!
I'M DOING GREAT!

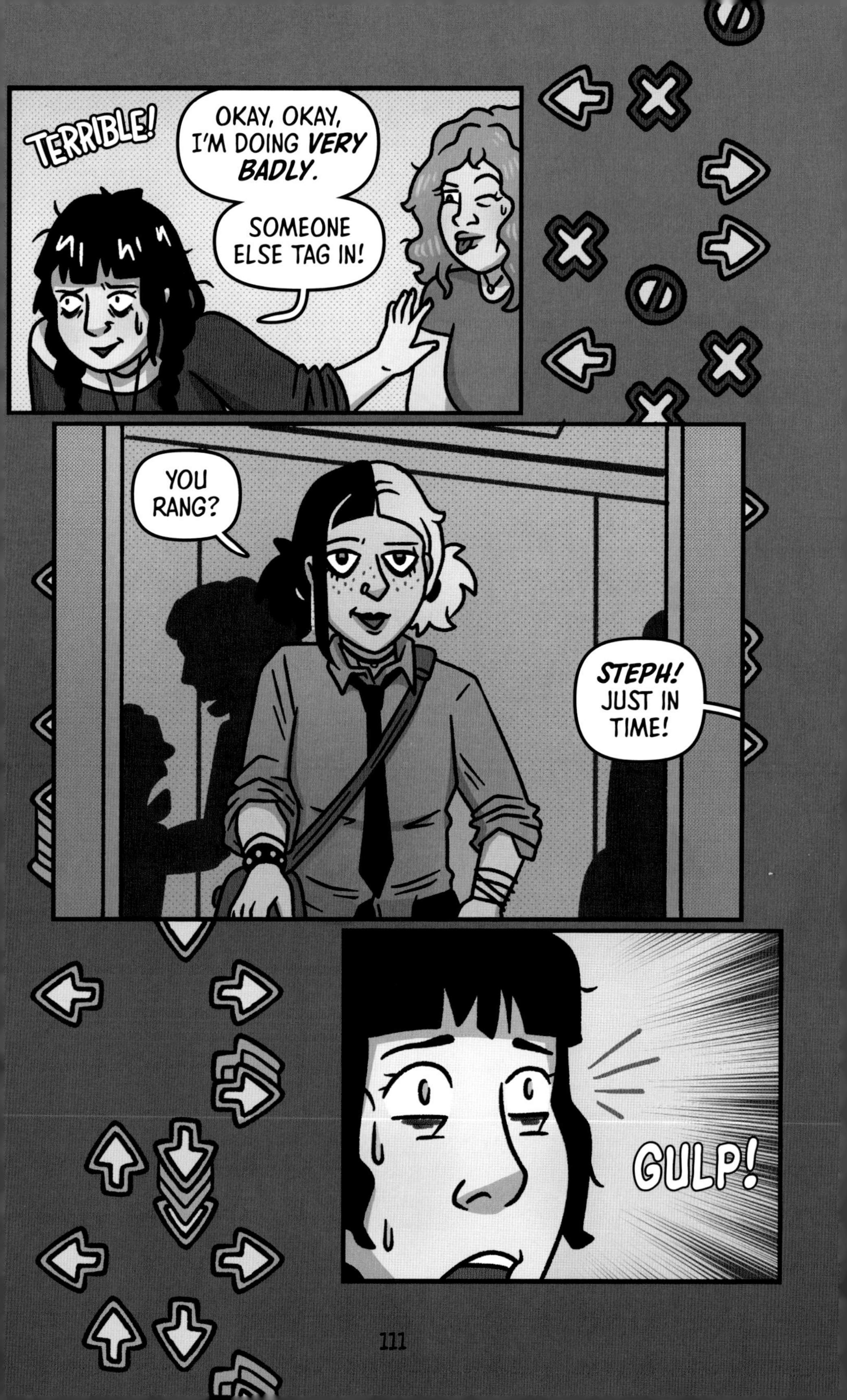

TERRIBLE!
OKAY, OKAY, I'M DOING VERY BADLY.
SOMEONE ELSE TAG IN!
YOU RANG?
STEPH! JUST IN TIME!
GULP!

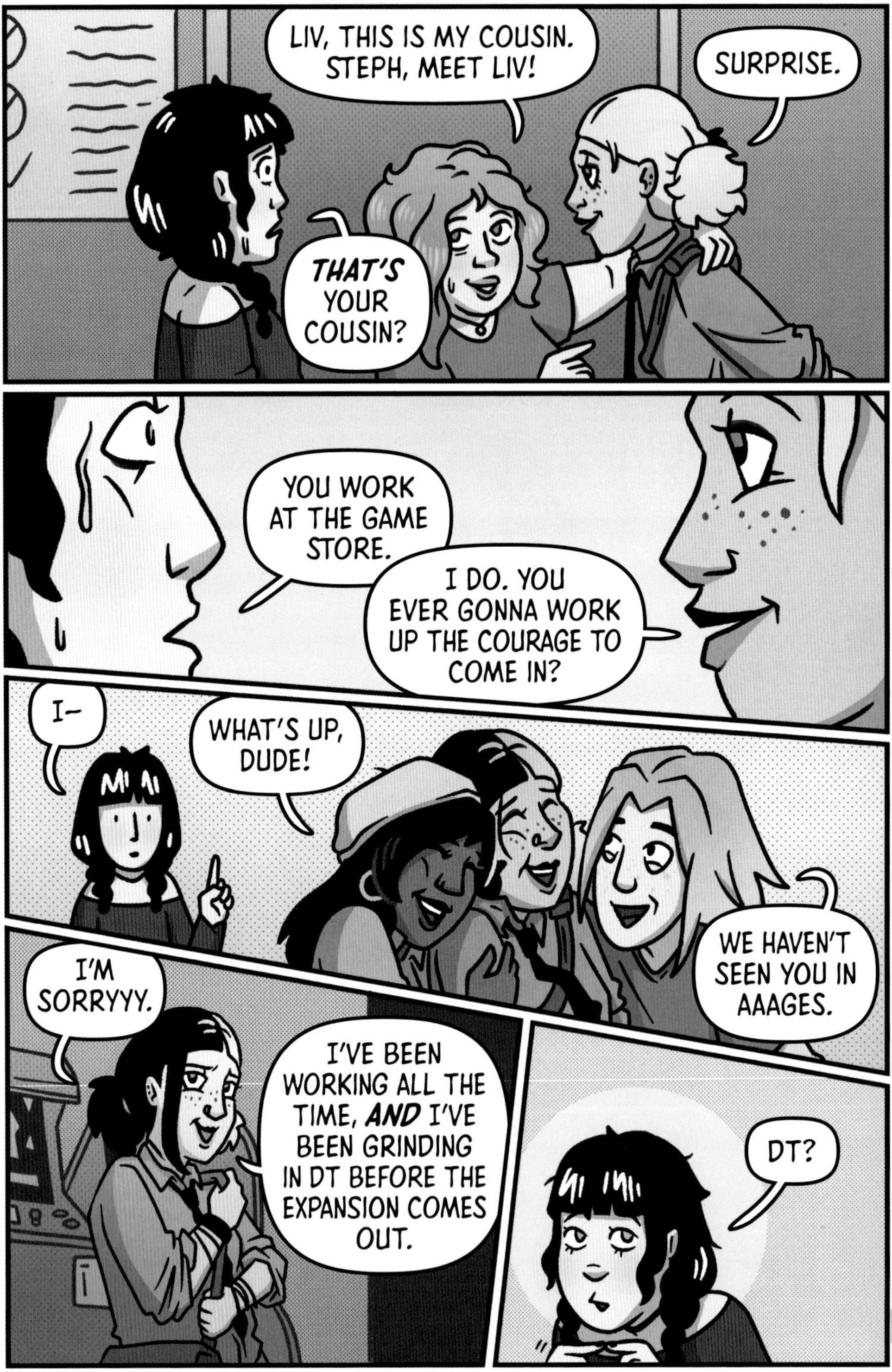
LIV, THIS IS MY COUSIN. STEPH, MEET LIV!
SURPRISE.
THAT'S YOUR COUSIN?
YOU WORK AT THE GAME STORE.
I DO. YOU EVER GONNA WORK UP THE COURAGE TO COME IN?
I–
WHAT'S UP, DUDE!
WE HAVEN'T SEEN YOU IN AAAGES.
I'M SORRYYY.
I'VE BEEN WORKING ALL THE TIME, *AND* I'VE BEEN GRINDING IN DT BEFORE THE EXPANSION COMES OUT.
DT?

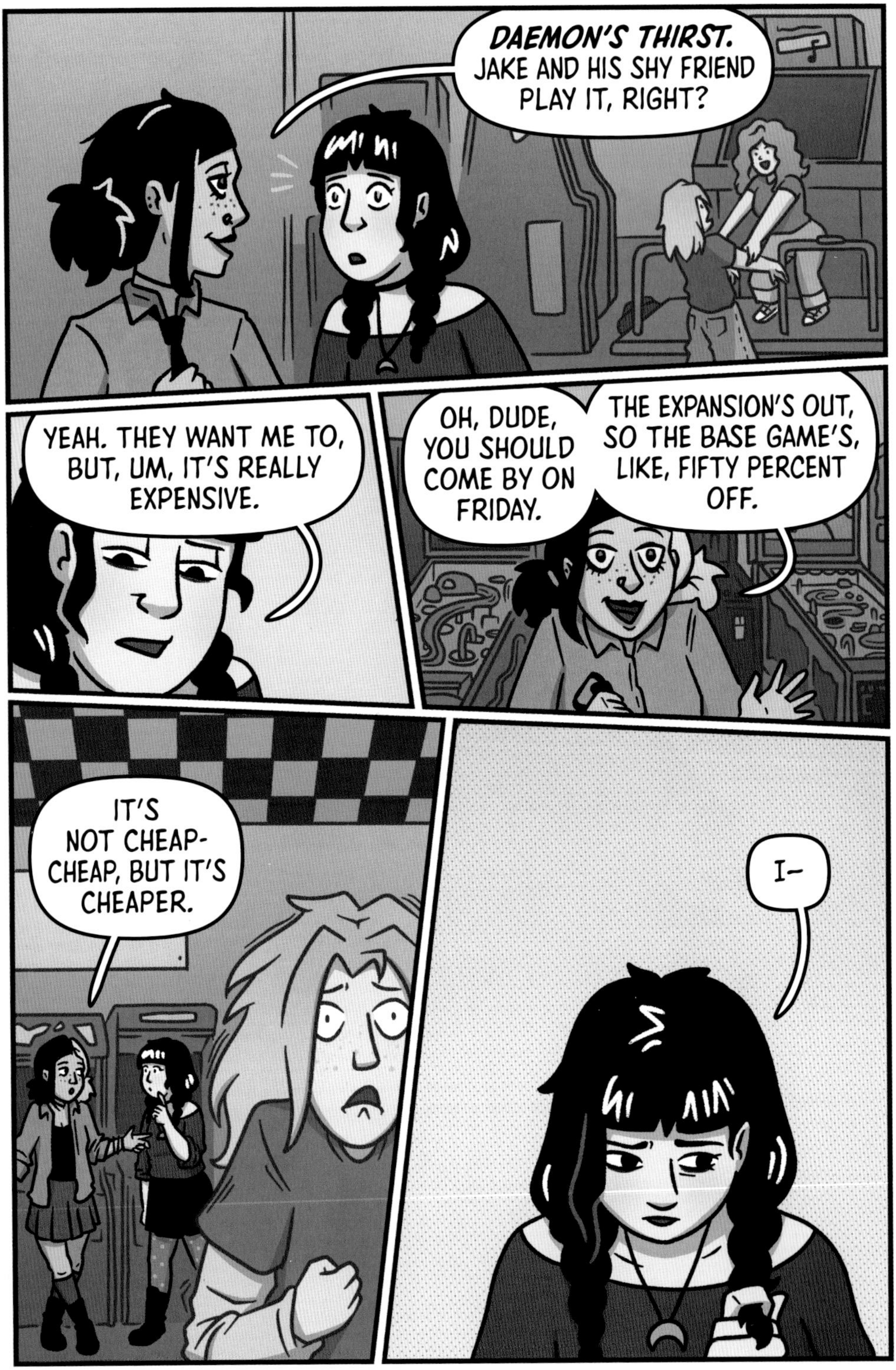

DAEMON'S THIRST. JAKE AND HIS SHY FRIEND PLAY IT, RIGHT?
YEAH. THEY WANT ME TO, BUT, UM, IT'S REALLY EXPENSIVE.
OH, DUDE, YOU SHOULD COME BY ON FRIDAY.
THE EXPANSION'S OUT, SO THE BASE GAME'S, LIKE, FIFTY PERCENT OFF.
IT'S NOT CHEAP-CHEAP, BUT IT'S CHEAPER.
I–

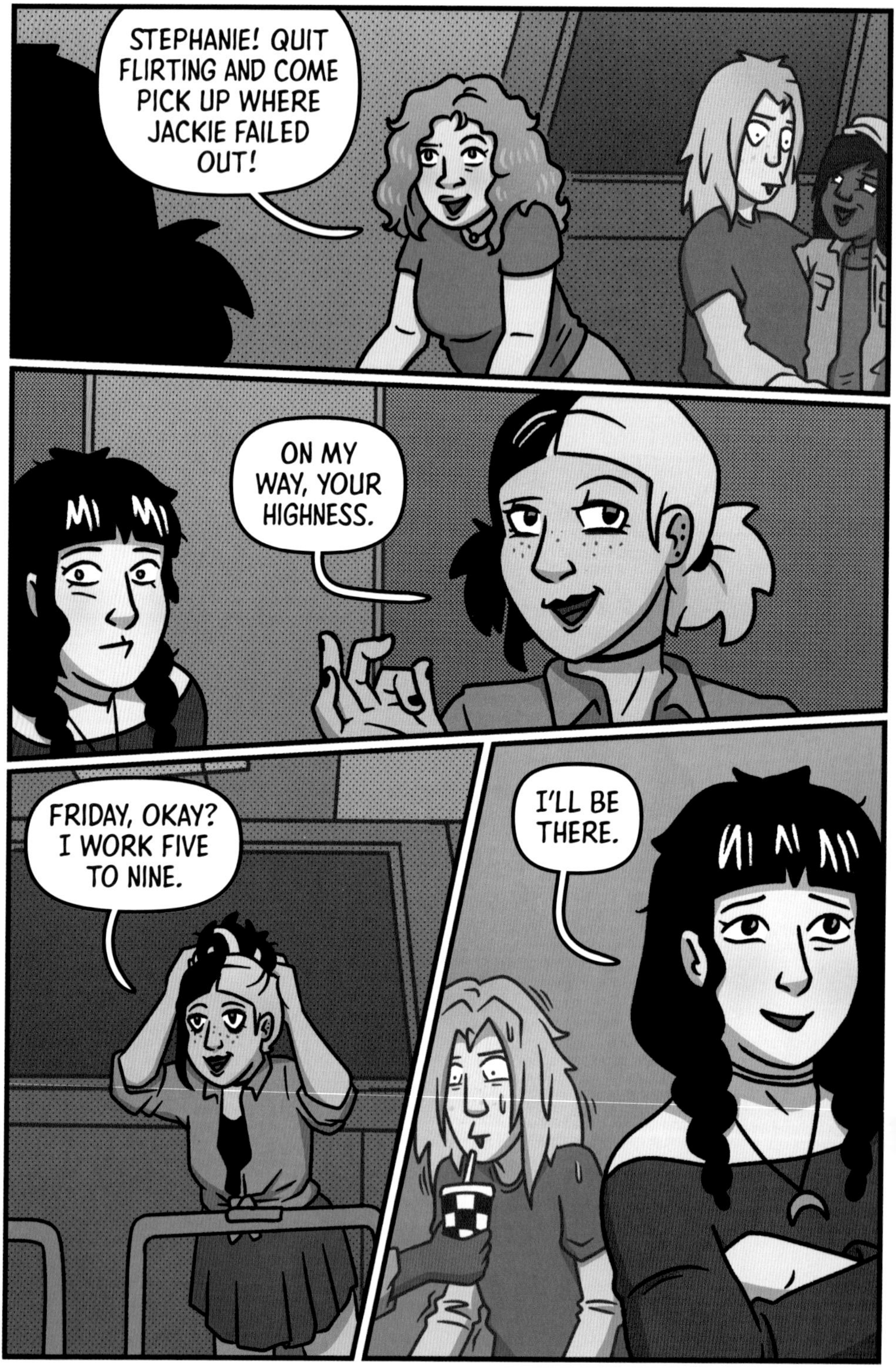
STEPHANIE! QUIT FLIRTING AND COME PICK UP WHERE JACKIE FAILED OUT!
ON MY WAY, YOUR HIGHNESS.
FRIDAY, OKAY? I WORK FIVE TO NINE.
I'LL BE THERE.

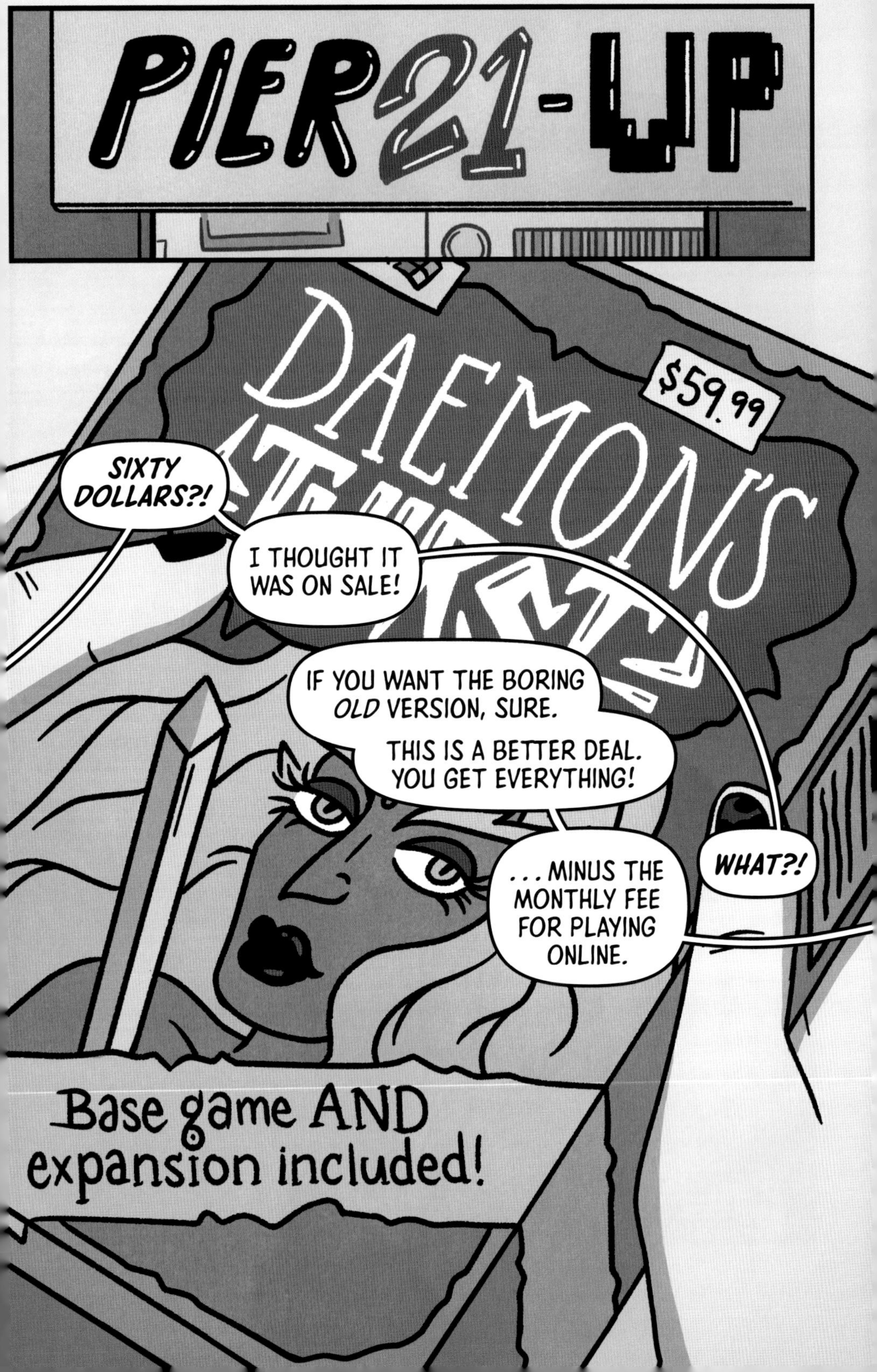
PIER 21-UP
DAEMON'S
$59.99
SIXTY DOLLARS?!
I THOUGHT IT WAS ON SALE!
IF YOU WANT THE BORING OLD VERSION, SURE.
THIS IS A BETTER DEAL. YOU GET EVERYTHING!
. . . MINUS THE MONTHLY FEE FOR PLAYING ONLINE.
WHAT?!
Base game AND expansion included!

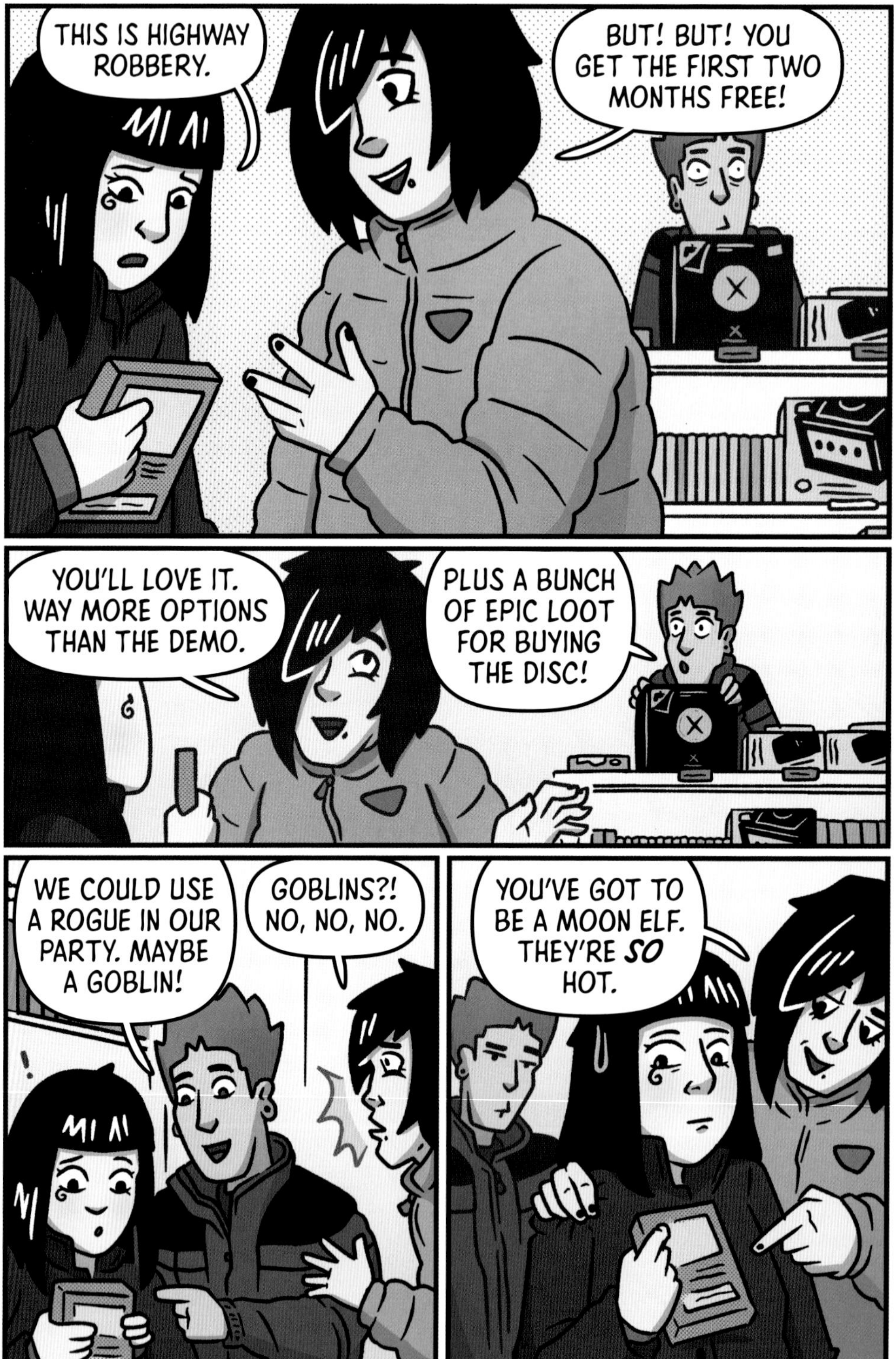
THIS IS HIGHWAY ROBBERY.
BUT! BUT! YOU GET THE FIRST TWO MONTHS FREE!
YOU'LL LOVE IT. WAY MORE OPTIONS THAN THE DEMO.
PLUS A BUNCH OF EPIC LOOT FOR BUYING THE DISC!
WE COULD USE A ROGUE IN OUR PARTY. MAYBE A GOBLIN!
GOBLINS?! NO, NO, NO.
YOU'VE GOT TO BE A MOON ELF. THEY'RE *SO* HOT.

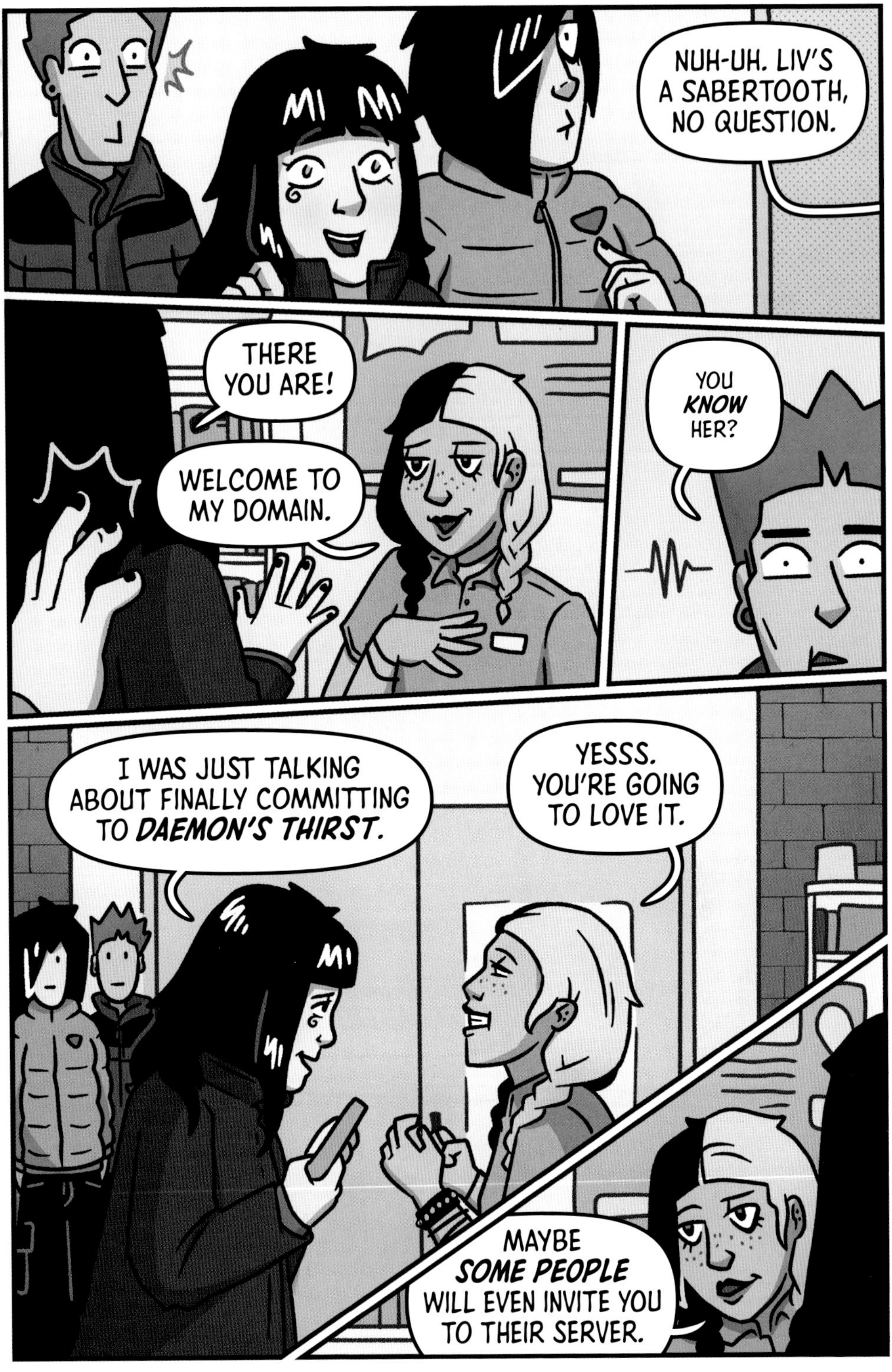
NUH-UH. LIV'S A SABERTOOTH, NO QUESTION.
THERE YOU ARE!
WELCOME TO MY DOMAIN.
YOU *KNOW* HER?
I WAS JUST TALKING ABOUT FINALLY COMMITTING TO ***DAEMON'S THIRST***.
YESSS. YOU'RE GOING TO LOVE IT.
MAYBE ***SOME PEOPLE*** WILL EVEN INVITE YOU TO THEIR SERVER.

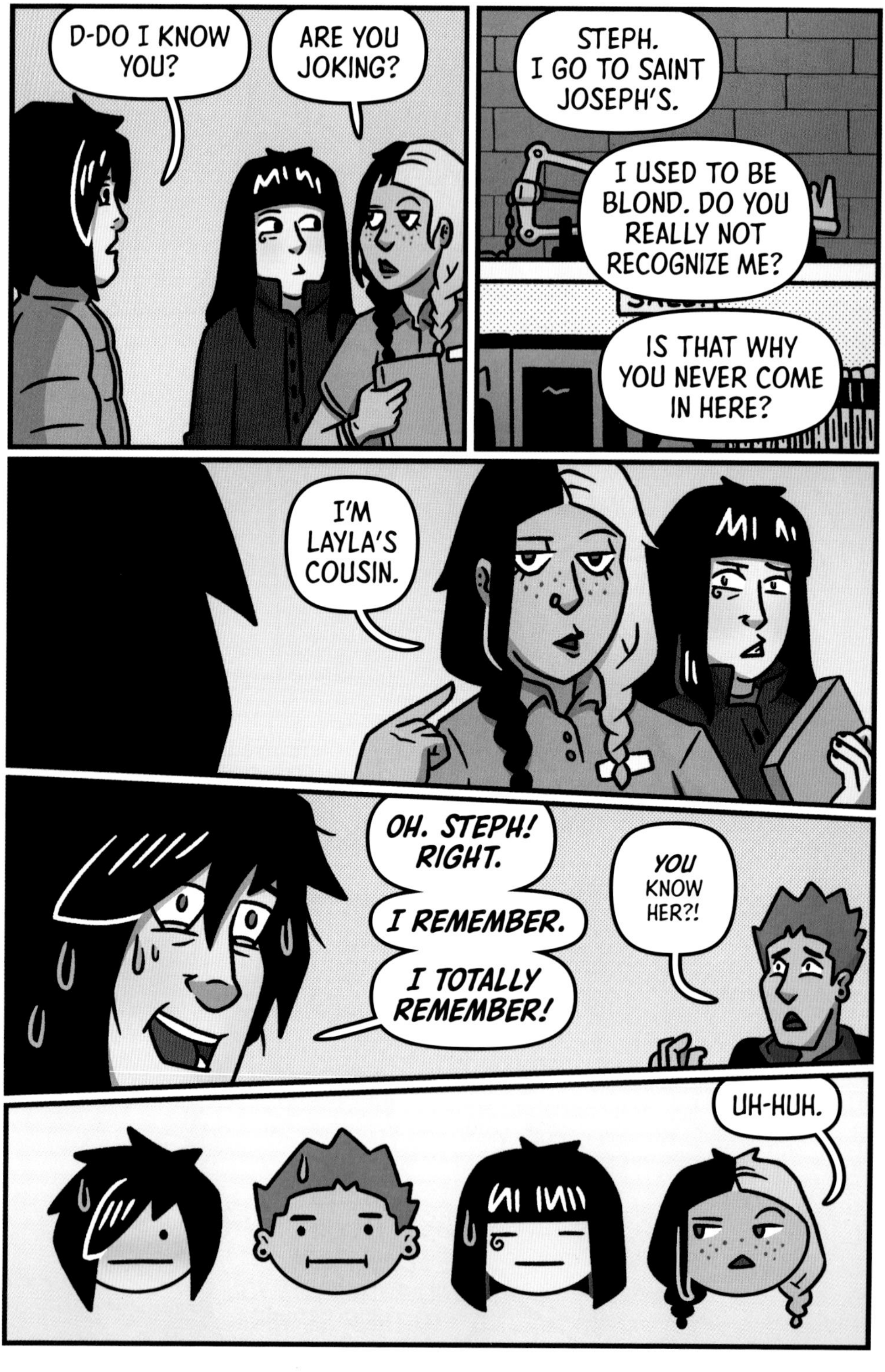
D-DO I KNOW YOU?
ARE YOU JOKING?
STEPH. I GO TO SAINT JOSEPH'S.
I USED TO BE BLOND. DO YOU REALLY NOT RECOGNIZE ME?
IS THAT WHY YOU NEVER COME IN HERE?
I'M LAYLA'S COUSIN.
OH. STEPH! RIGHT.
I REMEMBER.
I TOTALLY REMEMBER!
YOU KNOW HER?!
UH-HUH.

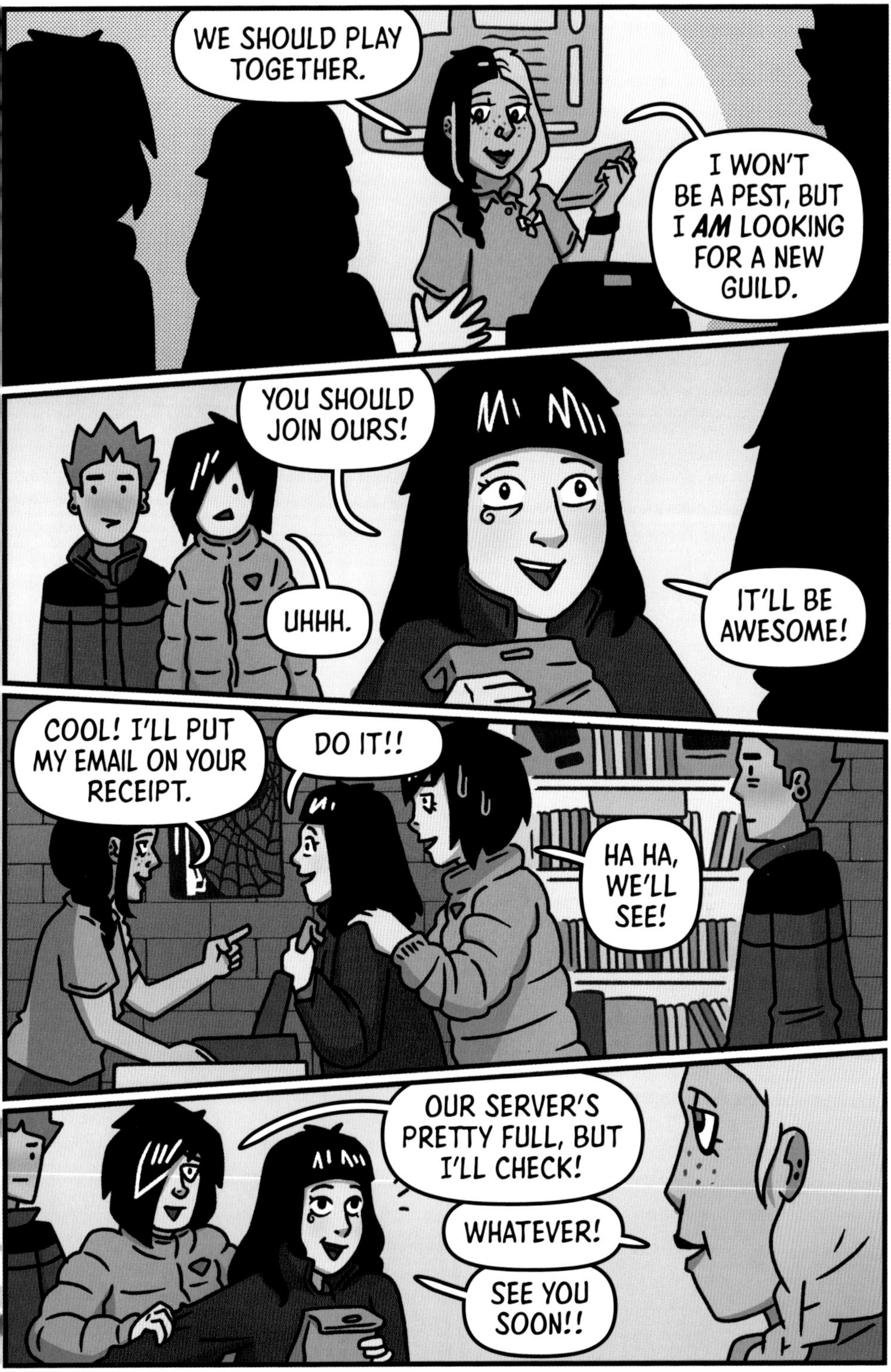
WE SHOULD PLAY TOGETHER.
I WON'T BE A PEST, BUT I *AM* LOOKING FOR A NEW GUILD.
YOU SHOULD JOIN OURS!
UHHH.
IT'LL BE AWESOME!
COOL! I'LL PUT MY EMAIL ON YOUR RECEIPT.
DO IT!!
HA HA, WE'LL SEE!
OUR SERVER'S PRETTY FULL, BUT I'LL CHECK!
WHATEVER!
SEE YOU SOON!!

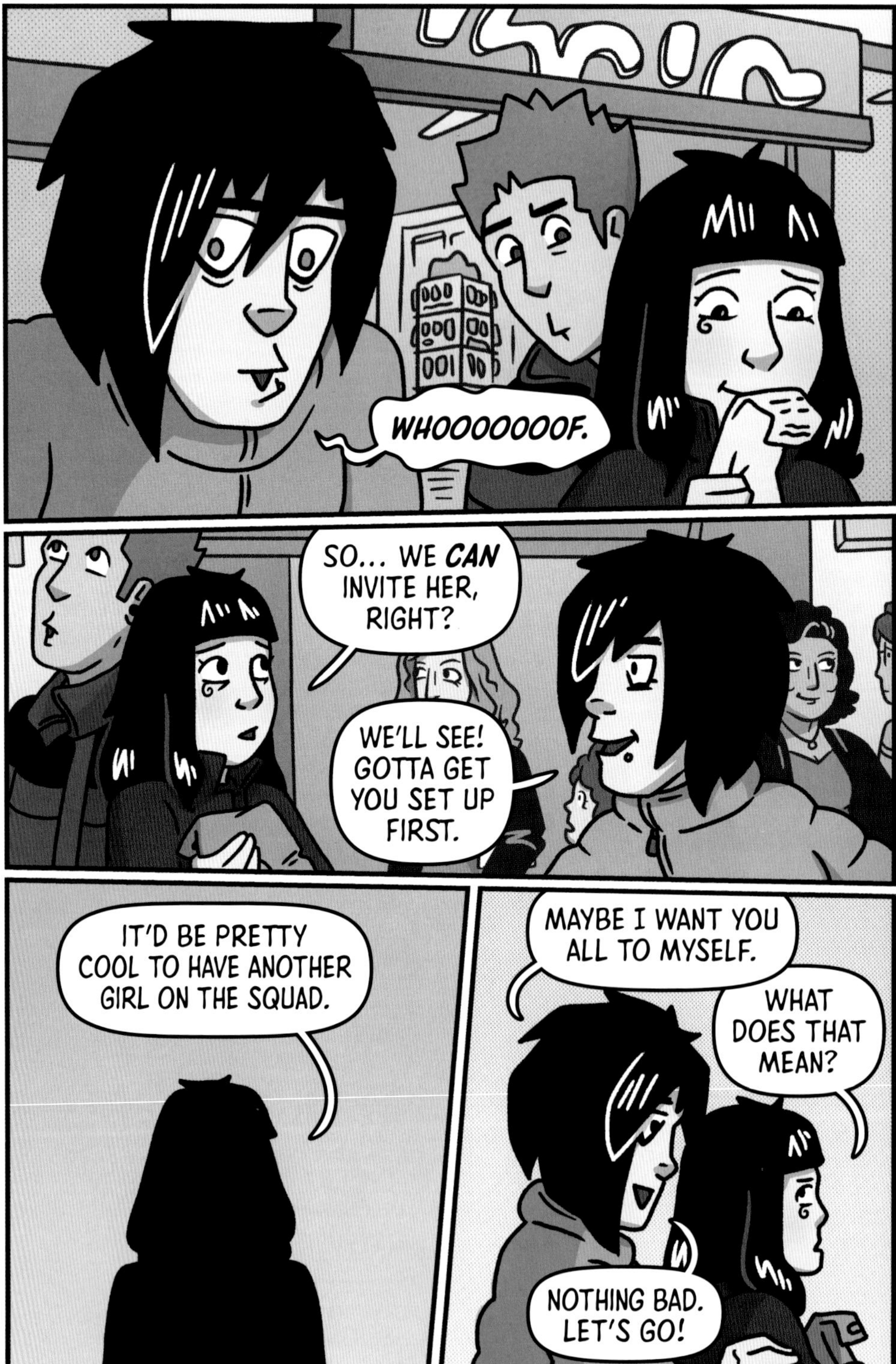
WHOOOOOOOF.
SO... WE CAN INVITE HER, RIGHT?
WE'LL SEE! GOTTA GET YOU SET UP FIRST.
IT'D BE PRETTY COOL TO HAVE ANOTHER GIRL ON THE SQUAD.
MAYBE I WANT YOU ALL TO MYSELF.
WHAT DOES THAT MEAN?
NOTHING BAD. LET'S GO!

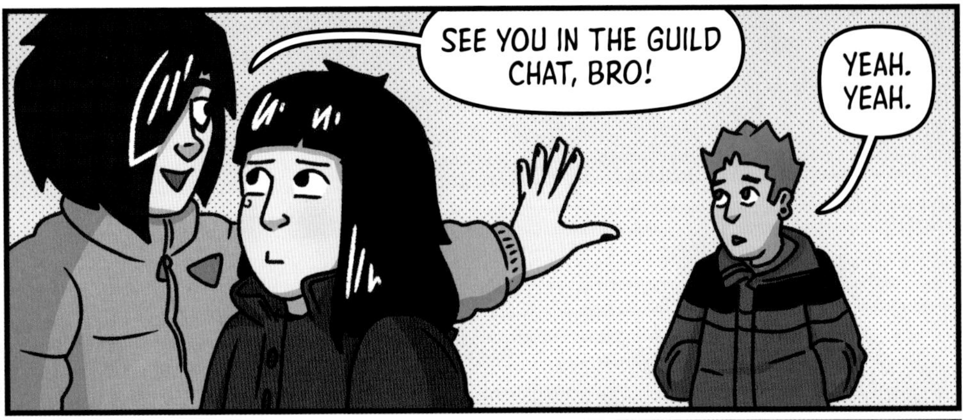
SEE YOU IN THE GUILD CHAT, BRO!
YEAH. YEAH.

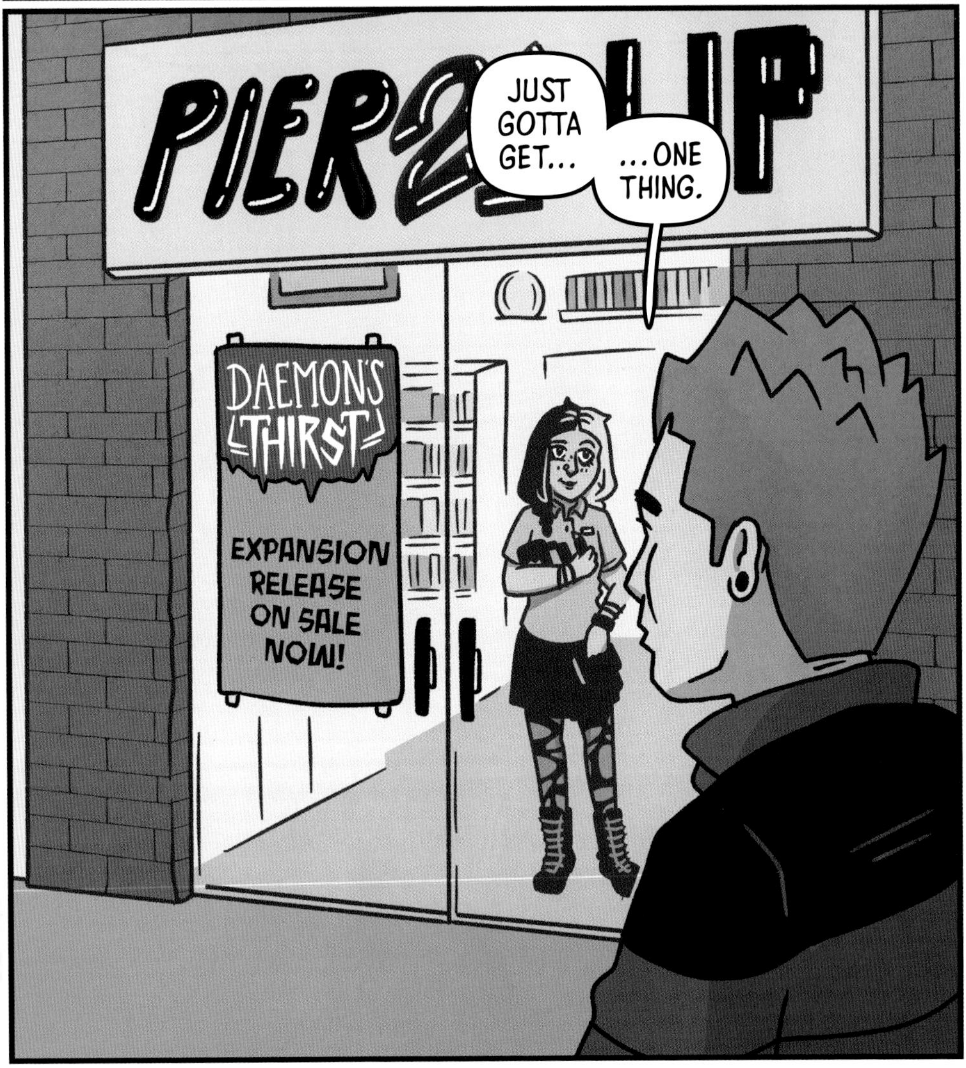
PIER
UP
JUST GOTTA GET...
...ONE THING.
DAEMON'S THIRST
EXPANSION RELEASE ON SALE NOW!

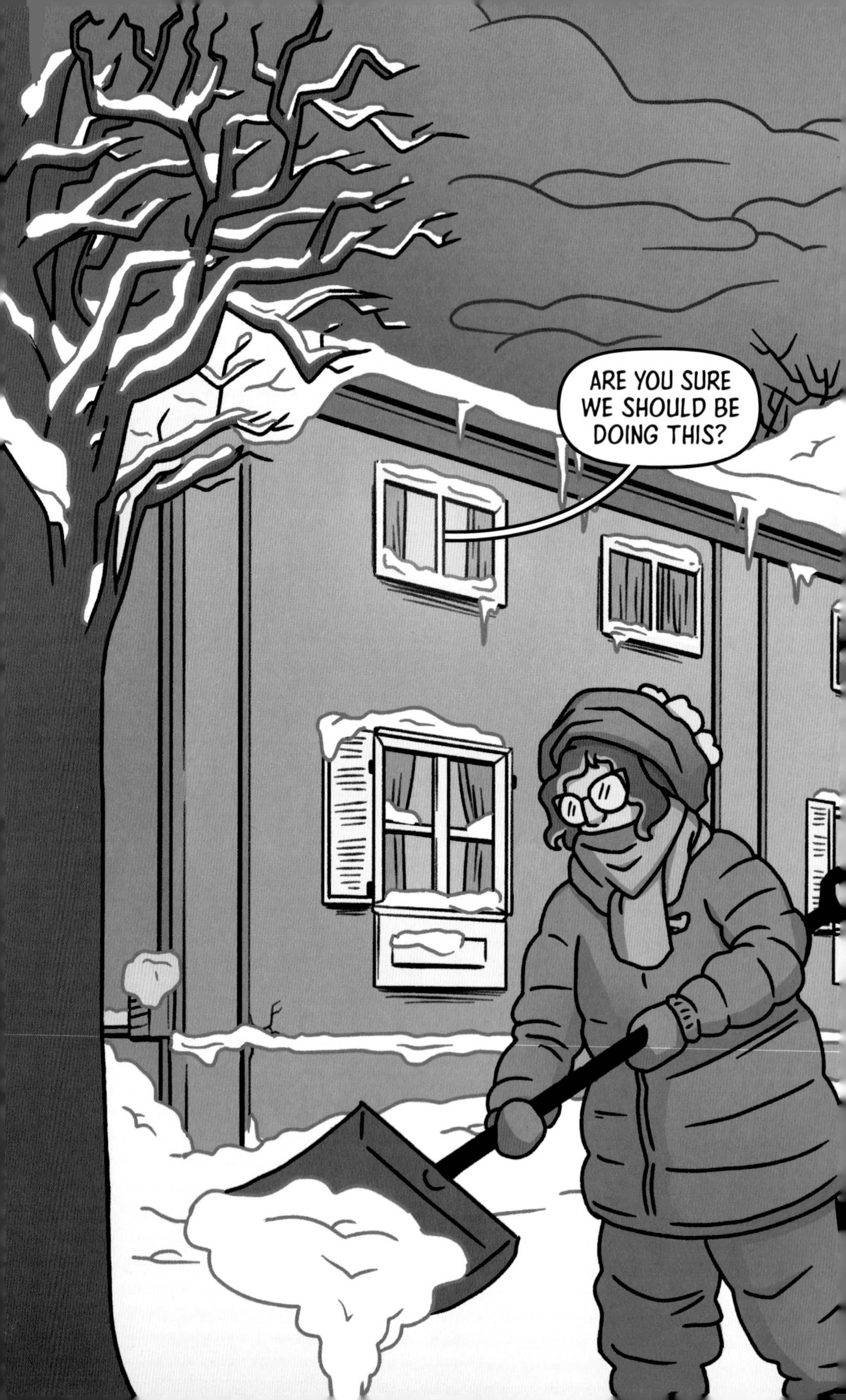
ARE YOU SURE WE SHOULD BE DOING THIS?

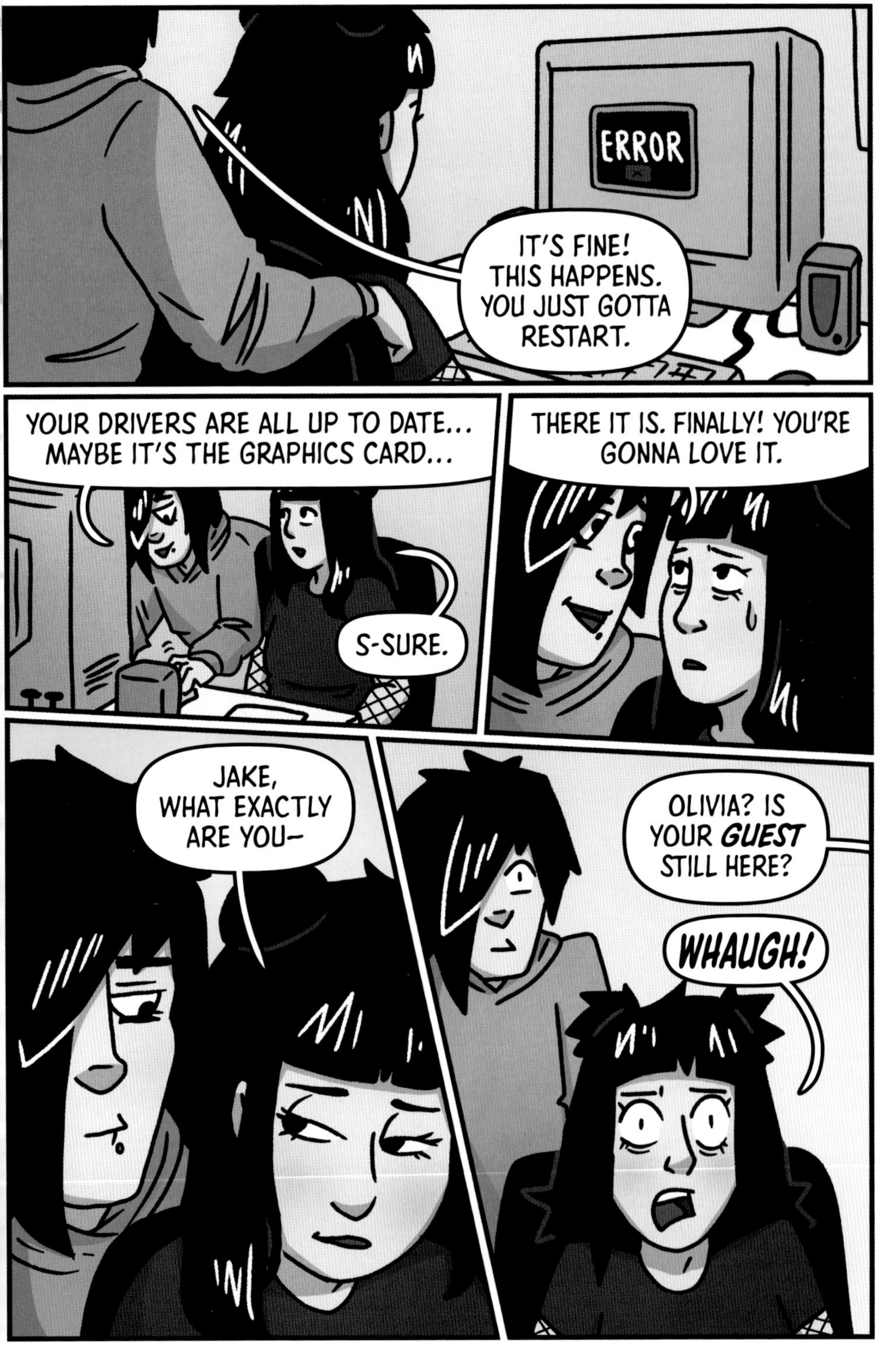
ERROR
IT'S FINE! THIS HAPPENS. YOU JUST GOTTA RESTART.
YOUR DRIVERS ARE ALL UP TO DATE... MAYBE IT'S THE GRAPHICS CARD...
S-SURE.
THERE IT IS. FINALLY! YOU'RE GONNA LOVE IT.
JAKE, WHAT EXACTLY ARE YOU–
OLIVIA? IS YOUR GUEST STILL HERE?
WHAUGH!

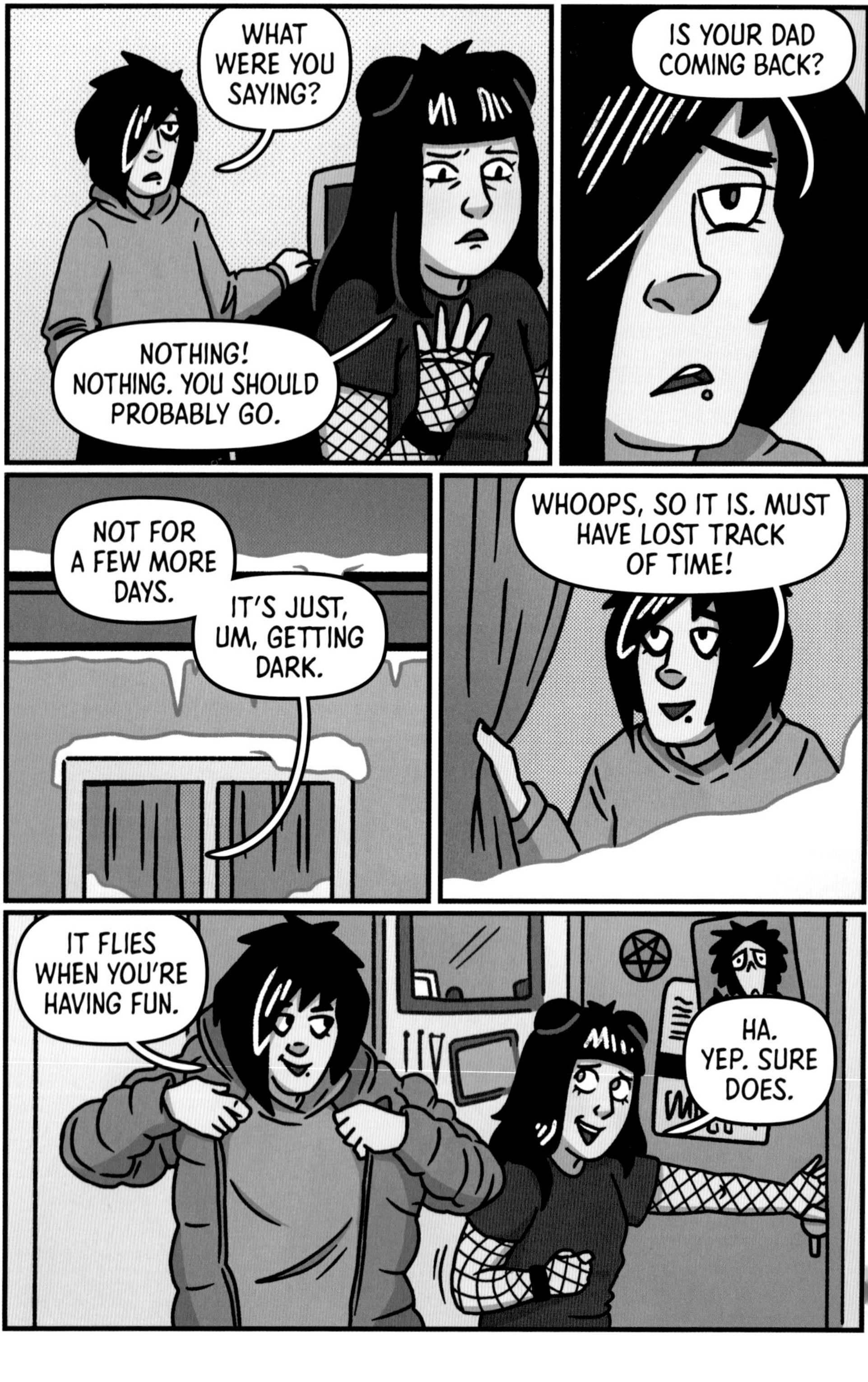
WHAT WERE YOU SAYING?
NOTHING! NOTHING. YOU SHOULD PROBABLY GO.
IS YOUR DAD COMING BACK?
NOT FOR A FEW MORE DAYS.
IT'S JUST, UM, GETTING DARK.
WHOOPS, SO IT IS. MUST HAVE LOST TRACK OF TIME!
IT FLIES WHEN YOU'RE HAVING FUN.
HA. YEP. SURE DOES.

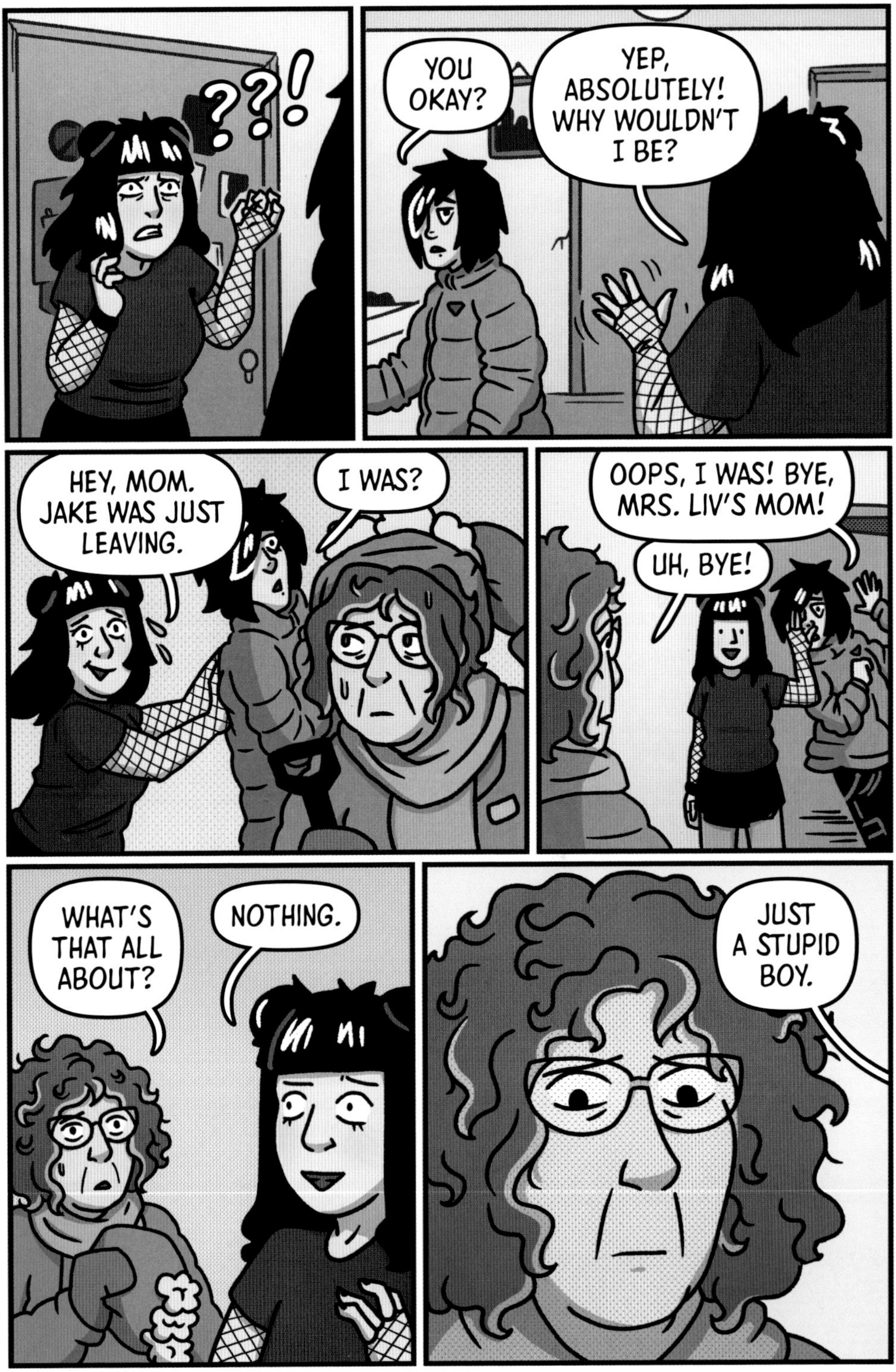
??!
YOU OKAY?
YEP, ABSOLUTELY! WHY WOULDN'T I BE?
HEY, MOM. JAKE WAS JUST LEAVING.
I WAS?
OOPS, I WAS! BYE, MRS. LIV'S MOM!
UH, BYE!
WHAT'S THAT ALL ABOUT?
NOTHING.
JUST A STUPID BOY.

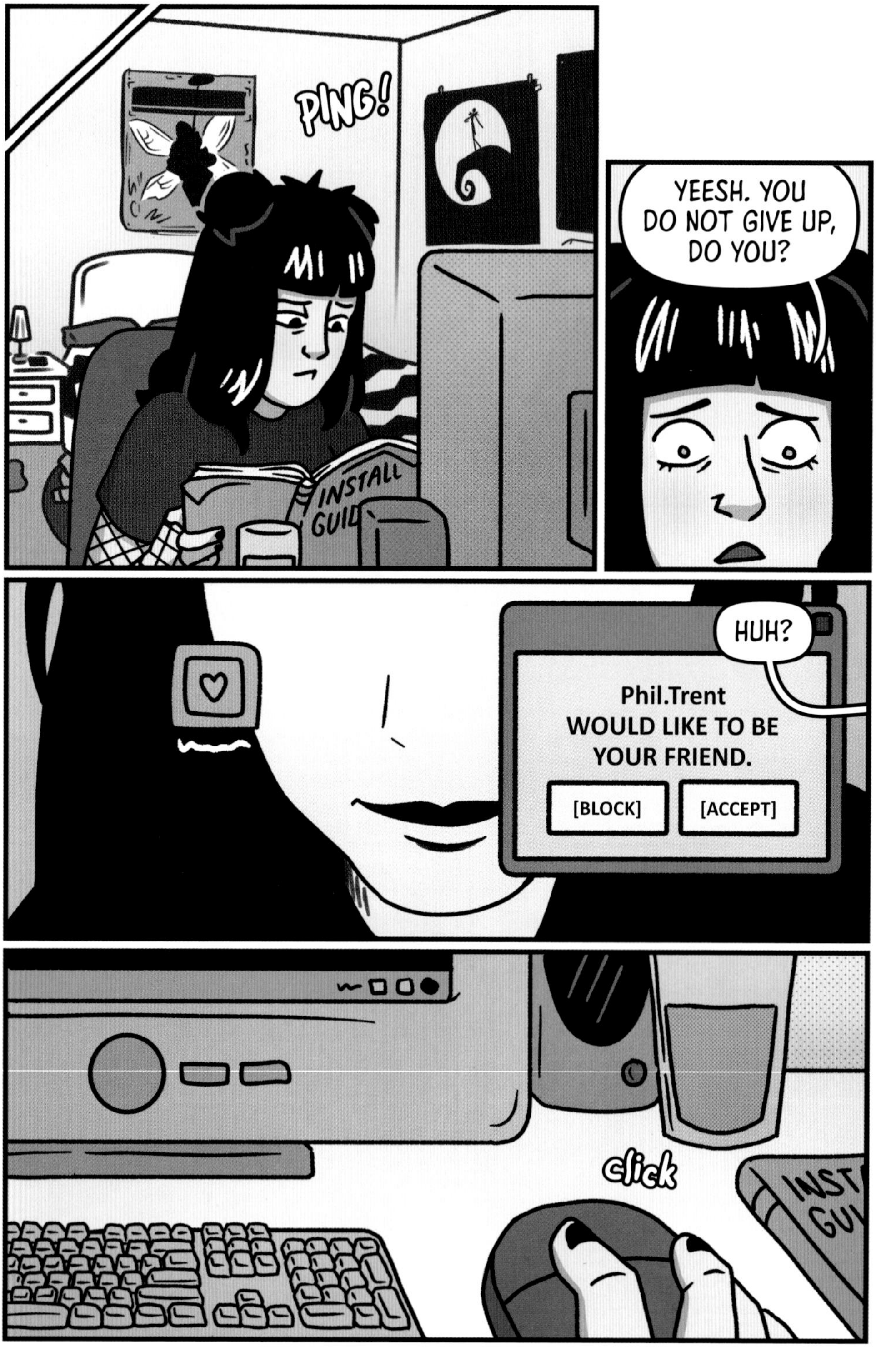
PING!
YEESH. YOU DO NOT GIVE UP, DO YOU?
INSTALL GUID
HUH?
Phil.Trent
WOULD LIKE TO BE YOUR FRIEND.
[BLOCK]
[ACCEPT]
click
INST GUI

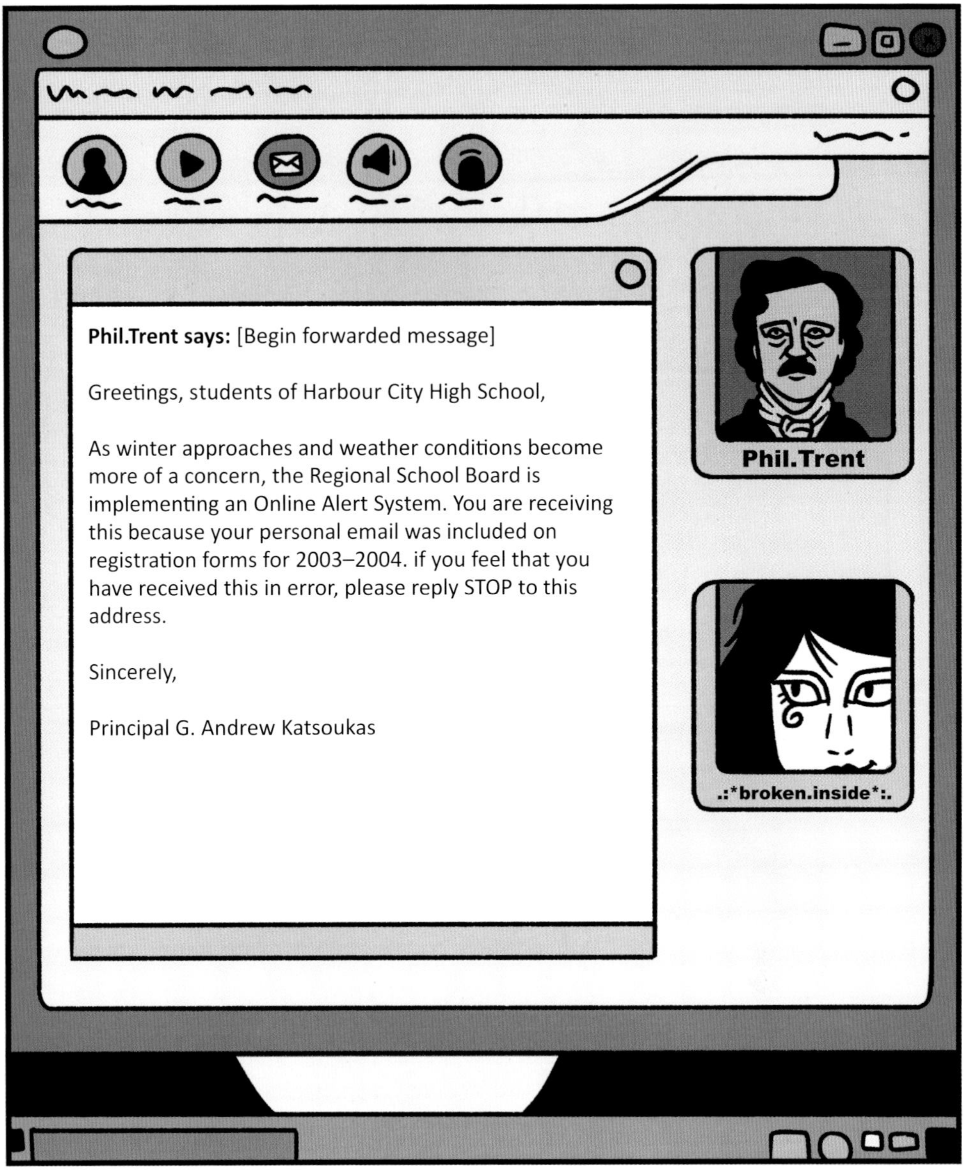
Phil.Trent says: [Begin forwarded message]
Greetings, students of Harbour City High School,
As winter approaches and weather conditions become more of a concern, the Regional School Board is implementing an Online Alert System. You are receiving this because your personal email was included on registration forms for 2003–2004. if you feel that you have received this in error, please reply STOP to this address.
Sincerely,
Principal G. Andrew Katsoukas
Phil.Trent
.:*broken.inside*:.

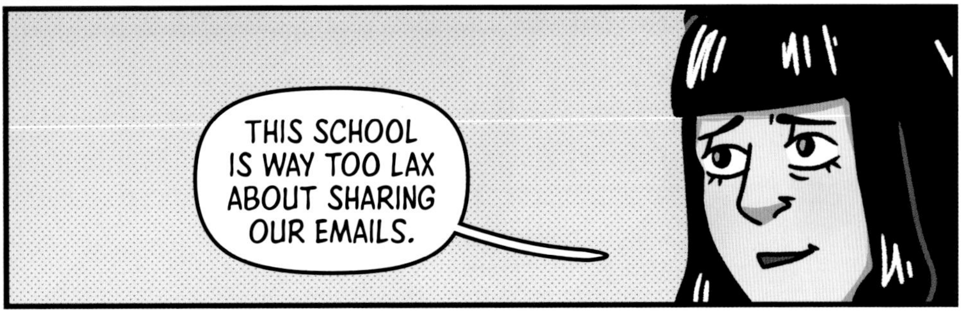
THIS SCHOOL IS WAY TOO LAX ABOUT SHARING OUR EMAILS.

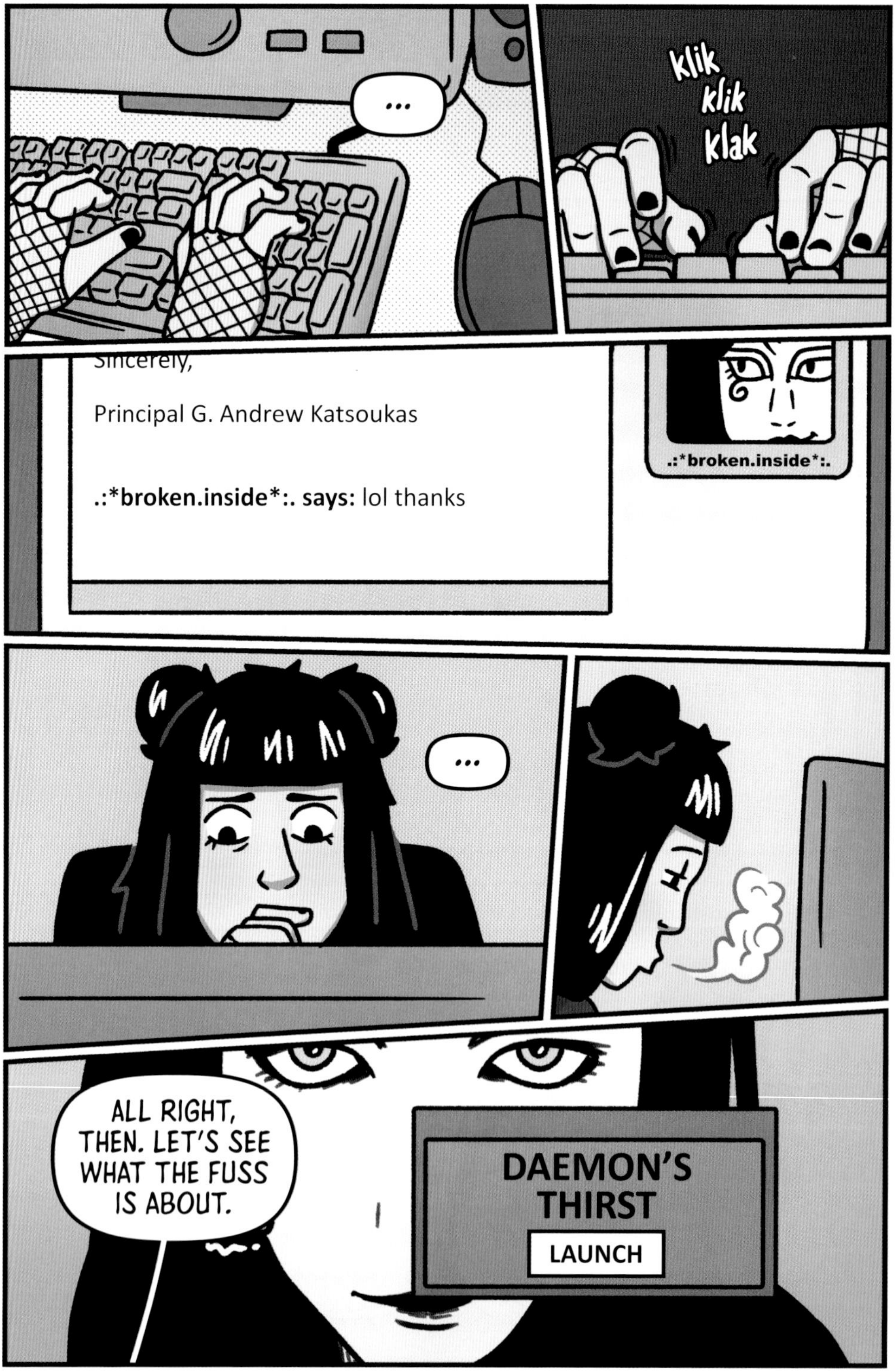
...
klik
klik
klak
Sincerely,
Principal G. Andrew Katsoukas
.:*broken.inside*:. says: lol thanks
.:*broken.inside*:.
...
ALL RIGHT, THEN. LET'S SEE WHAT THE FUSS IS ABOUT.
DAEMON'S THIRST
LAUNCH

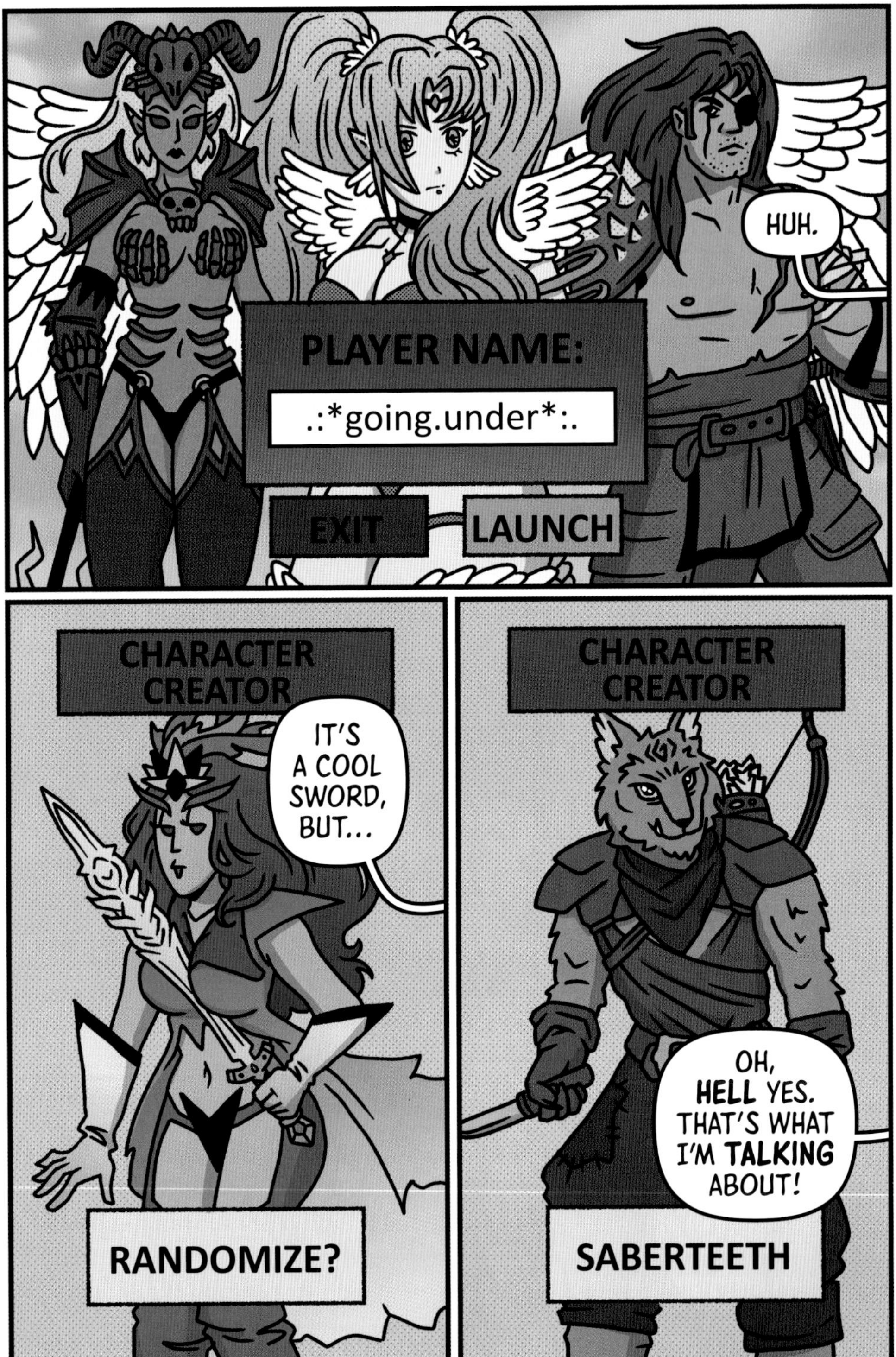
HUH.
PLAYER NAME:
.:*going.under*:.
EXIT
LAUNCH
CHARACTER CREATOR
IT'S A COOL SWORD, BUT...
RANDOMIZE?
CHARACTER CREATOR
OH, HELL YES. THAT'S WHAT I'M TALKING ABOUT!
SABERTEETH

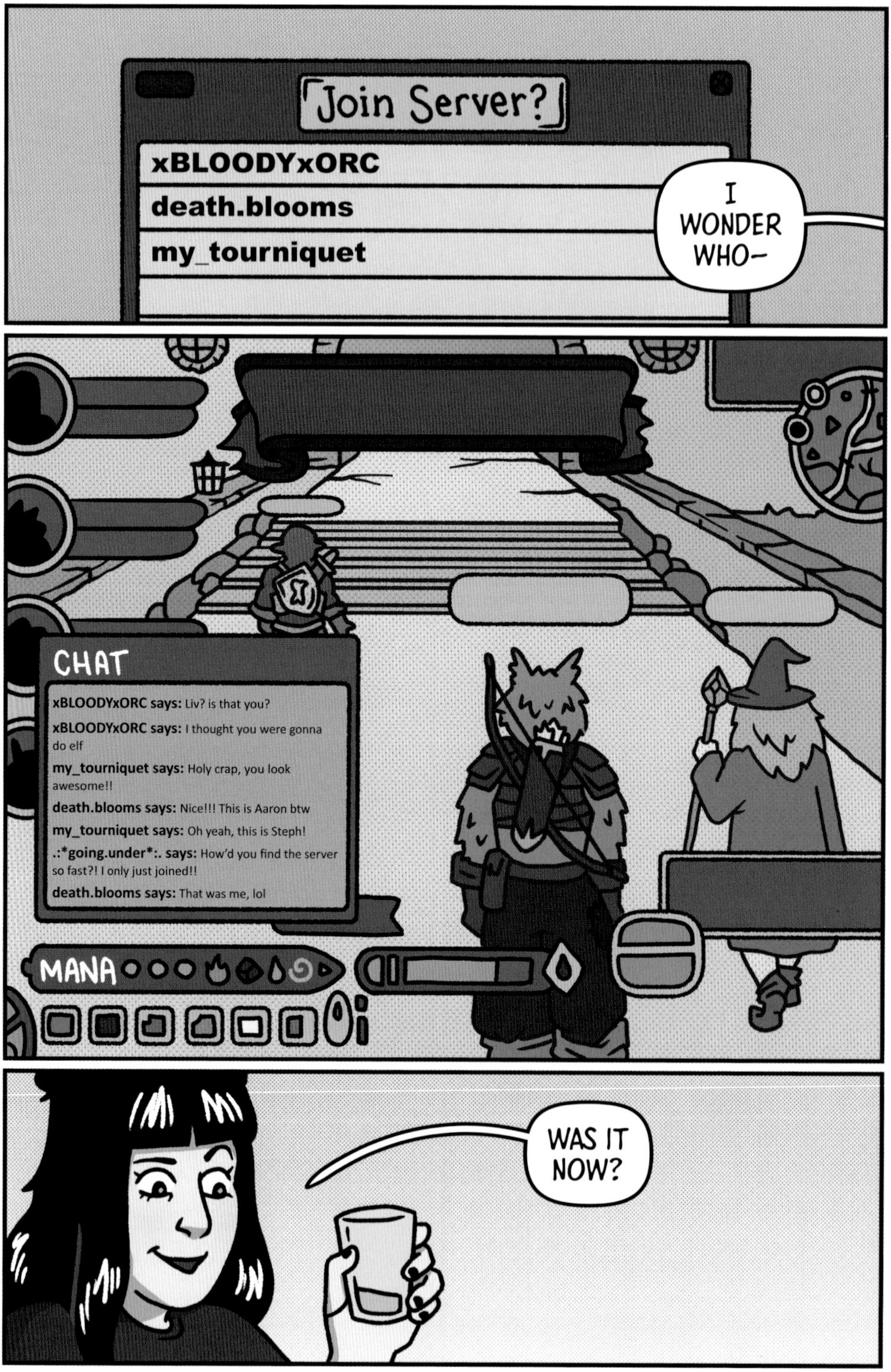
Join Server?
xBLOODYxORC
death.blooms
my_tourniquet
I WONDER WHO–
CHAT
xBLOODYxORC says: Liv? is that you?
xBLOODYxORC says: I thought you were gonna do elf
my_tourniquet says: Holy crap, you look awesome!!
death.blooms says: Nice!!! This is Aaron btw
my_tourniquet says: Oh yeah, this is Steph!
.:*going.under*:. says: How'd you find the server so fast?! I only just joined!!
death.blooms says: That was me, lol
MANA
WAS IT NOW?

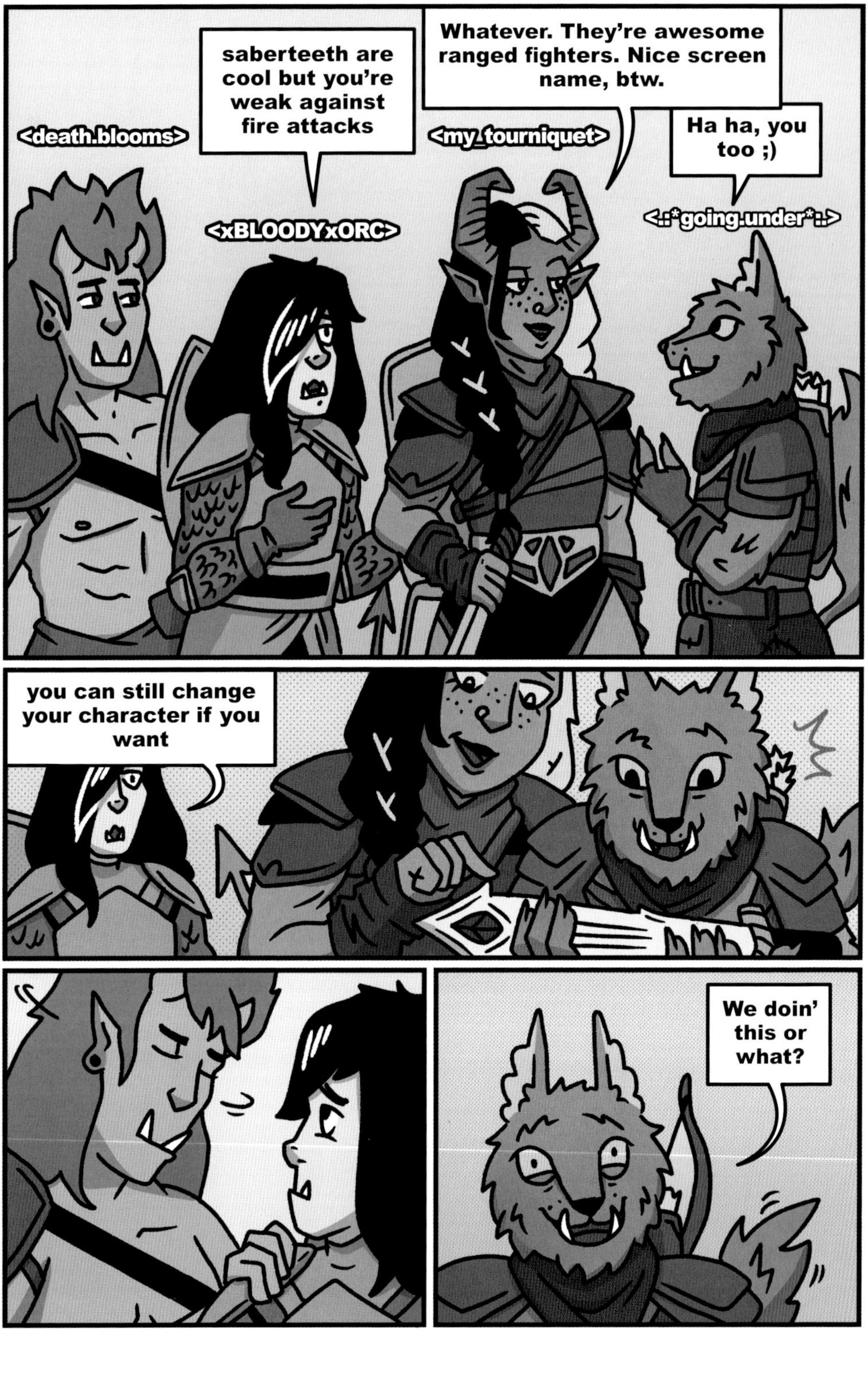

<death.blooms>
saberteeth are cool but you're weak against fire attacks
<xBLOODYxORC>
Whatever. They're awesome ranged fighters. Nice screen name, btw.
<my_tourniquet>
Ha ha, you too ;)
<.:*going.under*:.>
you can still change your character if you want
We doin' this or what?

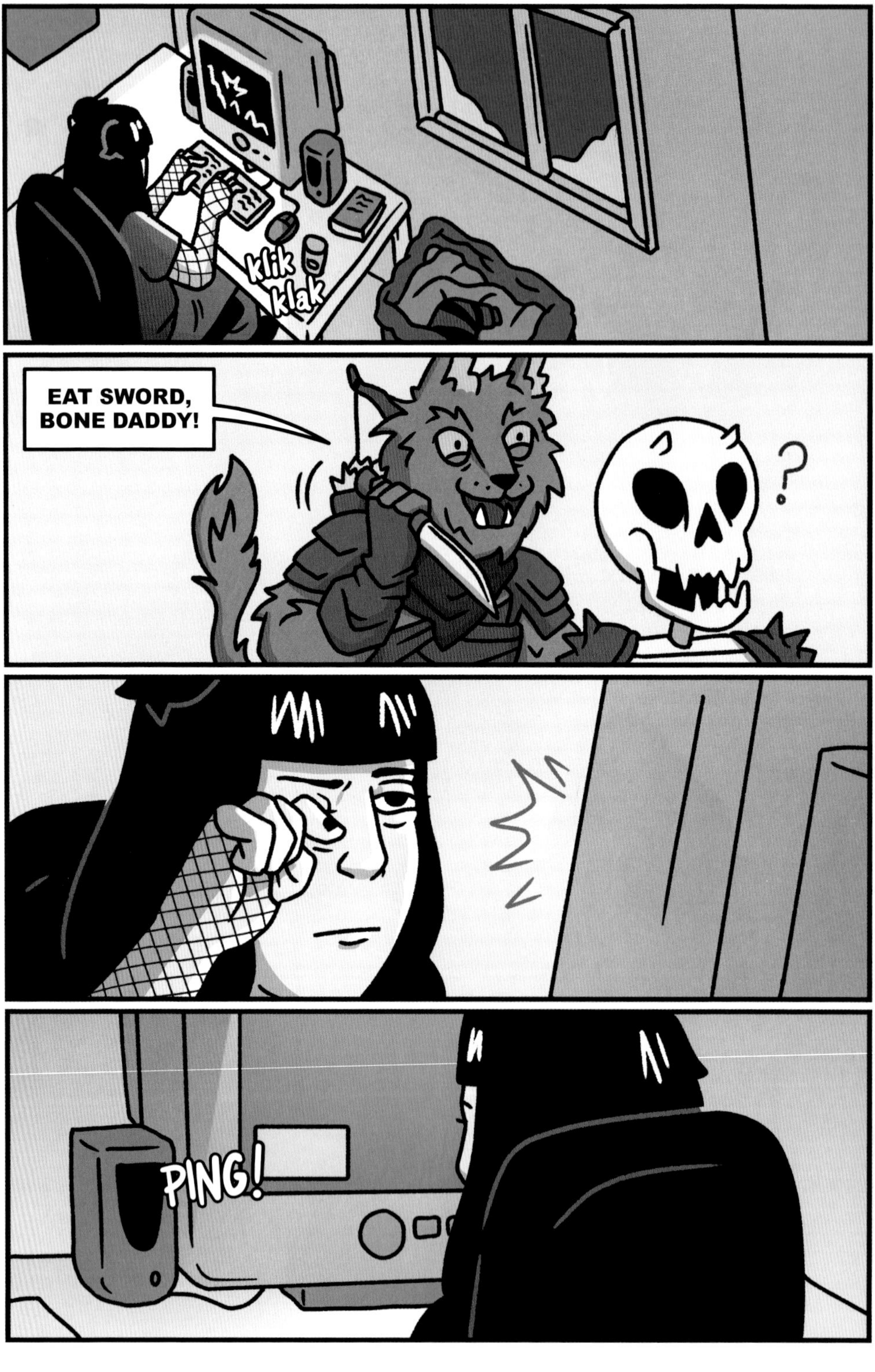
klik
klak
EAT SWORD, BONE DADDY!
?
PING!

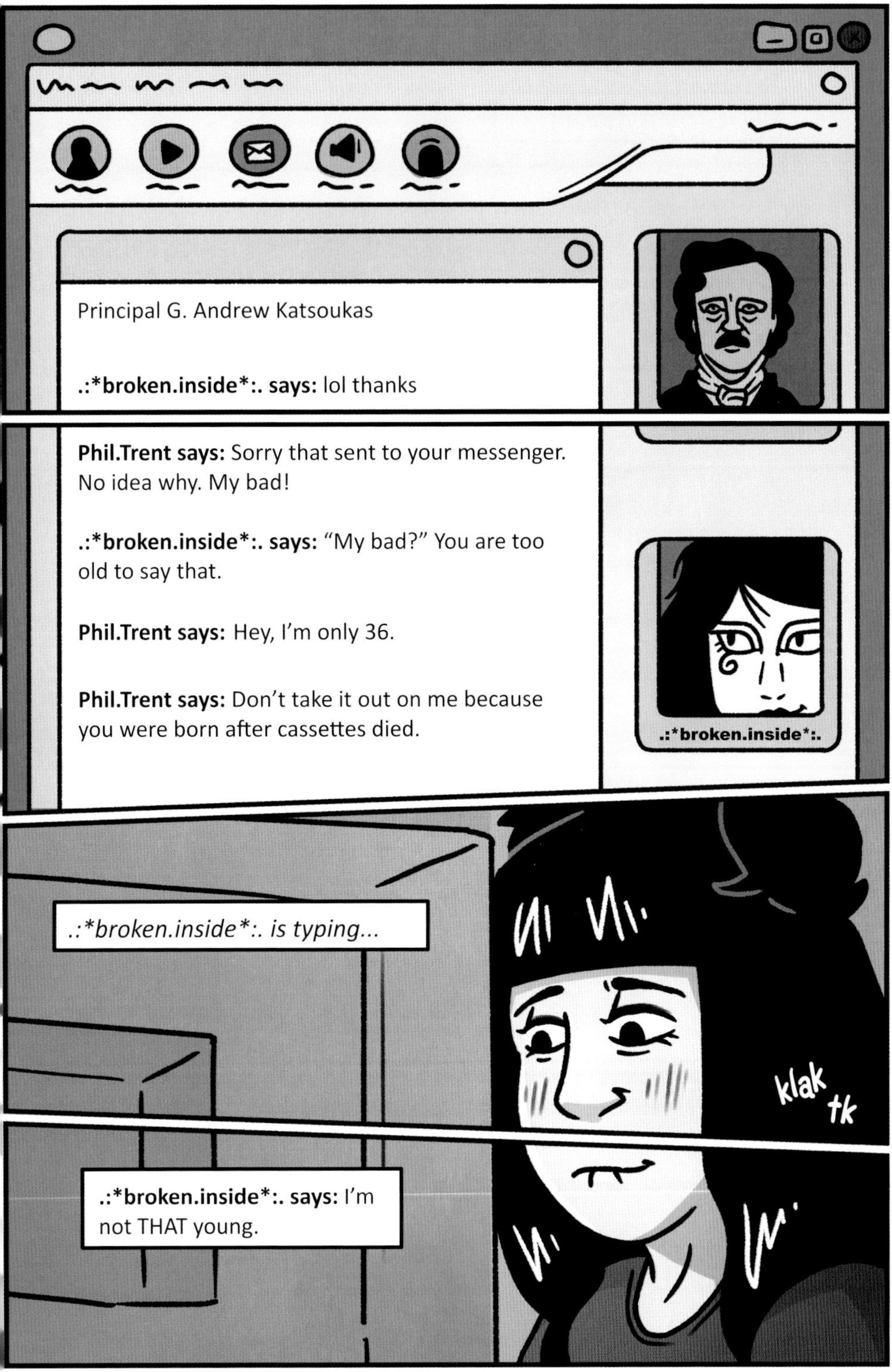
Principal G. Andrew Katsoukas
.:*broken.inside*:. says: lol thanks
Phil.Trent says: Sorry that sent to your messenger. No idea why. My bad!
.:*broken.inside*:. says: "My bad?" You are too old to say that.
Phil.Trent says: Hey, I'm only 36.
Phil.Trent says: Don't take it out on me because you were born after cassettes died.
.:*broken.inside*:.
.:*broken.inside*:. is typing...
klak
tk
.:*broken.inside*:. says: I'm not THAT young.

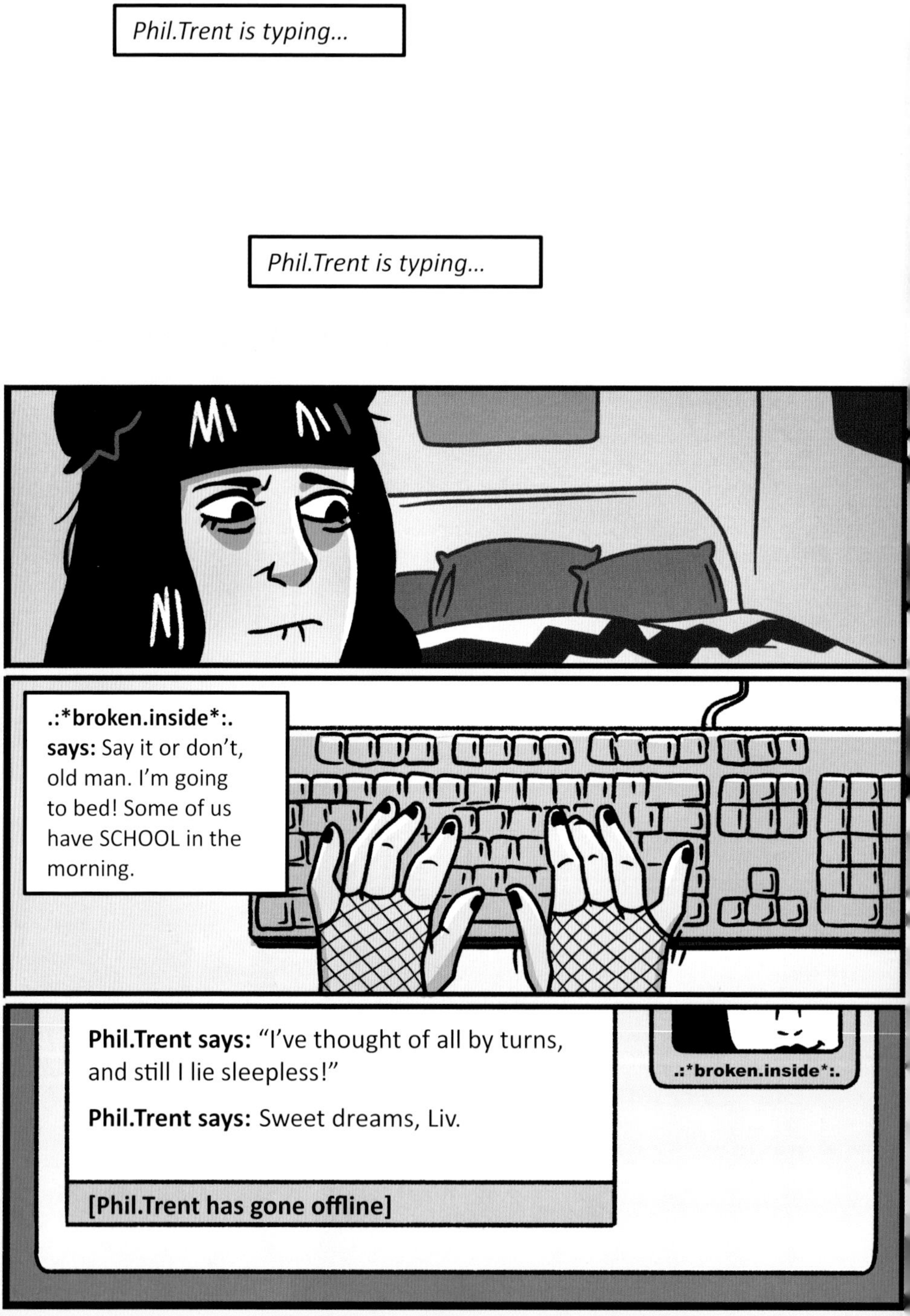
Phil.Trent is typing...
Phil.Trent is typing...
.:*broken.inside*:. says: Say it or don't, old man. I'm going to bed! Some of us have SCHOOL in the morning.
Phil.Trent says: "I've thought of all by turns, and still I lie sleepless!"
Phil.Trent says: Sweet dreams, Liv.
[Phil.Trent has gone offline]
.:*broken.inside*:.

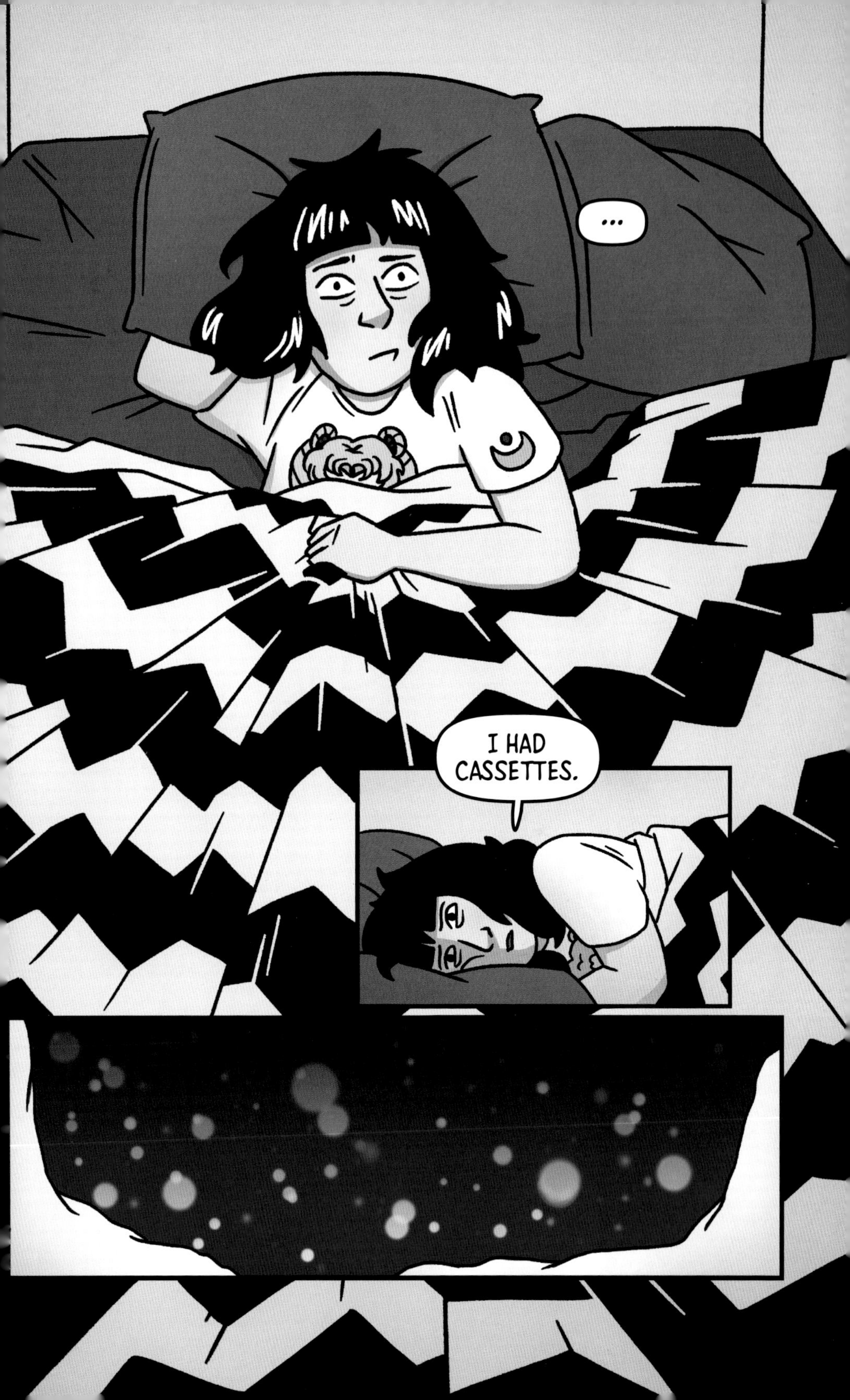
...
I HAD CASSETTES.

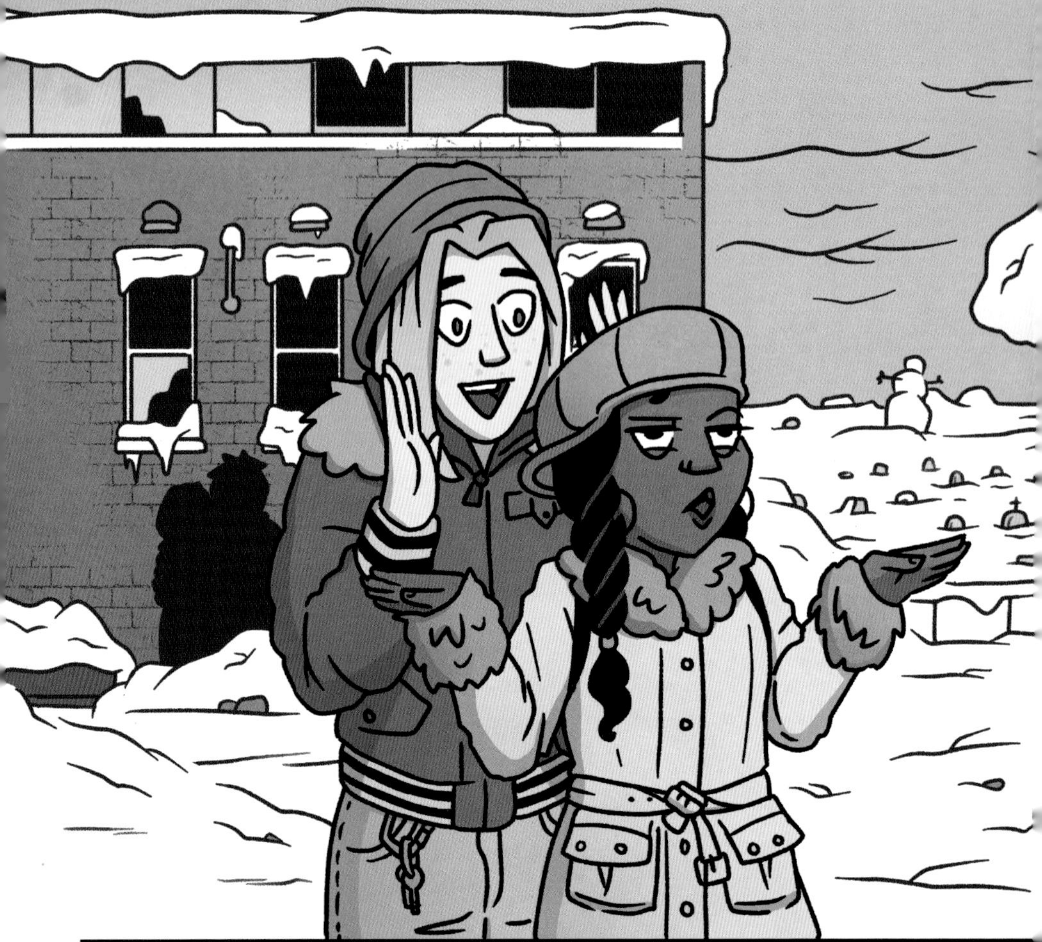

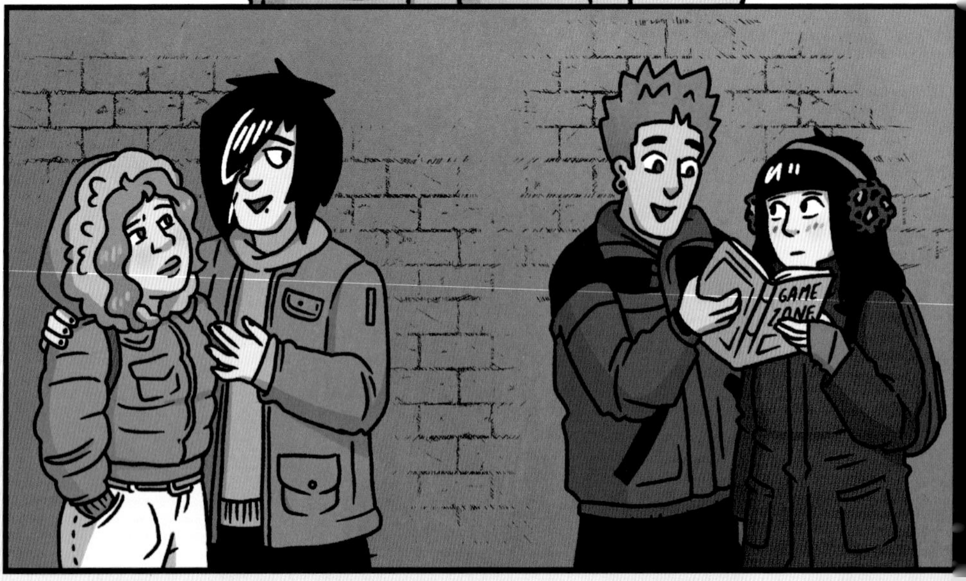
GAME ZONE

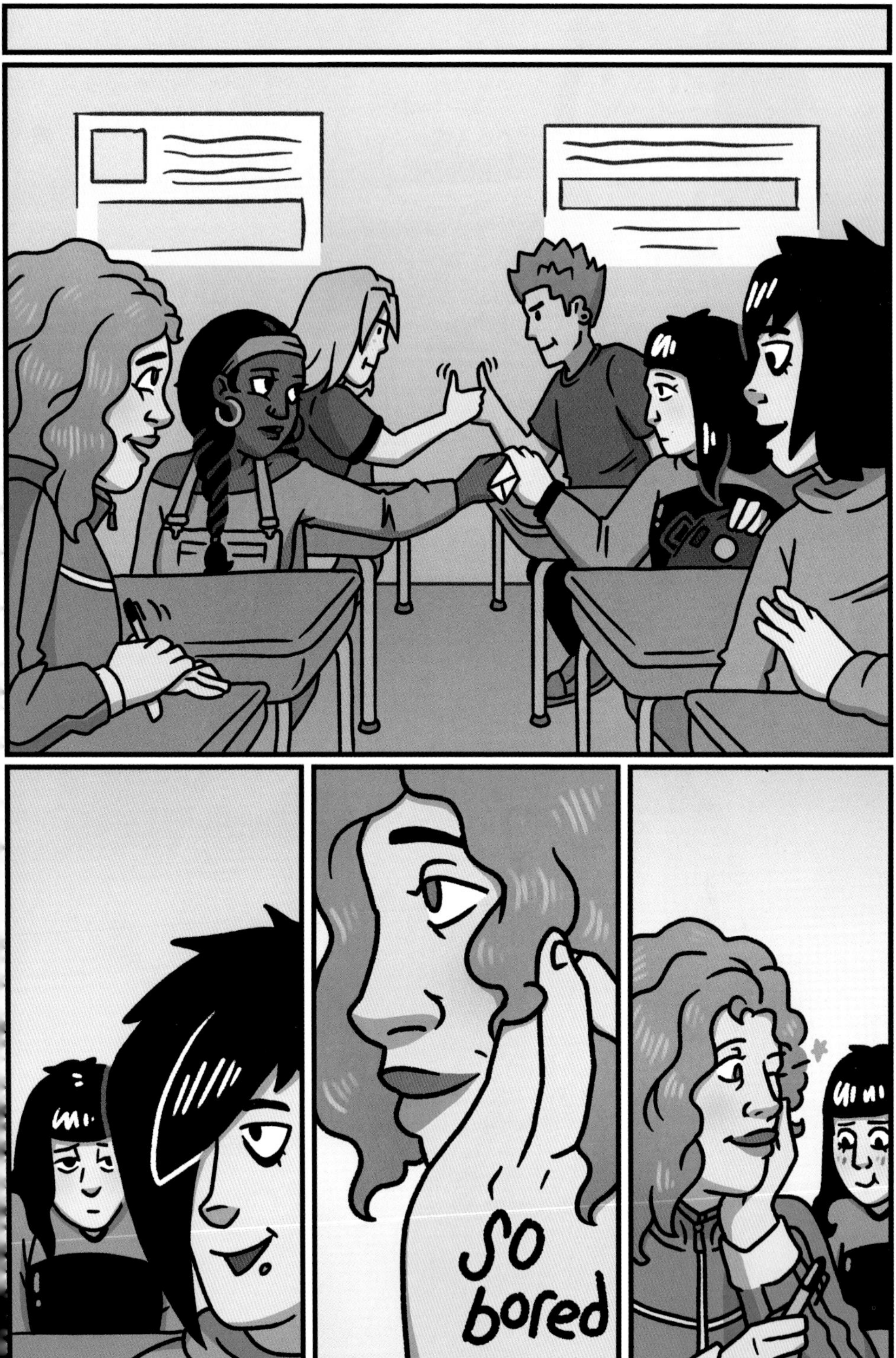
so
bored

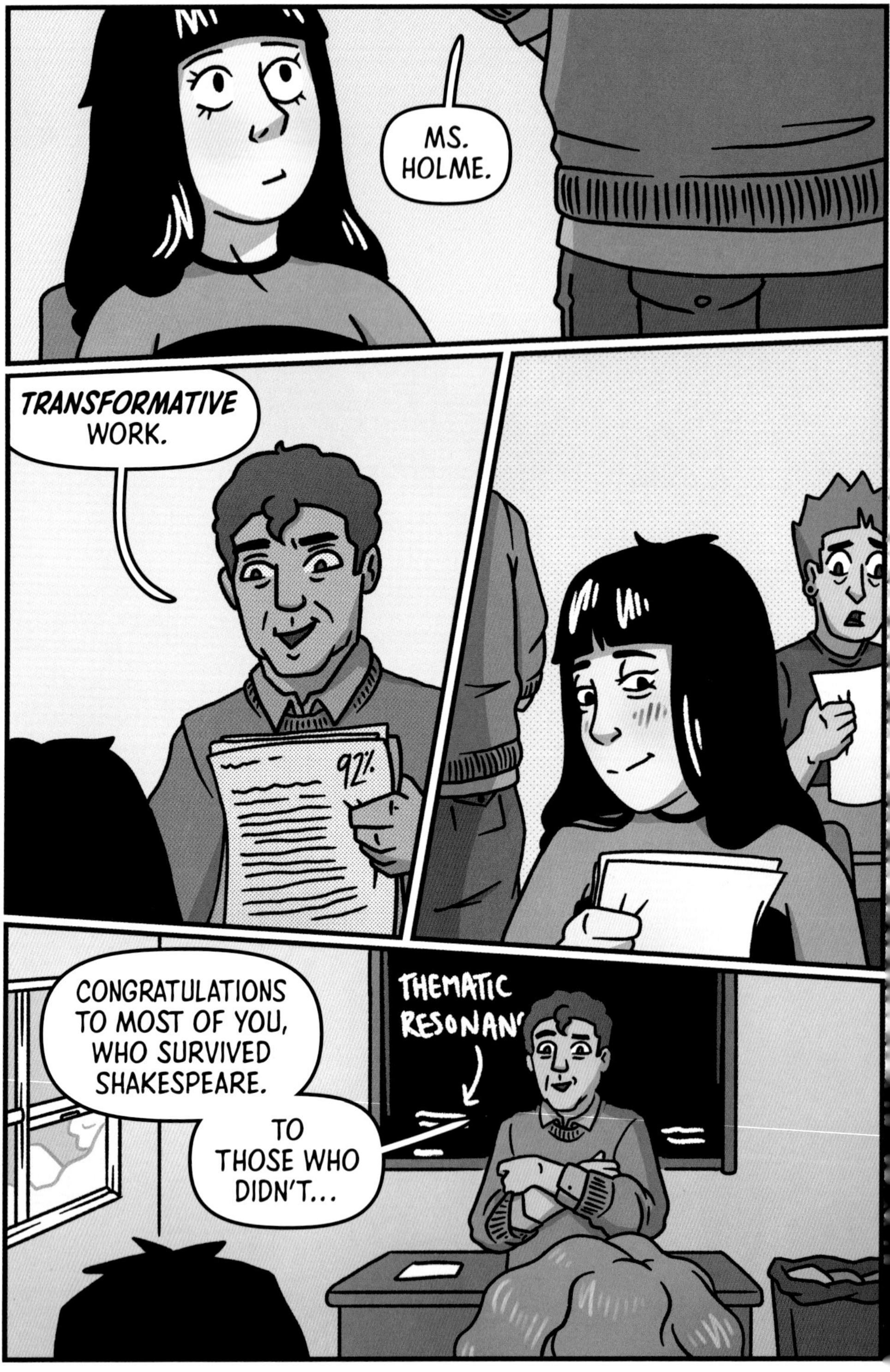
MS. HOLME.
TRANSFORMATIVE WORK.
92%
CONGRATULATIONS TO MOST OF YOU, WHO SURVIVED SHAKESPEARE.
TO THOSE WHO DIDN'T...
THEMATIC RESONAN

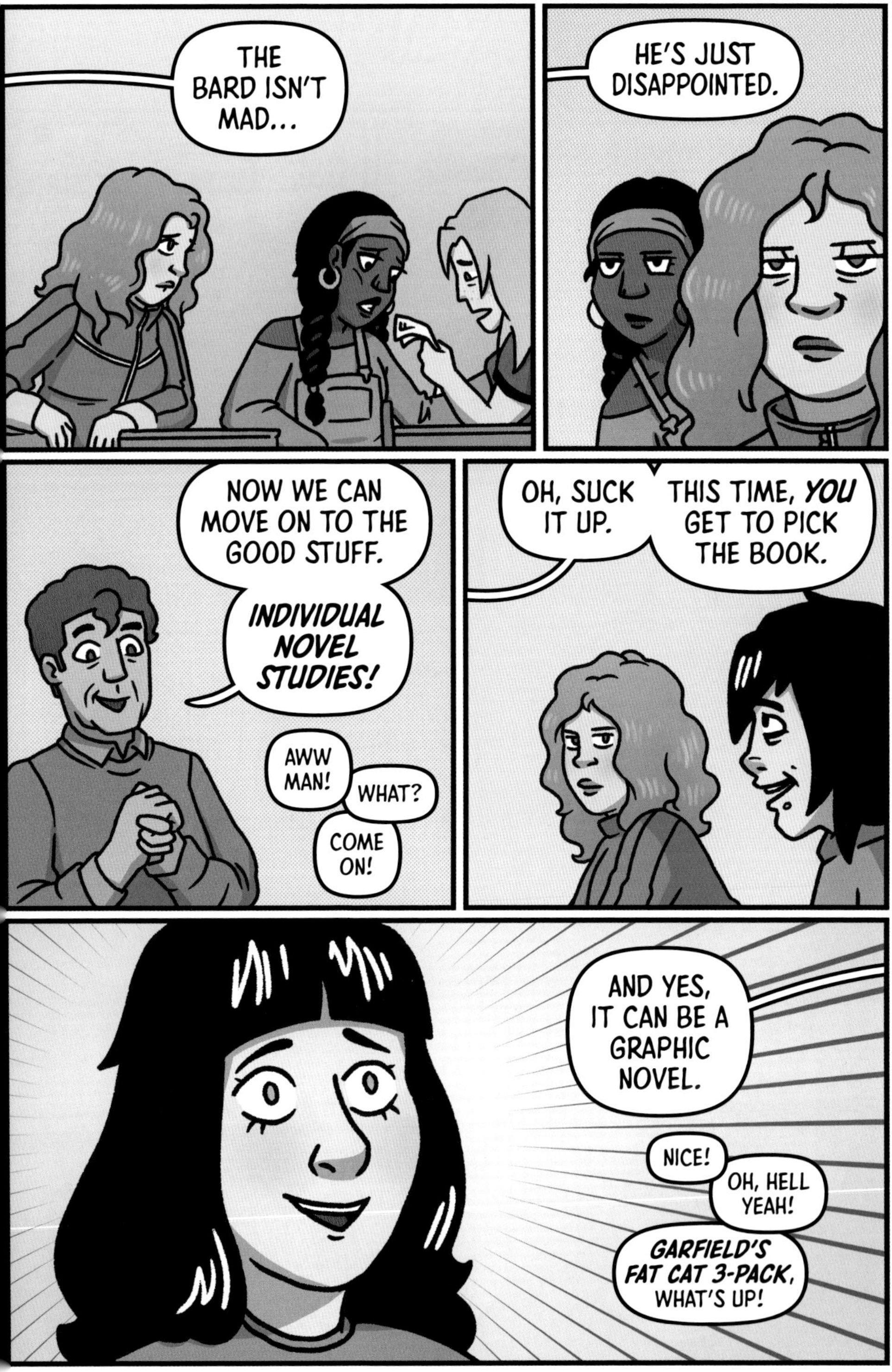
THE BARD ISN'T MAD...
HE'S JUST DISAPPOINTED.
NOW WE CAN MOVE ON TO THE GOOD STUFF.
INDIVIDUAL NOVEL STUDIES!
AWW MAN!
WHAT?
COME ON!
OH, SUCK IT UP.
THIS TIME, *YOU* GET TO PICK THE BOOK.
AND YES, IT CAN BE A GRAPHIC NOVEL.
NICE!
OH, HELL YEAH!
GARFIELD'S FAT CAT 3-PACK, WHAT'S UP!

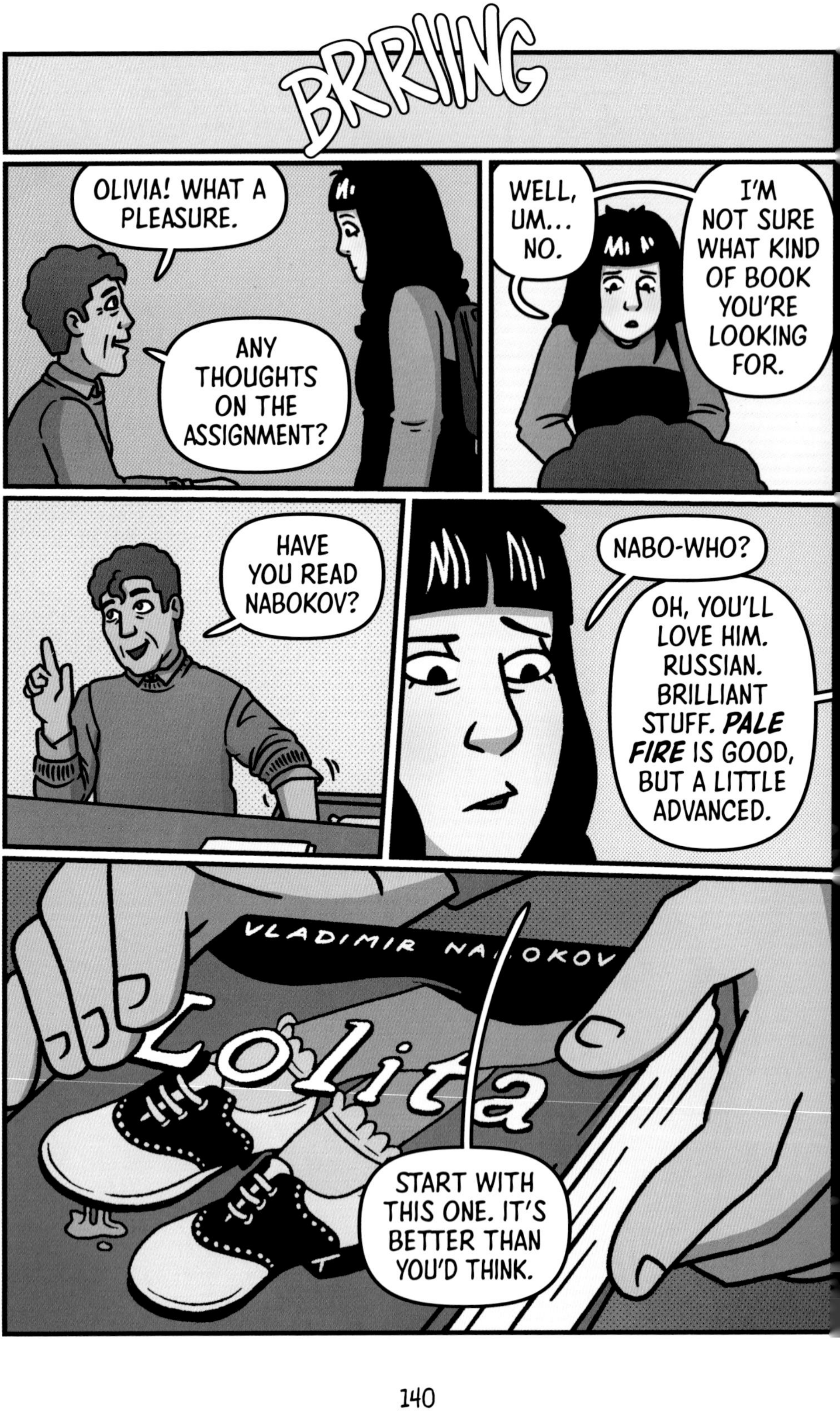
BRRIIING
OLIVIA! WHAT A PLEASURE.
ANY THOUGHTS ON THE ASSIGNMENT?
WELL, UM... NO.
I'M NOT SURE WHAT KIND OF BOOK YOU'RE LOOKING FOR.
HAVE YOU READ NABOKOV?
NABO-WHO?
OH, YOU'LL LOVE HIM. RUSSIAN. BRILLIANT STUFF. *PALE FIRE* IS GOOD, BUT A LITTLE ADVANCED.
VLADIMIR NABOKOV
Lolita
START WITH THIS ONE. IT'S BETTER THAN YOU'D THINK.

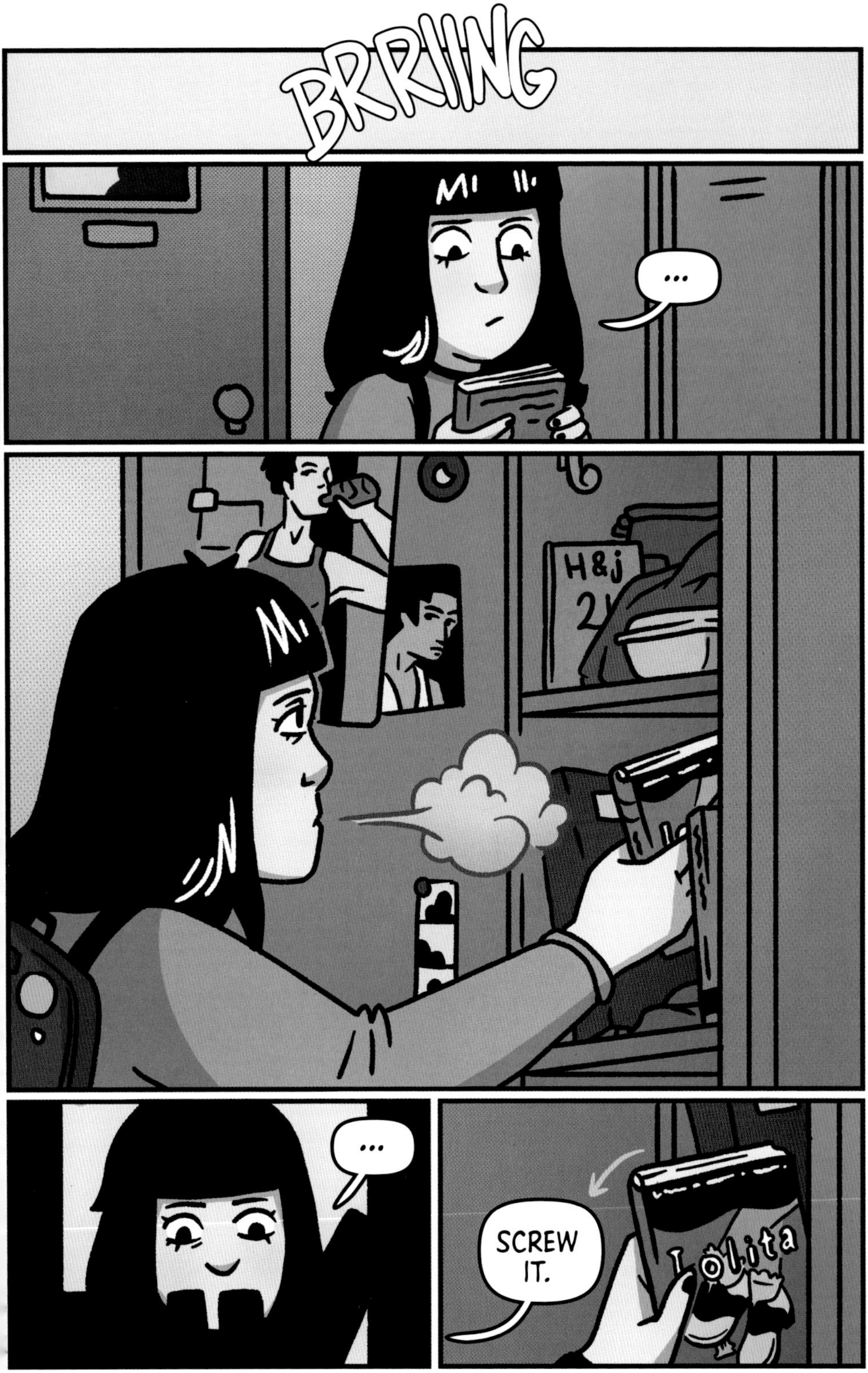
BRRIING
...
H&j
21
...
SCREW IT.
Lolita

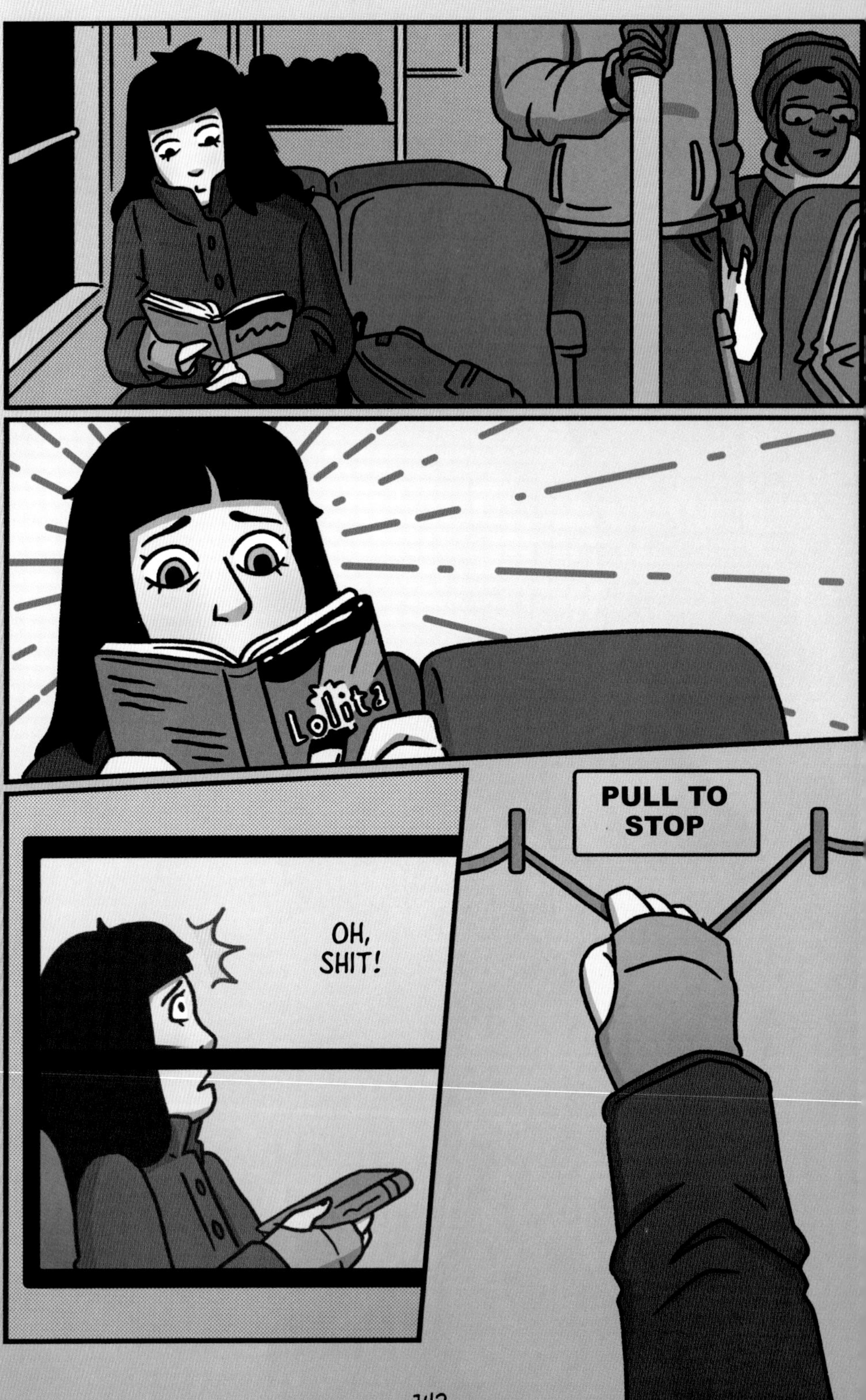
Lolita
PULL TO STOP
OH, SHIT!

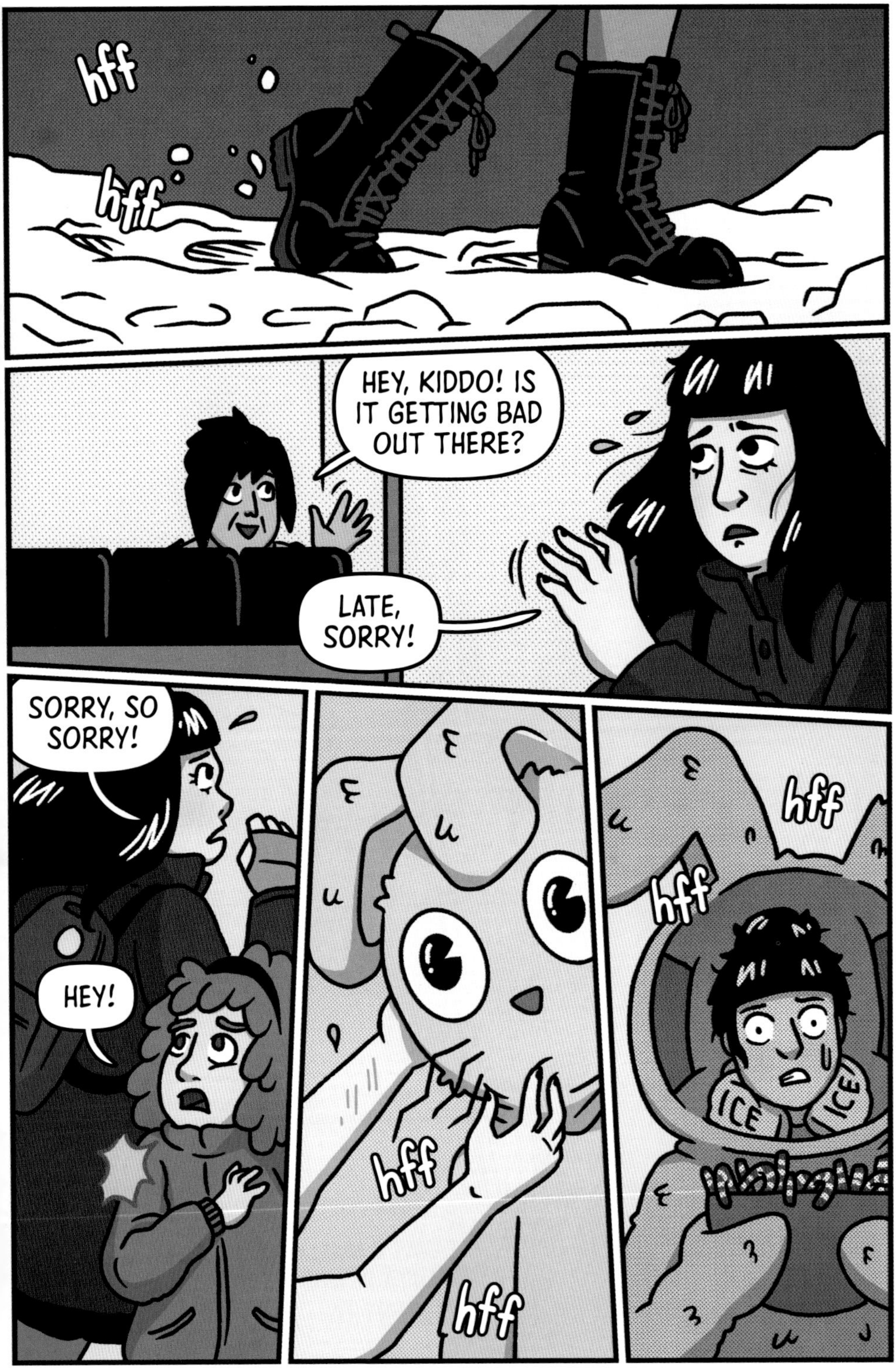
hff
hff
HEY, KIDDO! IS IT GETTING BAD OUT THERE?
LATE, SORRY!
SORRY, SO SORRY!
HEY!
hff
hff
hff
hff

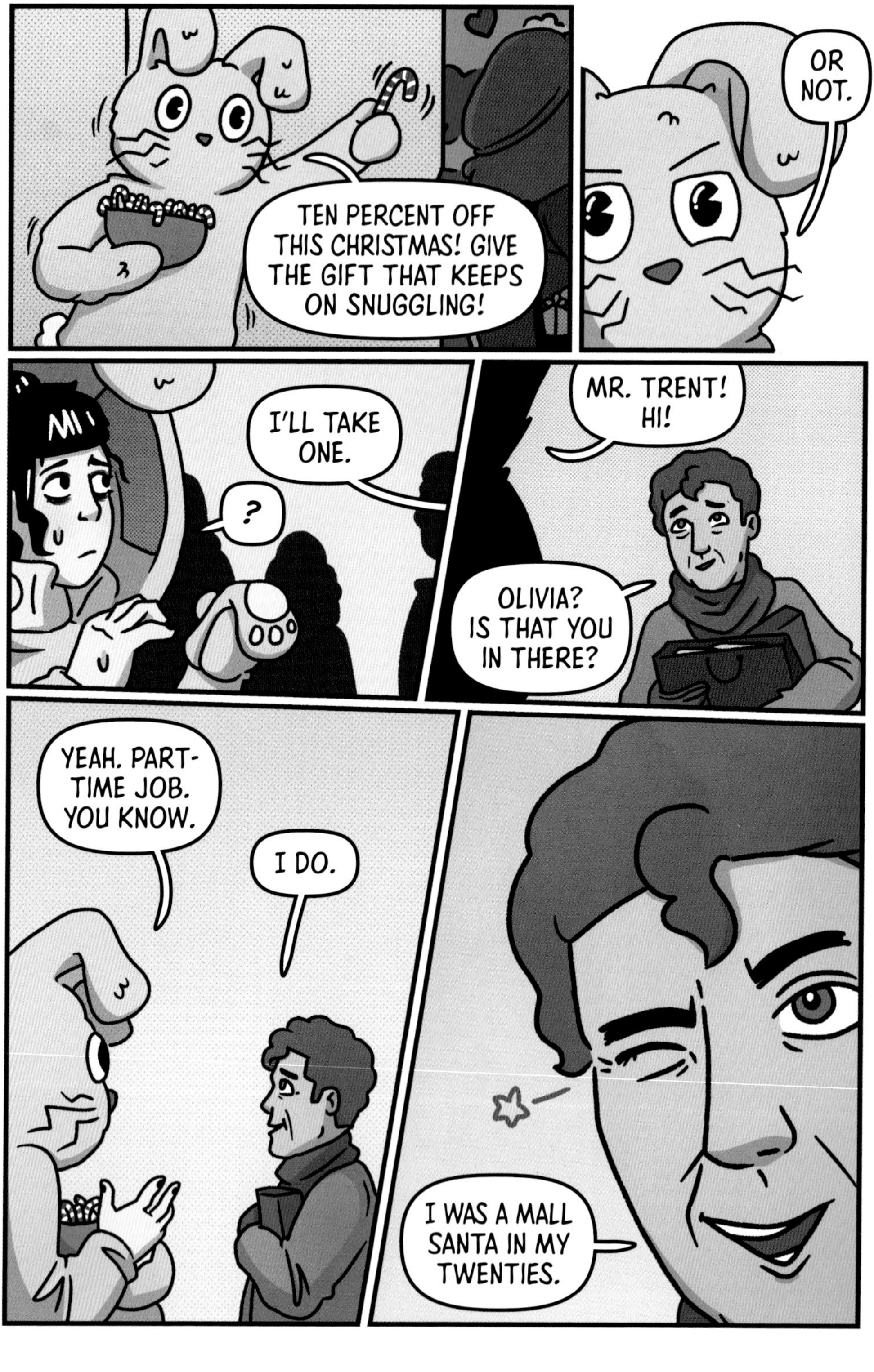
TEN PERCENT OFF THIS CHRISTMAS! GIVE THE GIFT THAT KEEPS ON SNUGGLING!
OR NOT.
I'LL TAKE ONE.
?
MR. TRENT! HI!
OLIVIA? IS THAT YOU IN THERE?
YEAH. PART-TIME JOB. YOU KNOW.
I DO.
I WAS A MALL SANTA IN MY TWENTIES.

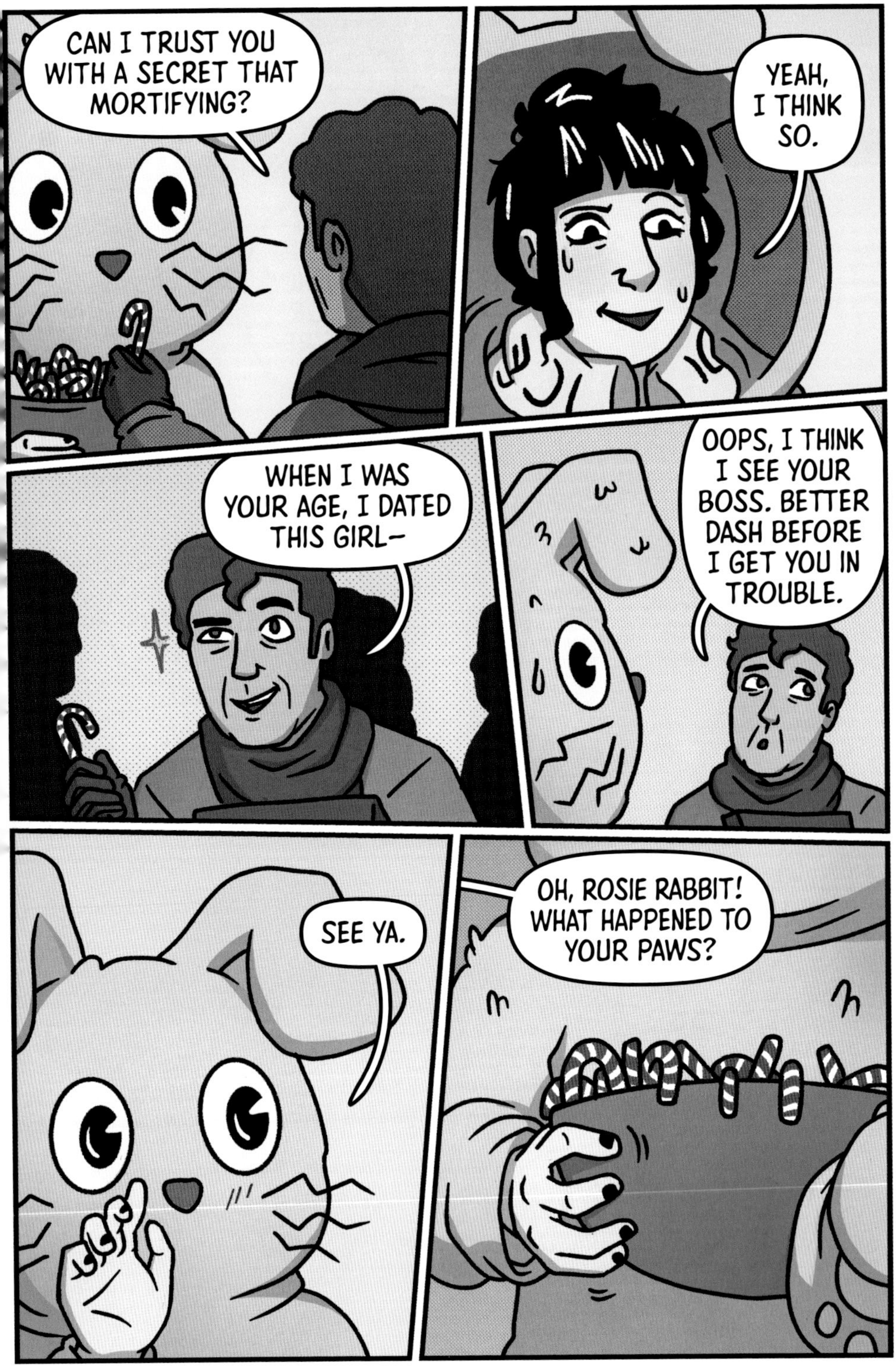
CAN I TRUST YOU WITH A SECRET THAT MORTIFYING?
YEAH, I THINK SO.
WHEN I WAS YOUR AGE, I DATED THIS GIRL–
OOPS, I THINK I SEE YOUR BOSS. BETTER DASH BEFORE I GET YOU IN TROUBLE.
SEE YA.
OH, ROSIE RABBIT! WHAT HAPPENED TO YOUR PAWS?

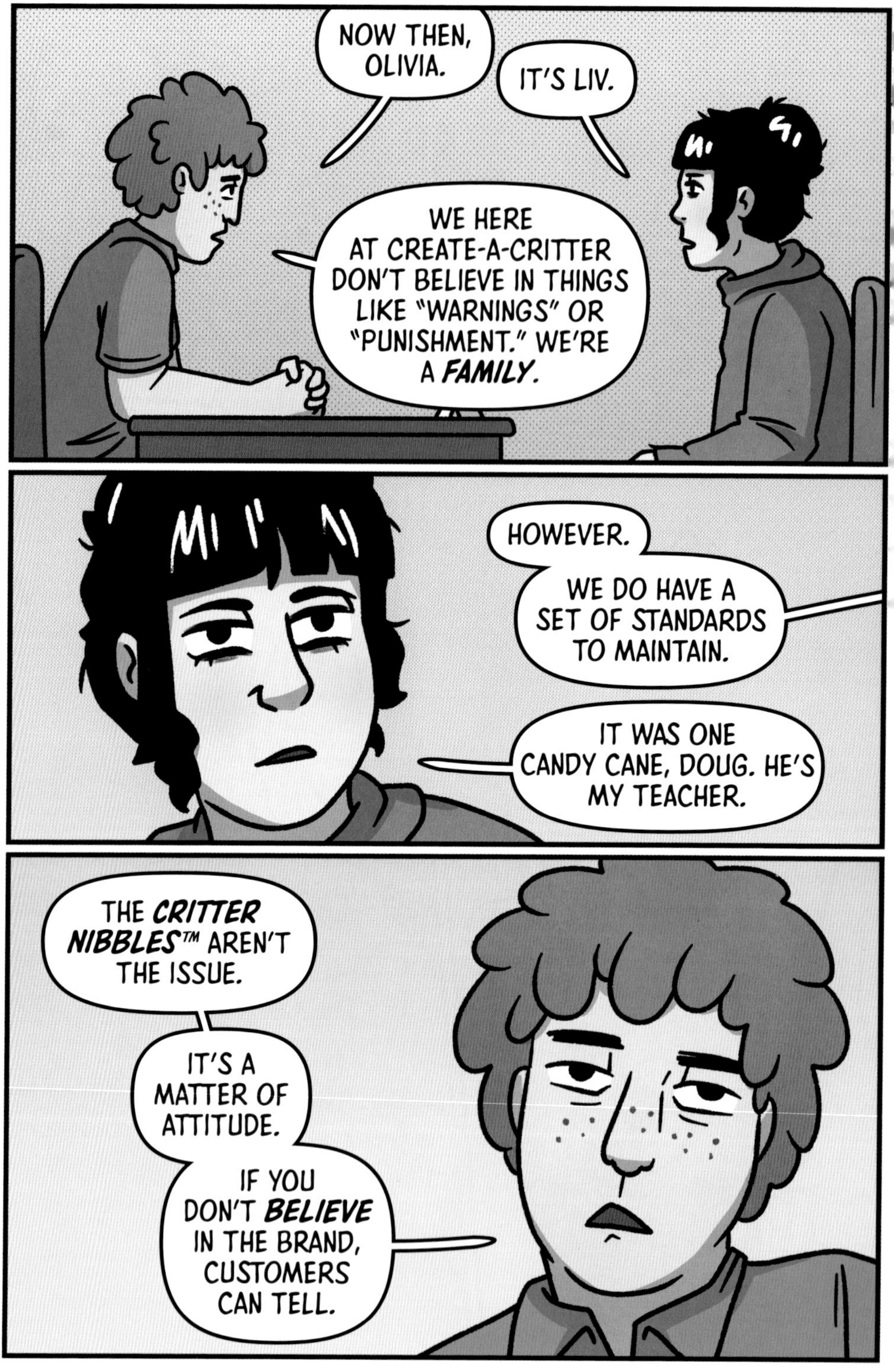
NOW THEN, OLIVIA.
IT'S LIV.
WE HERE AT CREATE-A-CRITTER DON'T BELIEVE IN THINGS LIKE "WARNINGS" OR "PUNISHMENT." WE'RE A *FAMILY*.
HOWEVER.
WE DO HAVE A SET OF STANDARDS TO MAINTAIN.
IT WAS ONE CANDY CANE, DOUG. HE'S MY TEACHER.
THE *CRITTER NIBBLES*™ AREN'T THE ISSUE.
IT'S A MATTER OF ATTITUDE.
IF YOU DON'T *BELIEVE* IN THE BRAND, CUSTOMERS CAN TELL.

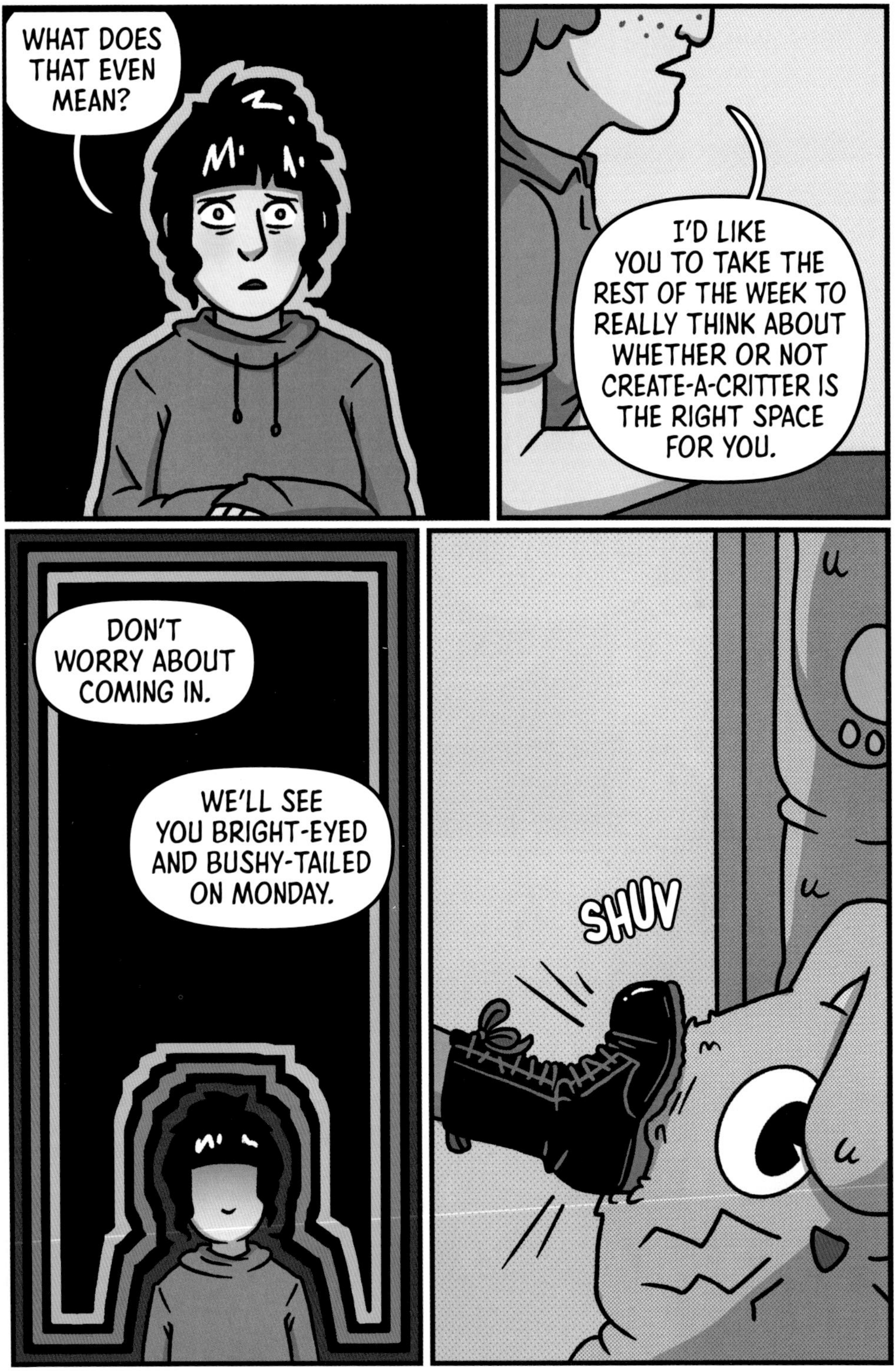
WHAT DOES THAT EVEN MEAN?
I'D LIKE YOU TO TAKE THE REST OF THE WEEK TO REALLY THINK ABOUT WHETHER OR NOT CREATE-A-CRITTER IS THE RIGHT SPACE FOR YOU.
DON'T WORRY ABOUT COMING IN.
WE'LL SEE YOU BRIGHT-EYED AND BUSHY-TAILED ON MONDAY.
SHUV

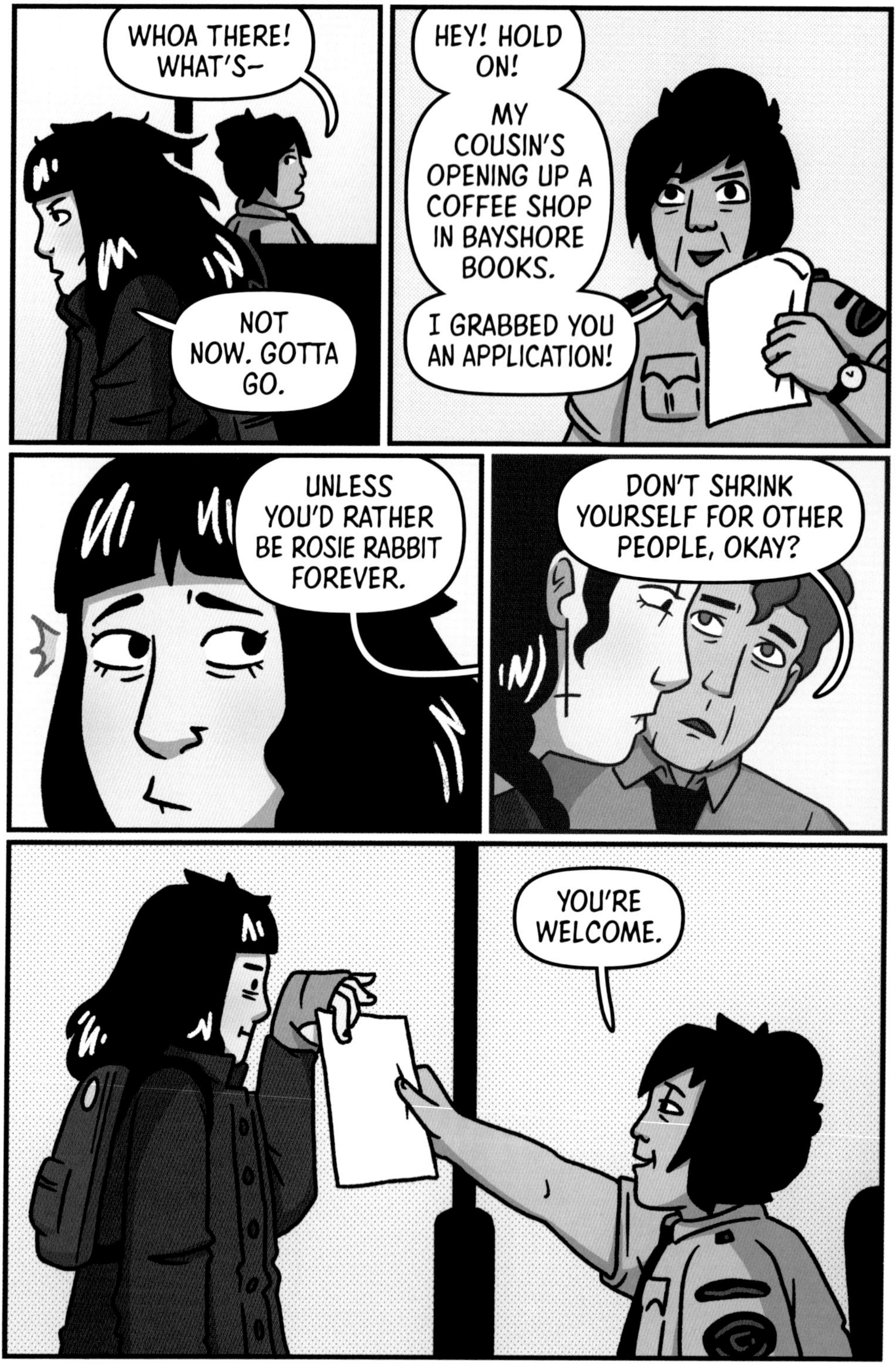
WHOA THERE! WHAT'S–
NOT NOW. GOTTA GO.
HEY! HOLD ON!
MY COUSIN'S OPENING UP A COFFEE SHOP IN BAYSHORE BOOKS.
I GRABBED YOU AN APPLICATION!
UNLESS YOU'D RATHER BE ROSIE RABBIT FOREVER.
DON'T SHRINK YOURSELF FOR OTHER PEOPLE, OKAY?
YOU'RE WELCOME.

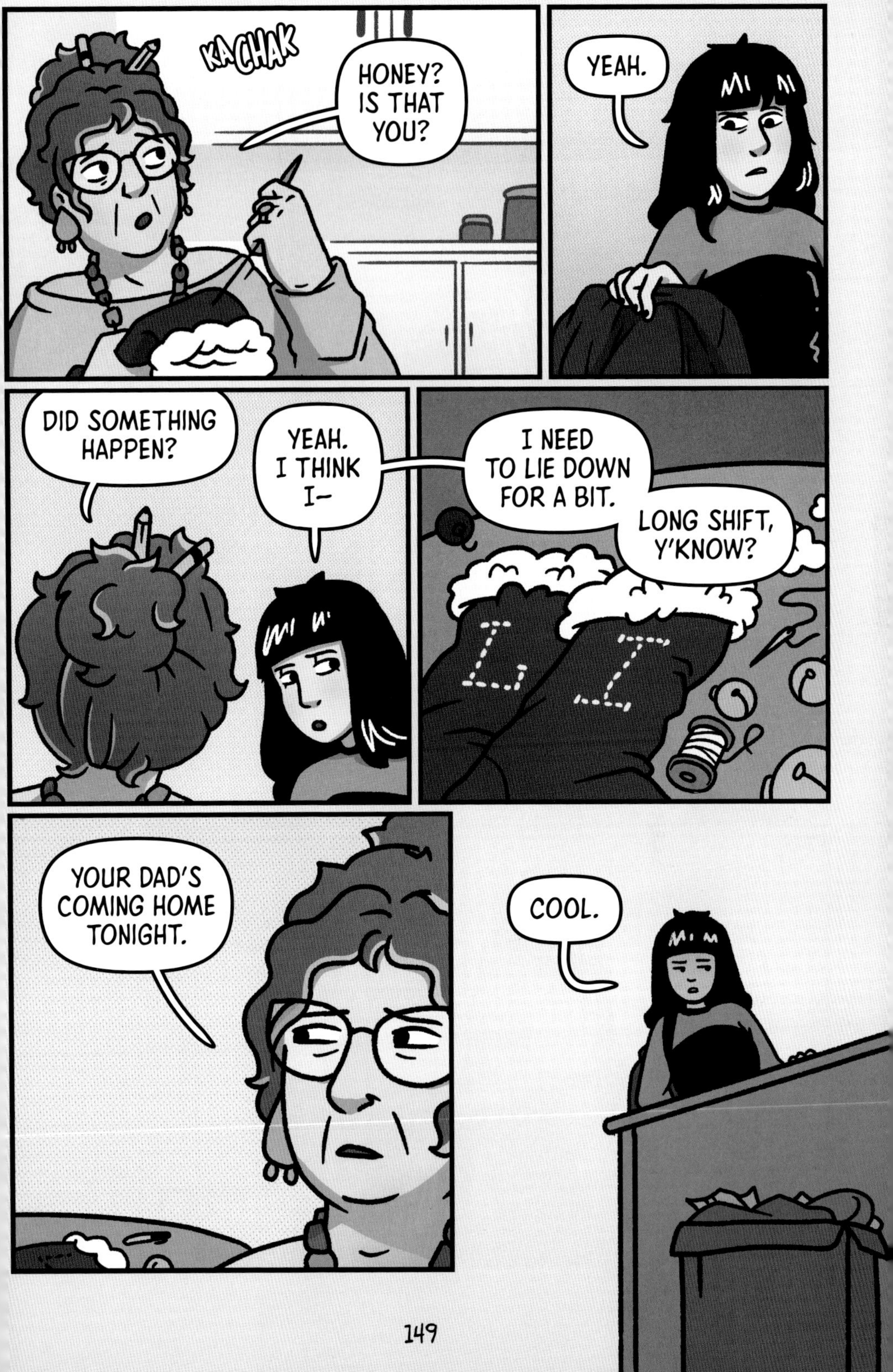
KACHAK
HONEY? IS THAT YOU?
YEAH.
DID SOMETHING HAPPEN?
YEAH. I THINK I–
I NEED TO LIE DOWN FOR A BIT.
LONG SHIFT, Y'KNOW?
YOUR DAD'S COMING HOME TONIGHT.
COOL.

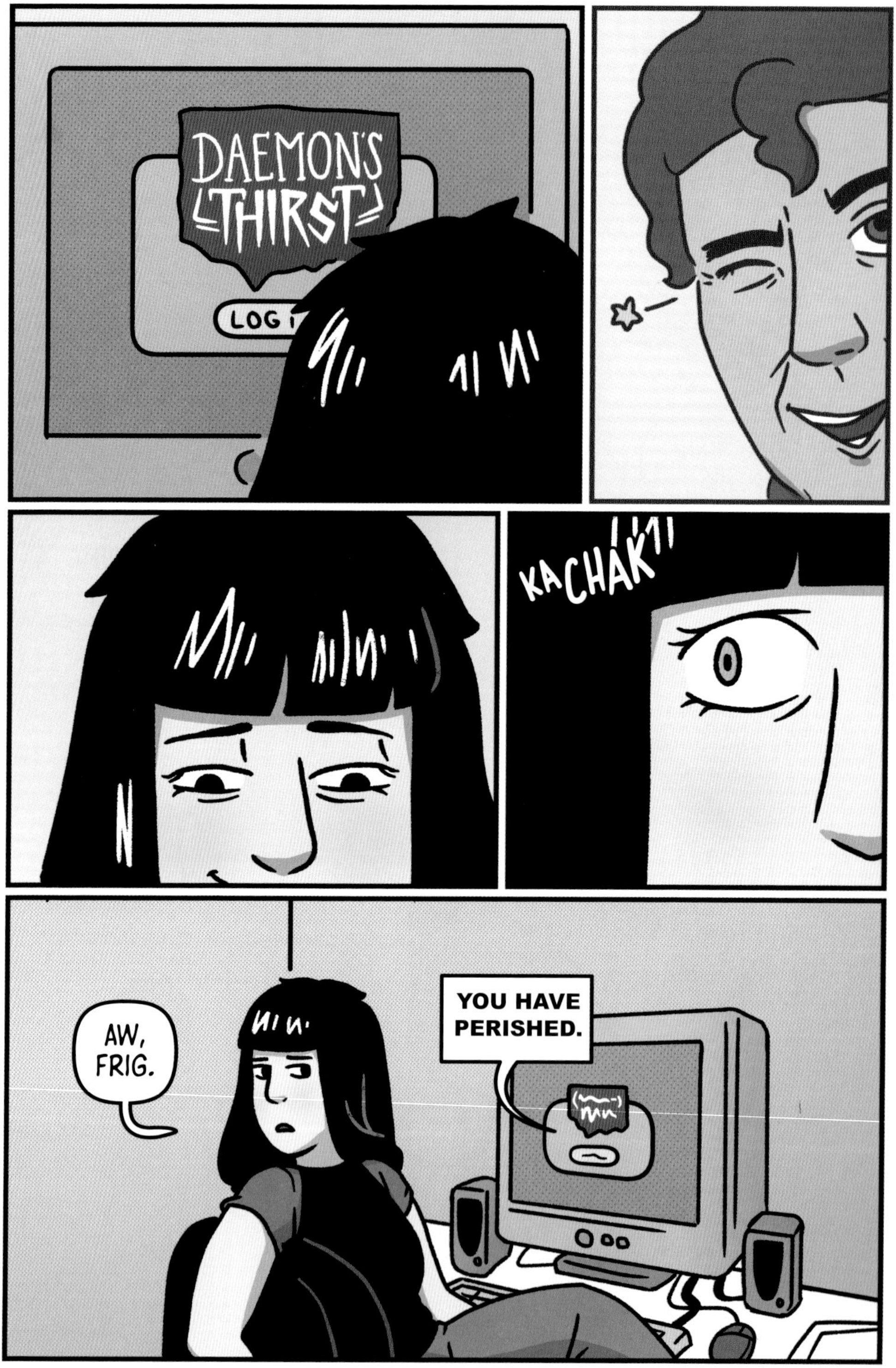
DAEMON'S THIRST
LOG I
KACHAK
AW, FRIG.
YOU HAVE PERISHED.

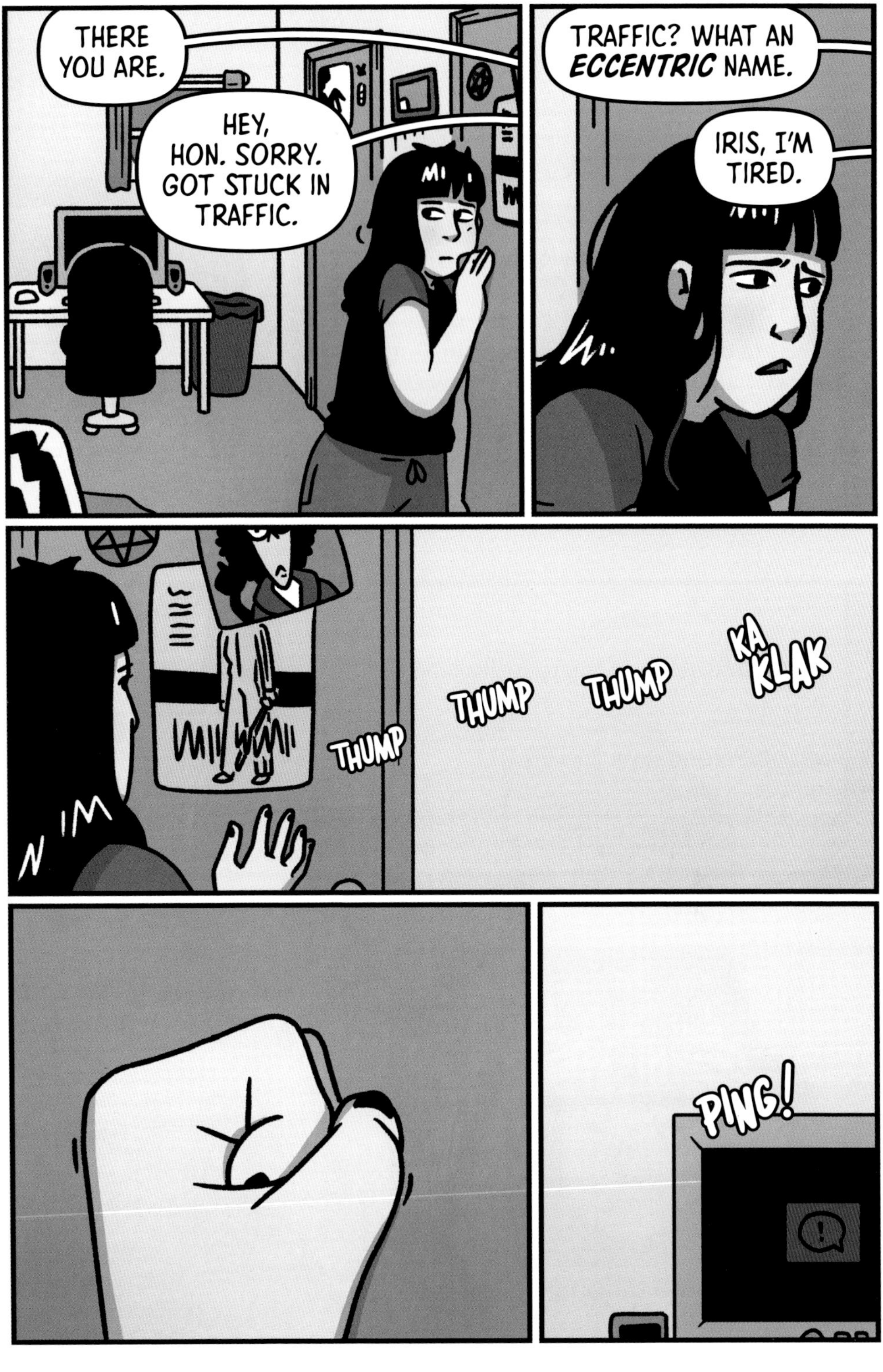
THERE YOU ARE.
HEY, HON. SORRY. GOT STUCK IN TRAFFIC.
TRAFFIC? WHAT AN *ECCENTRIC* NAME.
IRIS, I'M TIRED.
THUMP
THUMP
THUMP
KA KLAK
PING!

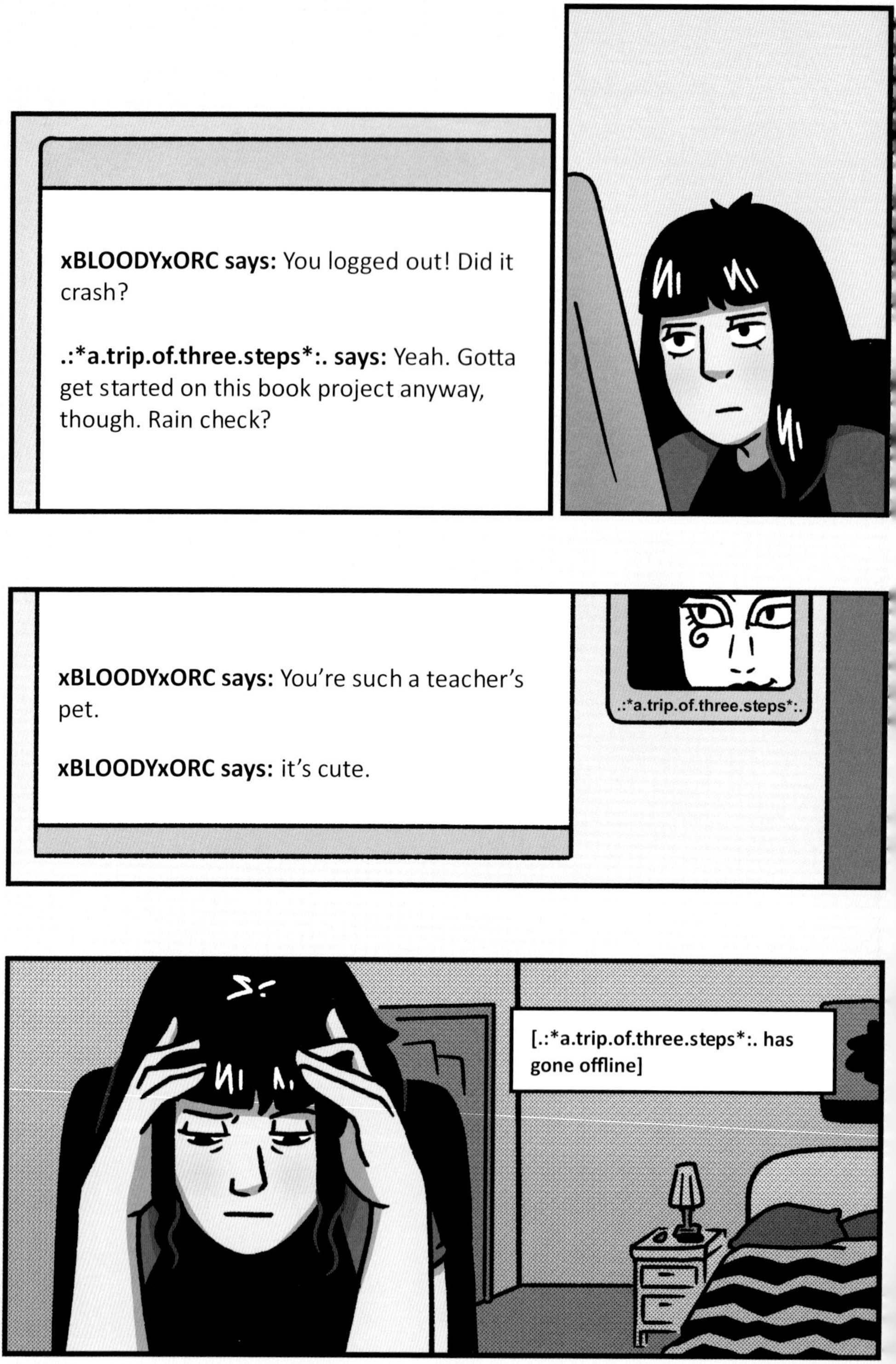

xBLOODYxORC says: You logged out! Did it crash?
.:*a.trip.of.three.steps*:. says: Yeah. Gotta get started on this book project anyway, though. Rain check?
xBLOODYxORC says: You're such a teacher's pet.
xBLOODYxORC says: it's cute.
.:*a.trip.of.three.steps*:.
[.:*a.trip.of.three.steps*:. has gone offline]

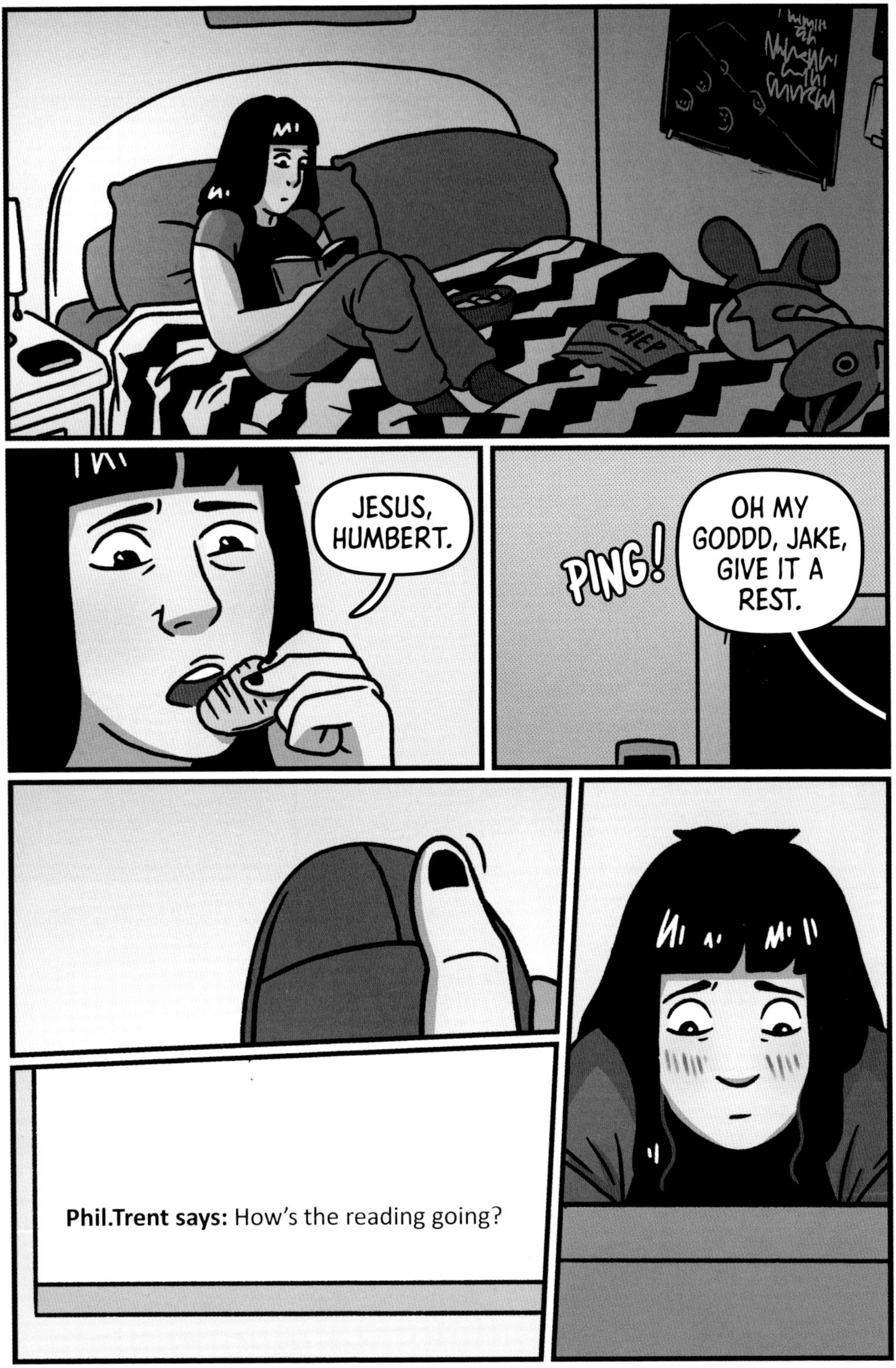
CHEP
JESUS, HUMBERT.
PING!
OH MY GODDD, JAKE, GIVE IT A REST.
Phil.Trent says: How's the reading going?

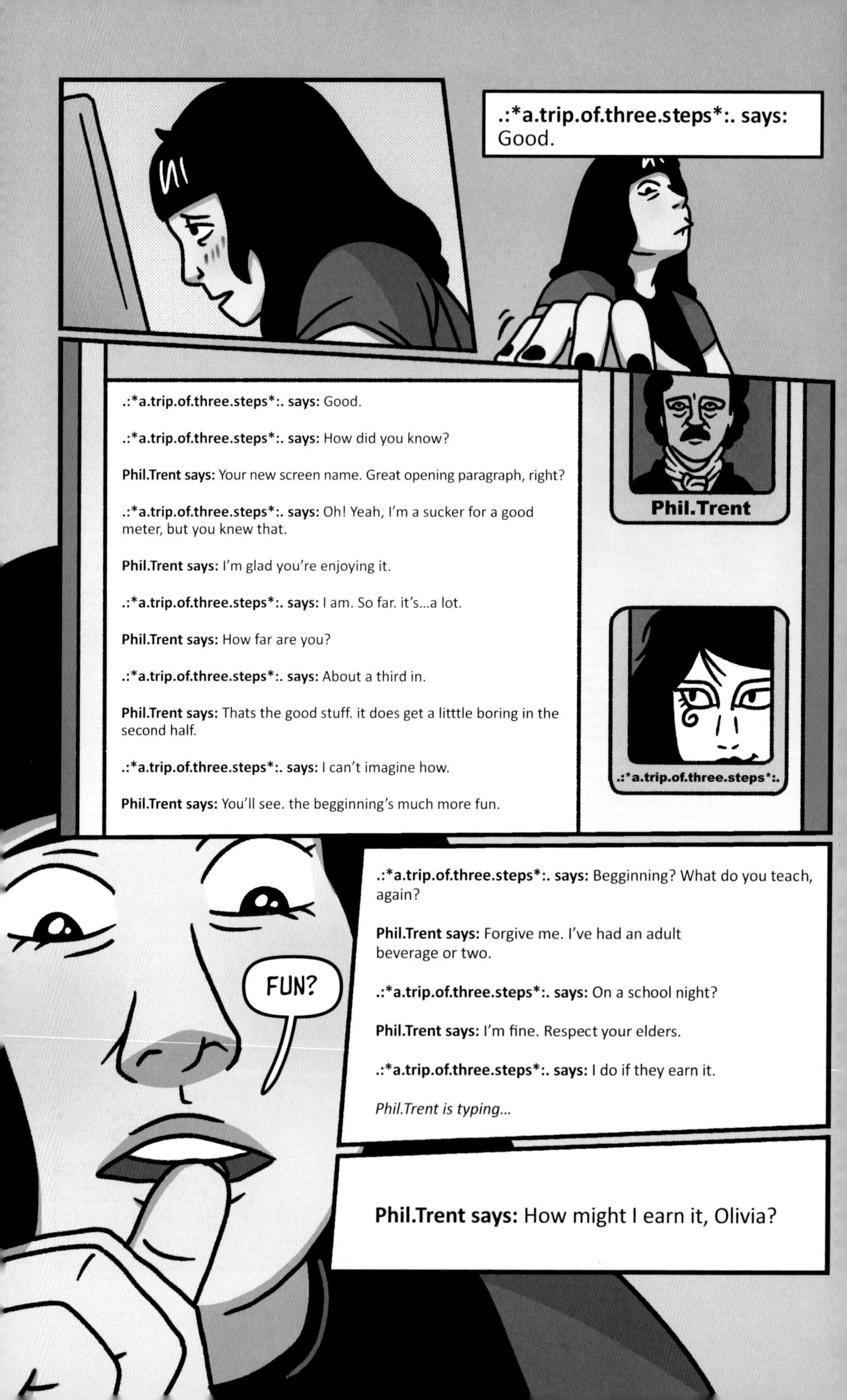
.:*a.trip.of.three.steps*:. says: Good.
.:*a.trip.of.three.steps*:. says: Good.
.:*a.trip.of.three.steps*:. says: How did you know?
Phil.Trent says: Your new screen name. Great opening paragraph, right?
.:*a.trip.of.three.steps*:. says: Oh! Yeah, I'm a sucker for a good meter, but you knew that.
Phil.Trent says: I'm glad you're enjoying it.
.:*a.trip.of.three.steps*:. says: I am. So far. it's...a lot.
Phil.Trent says: How far are you?
.:*a.trip.of.three.steps*:. says: About a third in.
Phil.Trent says: Thats the good stuff. it does get a litttle boring in the second half.
.:*a.trip.of.three.steps*:. says: I can't imagine how.
Phil.Trent says: You'll see. the beggginning's much more fun.
Phil.Trent
.:*a.trip.of.three.steps*:.
FUN?
.:*a.trip.of.three.steps*:. says: Begginning? What do you teach, again?
Phil.Trent says: Forgive me. I've had an adult beverage or two.
.:*a.trip.of.three.steps*:. says: On a school night?
Phil.Trent says: I'm fine. Respect your elders.
.:*a.trip.of.three.steps*:. says: I do if they earn it.
Phil.Trent is typing...
Phil.Trent says: How might I earn it, Olivia?

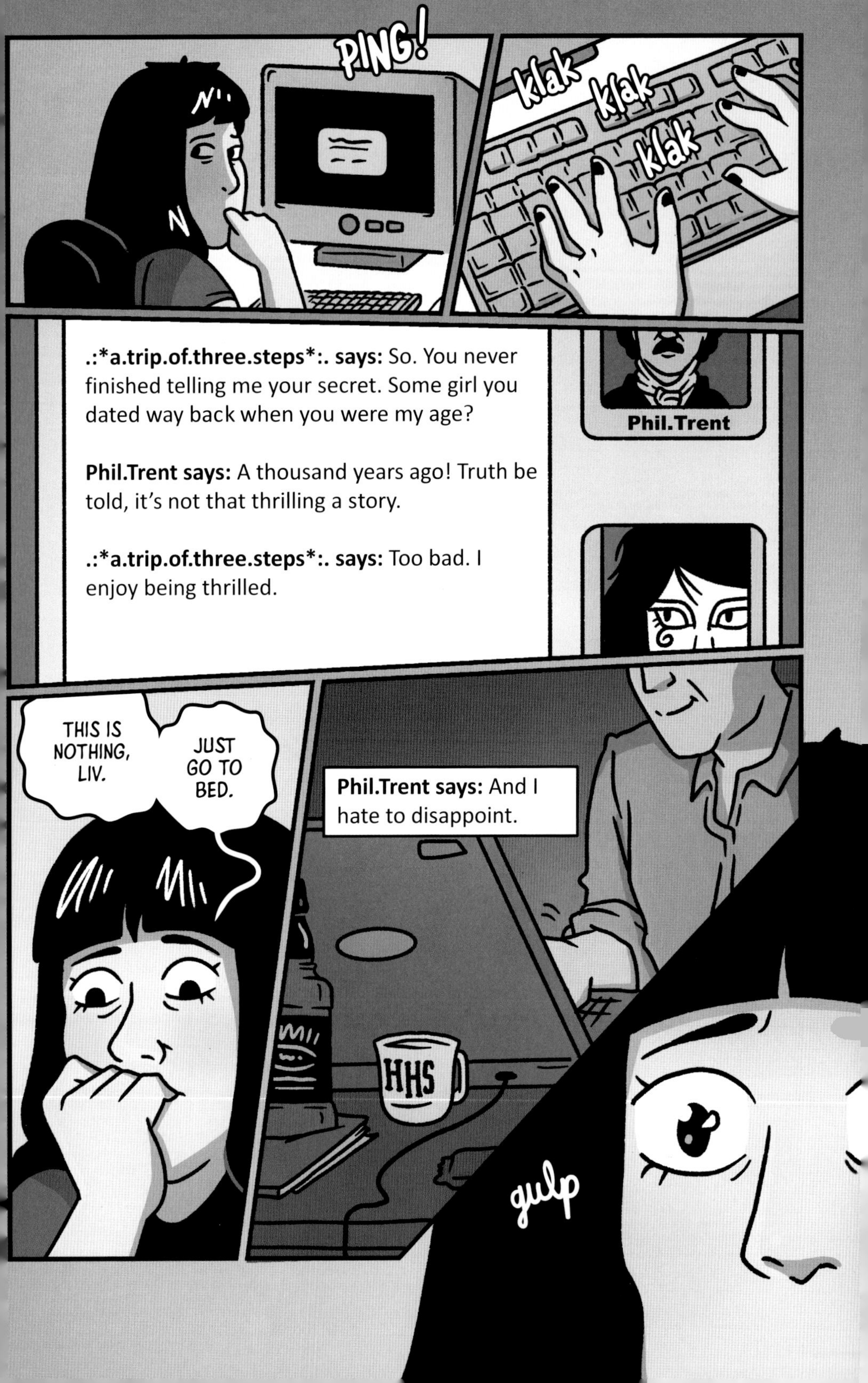

PING!
klak klak klak
.:*a.trip.of.three.steps*:. says: So. You never finished telling me your secret. Some girl you dated way back when you were my age?
Phil.Trent
Phil.Trent says: A thousand years ago! Truth be told, it's not that thrilling a story.
.:*a.trip.of.three.steps*:. says: Too bad. I enjoy being thrilled.
THIS IS NOTHING, LIV.
JUST GO TO BED.
Phil.Trent says: And I hate to disappoint.
HHS
gulp

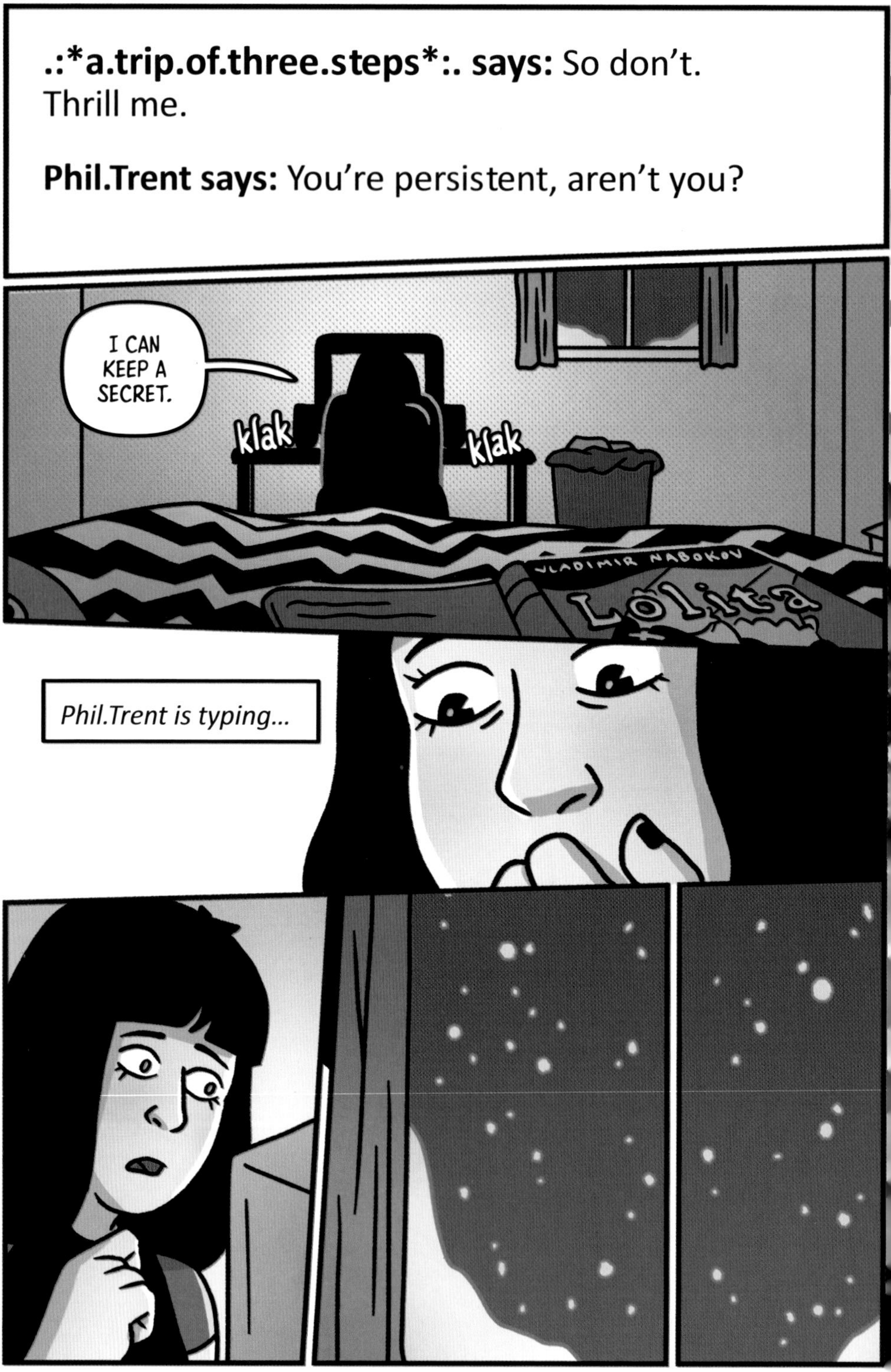
.:*a.trip.of.three.steps*:. says: So don't. Thrill me.
Phil.Trent says: You're persistent, aren't you?
I CAN KEEP A SECRET.
klak
klak
VLADIMIR NABOKOV
Lolita
Phil.Trent is typing...

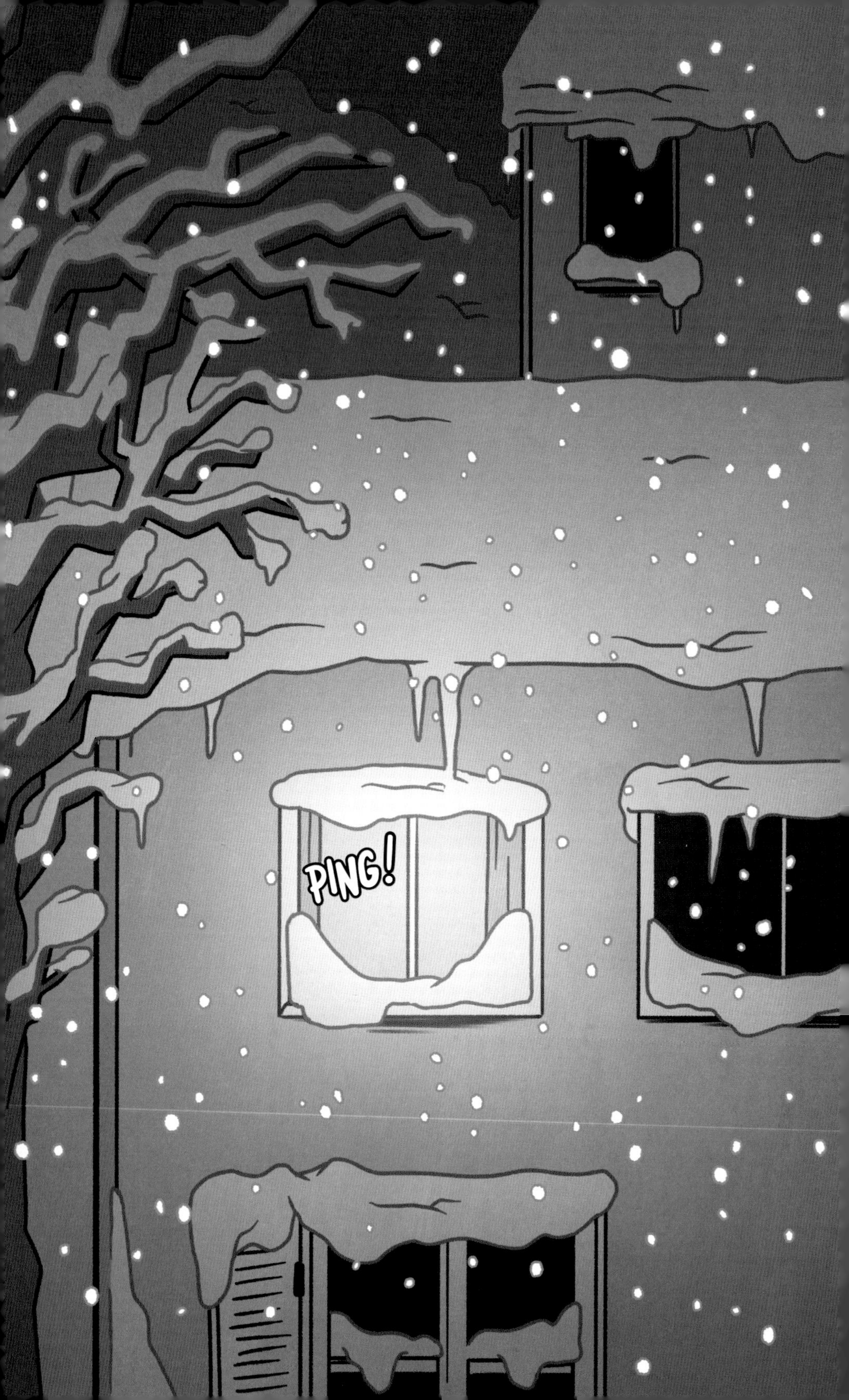
PING!

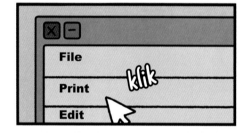

klik

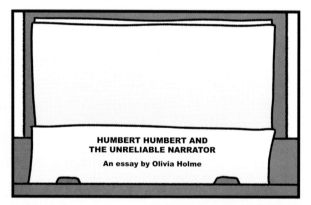

**HUMBERT HUMBERT AND
THE UNRELIABLE NARRATOR**

An essay by Olivia Holme

FZZT

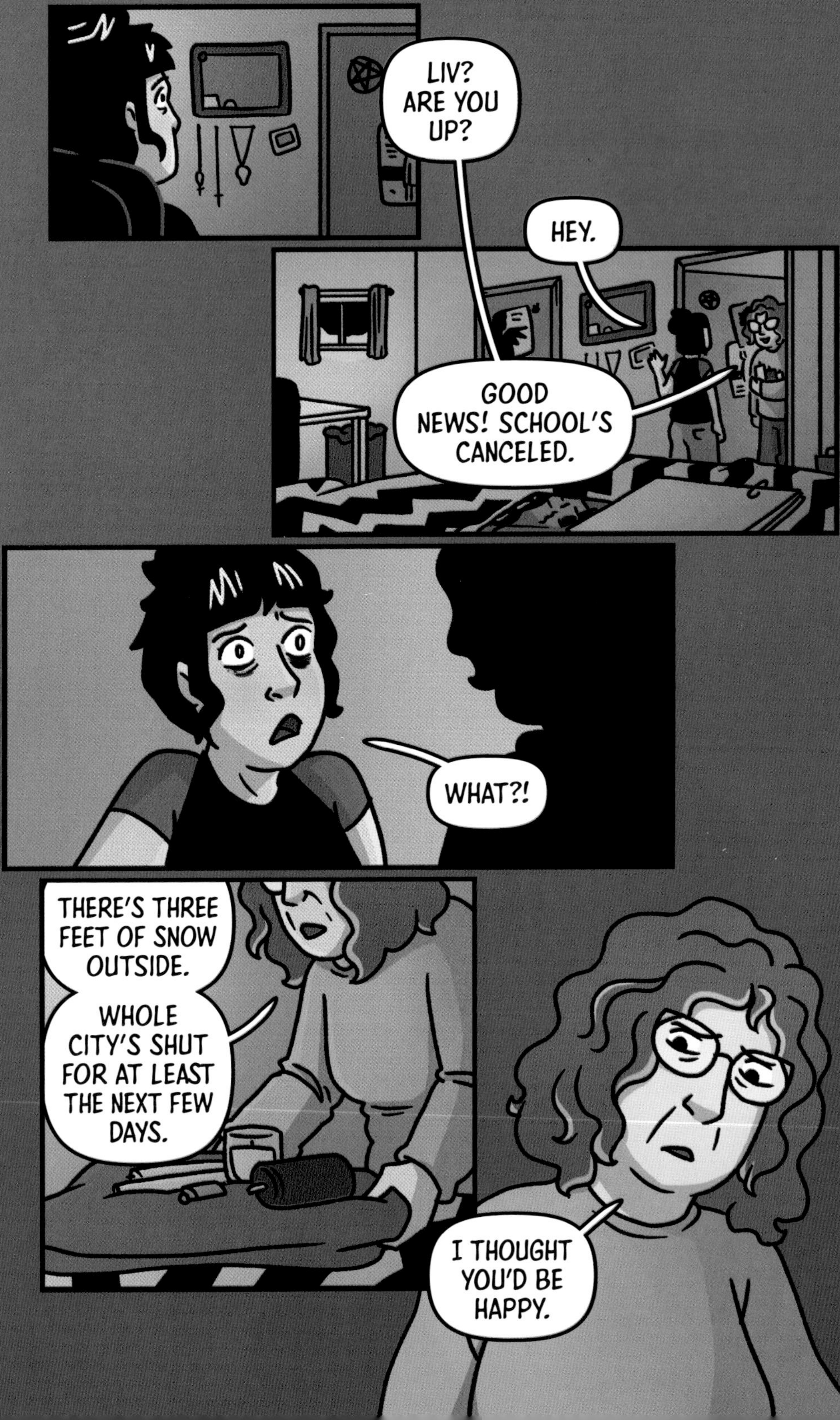
LIV? ARE YOU UP?
HEY.
GOOD NEWS! SCHOOL'S CANCELED.
WHAT?!
THERE'S THREE FEET OF SNOW OUTSIDE.
WHOLE CITY'S SHUT FOR AT LEAST THE NEXT FEW DAYS.
I THOUGHT YOU'D BE HAPPY.

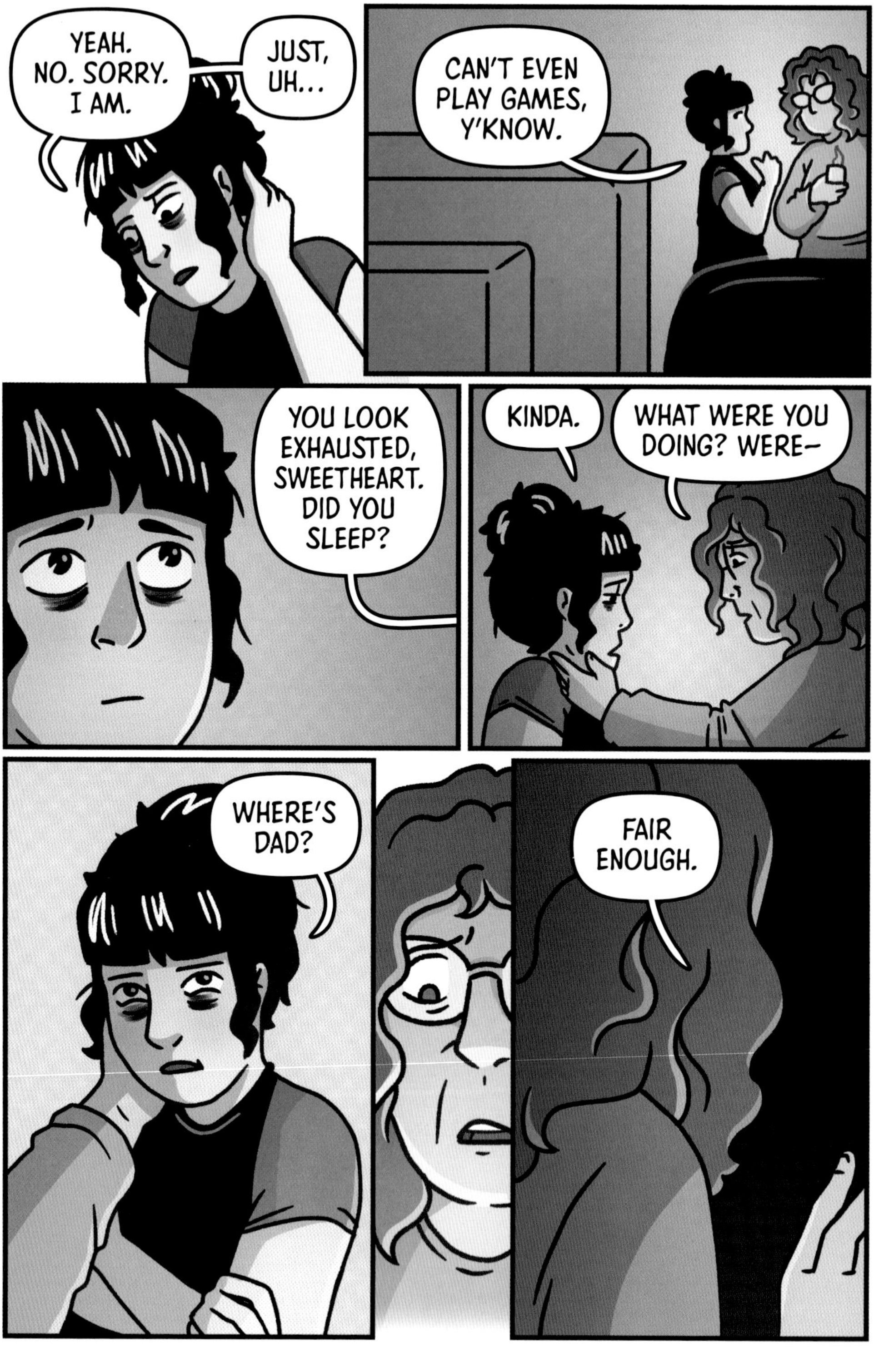
YEAH. NO. SORRY. I AM.
JUST, UH...
CAN'T EVEN PLAY GAMES, Y'KNOW.
YOU LOOK EXHAUSTED, SWEETHEART. DID YOU SLEEP?
KINDA.
WHAT WERE YOU DOING? WERE–
WHERE'S DAD?
FAIR ENOUGH.

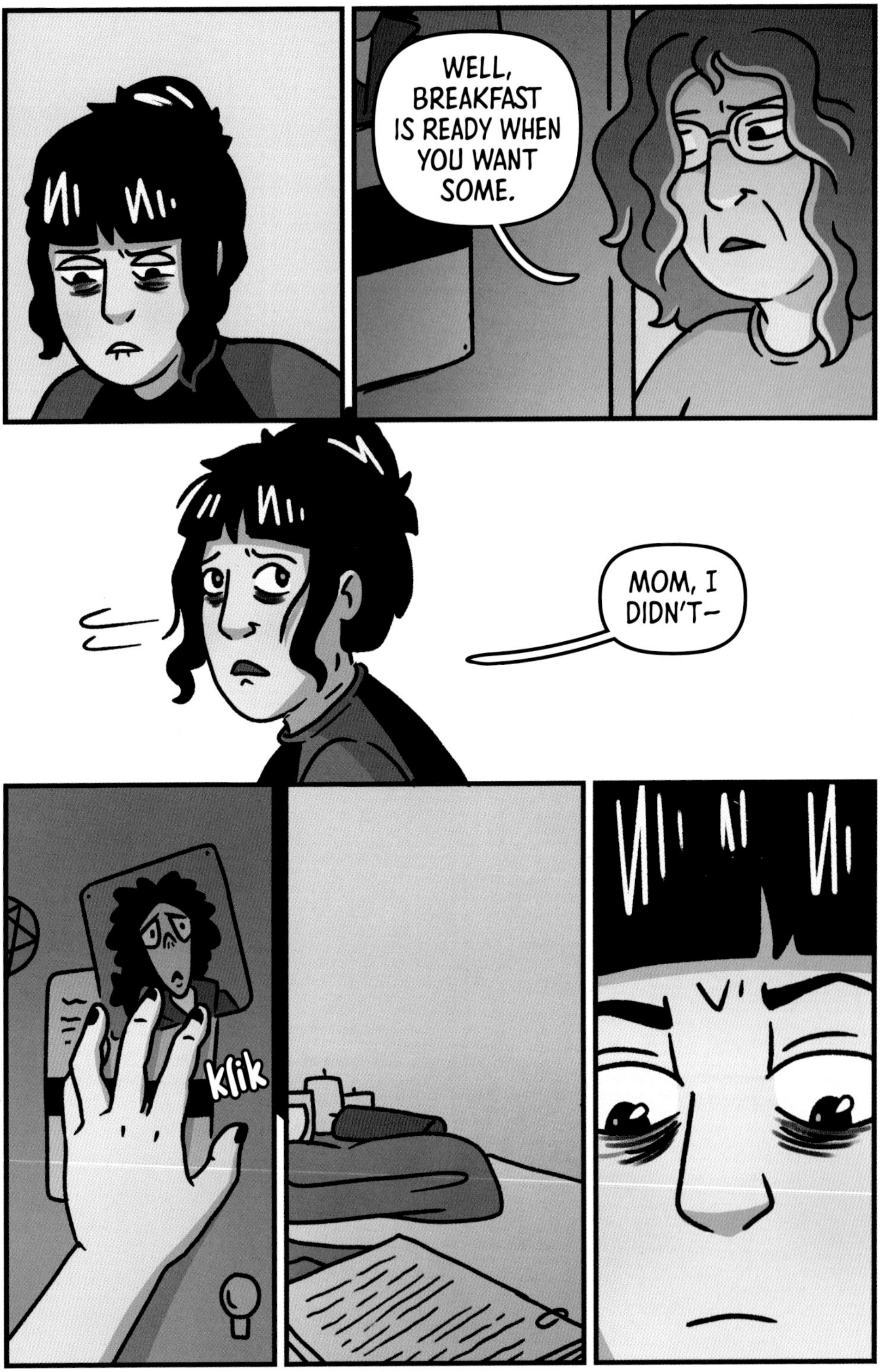
WELL, BREAKFAST IS READY WHEN YOU WANT SOME.
MOM, I DIDN'T–
klik

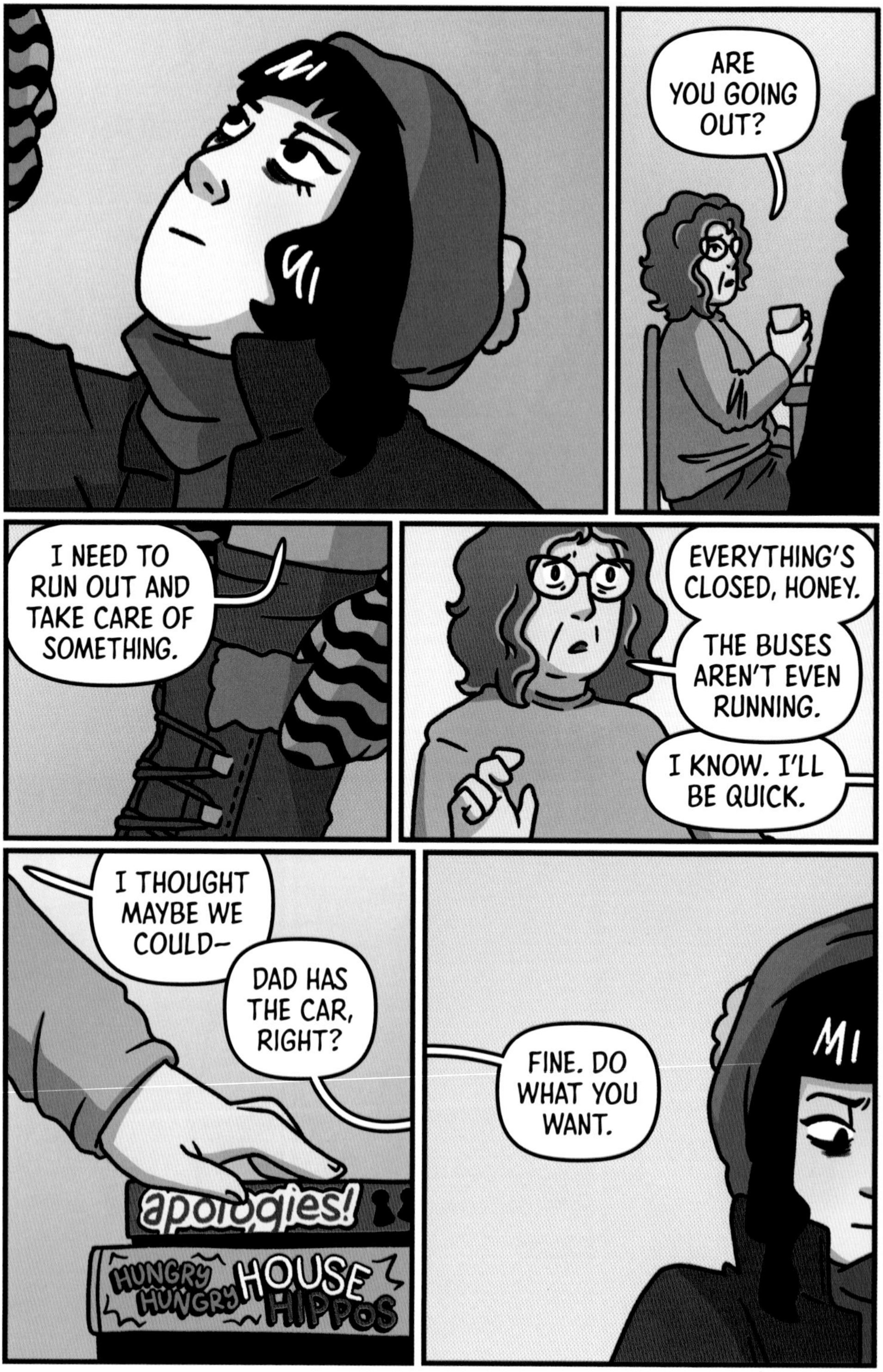
MI
ARE YOU GOING OUT?
I NEED TO RUN OUT AND TAKE CARE OF SOMETHING.
EVERYTHING'S CLOSED, HONEY.
THE BUSES AREN'T EVEN RUNNING.
I KNOW. I'LL BE QUICK.
I THOUGHT MAYBE WE COULD–
DAD HAS THE CAR, RIGHT?
apologies!
HUNGRY HUNGRY HOUSE HIPPOS
FINE. DO WHAT YOU WANT.
MI

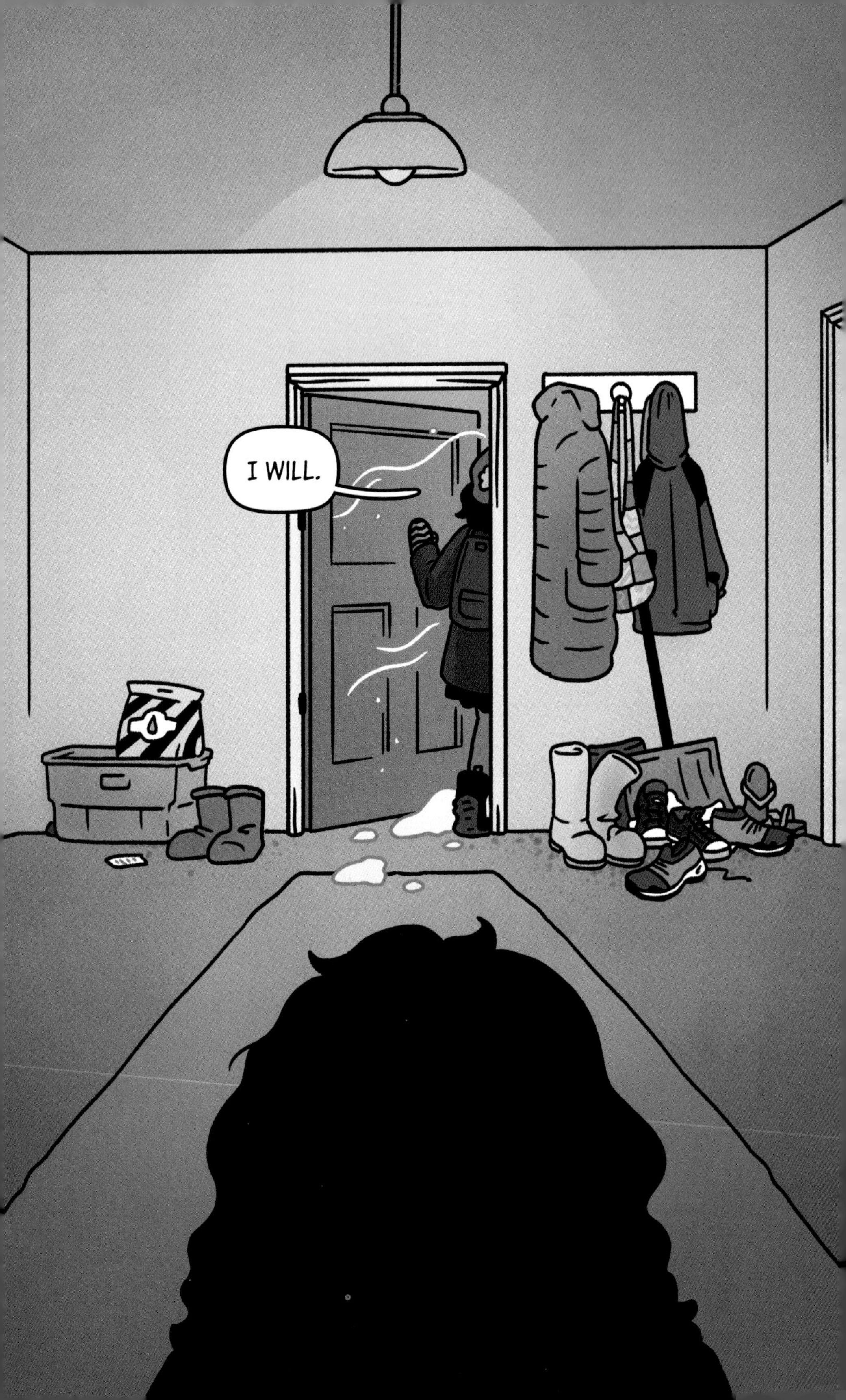
I WILL.

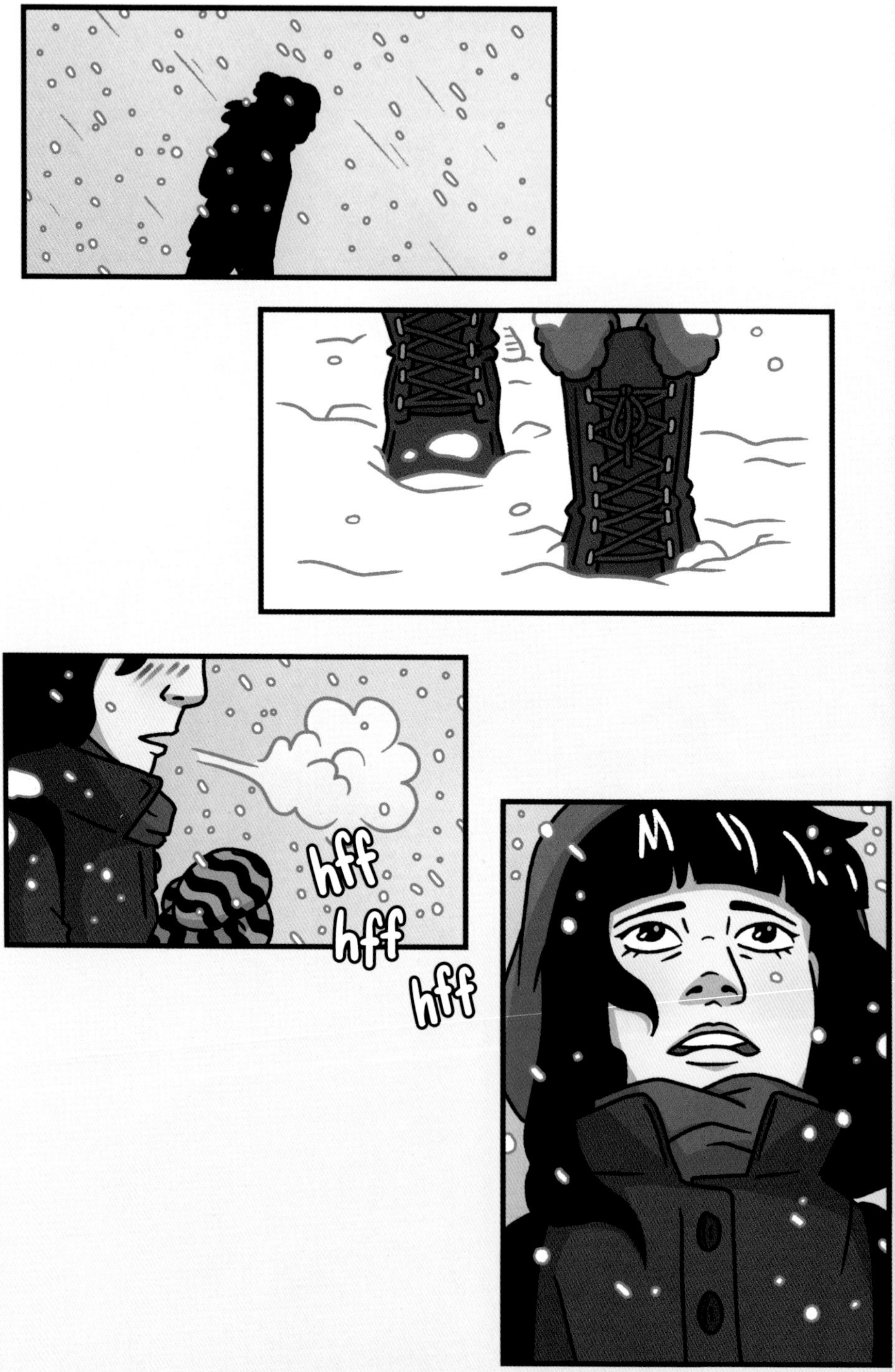
hff
hff
hff

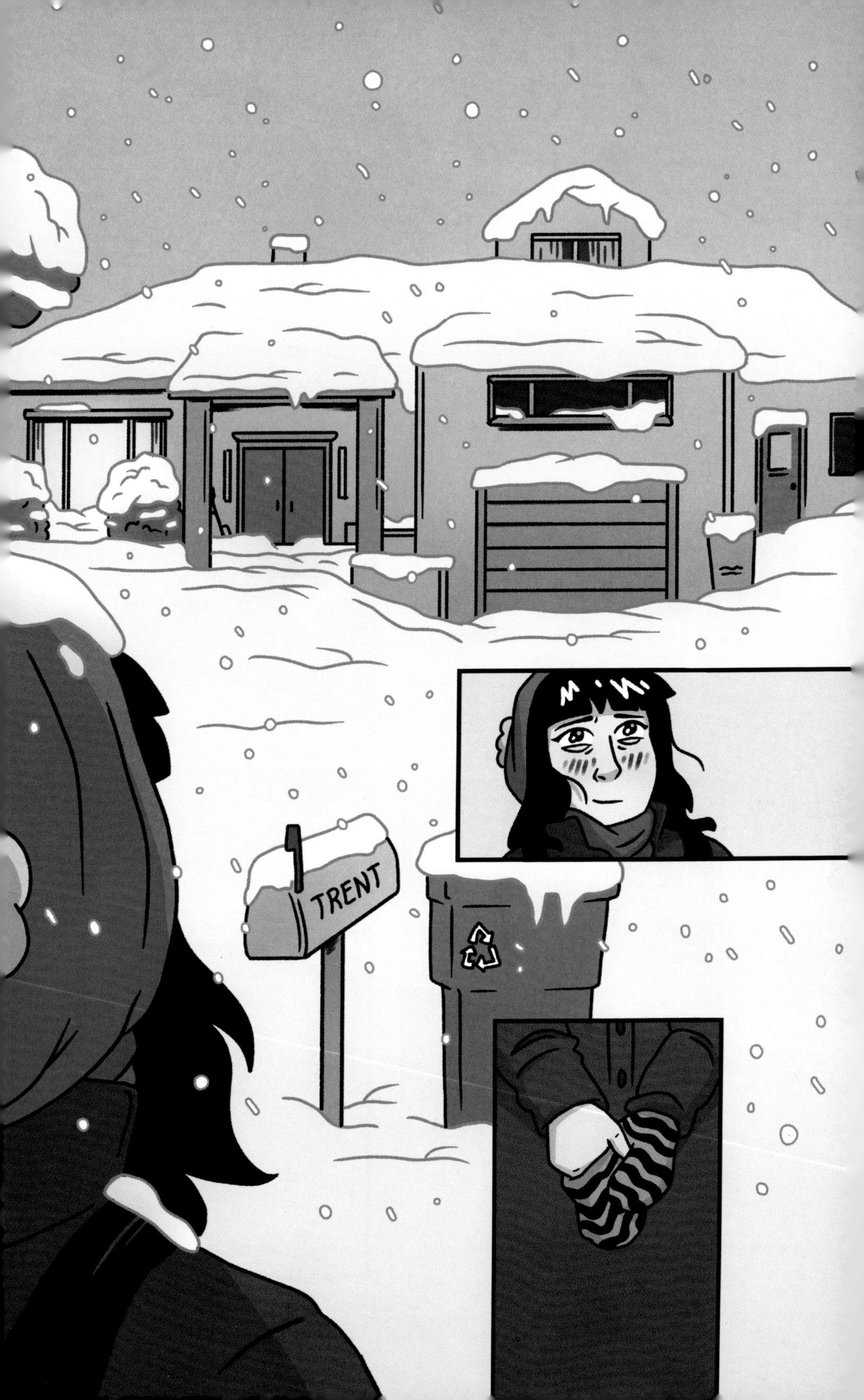
TRENT

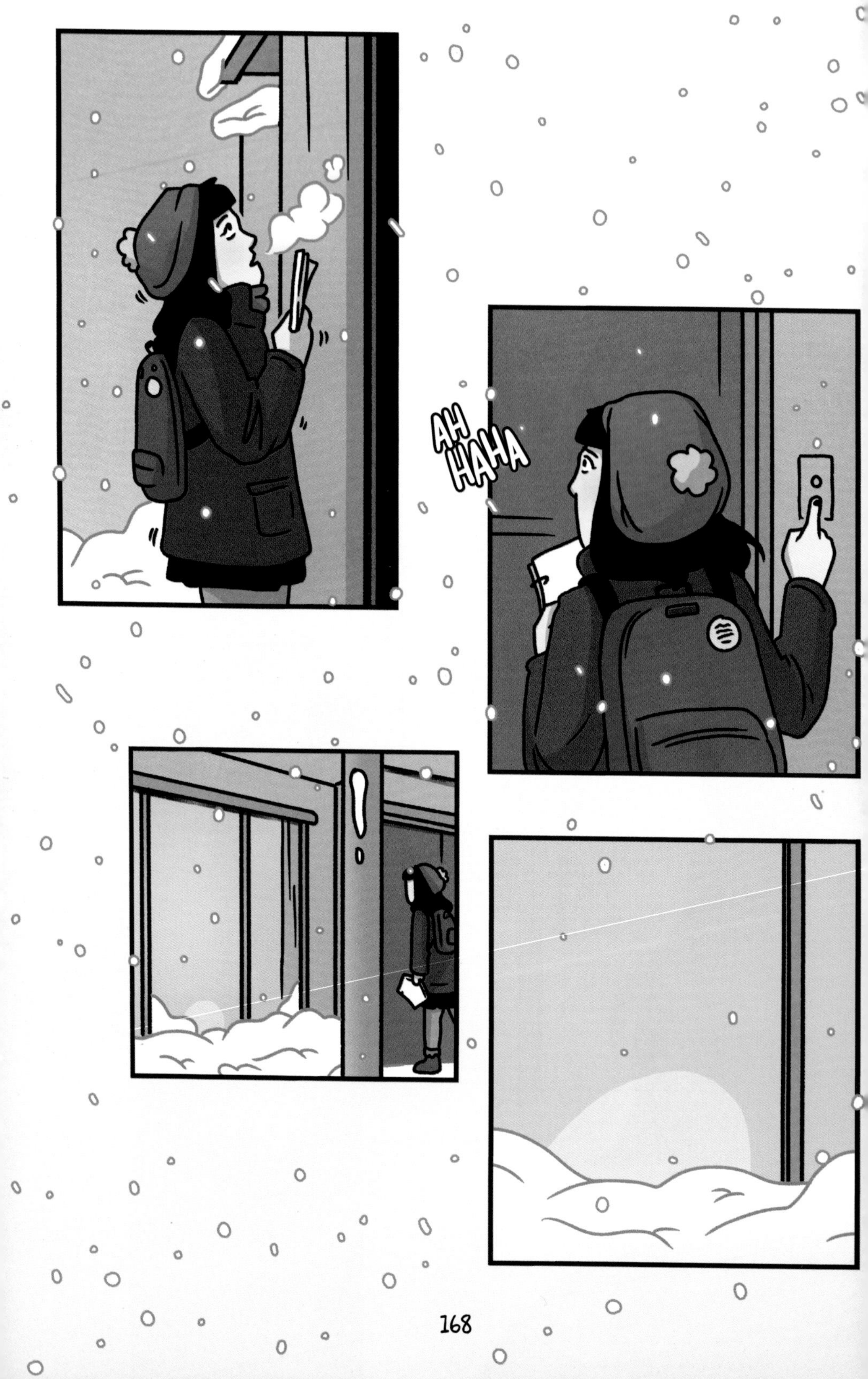
AH HAHA

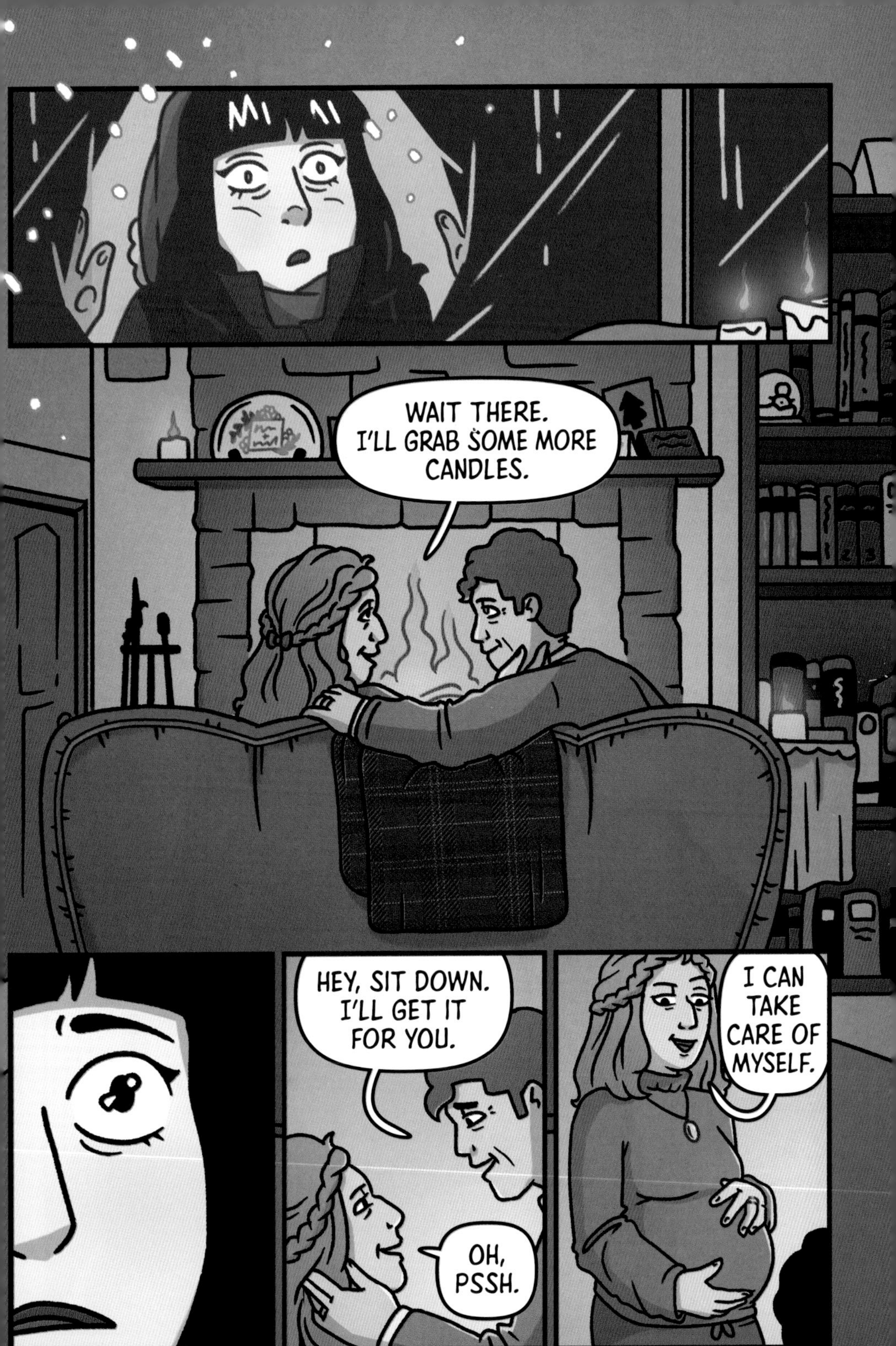
WAIT THERE. I'LL GRAB SOME MORE CANDLES.
HEY, SIT DOWN. I'LL GET IT FOR YOU.
OH, PSSH.
I CAN TAKE CARE OF MYSELF.

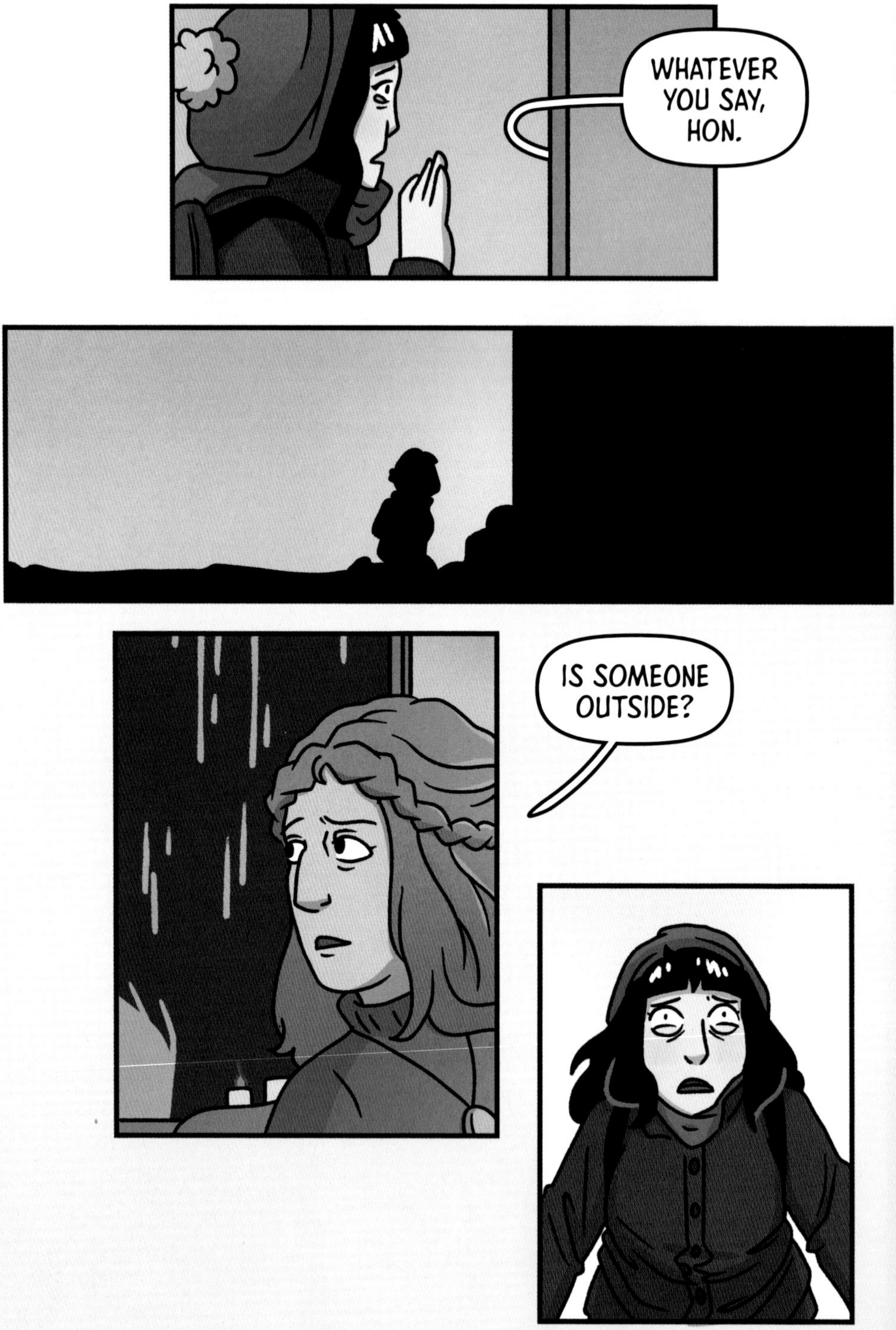
WHATEVER YOU SAY, HON.
IS SOMEONE OUTSIDE?

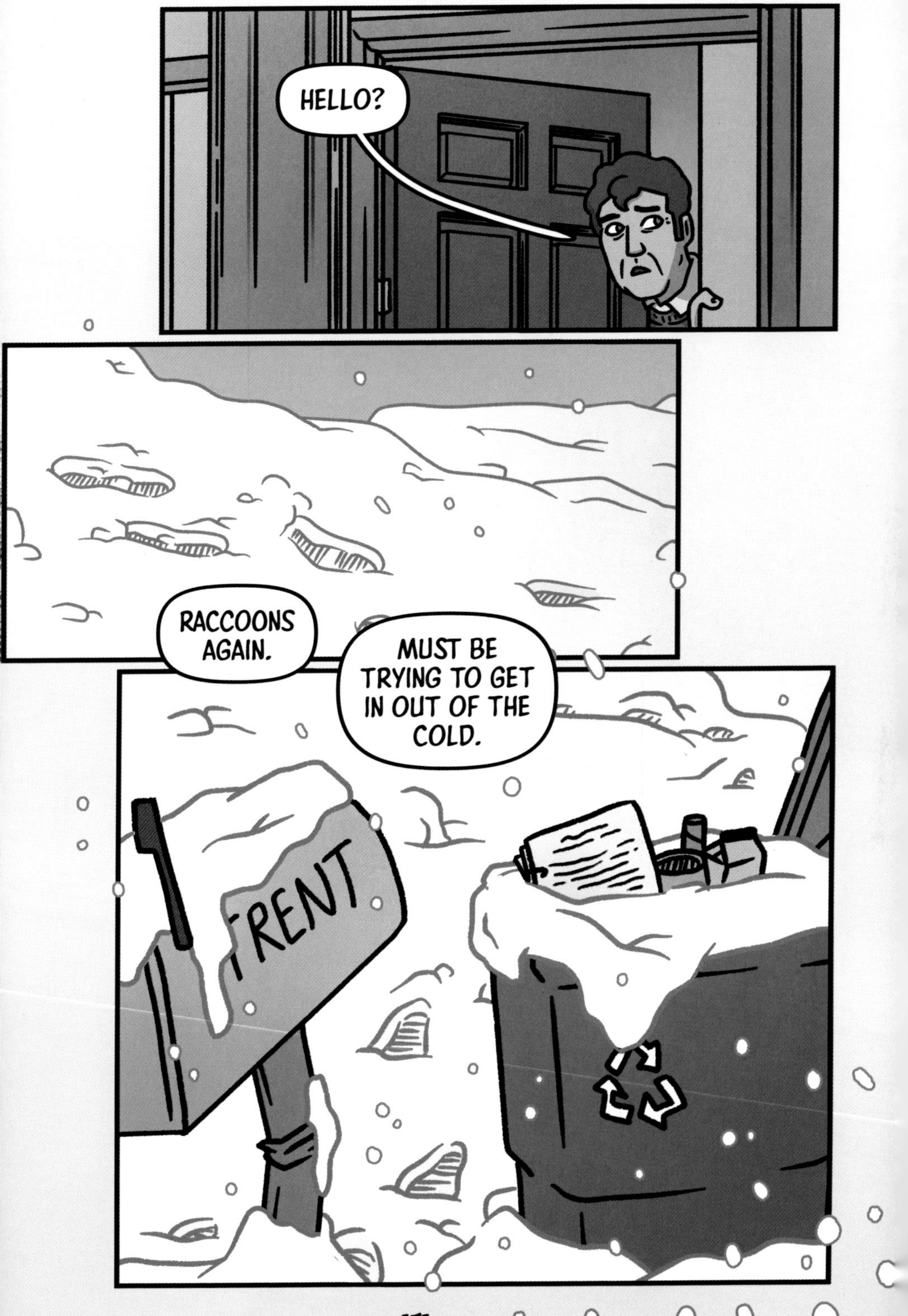
HELLO?
RACCOONS AGAIN.
MUST BE TRYING TO GET IN OUT OF THE COLD.
TRENT

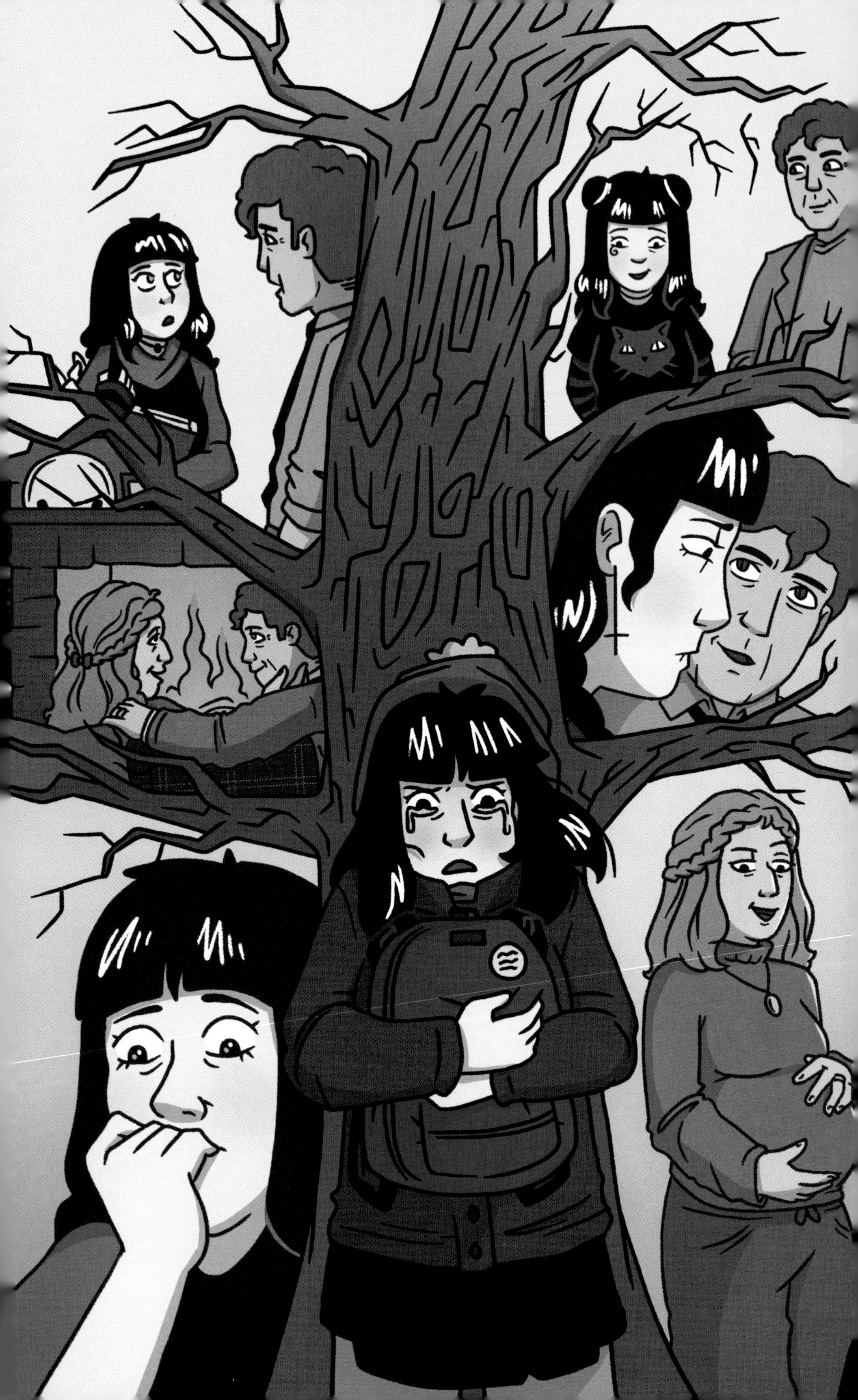

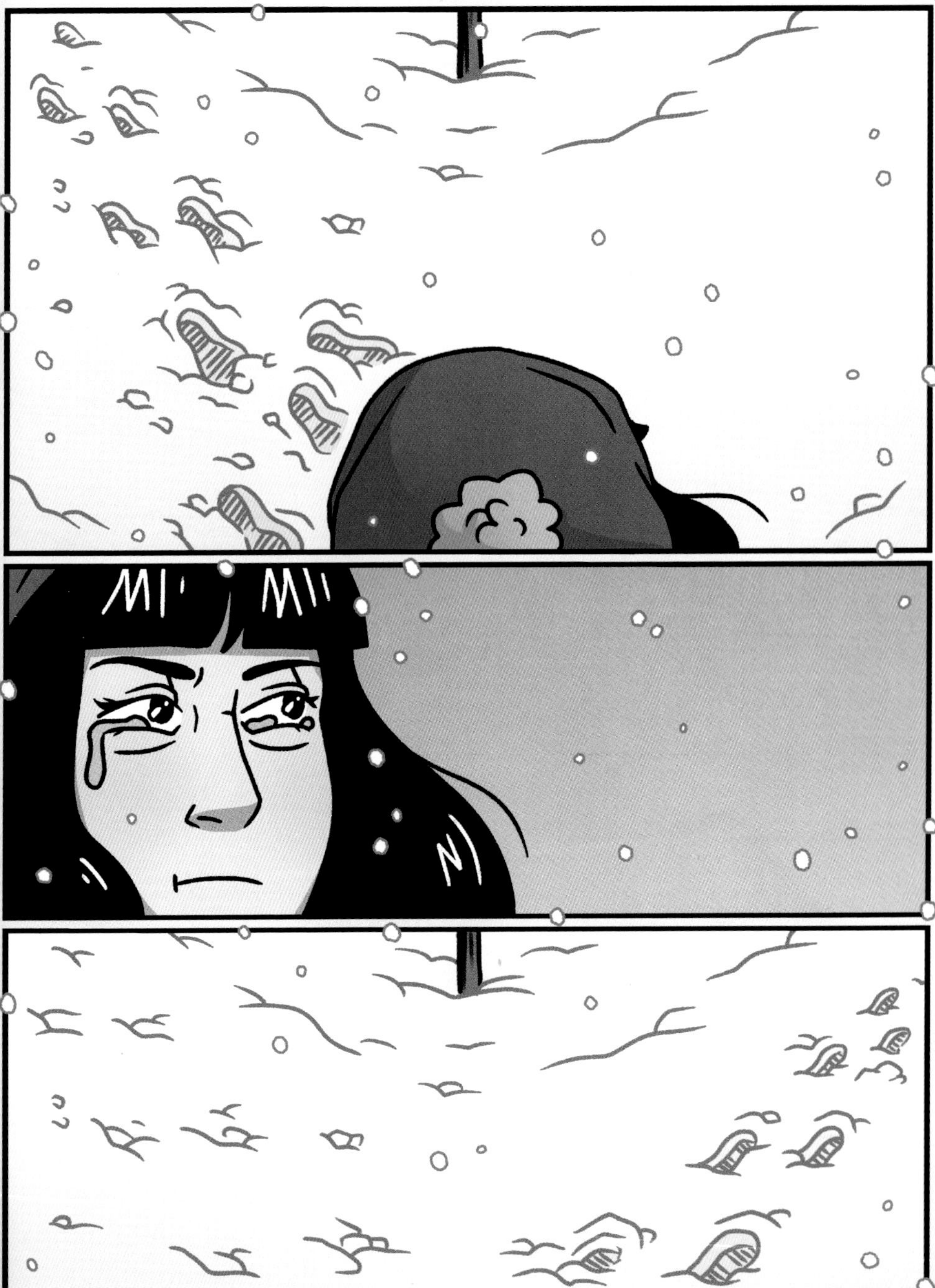

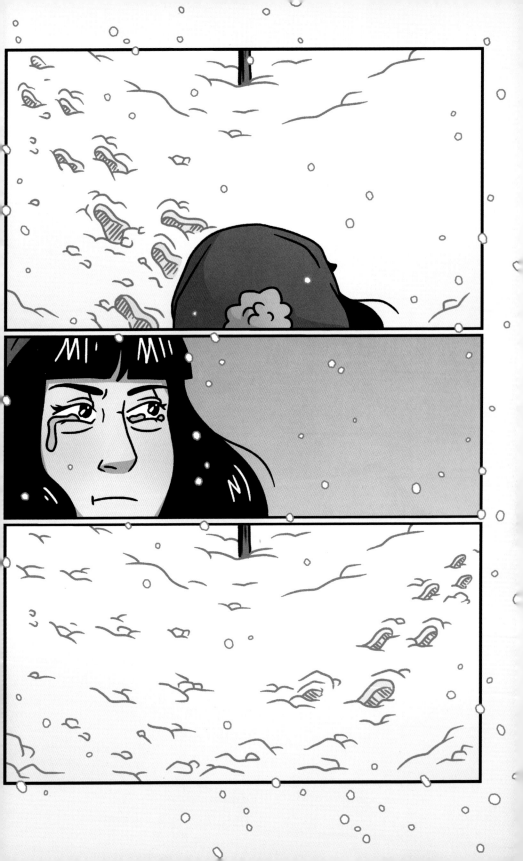

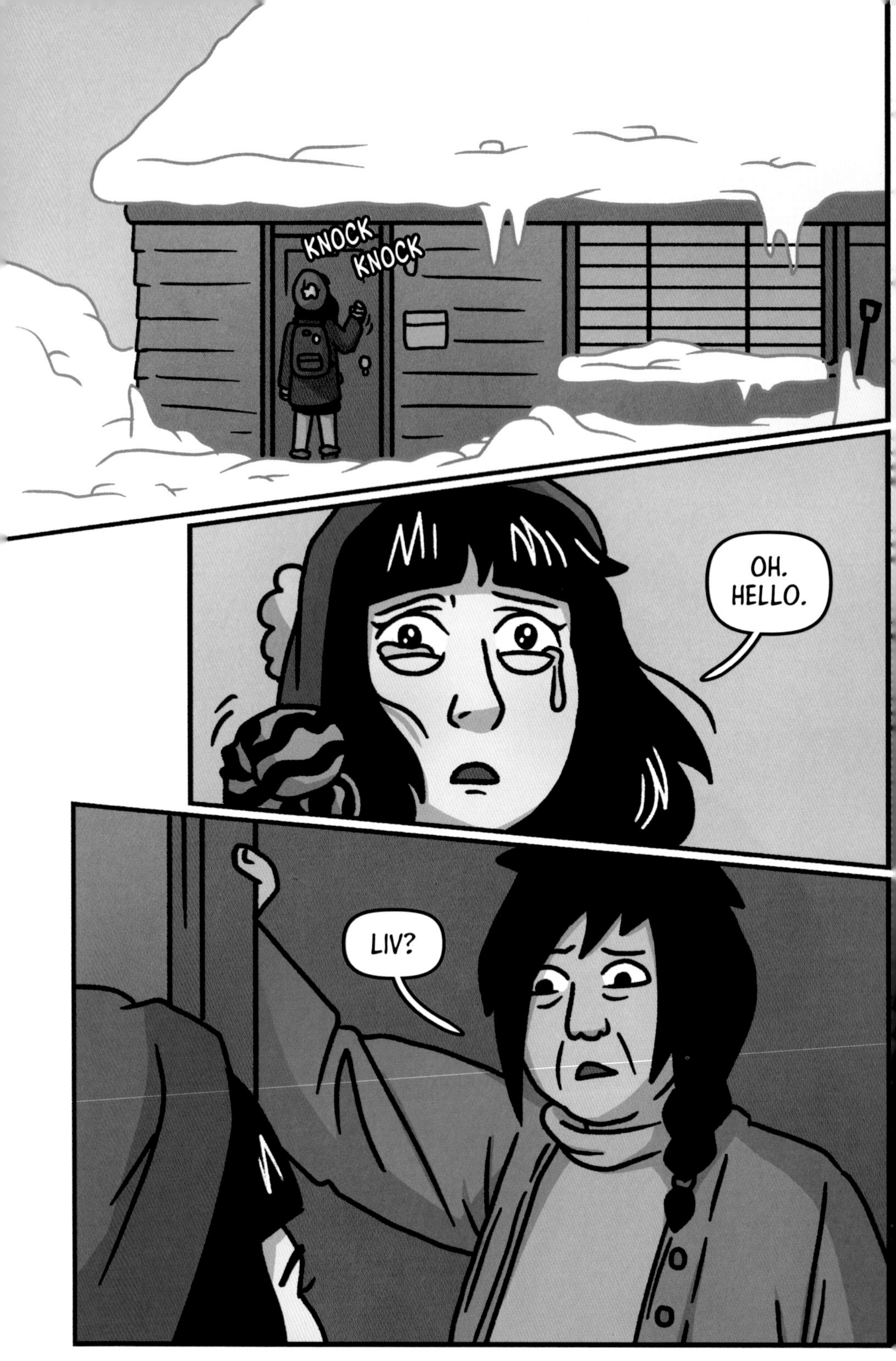
KNOCK
KNOCK
OH. HELLO.
LIV?

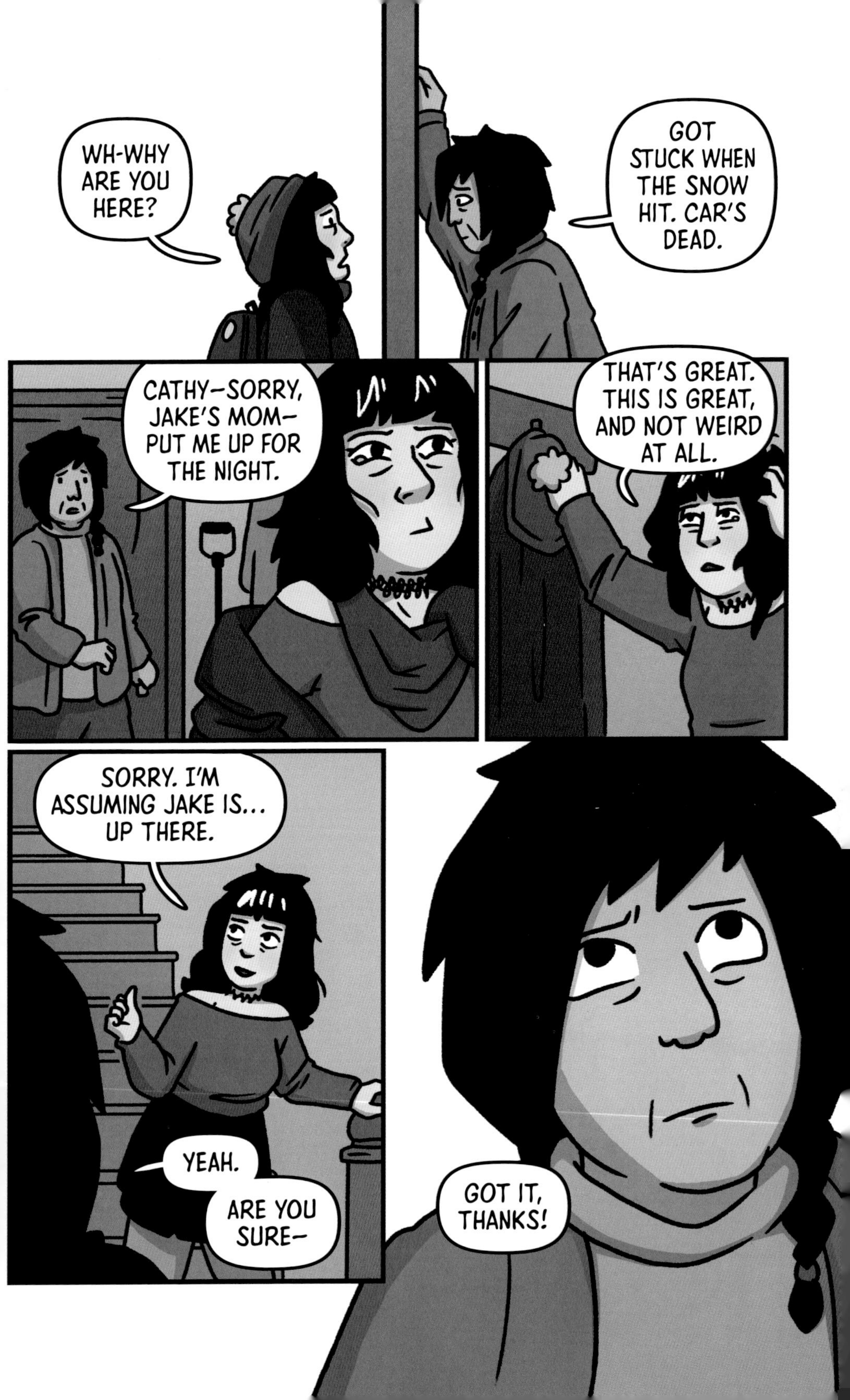
WH-WHY ARE YOU HERE?
GOT STUCK WHEN THE SNOW HIT. CAR'S DEAD.
CATHY—SORRY, JAKE'S MOM—PUT ME UP FOR THE NIGHT.
THAT'S GREAT. THIS IS GREAT, AND NOT WEIRD AT ALL.
SORRY. I'M ASSUMING JAKE IS... UP THERE.
YEAH.
ARE YOU SURE—
GOT IT, THANKS!

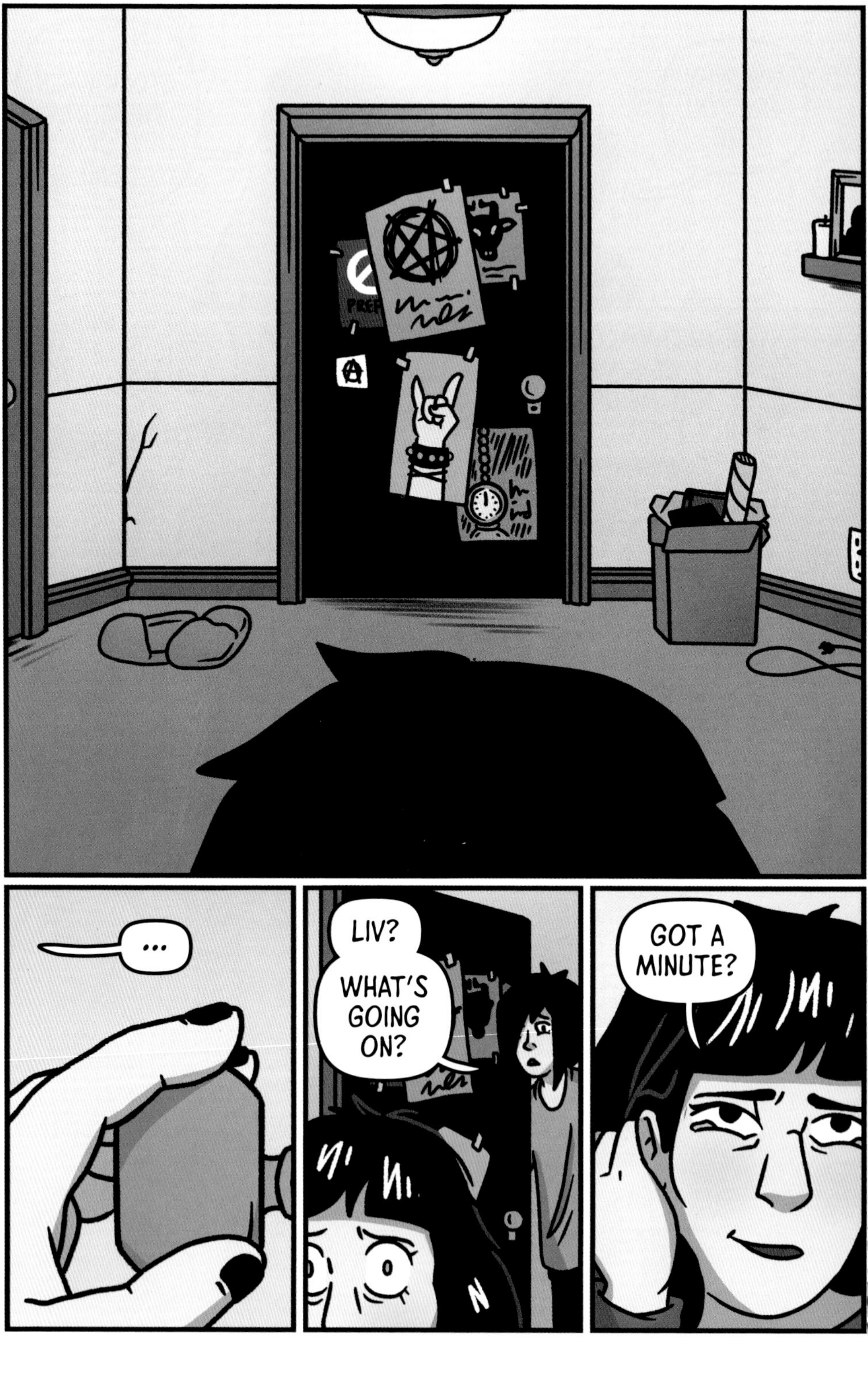
PREP
...
LIV?
WHAT'S GOING ON?
GOT A MINUTE?

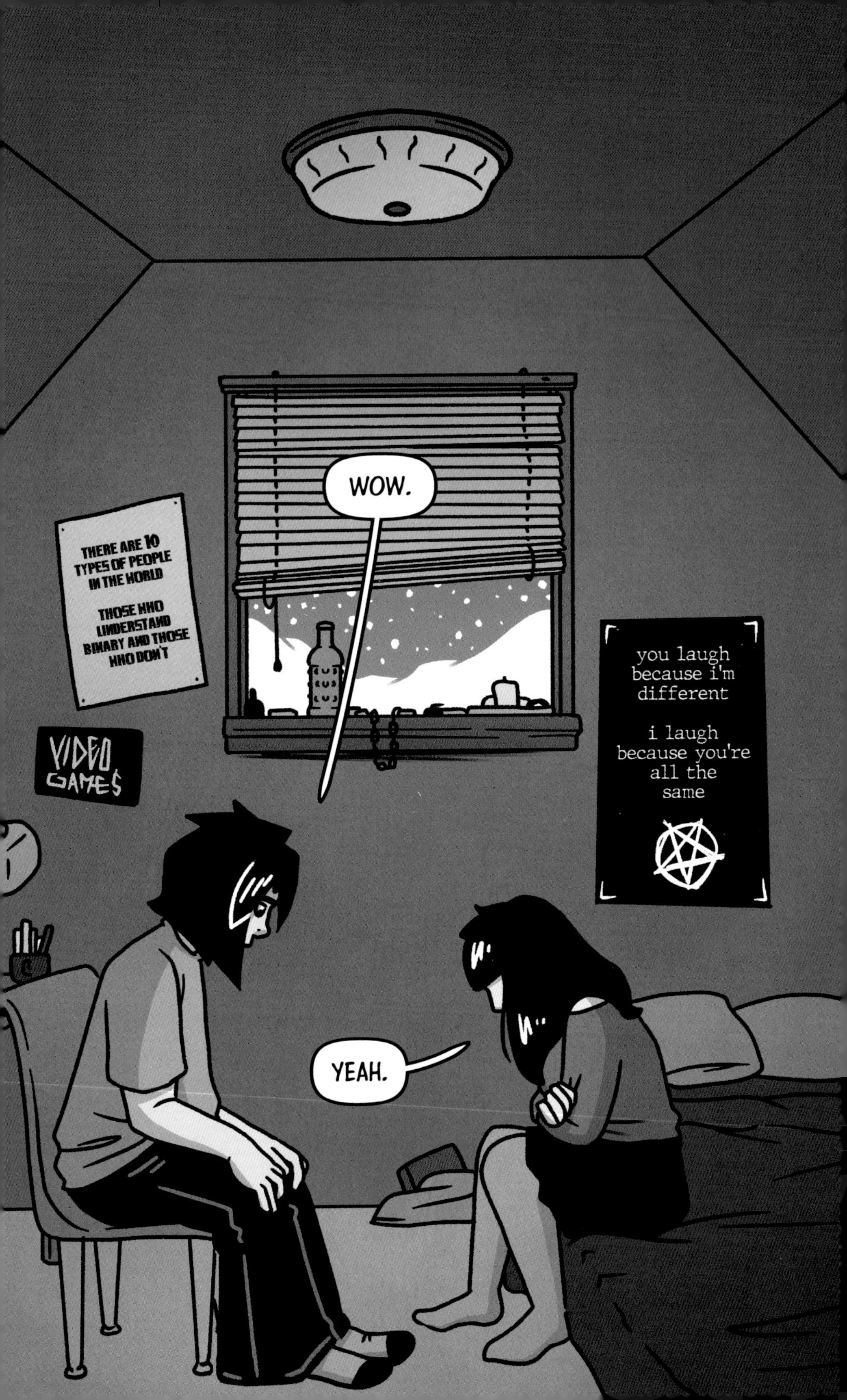
THERE ARE 10 TYPES OF PEOPLE IN THE WORLD
THOSE WHO UNDERSTAND BINARY AND THOSE WHO DON'T
VIDEO GAMES
WOW.
you laugh because i'm different
i laugh because you're all the same
YEAH.

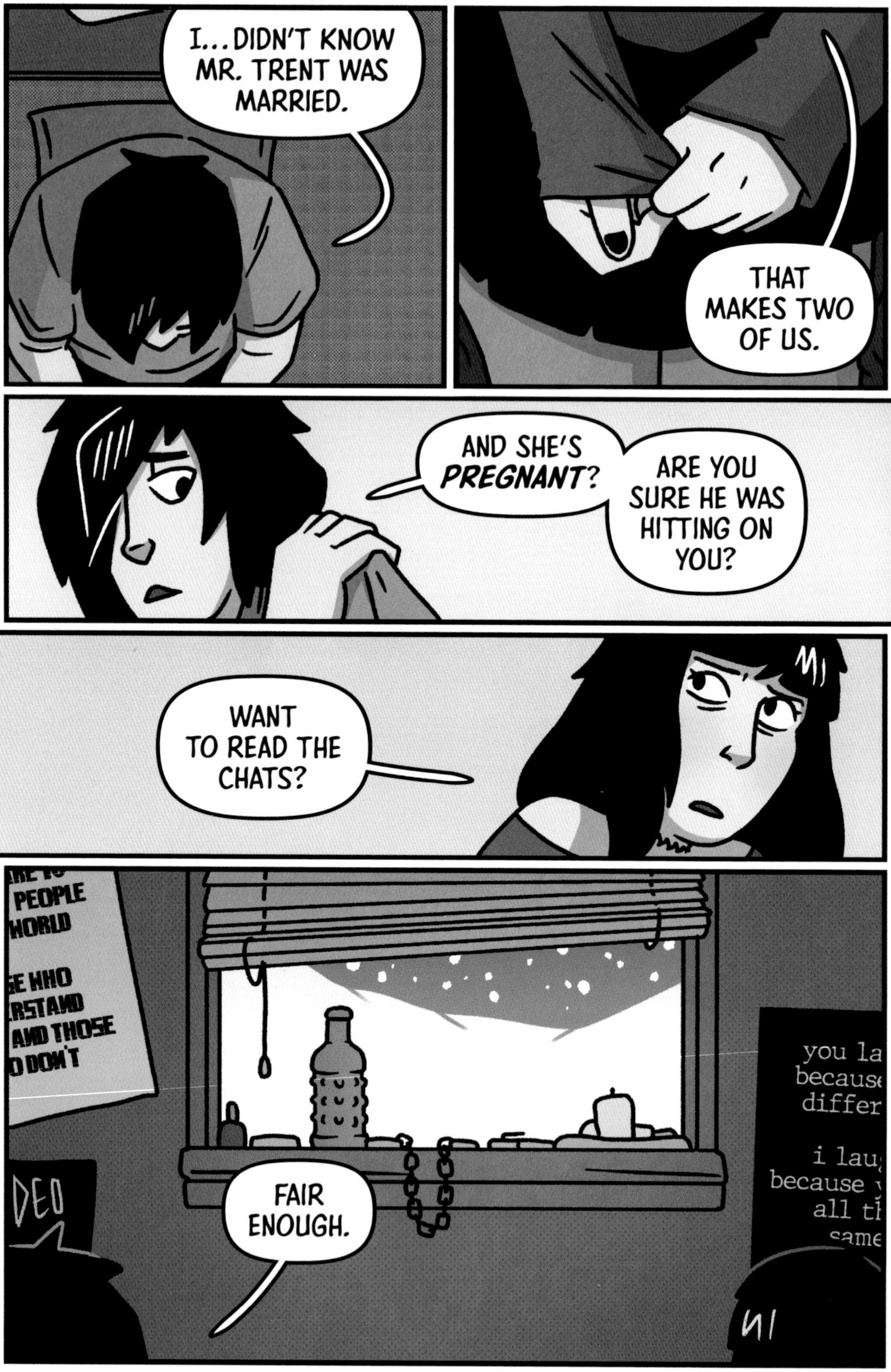
I...DIDN'T KNOW MR. TRENT WAS MARRIED.
THAT MAKES TWO OF US.
AND SHE'S *PREGNANT*?
ARE YOU SURE HE WAS HITTING ON YOU?
WANT TO READ THE CHATS?
FAIR ENOUGH.

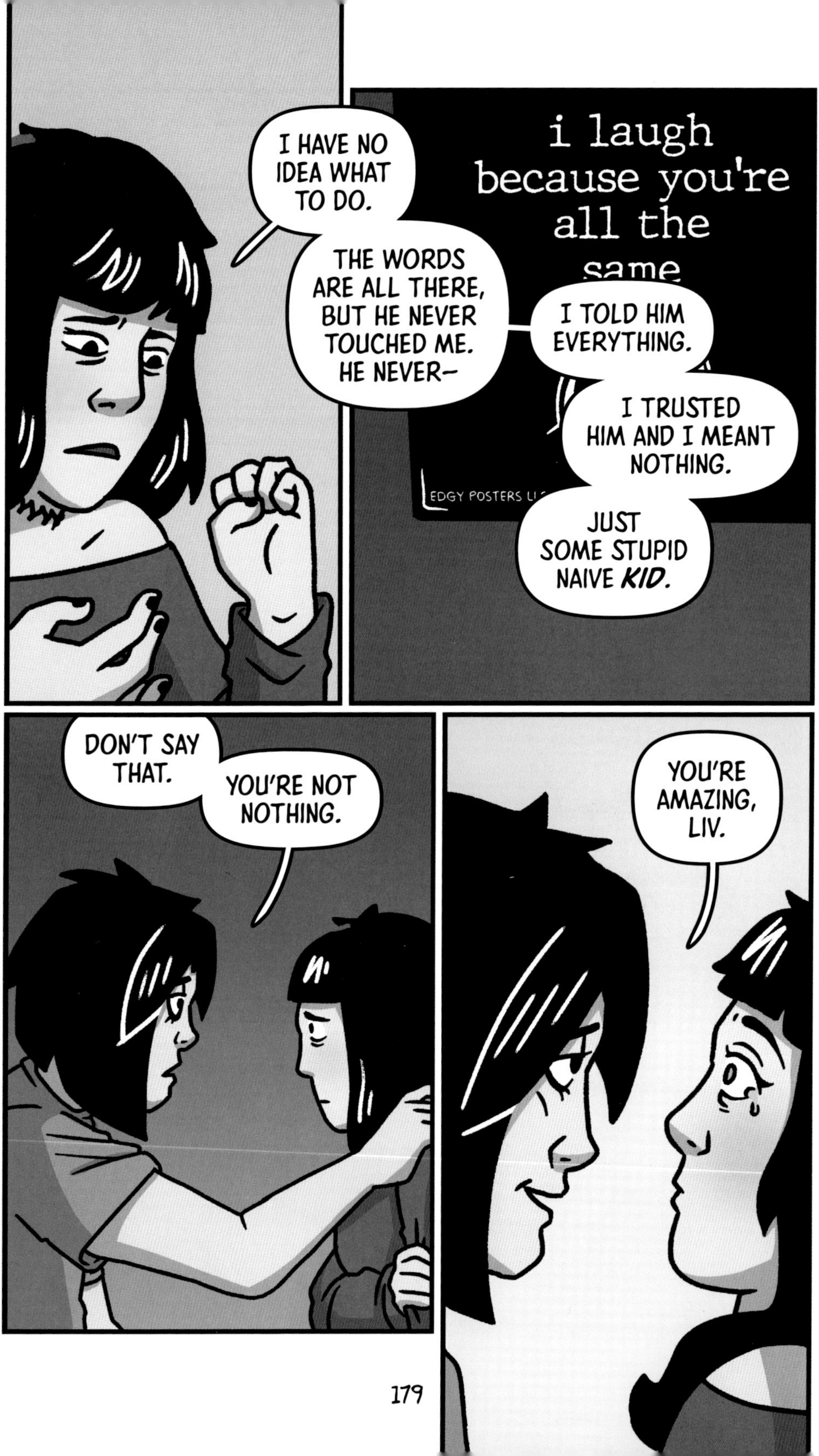
I HAVE NO IDEA WHAT TO DO.
THE WORDS ARE ALL THERE, BUT HE NEVER TOUCHED ME. HE NEVER–
i laugh because you're all the same
I TOLD HIM EVERYTHING.
I TRUSTED HIM AND I MEANT NOTHING.
EDGY POSTERS
JUST SOME STUPID NAIVE KID.
DON'T SAY THAT.
YOU'RE NOT NOTHING.
YOU'RE AMAZING, LIV.

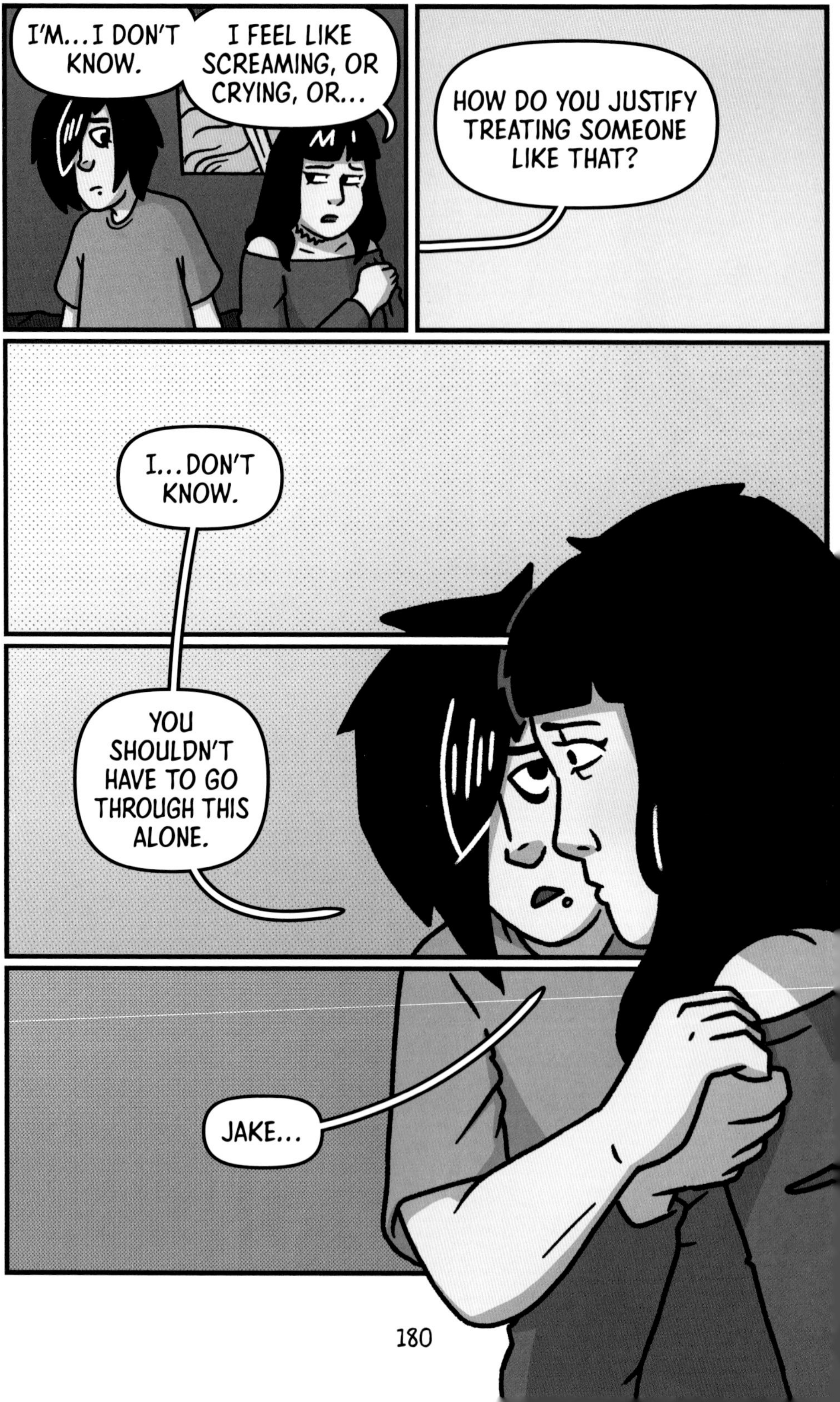
I'M...I DON'T KNOW.
I FEEL LIKE SCREAMING, OR CRYING, OR...
HOW DO YOU JUSTIFY TREATING SOMEONE LIKE THAT?
I...DON'T KNOW.
YOU SHOULDN'T HAVE TO GO THROUGH THIS ALONE.
JAKE...

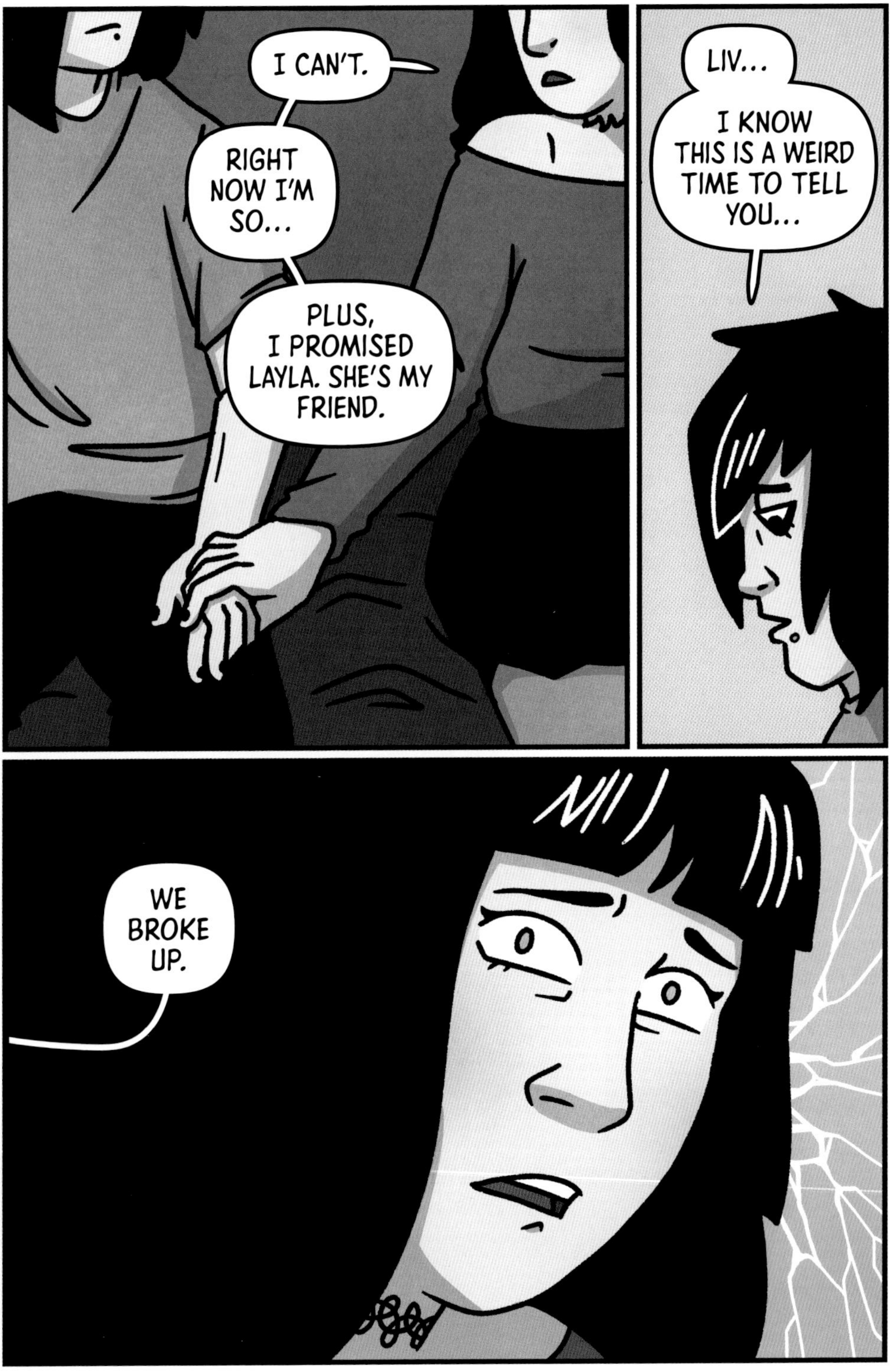
I CAN'T.
RIGHT NOW I'M SO...
PLUS, I PROMISED LAYLA. SHE'S MY FRIEND.
LIV...
I KNOW THIS IS A WEIRD TIME TO TELL YOU...
WE BROKE UP.

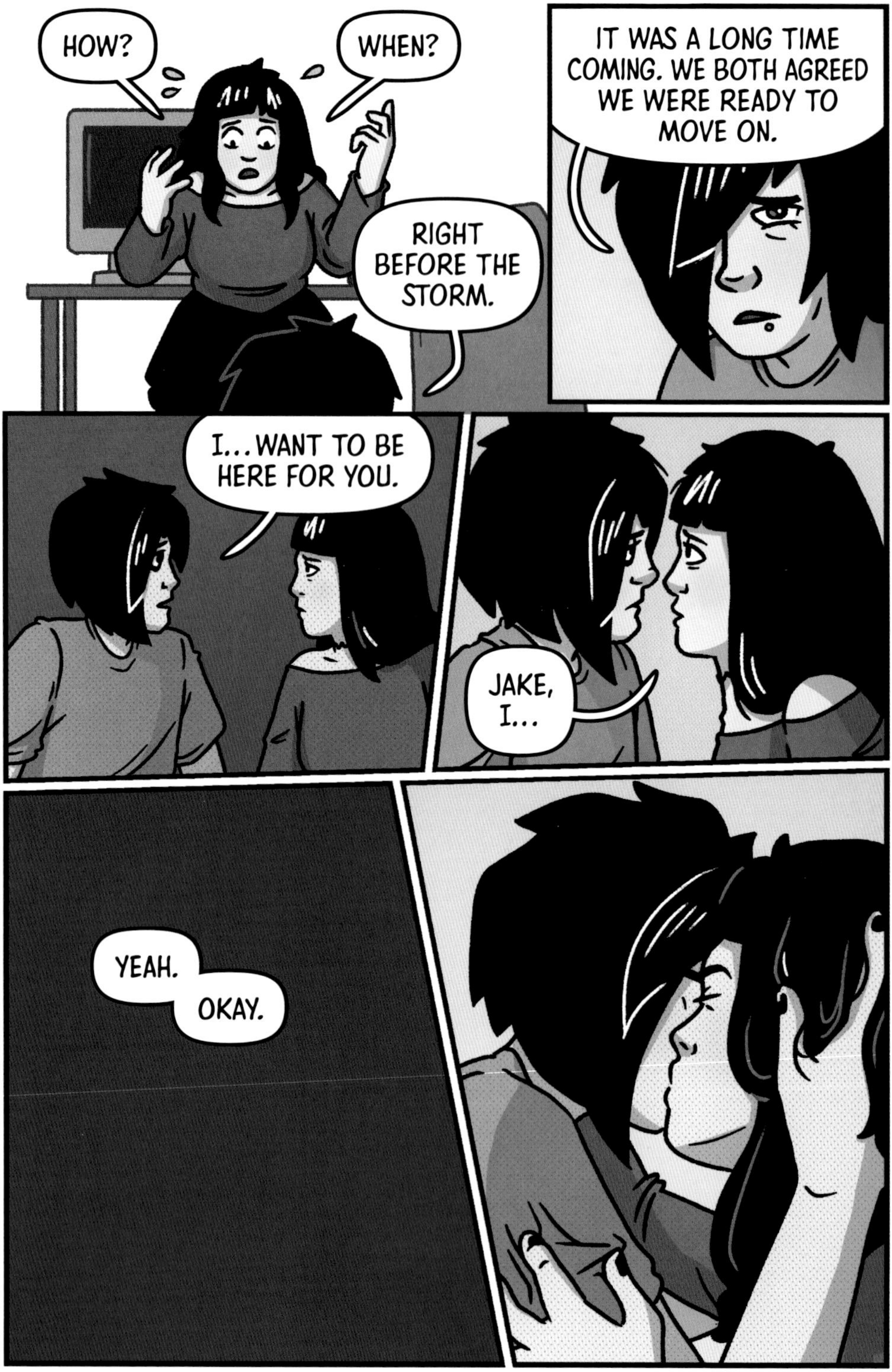
HOW?
WHEN?
RIGHT BEFORE THE STORM.
IT WAS A LONG TIME COMING. WE BOTH AGREED WE WERE READY TO MOVE ON.
I...WANT TO BE HERE FOR YOU.
JAKE, I...
YEAH.
OKAY.

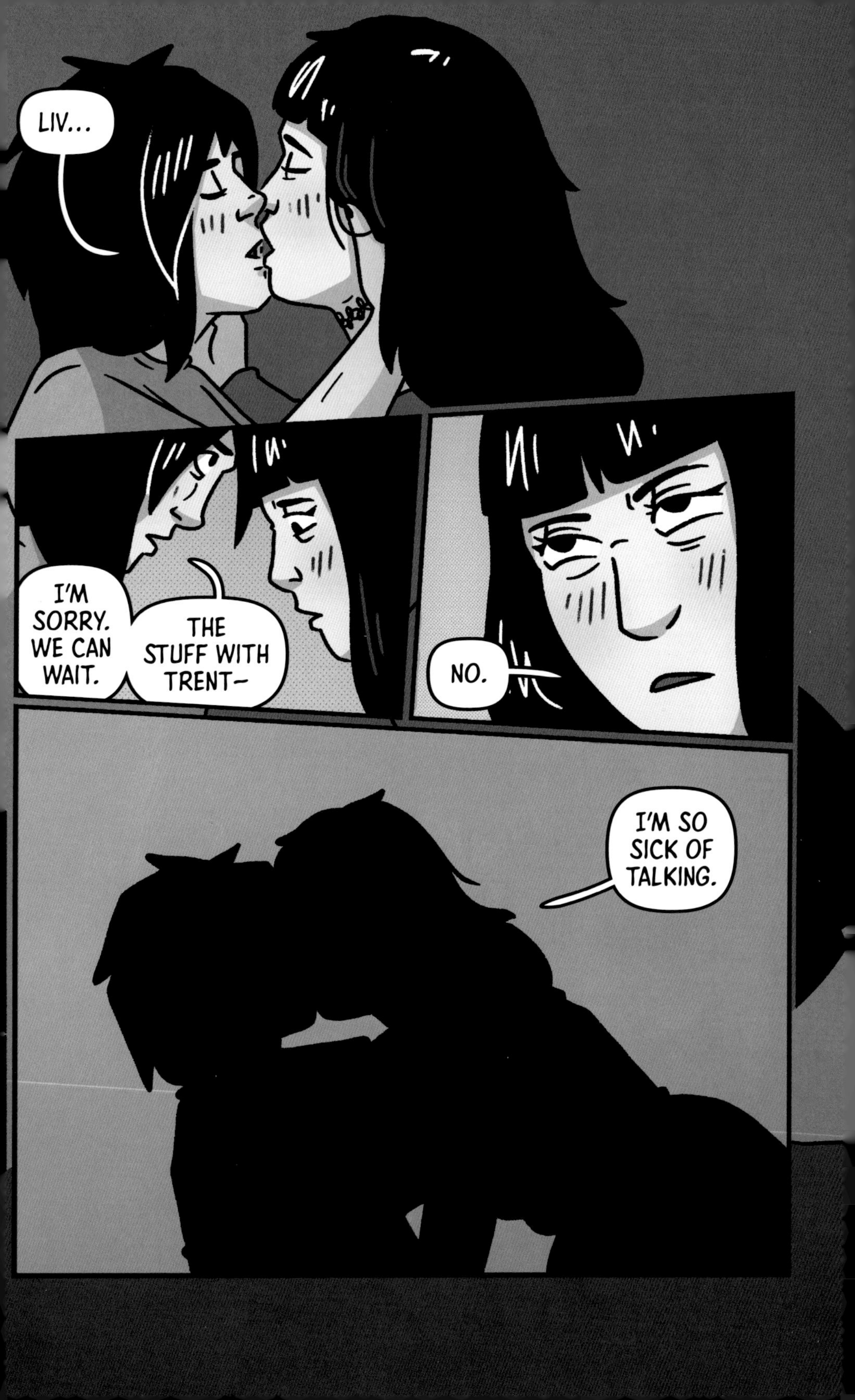
LIV...
I'M SORRY. WE CAN WAIT.
THE STUFF WITH TRENT–
NO.
I'M SO SICK OF TALKING.

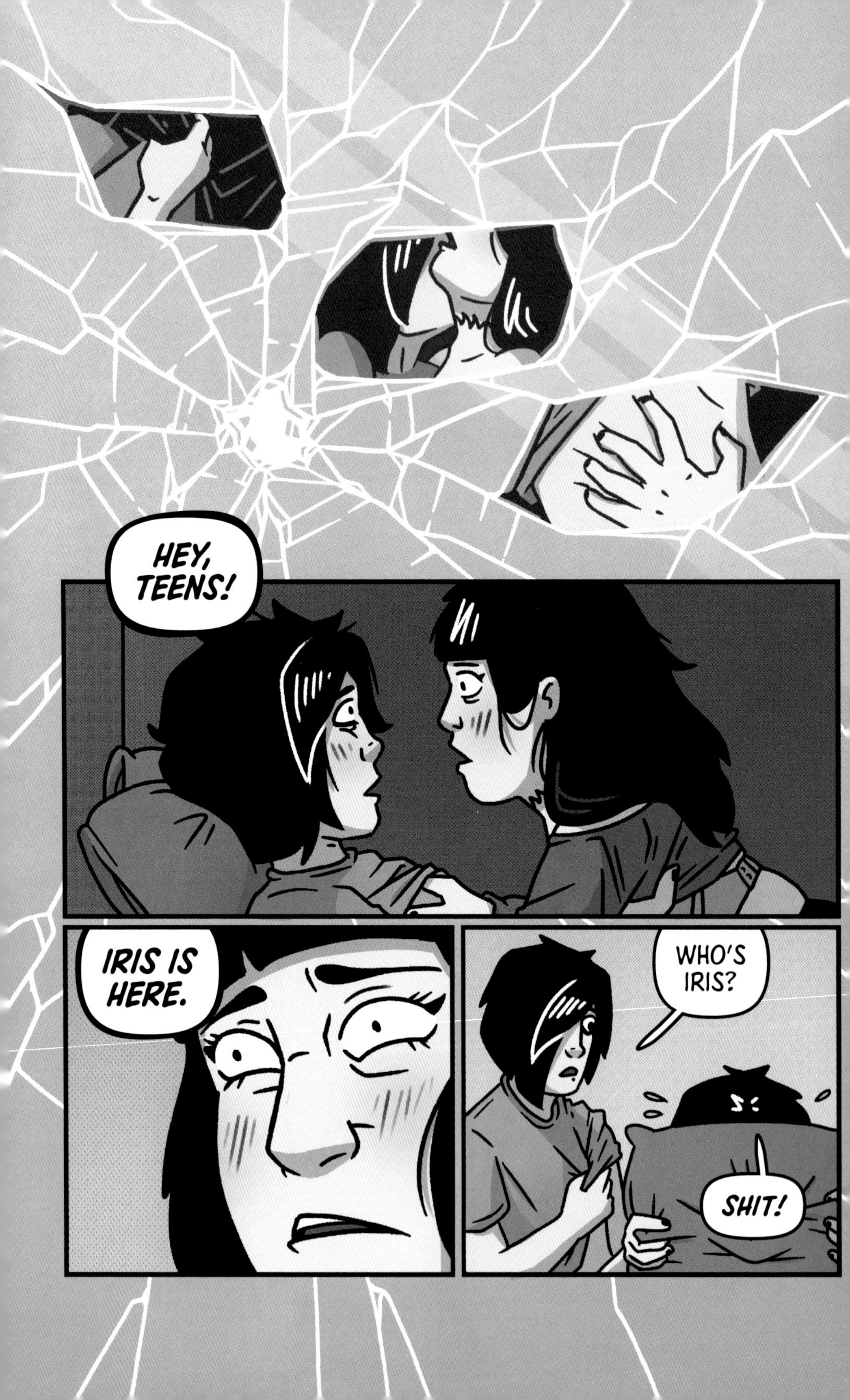
HEY, TEENS!
IRIS IS HERE.
WHO'S IRIS?
SHIT!

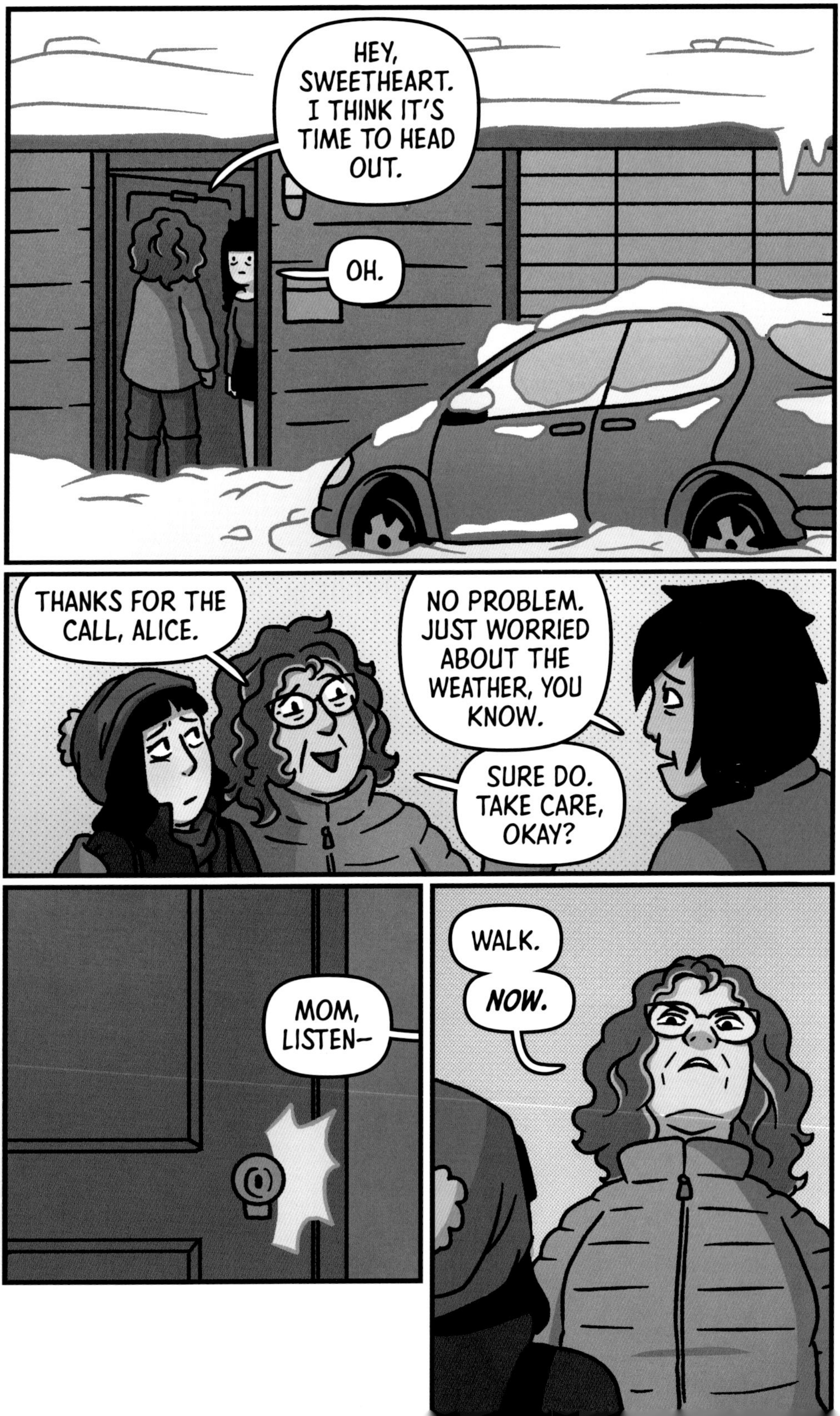
HEY, SWEETHEART. I THINK IT'S TIME TO HEAD OUT.
OH.
THANKS FOR THE CALL, ALICE.
NO PROBLEM. JUST WORRIED ABOUT THE WEATHER, YOU KNOW.
SURE DO. TAKE CARE, OKAY?
MOM, LISTEN—
WALK.
NOW.

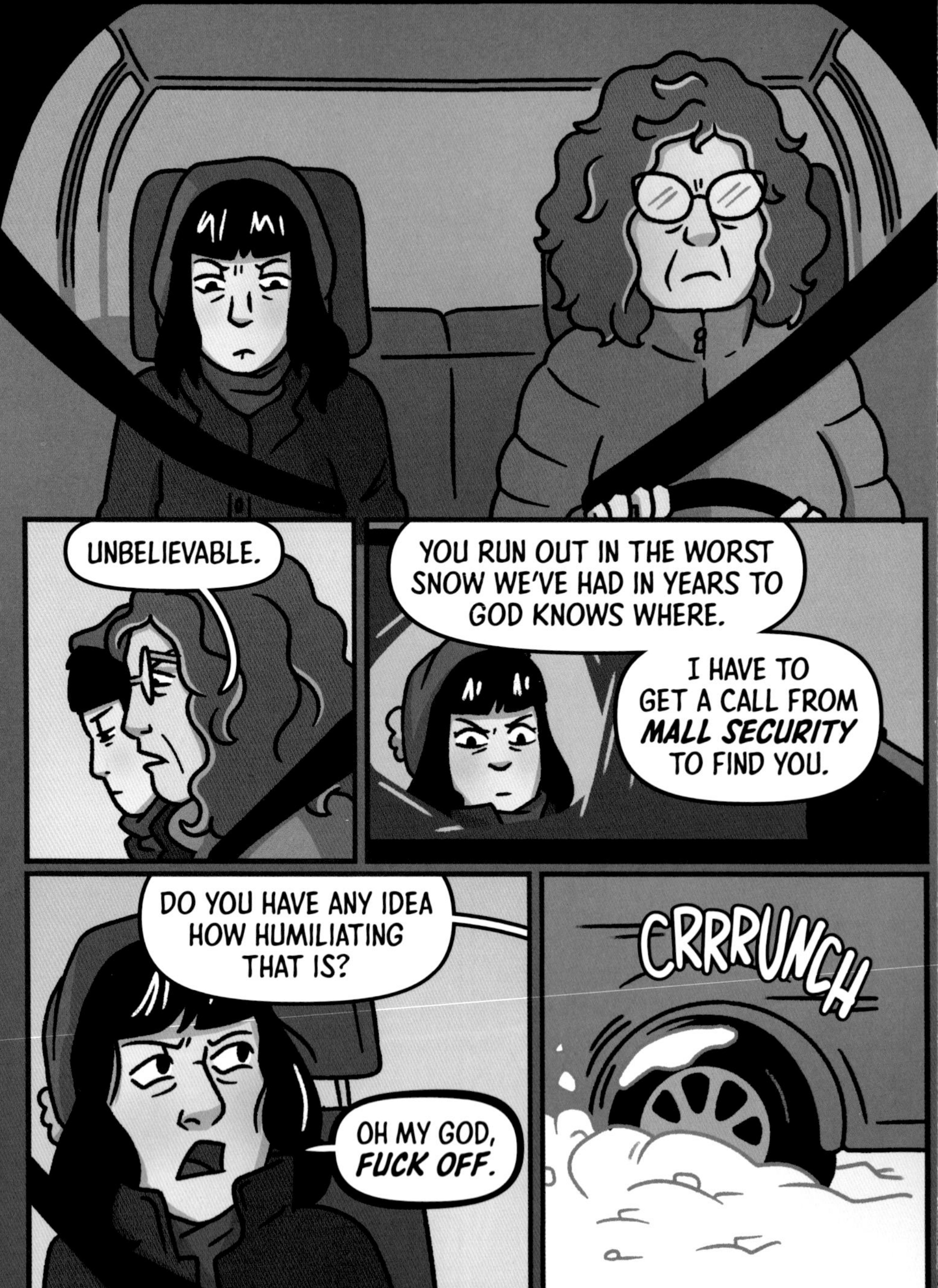
UNBELIEVABLE.
YOU RUN OUT IN THE WORST SNOW WE'VE HAD IN YEARS TO GOD KNOWS WHERE.
I HAVE TO GET A CALL FROM ***MALL SECURITY*** TO FIND YOU.
DO YOU HAVE ANY IDEA HOW HUMILIATING THAT IS?
OH MY GOD, ***FUCK OFF.***
CRRRUNCH

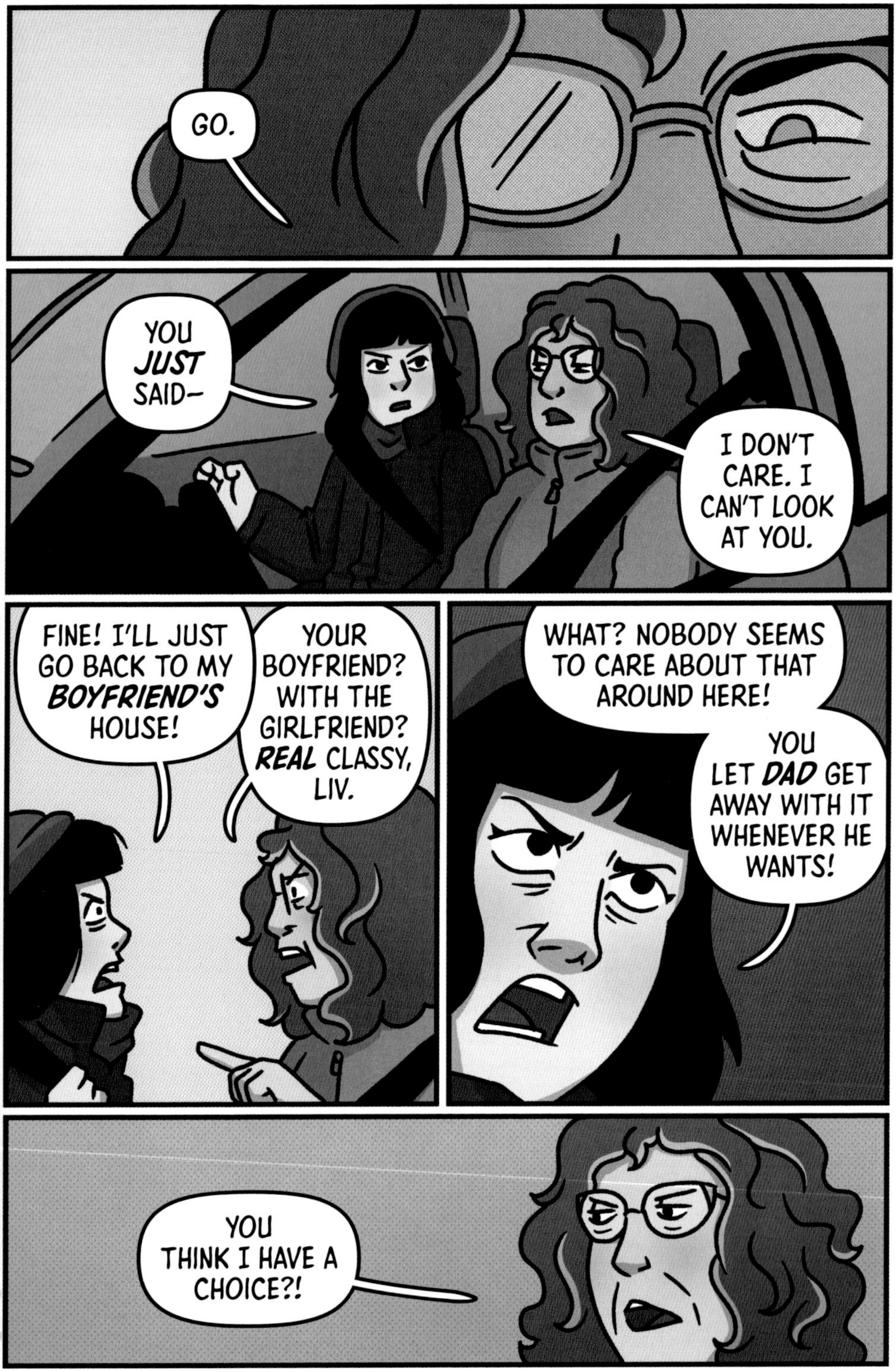
GO.
YOU JUST SAID–
I DON'T CARE. I CAN'T LOOK AT YOU.
FINE! I'LL JUST GO BACK TO MY BOYFRIEND'S HOUSE!
YOUR BOYFRIEND? WITH THE GIRLFRIEND? REAL CLASSY, LIV.
WHAT? NOBODY SEEMS TO CARE ABOUT THAT AROUND HERE!
YOU LET DAD GET AWAY WITH IT WHENEVER HE WANTS!
YOU THINK I HAVE A CHOICE?!

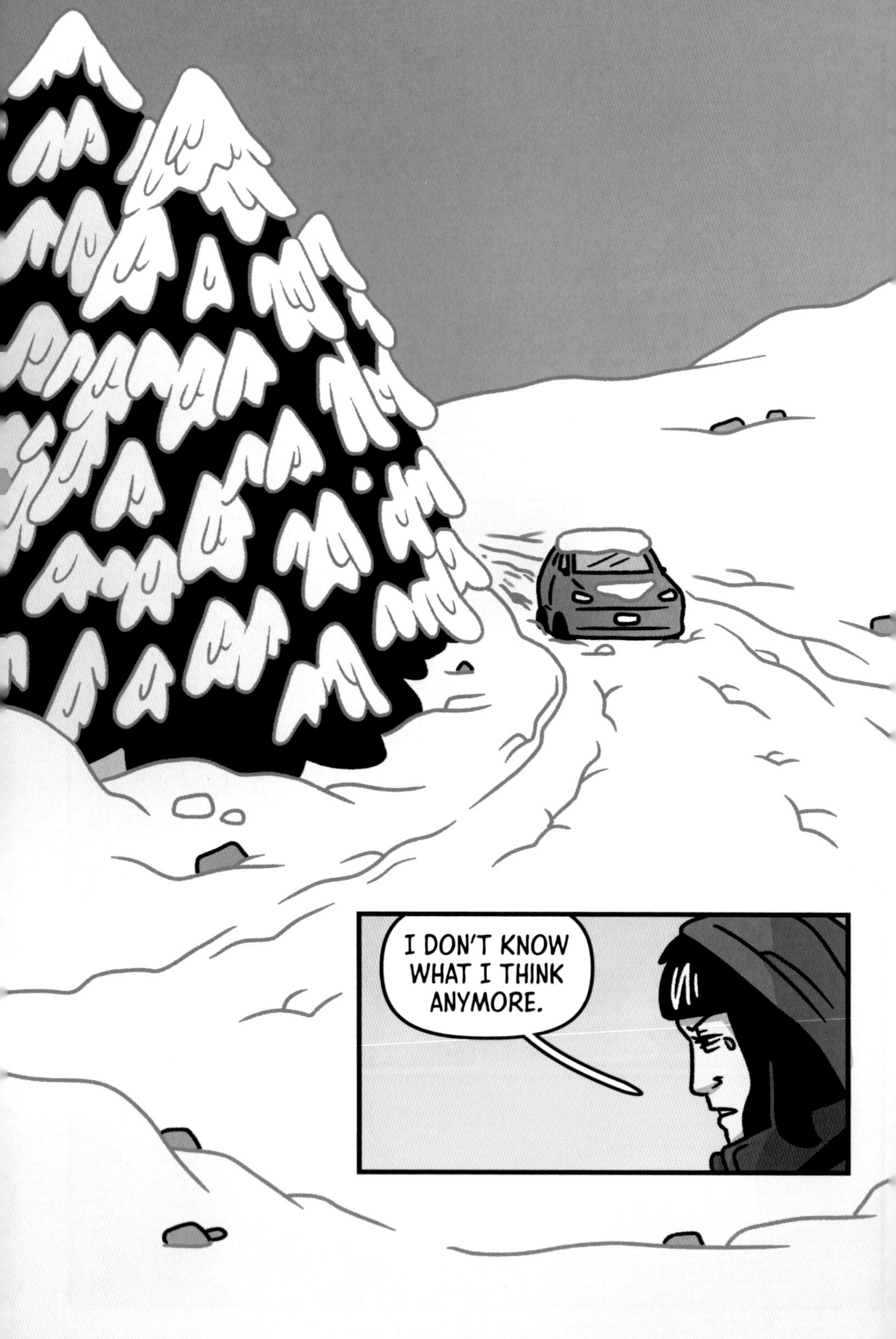
I DON'T KNOW WHAT I THINK ANYMORE.

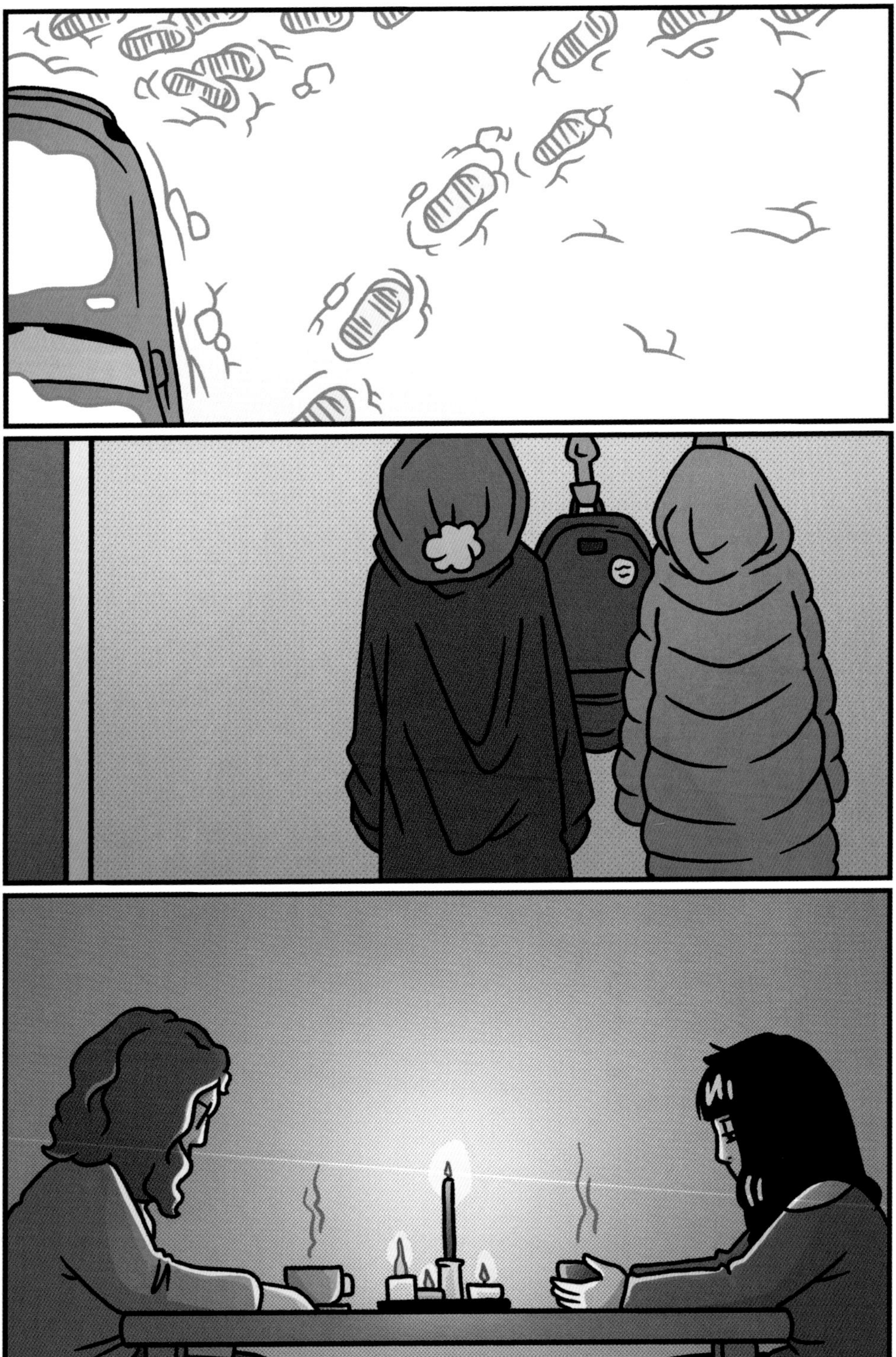

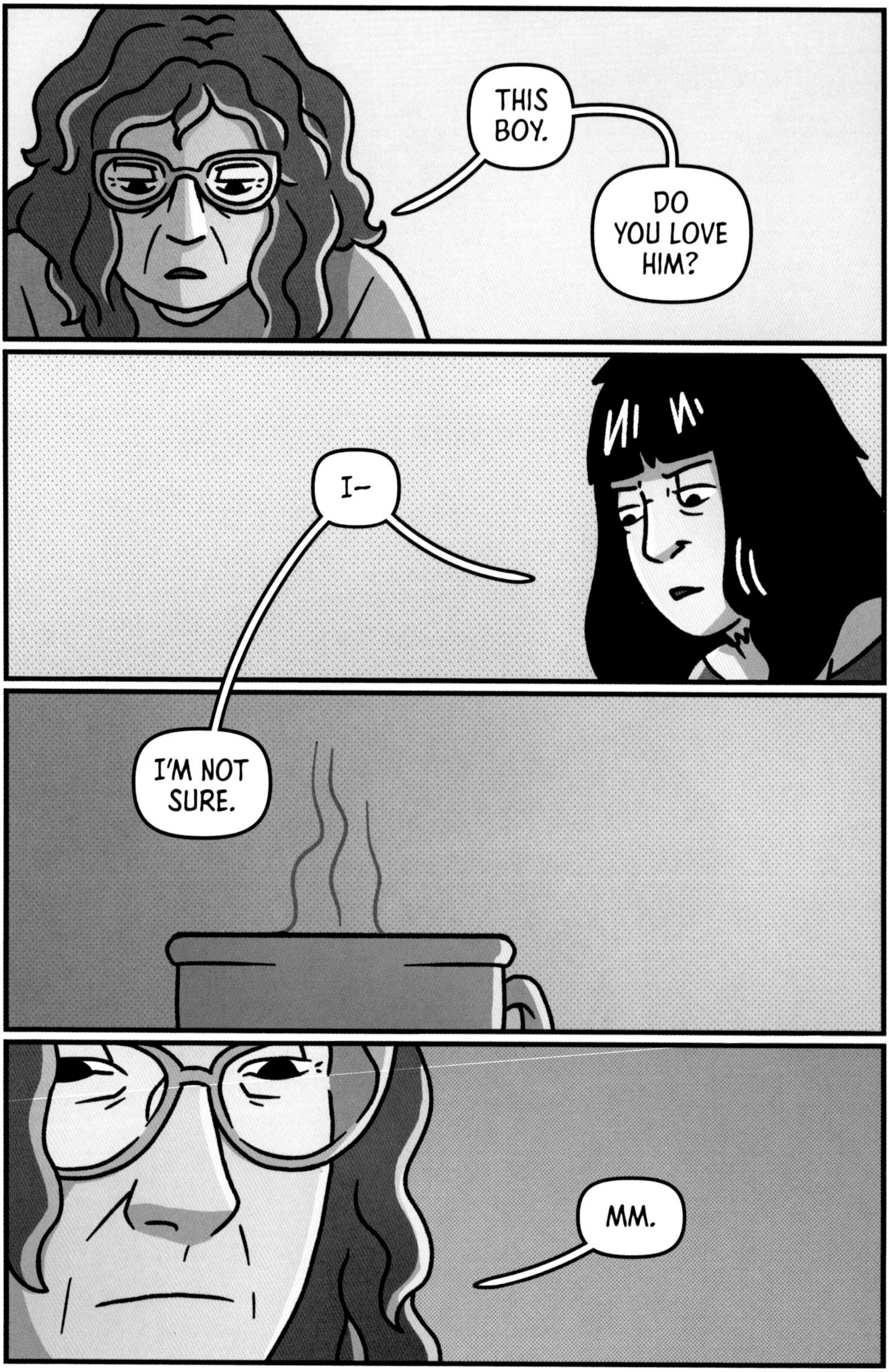
THIS BOY.
DO YOU LOVE HIM?
I–
I'M NOT SURE.
MM.

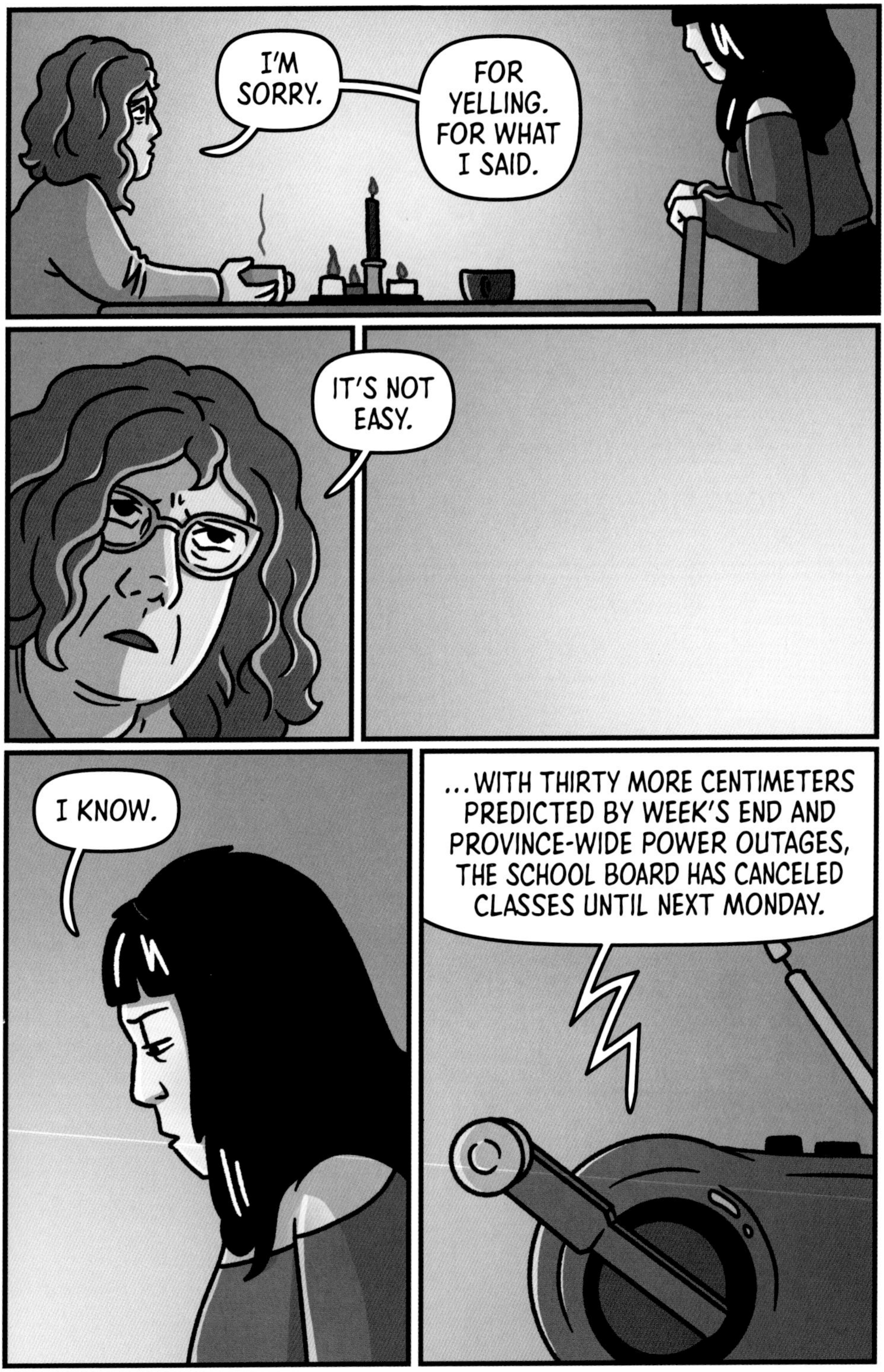
I'M SORRY.
FOR YELLING. FOR WHAT I SAID.
IT'S NOT EASY.
I KNOW.
...WITH THIRTY MORE CENTIMETERS PREDICTED BY WEEK'S END AND PROVINCE-WIDE POWER OUTAGES, THE SCHOOL BOARD HAS CANCELED CLASSES UNTIL NEXT MONDAY.

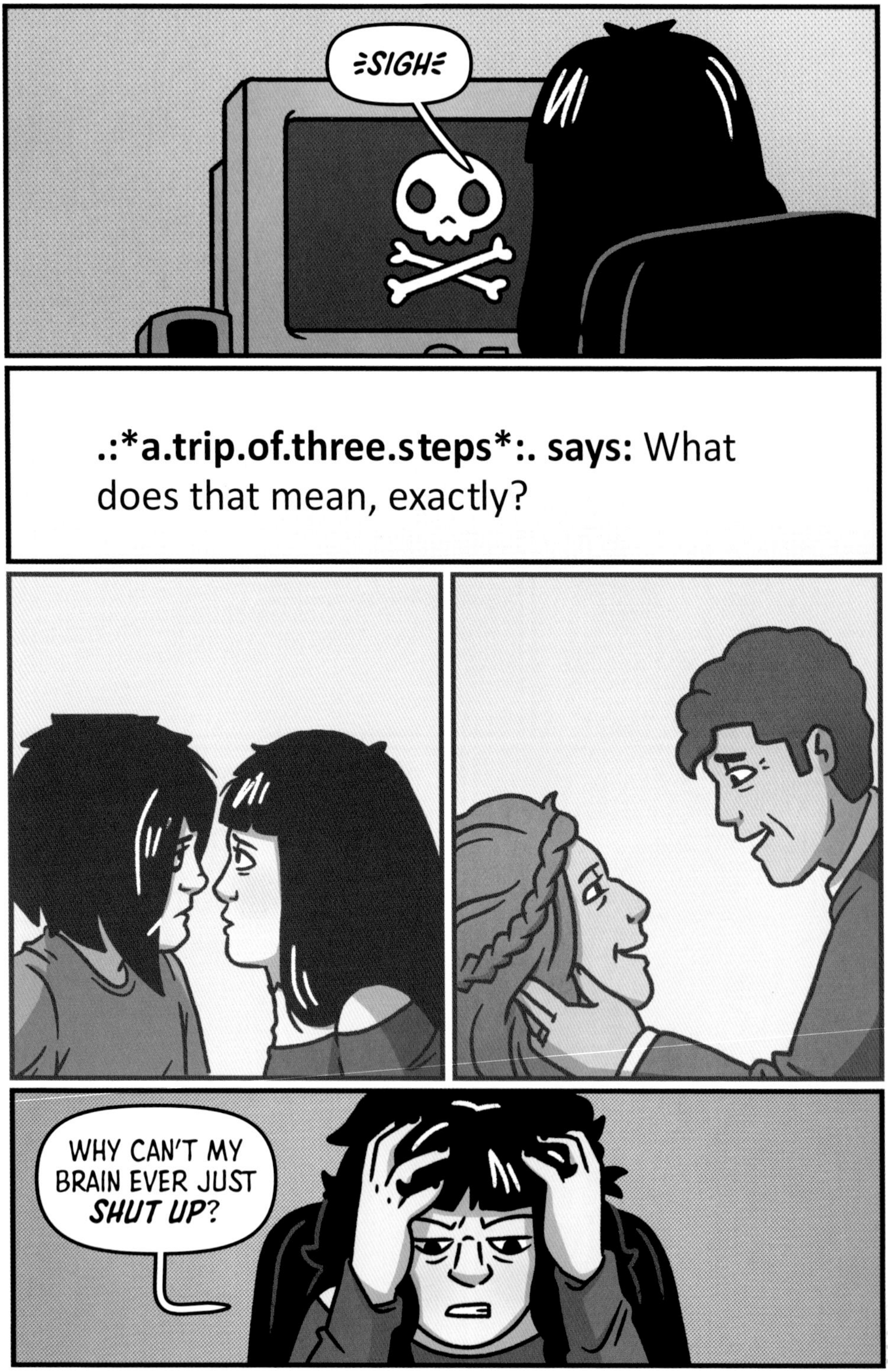
SIGH
.:*a.trip.of.three.steps*:. says: What does that mean, exactly?
WHY CAN'T MY BRAIN EVER JUST SHUT UP?

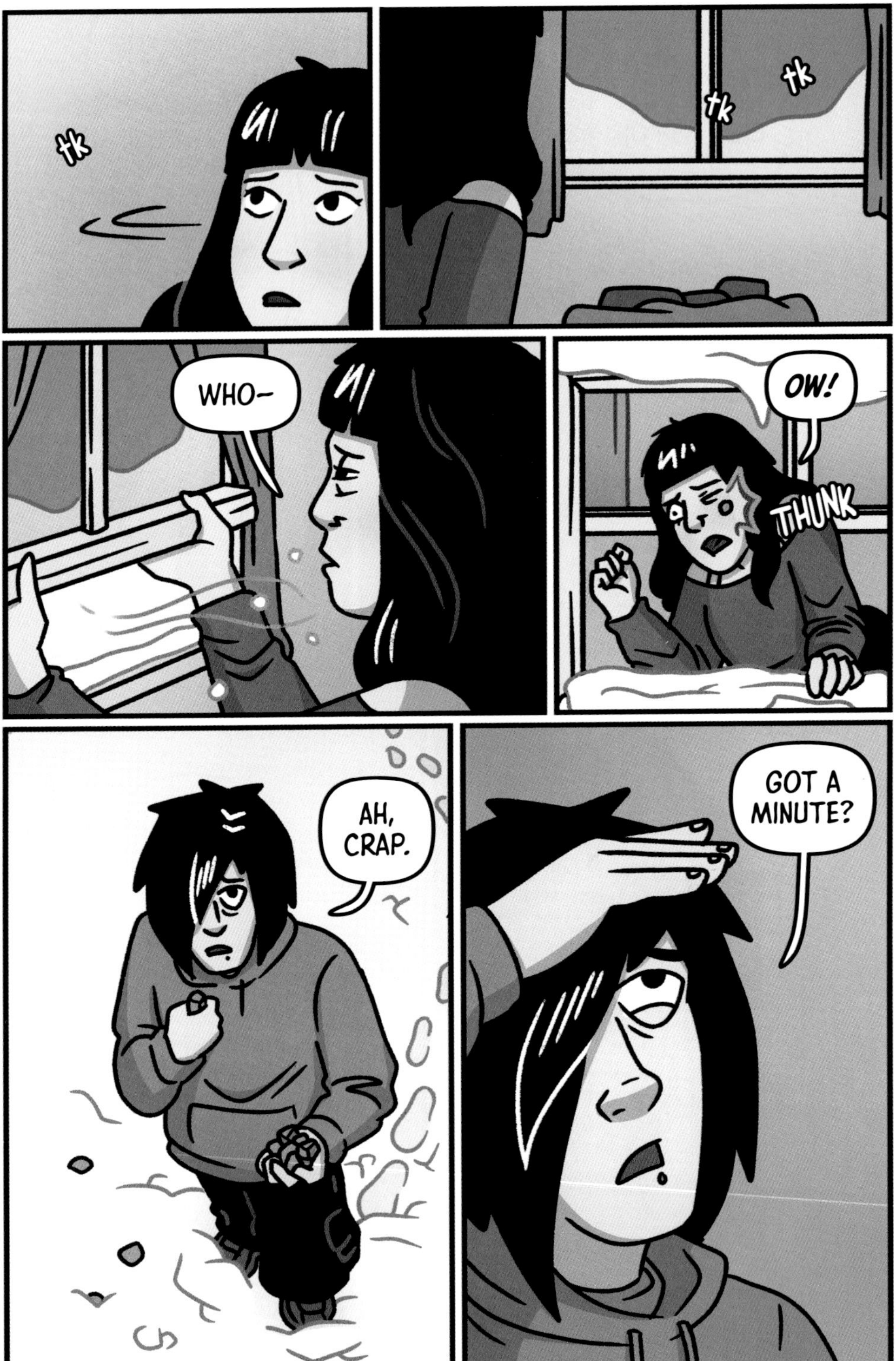
tk
tk
tk
WHO-
OW!
THUNK
AH, CRAP.
GOT A MINUTE?

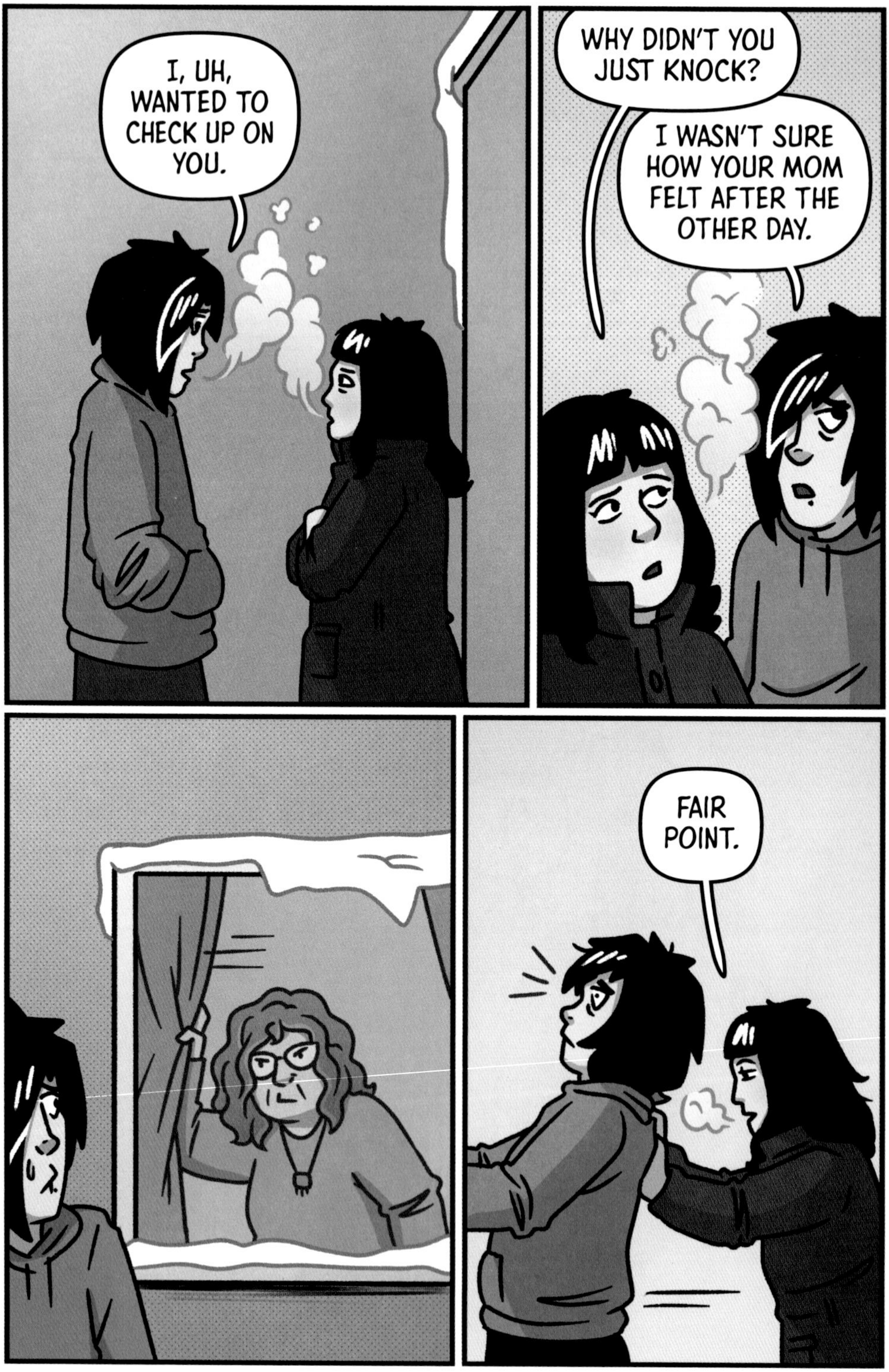
I, UH, WANTED TO CHECK UP ON YOU.
WHY DIDN'T YOU JUST KNOCK?
I WASN'T SURE HOW YOUR MOM FELT AFTER THE OTHER DAY.
FAIR POINT.

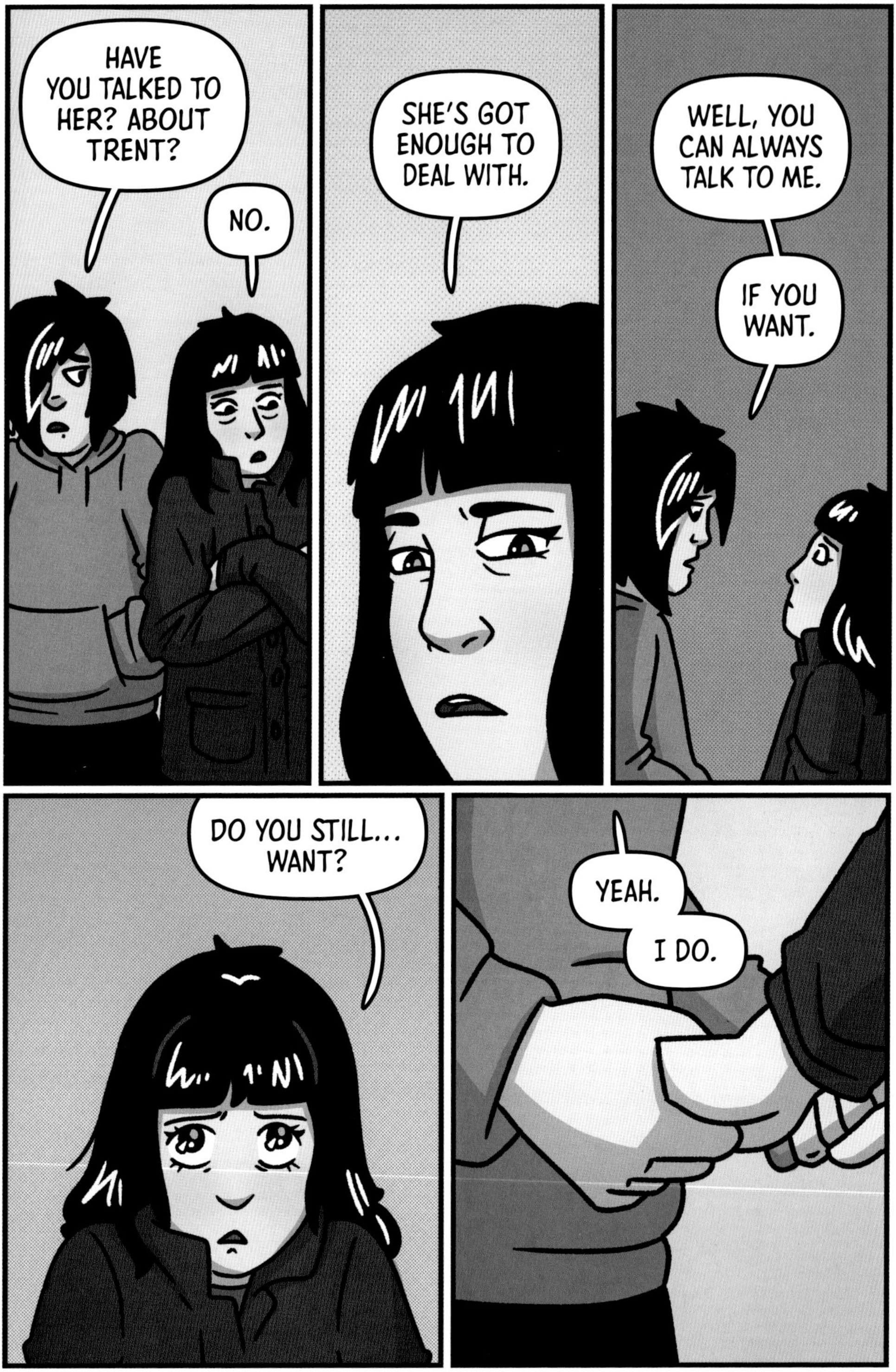
HAVE YOU TALKED TO HER? ABOUT TRENT?
NO.
SHE'S GOT ENOUGH TO DEAL WITH.
WELL, YOU CAN ALWAYS TALK TO ME.
IF YOU WANT.
DO YOU STILL... WANT?
YEAH.
I DO.

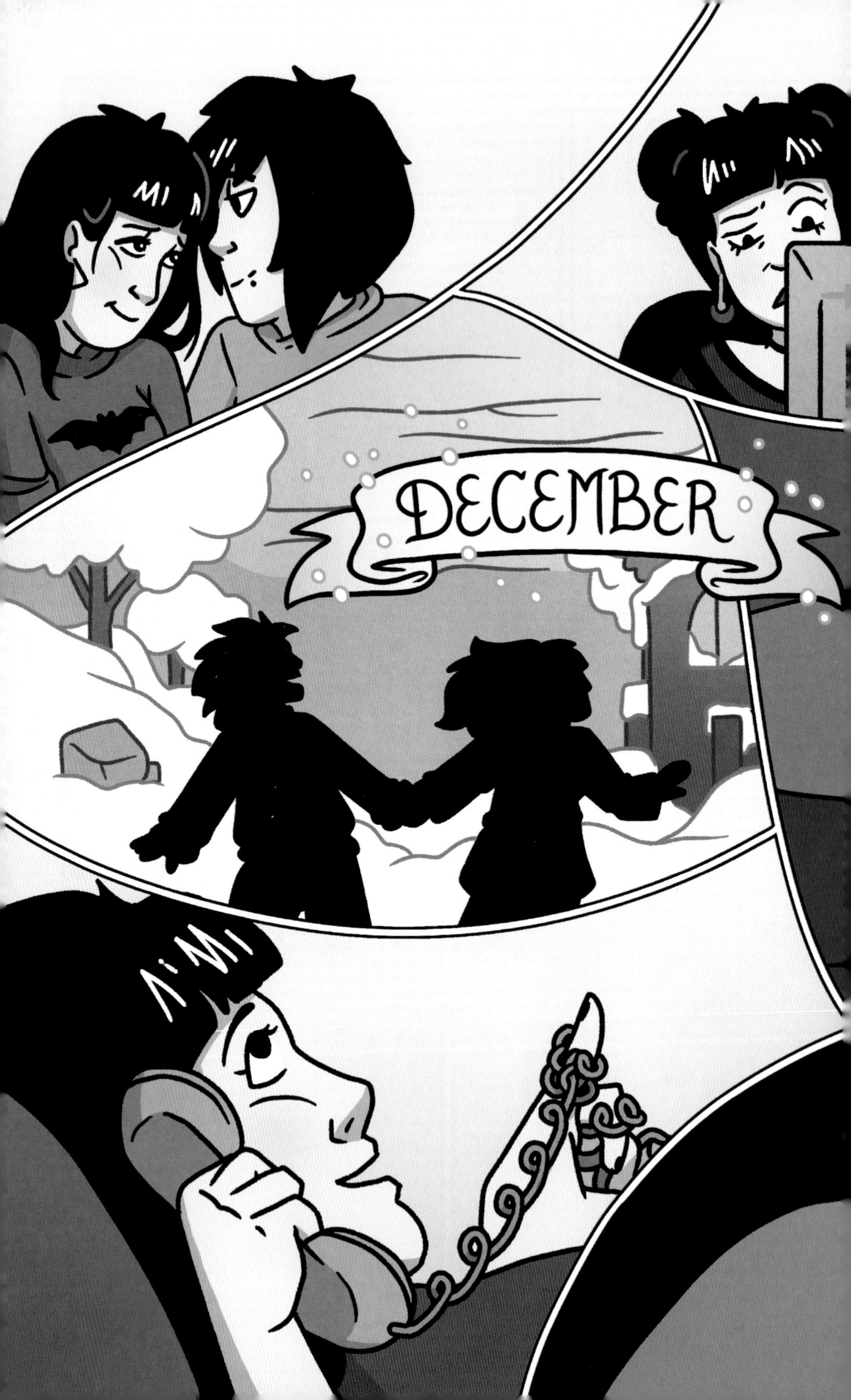
DECEMBER

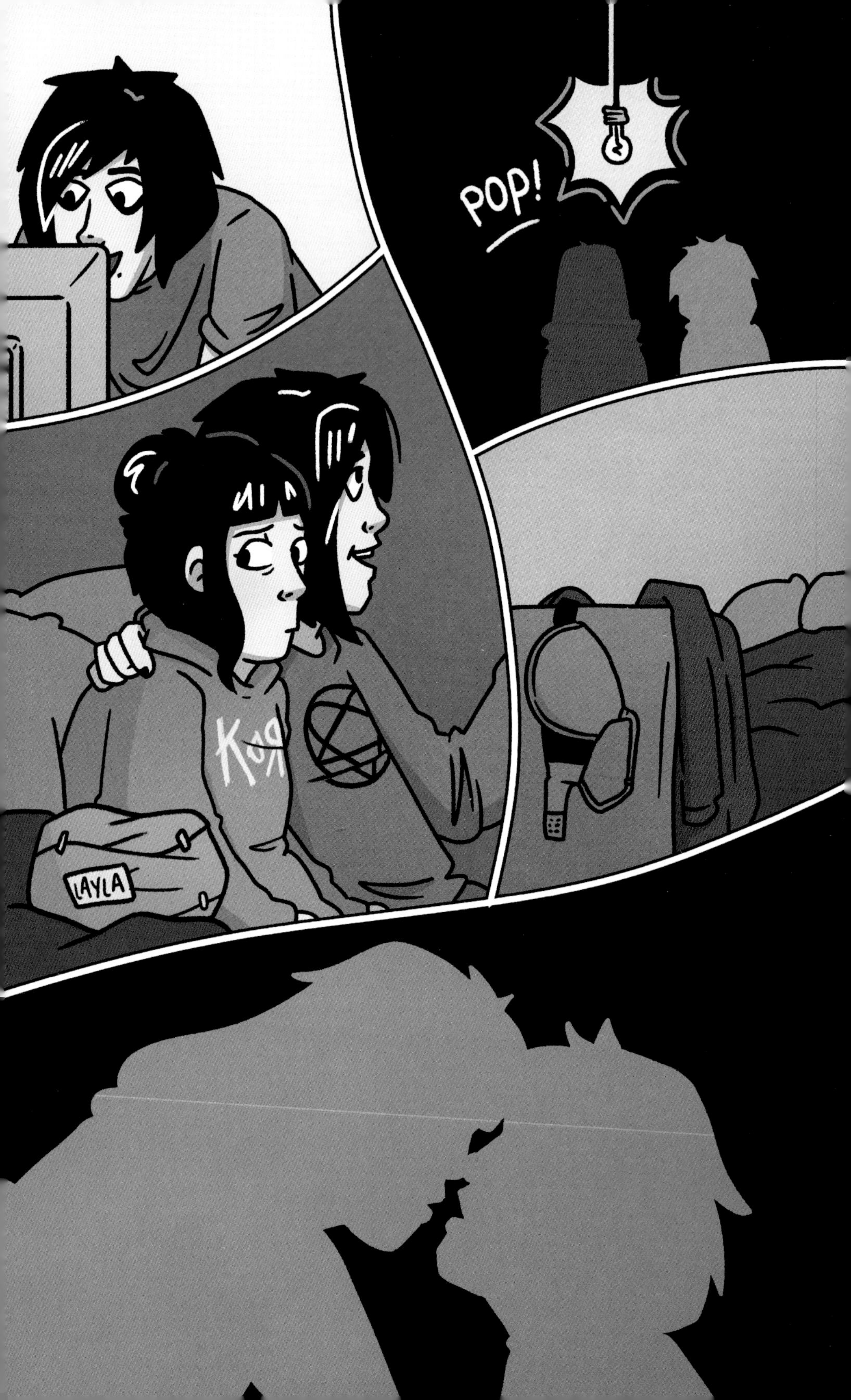
POP!
KoЯn
LAYLA

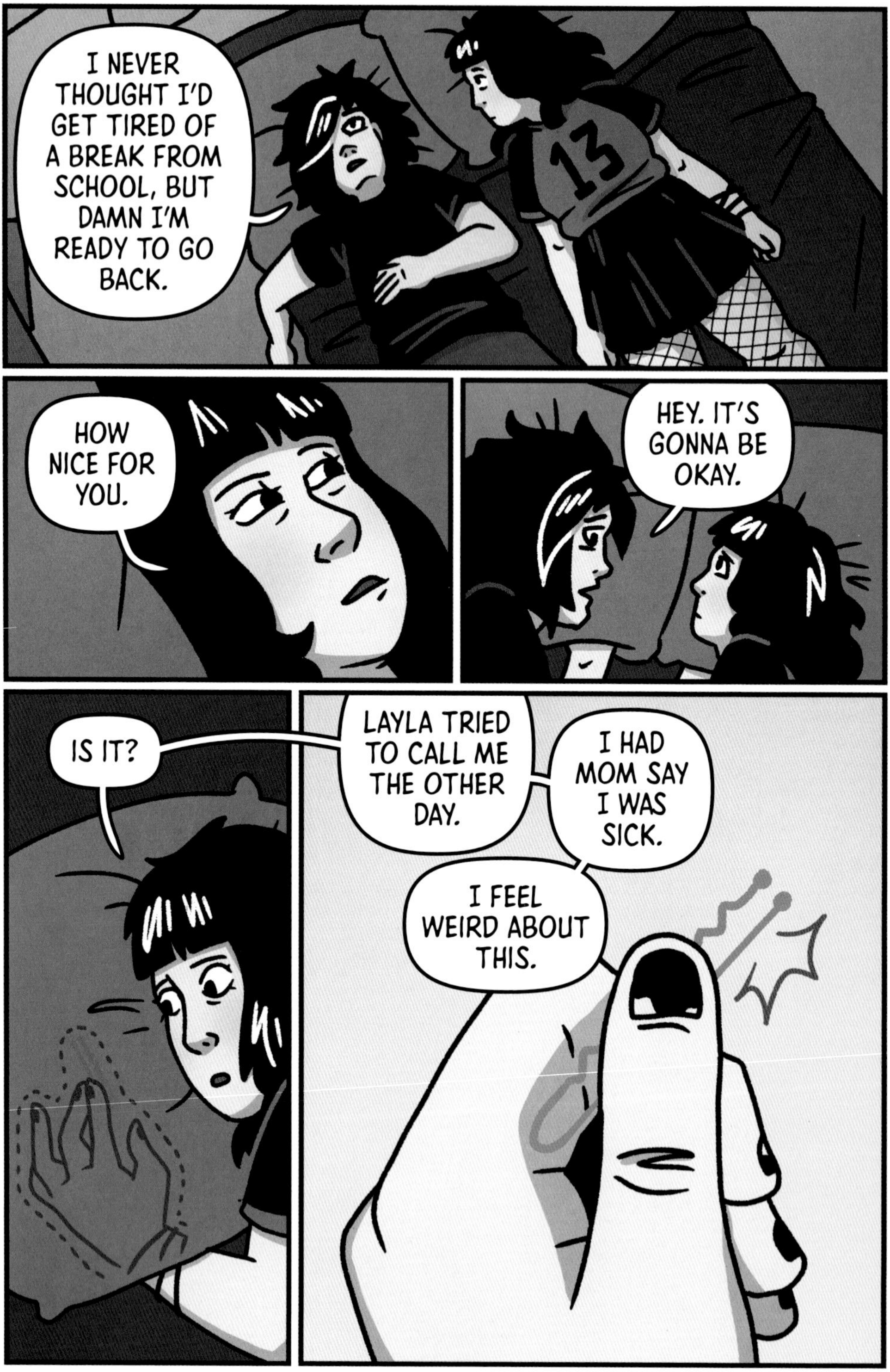
I NEVER THOUGHT I'D GET TIRED OF A BREAK FROM SCHOOL, BUT DAMN I'M READY TO GO BACK.
HOW NICE FOR YOU.
HEY. IT'S GONNA BE OKAY.
IS IT?
LAYLA TRIED TO CALL ME THE OTHER DAY.
I HAD MOM SAY I WAS SICK.
I FEEL WEIRD ABOUT THIS.

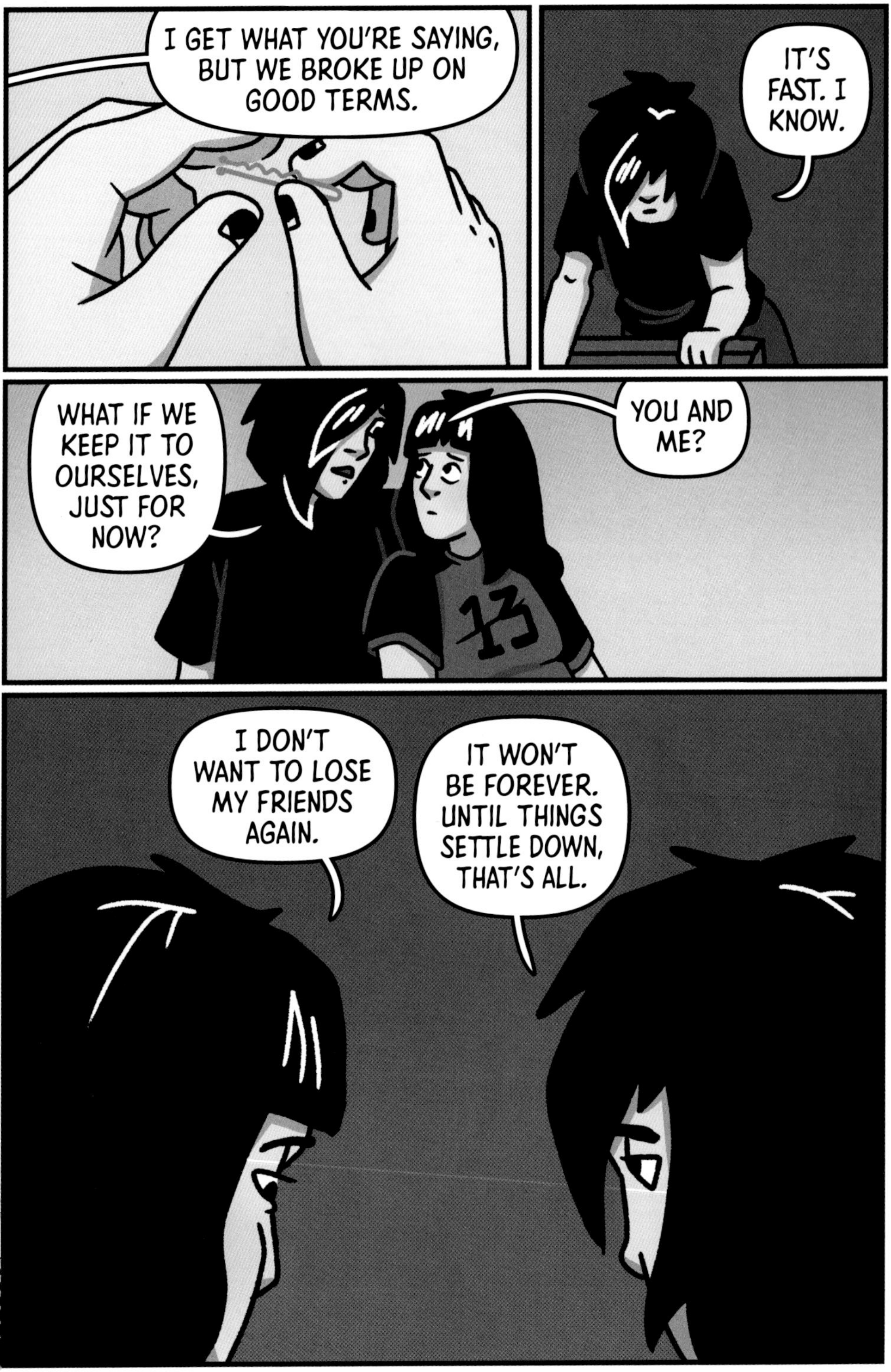
I GET WHAT YOU'RE SAYING, BUT WE BROKE UP ON GOOD TERMS.
IT'S FAST. I KNOW.
WHAT IF WE KEEP IT TO OURSELVES, JUST FOR NOW?
YOU AND ME?
13
I DON'T WANT TO LOSE MY FRIENDS AGAIN.
IT WON'T BE FOREVER. UNTIL THINGS SETTLE DOWN, THAT'S ALL.

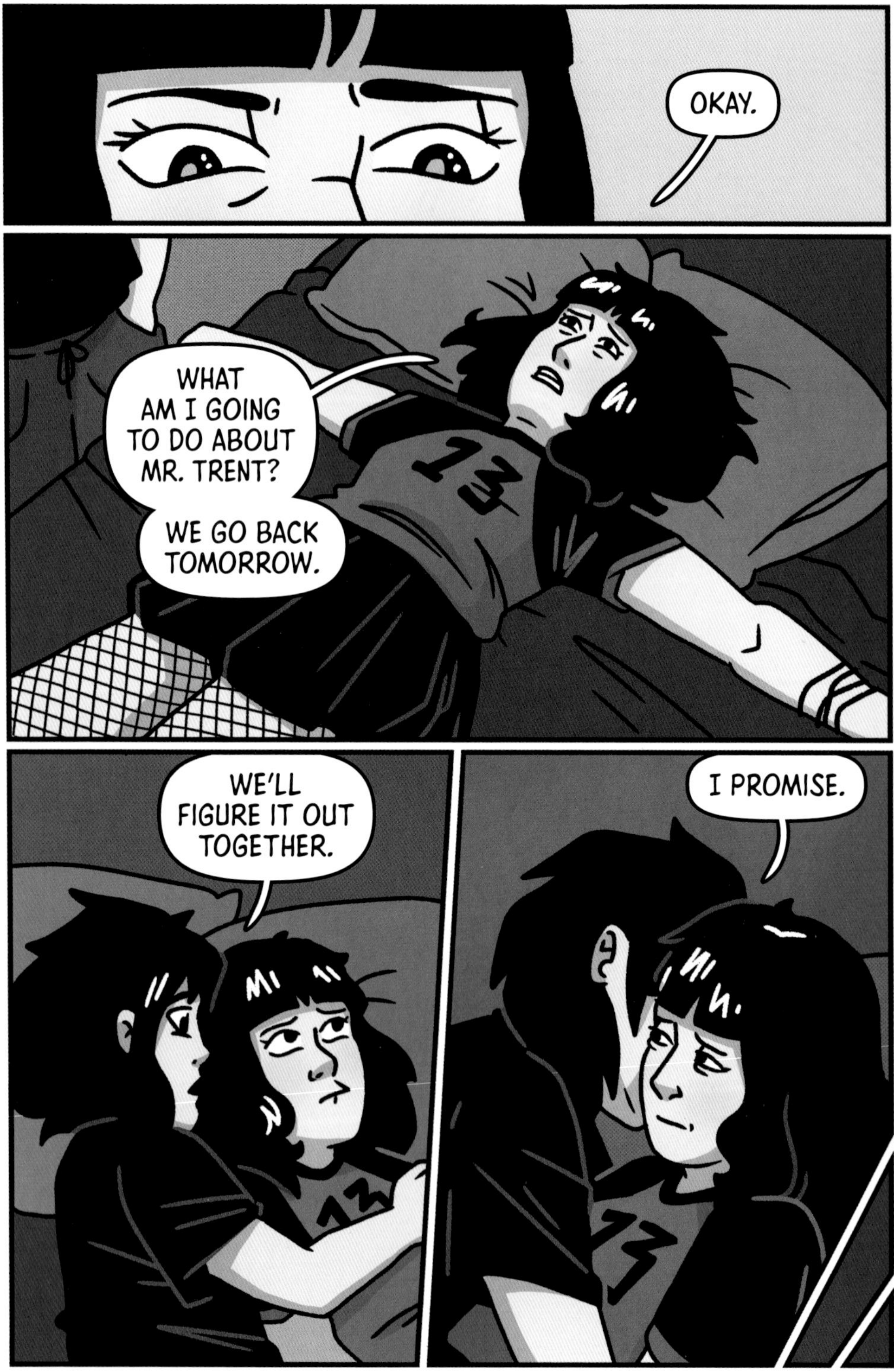
OKAY.
WHAT AM I GOING TO DO ABOUT MR. TRENT?
WE GO BACK TOMORROW.
WE'LL FIGURE IT OUT TOGETHER.
I PROMISE.

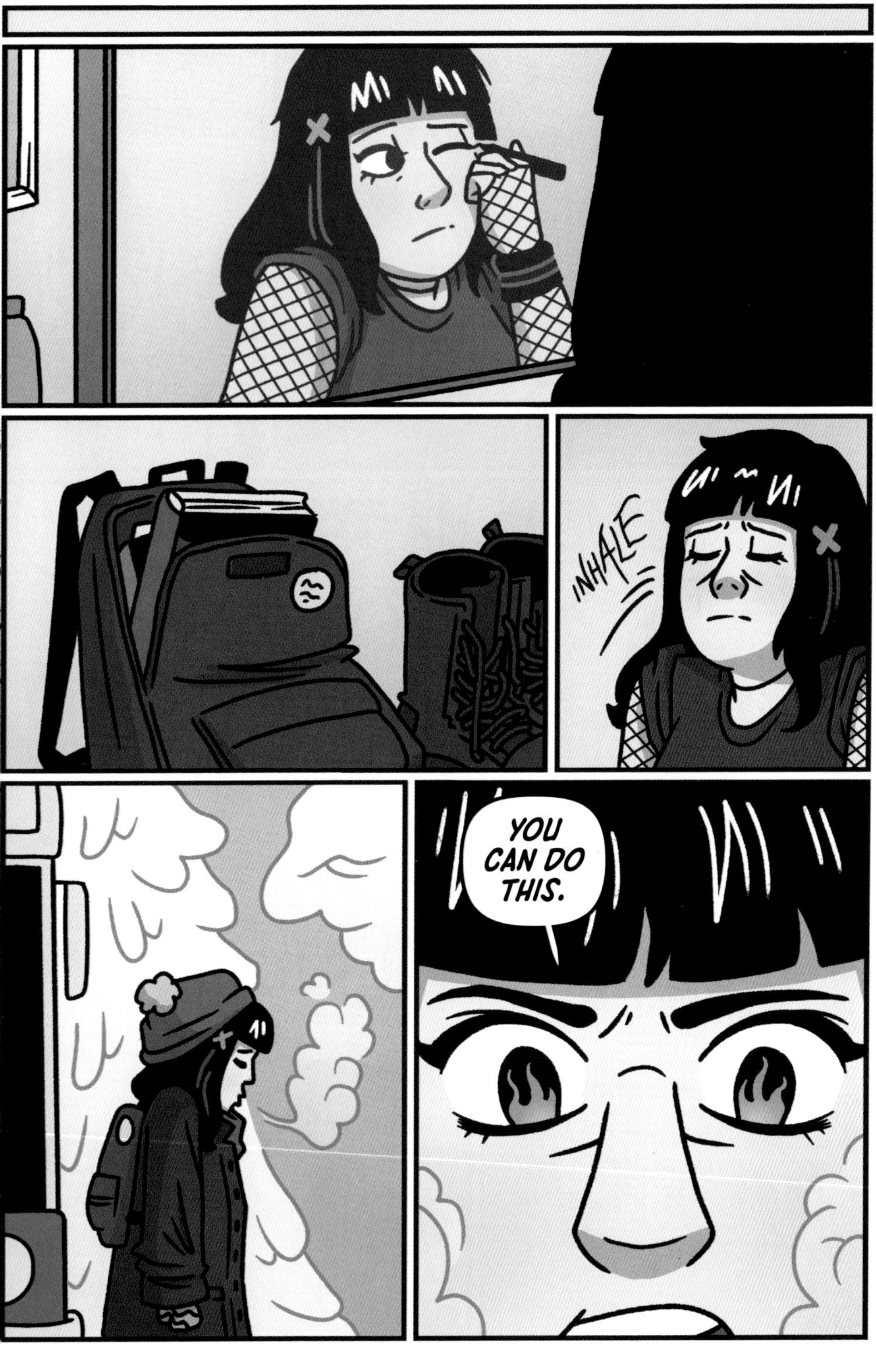
INHALE
YOU CAN DO THIS.

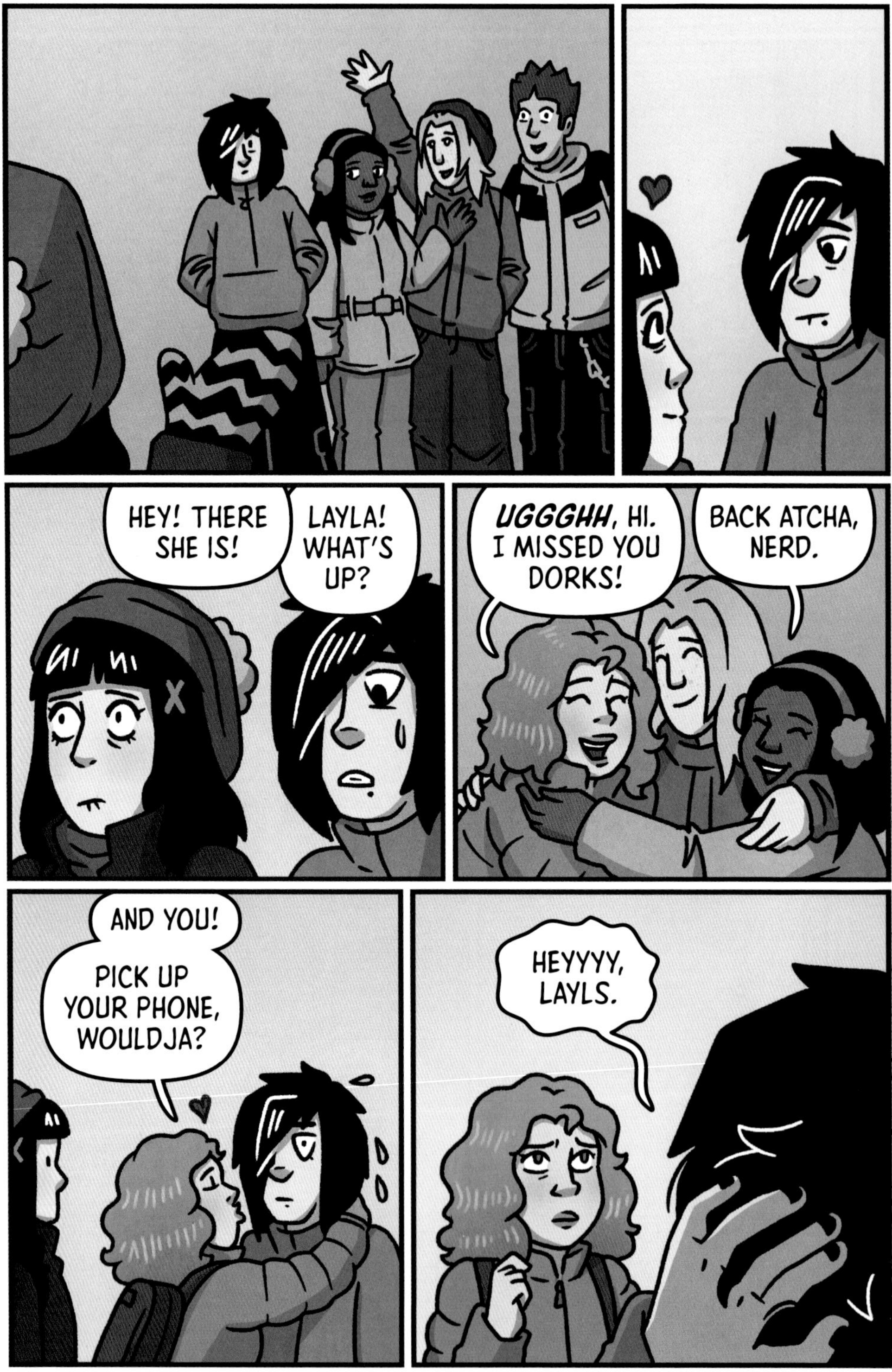
HEY! THERE SHE IS!
LAYLA! WHAT'S UP?
UGGGHH, HI. I MISSED YOU DORKS!
BACK ATCHA, NERD.
AND YOU!
PICK UP YOUR PHONE, WOULDJA?
HEYYYY, LAYLS.

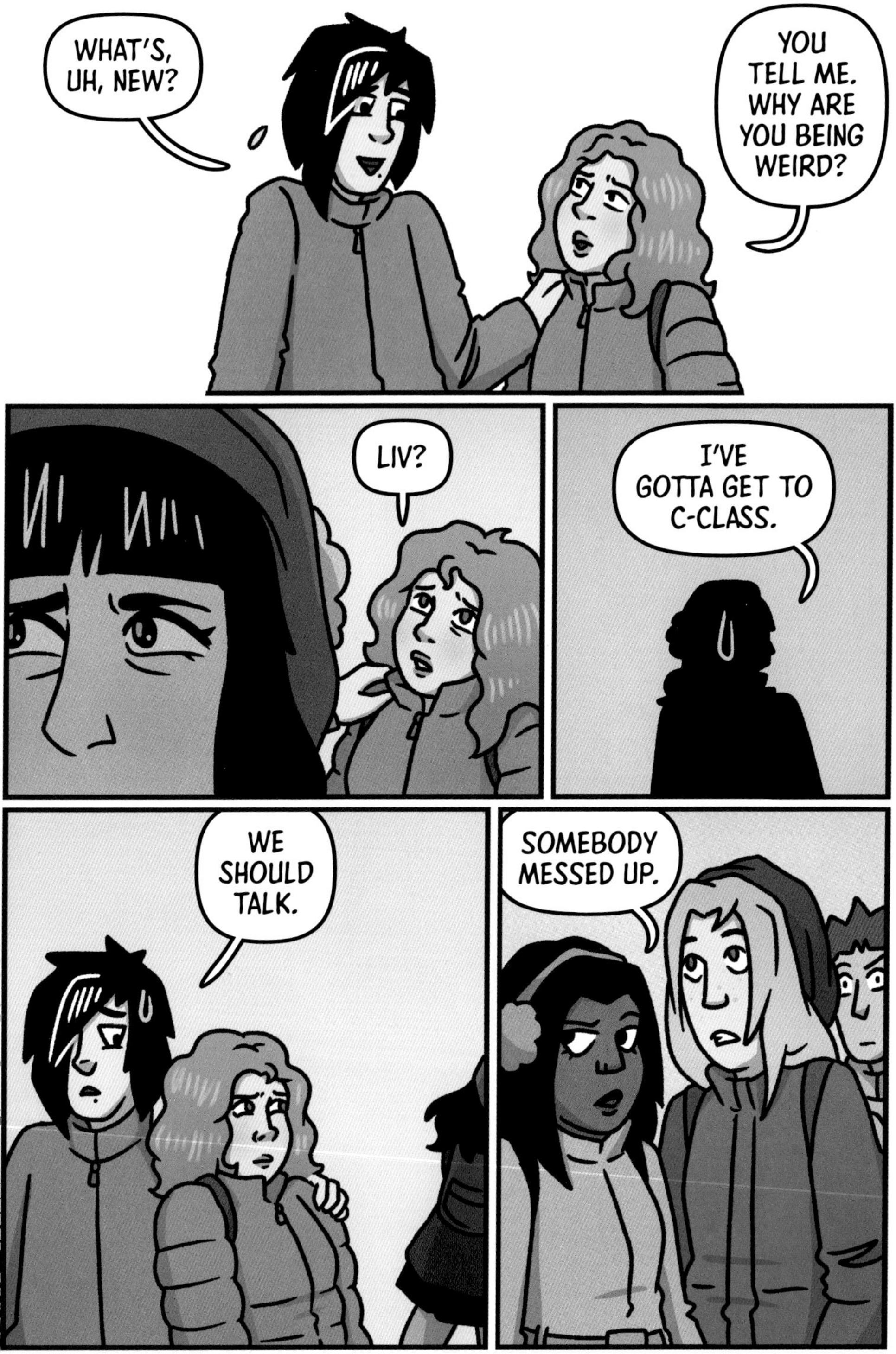
WHAT'S, UH, NEW?
YOU TELL ME. WHY ARE YOU BEING WEIRD?
LIV?
I'VE GOTTA GET TO C-CLASS.
WE SHOULD TALK.
SOMEBODY MESSED UP.

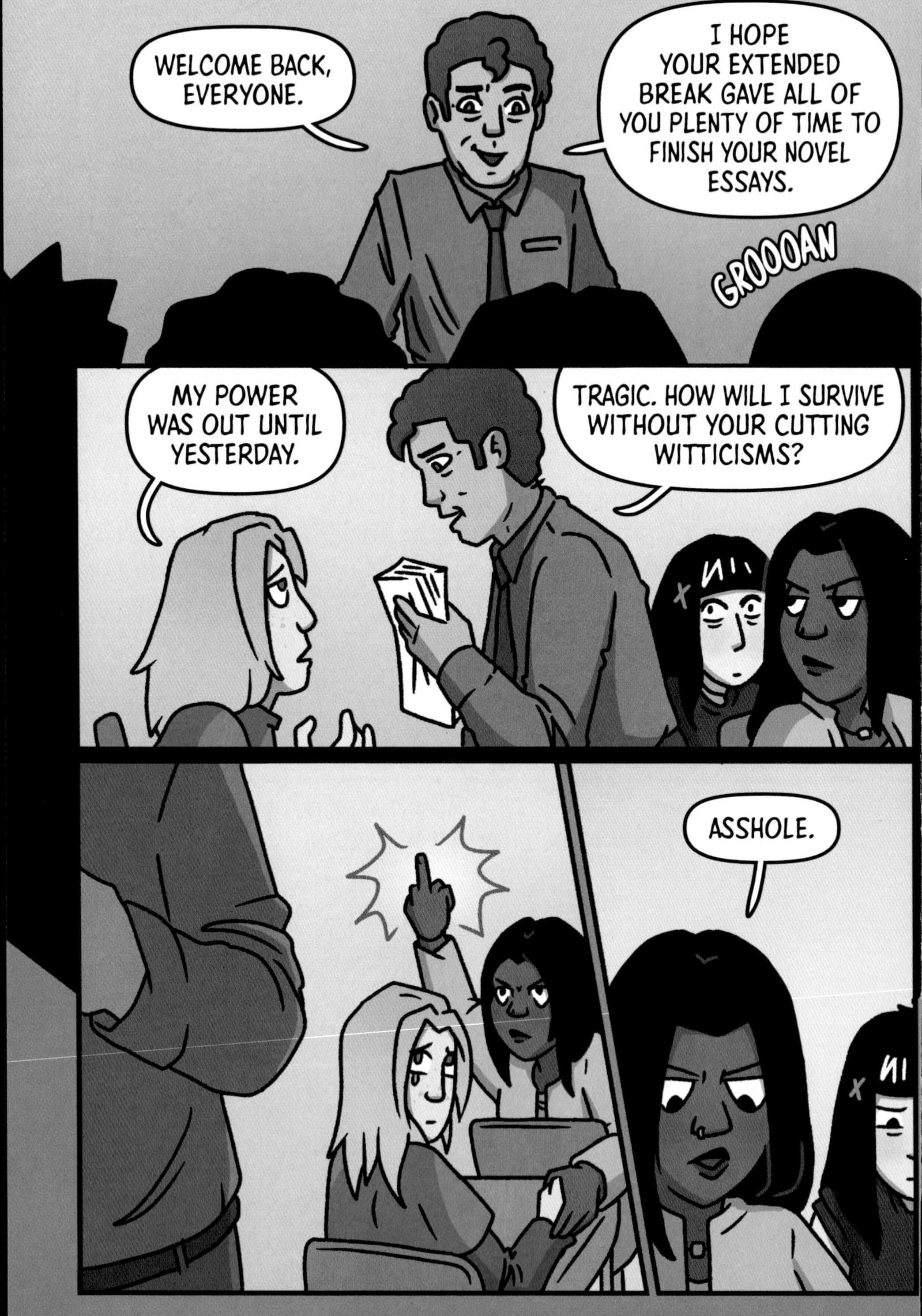
WELCOME BACK, EVERYONE.
I HOPE YOUR EXTENDED BREAK GAVE ALL OF YOU PLENTY OF TIME TO FINISH YOUR NOVEL ESSAYS.
GROOOAN
MY POWER WAS OUT UNTIL YESTERDAY.
TRAGIC. HOW WILL I SURVIVE WITHOUT YOUR CUTTING WITTICISMS?
ASSHOLE.

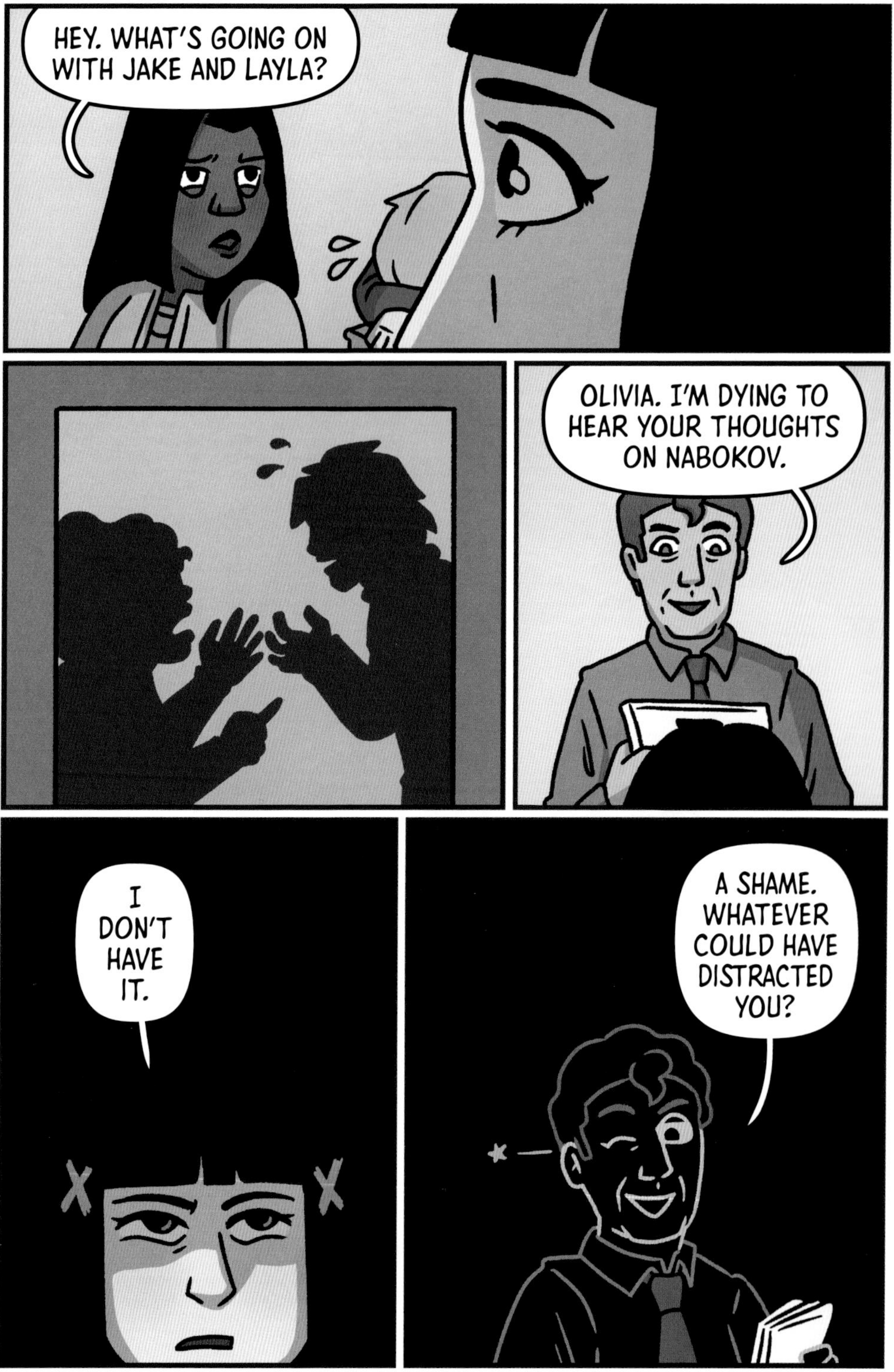
HEY. WHAT'S GOING ON WITH JAKE AND LAYLA?
OLIVIA. I'M DYING TO HEAR YOUR THOUGHTS ON NABOKOV.
I DON'T HAVE IT.
A SHAME. WHATEVER COULD HAVE DISTRACTED YOU?

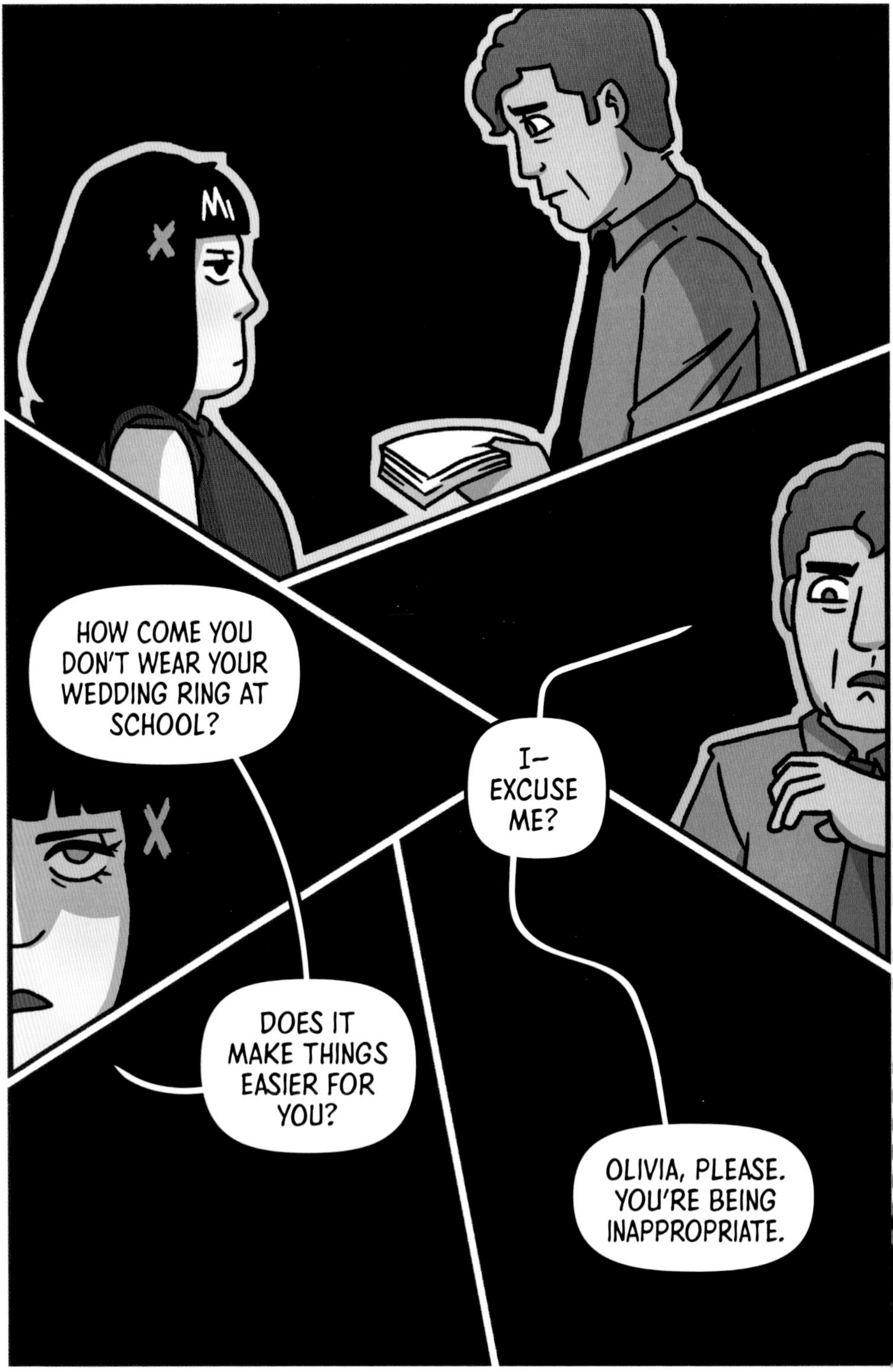
HOW COME YOU DON'T WEAR YOUR WEDDING RING AT SCHOOL?
I— EXCUSE ME?
DOES IT MAKE THINGS EASIER FOR YOU?
OLIVIA, PLEASE. YOU'RE BEING INAPPROPRIATE.

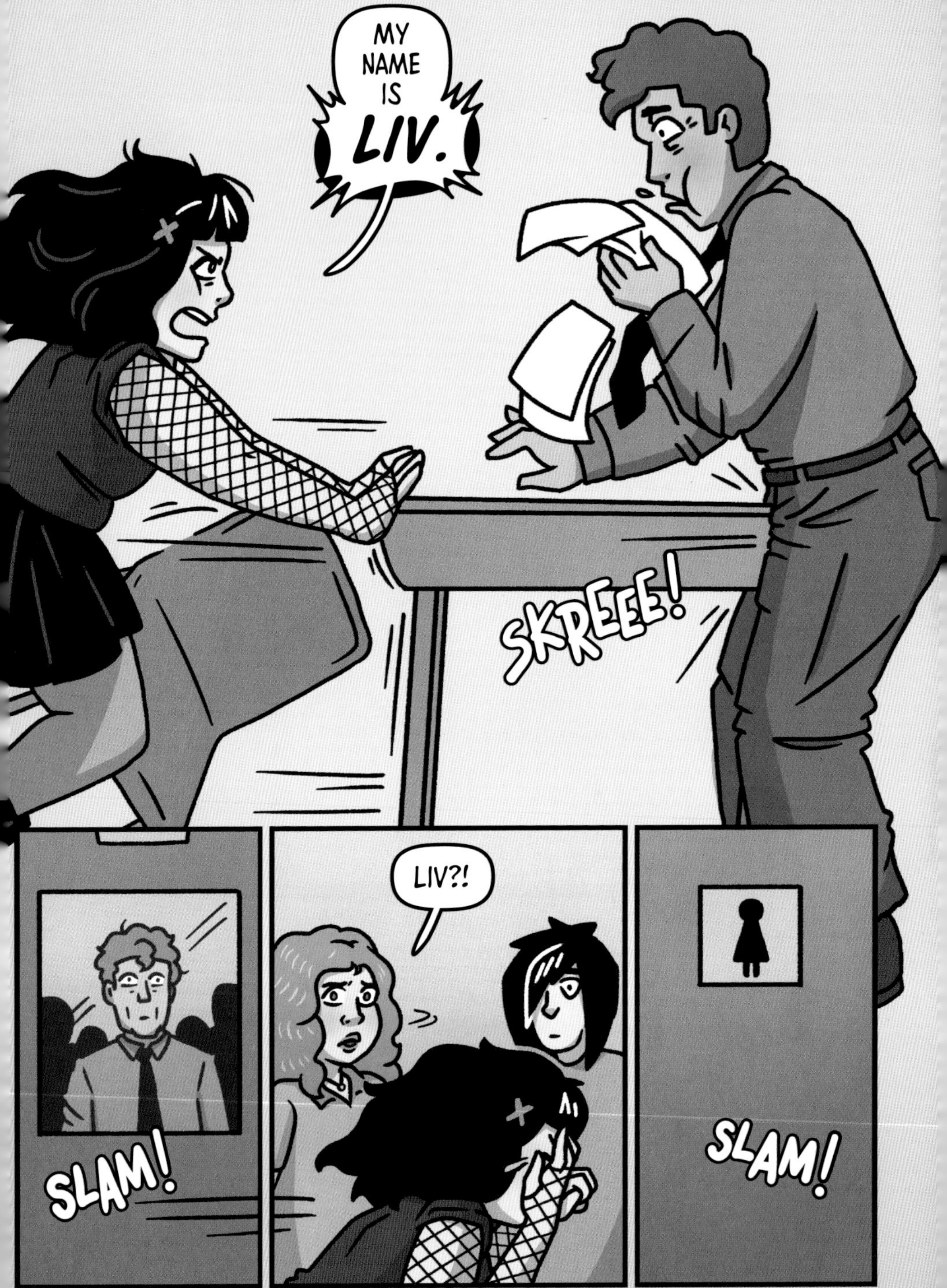
MY NAME IS LIV.
SKREEE!
SLAM!
LIV?!
SLAM!

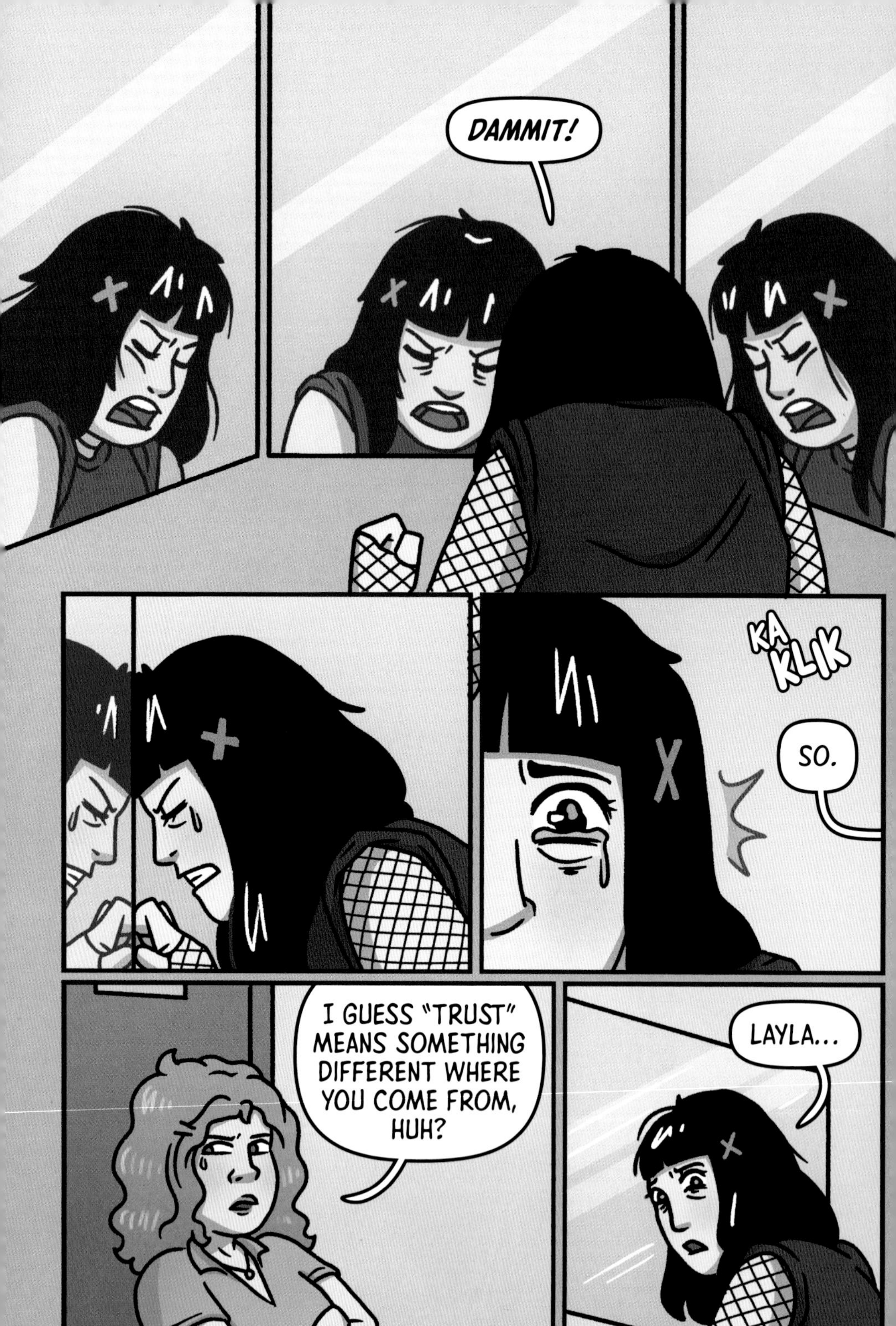
DAMMIT!
KA KLIK
SO.
I GUESS "TRUST" MEANS SOMETHING DIFFERENT WHERE YOU COME FROM, HUH?
LAYLA...

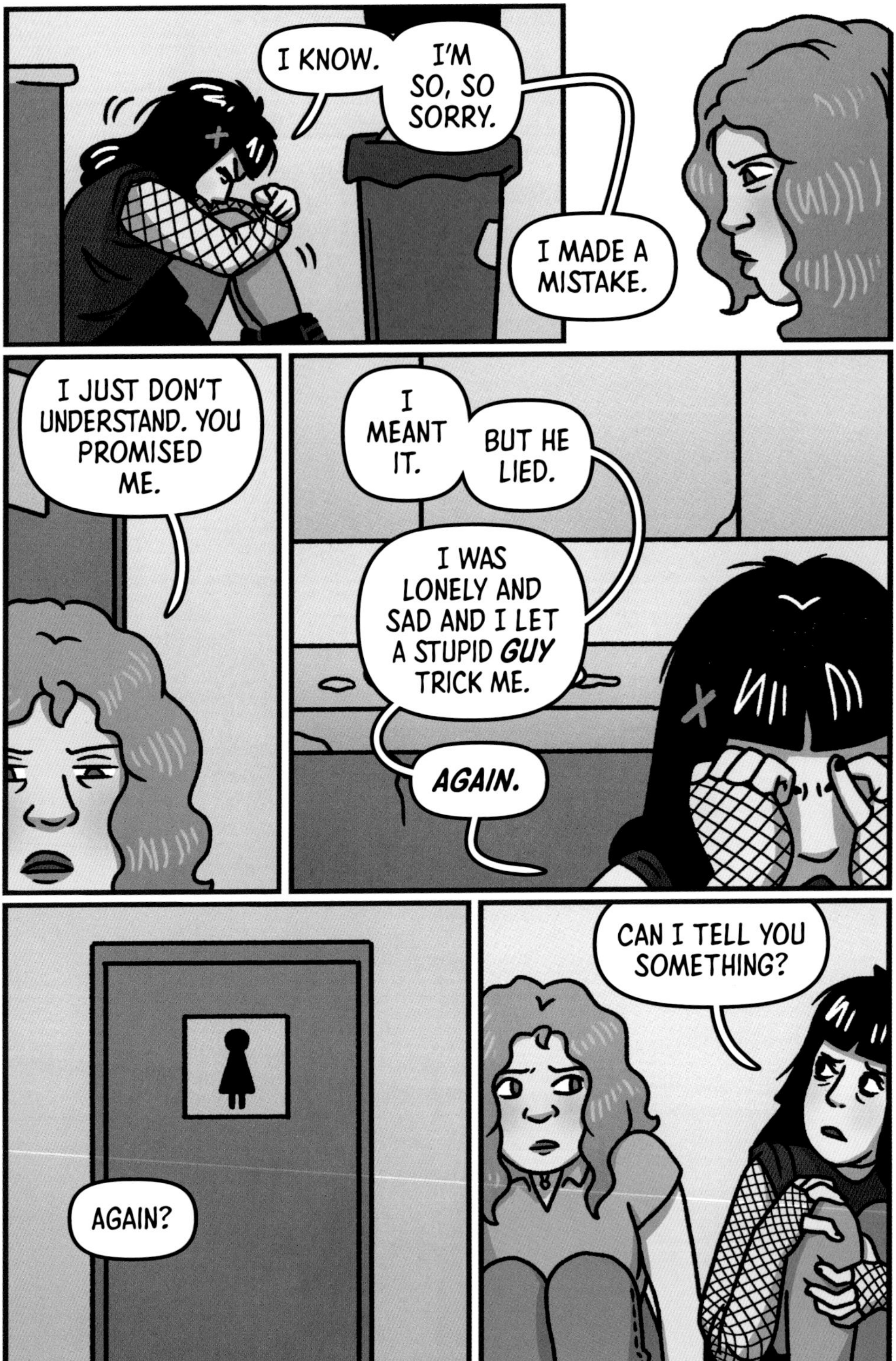
I KNOW.
I'M SO, SO SORRY.
I MADE A MISTAKE.
I JUST DON'T UNDERSTAND. YOU PROMISED ME.
I MEANT IT.
BUT HE LIED.
I WAS LONELY AND SAD AND I LET A STUPID *GUY* TRICK ME.
AGAIN.
AGAIN?
CAN I TELL YOU SOMETHING?

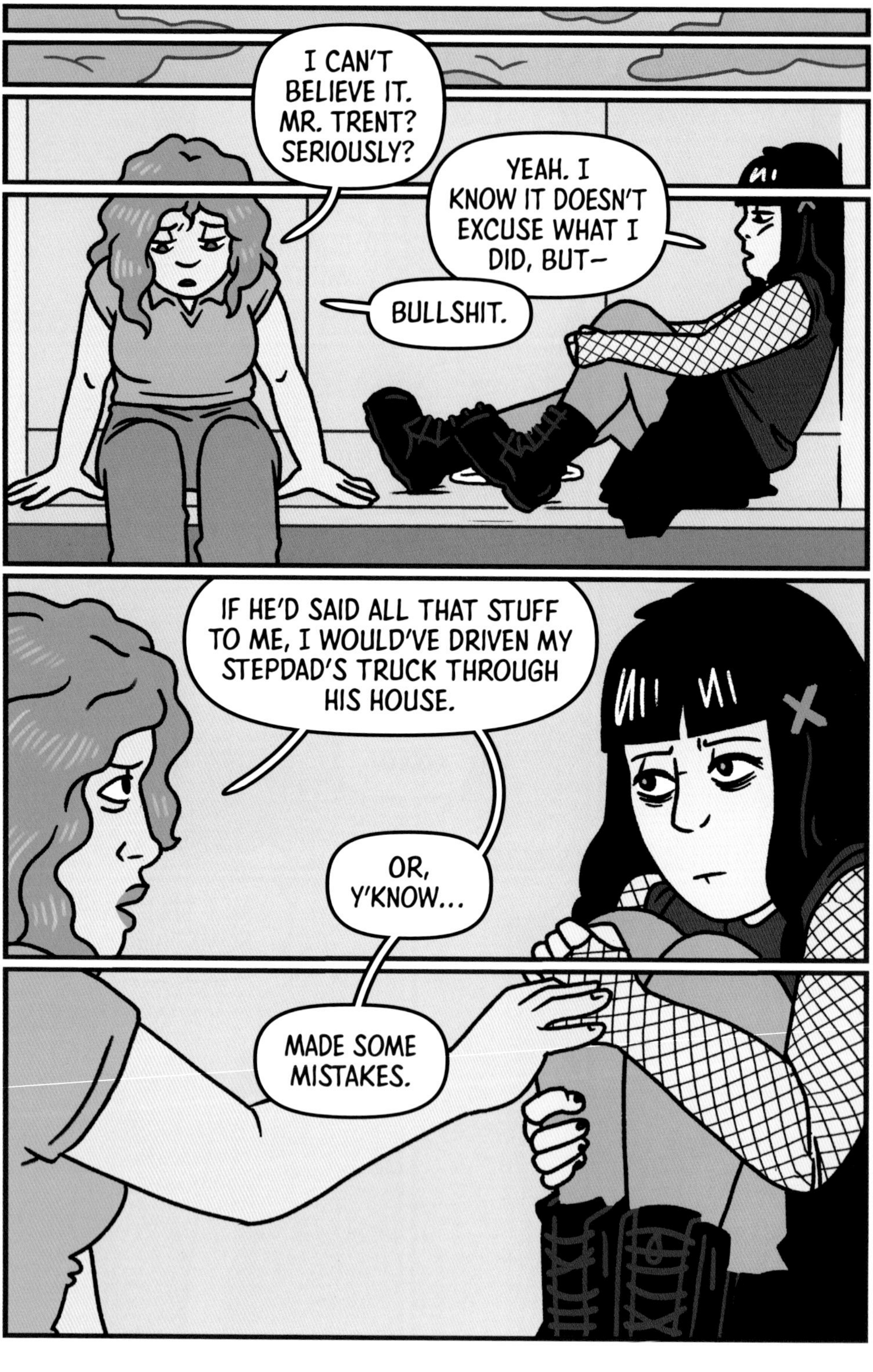
I CAN'T BELIEVE IT. MR. TRENT? SERIOUSLY?
YEAH. I KNOW IT DOESN'T EXCUSE WHAT I DID, BUT—
BULLSHIT.
IF HE'D SAID ALL THAT STUFF TO ME, I WOULD'VE DRIVEN MY STEPDAD'S TRUCK THROUGH HIS HOUSE.
OR, Y'KNOW...
MADE SOME MISTAKES.

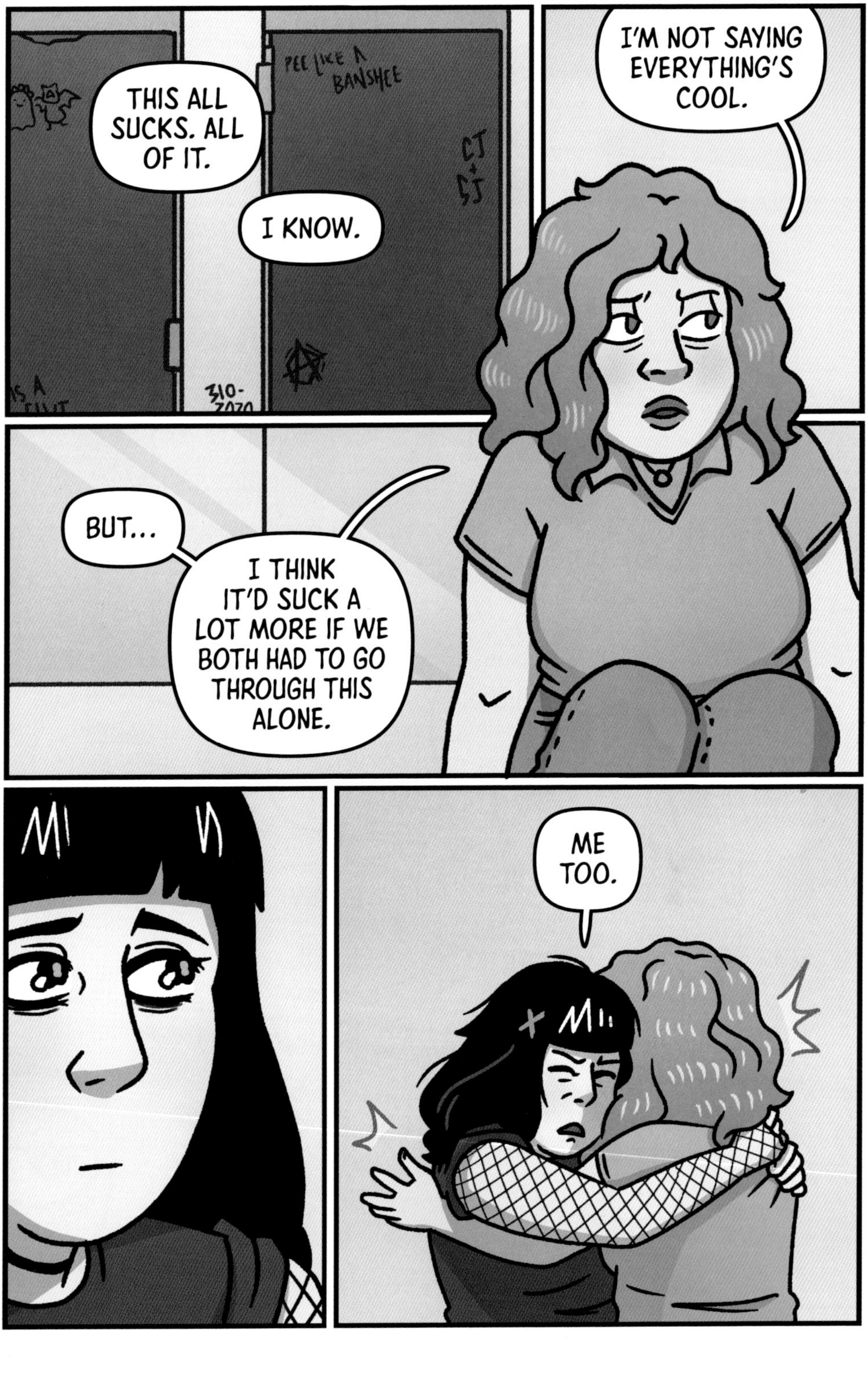
THIS ALL SUCKS. ALL OF IT.
PEE LIKE A BANSHEE
CJ + SJ
I KNOW.
I'M NOT SAYING EVERYTHING'S COOL.
BUT...
I THINK IT'D SUCK A LOT MORE IF WE BOTH HAD TO GO THROUGH THIS ALONE.
ME TOO.

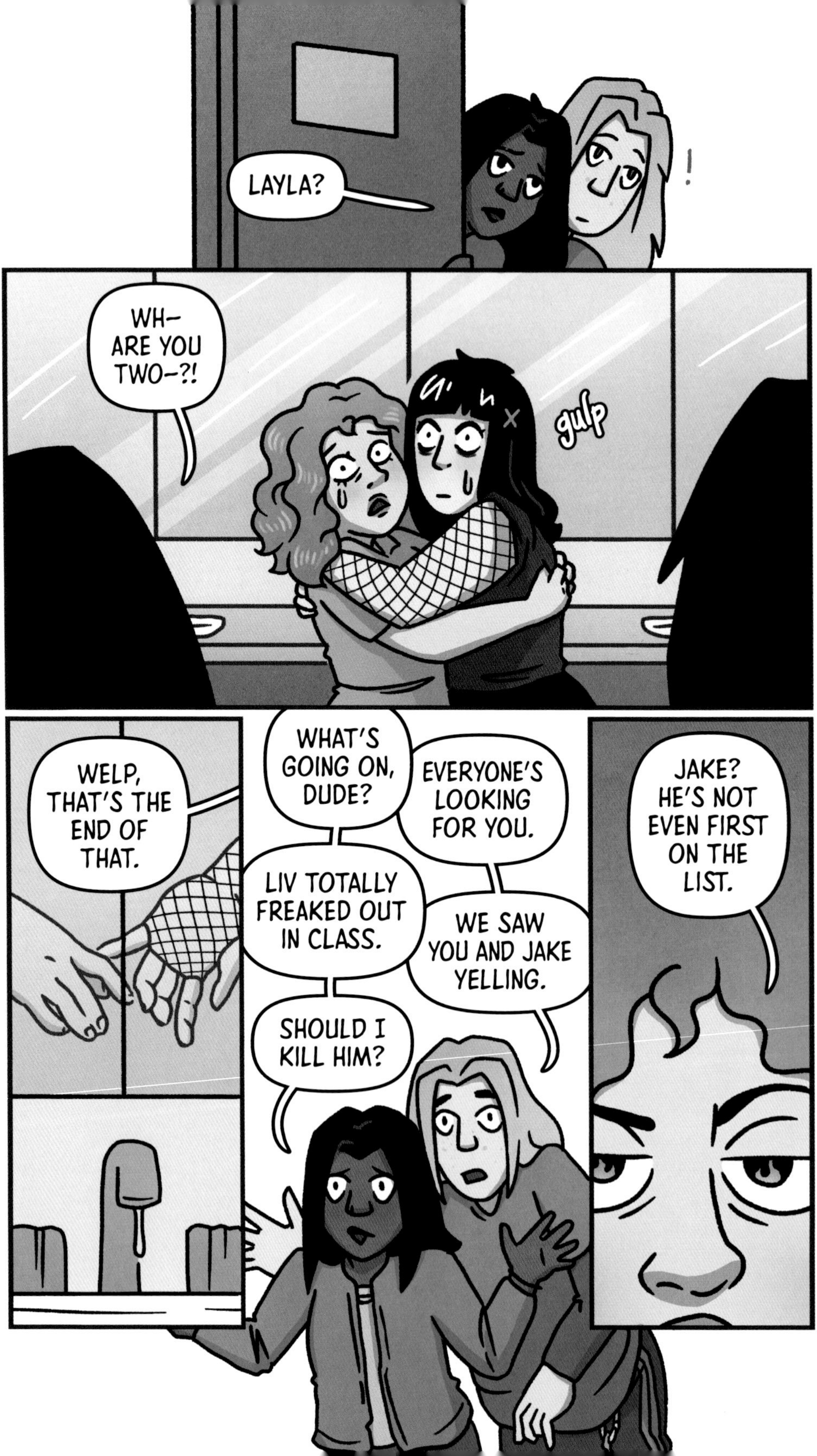

LAYLA?
!
WH– ARE YOU TWO–?!
gulp
WELP, THAT'S THE END OF THAT.
WHAT'S GOING ON, DUDE?
EVERYONE'S LOOKING FOR YOU.
LIV TOTALLY FREAKED OUT IN CLASS.
WE SAW YOU AND JAKE YELLING.
SHOULD I KILL HIM?
JAKE? HE'S NOT EVEN FIRST ON THE LIST.

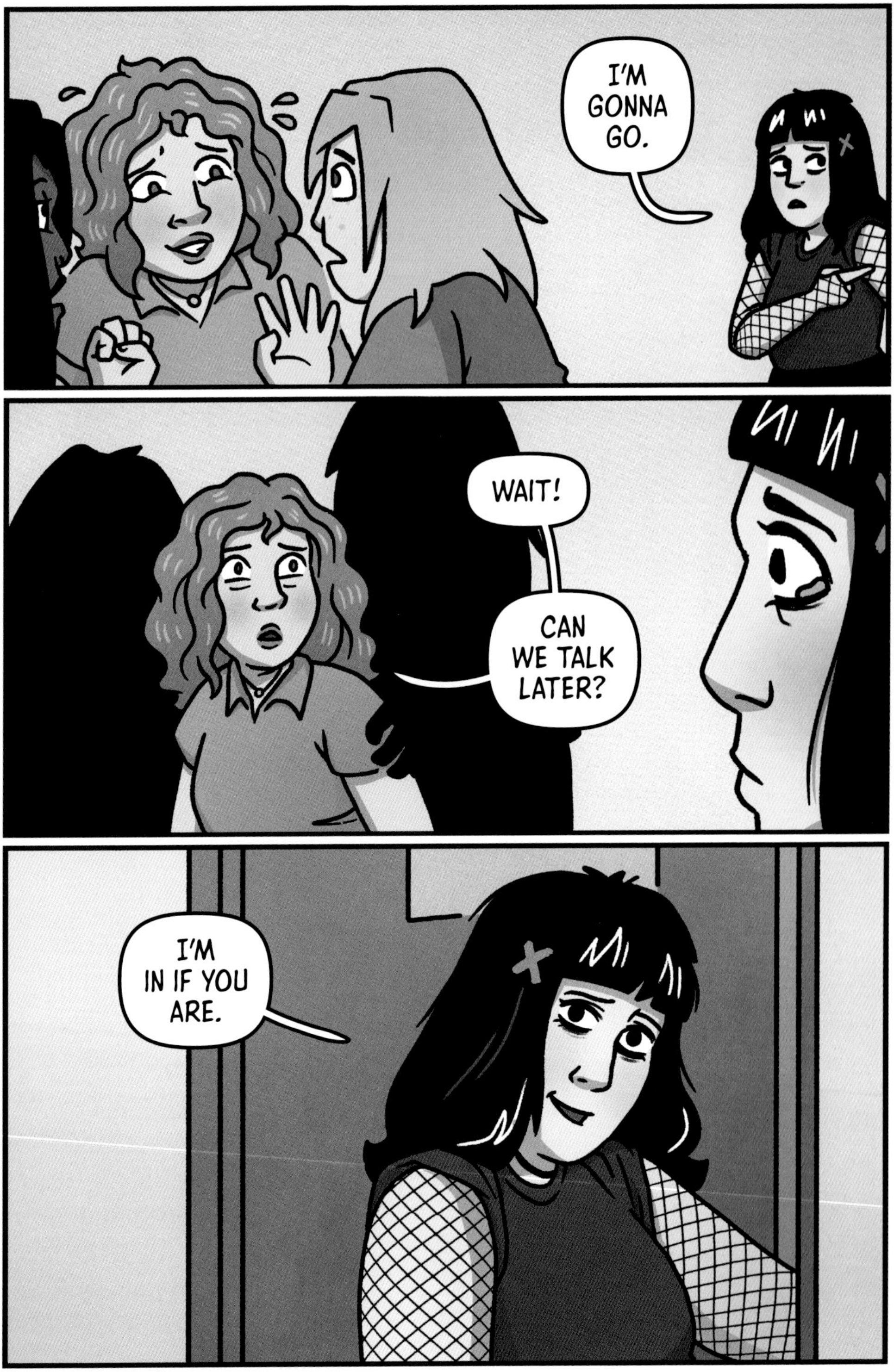
I'M GONNA GO.
WAIT!
CAN WE TALK LATER?
I'M IN IF YOU ARE.

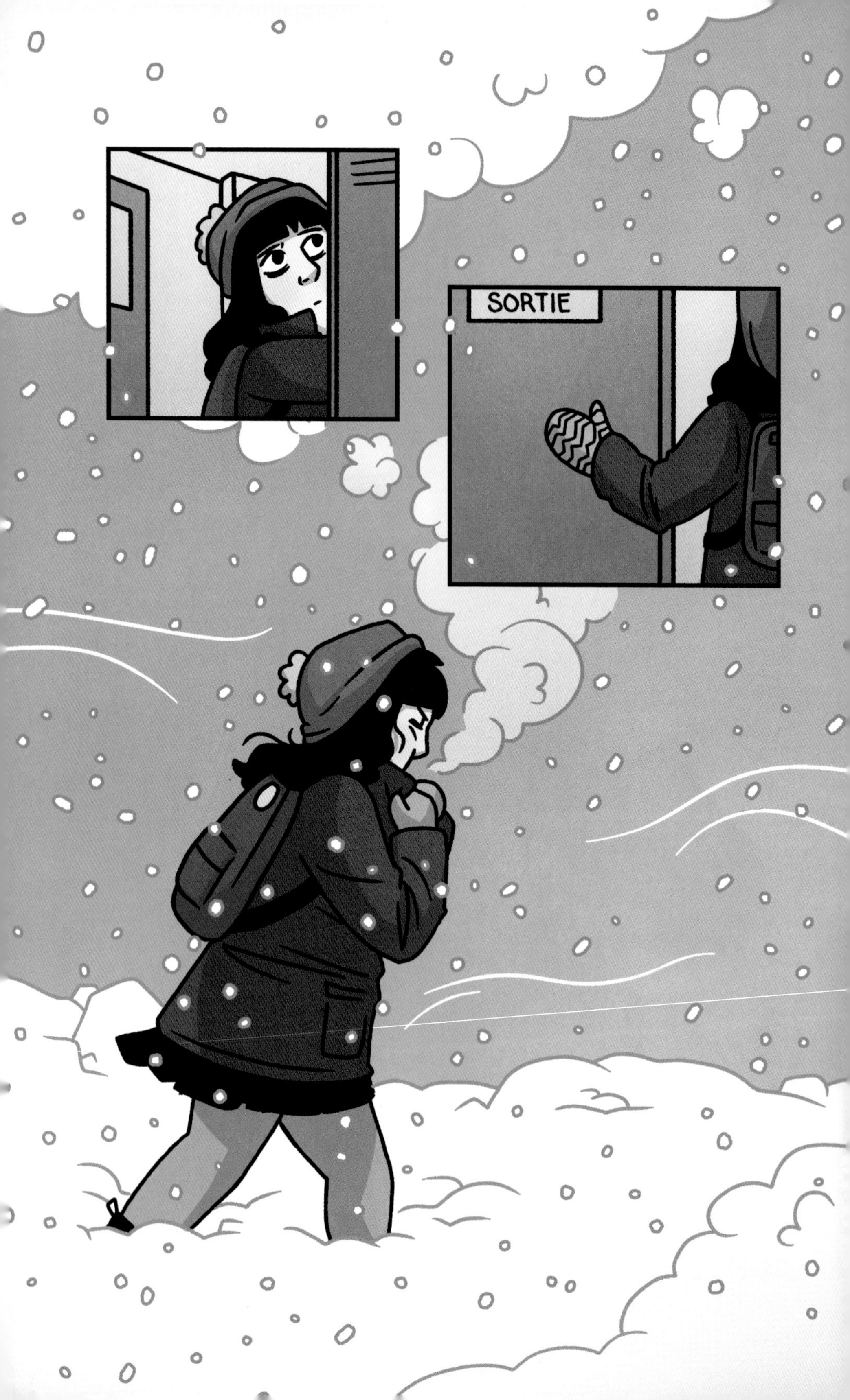
SORTIE

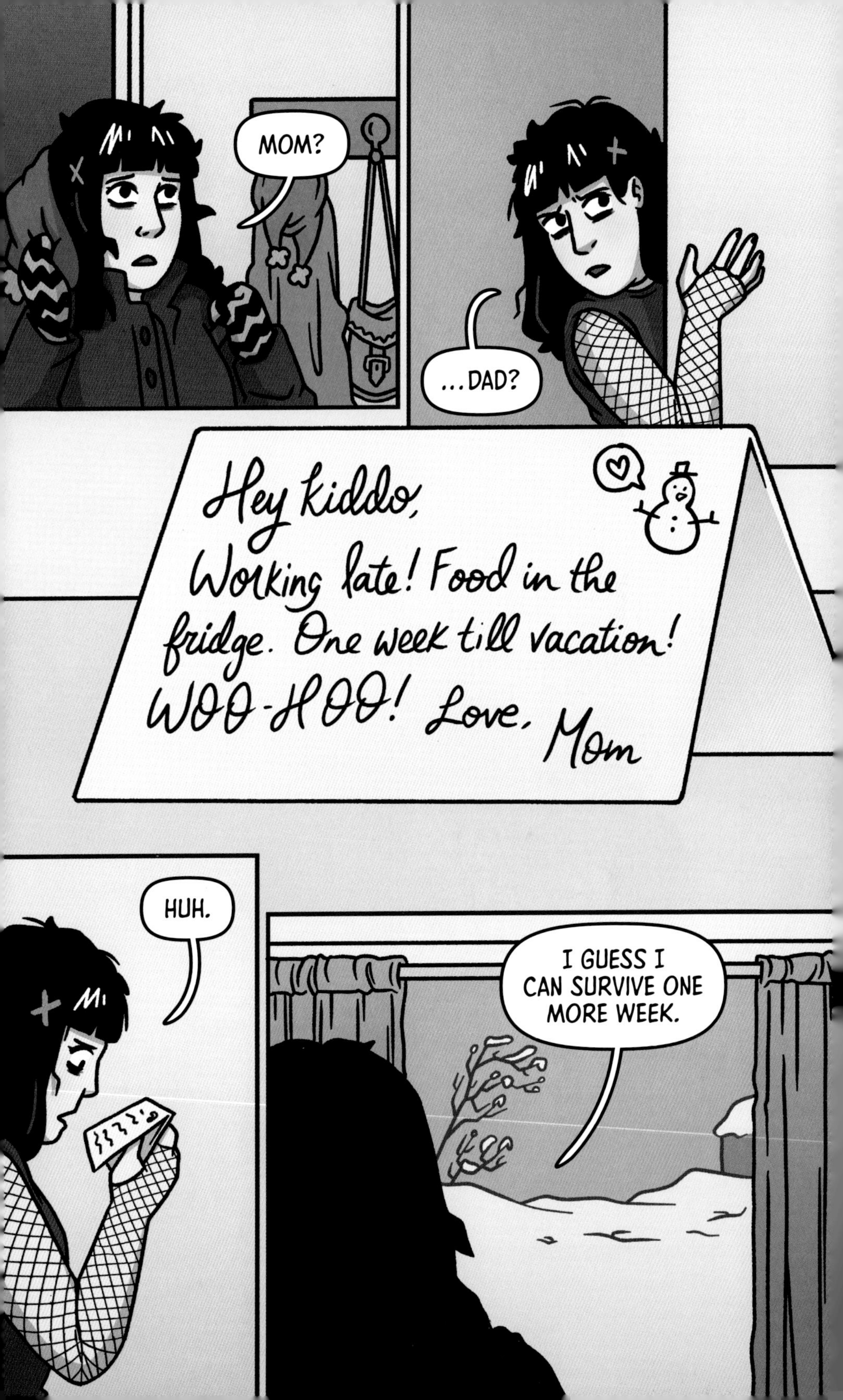
MOM?
...DAD?
Hey kiddo,
Working late! Food in the fridge. One week till vacation! WOO-HOO! Love, Mom
HUH.
I GUESS I CAN SURVIVE ONE MORE WEEK.

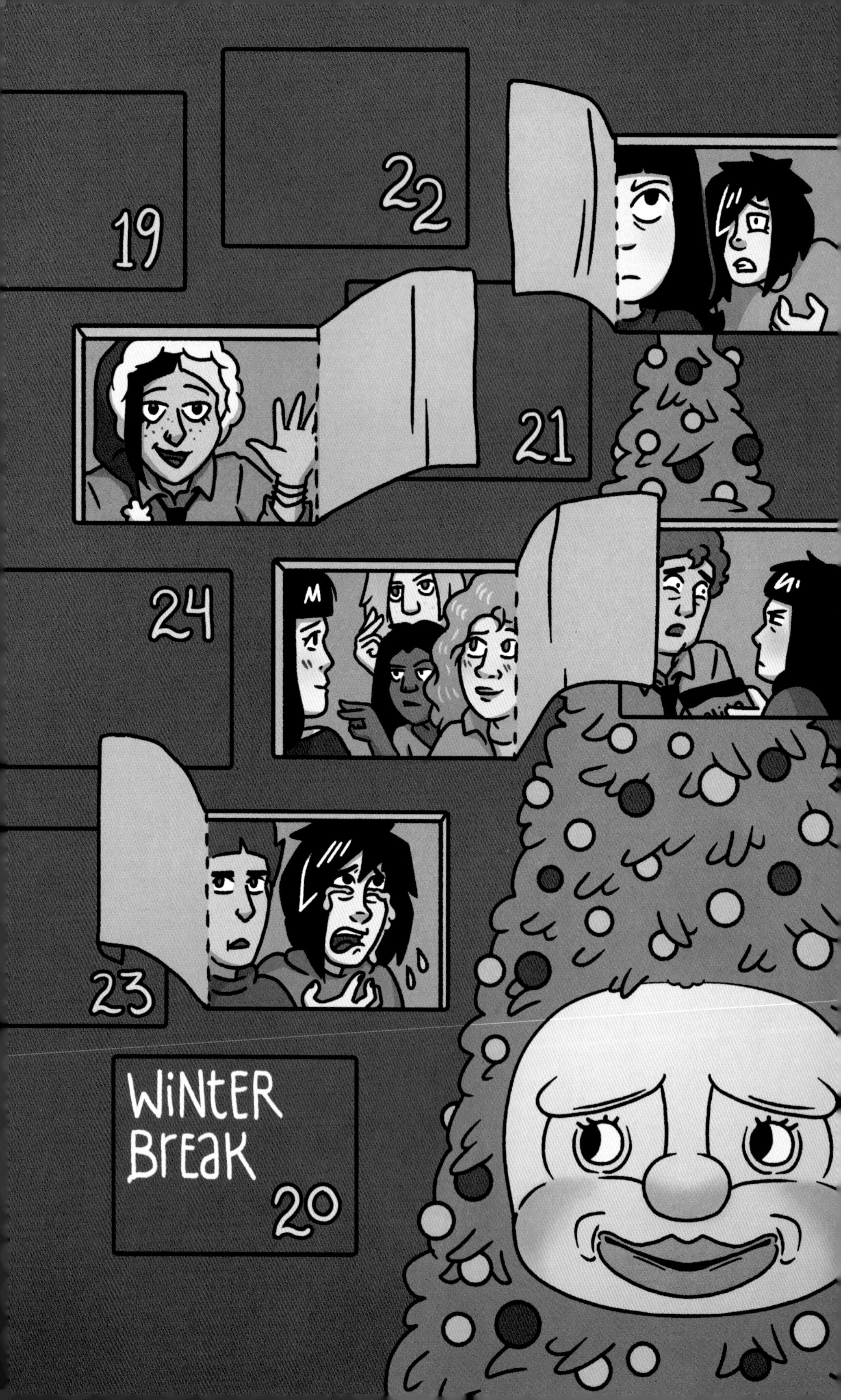
19
22
21
24
23
WINTER BREAK
20

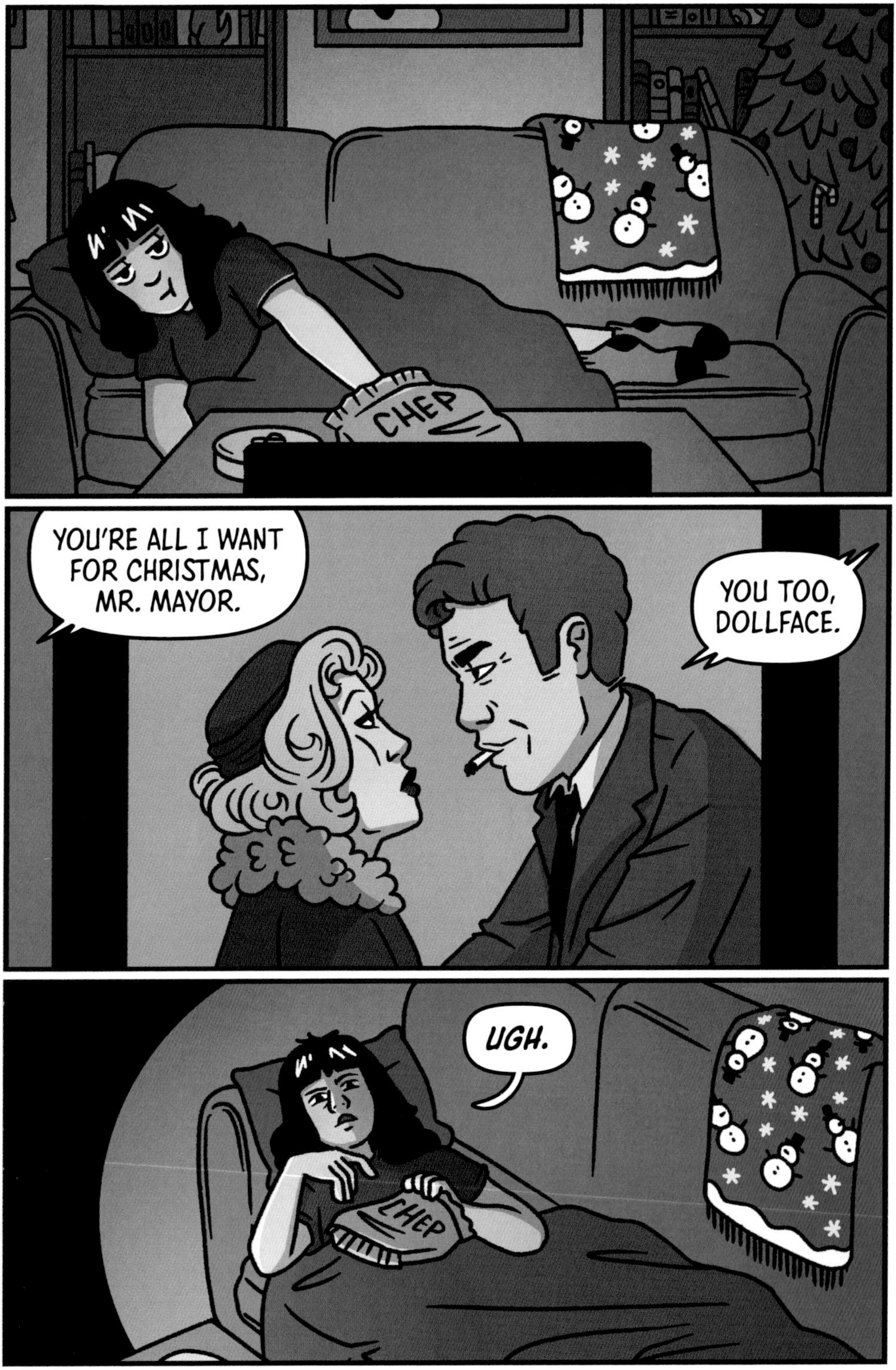
CHEP
YOU'RE ALL I WANT FOR CHRISTMAS, MR. MAYOR.
YOU TOO, DOLLFACE.
UGH.
CHEP

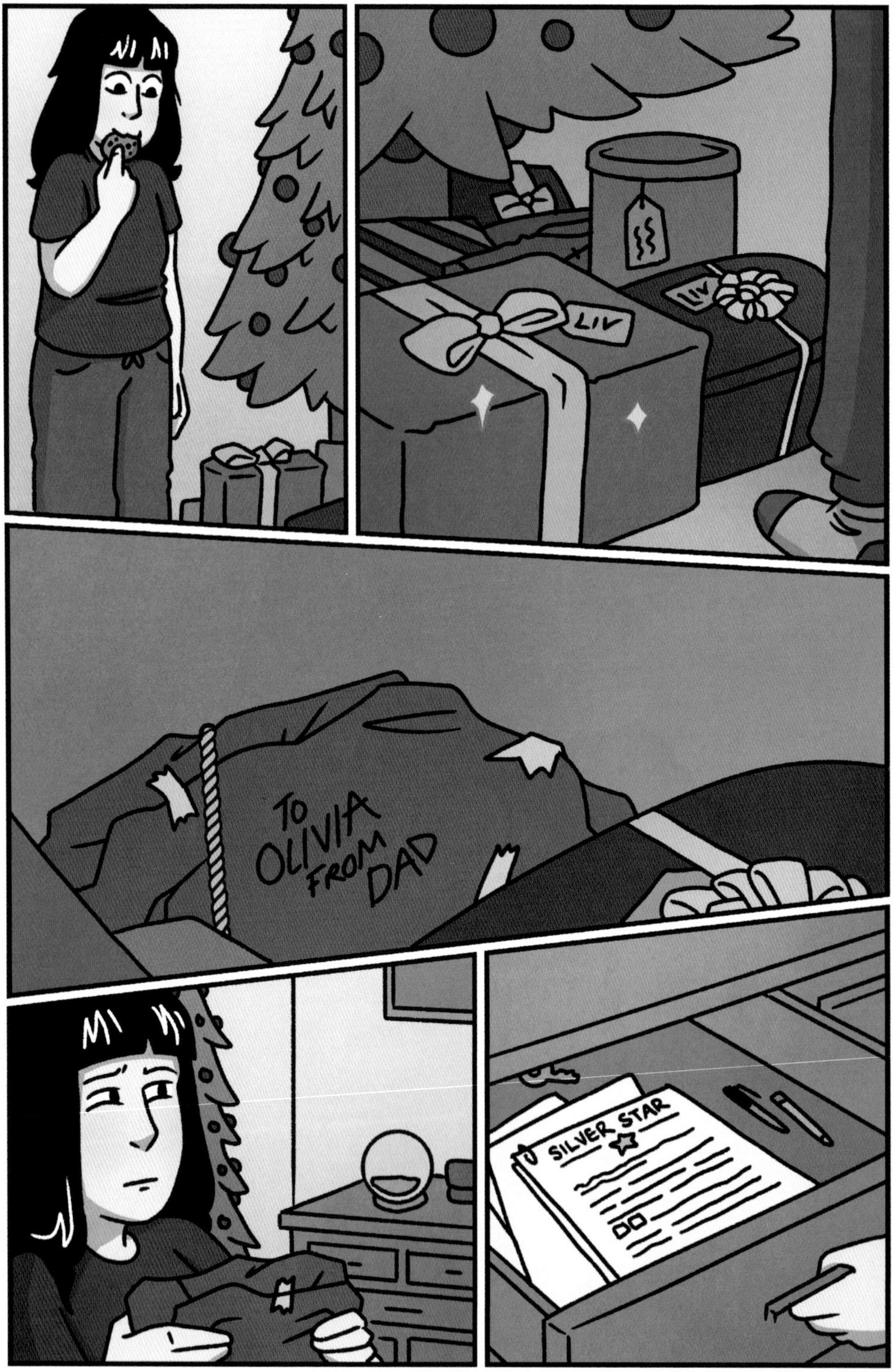
LIV
LIV
TO OLIVIA FROM DAD
SILVER STAR

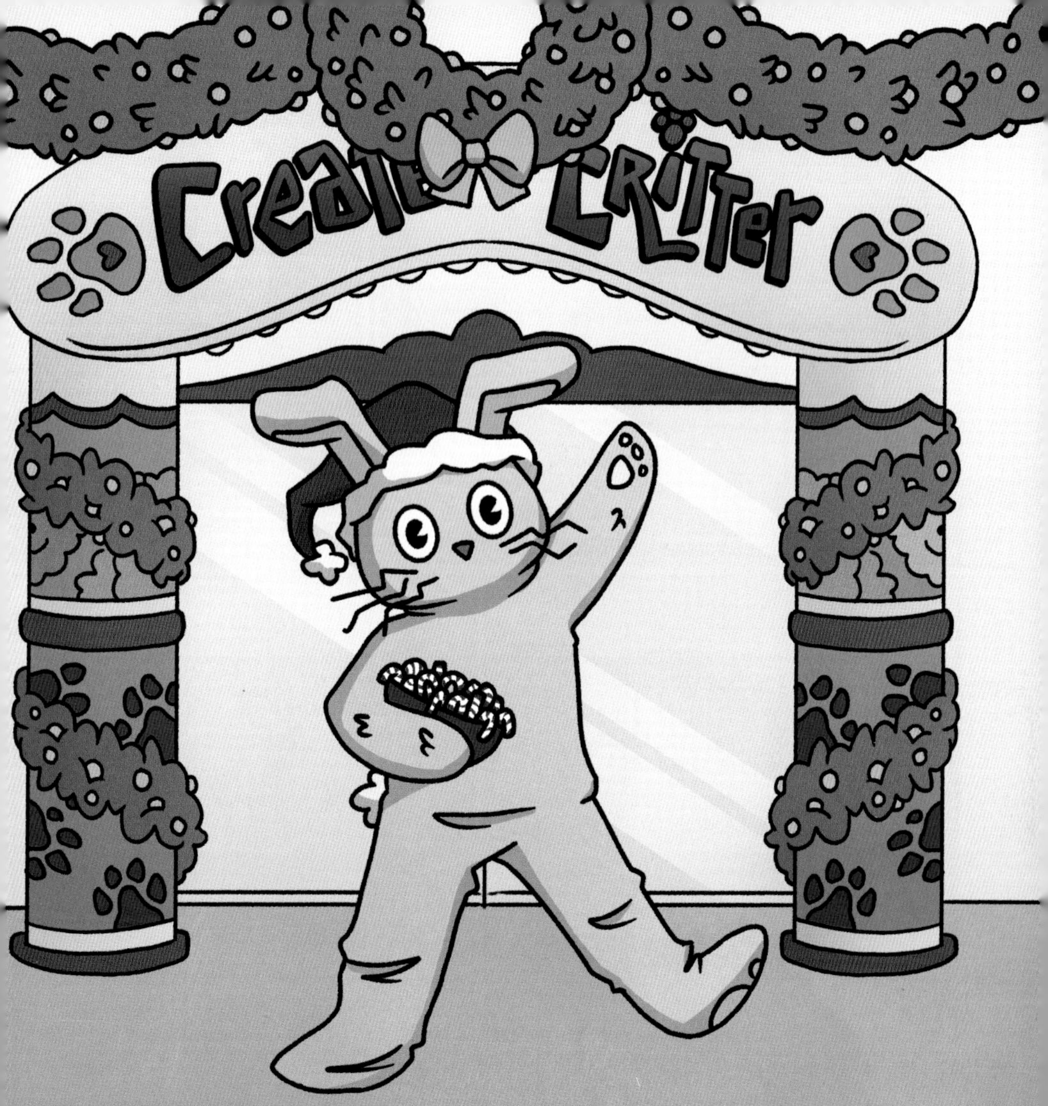
Create Critter

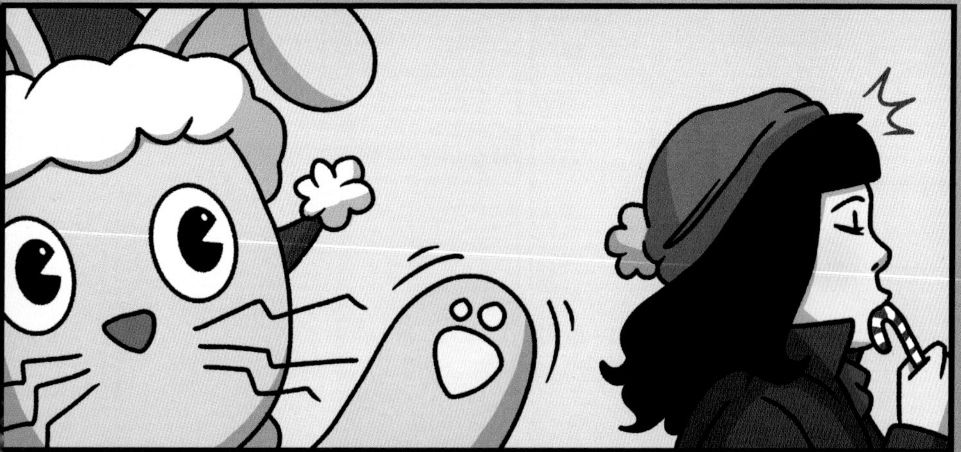

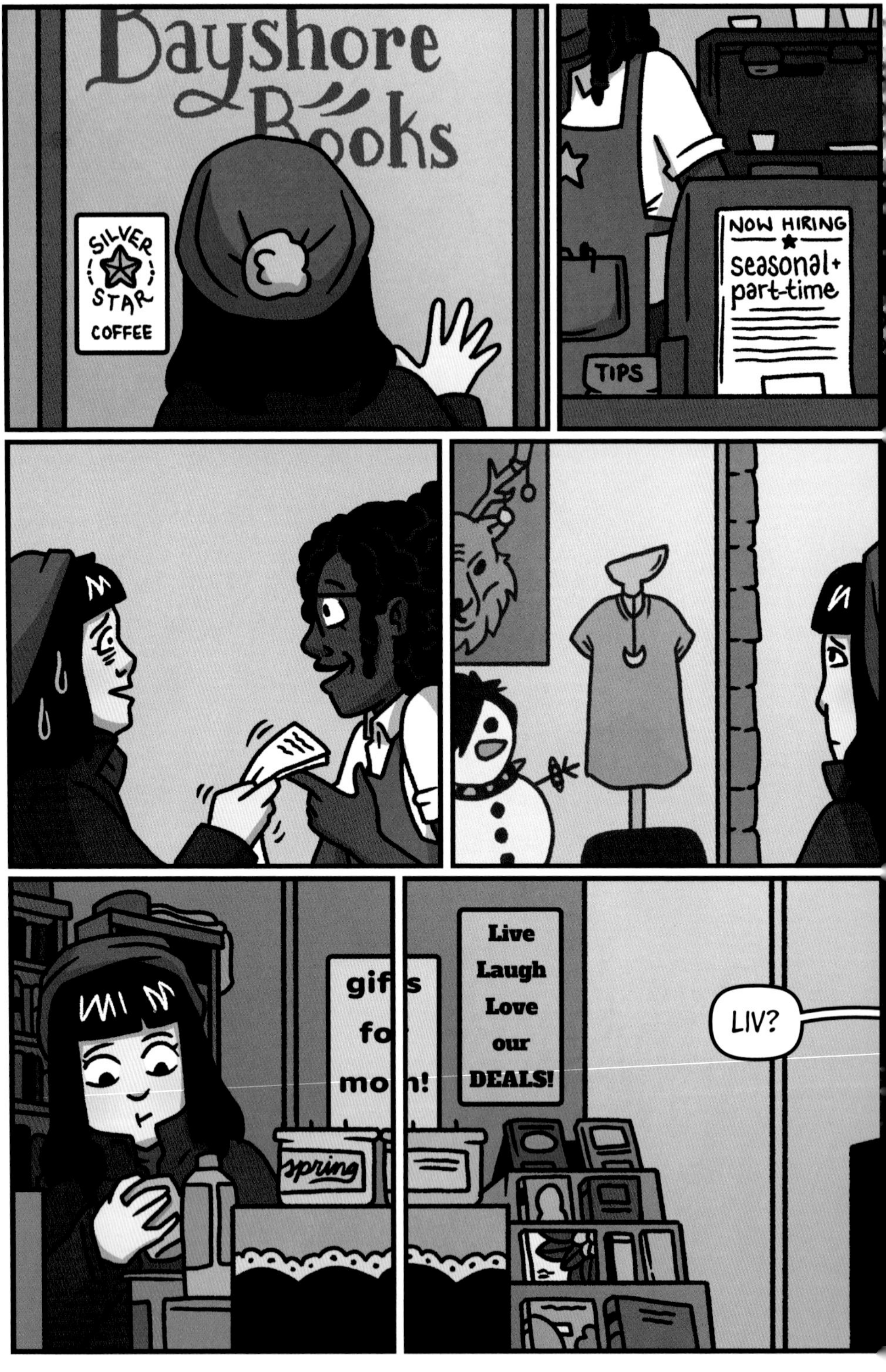
Bayshore Books
SILVER STAR COFFEE
NOW HIRING
seasonal+ part-time
TIPS
gif s fo mo n!
Live Laugh Love our DEALS!
spring
LIV?

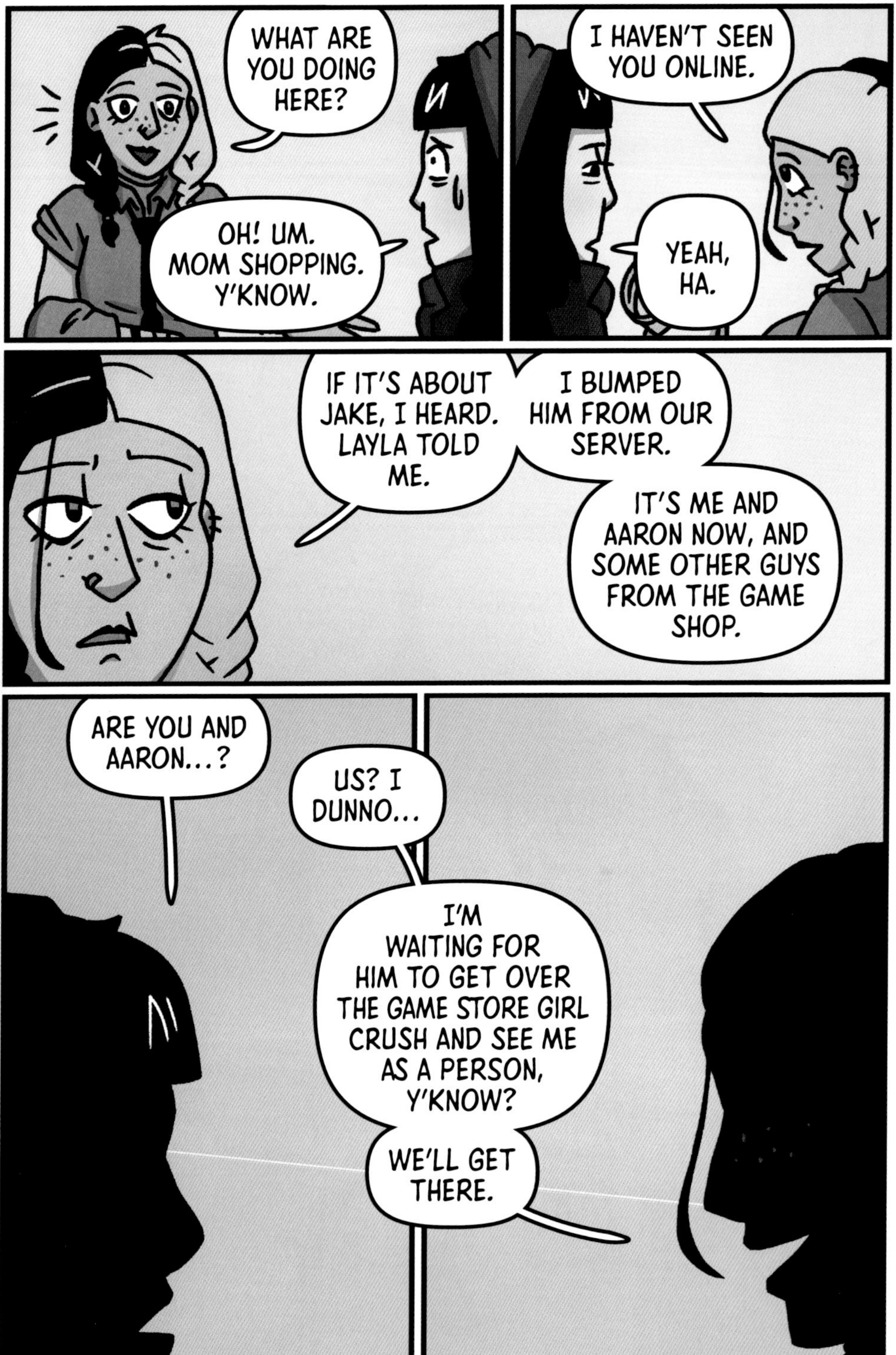
WHAT ARE YOU DOING HERE?
OH! UM. MOM SHOPPING. Y'KNOW.
I HAVEN'T SEEN YOU ONLINE.
YEAH, HA.
IF IT'S ABOUT JAKE, I HEARD. LAYLA TOLD ME.
I BUMPED HIM FROM OUR SERVER.
IT'S ME AND AARON NOW, AND SOME OTHER GUYS FROM THE GAME SHOP.
ARE YOU AND AARON...?
US? I DUNNO...
I'M WAITING FOR HIM TO GET OVER THE GAME STORE GIRL CRUSH AND SEE ME AS A PERSON, Y'KNOW?
WE'LL GET THERE.

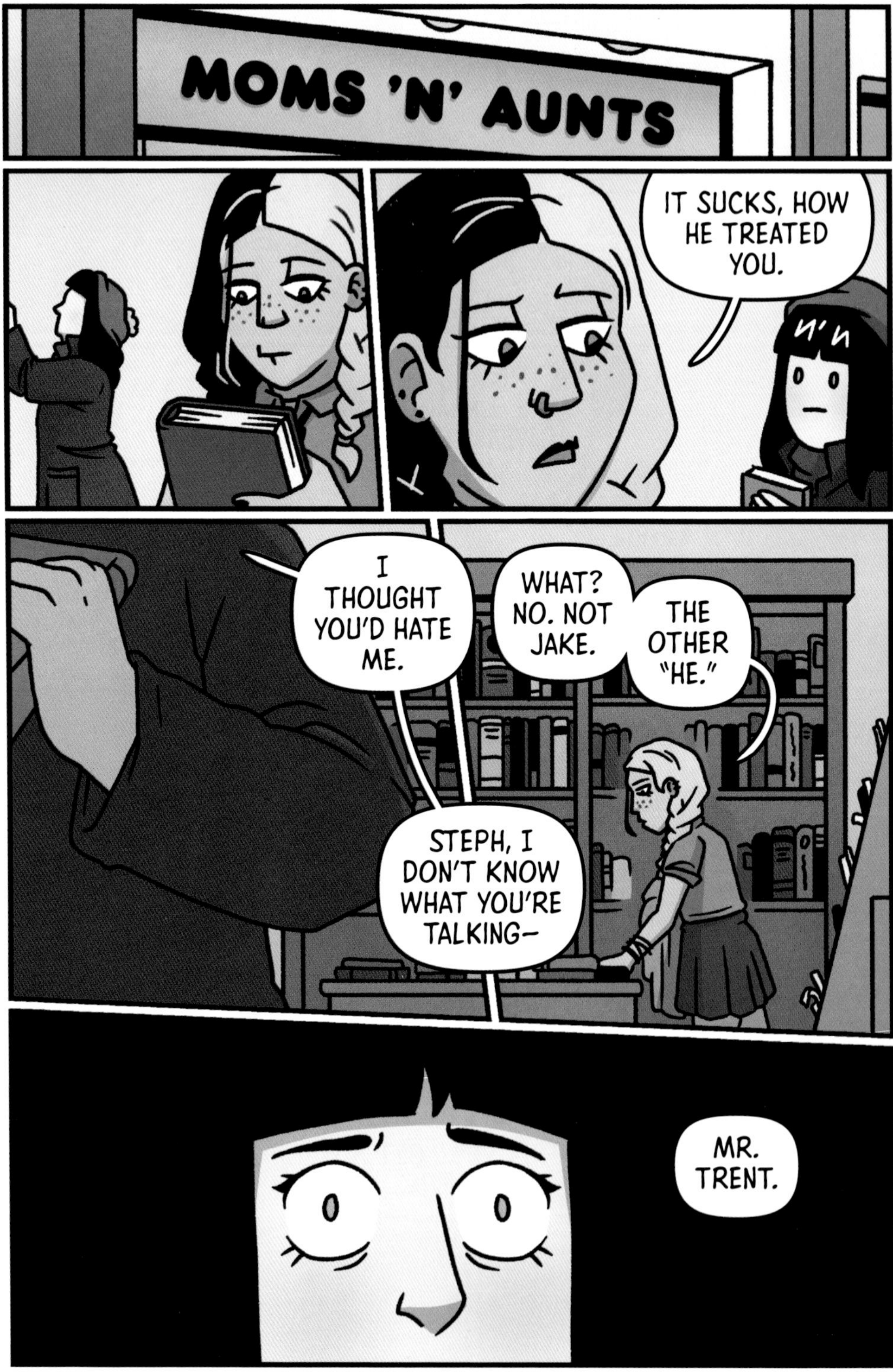
MOMS 'N' AUNTS
IT SUCKS, HOW HE TREATED YOU.
I THOUGHT YOU'D HATE ME.
WHAT? NO. NOT JAKE.
THE OTHER "HE."
STEPH, I DON'T KNOW WHAT YOU'RE TALKING—
MR. TRENT.

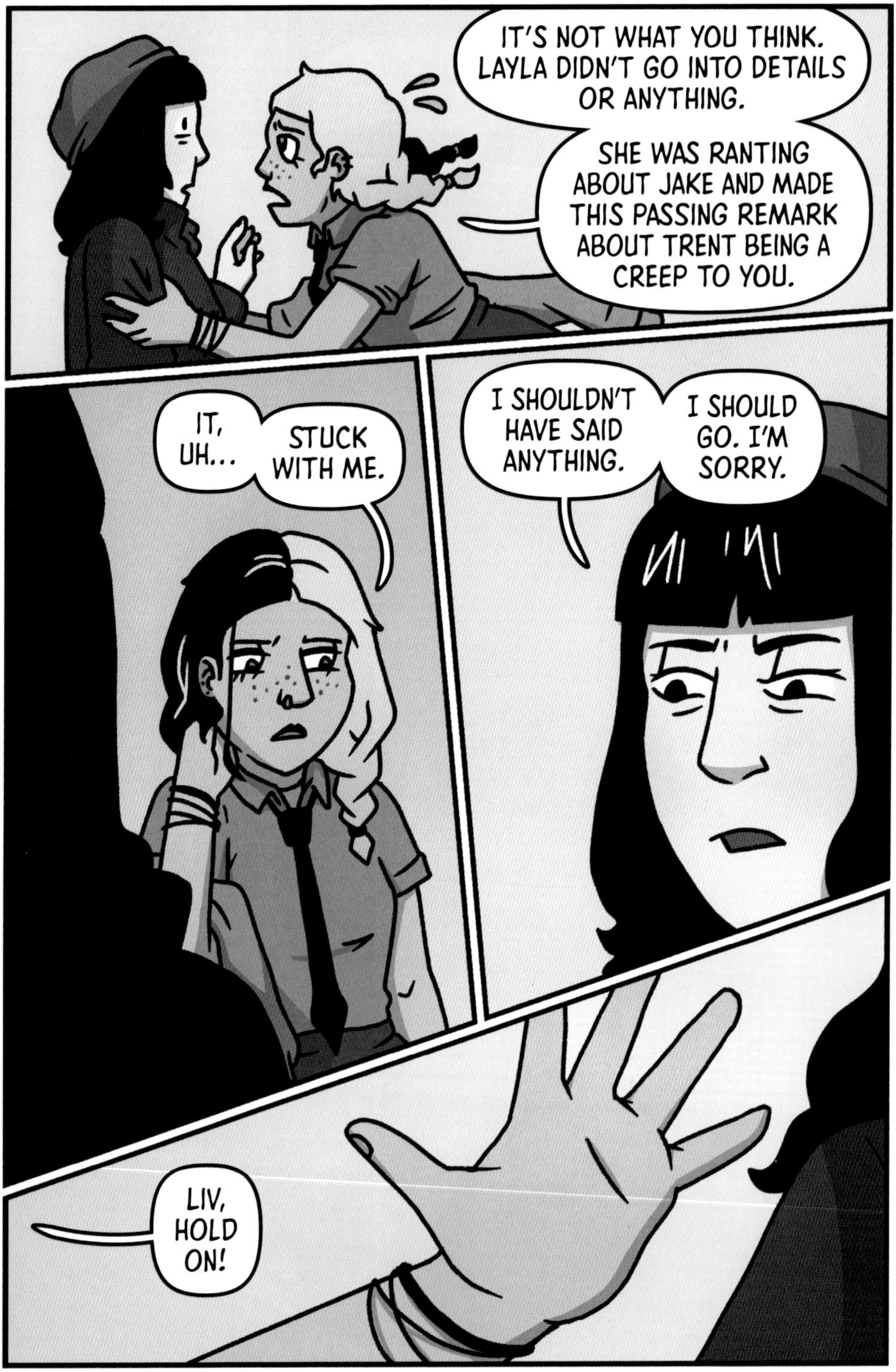
IT'S NOT WHAT YOU THINK. LAYLA DIDN'T GO INTO DETAILS OR ANYTHING.
SHE WAS RANTING ABOUT JAKE AND MADE THIS PASSING REMARK ABOUT TRENT BEING A CREEP TO YOU.
IT, UH...
STUCK WITH ME.
I SHOULDN'T HAVE SAID ANYTHING.
I SHOULD GO. I'M SORRY.
LIV, HOLD ON!

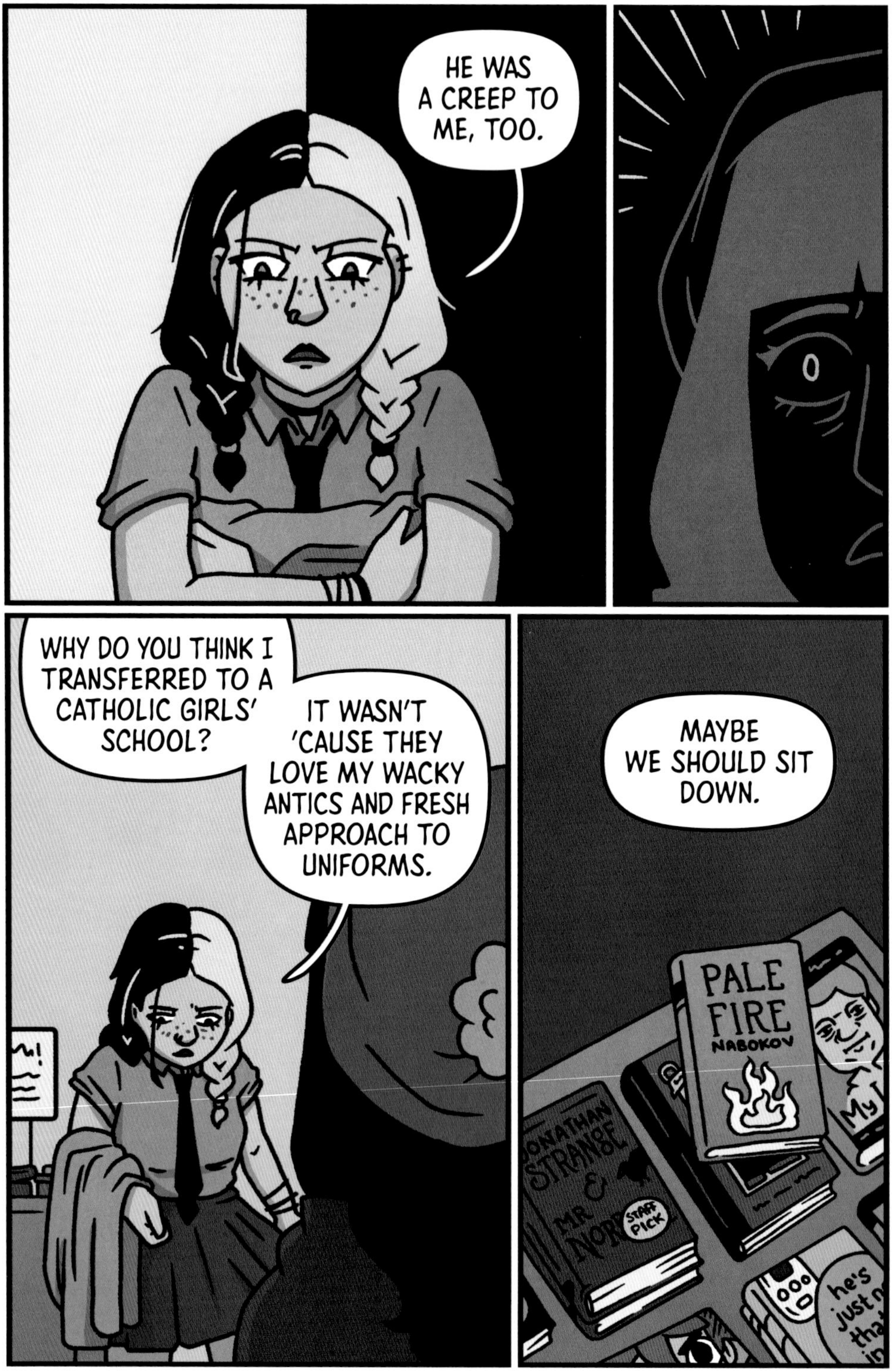
HE WAS A CREEP TO ME, TOO.
WHY DO YOU THINK I TRANSFERRED TO A CATHOLIC GIRLS' SCHOOL?
IT WASN'T 'CAUSE THEY LOVE MY WACKY ANTICS AND FRESH APPROACH TO UNIFORMS.
MAYBE WE SHOULD SIT DOWN.
PALE FIRE
NABOKOV
JONATHAN STRANGE & MR NORR
STAFF PICK

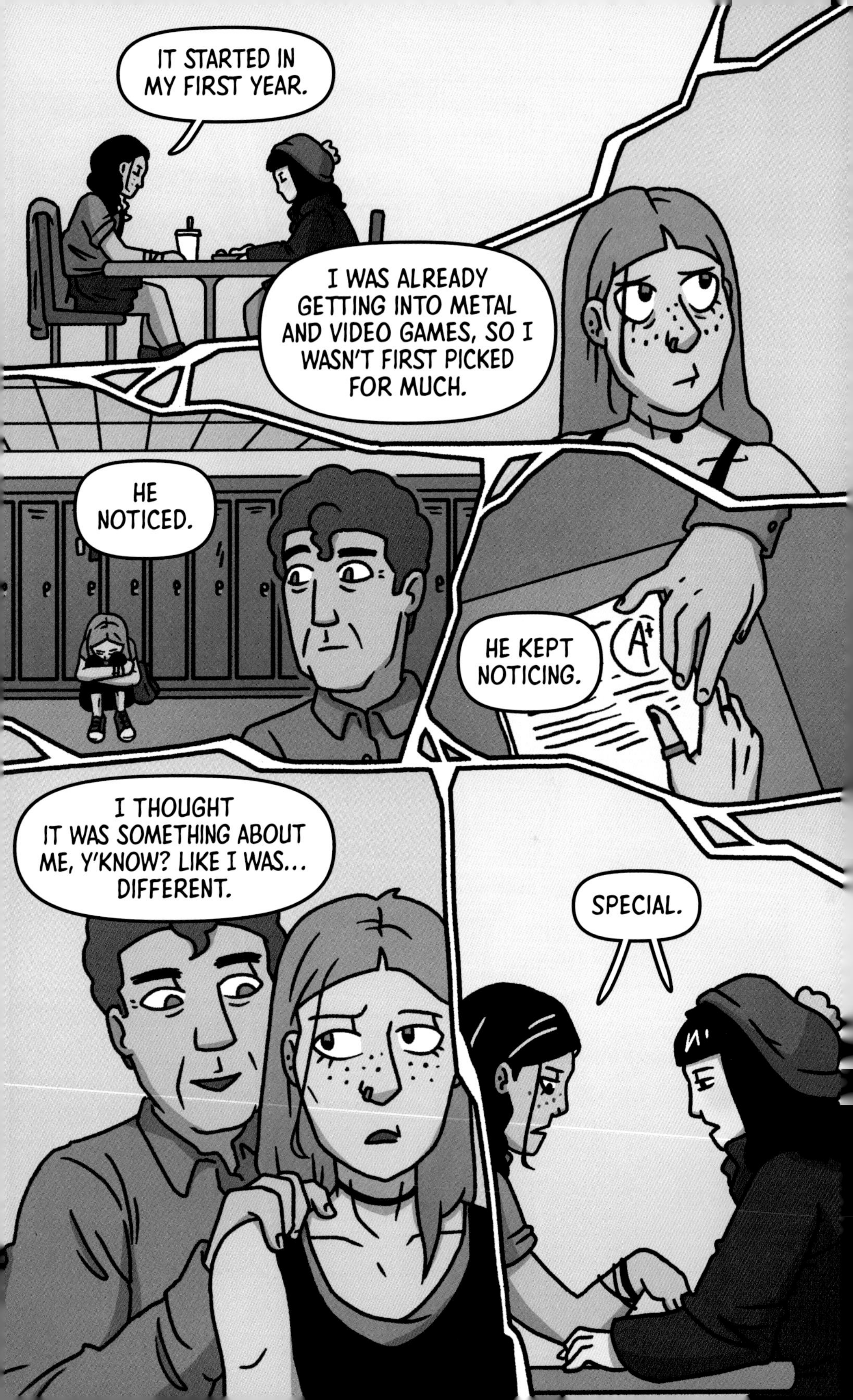
IT STARTED IN MY FIRST YEAR.
I WAS ALREADY GETTING INTO METAL AND VIDEO GAMES, SO I WASN'T FIRST PICKED FOR MUCH.
HE NOTICED.
HE KEPT NOTICING.
A+
I THOUGHT IT WAS SOMETHING ABOUT ME, Y'KNOW? LIKE I WAS... DIFFERENT.
SPECIAL.

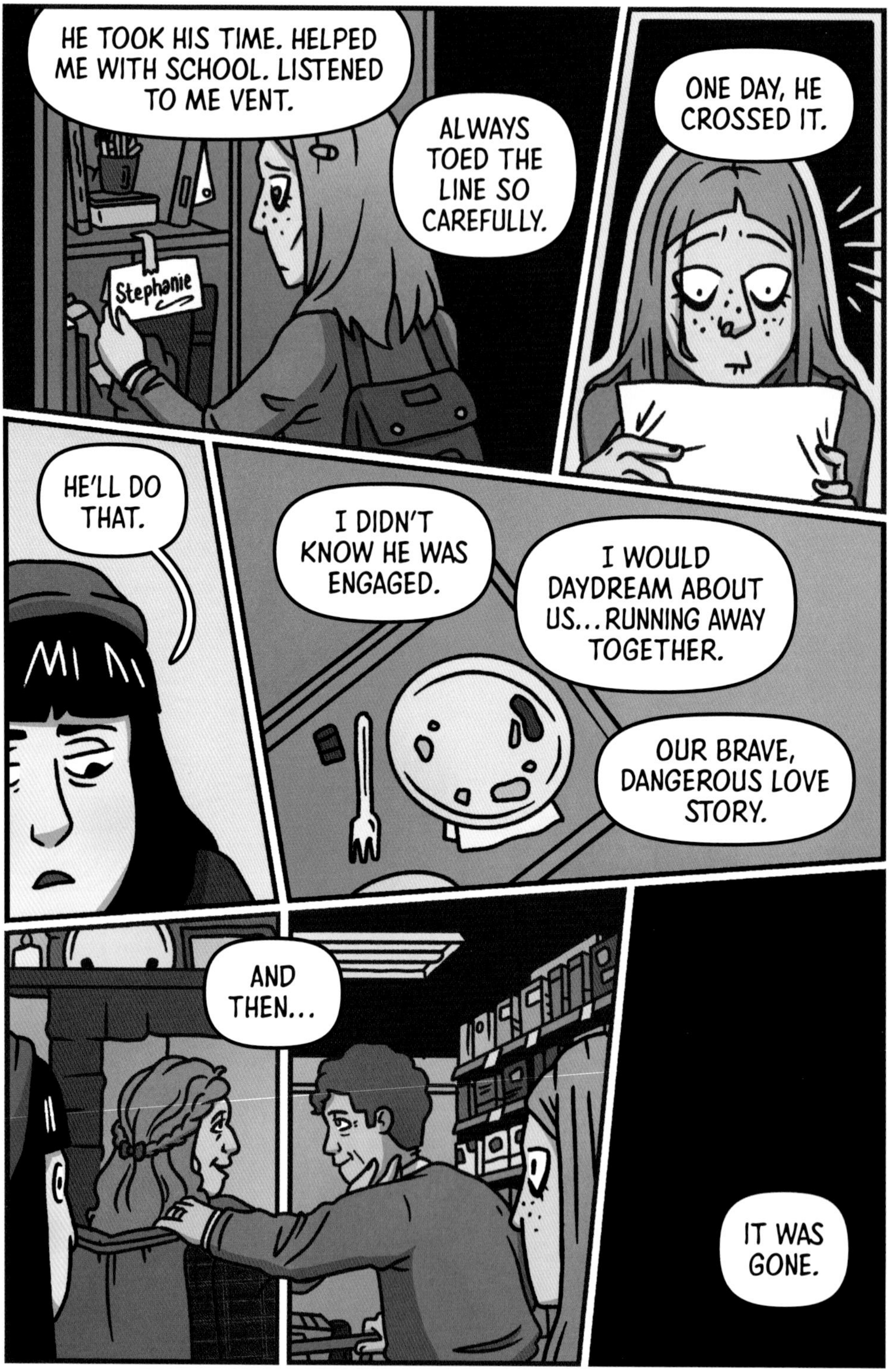
HE TOOK HIS TIME. HELPED ME WITH SCHOOL. LISTENED TO ME VENT.
ALWAYS TOED THE LINE SO CAREFULLY.
Stephanie
ONE DAY, HE CROSSED IT.
HE'LL DO THAT.
I DIDN'T KNOW HE WAS ENGAGED.
I WOULD DAYDREAM ABOUT US...RUNNING AWAY TOGETHER.
OUR BRAVE, DANGEROUS LOVE STORY.
AND THEN...
IT WAS GONE.

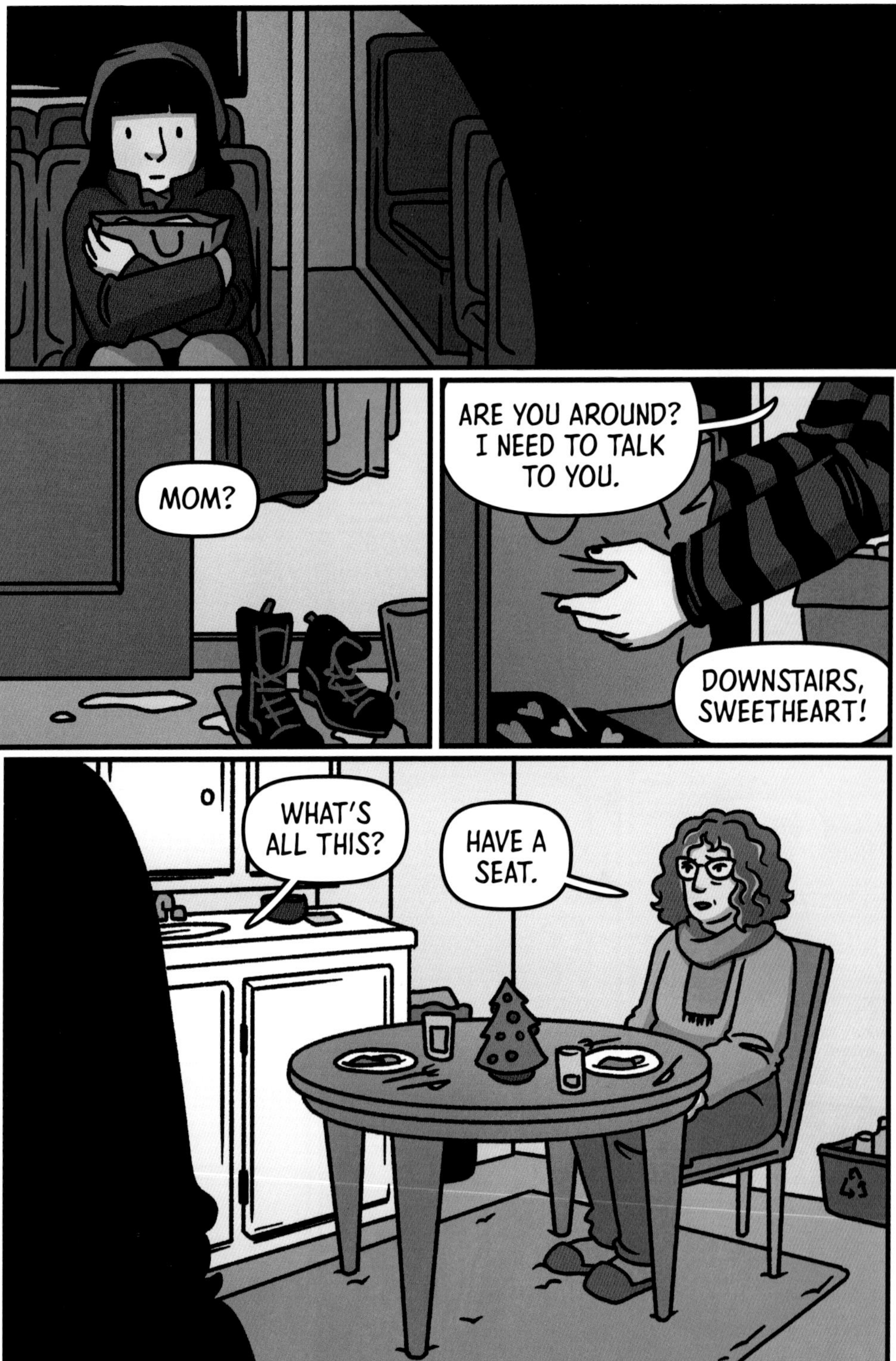
MOM?
ARE YOU AROUND? I NEED TO TALK TO YOU.
DOWNSTAIRS, SWEETHEART!
WHAT'S ALL THIS?
HAVE A SEAT.

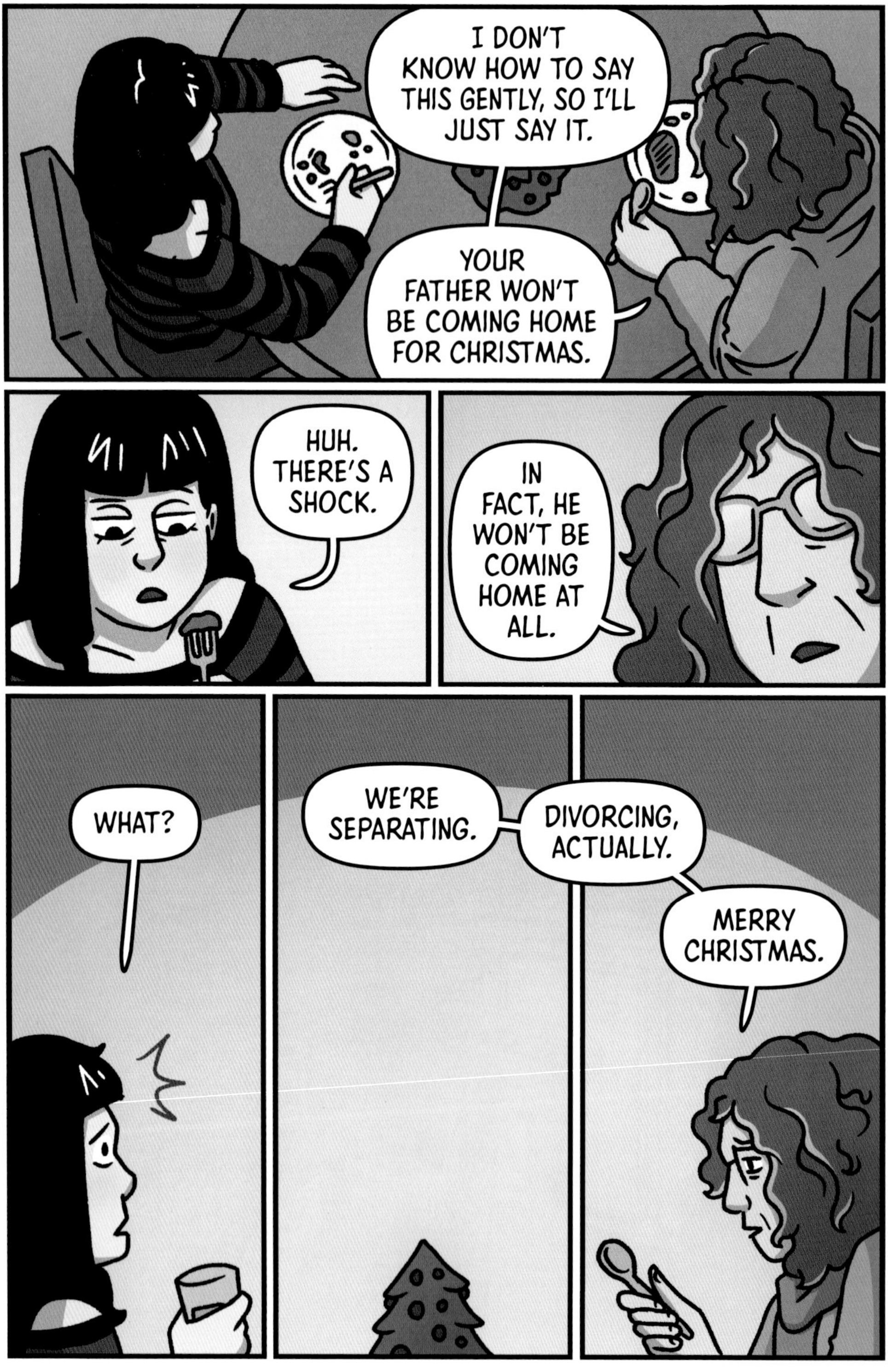
I DON'T KNOW HOW TO SAY THIS GENTLY, SO I'LL JUST SAY IT.
YOUR FATHER WON'T BE COMING HOME FOR CHRISTMAS.
HUH. THERE'S A SHOCK.
IN FACT, HE WON'T BE COMING HOME AT ALL.
WHAT?
WE'RE SEPARATING.
DIVORCING, ACTUALLY.
MERRY CHRISTMAS.

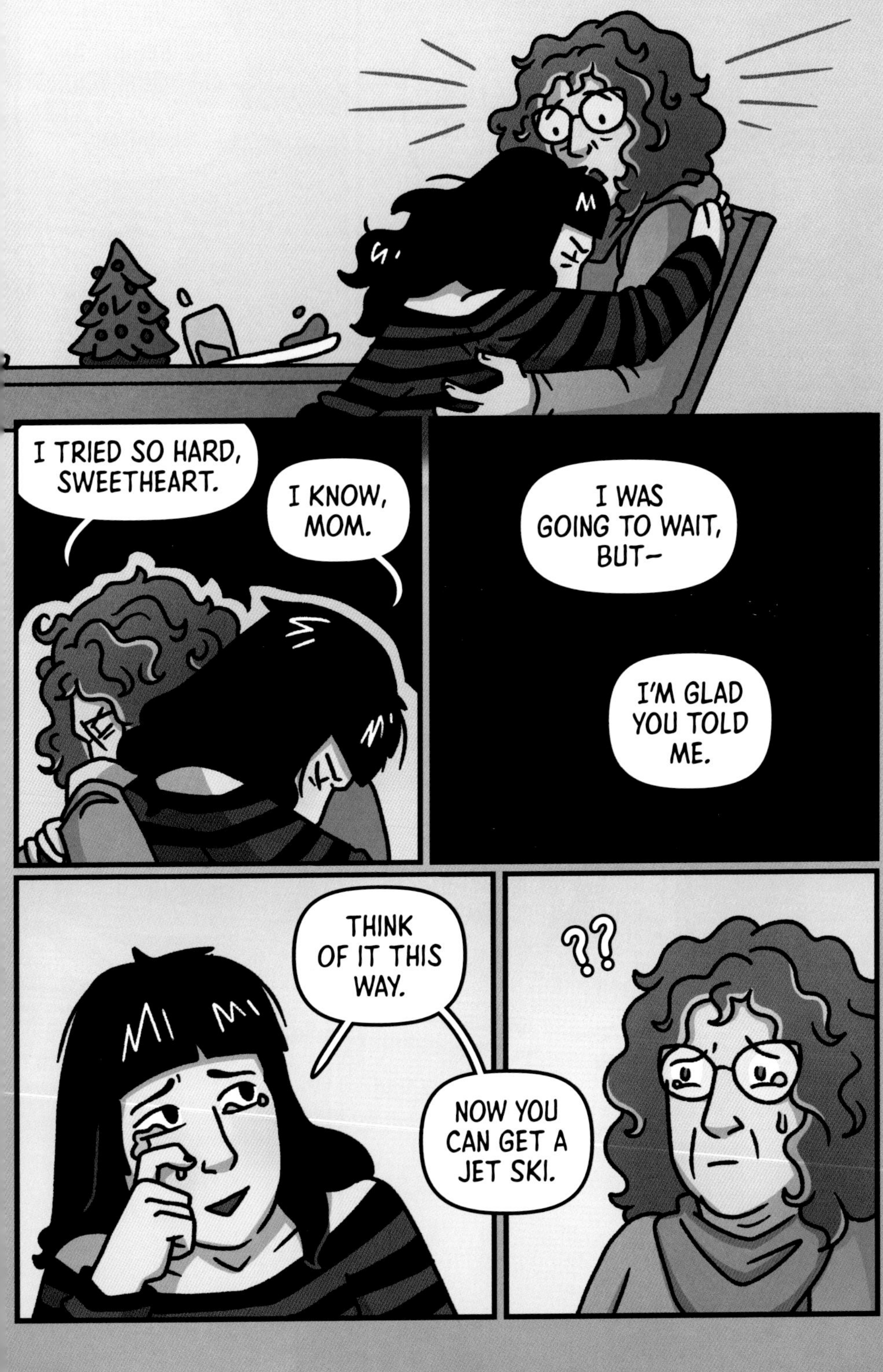

I TRIED SO HARD, SWEETHEART.
I KNOW, MOM.
I WAS GOING TO WAIT, BUT–
I'M GLAD YOU TOLD ME.
THINK OF IT THIS WAY.
NOW YOU CAN GET A JET SKI.
??

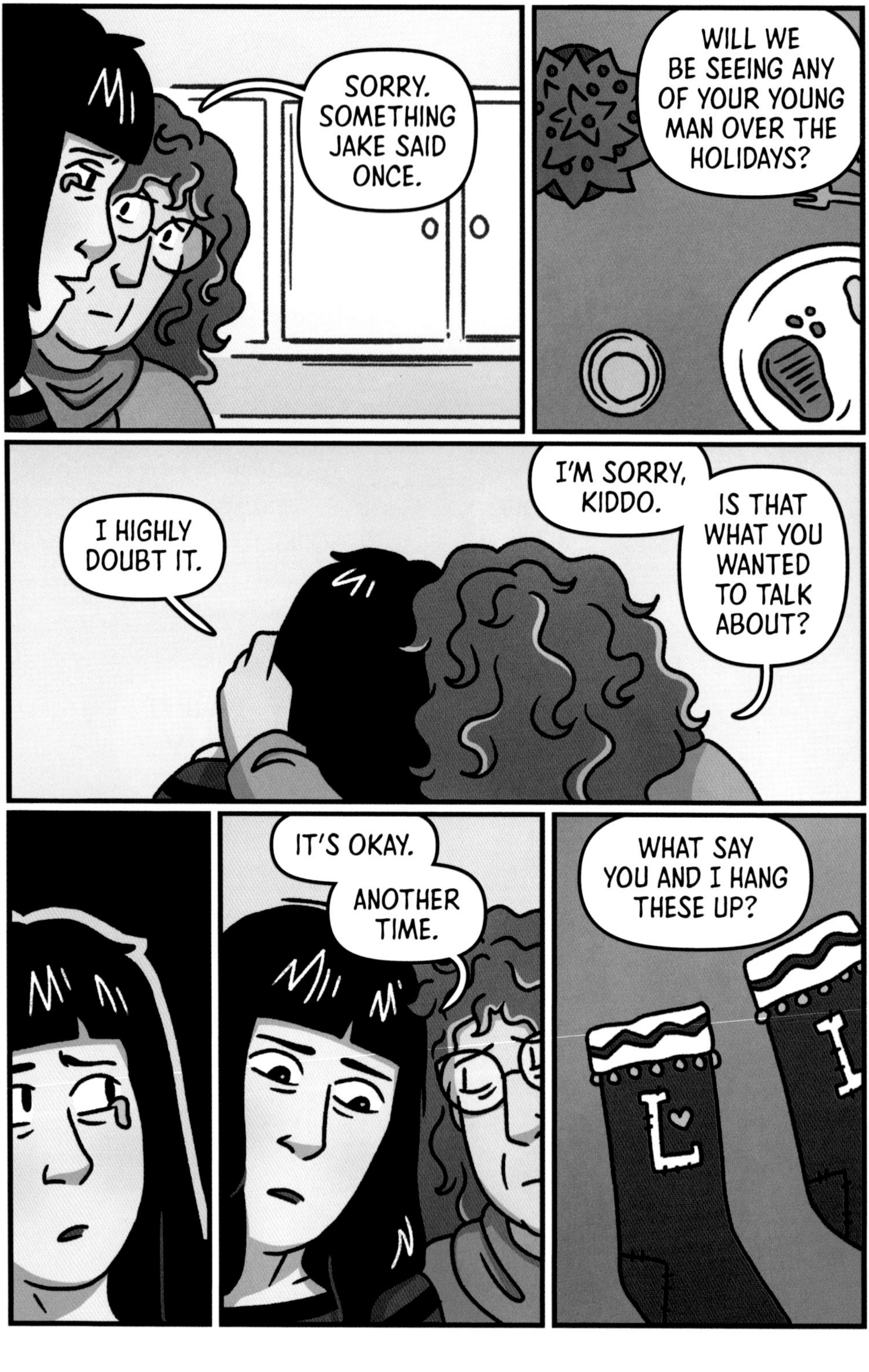

SORRY. SOMETHING JAKE SAID ONCE.
WILL WE BE SEEING ANY OF YOUR YOUNG MAN OVER THE HOLIDAYS?
I HIGHLY DOUBT IT.
I'M SORRY, KIDDO.
IS THAT WHAT YOU WANTED TO TALK ABOUT?
IT'S OKAY.
ANOTHER TIME.
WHAT SAY YOU AND I HANG THESE UP?

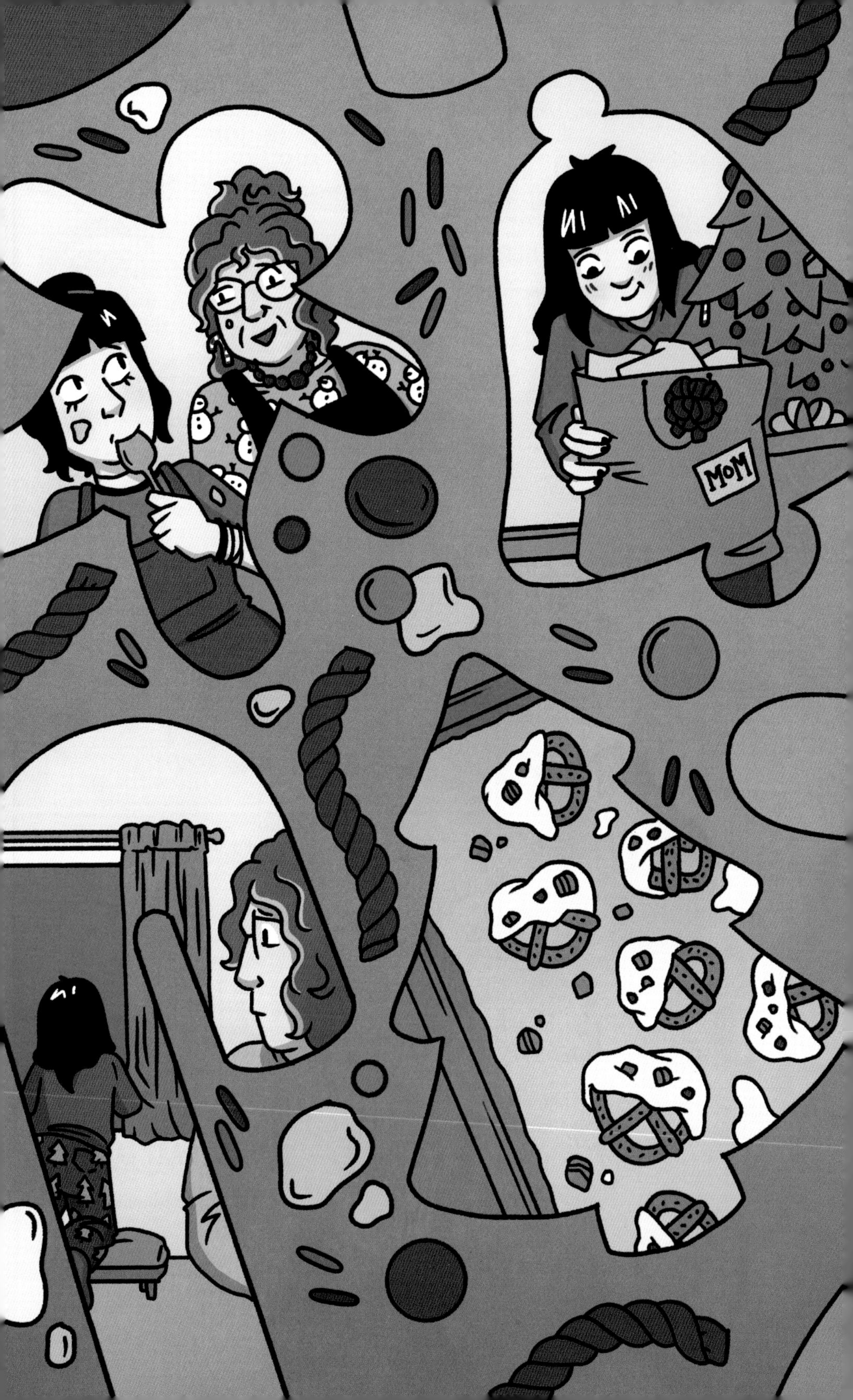
MOM

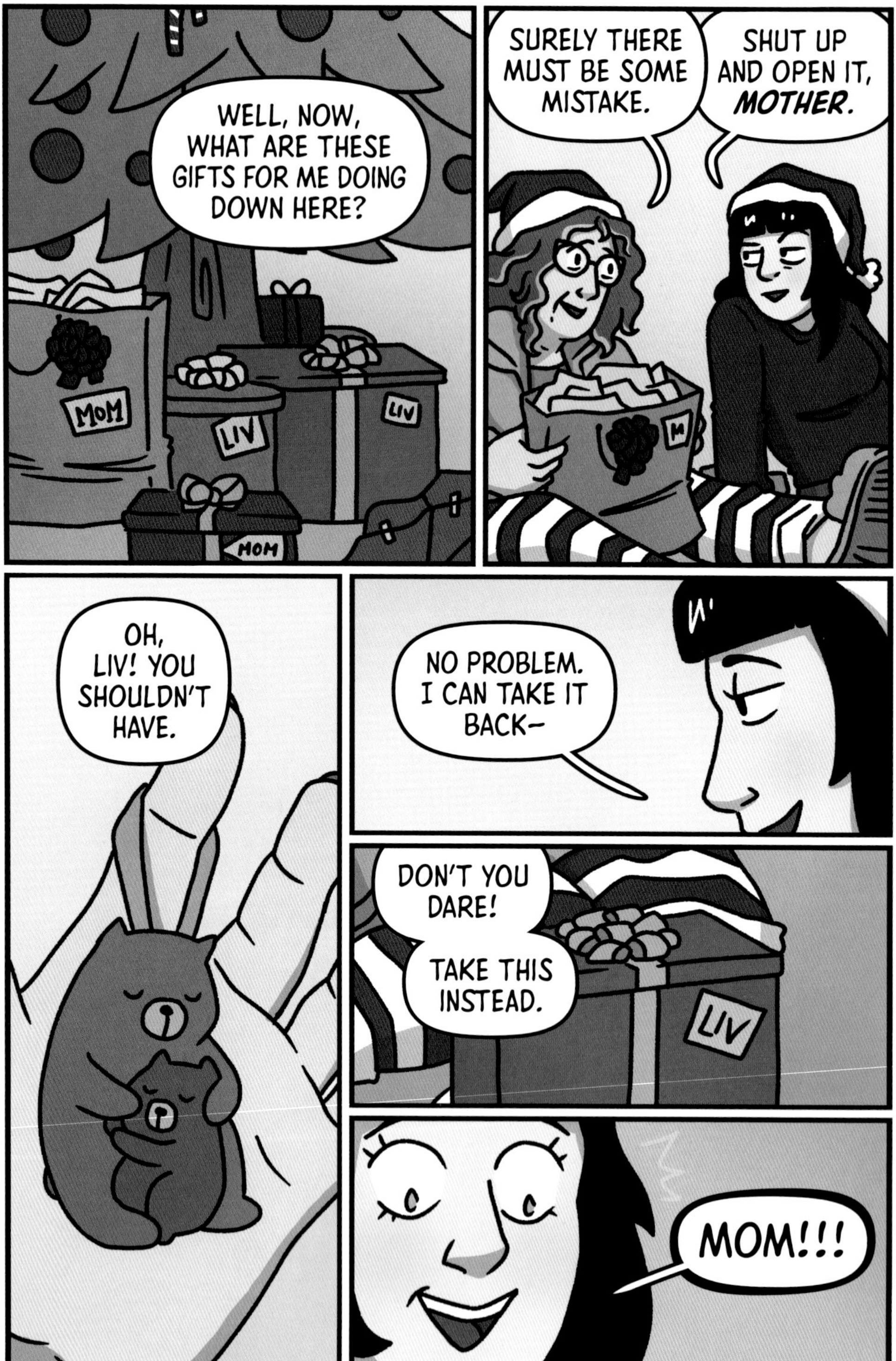
WELL, NOW, WHAT ARE THESE GIFTS FOR ME DOING DOWN HERE?
MOM
LIV
LIV
MOM
SURELY THERE MUST BE SOME MISTAKE.
SHUT UP AND OPEN IT, ***MOTHER.***
M
OH, LIV! YOU SHOULDN'T HAVE.
NO PROBLEM. I CAN TAKE IT BACK—
DON'T YOU DARE!
TAKE THIS INSTEAD.
LIV
MOM!!!

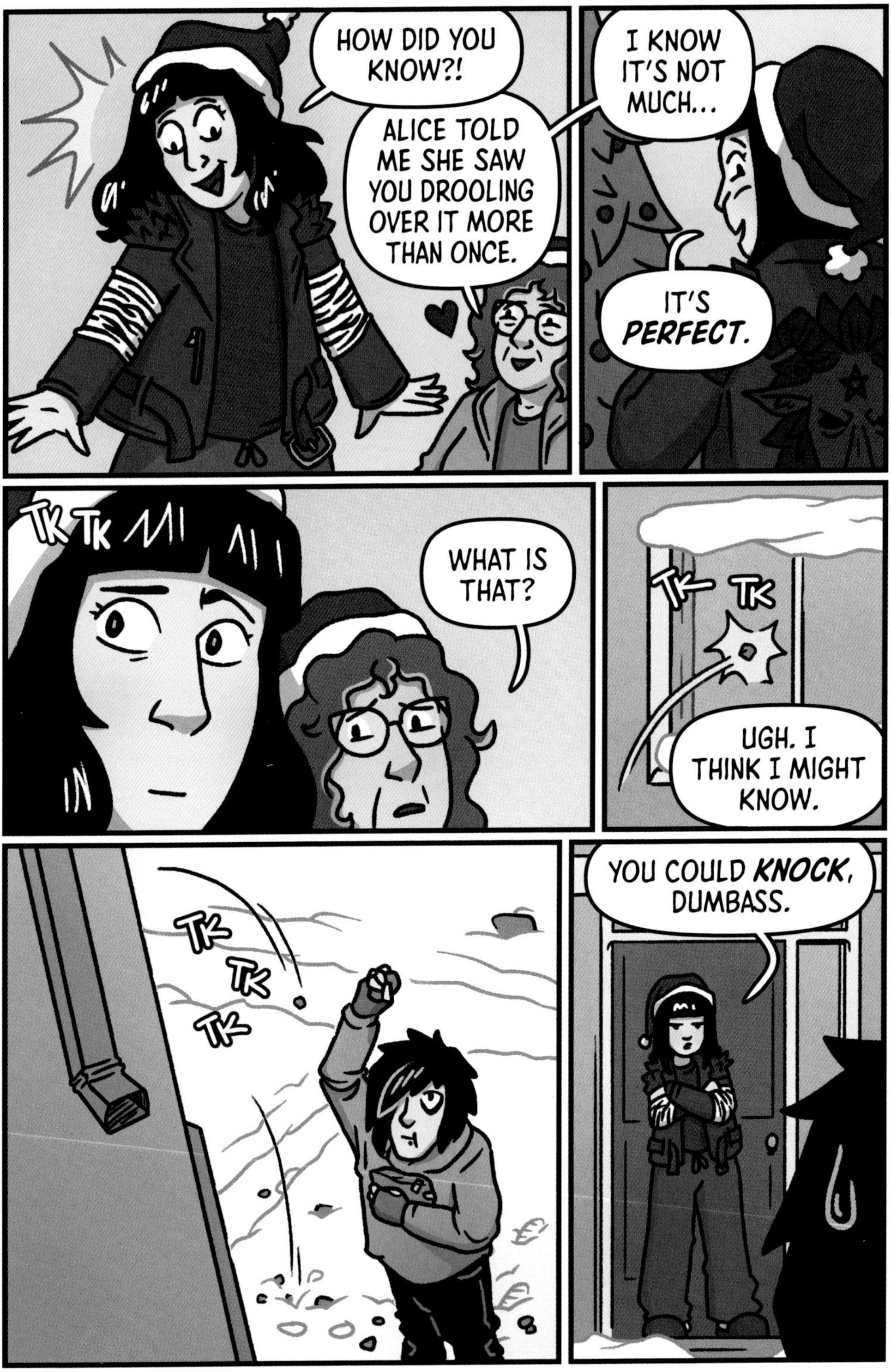
HOW DID YOU KNOW?!
ALICE TOLD ME SHE SAW YOU DROOLING OVER IT MORE THAN ONCE.
I KNOW IT'S NOT MUCH...
IT'S **PERFECT.**
TK TK
WHAT IS THAT?
TK TK
UGH. I THINK I MIGHT KNOW.
TK
TK
TK
YOU COULD **KNOCK,** DUMBASS.

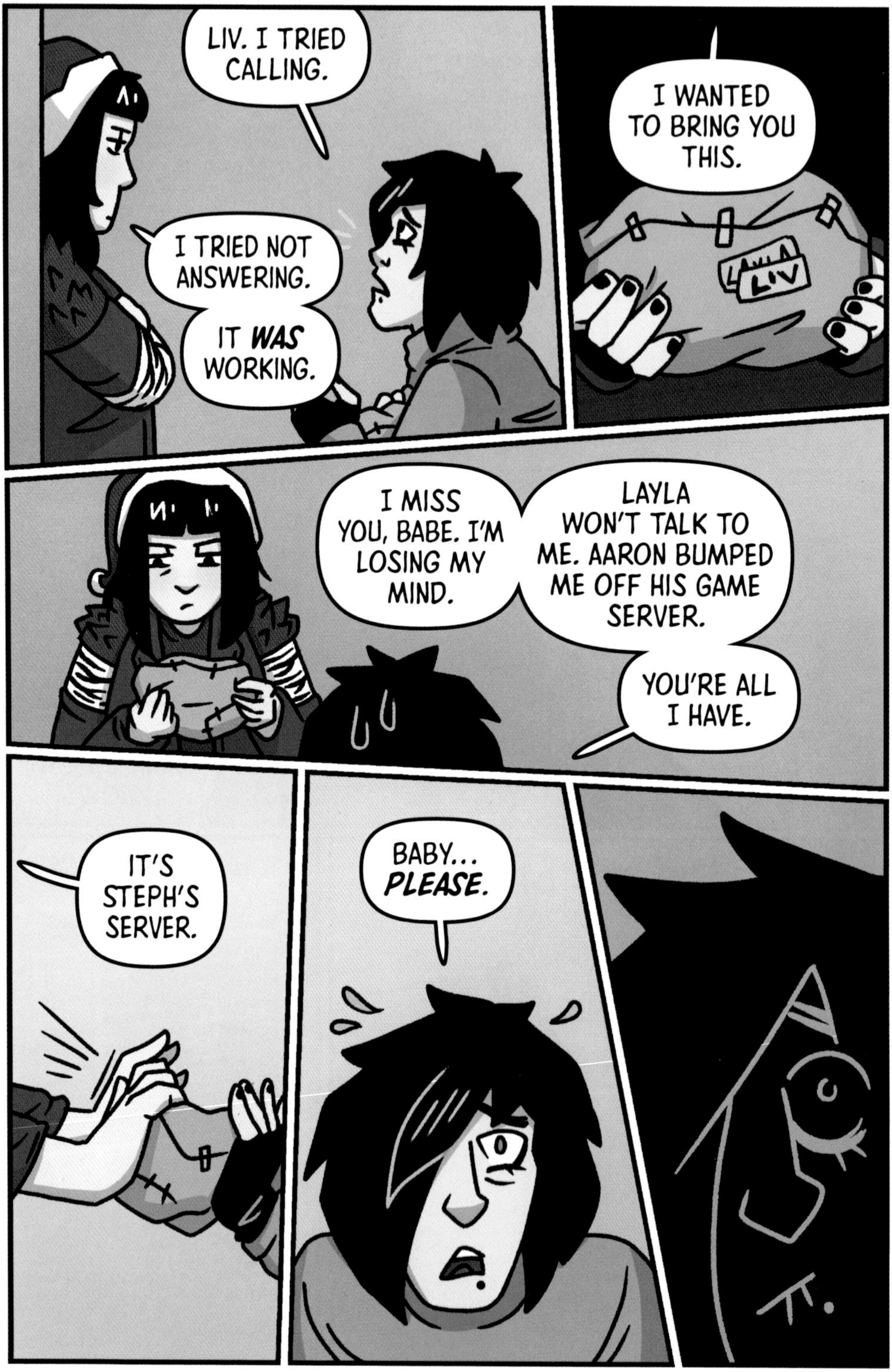
LIV. I TRIED CALLING.
I TRIED NOT ANSWERING.
IT *WAS* WORKING.
I WANTED TO BRING YOU THIS.
LAYLA
LIV
I MISS YOU, BABE. I'M LOSING MY MIND.
LAYLA WON'T TALK TO ME. AARON BUMPED ME OFF HIS GAME SERVER.
YOU'RE ALL I HAVE.
IT'S STEPH'S SERVER.
BABY... *PLEASE.*

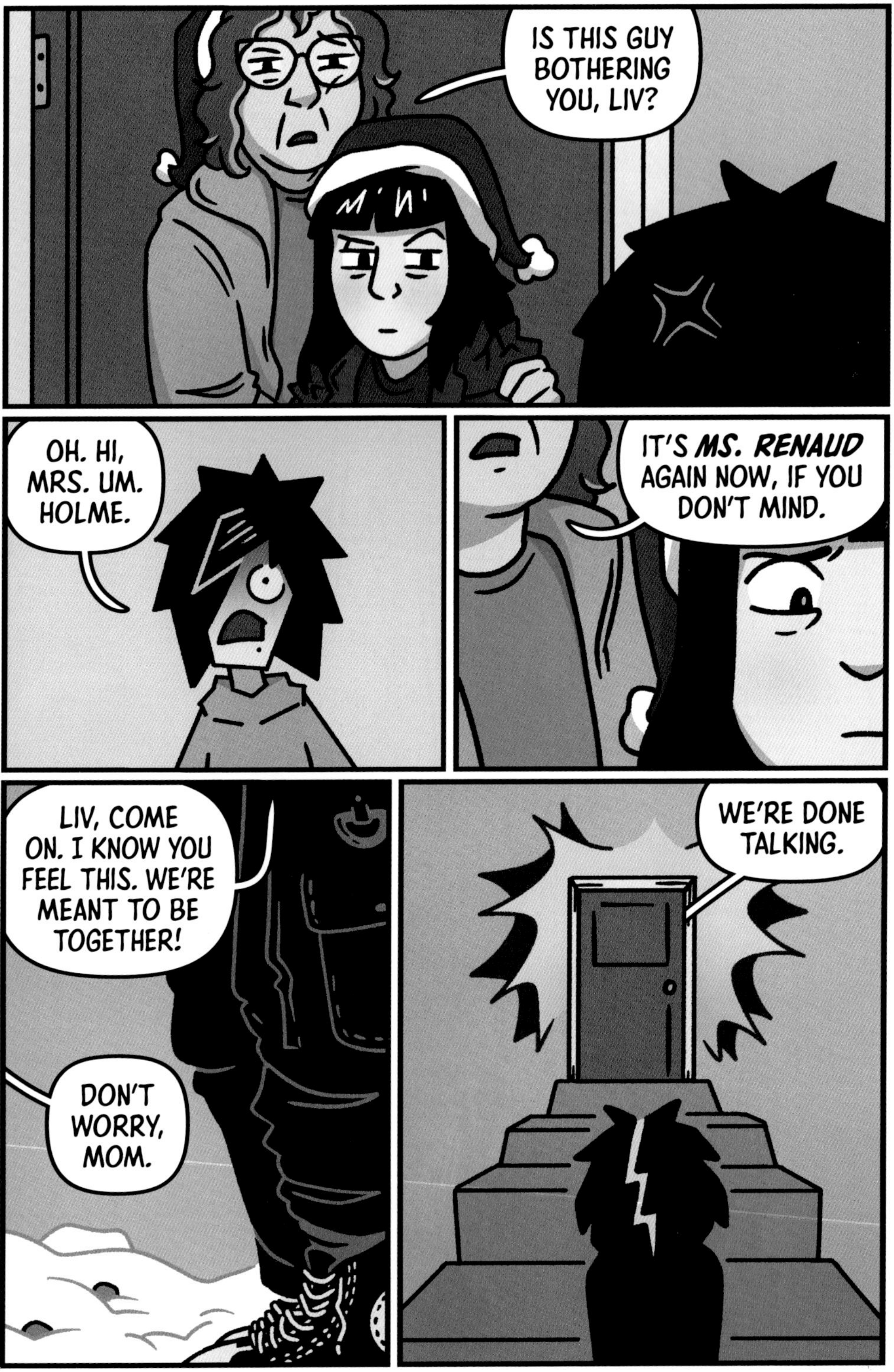
IS THIS GUY BOTHERING YOU, LIV?
OH. HI, MRS. UM. HOLME.
IT'S MS. RENAUD AGAIN NOW, IF YOU DON'T MIND.
LIV, COME ON. I KNOW YOU FEEL THIS. WE'RE MEANT TO BE TOGETHER!
DON'T WORRY, MOM.
WE'RE DONE TALKING.

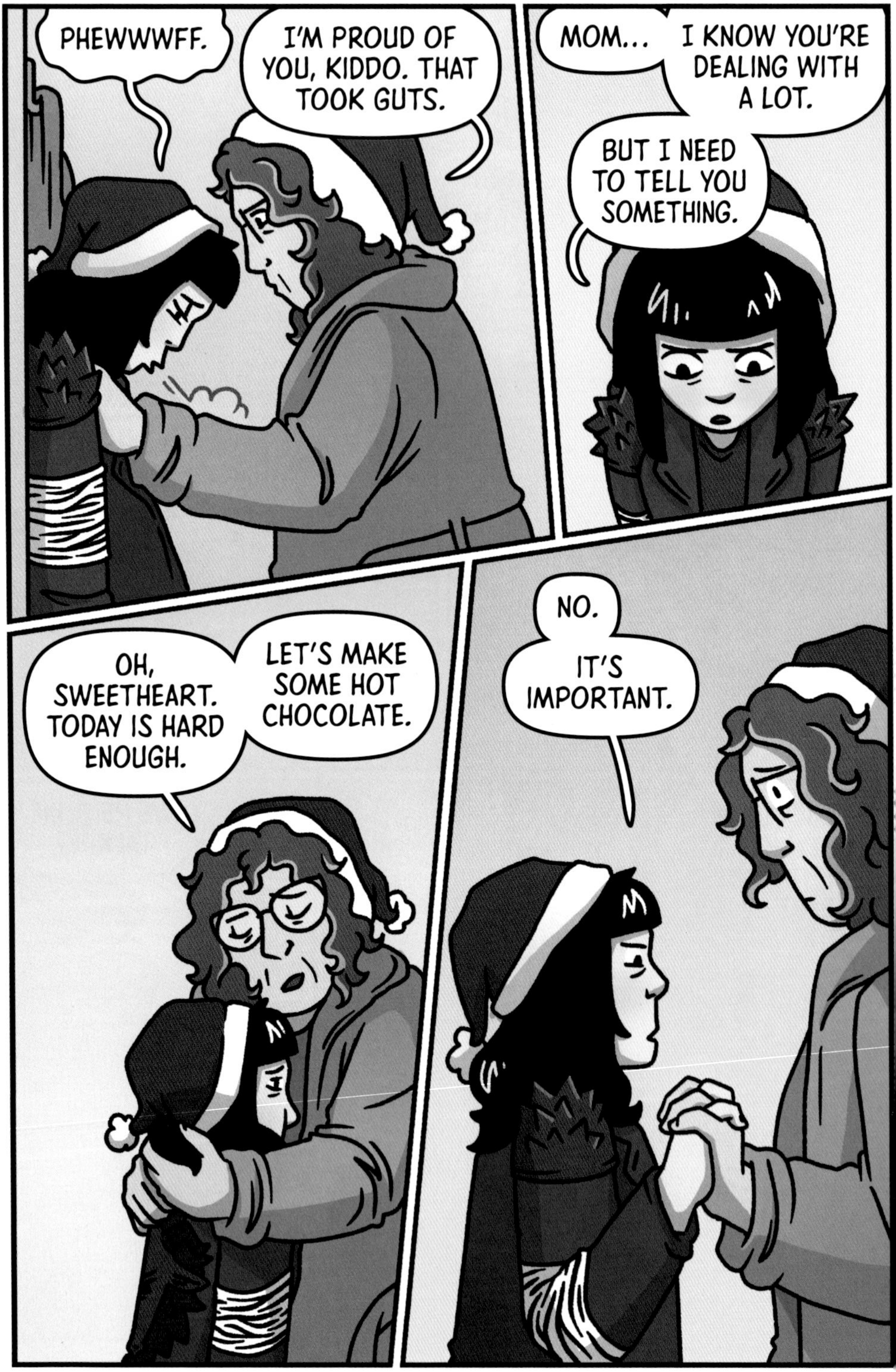
PHEWWWFF.
I'M PROUD OF YOU, KIDDO. THAT TOOK GUTS.
MOM...
I KNOW YOU'RE DEALING WITH A LOT.
BUT I NEED TO TELL YOU SOMETHING.
OH, SWEETHEART. TODAY IS HARD ENOUGH.
LET'S MAKE SOME HOT CHOCOLATE.
NO.
IT'S IMPORTANT.

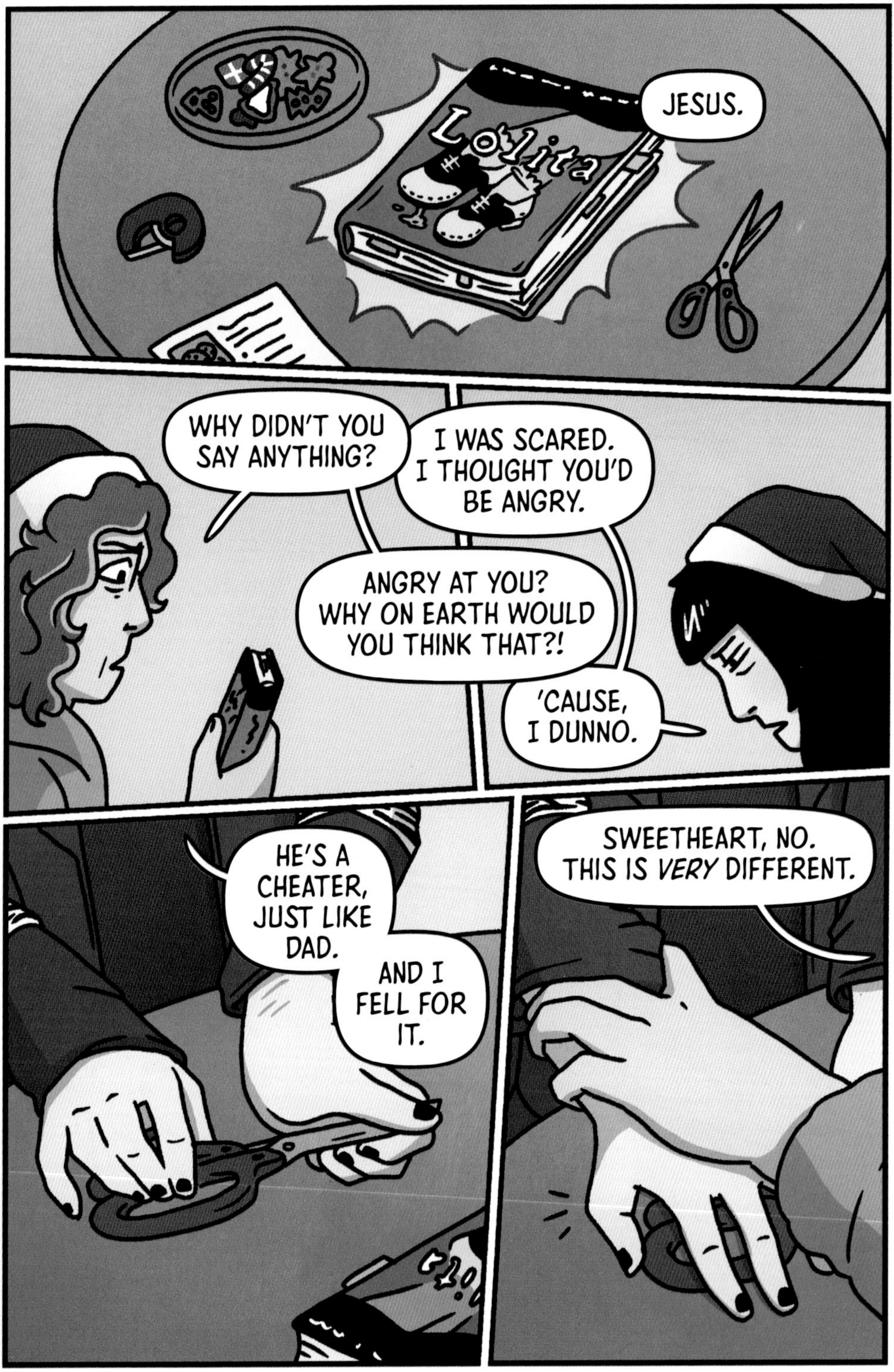
Lolita
JESUS.
WHY DIDN'T YOU SAY ANYTHING?
I WAS SCARED. I THOUGHT YOU'D BE ANGRY.
ANGRY AT YOU? WHY ON EARTH WOULD YOU THINK THAT?!
'CAUSE, I DUNNO.
HE'S A CHEATER, JUST LIKE DAD.
AND I FELL FOR IT.
SWEETHEART, NO. THIS IS *VERY* DIFFERENT.

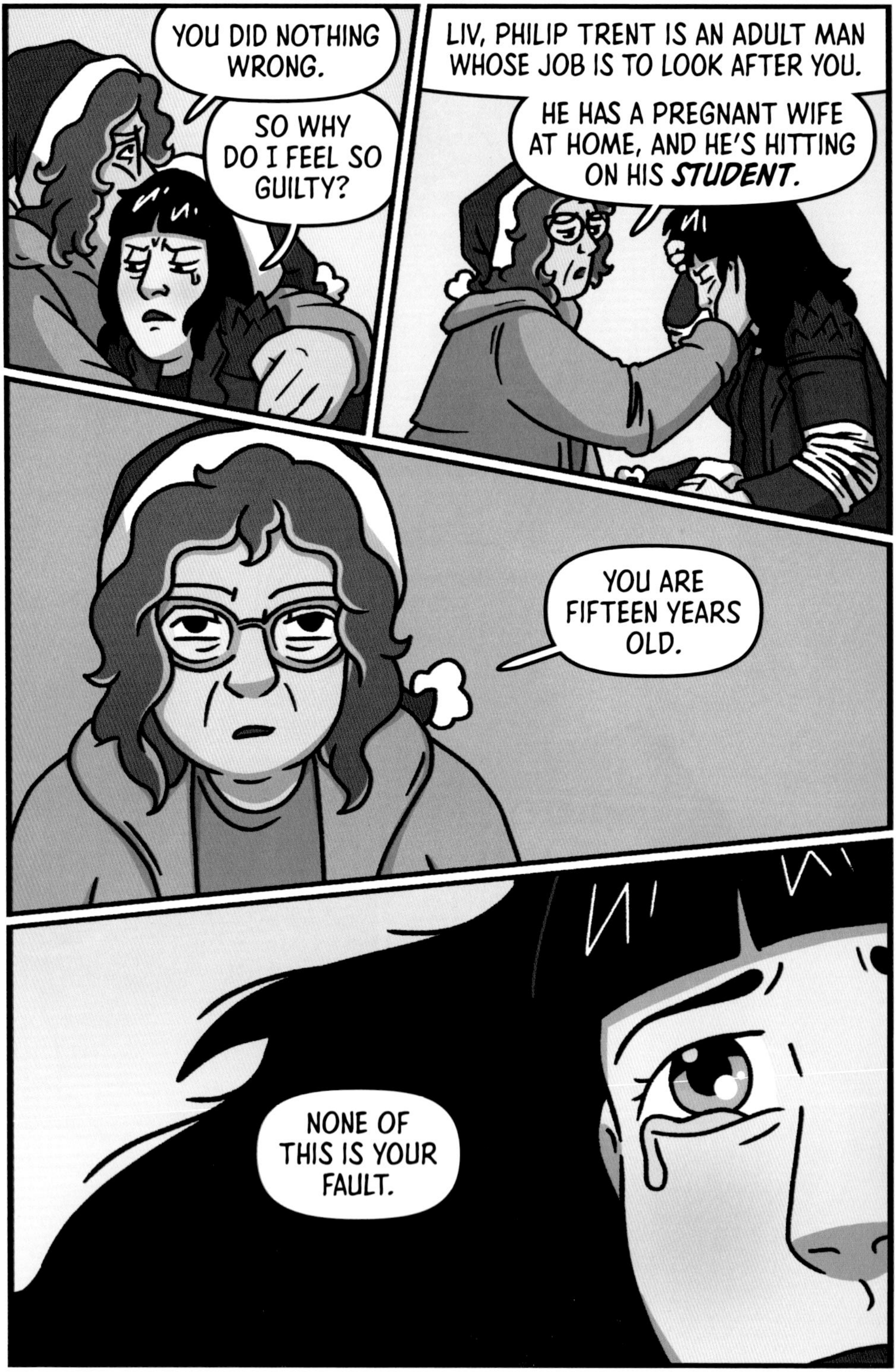
YOU DID NOTHING WRONG.
SO WHY DO I FEEL SO GUILTY?
LIV, PHILIP TRENT IS AN ADULT MAN WHOSE JOB IS TO LOOK AFTER YOU.
HE HAS A PREGNANT WIFE AT HOME, AND HE'S HITTING ON HIS *STUDENT*.
YOU ARE FIFTEEN YEARS OLD.
NONE OF THIS IS YOUR FAULT.

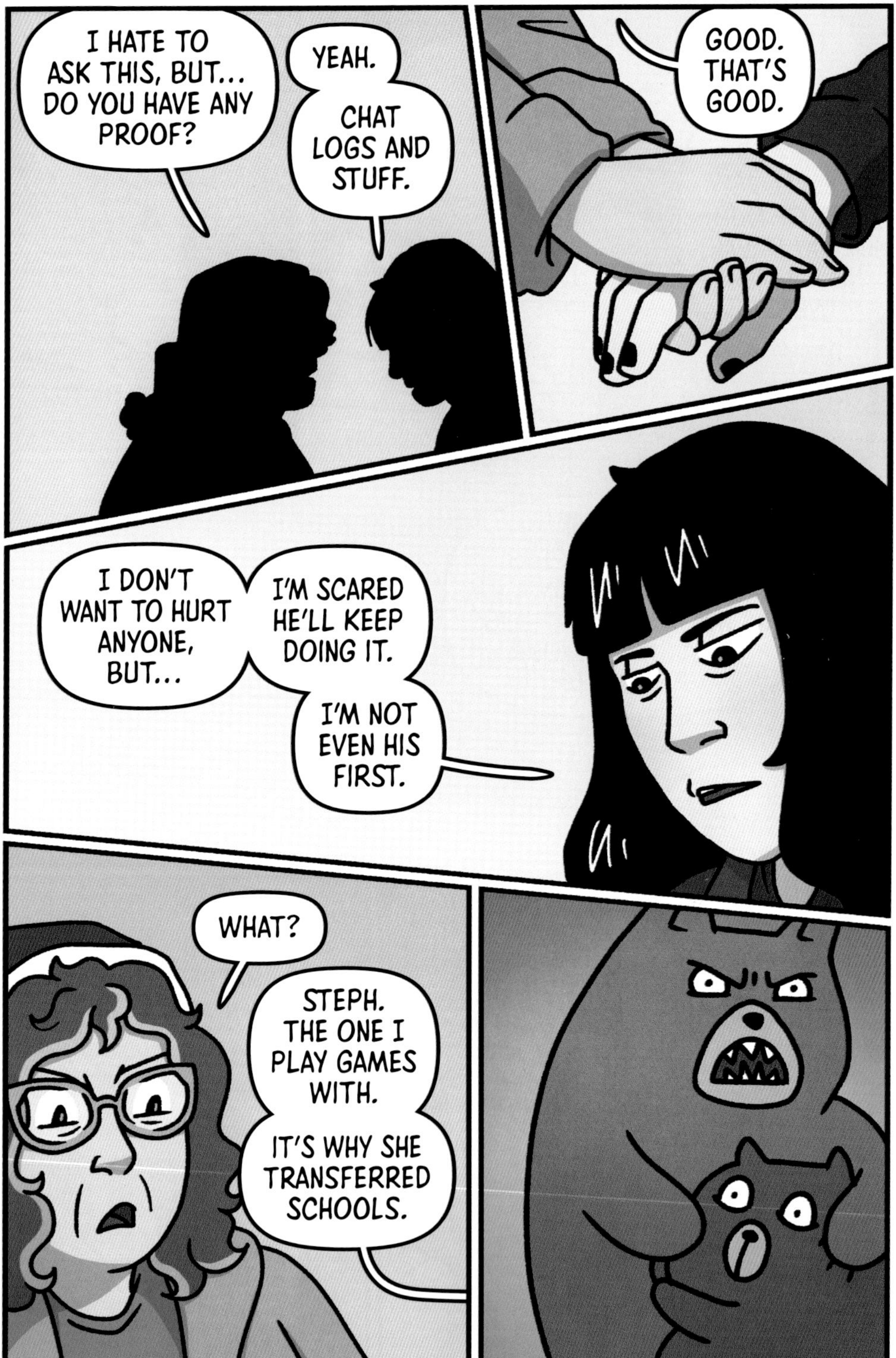
I HATE TO ASK THIS, BUT... DO YOU HAVE ANY PROOF?
YEAH.
CHAT LOGS AND STUFF.
GOOD. THAT'S GOOD.
I DON'T WANT TO HURT ANYONE, BUT...
I'M SCARED HE'LL KEEP DOING IT.
I'M NOT EVEN HIS FIRST.
WHAT?
STEPH. THE ONE I PLAY GAMES WITH.
IT'S WHY SHE TRANSFERRED SCHOOLS.

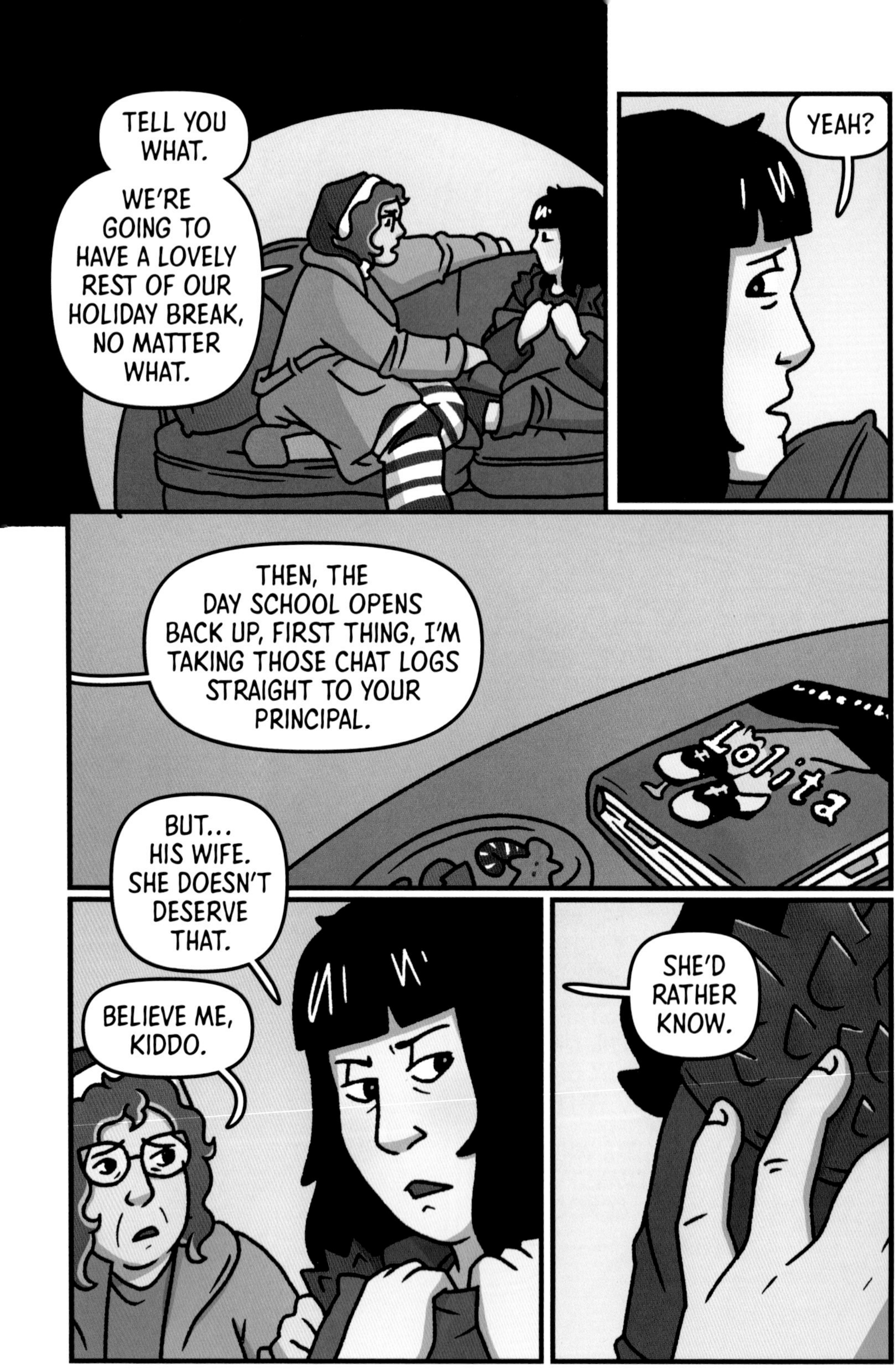
TELL YOU WHAT.
WE'RE GOING TO HAVE A LOVELY REST OF OUR HOLIDAY BREAK, NO MATTER WHAT.
YEAH?
THEN, THE DAY SCHOOL OPENS BACK UP, FIRST THING, I'M TAKING THOSE CHAT LOGS STRAIGHT TO YOUR PRINCIPAL.
Lolita
BUT... HIS WIFE. SHE DOESN'T DESERVE THAT.
BELIEVE ME, KIDDO.
SHE'D RATHER KNOW.

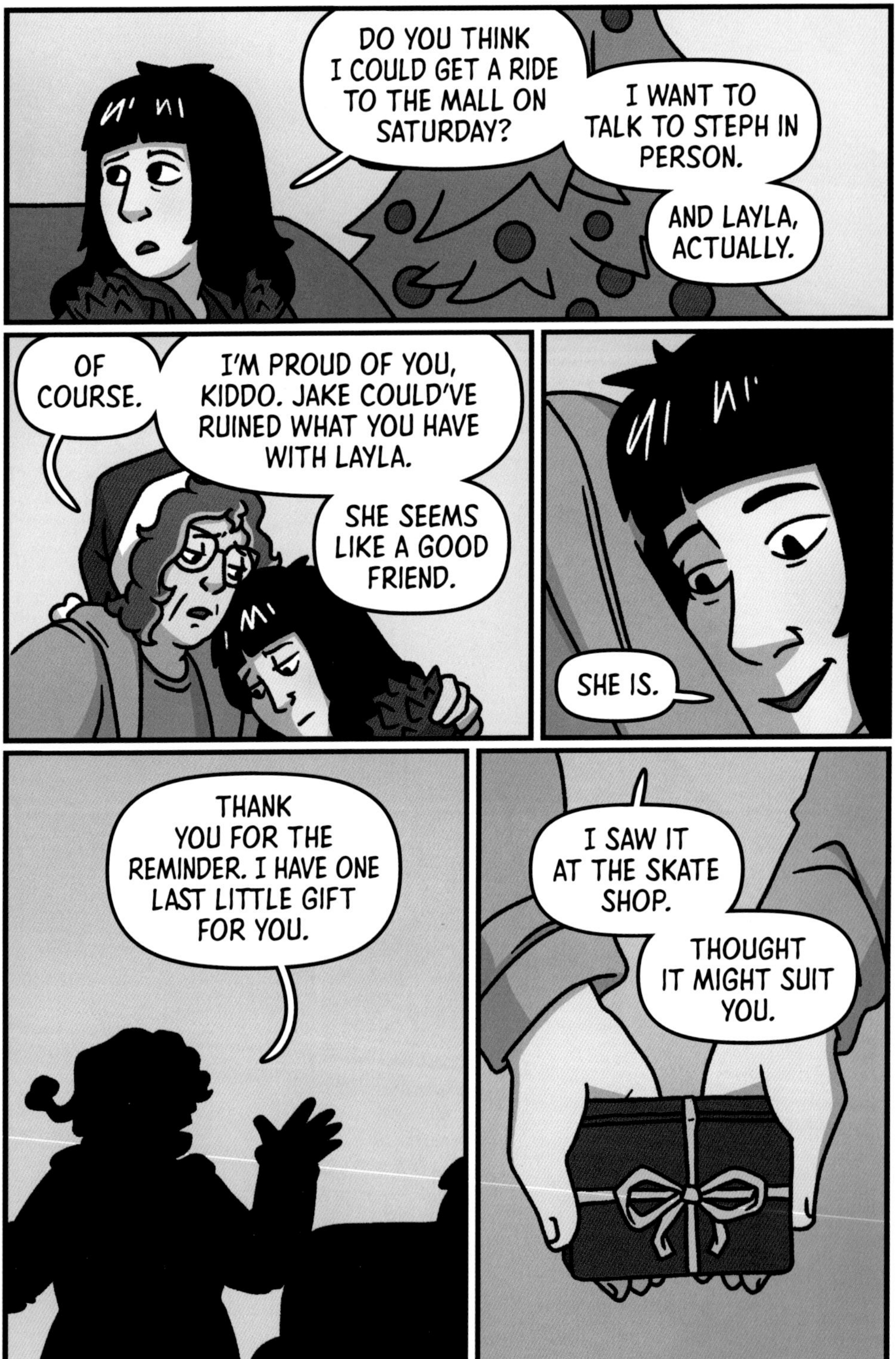
DO YOU THINK I COULD GET A RIDE TO THE MALL ON SATURDAY?
I WANT TO TALK TO STEPH IN PERSON.
AND LAYLA, ACTUALLY.
OF COURSE.
I'M PROUD OF YOU, KIDDO. JAKE COULD'VE RUINED WHAT YOU HAVE WITH LAYLA.
SHE SEEMS LIKE A GOOD FRIEND.
SHE IS.
THANK YOU FOR THE REMINDER. I HAVE ONE LAST LITTLE GIFT FOR YOU.
I SAW IT AT THE SKATE SHOP.
THOUGHT IT MIGHT SUIT YOU.

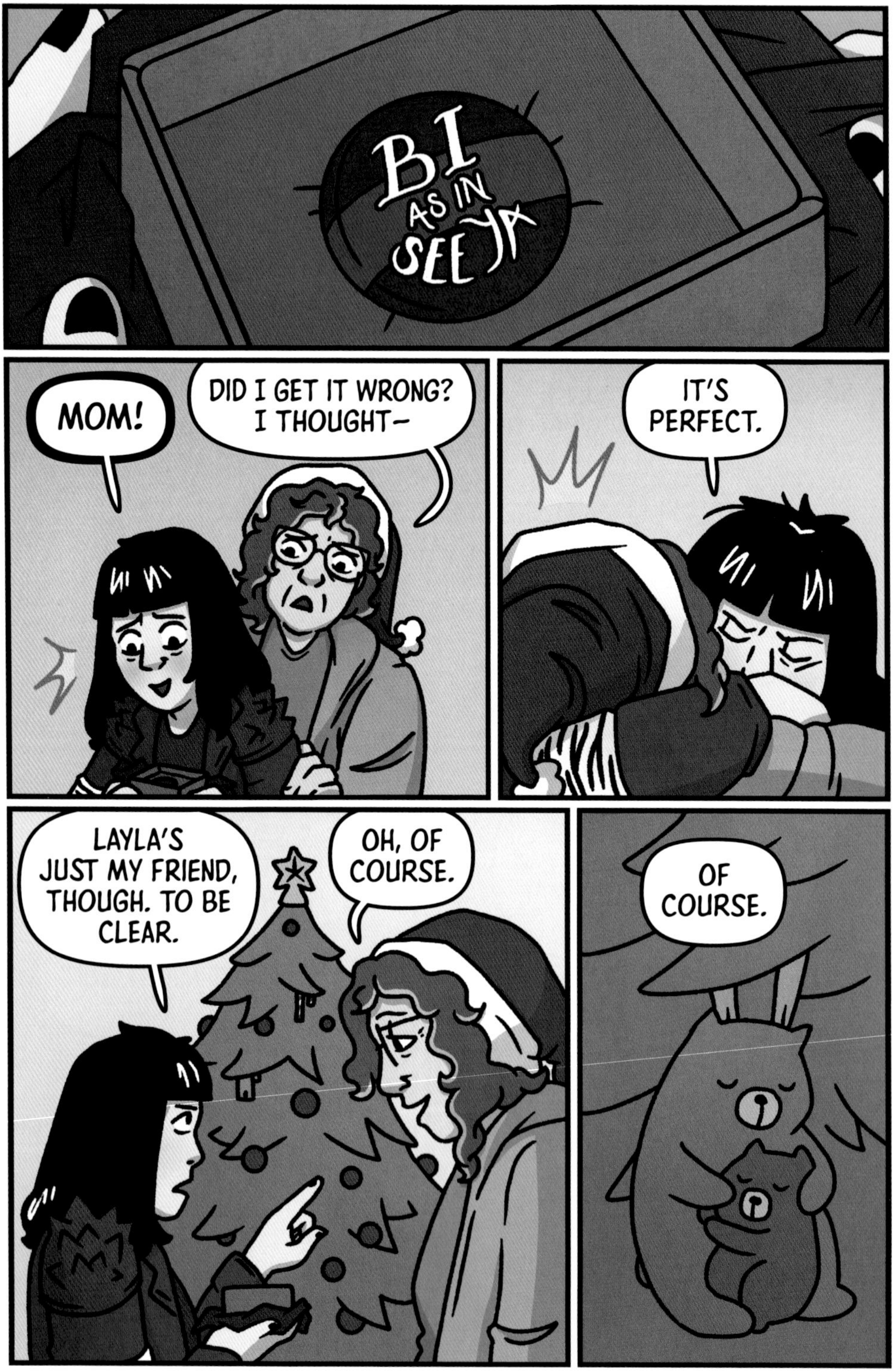
BI AS IN SEE YA
MOM!
DID I GET IT WRONG? I THOUGHT–
IT'S PERFECT.
LAYLA'S JUST MY FRIEND, THOUGH. TO BE CLEAR.
OH, OF COURSE.
OF COURSE.

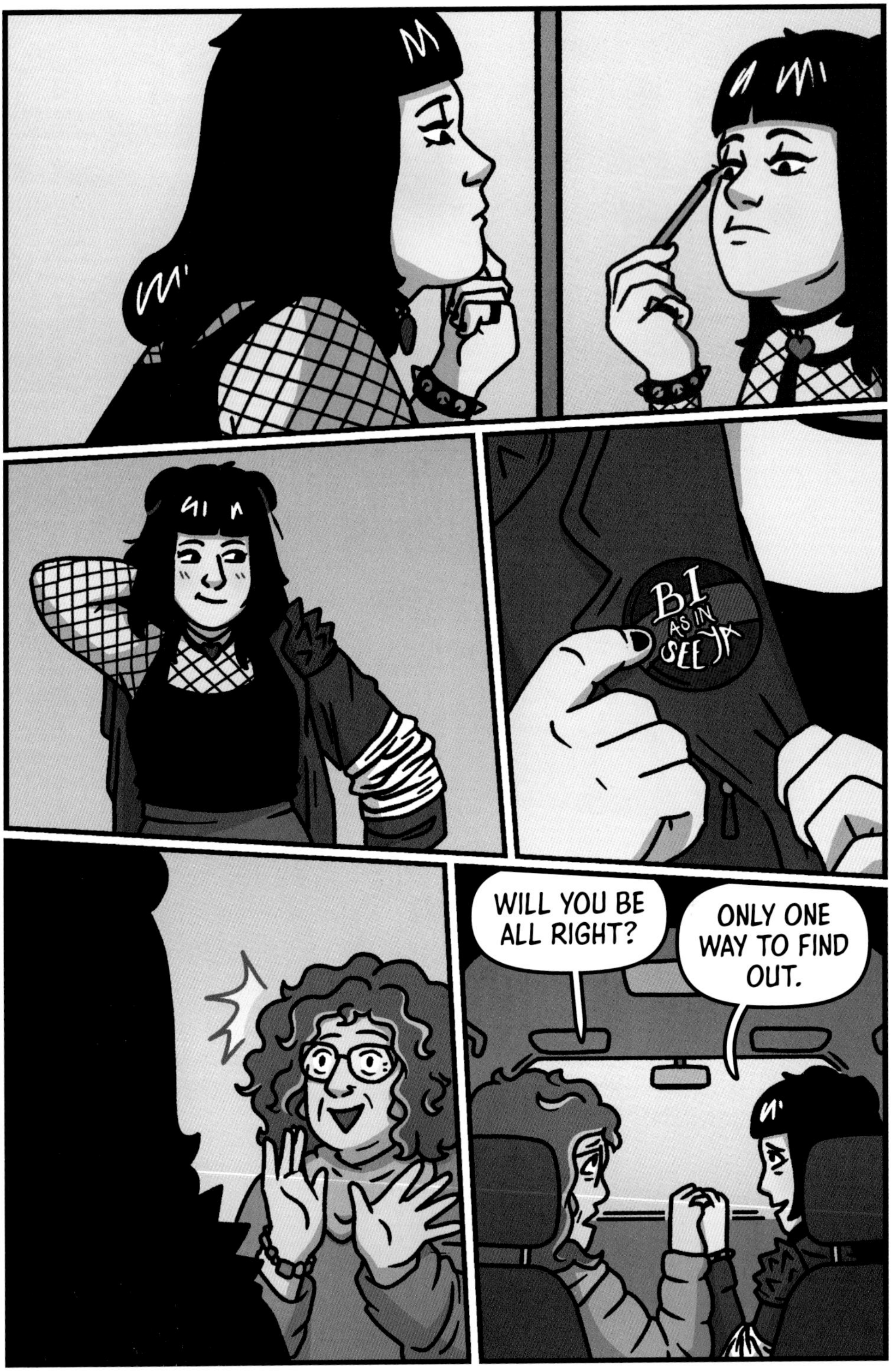
BI AS IN SEE YA
WILL YOU BE ALL RIGHT?
ONLY ONE WAY TO FIND OUT.

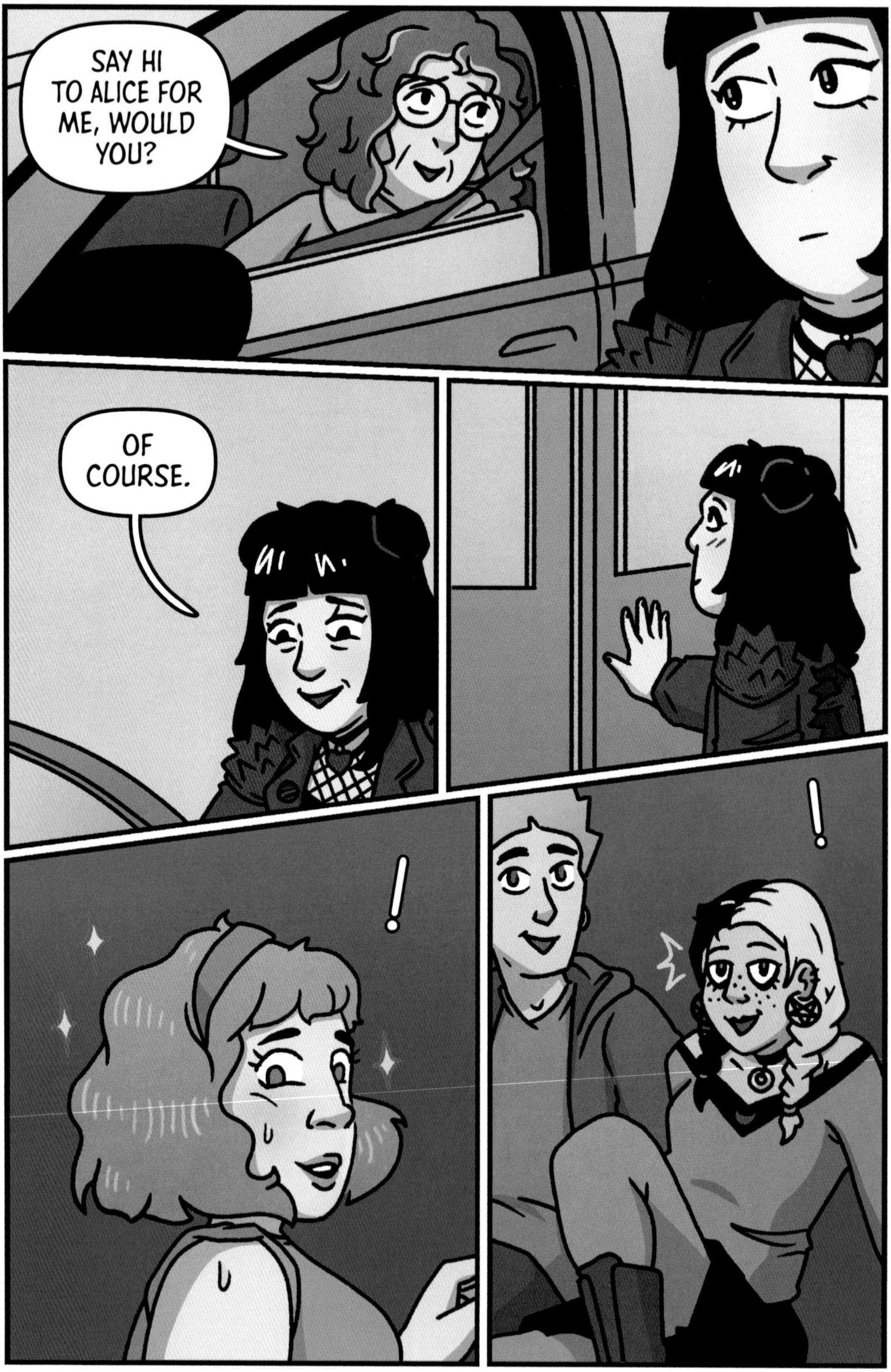
SAY HI TO ALICE FOR ME, WOULD YOU?
OF COURSE.
!
!

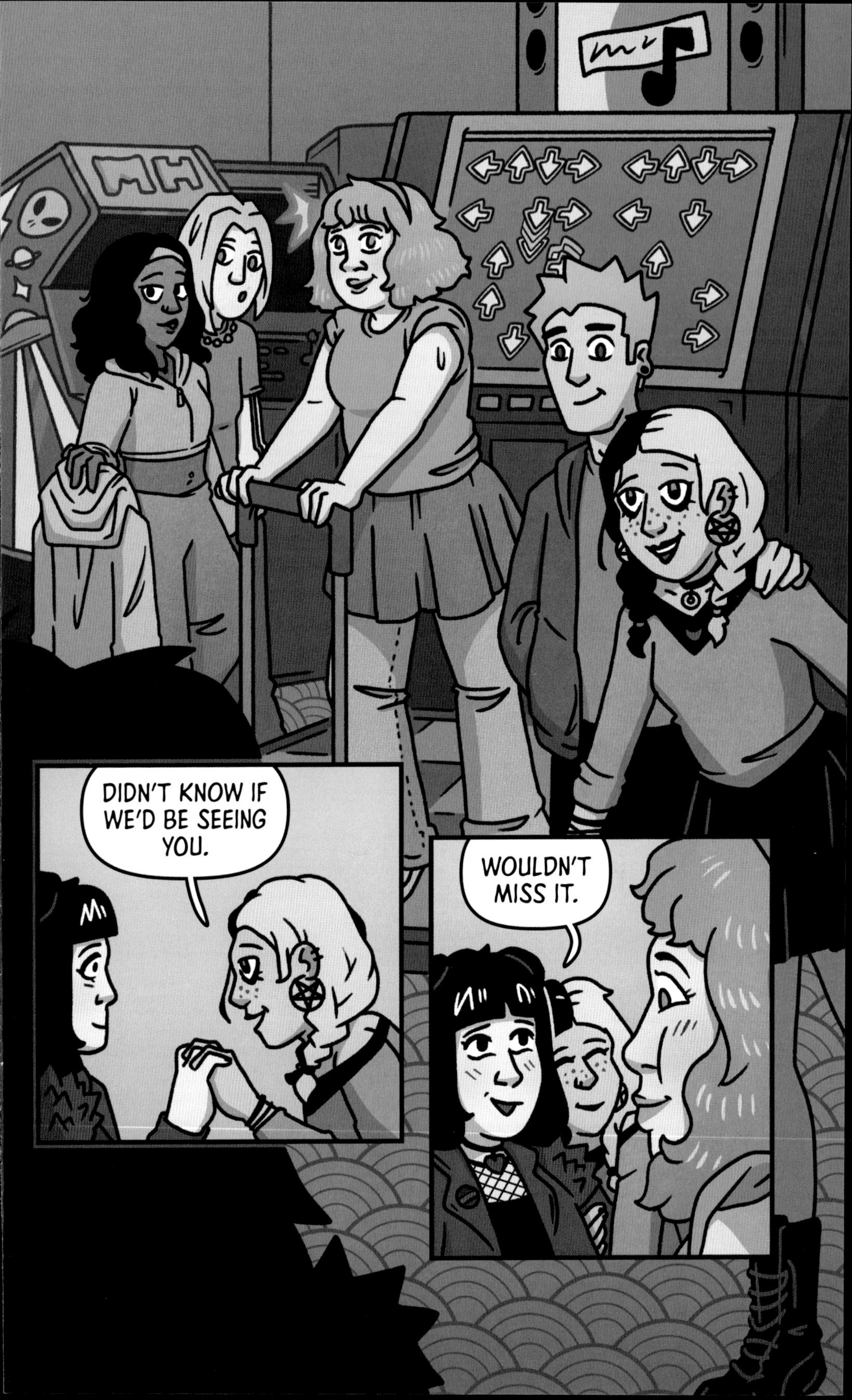
DIDN'T KNOW IF WE'D BE SEEING YOU.
WOULDN'T MISS IT.

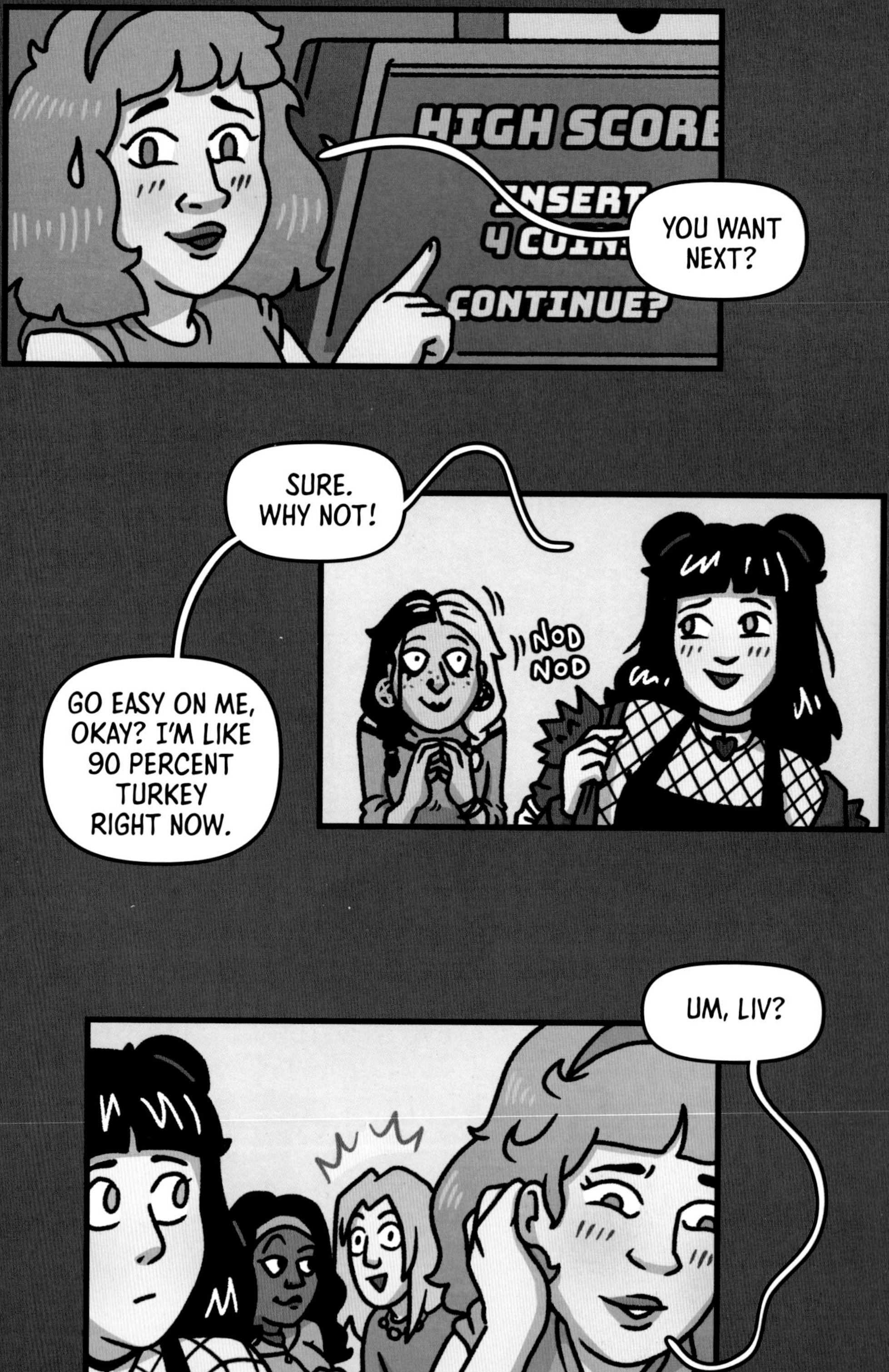
CONTINUE?
YOU WANT NEXT?
SURE. WHY NOT!
GO EASY ON ME, OKAY? I'M LIKE 90 PERCENT TURKEY RIGHT NOW.
NOD NOD
UM, LIV?

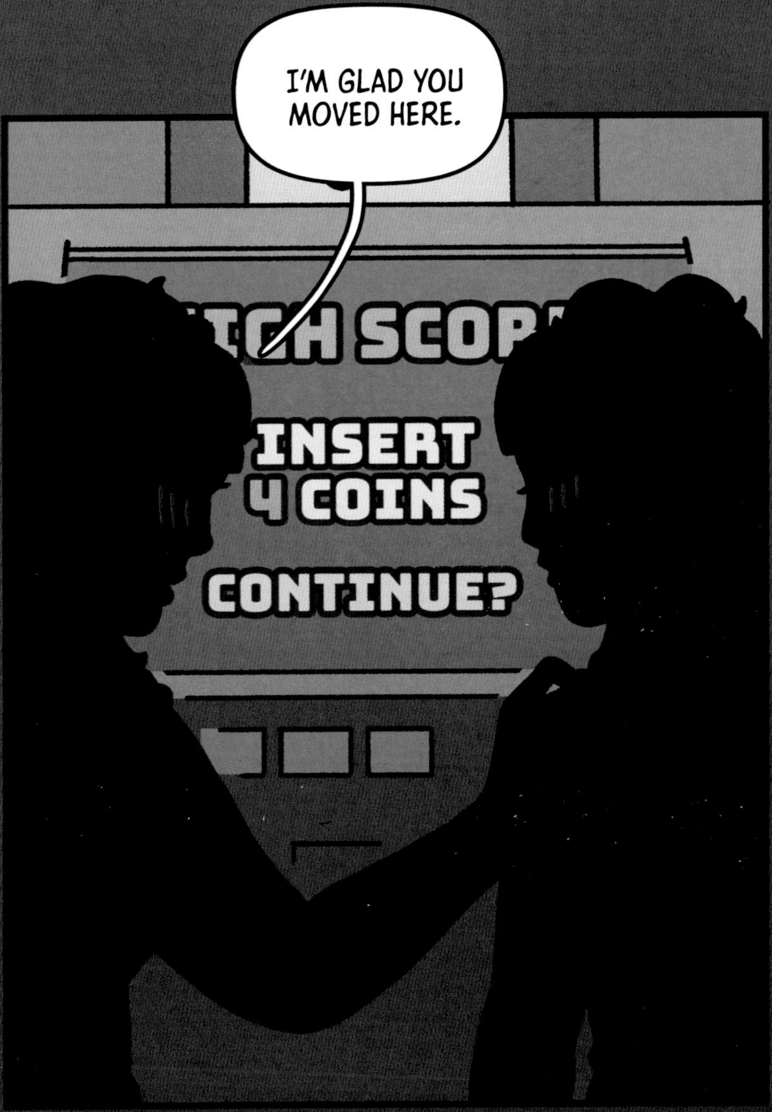
I'M GLAD YOU MOVED HERE.
INSERT 4 COINS
CONTINUE?

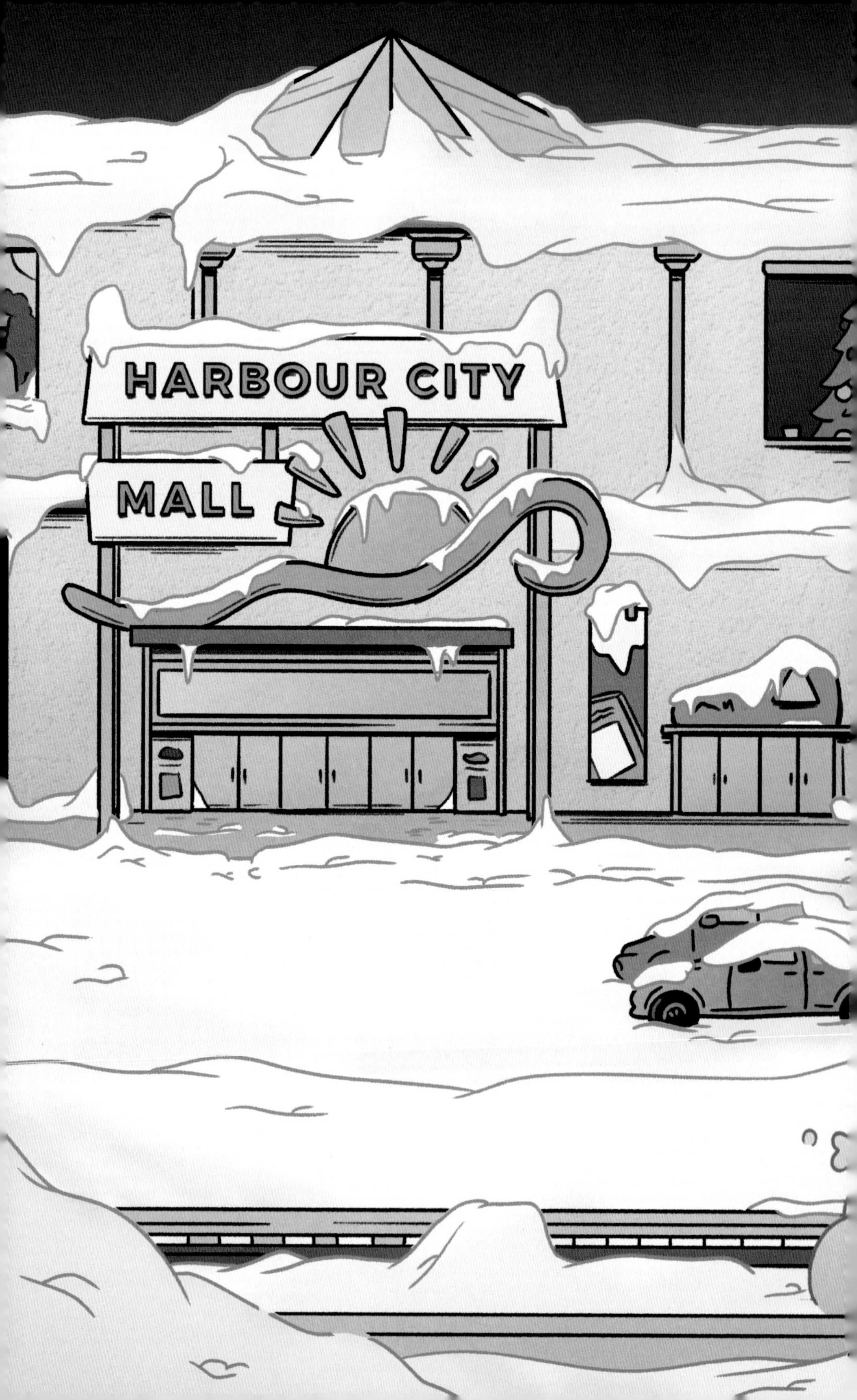
HARBOUR CITY
MALL

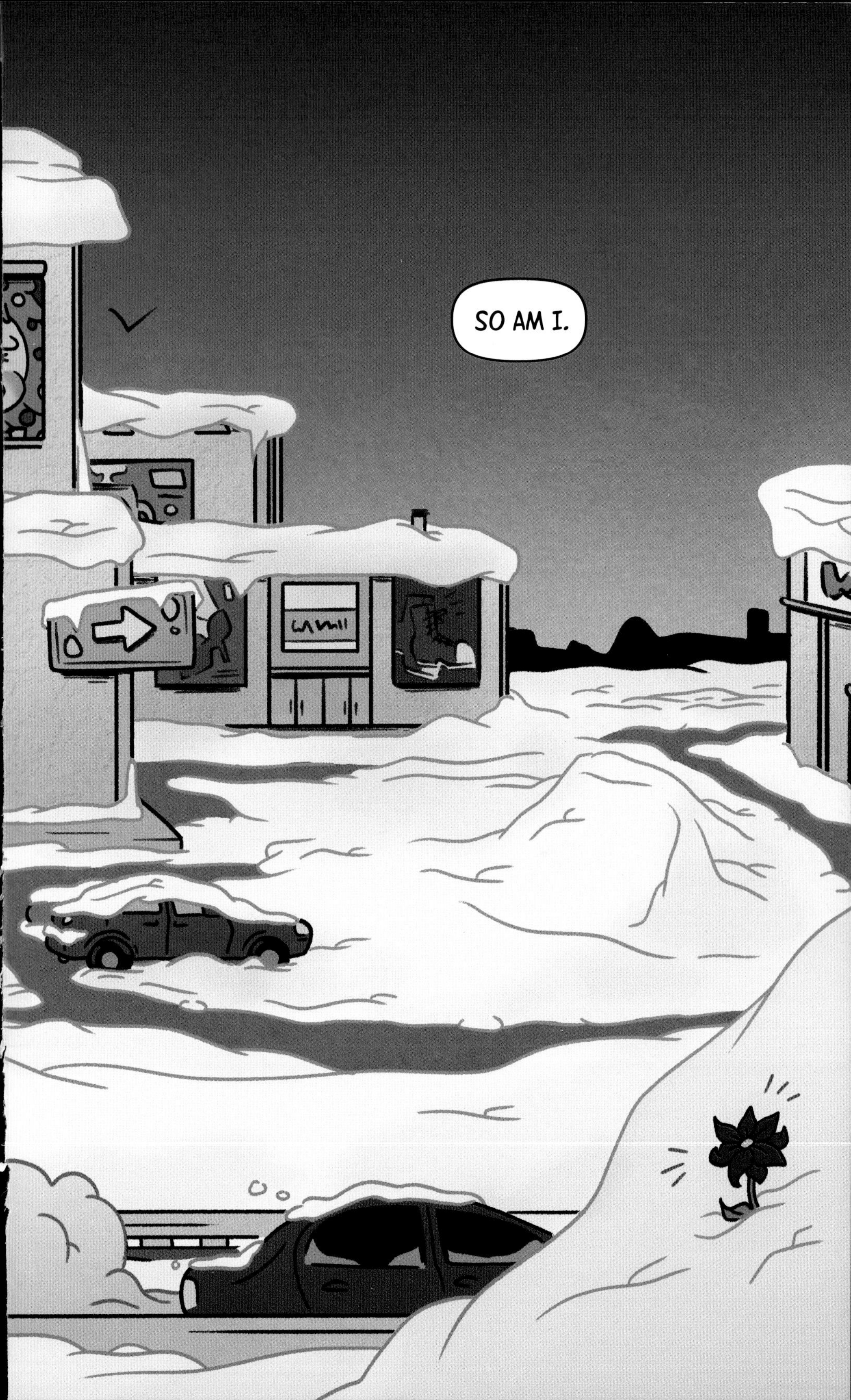
SO AM I.

ACKNOWLEDGMENTS

I HAVE TOO MANY PEOPLE TO THANK FOR THIS BOOK BECOMING REAL. I'LL DO MY BEST TO CREDIT EVERYONE, BUT IF YOU SO MUCH AS *LIKED* A POST ABOUT IT, FEEL FREE TO ADD YOUR NAME TO THE BLANK SPACE I HAVE PROVIDED. IF YOUR NAME CHANGES, AS SO MANY DO, JUST SCRATCH IT OUT. IT'S WHAT I'D WANT.

ALL MY LOVE AND GRATITUDE TO JENN LINNAN, MY FABULOUS AGENT; DEEBA ZARGAR-PUR, MY PATIENT EDITOR; TOM DALY, ART DIRECTOR EXTRAORDINAIRE; DIANA SOUSA, WHOSE COLORS BROUGHT *MALL GOTH* TO LIFE; AND ROBIN CRANK, LETTERER TO THE STARS. THE ENTIRE S&S TEAM, REALLY: DAINESE SANTOS, LIZ KOSSNAR, KENDRA LEVIN, JUSTIN CHANDA, JENICA NASWORTHY, AND BRENNA FRANZITTA. *SKÅL!*

I MUST ALSO THANK COHEN EDENFIELD, WHO LISTENED TO MY MANY RANTS ABOUT PREDATORY GROOMING AND STRIPED ARM-WARMERS DURING LOCKDOWN. CAL JOHNSTON, WHO GOT ME STARTED ON THIS JOURNEY. MEG, ZACH, AND OLLIE, WHOSE HOME REMAINS MY SAFE HARBOR. THE GOLF CART GANG AND THE BAD APPLES, MY INNER CIRCLE! WHAT WOULD I DO WITHOUT YOU?

THANK YOU TO MY PATRONS ON PATREON, WHOSE SUPPORT QUITE LITERALLY KEEPS ME ALIVE. JAMES, SLANEY, LOGAN, OTHER KATE, ABBEY, DORIAN, DANA, MATTIE, LASER, AND THE ABENE TWINS. THE ENTIRE TOPATOCO CLAN, THE NIGHT VALE CREW. THE HSHC AND GRS MONTREAL, WHO HELPED ME GET SOME THINGS OFF MY CHEST DURING PRODUCTION. JASON, ASHLEY, JOAQUIM, BECKY, RAINA, GWENDA, ERIC, RACHAEL, LEIGH, AND NATZILLA THE RAT KILLA. ADAM, THE ORIGINAL *KATE OR DIE!* STAN, EVERYONE WHO HAS EVER BEEN NICE TO ME, AND THE MANY, MANY, *MANY* ASMR*TISTS* WHOSE WORK I RELIED ON FOR THOUSANDS OF HOURS AS *MALL GOTH* TOOK SHAPE. I'LL POST LINKS ONLINE. THERE ARE DOZENS OF YOU. *DOZENS!*

LASTLY, TO _____ (INSERT YOUR NAME HERE), WHOSE SUPPORT IS THE REASON I KEEP GETTING TO DO WHAT I LOVE A DECADE-PLUS INTO MY CAREER. YOU BRING ME TO LIFE.